*Grand Conspiracy*

# Books by Janny Wurts

Sorcerer's Legacy

*The Cycle of Fire Trilogy*

Stormwarden
Keeper of the Keys
Shadowfane

The Master of Whitestorm
That Way Lies Camelot

*The Wars of Light and Shadow*

Curse of the Mistwraith
Ships of Merior
Warhost of Vastmark
Fugitive Prince
Grand Conspiracy

*With Raymond E. Feist*

Daughter of the Empire
Servant of the Empire
Mistress of the Empire

Voyager

# Janny Wurts

# GRAND CONSPIRACY

## The Wars of Light and Shadow

### VOLUME 5

SECOND BOOK OF
THE ALLIANCE OF LIGHT

HarperCollins*Publishers*

Sci Fi
WHAT

*Voyager*
An imprint of HarperCollins*Publishers*
77–85 Fulham Palace Road,
Hammersmith, London W6 8JB

The *Voyager* World Wide Web site address is
http://www.harpercollins.co.uk/voyager

Published by *Voyager* 1999
1 3 5 7 9 8 6 4 2

A catalogue record for this book
is available from the British Library

ISBN 0 00 224074 2
ISBN 0 00 224075 0 (trade pbk)

Typeset in Aldus and Belwe by
Palimpsest Book Production Limited,
Polmont, Stirlingshire

Printed and bound in Great Britain by
Caledonian International Book Manufacturing Ltd, Glasgow

*For Roderick MacDonald,*
*with profound thanks for*
*the opportunity to study*
*music under a master*

# Acknowledgements

Thanks to the following people, who gave
generously of their time and patience over the years
as this manuscript was written:
Jeff Watson, Mark Bereit, Bob and Sara Schwager,
Jane Johnson, Caitlin Blaisdell
and always,
my husband, Don Maitz.

# Contents

## Second Book

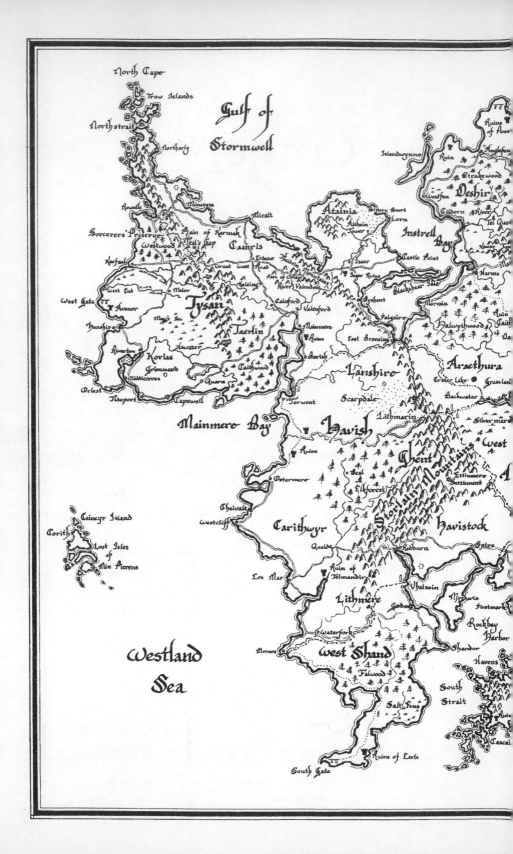

# Athera
## Continent of Paravia

### Age of the Mistwraithe

North Ward · Grimwood
Fallowmere
of Araithe
Perlorn
Etera
Mountains
hain
Fuel Rocks
amon
Darkling
Valgapre
Ithilt
Eastwall
Minderl Ruin
Kewar River
Ithamon
Caith
Ithwish Mountain
Escarp
Caolot
Bay of Eltair
Tharidor · Whitehold
rt
Warens
Atwood
Athlir
Atainn
East Halla
Telzen Ruins
Alestron · Kalesh
Adruin
dhalla
Mountains
Mirthlvain
Swamp
Orvandir
Mathiele
Methlas Lake
Durn
Ishlir
o Ganish
Sic Towers
nark
Forthmark
River Ippash
Ishth
Archer
Aland
Janish
Desert of Sanpashir
Ruins
Selkwood
Sanshevas
Werpoint
Crescent Isle
Minderl Bay
Minderl Strait
Baint's Point
East Gate
Alhar Ruins
Vaststrait
Northstor
Farsee
Eastialr
Tirans
Perdith
Tirans Ruins
Fissino
Telzen
Scimlade Tip
Merior
Sickle Bay
Sheddorn
Southshir

## Cildein Ocean

Los Lier

## South Sea

### Scale in Leagues

0    10    25        50                    100

| | |
|---|---|
| ⊠ | Sorcerers' Preserve |
| • | Cities |
| ⊻ | Second Age ruins |
| ✷ | City that did not fall in uprising |
| ⊓ | Worldsend Gates |
| ∫ | Standing Stones |
| ·—·—· | Kingdom Borders |
| ∿ | Rivers |
| ♠♠ | Forests |
| ⌂ | Marshes or Mires |
| ⋮⋮⋮ | Wastelands |
| ······ | Second Age Roads |
| ⌒ | Trade Roads |
| ⋀⋀ | Mountains |

*One child, four possible fates*
*looped through the thread of his life span.*
*He will grow to manhood.*
*Should he die in fire, none suffers but he.*
*Yours to choose when the time comes,*
*Fferedon'li.*
– from Fionn Areth's birth augury
Third Age 5647

# I. Opening Play

T he hard frost came to the downs of Araethura early, and the rains at their cusp laced crusts of ice through the peat stacks under the sheds. Indoors, with no fire lit to fend off autumn's breezes, the invasive cold settled at will. Crouched on her knees on the packed earthen floor beside her darkened cottage hearthstone, the Koriani enchantress Elaira cast aside her flint striker. She cupped her chilled fingers, blew on the caught spark. Well versed in the contrary nature of wet peat, she launched into strings of ridiculous endearments, coaxing damp fodder to nourish its struggling wisp of caught flame.

The fateful knock at her door, which shattered her peace, interrupted her then.

Elaira damped back her annoyance. The spill in her fingers fluttered out as she arose, resigned to the usual request for a cough remedy or a tincture to dose a sick goat. For seven years, she had lived alone, plying her herbal wisdom on the moorlands. Time had eased the innate distrust the local herders held toward practice of her craft, and families now came to her freely when trouble visited their livestock and farmsteads. While the leaves turned, and the season's late foraging sent her deep into the hills, such supplicants knew she was best found at home after sundown.

The dark in the cottage weighed like felt soaked in the sweet meadow scents of the herbs bundled to dry in the rafters. Elaira breathed in the oily must from her fleece jacket, just pulled from storage in her clothes chest. While she threaded between her sparse furnishings by touch, the pounding resumed, impatient.

'Daelion's bollocks, I hear you!' Elaira clawed under her collar, hooked out the silver chain that hung her spell crystal. The quartz as her focus, she invoked mage-sight to steer past the tumbledown stacks of herb hampers and clay jars, long since overcrowding the niche underneath the cluttered board of her work trestle. Barefoot and cold, she reached the door and fumbled with numbed hands for the latch.

Apprehension swept her, unbidden. For the crystallized span of a heartbeat, every fiber of her being clamored in primal, precognitive warning.

Then her roan gelding whinnied from the shed. His call was answered by a strange horse's whicker; a shod hoof chinked against rock, and a distinct chime of bit rings sliced the night. Innocuous sounds; yet their import snapped away the false calm she had wrested from whole years of disciplined solitude.

'Sithaer's begotten demons!' Elaira released her crystal, swept over by needling gooseflesh in the chill embrace of the dark. Those downsland herders who called needing help came on foot, or else they rode in astride scruffy moor ponies with hackamores braided from leather. Their mounts wore no tack with metal fittings. Nor did they ever fare shod.

Her left hand hovered, indecisive, while the knock resounded a third time. The rickety wood panel jounced in its frame and threatened the strapped leather hinges. Before the door gave way under punishment, Elaira tripped up the latch. Wind flung the panel against her braced shoulder and revealed what the fell night had brought her.

A Koriani enchantress stood on her threshold, ruffled into lofty disdain by the inclement Araethurian autumn.

She said, acerbic, 'Were you asleep with your bumpkin head under a blanket?' Searing displeasure rolled off her in waves and jutted the chin beneath her hood. Whatever her status, the buffeting elements had abused her like any other traveler. Her initiate's mantle was rumpled and splashed, the hemline snagged loose by a thorn brake. Bristled to yet more extreme irritation, the enchantress inspected the splinters stabbed through her expensive calf gloves. 'Beastly boards! Why haven't you found some needy laborer to come here and faire them smooth?'

Elaira clapped down a flyaway tendril of her auburn hair and cracked the offending door wider. 'Are you going to rail, or come in?' Her dread pulled awry by irrepressible devilment, she gestured toward the comfortless darkness inside, offering a shelter as rude in simplicity as any length of unsanded oak.

A purposeful rustle, as the woman outside raised her quality, layered silk above the muck-splashed ankles of her riding boots. 'Dear woman, how quaint.' Aristocratic accents packaged each word with precise and patronizing venom.

The rising winds sliced bitter and chill through that moment, as the unforgotten past encountered the present and irrefutably tangled. Elaira knew who had come. Her recognition raised sourceless panic, and then sharp rage, that the grasping demands of her order would destroy all the hard-won sanctuary she had found in the heart of these barren moorlands.

'First Senior,' she greeted, the requisite formality of high office like ice chips between her locked teeth.

Lirenda unclasped her mantle, her air of reserve an acid rebuff. 'No longer First Senior.' As if upbraiding a junior initiate for an insubordinate attitude, she admitted, 'The Prime Matriarch has rescinded my privileges.'

That was news; a political break of shattering magnitude, which implied a long fall from position and favor.

All blank practicality, Elaira shouldered the door closed before the raw winds could strip her bundles of dried herbs from the rafters. Her back to barred wood, she endured a tense interval, while the unintimidated gusts continued to howl and batter over the thatch. By her cot in the corner, the one window's shutter shivered and worked on its pins. The drafts through the chinks made no allowance for smashed expectations or shamed pride; the floor gave off its humble scent of dank earth.

'You do keep a candle, I presume,' Lirenda said at length. She smoothed her shed mantle over her arm, unwilling to risk the silk lining to the hazards of unvarnished furnishings.

'There's a tallow dip.' Beeswax was far too precious to burn in the barren isolation of the moorlands. Elaira crossed the cottage. Arrogance alone did not explain why a grand senior of the order should disdain simple use of trained mage-sight. While rummaging through a cupboard for a wick, Elaira could not strangle logic, or shake her sense of foreboding.

The implied disgrace of an eighth-rank enchantress defied all sane credibility. For over five decades, Lirenda had stood second in line behind the Koriani Prime Matriarch. Morriel was weakened by vast age, even dying, rumor said. There seemed no imaginable intrigue or expediency that might drive her to disown her sole groomed successor against the hour when her faculties would finally fail her.

Despite the moiled waters of Koriani high policy, Lirenda's arrival would not be chance, but tied like forged chain to the name that haunted every facet of Elaira's existence.

'What will you ask to know of Prince Arithon this time?' Her resentment sang through the gloom as she straightened, the tallow dip cradled between sweating palms, while the cupboard gaped open behind her.

For, of course, the Koriani Order would not have stopped meddling in the feud between the royal half brothers who had banished the Mistwraith. Their strengths and their sacrifice had restored Athera to clear sunlight, but that victory had been bought in tragedy. The possessed fogs of Desh-thiere had been battled to a standstill and trapped. Last stroke in defeat, its poisonous curse had left Lysaer s'Ilessid and Arithon s'Ffalenn entangled in unbreakable enmity. Their gifted talents of light and shadow had been turned one against the other, the violence extended to bloody war and cutthroat politics for a span of sixteen years.

Morriel's entrenched conviction that Arithon Teir's'Ffalenn was a threat and a danger to society would scarcely have changed since the spring's breeding intrigues had relieved Lysaer s'Ilessid of his proudly launched fleet of sail.

Silence; the descending wail of a gust overlaid by the secretive whisper of costly, town-loomed silk.

'Why else would you come?' Elaira accused outright. Steady as iron, and guarded in ways she wished she could trade for the cleaner oblivion of death, she crossed the cramped cottage and stooped to retrieve her dropped flint and striker from the hearthstone. 'At least, I should think dirt floors and rabbit stew could be found in more interesting company than mine.'

'You know the Shadow Master's whereabouts.' Lirenda tried a step, groped at the edge of the trestle, and stopped to the chink of bumped flasks. Her restraint spoke volumes, since her highbrow nature invariably met baiting with a show of superior authority.

Elaira snapped the striker. Against felted darkness, a spat tangle of sparks; their reflections touched her eyes, the unyielding, flat tone of wet slate in that moment when illicit love and compassion collided with inflexible duty. She must answer when questioned. Her initiate's vow demanded obedience; nor could she feign ignorance. The uncanny cord of awareness she shared with Rathain's prince had not faded one whit through seven long years of separation.

She wrung what stabbing satisfaction she could from the level force of her honesty. 'My reply won't be news.' Her shrug was blurred by the tenuous flicker as the new flame died on the wick. 'Your scryers could have spoken without the rank bother of spending a cold night under thatch that's infested with silverfish.'

Lirenda returned an expectant silence.

Compelled to elaborate, Elaira gave the striker another fierce effort. 'What would any thief do with jacked brigs, except sail them? His Grace of Rathain's been at sea for three months.'

The tallow dip caught. Marigold light flared over crude edges of wood, then the chipped rims of her hard-used Araethurian crockery, and lastly, in a wavering, unkind disclosure, the tatty, patched quilts and old fleeces tumbled over her cot in the corner. Elaira refused the embarrassment of an apology. Life here on the moor gave her all that she needed. Her roof did not leak, a comfort never to be taken for granted after her impoverished childhood. This tiny cottage had been her home since she had forsaken Arithon's company at Merior. Its unvarnished planks gleamed oiled yellow, walls and pegged furnishings left unadorned in their natural dappling of knots. The steam-bent wooden canisters, the iron pot, the stone knives, and the brazier which served her herbalist's vocation scattered their familiar melange across the trestle.

Yet, as if such cozy, workaday clutter had subtly slipped into chaos, the haven Elaira had claimed for herself no longer seemed safe or friendly.

An enchantress who held her in utmost contempt commandeered the stool which still wore the nicks of its origin in a cobbler's shop. All citybred elegance, Lirenda perched like a displeased cat, a slipped coil of hair unreeled down the white-marble skin of her temple. But for the marred elegance of travel-creased skirts, her composure was flawless, each limb arranged with the serenity of a sculptor's sketch for a masterpiece.

Which complacency struck a false chord in a fireless cottage with the change in the season howling through the chinks; Elaira suppressed a raking, fresh pang of unease. Lirenda had always deplored life's rough edges. For a sleek, cultured woman who demanded her bathwater scalding and her personal servants brisk and silent, a cottage in these moorlands on the biting edge of autumn posed an inconvenience akin to punishment. Without Morriel Prime's direct order, Lirenda would have foisted this sorry errand on one of her least-favored underlings. The fact that her misery kept no company bespoke an ominous secrecy.

Elaira shed the tallow dip on the table before her trembling drew unwanted notice. Rather than grapple with her building dread, she crouched and resumed the easier task of coaxing wet fuel to take fire. 'You can't really believe I could hold sway over Prince Arithon's movements.'

Lirenda insisted, 'You have a part to play, even so.'

Elaira recoiled. Her pile of birch shavings scattered as if by an arrow's aimed force, and the spark snuffed, spindled into a sullen ribbon of smoke. Jaw hard, her friable emotions buttressed behind a facade as determined as stormed granite, Elaira recouped her scattered kindling. She ground the flint against her worn lump of ore, distressed enough to start a conflagration on the sheer impetus of resentment.

Her Koriani oath constrained her, until the achievement of each inhaled breath taxed her separately to complete. The instant the blaze caught under her hands, she stood erect and faced her tormentor. 'Say what you mean.'

Lirenda fussed with the muddied silk draped across her braced calf. 'Why protect Rathain's prince? He stands accused of monstrous crimes. Avenor has gathered hard evidence. Lysaer's magistrates claim he used black arts and blood sorcery to fracture the cliff face above Dier Kenton Vale. You can't pretend not to know Lysaer's great war host was milled down and slaughtered wholesale under a shale slide.'

'That's six-year-old news. We're remote here, not fossilized.' Elaira cast the striker into the wood scuttle, silted under the flaked ash of the charcoal she hoarded to heat her brazier. 'Does the Koriani Senior Circle believe that's what happened? That Arithon engaged wrongful conjury?'

'The man's capable, certainly.' Silk rustled, an offended whisper against the diminished clang of abused tinware. Lirenda looked up at last, her eyes like poured oil in the primitive play of the firelight. 'His malice is documented. None can deny the massacre wrought by his hand. But you know him best. What defense could you possibly offer to exonerate him from those acts?'

'I would ask him,' Elaira said. To deflect her overwhelming desire to strike out, to smash through the porcelain-doll certainty stamped on Lirenda's features, she folded her forearms under the scruffy fleece lining her jacket. 'Whatever his Grace of Rathain did, then or now, he will have his own reason. I have never seen him lie for convenience. Nor have I known him to break from the sound tenets of his character.'

'Well then, your conviction won't prove any hindrance, at the least.' Satisfaction smoothed Lirenda's dulcet tones. 'The task your Prime asks should reward such sterling faith. Rathain's prince need do nothing else but confirm your belief in his incorruptible s'Ffalenn compassion.'

'What are you saying?' Blind panic flared into temper before Elaira could think. 'Have done with coy riddles. I won't stand being toyed with.'

'Very well.' Lirenda peeled off her gloves, her enameled veneer of deportment at odds with the rough-cut timbers around her. 'The Koriani Prime commands your assistance to create a living double who can pass in close company for Arithon of Rathain.'

'Ath's infinite mercy!' Horror leached the color that cold had burnished into Elaira's cheeks. Intuitively leaping ahead, she cried, 'You can't be thinking of young Fionn Areth as the unwitting subject of a shapechange!'

The ruthless affirmation Lirenda returned shocked beyond reach of all tact.

'What's happened to pity? *Has our Matriarch gone mad?* That's a monstrous act for an order whose founders aspired to healing and mercy!' Elaira interlocked whitened fingers. Hackled to a suicidal, insubordinate rage, she shivered, well aware her explosion must not venture beyond the briefest word of hot protest. 'What need on Ath's earth could be dire enough to cast a child into the breach?' Koriani interests, set against the Alliance's stew of power and trade intrigues made deadly ground for a game piece. 'Save us all; Fionn's naught but a herder's son with a blameless life left ahead of him.'

'You know that's not entirely true.' The superior tilt of Lirenda's chin lent her beauty the chill of an ice sculpture. 'Our scryers know the boy's birth prophecy. Why shouldn't the destiny groomed by our order be the one to lead him from obscurity?'

'That's heartless arrogance!' Elaira shoved away from the trestle, too riled to pause for the clash of disarranged contents. 'Whatever stakes ride on Arithon's life, no end could justify such callous misuse of an innocent.'

'The preservation of civilized society is all the reason our Matriarch requires. The Shadow Master's powers have already proven an endangerment. Your regrettable attachment won't change that hard truth.' Lirenda picked a caught thread from her hem, eyes narrowed with sulfurous disdain. 'Soft sentiment aside, this child is a cipher who happens to owe you a life debt. Your Prime is now laying claim to his sacrifice for the greater good of the Koriani Order.'

The statement held threat like a dagger in a sleeve, a signal warning that far more was at stake than the straightforward demands of obligation.

Bitterly, Elaira wished back the bleak anonymity of the darkness. The light left her exposed. Like a cat who toyed with a wounded mouse, Lirenda tracked every erratic interval of stopped breath, the telltale tremor of each flinching nerve as her adversary capped the volcanic burst of her fury. Both women were too well versed in the risks of venting unbridled emotion. Between them, only the tallow dip quavered. Too numbed now to notice the cold, light-headed as an unmoored leaf, Elaira battled the tug of a proscribed love that might recklessly come to cost everything.

Her streetwise instinct for survival gave warning the stillness had lasted too long. She moved on, bent, and tended the fire. While her cast shadow capered like a demon at her heels, she laid two logs of sweet-burning birch over the coals of spent kindling.

'What earthly good will be served through creation of Arithon's look-alike?' Elaira fenced words with dispassionate tact. 'No one familiar with his Grace's presence could mistake his living character for a herder boy wearing s'Ffalenn features.'

'We intend no replacement.' Lirenda laid her thin gloves on the trestle and arose. 'Morriel wishes Arithon of Rathain taken captive. To that end, she has ordered that his double should be raised as the decoy to draw out his enemies. If Fionn Areth stands trial for the Shadow Master's misdeeds, outraged politics will brand him guilty. We believe the threatened execution of an innocent will lure the Teir's'Ffalenn back ashore. He has an infallible heart, so you say. I know the arrogant pride of his line will not let him suffer another to die in his place. Whichever trait answers, his fate can be played straight into our hands on the puppet strings of his royal-born tie to compassion.'

Elaira felt as if every bone she possessed had been opened to let in the cold. 'What of Lysaer?'

The amethyst rings on fingers and thumb flashed to Lirenda's dismissive gesture. 'Be sure we'll find means to see him detained when the moment comes to take action.'

Dizzy, sickened, all but crushed by despair, Elaira snatched at straws. 'What of the child's parents? How do you intend to gain their consent, and how many scheming truths will you hide on your course to persuade them? It's a dangerous strait, to wear Arithon's face, with the merchant guilds now funneling gold to arm Lysaer's Alliance. Every headhunting band of unattached mercenaries is hiring itself out for the chance to spill s'Ffalenn blood.'

'Why should the boy's parents ever know?' Lirenda inspected the cot, her dark, cut-silk lashes pinned wide in disdain. 'These moorlands are isolated, long leagues from the trade road. Since the child is not yet six years of age, the sealed enchantment to remake his features can be tuned to unfold over time. No ignorant herder would distinguish the change from his normal growth to maturity.'

Outlined by the leaping heat of the fire, Elaira let her stunned silence speak for her.

'You have vowed to serve,' Lirenda reminded. Her regard turned fixed in cruel fascination; as if, deeply hidden, she had a personal reason to savor her victim's unfolding pain.

'I have vowed to serve,' Elaira agreed, her expressionless face feeling brittle as the crackled glaze on porcelain.

The clear, topaz eyes of her tormentor stayed pinned on her, unrelenting. 'But a vow is no guarantee of right action.'

'You *wouldn't* imply I've a choice in the matter?' Elaira let sarcasm ignite into venom. 'There's a herdwife who lets rooms. She's a wonderful cook. Stay here, and you'll get nothing better than a half portion of stewed hare with pepper.'

'Whatever unsavory supper you have planned, you need not share a morsel with me. I've dined already.' Lirenda poked under the mismatched layers of bedding, then fluttered her hand to disperse the dust that wafted from the grass ticking. 'Regarding free choice, your options are limited since the Fellowship can't intervene.'

She looked up, lips curved to a stabbing smile at Elaira's wooden stillness. 'Oh, be sure that's accurate. Morriel made certain no Sorcerers would meddle. The Warden of Althain is this moment immersed in rebalancing the protections on a grimward. His earth-sense is deaf. By the hour he emerges, through your help we'll have Fionn Areth's clear and willing consent.'

Elaira held firm through the wreckage of hope. While the wind moaned and hissed through the thatch overhead, she offset her distress with the tenacity taught by the arthritic old thief who had raised her. What use to dwell on the damning array of insupportable consequences? In the end, she must decide which part of herself to betray: the Koriani Order, with its merciless penalty for oathbreaking, which would obliterate her last conscious vestige of character. Or a price for survival that came dearer than blood: the coin of her love for a man who had become her very self, since one fated evening in Merior. Perhaps worse, she must violate a child's blind trust, misuse his very flesh as the vessel to shape the design of her Prime Matriarch's ordained purpose.

'You'll have a few hours to think and decide,' Lirenda said in dismissal. 'For the interval, I wish to rest.' She flicked out her mantle and arranged its rich folds over the cot's tumbled bedding.

'I thought we agreed, there was no choice to make,' Elaira bit back in acerbity. Staunch in the face of explosive despair, she added, 'If you're dead set on pursuit of this evil, say when you wish to begin.'

'Wake me in the hours between midnight and dawn.' Lirenda plucked out the tortoiseshell combs confining the sleek fall of her hair. 'At least, I presume by then the herder boy's parents will be snoring the soundest in sleep.'

Black hair cascaded in waves down the prim slope of her shoulders. Lirenda fluffed the crimped ends with crisp fingers, then settled herself on the cot, her limbs arranged in exquisite wrapped comfort in the thick folds of her mantle. 'You do stock valerian? Then mix a soporific. The steps will go harder if the boy cries in pain as the shapechanging is sealed. If you agree to keep your sworn faith with the order, be ready when the quarter moon breaks the horizon.'

Lirenda closed lids the delicate, shell blue of a songbird's egg, and settled herself into sleep.

So brief a time to measure a decision that held the potential to rock every facet of the world; Elaira reclaimed her seat and sank down in limp shock at the trestle. Around her, the tools of her trade seemed transformed into items of damning remembrance. Here, the stone knife that Arithon had once borrowed to slice the galls from an oak branch; there, the small chip in the enamel jar she had made in that fateful, first hour he had chosen to cross over her threshold.

Knotted round her wrist, warm against the sped pulse in her veins, she still wore his leather cuff lace, with its unassuming abalone beads. That treasured, soft length of deerhide had been left behind as a thoughtless gesture; in the safety of dreams, she still savored the competent, steadying touch he had used to bundle her rain-sodden hair and tie the length into a plait.

Each detail hurt now with unbearable force.

Elaira gripped the round stone she used for a pestle, a futile effort to draw comfort from the river-smoothed grain of the granite. The crossroads she faced was unalterably plain. She could fail to arouse Lirenda at moonrise; for disobedience of a Koriani senior's command, she would pay the ultimate penalty of losing all ties to conscious awareness. Forced enslavement would follow. The power of her free will would be called forfeit through the bonds of the initiate's oath she had sworn into the matrix of the Skyron aquamarine. That option offered her peaceful surcease through the painless void of oblivion.

The stone under her palms made her flesh ache with cold. Trapped in the knife-edged coils of irony, Elaira squeezed back angry tears. She could not live the lie. If she allowed her spirit free rein in defiance, *that would be the easy way out*. Her personal stake in the future might be absolved on a word of defiance, but Lirenda's uncanny sharp interest had laid bare the fallacy behind simple refusal.

Elaira set down the rock, reamed to the bone by the tireless drafts that sang through the chinks in her casement. She held no illusions. She was expendable. Her cooperative contribution became little more than expedience within the larger pattern of Koriani design. Should she yield up her identity, Morriel Prime would simply appoint her replacement. The Skyron crystal would retain a full record of her memories and experience. Given that borrowed template, another enchantress would study her perception of Arithon s'Ffalenn and replicate her personal insights of his character in her stead. Fionn Areth would come to suffer the same fate. The plot to arrange the Shadow Master's capture would proceed, with or without her consent to become the tool to enact his betrayal.

The jaws of the quandary bit insidious and deep. Elaira raged, helpless before the inexorable truth. She wanted to rise, scream and rant like a madwoman, then break anything within reach in a manic spree of vindication. There seemed no justice, that the greatest sacrifice under her power to make would spare no one and *nothing* but her own peace of mind.

She could wish she had chosen the good sense to die before this sorry hour should visit her. That misery recalled another night in chill drizzle, when she had walked the beachhead at Narms in fear for Arithon's safety. Then as now, she had railed against the order's restraint with seething rebellion on her mind. Unbidden, she remembered the warning a Fellowship Sorcerer had delivered, while in darkness and rainfall, the earth turned in balance, and the tidewaters ebbed from the bay: '*I was sent to you,*' Traithe had explained in gentle sympathy, '*because an augury showed the Warden of Althain that, for good or ill, you're the one spirit alive in this world who will come to know Arithon best. Should your Master of Shadow fail you, or you fail him, the outcome will call down disaster.*'

Tonight in Araethura, the burden of that scrying became as a spike through the heart.

Elaira looked inward in brutal self-honesty and understood that her personal integrity amounted to nothing. The Koriani sisterhood's supreme penalty for willful disobedience was no more and no less than a coward's rejection of responsibility. Her love could heal no one in witless obscurity. Cornered by obligations of duty and emotion, she perceived that the conscious road led to a thorny and desperate gamble. No matter the cost, she might go forward and embrace the most tenuous hope: the odds on a hell-bent course toward disaster perhaps might be routed by Arithon's sharp penchant for cleverness.

Fionn Areth's adult future might rest on that razor's edge of possibility. She dared not entrust a replacement to act for her. Another initiate appointed in her stead might eclipse that slim chance for reprieve. Yet for Elaira to stand vigil to guard that small opening, she must first keep cold faith with her order. She must place both the child and the man in jeopardy to preserve her stake in the outcome. And if the s'Ffalenn gift of ingenuity did not prevail, she must in turn live out the appalling consequence.

Held firm by her street waif's obdurate tenacity, Elaira fixed her resolve.

'I will trust you,' she murmured to a prince whose own burden of adversities drove him unhearing leagues out to sea. 'Before my own peace, I will not bow to failure. You must be the axis upon which Morriel's wicked plot stands or falls.'

Sucked hollow by a dread that threatened to break her, Elaira masked her face in chapped hands. For nearly an hour she listened against hope to the empty wail of the winds. No Sorcerer answered her silent appeal. The Fellowship had once given their promise that Arithon s'Ffalenn was qualified to withstand any dangers that might arise through her bound service to the Koriani Order. Yet their steady, wise counsel lay far beyond reach on this night. She must carry on alone and suffer the risk that their judgment at Narms still held true.

Outside the casement, a spill of washed silver reflected the first rise of the moon. Elaira exhausted every filthy word she knew, then mastered her bitter distress. She put aside the insidious dread, that the Teir's'Ffalenn might prevail; he might escape Morriel's snare and stay free, and never understand or forgive the betrayal she now chose to enact out of faith.

'Ath's mercy on us both, if that happens,' Elaira whispered.

Worst of all, she feared for the agony she might inflict on a man whose strengths had been expended again and again in the desperate cause of necessity. Choked by hot tears that were useless to shed, she rummaged through her stores and boiled water to brew an infusion of valerian. Let her vindictive bustle of noise awaken the former First Senior.

Lirenda stirred, raked back onyx hair, and blinked like a milk-fed lynx. 'There could be compensation,' she murmured as she measured the steel in the junior initiate's smoldering composure. 'When Arithon's taken, you might ask to keep his shapechanged double for your servant.'

Elaira said nothing, the response to such baiting beneath her utmost contempt.

'Well, I might ask for him then. Such a tempting potential for amusement and irony! He could bleach my soiled linens and brush my suede shoes.' Lirenda uncoiled from the cot in disaffected exasperation. Her feint had provoked no sign of insolence or challenge, disappointing proof that tonight the mouse was too wise to play for the stalking cat. 'We'll need an hour to set preliminary wards and ready a circle for grand scrying.'

Elaira bowed her head and gave her, not words, but a curtsy that swept to the floor. There existed no half measures. Her irreplaceable integrity and the desperate plight of Fionn Areth's future must rest in Arithon's hand. Her vindication now stood or fell on the strength of the Shadow Master's character, to defang the jaws of Koriani design and upset the Prime Matriarch's plotting.

# Sentinel

As Lirenda had arranged by scheming design, on the one fated hour when the half-moon arose over the moors of Araethura, the Fellowship of Seven had no hand free to delve into her order's machinations.

Yet the boundaries the Sorcerers maintained to keep faith with the terms of their sworn compact were far from weakened or hamstrung. The wild lands under their charge remained free, and the ward rings they guarded held true. The Law of the Major Balance they lived by had never been breached or broken in two ages of recorded history.

Too often, past and present, the foundation of that integrity remained steadfast at punishing cost. As the presence of the Paravian races had waned, the Fellowship had been left as caretakers of Althain Tower, with all of its attendant perils and additional obligations.

Not the first fortress built, but among the oldest, and by lengths the most well defended, the tower had been raised at the dawn of the Second Age. Those times had seen the world's brightest hope plunge awry, when the primal purity of Ath's song of creation had turned, and the maligned power of the dragons' true dreaming had spawned new life out of discord and conflict. The Paravian races sent to the world to bring healing had been met with slaughter, the shining grace of their example brought down in sorrow and bloodshed. Ripped raw with wounds and punishing grief for a triumph undone in doomed war, the Ilitharis Paravians had fitted and sung the keep's mortised stone with grand conjury. Antlered heads bent, torsos and haunches straining to shift half-ton blocks on log ramps, they raised the blunt-fisted height of this turret at the edge of the Bittern Desert. Here, where the winds still sang their laments for a grasslands spoiled by drakefire, and the spring rains fell too seldom to ease the imprinted horror of the dead torn down in battle; as if the land itself refused to relinquish its pain for the unicorns who had held the front line. Pure spirit made flesh, they were the promise of Ath's unconditional redemption. Conceived as a gift, they had died as a sacrifice, unable to contain in pure love the aberrated creatures that had, for need, been cleansed from the face of Athera: a graceless expedient of survival last enacted by scouring conflagration.

Now the old, warded granite housed the records of those all-but-forgotten years: the Names of those Paravians slain, and the memories of their passing by sword and by fire; by claw and cruel fang; and never least, loss, and bloodshed grown too overwhelming to endure. The tower's fast vaults held ancient wonders. Here resided the bright and dark threads of Athera's history – the faded maps and primal ciphers; the arcane keys to earth's mystery – a detailed body of knowledge that could unlock the bound gates of time. Through the years, as the Mistwraith had choked out the sunlight, the Paravians departed from the continent. On leaving, the eldest centaur guardian had oathsworn the Fellowship Sorcerers to safeguard the legacy of Althain Tower's contents.

That trust had endured for five centuries. Nor was the tower ever left untenanted those beleaguered, rare times when its Warden passed beyond reach of the earth link. The mighty endowment of vision he possessed had been ceded by the last Paravian. Its tied power married Sethvir's awareness to all that transpired in the world. Few could have endured that grand flux without losing their minds to insanity. Sethvir had done more, had embraced and encompassed the whole by surrendering every aspect of his being to address the needs of Athera.

Forgiveness for an unspeakable past had come to him in that moment, that his heart had mastered the challenge.

On the night hour Fionn Areth fell prey to Koriani design, the discorporate Sorcerer Luhaine kept displeased vigil. His ingrained penchant for fussy detail could never match Sethvir's broad perception. A cast-iron pessimist, Luhaine grumbled. He had never loved solitude; his natural preference bent toward comforting lectures when he faced untidy loose ends. Nor would he compromise his innate, plodding accuracy, a trait that often abraded his colleagues to fits of exasperation.

Had Luhaine still been enfleshed, he would have vented his stress by stuffing himself on muffins and butter. Left to life as a shade after a catastrophic mishap, he could only shed aimless static, his frustration built to a fulminating crescendo by the second month of his tenancy.

'Far better for everything if those meddlesome Koriani had never set foot on Athera!' He hissed past a balustrade in the Second Age library, goaded to a brisk, snapping breeze since the Prime Matriarch's instructions had dispatched Lirenda to Araethura.

Elaira's renewed role in her sisterhood's affairs boded the worst sort of trouble. The Fellowship Sorcerers were already spread thin. Their concern now redoubled since the Koriani had failed in their first attempt to take Arithon as their order's string-puppet captive. Luhaine knew best of any: their ancient Prime Matriarch would not abide her defeat. The enchantresses' current intervention in Araethura gave warning of a new strategy, with no Fellowship Sorcerer at hand to track their intent through surveillance.

Nor was Luhaine complacent. He spun drafts of chill air down seven flights of stone stairwells, whipping the settled dust of two ages into tight, frenzied spirals in his wake.

He stormed past the landing, a miniature tempest that shrilled through the cracks in the strapped oak doors to the storeroom, which held the Second Age talismans and artifacts. Among the locked coffers and shrouded sword hilts, alongside the ash shafts of arrows with points of chipped crystal, and the gem-studded shields whose arcane properties included wards for the banefire of dragons, he sought the one item fashioned by Fellowship hands.

The golden hoop had been wrought by Ciladis the Lost shortly after the Mistwraith's invasion. The gentlest, most sensitive of the Sorcerers had endowed his creation with a cipher of scrying to forecast the revival of pure sunlight.

The device had never been observed to perform its prime function. Sethvir had banished the sunloop to storage on the sorrowful hour when Ciladis had passed beyond contact, his search to locate the vanished Paravians ended by his disappearance. Sore grief remained. Despite repeated efforts to trace Ciladis's whereabouts, no Fellowship Sorcerer ever learned what fate had befallen him. Althain's Warden had shelved the sunloop out of heartache, an inadequate gesture to distance the agony of an unresolved mystery. Remembrance still haunted, of the small-boned, walnut-skinned colleague who had immured himself for silent, futile hours, sifting phantom auguries and combing the infinite loom of existence for reprieve from the fogs of Desh-thiere.

Luhaine sought the sunloop now for reasons of acid efficiency. In that hour, the device's fine-tuned spells of observation offered his best means to trace the events that might threaten the land held in trust by the Fellowship's compact.

Through the advent of midnight, the first-level storeroom lay cloaked in darkness, its sole arrow slit masked by the board ends of shelving, and Sethvir's scrawled spells against rot. Cold air poured in, an invisible black current that sheared like a blade across Luhaine's purposeful presence. The tidy, round chamber held no trace of mice, only the bracing, spiked scent of frost riming the stalks of dried meadow grass. Sethvir might disregard his personal appearance, but his catalogues and antiquities were maintained with immaculate care. No dust layered the floor. Ancient records did not molder, and the oiled leather scabbards on ceremonial knives did not deteriorate from dampness.

Luhaine wended his way between the bound coffers and wrapped armrings, bagged in flannel against tarnish. Here lay the massive, gold-banded horns once carried by centaur guardians, the rims chased in runes with Names of forests that remembered the first song of Ath's creation. Amid crowns once worn by Paravian high kings, and the crystal and bone flutes the Athlien played to honor the rise of summer stars, Sethvir kept the jeweled scepter that had belonged to the brightest of their kind, Cianor, who was named Sunlord. But in this hour of the world's need, the fire-wrought bronze dragons that bore the spoken powers of prophecy lay dormant, sleeved in pale silk. In passing, Luhaine shared the echo of memory, a sigh out of time for past glories.

Even he must bow to the history enshrined in this place. The treasures housed at Althain were the stuff of past legend, with their marvels and wonders, and their uncanny perils to entrap the unguarded mind. Luhaine ranged the collection in wary respect, despite his hurried passage.

He found the sunloop in its mother-of-pearl stand alongside the whistle the Masterbard, Elshian, had carved from a tine of Shehane Althain's right antler. The placement gave testament to Sethvir's remorse. One blast from that whistle would frame a note to defy time and space, and dispatch help from the tower's current Warden. As if, in hindsight, the Sorcerer who normally shouldered the post regretted not sending the artifact with Ciladis against the perils of an unknown journey.

Too late now, to wish past mistakes might be salvaged. The Fellowship Sorcerers themselves were shorthanded, with one of them crippled, and another, even now, gone past the veil into mystery. Blunt-nosed, ever-practical Luhaine settled, a viselike well of cold coiled around the sunloop's filigree stand. A nimbus of light clung and shimmered off the delicate metalwork. The cast-gold circle still held the unearthly elegance that set Ciladis's character apart. Abalone inlay threw off misted rainbows where the far-flung spells of vision ranged dormant, a whisper of suggestion smothered within a cruel and unanswering silence.

As always, the radiant grace of the sunloop made Luhaine feel coarse as old smoke. Still worse, the faint sense of shame and betrayal, as he tapped into the gossamer web of fine energies and changed the significating rune from a figure of joy to one that harkened to discord. Light plunged into darkness as the spell's focus reversed its original polarity.

The scene that formed in the loop's clouded center showed him the prelude to ruin . . .

The visioning revealed the white-marble floors of Avenor's grand hall of state, rebuilt from ruin in Tysan. Under the costly, clean glow of wax candles, two high officials conferred.

One hulked solid as weather-beaten rock from his hard-bitten years of field service. An unshakable presence, with his clipped beard and wedged forehead, Lord Harradene had served as Etarra's Lord Commander at Arms since the death of his predecessor at Valleygap. The other beside him, who flourished a sealed requisition, was dark haired and neat as a ferret. His gold-trimmed surcoat might be cut fine as a courtier's, emblazoned with the sunwheel of Avenor's royal guard, but the sword and steel dagger that hung at his waist showed the battered, dull scars of hard fighting. Young for his high position at court, he spoke with a brisk, sharp-tempered confidence, to which the older veteran deferred.

'I presented your petition.' A furtive flash of teeth, though the eyes remained inimically still as poured nickel. By the sliced vowels of the man's accent, Luhaine identified Sulfin Evend, lately invested as the supreme commanding officer to spearhead Prince Lysaer's armed offensive.

The speaker resumed with a focus that matched his purposeful bearing. 'His Grace of the Light has heard your appeal. Your men will not quit the field before winter without chance to snatch back the victory.'

Lord Harradene's thatched eyebrows rose, dislodging a scowl like a logjam. 'We'll get more troops? That's laughable! They can't possibly arrive before the cold weather puts fodder in critical shortage.'

Sulfin Evend's nerveless response affirmed his reputation for sharp swordplay and vicious strategy. 'His Grace won't send troops.' Light shifted like misted pearl over his silk as he strode past the niche of a casement.

Harradene flanked like a shambling bear, canny enough not to waste words.

But Sulfin Evend quickened for challenges; his razor-sharp smile provoked. 'Avenor's treasury's too tight. The trade guilds all know it.

They've seized up their ears and their purse strings. The ones with paid spies are all squalling like stoats. Can't be more funding until our Prince of the Light inspects his shipyard at Riverton and sets the launchings there back on schedule.'

Before Harradene's bull-roaring protest gained force, the lean fingers, with their ancestral gold ring, snapped up the sealed state parchment. Sulfin Evend's grin widened, oiled as the fox with a chicken clamped in its teeth. 'Don't let your joy spoil the fun. The Prince Exalted has granted you means to roust out your pesky clan renegades. You now hold permission to set fire to Caithwood to clear out the cover that hides them.'

Lord Harradene's beard split in half as his jaw dropped. Then he shouted and clapped Sulfin Evend on the shoulder. 'Tell your Exalted Prince I'll be more than delighted to oblige.'

Uncoiled like fluid ice from the gleam of the sunloop, Luhaine flounced in agitation. '*Prince Exalted*,' he muttered. 'Aren't we getting high-and-mighty, and just a *bit* large for our breeches?' He spun off the shelf, rattling the wired fastenings of Sethvir's oak-paper tags. 'And *burn Caithwood?*' Luhaine seethed on toward the locked and barred door, hurled his essence through the keyhole with a force that raised a shrill whistle. 'Just try, you self-righteous, arrogant ignoramus! It gives me *great* satisfaction at last to be handed the Ath-given license to stop you.'

Past the stubs of the candles in their wrought-iron sconces and down the foot-worn spiral stair, Luhaine ranged like a self-contained wind devil. He passed the commemorative statues of departed Paravians arrayed on the tower's ground floor. The poised flutes of sunchildren lent fretful voice to his passage. Stone unicorns reproached with their fixed, sightless eyes, the shine on raised horns like the gleam of dropped tinsel in the late-day glare through the arrow slits. Massive, carved centaurs endured in marble majesty; their jeweled caparisons and linked chains and gold braid rippled to Luhaine's distress.

The Sorcerer despaired for the timing.

Threat to Caithwood must perforce overshadow his concern for Koriani malfeasance in Araethura. Sethvir was beyond reach, gone to stabilize the protections that guarded the grimward in Korias. Since time flowed differently inside that dire vortex, no one could predict his return. Disdainful of oaths, Luhaine whined past a carved cornice.

A blind fool would have realized Prince Lysaer would not recall his crack troops from the field. Not without one last flourish to bring Caithwood's clan defenders to their knees.

Luhaine slipped through the wards that secured the trapdoor leading to Althain's dungeon. His annoyance raised hoarfrost on the black-iron pull ring, and the oiled chains and counterweights geared to move the massive slab sang back in disturbed notes of dissonance. Sieved through by uneasy, ozone-rank air, Luhaine flowed down another stairwell. He emerged in the blue-tinged glow cast by the third lane focus circle the Paravians had inlaid in white quartz and onyx over a bedrock foundation.

With candles unlit, and the vaulted ceiling in darkness, the pale marble walls loomed like a veil of merle smoke. The spiraling flux of the lane's background flow raised tingling eddies against Luhaine's unshielded spirit. He passed the carved gargoyle that overlooked the east radiant, its beeswax candle left untrimmed by Sethvir in his rushed hour of departure. Luhaine claimed his favored perch on the statue that stood watch pointing north. Between its curved horns and the bronze socket for the taper, he poised, a distilled point of cold amid the faint web of light swirling from the pattern's vortex.

Ath help the Fellowship's straits, risk of fire in Caithwood left no other option than to recall Asandir from the field.

Luhaine spun thought and imprinted the fine energies like a spider spinning in light. His summoning ward stitched ephemeral frequencies into Name for the colleague he wished to contact. A Fellowship ward seal tied the call to the east wind, for guidance. The construct of bound energies would disperse down the third lane, then be picked up in turn by the seasonal breezes that ranged across latitude, driving the currents that spawned the cyclonic winter gales. The shed leaves of turned trees and birds in migration would imprint the resonance of the spell and expand its range, until the designated Sorcerer heard his Name in the air and responded.

Small use to mourn, that no such broad summoning had managed to locate Ciladis.

Brooding to the bent of his maudlin thoughts, Luhaine cast free his small binding. The Paravian rune circle flared delicate gold as the field magnetics of Athera accepted the minuscule burden of its signature. Last anyone knew, Asandir was at Methisle fortress to help contain another outbreak of *methuri*. Unless the aberrated creatures held the isle under siege, the Sorcerer should return to Althain Tower on the tide of the lane surge at dawn.

## Autumn 5653

# Pawn

On the moors of Aracthura, the stars wheeled their inexorable passage across the black arc of the zenith. Midnight gave way to the small hours of night when the child, Fionn Areth, stirred and opened his eyes, unsure what dream had awakened him. The loft he shared with his siblings hung in darkness. Two older brothers had filched the wool blankets. Left to snuggle in a tangle of stale sheepskins, the younger ones lay twined like two mop-headed puppies.

Outside, the winds scoured over the moorlands. Drafts hissed through the boards where vermin had hollowed out nests in the thatch. The rafters smelled of damp, musty broomstraw, and the grease left from boiled mutton stew. Fionn Areth shoved back his tangled black hair. The ends needed cutting, an embarrassment he resisted, since his mother would use the same shears she kept sharp to fleece the steading's herd of goats. Ungroomed as the wind-tousled ponies on the moor, the boy levered himself up on one elbow.

'Pisshead,' grumbled the small brother he disturbed. 'D'you have to thrash about like a nanny with the gripes?'

'Stuff your face,' Fionn whispered. While his sibling muttered and subsided back to sleep, he listened, certain that someone nearby had just spoken and called him by name.

Below the loft ladder, the banked embers in the grate flared sullen orange as cold air eddied down the flue. The single-paned casement held whorled scrolls of frost, etched brilliant silver by moonlight. No one else stirred. His father's saw-toothed snores rumbled uninterrupted

21

through the downstairs doorway.

The call came again, no true sound, but a beckoning presence that prickled the nape of his neck. Fionn Areth shivered. He sat up. A prodding compulsion would not let him keep still. Careful not to jostle the sprawled limbs of his brother, he clutched his nightshirt against his thin chest and slipped from the warmth of the sheep fleece. His bare feet made no sound as he padded through darkness and groped his way down the ladder.

Gripped by the force of an uncanny summons, he reached the ground floor. A pause, while the arthritic herd dog by the hearth raised her muzzle to lick at his fingers.

'Stay, Bounder,' he commanded, and crept on.

The dog slanted her black-tipped ears and whined. She was too well trained to disobey. Quivering unease rippled her brindle coat, and her liquid, dark eyes tracked the boy's progress past the baskets of carding left piled beside his mother's spinning wheel.

'Bounder, stay home.' Impelled by an urge that seemed spun from dreams, Fionn Areth pushed up the door bar and latch, and silently let himself out.

The stone step was ice beneath his naked soles. More curious than cold, the boy stooped to scratch his scabbed shin, the one he had scraped while chasing a cat over a deadfall. The wind flapped his nightshirt and tousled his hair. Dry leaves still clinging to the crown of the scrub oak stirred like the whispers of old men. The ash trees beyond were already shorn. Their shadowy, thin skeletons flung contorted silhouettes against the stone wall by the hay byre. Stars burned in the autumn-still silence, while a risen half-moon lit the grass to a glittering, frost carpet of silver.

A little afraid, Fionn Areth fetched the stick he used to feign swordplay. His birth augury promised him battles and fame, or so he bragged when the herd families gathered and his peers drove the goats in for counting.

Already he could swing with a force to whistle air. When he slashed against the wind he imagined the sharp whine of tempered steel. Pressed on by his spurious craving for mischief, he decided to visit the orchard. On such a mad jaunt, he could fight shadow armies and spar with the crabbed boughs of the apple trees.

He gained a new scrape scrambling over the wall. His mother would scold if she noticed. Nor would she let him run wild at night, undressed and without his warm jacket. The gusts bit and burned across his bare skin. Fionn Areth gnawed his lip, unsure. All at once, his bed in the loft seemed more inviting than battering a stupid old branch with his stick.

'Fionn Areth!' The call came pure as struck glass out of the air just behind him.

The boy spun around.

A lady in shimmering violet robes stood limned in the moonlight by the hay byre. She cupped a jewel as cool as a glacier. Her long hair was braided and pinned into a coil the gloss black of a raven against her cameo skin.

Fionn Areth cried out. His terror redoubled as the crystal in the lady's hands exploded into blank darkness. Sight became blinded. Ears became deaf. Launched to reflexive flight, the boy dislodged a rock from his perch on the dry wall. He overbalanced, fell, while the blackness expanded. Swallowed and suffocated, he never uttered the scream that struggled to burst from his throat.

Elaira caught Fionn Areth's limp body before the child struck the ground. 'Merciful maker, that was ill done!' She glared past the dark, tousled head now cradled against her shoulder.

Unperturbed, Lirenda shielded the Skyron aquamarine inside a fold of her mantle. 'I'd think you would thank me. If not, then you needn't have argued my preference for sending him out on valerian.'

'You could have broken his bones, or much worse,' Elaira snapped. 'If he takes any harm from your cavalier handling, may Dharkaron Avenger demand due redress in his name.'

'Don't welter in pity. We have what we came for.' Dark-lashed topaz eyes examined the child's slack form with contempt. 'You'd rather he shouted and roused the herd dogs to alarm? I'd thought we agreed that our task would go better if the household stayed soundly sleeping.'

'The poor boy's half-frozen,' Elaira flared back. 'If we had to draw him outside through a dream summons, you could at least have left him a moment of clear thought to find himself suitable clothing.'

'Loan him your jacket if you fear he'll take cold.' In malice, her senior added, 'You're sure to catch fleas for the kindness. Though given the uncivilized life on these moors, I suppose you'd have memorized the sigil of remedy for vermin out of necessity.'

'We don't have your city population of rats,' Elaira pointed out, her jacket already stripped off. 'They breed more pests than the herd dogs.'

Lirenda picked a disdainful course between the broomstraw and briars, skirts raised to keep runs from the silk and her work satchel slung from her shoulder. Her kid boots she could do little to spare; the path through the orchard was a rut of gouged mud, slotted by goats and heaped with dung dropped by the steading's milch cow. 'Just don't lag behind. We need to be finished before Althain's Warden completes the new seals on that grimward.'

Elaira ignored the admonishment. 'Shame on us if Sethvir's awareness is all that holds our order to common decency. Forgive me,' she added to the child as she wrapped his sturdy form in the fleece still warmed from her body. On impulse, she retrieved his dropped practice stick and leaned it against the wall where he could find it. 'The seeress who cast your birth prophecy was most wise. You'll need to start young to master the skills of a warrior.'

'Stop wasting time!' Lirenda poised by the canted gate of the orchard. Sulky irritation sharpened her face as the moorland elements played havoc with her costly clothes and fine grooming. 'I want the seal wards in place before our young decoy sits up and recovers his wits.'

'Should he waken, I'll manage quite well without help.' Mud and briars posed Elaira no hindrance as she followed in Lirenda's footsteps. She dawdled where she could, well aware that her peer's flighty nerves stemmed from worries of Fellowship vigilance. Asandir and Traithe might be engaged in distant lands across the continent. But the discorporate mage Luhaine would not stay diverted at Althain Tower for one second longer than Sethvir required to emerge from the grimward and reclaim the lapsed gift of his earth sense. Until Fionn Areth yielded willing consent, one Sorcerer's notice could make ruins of Morriel's plot.

Elaira dragged her feet as much as she dared, though she guessed her effort was futile. Lirenda was always meticulous in allowing a wide margin for mischance. The spiteful satisfaction offered small recompense, that for each minute the Koriani senior was delayed, the wind tugged wild wisps from her knotted, jet braid and chapped her pampered complexion.

Under the blown ink boughs of the orchard, the grasses lay tangled and damp. Frost-withered dock stalks crunched underfoot. The faint, silver foil of moonlight stamped through knotted trees and lapped light upon shade like ethereal wisps of cast floss. The wind smelled of winter in waiting. Each ice-sharp gust razed and rattled through the bare branches. The stars were snagged pinpricks, their beauty no boon on this night. In Elaira's dark thoughts, cruel rain and black storm should have dogged every step since the demands of her vows forced compliance. Had her voice been her own, she would have screamed for Fionn Areth to waken and flee, and call down the wrath of his family.

No saving slip of good fortune arose. The stayspell held the boy quiet without mishap, until Lirenda found a clearing where a deadfall had been hewn down for firewood. The hollow where the roots had torn free offered shelter and natural seclusion.

'Lay the child there.' The disdainful flick of a finger indicated the boy's head should orient northward. Under the waning moon, Lirenda seemed a carved ivory figure, mantled in ebony silk. She opened the satchel and unveiled a weighty, terminated rock crystal, chosen to channel the spells of transformation. The bared quartz seemed a flame's heart sculpted in ice, paned in frost-polished facets. Like every major focus held in Koriani service, the stone had been mined on a world far distant from Athera. The etched mapwork of its natural formation had been buffed to a polish to obviate any unwanted features of character. The jewel was conformed as a tool, subservient to the order's dedicated cause to further the needs of humanity.

Sick at heart, Elaira settled the boy on a soft patch of grass. 'He'll need to be conscious,' she reminded. Dread lent her a stripping new edge of hostility. 'That's if you're still planning to go through the pretense of asking for his consent.'

'Wards first.' This was no sheltered sisterhouse tower, where the metallic, formed rings of runes and spell seals laid down permanent defenses. Lirenda shot back a reproachful glance as she knelt beside Fionn Areth. She set the quartz point to one side, then unpacked an assortment of thin copper rods. These she assembled into a pyramid. A wide silver ring stained black with tarnish formed the structure's apex, its position arrayed above the boy's forehead. 'Set the perimeter guard spells,' she commanded, her lashes half-lidded in concentration as she placed the large crystal point downward in the cradling band of dark silver.

Elaira accepted the four directional tetrahedrons of cut hematite, then the pairing rods of black tourmaline whose screening virtues would defend against psychic attack. She cupped the burden of each separate mineral and invoked the focus of her personal quartz to recharge their properties of alignment. In a ritual older than written memory, she began the steps to lay out a circle of protection. East, to south, to west, to north, she demarked the points of direction. The tourmaline wands she placed like black arrows beyond the outer perimeter; at the base of each one, the hematite tetrahedrons, heavy to the hand as dark lead. If the properties of the tourmaline became overwhelmed, the next crystal in line would send harmful influence to ground before any breach could disrupt the innermost circle.

Invocation and seal raised a small spark to stand sentinel at each point of the compass. '*Anient*,' she intoned, the Paravian invocation for unity. The summoned flecks of light bled round the ring in an active spiral, deosil. South met west, west meshed to north, north arced to east, and east closed the circle back to the point of origin, aligned by the glimmer of the polestar. A soft halo of phosphor glowed faintly pink and joined the four arcs into an unbroken figure.

'*Fariennt tyr*,' Elaira invoked over the traced runes of the set seal. 'So be this construct, as I have defined.'

'Begin.' Lirenda engaged the energy closure, and the wardspell meshed into completion. She leaned over the rods supporting the large crystal and scribed a symbol into the base. A whispered invocation and a breath keyed the cipher's activation. The quartz flared a sultry, actinic yellow. As its matrix imprinted and magnified the transmission, a pale flower of illumination touched the skin at the center of Fionn Areth's forehead.

Lirenda murmured the incantation to waken only the mind. The words of her litany were framed in a tongue whose origins came from a world far removed from Athera.

Young Fionn Areth opened his eyes, but not to the autumn night he remembered. No moon shone above him, no stars. He did not perceive the bare branches of the fruit trees that shivered in the moan of cold winds. The spell seal cocooned his conscious awareness, and his senses stayed suspended, netted into disembodied quiet. The etheric web of a jewel's charged lattice enclosed his sight like glass walls.

'Where am I?' His voice fell echoless and flat, splintered against that imprisoning silence.

'You are in dreams, but awake,' a woman's voice answered. Her vowels struck through consonants edged with high-pitched harmonics.

Too distanced to be frightened, Fionn Areth searched the planes of the crystal's lit heart, trying to make out the speaker. 'Where are you?'

'Here.' Her laugh rang like glassine slivers of ice. 'You shall see.'

A shimmer bit through the blank vista of perception; and he made out a dim figure muffled in dark purple silk. Veils of softer violet light shimmered amid the radiance thrown off by the activated quartz. Fionn Areth beheld a dark-haired woman with a face of marble serenity. She had lips of bleached coral and hands too ethereally fine to have toiled at birthing goats, or spinning fleece, or stirring an iron pot to render raw fat into tallow.

'I know who you are,' the boy ventured, determined not to be craven under her steady regard. Her brows were fine arches, and her eyes the rich, ruddy amber of the whiskey his father bought from the backwater traders. 'You're an enchantress. Why have you brought me here?'

'To ask if you're ready to lay claim to the fate your tribe's seeress prophesied at your birth.' The lady's amused gaze seemed to measure him. 'Are you brave?'

'My sisters don't think so.' Fionn Areth gave their opinion his scornful dismissal. 'I had to climb to the top of the ash tree by the brook to show them that girls don't know anything. Are you like Elaira, the enchantress who saved my life the night I was born?'

'She is there,' said the lady, and pointed.

Fionn Areth noticed the second figure then, this one clad in the laced leathers and jacket she wore when she called bringing simples. To the woman he recognized as a friend, he need not cling to appearances. 'You look sad. Why is that, lady?'

Inside that prison of crystalline walls, Elaira stepped forward. The spectral light made her features seem strained. The rich, russet highlights in her hair were erased, as if she had become but a shadow of herself in that place of carved ice and moonlight. 'I am saddened, Fionn. The time's come when I'm asked to give over your birth debt to the higher power of the Koriani Order. This cannot be done without your consent, but Lirenda insists you are old enough. She would have you speak and arrange for the terms of your sacrifice.'

'What do I say?' Fionn Areth asked, plaintive. 'I could give her my knife, but Father told me if I lost it, I couldn't have another for a year.'

Elaira wiped leaking eyes with the back of her wrist. 'Keep your knife, Fionn. The lady wants nothing more than your word. Say if the Koriani Order may lay claim to your fate in my stead.'

Fionn Areth's eyes narrowed. 'She wants this, the lady?' He considered with the gravity of a child too young to respond as an adult. 'My mother would say to give nothing for free. What will the Koriathain trade in return?' His voice firmed as he stiffened his small spine. 'I'm going to need an expensive, sharp sword.'

'You shall have the very best, fabricated by the hand of a master armorer.' Lirenda gestured encouragement with the magnanimous assurance of one who had never eaten someone else's table scraps or missed a night in cosseted comfort. 'Not only that, but a tutor at arms will be sent to Araethura to school you. Give your consent, and our bargain is sealed.'

'Do I get a scabbard too?' Fionn Areth said, distrustful enough to be shrewd.

'A scabbard, of course, child.' Impatient with young ones, Lirenda tapped her foot. 'You have only to give your consent.'

'Then yes!' Fionn Areth followed his shout with a whoop that rattled his dream to echoing exuberance.

But for Lirenda's twisted plot, plainspoken speech was insufficient. 'Swear, then. Heart and mind, give me your formal permission for the record to be set in crystal.'

Elaira turned away, unable to watch, as, still fearless, the boy gave away his autonomy. The words of his oath rang through the frost-cloaked silence of the night. In too brief an instant, the act stood complete.

Tied by consent to a Koriani quartz focus, Fionn Areth now belonged to the order as irrevocably as any young initiate inducted for vows of life service.

In the orchard, released from the grip of spelled dreams, Fionn Areth's body fell limp inside the fleeces of Elaira's borrowed jacket. For a drawn-out moment, the unnatural trance kept his pupils dilated, their depths an uncanny, fathomless black in the frigid spill of the moonlight. Then Lirenda inscribed the seal for deep sleep. The boy's wide, staring eyes hazed from focus and fluttered closed. His lips parted in a sigh, while an uncaring breeze bearing winter in its weave flicked the jet ends of his hair. A pen stroke ruled against darkness, the beam of pale light from the crystal seemed to drill through his unmarked forehead.

'He's sworn oath of debt.' Lirenda's satisfaction held triumph, a chilling indication that Morriel's command matched the grain of her personal involvement. In a guarded move, she raised lily-scented hands and tugged the hood of her mantle to shelter her high-cut cheekbone. 'Not even the Fellowship of Seven can argue the validity of a vow sworn and sealed as a bargain.'

'You should be proud.' Elaira made no effort to curb her raking sarcasm. 'Your victim is only six years of age, and a tutor and a sword are a paltry return for enslavement.'

'Given the choice of a life raising goats, I much doubt the child's going to care.' Lirenda's rose lips bent upward in secretive satisfaction. 'Don't think you're finished here.'

Elaira huddled, shivering. She knew very well that the coming spells of transformation should not require her presence. This spiteful play to force her participation framed a more than disturbing oddity. Raised on the street as an orphaned child, Elaira had never welcomed authority. Now, her deep, primal instinct gave warning: the strained relationship shared with her senior had somehow grown beyond the surface disparities of social station and character.

A closer study of Lirenda's demeanor revealed where rice powder and eye paint could not quite mask her evident strain. The flesh over its beautiful template of bone seemed fine drawn, as though for weeks her sleep had been restless and her thoughts a turmoil of distress.

In a sure burst of insight, Elaira said, 'What has Arithon s'Ffalenn ever done to antagonize you?'

Lirenda recoiled. Her amber pale eyes flicked up in a match flare of rage. 'How dare you!'

Chilled as she was, and sick with self-loathing, Elaira damped a grin of ripe devilment. 'Touché. He's difficult. I know far better than any. Was his influence why Morriel set you aside in disgrace?'

'That's none of your business!' Lirenda's frustration rankled, that she no longer wielded the ranking prerogative to quash prying questions and insolence. 'My right to the privileges of prime succession shall not stay in question for long. Have a care. Cross me again, and your lot could be miserable.'

'I'm miserable now,' Elaira pointed out. 'You'll need to threaten with more imagination if you're expecting me to act cowed.'

Lirenda stroked manicured fingers along the inverted base of the quartz point. 'You will provide the focal point for this shapechange.' Her catty, three-cornered smile showed teeth. 'As you once did for Morriel's scrying at Narms, you will shape me a reflected image of Prince Arithon's features. Your memory will provide the template to guide Fionn Areth's transformation until the last seal is complete.'

'Touché,' Elaira repeated with self-derogatory bitterness. 'Beware whom you cross. The s'Ffalenn royal line has never taken kindly to meddling interference from anyone.'

'I know.' Lirenda turned away and began to link the first sigil. 'If you're worried for the child, the strength of our order will eventually come to shelter him. His skill at arms can be turned to training the boy orphans for posts in the garrisons and the trade guilds' guard.'

'A fine, useless talent,' Elaira bit back, her pain and her rage too large to mask behind shallow insults or platitudes. 'If Arithon's to become the Matriarch's captive, and Lysaer's Alliance clears the woods of the clanblood who harry the trade routes, pray, who will be in the market to pay hired swords? No one will have enemies to burn out and kill.'

'That's enough!' Lirenda's stiffened posture gave warning. 'We have a task to finish.'

Elaira tossed her a gesture to begin, one that on street terms doubled as obscenity. 'You first. The opening sigil is yours, thank blazes. I'll enjoy the moment to the fullest when the fire of s'Ffalenn vengeance grabs you by the throat and strikes at every one of your weaknesses.' She knelt in chill grasses, arms wrapped to her chest, then closed her eyes to recall the male face that had long since become a branded part of her being. Before she took the irrevocable last step, she let fly the full force of her anguish. 'Just so you understand, when we're done, I'm going to buy gin from the first herder I see and drink myself blind, heaving drunk.'

A knifing blast of north wind shrieked over the byre and rattled the trees in the orchard. Elaira engaged the focusing properties of the small quartz crystal at her neck. Then, with the cold roaring through her like a cataract, she framed Arithon's likeness with all the detail she remembered: the fall of sable hair and the sharp angles of cheekbone and jaw. The lips which smiled too seldom, and the eyes, their green depths masked by ironies and a guarded defense too wary for most minds to fathom. Through a hazing shimmer of tears, she set perfect recall of the Shadow Master's features into the ice veils of the crystal suspended over Fionn Areth's face.

She tried to hear nothing else but the wind, to let the thrash of whipped branches batter all thought from her mind. But her fickle ears gave her clarity instead: every rolling, studded consonant and silver-toned vowel of the shapechanger's incantation. She clamped her fists against her clenched jaw, torn screaming inside by the insidious progression of the spell. Lirenda remained unmoved throughout, her diction as carved frost while the crystal came alive at her bidding. Hard bars of light beamed from the quartz point. These fell and diffused a spectral mask over the unformed features of the child. The dichotomy burned: through the light-cast image of Arithon's face, a sleeping boy's innocence, forced passive under ties of cold sorcery. In despair born of horror, Elaira stood witness as the webwork of whorled power matched spell rune to set seal, then sank like ribboned wire under blameless skin and bone, there to seed the slow elements of change.

Small differences which would not conform over time struck her now with wounding impact. As if in this one, trapped moment of existence, she must relive each nuance of Arithon's form and measure the particulars anew: these grubby boy's hands would mature to match the broad, sturdy frame of the herder stock of his birth; fingers that would never spin the filament of bardic melody from the wire of a lyranthe's string. The unmarked right forearm and small, callused palm, to stay unmarred by the welt from the light bolt which had seeded the geas of Desh-thiere's curse. The wrists and the ankles that would remain unscarred, never torn by the welded shackles and chain imposed by the blood feud with s'Ilessid begun on the worlds beyond West Gate. Elaira could but ache for the discrepancies that enemies would miss in the engrossing, blind fervor of hatred.

Through revulsion that mounted into lacerating pain, she knew that

Arithon's likeness could never make even a second-rate substitute for
the character that was the living man.

Long before the finish, when the flare of blue light sealed the ending
cipher, her eyes spilled shamed tears. Undone at long last by her pity
for the boy and her remorse for the suffering her decision must come
to cast upon the grown man, Elaira knelt with blinded eyes. The hot
bloom of power extinguished in the heart of the crystal; the small star
of light vanished from the center of Fionn Areth's forehead. Elaira knew
the critical moment was past. The shapechange to replicate Arithon's
appearance had been accomplished beyond any chance of reprieve. Years
might elapse before this night's work reached completion, but the final
outcome was set.

Grief for that irrevocability lanced her. Sickened for the part her
vows had forced her to play, Elaira missed the odd look of riveted
fascination Lirenda fixed on the template image of the Shadow Master
still imprinted within the focal matrix of the dimmed quartz.

The portrait was one drawn by love, in each accurate detail a true
map of Arithon's character. Through the interval while Elaira recovered
herself, Lirenda beheld the features of the man as few others living had
seen him. Hooked to inadvertent, rapt fascination, she strove to brand
the s'Ffalenn likeness in mind for a later, more leisurely study.

Night by then had waned to the charcoal hour before dawn. The moon
rode the horizon like yellowed ivory, with all but the brightest stars
faded. The grasses lay rimed and bearded with new frost, and the wind
dropped, leaving the air gripped fast in a stilled and penetrating cold.

Elaira awakened to the fact she was shivering. 'We should be gone
before the herd dogs awaken.'

Lirenda stirred, gathered up the chill quartz, and folded the supporting
rods. 'We can't abandon the boy to find his way home.'

Galled that anyone should think her so callous, Elaira stood up. 'I'll
carry him. A veiling of stayspells over the house would be a kindness
as I take him inside. The wife's goodman sleeps lightly, and there's a
crippled old sheep dog who sleeps on the rug by the hearth.'

'No doubt the stair squeaks as well?' Lirenda said, scornful.

'They'll have a ladder,' Elaira corrected. 'These are simple folk, who
trust a dog before locks and keys to safeguard their threshold.' She
shook out damp leathers and knelt to gather up the sleeping child.
'The cottage that has stairs isn't found on these moors. Babes sleep
with their mothers until they're old enough to climb.'

'Well, don't leave your jacket behind out of pity,' Lirenda dismissed, an acerbic lift to her brows. 'I'd prefer that nobody knows
we were here.'

'Don't worry.' Elaira straightened up, a set to her jaw that betrayed her cutting distress. 'The last thing I want is to acknowledge our night's work to anyone with a conscience.'

She turned toward the hay byre, the boy's limp form cradled awkwardly in her arms. His face was his own. No trace showed yet of the profile he would bear at maturity. Through the course of those years, Elaira resolved, she would be far from Araethura. And she had misjudged, when she warned her senior that she would get puking drunk. The sickness inside her need not wait for spirits. Once Fionn Areth was tucked safely back in the loft with his sleeping siblings, she was going to snatch shelter in the nearest thicket and heave her guts inside out.

She reached the cottage doorway, churned-up with self-loathing that made her long for oblivion. As she freed a stealthy hand to raise the string latch, she wondered whether the boy would ever learn that his face was the gift of Koriani intervention, or if he would someday come to know the s'Ffalenn prince he was designed to decoy to captivity.

# Daybreak

Still infirm, confined by her weakness to her wide bed in the Capewell sisterhouse, the ancient Prime Matriarch receives word from her lane scryer that the first step in the plan to take Prince Arithon captive is in place; Lirenda's task in Araethura is accomplished, and Fionn Areth's transformation a sealed future . . .

Clad in muddy leathers and a green reck of bog mire, the craggy Sorcerer, Asandir, rummages through Sethvir's pantry at Althain Tower; over rinds of molded cheese, stale bread, and one forlorn sack of rice that hosts a new litter of field mice, he makes disposition to Luhaine, 'Since I can't survive on air and conundrums, that settles our dispute. You'll stay. I'll go to Caithwood and serve due redress against townsmen who believe trees can burn for the cause of misguided politics . . .'

Just returned from an errand in the Kingdom of Havish, Mearn s'Brydion, youngest brother and envoy of the clanborn Duke of Alestron, makes landfall at Middlecross; informed there that Prince Lysaer plans a royal inspection of the Riverton shipyards, he smiles in sharkish pleasure, then chooses to play the advantage of timing and let his demand for an inquiry coincide . . .

**Autumn 5653**

# II. Infraction

Asandir thumped back the lid of the battered wooden clothes chest, which held the few personal effects he kept at Althain Tower. Craggier, and cross-grained as beached driftwood from the harrowing events that had taxed him to infirmity last season, he chose a formal cloak of heavier wool, a deep enough blue to be taken for black, with borders edged in bands of silver foil ribbon. The rich color brought out his lingering pallor.

To Luhaine, attendant upon his preparations like a cloud of morose, glacial air, the detail became the caustic reminder of a convalescence cut short by necessity. 'You know you ought to be resting.'

Asandir paused. Recovery had left him just short of rail thin, the creases around his eyes knifed into dry flesh, and the rubbed ivory knuckles of each capable hand embossed through his blue-veined skin. Yet workworn as he appeared, the Sorcerer who shouldered the Fellowship's field work retained his uncompromised will. His gray eyes held the etched clarity of lead crystal, as he countered, 'You could have asked my leave when you lent Sethvir the use of my black stallion.'

'In fact, I could not,' Luhaine said, plaintive. 'At the time he departed, you happened to be comatose.'

That line of defense died into an unsettled quiet, neither of the Sorcerers anxious to pursue the confrontation head-on. Though Sethvir spent little time in his private quarters at Althain Tower, the chamber was cluttered as a junk stall. Mismatched chairs had acquired heaps of horse harness. Two marble plinths were piled with snake skins, spancel hoops of oak, a tea canister missing its top. The spare pallet held skeins of wool yarn, brought in to remedy a straw hamper stuffed to bursting with holed stockings. Their odd, distorted imprints came and went in the dance of shadows cast by the candle set on a tin pricket.

Asandir knelt on the scarlet carpet, a lit form against the gargoyle shapes sculpted from the surrounding gloom. Nor did he accept Luhaine's comment as he rummaged through the bottom of the clothes trunk. 'Even unconscious, I would have heard you speak. You know that.' He unearthed an item that chinked metallic protest.

'At least with no horse we forced you to rest until you regained strength to walk. Do we have to go through this all over again?' Luhaine huffed aside from the grounding threat of steel as his colleague raised a black-handled hunting knife and tested the edge with his fingertip. 'If you knew how it felt to live as a shade, you'd stop doing that.'

'You're right.' Asandir snicked the blade back into its sheath. Draft fluttered the dribbled candleflame as he added the knife to his select pile of necessities. 'Out of body, I'd have small use for skinning a deer.' The invasive smell of vacancy and dust made petty argument seem a welcome affirmation of life. 'An unnecessary sacrifice, whatever your case, had you taken a moment and asked the bread mold and field mice to feed anyplace else but the pantry.'

Luhaine snorted. 'The Prime Matriarch has launched a new plot, and you're bound in knots for a miserable few rinds of spoiled cheese?'

Asandir stood. Large boned and imposing as an ocean-flying albatross, with the same matchless grace when he moved, he folded one arm and tucked his other fist beneath the clean-shaven jut of his chin. 'Luhaine?' he asked with piercing mildness. 'What under Ath's sky have the Koriathain done this time?'

Stripped by a glance keen enough to shear granite, Luhaine regretted his impulsive choice to broach that particular sore subject. 'I don't know yet,' he hedged. 'Once Sethvir returns, I'll hope to be freed to find out.'

Asandir grunted. Unfazed by his colleague's transparent evasion, he knelt and bundled his supplies into a weatherproof blanket roll. 'Whatever unpleasant hunches you harbor, I could venture to Capewell and confront the Prime's purpose headlong.'

'That shouldn't be necessary.' Rather than reveal the shattering ill turn, that Morriel's interests had broken Elaira's retreat at Araethura, Luhaine breezed toward the doorway. 'Sethvir ought to find his way back before solstice. Koriani sigils can't trace Arithon at sea. Since his fleet sailed from Innish with provisions to last through midwinter, the matter should bide until then.'

And must, Luhaine raged in concealing silence; with six camps of Alliance armed forces blocking the safe sanctuary of half the clan bloodlines in Tysan, Caithwood's trees perforce must claim preference.

Blessedly practical, Asandir tied the last thong on his bundle and snuffed the failing candle. 'Then I'll enjoy being spared the company of a bedridden harridan with a grudge.' Faced with a second, urgent transfer by lane force, then an overland journey to be started afoot, the bent of his thoughts swung full circle. 'Sethvir needs my horse before I do in any case. That stallion's the only flesh-and-blood creature I trust to stand firm through a flux of grand conjury.'

Luhaine called in droll gloom through the doorway, 'I'm forgiven in advance if you're tossed off the back of some clansman's borrowed hack?'

Asandir straightened, a lank scarecrow in black leathers. His shoulder-length hair shone like loomed cloud in the fading light through the arrow slit, and his sudden, rare laugh shattered echoes off the ancient Paravian stonework. 'You're absolved if I happen to fall off a nag.' He raised a lean leg, kicked the trunk shut, and strode clear of Sethvir's belongings. 'But for the rest of the secrets you're brooding like eggs, I'll hold mercy under advisement.'

The sundown surge of the lane tide carried the Fellowship Sorcerer southward to Mainmere. The circle that delivered him lay under the gloom of near dark. Stars bloomed like punched sparks on a cobalt zenith, and wind-combed, thin cirrus overhung the ink waters of a restless, tide-roiled estuary. Asandir stood motionless and allowed his reeling senses to reorient. More worn from the transfer than he liked to admit, he sorely missed the warm presence of his horse, and the satin black shoulder that usually braced up his balance on arrival.

He willed himself steady, while around him the raised play of lane force subsided. The bleached, weathered runes laid into rinsed bedrock sparked and flashed as the discharge bled off, actinic white to a whisper of blue, before fading through the spectrum of ultraviolet into the ordinary night.

An owl called, mournful. Beyond the stilled circle, the tumbled-down ruin of the Second Age fortress slept under its shrouding of vine. Past memory ran deep through the rain-scoured granite. Where the wide grasslands of the coast joined the sea, unicorns had once run like braided light on the hilltops, gathered for their seasonal migration.

The songs of the sunchildren followed their course, while the joyous feet of the dancers had circled, waking the mysteries of renewal each cycle of equinox and solstice. The coming of mankind at the dawn of the Third Age had woven new thread through that ancient tapestry. From Mainmere, at midsummer, to the landing at Telmandir, the painted boats of townborn celebrants had rowed south under torchlight for the water festival. Each year, humanity made way for the passage of mysteries that were Ath's gift to this world, their presence too bright for mortal endurance, outside of those families born into the time-tested strength of clan lineage.

Now, no burning torches etched the wavecrests like copper engraving. Nor did the memory of vanished powers linger, except in the unquiet peace of broken stones, and in the leashed sorrow of the Sorcerer who addressed them to settle the trace resonance of his urgent passage. He paid the abandoned fortress his respect. Despite the precision of Sethvir's kept records, and the writings of the Paravian loremasters, Mainmere wore legends whose truths were no man's to unlock.

The centaur mason Imaury Riddler was said to have placed a wisdom in each of the megaliths set into the primary foundation. At need, stone would answer, latent power unchained in whispered response to the step of the one who faced the hour of Athera's most deadly peril.

Tonight, for Asandir, the dark rocks stayed silent. Only the storm-tattered crowns of the beech trees spoke on the stiff inland breeze, the first warning of winter borne on the dying taint of turned leaves.

Nor was the Sorcerer alone in that place.

As he strode from the quiescent white runes of the focus pattern, three forest-bred clan scouts stepped from the brush in cool, unafraid expectation.

'Kingmaker,' greeted the erect elder in the lead. 'My Lady Kellis, Duchess of old Mainmere, bids you welcome. In her name, how may we serve the land?'

Asandir's arched eyebrows showed surprise for the pleasure of the company. 'She knew I was coming?'

'She believed someone must.' The lead scout reached the Sorcerer, arm extended for the customary wrist clasp. In clipped speech, he explained, 'The grandmother seer who made simples at the Valenford crossroad was burned last month by the Alliance of Light's Crown Examiner. She screamed as she died that her vision showed burning trees, and sunwheel soldiers wielding torches that opened the sky to a rain of scorched blood. The duchess was worried Caithwood might be threatened. She set us to watch in case help came.'

'Daelion have mercy for the wrongful death sentence given that misfortunate seer! I'm here,' Asandir affirmed, taller by a head, his blanket roll rammed under one elbow. Shock lent a quickened spring to his step as he let the scouts lead him onward.

'So is Caithwood endangered?' asked the woman among them, bitter with worry as her lanky, cat's stride carried her through the maze of razed battlements.

Asandir followed through tufted bull grass toward the steep, crumbled stair to the sea gate. 'Yes. Though the sealed orders from s'Ilessid were sent from Avenor only this morning. You have horses?'

'Even better.' The woman pointed toward the broken-down archway that funneled the hail of another voice, cautious above the muted splash of water off a bulwark of tide-washed stone. 'We've got a smuggler's boat from the river delta waiting. Her master's a canny old fisherman who's moved raided goods out of every deep cove in the forest. Where do you wish to make landfall?'

His descent economical on the mossy, cracked slabs of the stair, Asandir gave his answer. 'The haven you have nearest a camp with fast horses, if I'm to spare more than green trees. How many refugee families are hiding south of the trade road?'

Just as sober, the scout captain replied, 'All of them.'

Asandir's response held barely leashed rage as the small party arrived on the landing. 'Then thank that seeress's unquiet shade for our chance of keeping them alive.' He stepped from the crumbled breastwork into the battered fishing sloop held in waiting by a boy draped with cod-fragrant oilskins.

'Grace, for your presence,' he murmured in blessing, then assumed the dew-damp seat by the thwart. The bilge swirling under the boards at his feet stank of fish, and the prow held a heaped mound of trawl nets. To the balding, barrel-round man who surged to loose jib and mainsails, Asandir made direct inquiry. 'Would you mind being loaned an unfair advantage?'

The fisherman's teak face split with laughter. 'Ye'd call down a gale? Toss up yer dinner, don't come crying to me.'

'How much can your craft handle?' Asandir wedged his blanket roll out of reach of chance spray, while the boy and two of the duchess's older scouts clambered in at his side. The woman stayed behind, her farewell brief as she shoved off the battered craft into the rip of the tide.

The dour helmsman grunted. 'I'll warrant my dearie's canvas and sticks'll take more abuse than your belly. We'll do ten knots, if the old besom's pushed.'

'So, we'll see.' Grim since the news of the witch's burning, Asandir touched the scout silent. He chose the heading for the helmsman himself, west-northwest, for the cove that lay nearest the trade road, which carved a diagonal scar through Caithwood and the low dales of Taerlin.

The fisherman stared at him, his meaty hands guided by instinct as he hauled in the mainsheet. Still regarding the Sorcerer, he called to his crew, a grandson or nephew by the look-alike stamp of young features. 'Lad, clew in the foresail.'

His corded shoulders bunched as he made his line fast and hauled the boat's tiller to port. The bow swung, sheered up a dousing sheet of spray while the headsail and main clamored taut. The hull rolled, settled into a steep heel, bashed and thrummed by the sucking drag of ebb tide. One squinted eye on the set of his canvas, the fisherman spoke at last in mild censure, 'Can't keep yon heading until the slack water at midnight. Current's too stiff, no matter the lay of the wind.'

'So we'll see,' Asandir repeated, his lean mouth pared thin with irony. He tucked his blanket roll under his shoulders, then reclined against the shining, wet wood and shut his eyes.

The older of the two clan scouts huddled into his fringed jacket and repressed the urgency to speak out of turn and disturb him.

Asandir sensed the man's fretting. His speech came mild against the hammering tumult of wave and wind as the sloop fought the rip for her heading. 'If your people have no horses tucked away near that landing, rest assured that I can make other arrangements.'

'That's well.' Relieved to the point of embarrassment, the scout shifted aside for the boy, who moved forward, dripping, to find a cranny amid the wadded netting. The scout's fox-thin features stayed trained toward the Sorcerer, pinched with frowning concern as he strove for politeness and subtlety. 'In case you don't know, there's an Alliance war camp billeted next to the trade road.'

'No setback at all.' Asandir seemed removed, even distant, the seamed map of his features written in calm that verged on the borders of sleep.

That appearance deceived. Behind closed eyelids, the Sorcerer extended his awareness. He cast his trained consciousness outward in a web that missed nothing, from the skeined lines of force that guided the winds, to the deeper tie strung between moon and water, which commanded the pull of the tide. His mind tracked each wavecrest. He knew the purl of scrolled sound as salt water splashed into foam, each single event one word in a language his ear understood. He sensed the invisible, lightning tracks of magnetic current where the earth's lane forces coiled through Mainmere and trailed a cascading signature of charged energy through the deeps.

His listening encompassed the fish in the shoals, and the gulls that bobbed, wing-folded in sleep on the swells. The sands of the seabed were singly made known to him, each grain by Name, their collective chord of existence laced through by streamered beds of kelp and live coral. The breadth of his thought embraced the four elements, and all else that touched upon the path of the fishing sloop's crossing. To each varied and interlocked facet of existence, he gave solemn greeting, his tacit recognition a gift that awakened acknowledgment in turn. Through the vast stillness his announcement of presence engendered, he made known his need, then asked leave for the sake of the green trees threatened in Caithwood.

His answer came back as a white flood of power that sang through flesh and bone in sweet resonance. On a phrase, he could have bidden the sea to launch from its channel and punch through the sky like a fist. Fish and birds, all would rise for his cause; even the staid stone and sand on the bay floor would unbind in an explosion of volatile force.

Such was his strength, he asked none of these things.

Gentle as a filament spun out of starlight, he aligned his intent: to see one patched Torwent fishing sloop to the far shore, his course a shot arrow of desire that blazed west-northwest and marked the wide cove where the trade road from Valenford crossed under the eaves of the forest.

To that vectored appeal, he set mindful stays of limitation: that no life be harmed, and no bird become tossed or ruffled in flight from the recoil of contrary elements. That the tide's rush through the estuary not falter, nor the anomaly his need would spin through the world's wind unleash a stressed vortex that might seed a storm or drought later. He understood the flow of power, from force of element to breathing life, in all aspects of interlocked complexity. Rooted in wisdom, he shaped the offered gifts of the land with a feather touch of clean subtlety.

Nor did he invoke any power but his own to spark his laid pattern of conjury. To an adept of his experience, the charge contained in just one grain of sand could lay waste to the entire planet; therefore, he would not disturb the spin of any one fragment of matter. A single deep breath, a precisely aimed thought, he engaged the quickened awareness of his spirit and plucked, like a harp string, the subliminal current of light and sound which gave substance its material polarity.

Power answered through the greatest recognition of them all, the chime of affirmation that defined his own Name on the loom of unified existence.

'*An*,' whispered Asandir, the Paravian rune one that marked all beginnings since song first gave rise to Ath's creation.

A ray of touched force flicked the air like a moth's wing and deflected a kink in the clasp of gravity that linked Athera in her partnered dance with the moon. At Asandir's directive, the twist became a spiral that touched water and air as a tuned breath might test the highest note on a flute.

Then change threaded through the coils of his conjury. The barest, soft shudder brushed the planks of the sloop as the bay arose in a swell of gleaming phosphorescence and nudged her. Changed breeze kissed her sails to a sullen flap of canvas, and the Torwent fisherman shot straight.

'Ath's deathless mercy!' he gasped, shaken white as the helm went slack in his startled grasp.

Eyes still closed, his face wholly serene, Asandir smiled. 'Not so far from plain truth,' he said gently.

The wave at the sloop's stern continued to build, rolling smooth and green, but not menacing. The small craft sheered ahead like a bead spilled down glass, her course west-northwest, though the tide roiled southward, its flow unimpeded by the loop newly wrought through its ebb. Then that first shifted breeze built into a gust that backwinded the headsail and clapped the main into banging frenzy.

'Slacken the sheets!' cried the captain to the terrified boy. 'Move smart, don't you see? This unnatural wind's going to swing dead astern.'

'Twenty points to starboard, in actual fact,' said Asandir in mild correction. He opened his eyes, which shone silver-gray as a rain pool touched by the moon. 'I thought you'd want steerage, since the standing wave we're riding will bear us on at eight knots. You'll get just enough breeze to keep headway.'

'Aren't like to toss supper, then.' The fisherman rubbed his rope bracelets, his unsettled nerves transformed to trembling awe. 'Who could've guessed? You've made us a passage so smooth a babe wouldn't roll off the foredeck.'

'We'll make landfall by daybreak,' the Sorcerer affirmed. His seamless act of grand conjury was dismissed as nothing outside of the ordinary. 'Bucking the tide to windward, my spare clothes would get soaked. No one could have snatched an hour of sleep, besides.' He folded lean arms, chin tipped to his chest, evidently prepared to take his own counsel in earnest.

The boy hauling lines stood stunned and mute; the seasoned clan scout gripped the rail in queer exultation. His forestborn sensibilities could scarcely encompass the rolling mound of water that propelled the sloop steadily toward Taerlin.

An hour slipped by. The moon rose in the east like yellowed parchment. Asandir dozed, while tide and wind danced, flawless, to the unseen tapestry of his will. The fisherman manned a helm that answered his touch like poured silk, and for him, the resentment cut sharply as grit ground into a wound.

'How can you sit like a beggar and accept this?' he charged the clan elder, crouched at the thwart with his hands lightly clasped to his weapon hilts.

The younger scout spun from his contemplation of spelled water with a fierce, quelling motion for silence. 'Mind your talk, man! Dreaming or not, yon Sorcerer hears what concerns him.'

'So he does. Should that matter?' The fisherman jabbed argumentative fingers toward Asandir's motionless form. 'If wind and tide can be turned on mere whim, why not act in kind to save children?' Longtime friend of the clans, he had given passage to the pitiful bands of refugee families who fled Tysan to take sanctuary in Havish. 'Your people deserve better help in misfortune.'

'Oh, be careful,' charged the elder, tense now as the scout, and braced with same trepidation. He, too, had known the grief of the young mothers, and the misery of small babes displaced and chilled and afraid.

The toll of ravaged lives brought by the Alliance campaign to drive the clan presence from Caithwood showed no sign of abating. Dogged by an outrage too sharp to contain, the fisherman would not stay silent. 'Why not choose to spare human lives instead of a stand of inanimate trees?'

Asandir turned his head, his cragged features not angered; yet the opened, gray eyes were tranquil no longer. 'Our Fellowship has no license to use power to influence mortal destinies.'

'That's a damned heartless platitude!' the fisherman shot back. 'The ships stolen from Riverton will scarcely be enough to stem the inevitable slaughter.'

Wholly mild, Asandir saw past temper to the seed of a deeper, more subtle anguish. 'I see you've met his Grace of Rathain?'

The fisherman responded as though goaded. 'Our village sheltered him when he crossed out of Tysan. He came soaked to the skin, exhausted from beating a course against head winds. He'd been ill. A blind fool could see he was in no shape to make passage, and the fat prophet with him was too seasick to offer him any relief at the helm.'

Asandir drew a slow breath, the rise of his chest the sole movement of his frame as he marshaled his patience to speak. 'Arithon of Rathain is safely offshore where the Mistwraith's curse cannot touch him.'

'Rumor claims you opened a grimward in his behalf.' The fisherman twisted the braided, rope talismans that circled his sun-browned wrists. 'I say, if that's true, you could have done more, and more still for those families hounded by Prince Lysaer's campaign of eradication. Folk born with mage talent suffer as well. Not just forest clansmen in Tysan will be dying while you gad about sparing trees.'

The scout gasped. 'Merciful Ath, we're not ungrateful! Kingmaker, forgive. Clanblood has asked for no intercession.'

Denial or warning, the words came too late. The Fellowship Sorcerer gripped the thwart and sat up, a stark, lean shadow against the silver-webbed foam sheered up by the sloop's sped passage. He linked his large-knuckled hands at his knees. His unshaken calm in itself framed a dangerous presence, while the waters off the stern rose green at his bidding, and the winds curved the sails, whisper light and responsive to the tuned might of his will.

'Our use of grand conjury is not subject to whim,' he stated. 'Crowned heirs who bear royal ancestry act as our agents, under the strict terms of the compact our Fellowship swore with the Paravians.' That intercession spanned more than five thousand years, when sanctuary had been granted to humanity at the dawn of the Third Age. As if that agreement was not all but forgotten, or its tenets misconstrued for the gain of town politics, Asandir resumed explanation. 'Prince Arithon's born compassion is our granted legacy, no less than King Eldir's gift of wise temperance. As rulers confirmed under Fellowship sanction, they have the right to receive our assistance. But they must ask. And then we can act only by the Law of the Major Balance, inside a prescribed set of limits.'

A brief pause, while the Sorcerer's terrible bright eyes turned down and regarded the linked clasp of his hands. 'I opened a grimward for the sake of Prince Arithon's safety,' he said, steel and sorrow gritted through the admission. 'Thirty-eight sunwheel guardsmen pursued him inside, driven on by duty and hatred. Of those, only one escaped with his life. Willful pride and rank ignorance brought the rest to their doom. Their deaths were chosen, not forced.'

'Why could you not save them?' the fisherman pressed. 'The power was yours.'

'The power is mine,' Asandir affirmed. 'But not then or ever, the arrogance to enact intervention!' He sat sharply forward, stern as chipped granite. 'The compact was sworn on mankind's behalf, but its tenets were designed to guard the land. Paravians hold our vow against greed and misuse. That grants no authority to impair human freedom, however the trade guilds cry tyranny. We take no license to enact judgment on others, *except as the weal of this world becomes threatened*. Town councils ignore this, yet the bare facts remain. Humanity exists here on sufferance. Forget at your peril! Your race would be homeless without our sworn surety that Athera's great mysteries stay sacrosanct.'

'You're saying—' began the fisherman.

Asandir cut him off, ruthless. 'We who are bound know better than any how a yoke chafes and how spirit can languish without the grace of free will. By Fellowship *choice* no child born under sky in this place is destined to live as a pawn!'

'I don't understand,' the fisherman whispered, mollified at last by the unsheathed pain he had aroused in the Sorcerer who confronted him.

'You couldn't know, but our people remember.' The gray-headed clansman stirred in the uncanny stillness that locked the air, between the lisp of turned waters and the matchless, steady breath of the wind, which even now held to the intent of Asandir's unimaginable control. He glanced at the Sorcerer, who granted a sharp nod of leave. 'The Fellowship of Seven were drawn here, long past, by the dreams of the dragons that no mind in creation can deny. They were charged and tied by a ritual magic wrought from drake's blood to ensure Paravian survival. That oath taking gifted them their knowledge of longevity. Record among the clans says their lives stay the course of a service that could last to the ending of time, if need be.'

'The drakes claimed us through the flaw of our own violence, and by the stain of slaughter already on our hands,' Asandir qualified. 'We were called as a weapon to destroy the drake spawn that could not be weaned from unconscionable killing. Only when Paravian survival is assured will our lives be set free once again.'

There passed an interval when only the wind spoke. The gruff, weathered fisherman could not bear to turn his head and suffer Asandir's magnanimous acceptance. Moonlight edged the tableau in metallic, cold lines, and the lisp of the waves carried the salt tang of primordial beginnings. The Sorcerer sat, rock patient throughout, while the occupants of the sloop who still owned their mortality came to terms with the history of his Fellowship.

'I have never understood,' the young clansman ventured, made bold by the Sorcerer's mild tolerance. 'When the drake spawn were contained, or put down in the wars, were you not given liberty to break the drake's binding and reclaim your own will once again?'

Asandir looked up, his eyes bleak with remembrance and his shoulders too straight against the moving weave of the wavecrests. 'We had only the *methuri* left to attend. They posed a minor threat, and Ciladis, who hoped to transmute their warped offspring, saw no need to hasten their final disposition. We all failed to foresee how our obligation would compound on the hour that refugee humanity discovered this world of Athera.'

Now the fisherman looked puzzled. Perhaps out of weariness, the Sorcerer chose to unveil the depth of the Fellowship's tragedy. 'The terms of the compact reinstated the drake's binding all over again.'

'But why?' The fisherman's incredulity clashed like snarled thread with the Sorcerer's shaded, soft sorrow.

'Because once, we were a large part of the reason why humanity needed refuge in the first place.' The confession was a bald-faced statement of fact, devoid of self-pity or guilt. Long since reconciled to the horrors of past history, Asandir seemed a figure carved out of oak. The sliding foam of the wake, and the stitched needles of reflection the night's moon and stars streaked across heaving waters were made to seem transient by comparison. 'We impair no man's free will by the Law of the Major Balance, that we are charged never to violate. But our peril in these times holds a razor's edge. For you see, if the Mistwraith's curse that drives the two princes to hatred wreaks havoc enough to break the compact, the guiding charge of the dragons will reclaim us.'

The pall of the quiet held nothing of calm, as the old fisherman shrank at the helm of his boat, and the boy slept, oblivious, curled in oilskin. The elder clansmen for decency averted his face, aware as his younger scout was not of the weight of admission forthcoming.

'You don't understand, still?' Asandir's remonstrance came gentle, grief and tears bound in iron that must meet the crucible unflinching. 'It's the fear we live and breathe with each waking hour since the Mistwraith breached South Gate five centuries ago. If mankind upsets the balance, if the grand mystery that quickens renewal and life here ever comes to be threatened, then the Paravians who are Ath's blessed gift to heal the dragons' transgressions will fade from Athera forever. Our Fellowship will be called to act ere that happens. We will be forced to carry out the directive the drakes set upon us, *to ensure Paravian survival no matter the cost of the sacrifice.*'

All the subtle, deft power that now cajoled wind and tide potentially turned to destruction, even to arranging the extinction of the one race whose wants and ambitions brooked no restraint. Spoken language fell short of expression; renewed anguish seemed chiseled by the unconscionable memories stamped into the Sorcerer's lined face.

Yet no resonance of bygone sorrow could prepare for the impact as Asandir concluded in stripped pain, 'We could be forced to call forfeit our redemption, don't you see? *If the compact is broken, then our Fellowship must enact the annihilation of humanity all over again.'*

Only this time, they would be compelled to the act of mass slaughter in full cognizance, causation set into a lens of awareness refined by ten thousand years of arcane wisdom. Sympathy faltered, and language became inadequate to express that stark weight of remorse. No mercy could soften the cruel edge of the paradox. Nor did means exist on a boat under way for the Sorcerer to recoup his privacy.

Sorry at last for the temerity of his questioning, the fisherman wept at the helm. The clan scouts maintained staid and dignified silence, while Asandir showed the grace of a humbling courage to grant them release from embarrassment. In unstudied diplomacy, he settled back on his blanket roll and slept.

He stirred once, at slack tide, to fine-tune the draw of the water that propelled the sloop on her heading. No one spoke to interrupt his dialogue with the elements. The boy was roused up to handle the lines, and the sails were hardened upon the opposite tack to steady the keel against the shift in the current. When the last sheet was cleated, the Sorcerer moved his blanket roll to windward. Again he dozed, his large hands abandoned like driftwood in the hollow of his lap.

Dawn brightened the waves to opaque, leaden gray. Gulls dipped and called against a sky like smoked pearl, layered with shredding drifts of light fog. The merciless light touched the Sorcerer's face and revealed his exhaustion, demarked in pinched lines, and sharp angles where the bone pressed against his thinned flesh. No one rushed to be first to awaken him, even when the shoreline of the estuary loomed ahead, notched with the torn sable outline of the forest he had come to spare from the torch.

Asandir needed no prompting in any case. Cued by the lift of the swell as his binding drove the sloop toward shoaling waters, he spoke the Paravian rune of ending and dismissed his ties of grand conjury. Wind and wave subsided. The small craft bobbed in the chop of a north breeze, freed to make landfall under the skill of her helmsman. In the rush toward shore, Asandir proved he knew how to handle a line. Nor was he proud. When the sloop reached the shallows, he thanked the fisherman for his passage and traced a ward sign of blessing on the craft's planks and tackle. Then, with no fanfare, he stripped his dark leathers alongside the two clansmen and breasted the waist-deep surf to set foot on the beach of Taerlin.

The first ray of sunrise spun the mists to raw gold as the party of three pressed into the deep shade of Caithwood.

A day on foot carried the Fellowship Sorcerer and the two clan scouts across seven leagues of wilds to the grooved rut of the Taerlin trade road. Sheltered by brush that rattled in stiff, northern gusts, the small party took covert stock of the Alliance encampment, tents and picket lines and supply wagons packed like a logjam along the verge of the thoroughfare. Here, the patrols of headhunters that swept Caithwood requisitioned their supplies, and caravans en route to Ilswater and Quarn picked up Alliance outriders and the armed escort they needed to ensure their safe passage through the forest.

'They've dug in tight as ticks, since the summer,' the older clansman said, bitter for the timber that had been cut to raise the rough quarters to shelter townborn officers.

The land bore the scars of that thoughtless inhabitancy from the trampled, bare quadrangles cleared for field drills to the grass and vegetation milled into pocked dust by the voracious foraging of livestock. The surrounding ravines had been picked clean of firewood. Streamlets ran turbid from the bucket brigades sent to fetch cooking and wash water, and everywhere, the slanting, low sunlight glanced off the war-polished steel of weapon and helm and horse armor.

'They keep a company of heavy cavalry,' Asandir said, surprised. 'Why? Lancers can't be much use in the deepwood.'

'Those are assigned to move slave coffles.' The elder spat on the clean, growing earth. 'Double bounties are still paid for male clansmen, when they can be captured alive. You didn't know? There's an established auction at Valenford, now, where galleymen go to buy oarsmen.'

A chilling, subtle change swept the Sorcerer's bearing. He knelt, all grim purpose, and untied his blanket roll, while an oblivious horn call sounded below and signaled the change in the watch. Several chattering grooms in sunwheel livery led a clutch of saddled remounts to water, unaware that their routine was watched.

'You don't plan to go down there,' the young scout broke in, his hands gone damp from overtaut nerves as he watched the Sorcerer shake out his formal mantle. The deep blue wool and fine silver ribbon stood out like a shout in the sun-filtered shade at the tree line. 'Archers and crossbowmen guard the perimeter with standing orders to kill. We've lost lives, trying to fire the grain stores in that accursed encampment.'

'We aren't going down there,' Asandir reassured. 'But I find I have a point to make, and that changes the grounds upon which we borrow three horses.'

The young scout sucked in a startled breath, while the elder expressed disbelief. 'What use could we possibly be to your cause?'

'Why should you devalue your worth?' Asandir glanced up, his eyebrows bristled in rebuke. 'Innate power walks in a company of three. Your presence joined to mine cannot but add depth to the impact of my demand.'

Done tying up knots, the Sorcerer straightened. He cast his long mantle around his broad shoulders, then issued his instructions, the lit gray of his eyes turned baleful as storm, and his purpose no mortal's to gainsay. 'Forget you bear weapons. We go empty-handed. I am going to raise a sphere of resonance that will forestall every aspect of violence. Its force will protect, but cannot discriminate. On your peril, remain at my back. Say nothing. Do nothing, no matter what threat arises. The solidarity of our defense will be underwritten by no other power than peace. Above anything else, I need you to stand fast. You must not give way to your hatred.'

Impatient, he broke from the dappled verge of the wood and strode down the slope in plain view. The two clansmen followed. Their bold disregard for enemy sentries with crossbows posed an affront that brooked no appeal.

They were spotted at once, set in sharp relief by the sunlight that poured molten brass over the browned stubble of the hillside. The first surprised shouts were cut through by an urgent challenge. 'Halt, you! Hold fast and declare for the Light!'

Asandir paid the officer in authority no heed. Straight as Dharkaron's Spear in his blue-and-silver cloak, he continued another three strides, his uncovered head like lit ice against the shadowy backdrop of evergreen, and his hands hanging loose at his sides. He stopped as he pleased. His falcon's stare fixed on the party of horses and grooms, at large on the bank of the streamlet.

Down the mild grade, the Alliance crossbowmen knelt and notched quarrels in flurried alarm. They brought weapons to bear, the bitten reflections off lethal, aimed steel chipped glare through the dust-hazed afternoon.

'Stand firm,' the Sorcerer reminded the sweating clansmen beside him. He did not glance at the archers, but maintained his obstinate survey of the grooms' innocuous activity on the streambank. 'On my word, you will come to no harm when they fire.'

'Release at will!' cried the officer, in determined adherence to duty.

The discharge of the trigger latches mangled the drawn stillness, creased by the waspish whine of launched quarrels. Asandir made no move to cast spells. He uttered no word of invocation. Yet the air in his presence acquired a sealed calm, as potent as the tensioned silence that channeled the strike of bolt lightning. The quarrels arched up; descended in deadly convergence. Ten paces before the Sorcerer's stilled form, they crossed the unseen boundary of his influence. The steel tips blurred out of focus, then shocked the charged air into spherical halos of gold sparks. All impetus died. The metal sang out in a queer, wailing dissonance, then dropped like shot stone back to earth.

At the same moment the horses led to drink at the streambed flung up their heads in excitement. Eyes rolling white, they reacted with one mind and shied sidewards. Hooves bit the muddied earth like balked thunder as they ripped their reins from the stupefied grasp of their grooms and bolted upslope toward the Sorcerer.

One last quarrel burst into a splash of fine static and crashed, limp, at Asandir's feet. No others followed. In the crease of the valley, the outraged captain who ordered a second volley toppled out of his saddle. His ranked rows of crossbowmen crumpled also, fallen facedown in a faint. The freed horses hurtled past their sprawled bodies. Glossy and fit, the beasts pounded uphill. Their initial madcap dash unraveled into a brisk trot, and equine ears perked forward, inquiring.

'Choose yourselves a mount,' Asandir instructed the two clansmen. Their appalled uncertainty awoke his swift smile, then a near laugh as a shouting, pointing knot of men convulsed the Alliance camp to fresh turmoil. A wedge of mounted lancers disgorged from their midst, still strapping on their snatched armor and grabbing weapons from squires and page boys. Their rush was spearheaded by an officer in a streaming, loose surcoat. Ahead of his company, he spurred his bay gelding upslope in a howling charge.

Asandir held his ground. Unconcerned, he addressed the loose horses. The sound of his voice soothed their volatile nerves. Reins trailing, the mare in the lead subsided back to a walk. She ambled the closing, final strides to nuzzle his outstretched hand, her equine disregard all but flouting the mounted Alliance horsemen boring in at an earthshaking canter. Forced to swing wide to avoid trampling downed archers, the irate captain lost nerve, if not outrage. He dragged his gelding to a headshaking halt, half-strangled by the folds of his unbelted garment.

'We're borrowing these horses,' Asandir informed. 'They'll come back sound and cared for.' Behind him, the two scouts caught trailing bridles and checked girths, then vaulted astride.

The Alliance officer yanked an arm from snagged silk and gestured an impatient advance. 'Surround them!' The men at his heels reined aside, fanned out, then circled and closed in, lances leveled at the intruders. Reassured as his cordon settled in place, the officer vented his temper.

'What's harm to three hacks, when you've dropped our best squad of
archers in their tracks by means of black sorcery?'

'They're sleeping,' Asandir corrected point-blank. He flipped the reins
over the mare's chestnut neck, tightened the girth, then adjusted the
stirrups two holes downward to accommodate his lean length of leg.
As the captain at arms clapped a fist on his sword hilt, he added, 'I'd
advise you not to try violence.'

'To Sithaer with your counsel!' The captain closed his mailed fingers
and hauled steel in a screeling wail from the scabbard. 'Take them down,
on my signal.'

Time hesitated, blurred, and for one binding moment, a flushed heat
like a wind passed through the nerves and flesh of every man in the
Sorcerer's presence.

A white puff of steam plumed from the officer's mail gauntlet.
He yelled, instantaneously scalded, and cast down his scarcely drawn
weapon. Those mounted companions called to act on his order gasped
in dismay as he ripped back burned fingers. The sharp jerk at the rein
and the smell of singed flesh caused his horse to snatch the bit and kite
sidewards. Loose clothing billowed. A seemingly stray breeze flipped
the flapping surcoat over the disgruntled officer's head. The beleaguered
man fought to untangle himself without tumbling out of his saddle.

Asandir looked on, guileless. 'That attack was unwise. Your men
would do well to avoid your mistake. I further suggest you disband
this Alliance encampment. Pack up your gear and your tents, and let
all the captives in your compound go free.'

Flushed with torment as his blistered fingers bore the weight of the
rein to control his plunging horse, the captain threw back a murderous glower. 'You hold no authority to revoke the direct command of
Avenor's Prince of the Light!'

'Perhaps not.' Asandir flicked the heavy, rich weight of his mantle back over nonchalant shoulders. The silk lining shone numinous
silver against the forest's turned foliage. 'But your s'Ilessid idol has
overstepped prudent limits and threatened the green life of Caithwood.'
Unwilling to grant any pause for rebuttal, the Sorcerer set foot in the
mare's stirrup and mounted. 'Such desecration will not be permitted.
By terms of the compact *I will act.*'

'How? By sending more archers to sleep?' the officer sneered in vain
effort to bolster his men, who were fast losing the courage to stand
firm. 'Or will you just singe a few fingers?'

'More than that. I am going to awaken the somnolent awareness of the
trees.' Asandir closed his heels and stepped the horse forward, trusting
the two clansmen would have the good sense to stay close and follow

his lead. To the captain at arms, helpless to prevent him as he and his party spurred past, he delivered his mild ultimatum. 'On that hour, woe betide any two-legged creature in this forest who unsheathes cold steel or kindles a fire for harm's sake. Remember my warning. The mind of quickened wood has no heart and no conscience, and no kinship at all with the needs of hot-blooded animals.'

Five days later, under pearl mists of drizzle, Asandir walked alone. His scout escort had departed, sent on as his emissaries to inform the scattered clan encampments of Prince Lysaer's intent to fire the timber in Caithwood. They would spread word of the Sorcerer's course of action to avert that looming catastrophe, and also deliver the list of necessary precautions to be observed by every man, woman, and child.

Asandir moved afoot on his long panther's stride, the reins of a different horse hooked in slack loops through his fingers. This mount was a scrub-bred bay with surly teeth and an unkempt autumn coat. By inclination it did not balk at thick brush; nor did it fear to tread through the mossy, rank mud of black mires and the tumbled, round rocks of swift streamlets. In its cantankerous company, the Sorcerer ventured the deepest heartwood of the forest. His sifting search sought out the most ancient tree, the one he must win as his ally to configure and catalyze the awakening.

Such a patriarch tree embodied far more than the accumulated wisdom of advanced years. Its ancient being would span the four elements, the deep taproots twined with earth and water; its upthrust limbs of vigor and majesty would be anchored in the transformative fire of the sun and the windy, wild force of the air. A king tree was not given to reveal its true nature. By the elusive manner of its kind, it could only be found through the riddle of subtle communion with its fellows.

Asandir paused, as he had many times in the dull, gray chill of the morning. He touched the horse still, though it snapped at his wrist. 'For shame,' he murmured into its laid-back ears; then he listened. Amid the splashed tapestry of sound caused by water drops kissing moist leaves, he measured the tap of their fall on the earth. The palm of the hand he held flattened against the trunk of a middle-sized oak became like an eavesdropping ear at a keyhole.

For there was language embedded in the dreaming awareness braided through these acres of live foliage. Word and syntax were tapped in the endless percussion of interlaced twigs. In the sticky, slow river of the sap flowing beneath his touch, the trained mind could read the imprinted secrets that passed from one tree to the next, their world of overlaid messages given amplified breath by the unending conduit of weather: of the wind and the free-falling water.

Nor was the questing touch of this Fellowship Sorcerer any stranger to Caithwood's vast silence. Asandir himself had once bespoken the world's trees to anchor a spell of homing. The signal had been sent to recall Kharadmon from the far-distant world of Marak, from which Desh-thiere had launched its first invasion. The ghost signature of that conjury still lingered, imprinted yet in the live congress of the greenwood. Welcomed by a surge of recognition, Asandir returned tacit greeting. Guardian that he was, and for all that the drake's binding had made him, his listening presence was admitted with forbearing tolerance.

*North*, he sensed. The whispered flow of information meandered that way, from saplings to stands of mature growth trees in full prime, to the twisted, skeletal ruins of the eldest, with their scraping crowns of stripped branches.

The Sorcerer shifted his grip on the reins. He urged the horse onward, then strode like a wraith in his soaked, dark leathers and ducked under a leaning stand of conifers. The loamy forest floor cushioned the sound from his footfalls. Green needles hoarded the insipid wet, each laden branch strung with clutched hoards of diamonds. Asandir bent, picked up the tattered, black shells of last season's cast-off fir cones. *North*, was repeated in the winding energy of spiraled petals from which fragile, winged seeds had departed.

He moved on. The horse at his heels snatched an opportunistic nip at his sleeve, but collided with the elbow he moved to intercept the tender flesh of its muzzle. It subsided, sullen, ears flopping. The squelch of each hoof into saturated moss stamped a pockmark of noise in the liquid symphony of runoff. The rain fell, dimming the light to dull mercury. Asandir's hair held the wet like dewed cobweb, and the shadowy density of the trees wore the gloom like a scene viewed through a smoked mirror.

Set into the layered weave of the wood, a cameo cut from milk porcelain, an ancient beech flagged Asandir's attention. The roots grasped the earth in an embrace that felt boundless and mighty as time, and the limbs framed a vaulted arch for the pearlescent sky. Asandir paused. He gave the old tree his intent, sweeping survey, as if the unveiling powers of his mage-sight would decode the manifest of its destiny in Ath's primal language of sound and light.

This beech he knew from all other beeches, and it was not the one tree that he probed for: the giant that guarded the heart strength of Caithwood, whose prodigious endowment would be masked and cherished, kept hidden like a cached treasure. Ties of loyalty would reside in this tree as well, and for the ingrained pride of its kind, it would not lightly unveil the trust of its sovereign's identity.

Asandir untied the tether rope knotted to his mount's neck and secured the animal to a deadfall. The horse had long since grown accustomed. Too shrewd to expend restless energy, it tipped one shaggy hoof, slanted a hip, and shut its eyes, relaxed to the point where its lower lip dangled. The Sorcerer was not fooled. He was careful to stay well clear of its heels as he settled himself in damp moss. There, he reclined, with his head cradled amid the branching divide where the trunk of the beech engaged its splayed grip on the earth. He, too, shut his eyes, but not to subside into sleep.

Instead, he embraced the dream of the tree, stately, slow, a step in four attenuated beats that marched to the change in the seasons. He drifted there, an immersion into a peace so beguiling, danger lurked for the unwary. The thick crawl of sap lay far removed from the pulse of a red-blooded heartbeat; recast to the dance of a rooted perception, the endurance of a winter's freezing winds became as poisonously gentle as a soundless, caressing fall of snow. All threads of human personality could unravel, lulled into forgetful slumber, and then drawn into deep coma that would spiral beyond the threshold that marked life from death. A mind trained to power embraced at its peril the engulfing, staid majesty of the greenwood.

The Fellowship Sorcerer took precautions and wove a small spell as an anchoring link to the sun. Should he lose his purpose and drift into languor, too much at one with the sugared tides of sap that subsided below ground for winter, the advent of nightfall would recall him. Earth's shadow would snap that frail linkage. A jarring cry of dissonance would run through his nerves as that binding gave way into chaos.

Should he fail to harken, his bones might be found, clutched at length in the ingrown embrace of the beech. His mind would be absorbed, welded into the current of dreaming that made up the leafed weaving of Caithwood.

Asandir let go of awareness without hesitation, without fear, with no marring note of unease. He immersed his whole being into the slipstream of life that was the joined multitude, root, trunk, and bough, that comprised the forest of south Tysan. In fullest command of all that he was, unencumbered by barriers that would cloud true perception, he *became* at one with the gnarled old beech.

The dream claimed him wholly. He was knotted root, tasting the mineral-rich darkness of earth. He was leaves, speaking the summer's endless, whispered promise of tranquillity. In the grasp of winter's gales, he was bare branch and twig, drumming the untamed tempo of the elements. He was pollen, sifted under spring sunlight, and the spanging snap of bitter frosts. The old beech's memory extended like fog past the dawn of Athera's Third Age.

Beneath the layering of the tree's individuality ran the currents that interlinked its being with its neighbors; and theirs, to their neighbors, until the forest's webbed consciousness extended its reach to encompass the far borders of the wood. Asandir rode that tranquil sea of soft whispers, loomed from the speech of blown leaves in the wind, and braided amid the gossamer filaments of root hairs. He sensed flowing water, and the tidal pull of the moon; the warm, flooding canopy of sunlight. He knew the blind, reaching growth of the acorn, and the ground-shaking fall of the elder trunk, claimed by rampaging tempest. The lives of the trees entangled in dream like the trackless silence of owl flight.

Deeper, the flow of arboreal awareness lost its seamless, broad fabric of communion. A directional tide stirred the fathomless depths, spiraling outward in tacit connection with the mystery that encompassed Ath's creation. Within that singing band of unity, Asandir found the signature he sought, encoded in language of sound and light, and steeped in the gentle nurture that was the wise province of trees.

He knew the wood's heart, the given Name for the patriarch tree whose great presence could be called to awaken the dream of the forest, and make its form manifest in the minds of animate beings. Granted the key he required to arrange for the defense of Caithwood, the Sorcerer withdrew his consciousness. A whispered act of will freed him back into separation. Such was his care, he left no disturbed ripple to mar the transmission of spirit language. Within the core wisdom of everlasting silence, that ageless current passed yet on the unquiet air, leaf to leaf, tree to tree; and sky to earth at the behest of sun's fire and cloud's rain.

# Handfasting

Seventy-five leagues northward, far removed from the chill of woodland nightfall in Taerlin, candlelight rinsed the carpeted chamber where the oldest daughter of the Lord Elect of Erdane perched on a brocade stool. Her lush skirts spilled a lake of pale rose silk and gilt trim around her primly crossed ankles. Walnut hair fanned over her shoulders, combed into a shining cascade of warmth by the lady's maid who attended her.

'Oh, Ellaine, to be so fortunate!' From a nearby stuffed chair, with a pert, dimpled chin perched on cupped palms, her younger sister mused on, 'Having a prince ask for your hand in marriage! I could burst from the excitement.'

The tortoiseshell comb slid, streaking sparks of static in the dry air, while the candle's rinsed glow raised Ellaine's skin to a flush and glinted off lips like ripe peaches.

The sister's spun fantasy gushed on through bright hopes and girlish dreams. 'You'll go to Avenor and wear diamonds and ermine, and we will all die of envy.'

'The contract's just signed,' Ellaine contradicted in her sweet, retiring alto. While the maid tipped her head to run the comb at Ellaine's nape, her muffled voice showed apprehension. 'A thousand things could go wrong.'

Her thoughts skittered and fled like dropped pearls. She tried not to think of the horse with the blue-and-gold trappings just arrived, with a train of liveried attendants. The turmoil of their stabling still upset

the evening calm of the yard. Dogs barked in the streets. Every hall in
the mayor's mansion reechoed with the fast-paced dialect of strangers.
Ellaine's damp fingers clamped in her swathed lap. Belowstairs, her
mother and father stood to receive the royal suit and exchange courtly
courtesies until the moment of her formal presentation.

'You could worry yourself silly!' A moue on her cupid lips, the
younger sister masked a giggle as the maid crossed her line of view.
'The trade guilds would scarcely see you lose such a prize! Father's
done nothing but count the coin for your dowry for at least the past
six weeks. Believe it. You're going to stop hearts.' The maid gathered
up the smoothed waves of hair and deftly separated the shining mass
into neat strands for braiding. 'You're not *thinking* of shaming us all
by throwing a scene as he meets you?'

Ellaine swallowed. 'No.' Erdane was no eastland city, to encourage
its women to bold acts of freedom and independence. 'But you know
there will be unkind comparisons drawn.'

She would not speak the name of Lysaer's first princess, who had
been Etarran, beautiful and proud and spirited as a wild lioness. During
her winter's stay at the palace of Erdane's mayor, the girls had known
Lady Talith well enough to measure her mettle. She had made no secret
of her penchant for the blood sport of palace intrigue. Small good her
rebellious intelligence had done her in the end; even her sharpened wit
had become eclipsed by the Prince of the Light's blinding majesty.

The maid's firm fingers braided Ellaine's hair, unconcerned, as the
sisters took stock of the recent tragedy that cast a dampening chill on
the hour's anticipation. The late Princess of Avenor now lay six months
dead, a suicide who had plunged from the high tower battlement that
fronted her husband's hall of state.

'She was barren and in despair,' the younger girl insisted, while the
maid's efforts bundled her sister's dark tresses in consoling, brisk tugs
that pulled at her small furrows of worry. 'All you need do is give the
prince heirs. You'll wear pearls and fine gowns and be comfortable for
the rest of your life.'

Other benefits remained politely unspoken, that Ellaine's promised
marriage would also bring Erdane the strength of Lysaer's royal protection. The city would claim the prince's defense against the machinations
of the Master of Shadow, and also a field-trained division of sunwheel
troops to secure the trade roads through Camris.

The indolent young sister lifted no hand to help as the maid stretched
and caught up the silk cord for tying: dusky rose, to match the dress,
wound in twisted gilt threads for strong accent, and tasseled with a
dropped spray of pearls. She laced its rich length through the end of

the braid, then coiled the magnificent, shining rope into a headdress to crown Ellaine's heart-shaped face. Elaborate grooming did not settle her nerves. Refined brows and doe eyes flickered in trepidation as a foot page tapped at the doorway.

'His Lordship the Elect asks that the Lady Ellaine come down for the presentation.'

'Stop frowning, you goose!' teased the sister. 'And leave off measuring yourself against Lady Talith. You don't keep forward habits. Nor do you delight in ambushing old, scarred captains at arms in their bathtubs. You won't gad about playing fire with politics, or get yourself abducted by a sorcerer.'

The maid patted down the last wisp of strayed hair. She garnished the piled glory of coiled braid with a gold-and-ruby pin, her earthbound steadiness in contrast to the sister's girlish trills of excitement. 'What will you do but have beautiful, strong babes for the realm? If you *dare* throw a tantrum, be sure I'll run ahead of you, begging to go in your place!'

That won the small, bowed ghost of a smile, and a loosening of clammy fingers. Ellaine arose. The pearls on the gold-and-rose ribbon dangled jauntily down the determined line of her back. Primped to a crescendo of magnificent good looks, and finished in the exacting deportment expected of the daughter of a westland city mayor, she dredged up a playful wink for her sister that unveiled the thoughtful, inner fiber of her courage. 'You shan't go in my place. If our father wishes me to wed royalty, I'll find the grace somewhere to make the best of the prosperity bestowed on our family.'

The younger sibling laughed, adoring as she watched the maid smooth and arrange the folds of the magnificent rose dress. 'Well, I'll just have no choice but to stay home and wilt from sheer awe.' She levered herself out of her nest of upholstery, kissed her sister's cheek, and whispered her most sincere wish for good luck and happiness.

'Thanks. I'll need everything.' Ellaine sucked in a final, deep breath, then sailed out the door and descended the long, curving stair to the salon.

The man who awaited her presence was dressed in shining silk in royal colors, and cosseted in her father's best chair. His lean hand curled on the stem of a glass of Falgaire crystal. As he smiled his appreciation for the quality of the vintage, he turned his gray head; and Ellaine paused, consternation masked behind manners. This was not the vigorous, fair-haired prince she had been led to expect.

Dry-skinned, sallow, and elderly, the rail-thin Seneschal of the Realm arose on stilt legs. He set the wine flute aside, while her father spoke her name and beckoned her forward. Avenor's aged envoy accepted her offered hand, his grasp cold and dry as he recited a prepared speech of welcome and acceptance. 'His Grace, the Lord Prince of the Light, sends his most sincere regrets. He has a war campaign to wind down in the wilds of Caithwood, and an inspection of the shipyard at Riverton overdue since the closing of summer.' The royal official blinked pouched, hound's eyes, apologetic and stiff, no doubt recalling the past princess's lightning wit, and the abrasive fight she had raised each time conflict arose with the Shadow Master's allies.

Soft civility before her predecessor's razored style, the Lady Ellaine masked her personal disappointment behind the decorum of her upbringing. She did not interrupt, but listened in patience as the seneschal finished his delivery. 'The safety of the realm must come before his Grace's preference and pleasure, as my lady must understand, who will become his crowned consort in the royal seat at Avenor.'

Ellaine endured the seneschal's bony, chapped clasp and dipped into a flawless curtsy. 'His Grace is excused. Please extend him my heartfelt wishes for a swift close to the strife in south Tysan.'

'He has sent the traditional gift in token of his regard.' The seneschal snapped his fingers. The page boy posted by the door stepped forward, bearing the royal offering.

She accepted the gold-edged coffer with shy grace and opened the lid. The inside was lined with damascened silk, and a plush velvet cushion. Against the shadow-soft nap, the sudden dazzle of gemstones cast back sliced light like a cry. Ellaine murmured polite thanks for the gift, a diamond-and-sapphire pendant hung on a massive chain of roped pearls. Though the piece was an emphatic exhibition of wealth, a male statement of property sent by a prince to the mark his personal claim, her smile to the page boy was genuine. 'Would you help with the clasp?'

The boy bowed, obedient, the gold fastening easy work for his admiring hands. The scintillant, dark jewel and sharp fire of the diamond lay too hard, too weighty against the delicate rose-and-gilt gown. Yet the girl handled herself well under the yoke of the twisted pearl chain. 'Tell the prince I am pleased.'

Her father stepped in, his thanks more effusive, while the mother whisked her daughter away like the cosseted asset she had become. Erdane's ambition and welfare would rise on her ability to pleasure Avenor's prince. The Seneschal of the Realm accepted the hospitality of the mayor's mansion, the discomfort that lingered after duty was discharged smoothed over in smiles and diplomacy.

The lady handfasted to wed the Prince of the Light in the month after spring solstice was a sweet child, with skin creamy rich as a white, summer peach, and sloe eyes like melted chocolate. Yet for all her unspoiled beauty and innocence, she was no match for the sultry wit of her late predecessor.

Lysaer's political choice was too evident: the wife selected to bear Tysan's royal heir was a biddable broodmare, not a mate who could stand as an equal partner in his cause to destroy the Master of Shadow. The nuptials to come would not interfere with his formal promise. The Prince of the Light had sworn to cleanse Athera of the tyrannies perpetuated by the Fellowship's compact and to eradicate the practice of sorcery. True to sovereign integrity, after Talith's embarrassments, he had ensured that no spirited wife would swerve him from the pursuit of his chosen destiny.

# Triangle

Ivel the blind splicer rubbed his nose with the back of a horny fist, eyes rolled like fogged marbles toward the impatient presence of the Riverton yard's master shipwright. He spat, then resumed tying an endsplice into a hawser. With rankling sarcasm, he said, 'Should we bathe? Clean our teeth?' Rope plies whipped into herringbones under flying, competent fingers as Ivel bared his gapped teeth in a grin of challenging mockery. 'Or should we just sweep up the shavings so his Grace's velvets won't soil? Personally, someone should shoulder the broom so we don't pain our knees when we grovel.'

The gripe concerned the scheduled royal inspection. Granted Ivel's natural penchant for mischief, the comment's disastrous timing was aimed to reap a storm of agonized embarrassment.

Feet planted in the scrolled flakes of spruce that blew like shed leaves from the sawpits, the burly master shipwright he tormented was no man's easy mark. Cattrick maintained his cast-iron calm as naturally as he drew breath. Clad in his best scarlet cloak against the winds that foreran the change of the season, he matched the splicer's wicked thrust with his own stamp of spiteful courtesy. 'With all due respect, I must leave your question to the voice of higher authority.'

Goading on Ivel's insolent disregard for rank, the yard's master added, 'That's presupposing his Grace cares to answer a commoner's impertinence in the first place.'

Stonewalled behind a laborer's grave deference, Cattrick bowed to

61

the glittering royal person, just arrived with his guard and his retinue for his long-deferred tour of the shipyard.

Ivel slapped his knee, the report of his callused palm like a whipcrack. 'Hah! I thought as much! Anybody who hasn't got the healthy stink o' tar is bound to wear jewels and airs. So that's his exalted self, the Prince of the Light, standing stiff-backed and pompous beside you?'

Cattrick pretended a cough behind the muffling sleeve of his shirt.

Lysaer s'Ilessid was all frigid formality in cloud white velvet, sewn like coarse rain with diamonds and sprays of small seed pearls. The statesman's panache he wore like steel armor let him meet Ivel's derision without astonishment.

Yet the rowdy splicer interrupted again before even the royal guard could intervene. 'Tell me, should I prostrate myself and press my face in the dirt? Or in the name of efficiency to your royal design, would you rather I finished this hawser?'

Silence ensued, more thunderous than the hollow boom of the caulkers' mallets which impacted the scene with the racketing crescendo of industry.

The lantern-jawed guard to the prince's left was first to reach for his sword hilt.

'No,' Lysaer snapped. His raised hand averted the tensioned response as his other two bodyguards rocked on their toes to charge forward. 'Let the craftsman be. He may mock, but his rank tongue harms nothing.' The prince advanced a step to distance his person from the zeal of his armed protection. Against weathered board sheds and the trampled mud of the yard, he seemed a figure displaced. Hazeless sunlight fired his gold hair. The stark purity of white velvets and diamonds amid the workaday grime of the ropewalk appeared as incongruous as a snowdrift arrived out of season.

To Ivel, the prince said, 'Bide in the grace of my tolerance and continue to place your best work into splicing new ropes for my ships.'

Ivel spat. His ejected gobbet landed just shy of the elegantly shod royal toe. 'My best work,' he said carefully, 'is saved for my leave time with wenches. And the joins in my lines will hold only as true as the quality of the hemp you import for their making. Supply's been second-rate, and your pay could be better.'

Lysaer blinked. A solemn corner of his mouth twitched. Then he laughed and swung his piercing regard back to his master shipwright. 'Am I given to understand my treasury's funding for this yard is fallen short of sufficient?'

While the gulls wheeled, crying, to a shift in the breeze, and the harbor bell pealed to signal the turn of ebb tide, Cattrick played his narrow-eyed survey across the row of ribbed hulls, the smoking brick chimneys of the boiler sheds, and the raw lengths of lumber, interlaced into stacks for the air to season the planks. He said, noncommittal, 'Your Grace, you've read the reports. We've had setbacks aplenty since the upsets involved with your rout of the Shadow Master last springtide.'

The offshore pursuit of that quarry to the Isles of Min Pierens had told worst, with no authorized crown officer left at Avenor to rectify the flow of supply and demand. The stalled requisitions, the delays, the missed deadlines which sprang from the bottleneck were inked in hard figures by the scribes. If Prince Lysaer had come properly primed for this meeting, he must already know the details: quality had suffered to meet the decreed royal schedule. The accounts contained each laborious detail: the lists of forged fittings bought lacking the ideal, tested temper; of the green spruce that had dried too checked to be steam-bent; of the varnish that bloomed and then flaked from the brightwork, inviting premature rot.

When Lysaer s'Ilessid declined the proffered opening to shoulder his due part, Cattrick picked words with a deference at odds with the powerful, bear's bellow he used to command his skilled craftsmen. 'It's scarcely my place to fault the crown treasury, your Grace. The inspection will show you our shortfalls.'

Lysaer's relaxed smile returned like lost warmth. As if the blind splicer had caused no sour note, he gestured his readiness to proceed.

For Cattrick, that day, the hard edge to the breeze forewarned of the keen chill of winter. He led the prince and his three guardsmen through the shipworks the same way he measured his planks: with direct and exacting attentiveness. The steam boxes puffed like somnolent dragons. The shadows cast from raw ribs and keelsons, and the golden lengths of spruce being shaped in the sawpits seemed glued into the abundant, rich scents of salt air, pine pitch, and hot tar.

Lysaer did not rush. Nor did he expect to be spoon-fed the facts. As though his jewels and spotless white velvet represented no difference of station, he engaged the laborers in conversation. He shook the men's hands as though they were not coarsely clad, rinsed in running sweat turned sticky with shavings and filth. If his majesty stunned them, or his unearthly grace, he gave no credence to awe. Nor did he seek either fault or restitution for the stupefying losses set in train by the Shadow Master's plotting.

The spontaneous contact touched off admiration and camaraderie. The laborers opened and laughed. Through their loosened ease, the Prince of the Light learned the workings of the yard in utmost, gritty detail. He found Cattrick's steady competence was held in respect. At each site, he tested and observed and moved on, while the rapport that he engendered between disparate men gained focus and became a unified cord of tied force.

Few could escape the drawing pull of the Prince of the Light's bright charisma. From the dusty boys who shoveled the shavings from the sawpits, to the ox goads who kept the creaking wheels of the ropewalks slowly turning, to the sailmakers in their swept loft, stitching yards of oak-dyed canvas, the craftsmen sharpened to purposeful unity. Their industry flowed with their source of inspiration. At one crook of Lysaer's diamond-jeweled finger, each one appeared ready to throw down his tools and beg for a place in armed service. The adulation was euphoric, as if within the prince's magnetic presence, plain sunlight shone brighter, and the toils of exertion came sweetened, enriched to scintillant meaning.

Cattrick watched the transformation. The lined, wary squint never left his expression, and his broad hands stayed jammed in his breeches. He volunteered little, but gave answers like ruled lines to those questions Lysaer posed directly. Afternoon wore away toward sundown. The shadows lost edges, elongated to the texture of torn felt, and blended without seam into twilight. The royal party climbed the outdoor stairway to the sanctum of Cattrick's chartloft. There, huddled under the glimmer of cheap tallow dips, they reviewed the close-guarded leaves penned with the lines of ships' plans.

The moment was inopportune for interruption, yet one came in the form of a riled yell from the royal man-at-arms posted on watch outside.

A voice pealed through commotion, demanding. 'Damn you, I'm an ally! If you don't want a fight, put up your fool sword. One grunt's length of steel is scarcely enough to keep me from going inside.'

Something responded with an indignant clang.

'Told you,' said the intruder, disgusted. 'Now use the brains that Ath gave a mule and don't try to stab me in the back.'

Speedy, light footsteps ascended the stair. An imperious fist banged on the door, and the latch gave way and flew open.

Mearn s'Brydion, youngest brother of the clanborn Duke of Alestron, arrived at the entry, slit-eyed and poised as a cat with a bristled tail. His gaze fastened instantly on Lysaer. 'You know how far and long I've had to ride to gain your ear for this audience?' Neither honorific nor apology was offered in his testy habit of old clanblood arrogance and quicksilver, unvarnished nerve.

He strode in. Leathers left sweat-damp and redolent of horse cracked to his brisk stride. Brown hair peeled up and spiked by chill wind threw sliding lines of shadow across his frowning agitation. 'Your lady is dead.'

For the second time, Lysaer's raised arm checked the defensive rush of his bodyguard. 'That's surely no news, though you were in King Eldir's court, I understand, on the day I blessed and settled her ashes.'

Mearn bore in like a terrier. 'If I was in Havish, that doesn't change that you honored her shade four months after the hour Princess Talith passed the Wheel!'

Resigned, Lysaer straightened from his perusal of a chart. Unruffled by the hard length of his day, he confronted the s'Brydion style of ripping censure with calm like grounded bedrock. 'Should you concern yourself?'

Mearn reached the edge of the trestle, stopped. He planted gauntleted fists on the edge. The studs bit into creaking wood as he leaned and bore down on his knuckles. 'Your seneschal claims she committed suicide.'

His blue eyes serene, Lysaer replied, 'I believe him.'

For one second, two, prince and clansman locked stares, the former all fired, untarnished elegance, and the latter rumpled and taut as stressed cord. Cattrick looked on with folded arms, while the tense royal guardsmen stood by with mailed hands welded to their sword grips.

Then Mearn spun about in abrupt, liquid grace. 'You believe him.' He paced, the short, blunt spurs on his boots flicking off small points of light. He expected no answer. When he reached the shuttered window, he faced about and braced his angular frame against the sill. 'They say on the streets that you have pressed suit for the Mayor of Erdane's eldest daughter.'

'My offer for her hand in marriage has been accepted.' Lysaer was not smiling. His jewels might have been frozen stars, so controlled was his breathing. 'The official announcement will be made next week.'

Mearn pushed back his cuffs and latched his thumbs through his sword belt. He might not bow, had never acknowledged Lysaer's claim to title. As the scabbard and sheath at his hip were not empty, no man present dared mistake his clanbred defiance of court etiquette. 'Well then,' Mearn said, 'since you're to marry so soon, you must understand the personal edge to my impatience. I've stood as my brother's ambassador for seven years. You'll agree, it's time I returned home to Alestron and settled myself with a wife.'

Before Lysaer could speak, he jerked up his chin. 'No leave is asked. I'm not one of your subjects.'

Lysaer smiled in carved, regal tolerance. 'No need to stand upon thorny clan pride. I never made such a claim. Please give your brother the duke my regards and the blessing of the Alliance.'

The words held dismissal. A polite man would leave. Mearn remained planted like immovable oak, his eyes pale ice in the gloom.

Lysaer chose diplomacy and ignored him, bent back to review the outspread leaves of scale drawings. He asked questions of Cattrick, who resumed answering with unruffled brevity. Minutes flowed into another hour. The shutters fretted in the play of the sea breeze, and the half-burned-down tallow dips gyrated to the wayward tug of the drafts. Outside, the yard workers indulged their light spirits, keyed to fast talk and euphoria. They seemed reluctant to leave. Their royal visitor was held by some to be god sent, and the rumors of miracles and divine favor gained fresh force with each passing month. Through Cattrick's clipped consonants, the foreman's exasperated remonstrance mingled with the metallic clangor of tools being put away. 'Well, don't just gawp with yer jaws hanging open. Damn fools. Honest citizens might think this was a boys' brothel, the way you lot hang about, staring at a closed doorway.'

'You wishing?' somebody whooped, half-choking with laughter, and the clutter of voices diminished as the yard at last settled to the night watch's step and the wash of the first riptide breakers.

The parchment drawing of a brig's revised lines remained spread on the table as Lysaer finally straightened to end his detailed inspection. Others, loosely rolled, not yet tied with string, lay in a jumbled heap to one side. Mearn still held his place, a taut form melted into close-woven shadow. His watching eyes caught the unsteady light like pinned sparks as the royal men-at-arms regrouped for their charge's departure.

White velvet and diamonds lent Prince Lysaer a wintery majesty as he voiced his commendation for Cattrick's watertight management. 'The neglect brought on by my absence will be put right the moment my handfasting to Erdane's daughter can replenish the funds in the treasury. Rest assured, her dowry will bring in enough gold to amend the quality of your raw materials. You'll have whatever sum you name then. Make an itemized list and send it under seal to my seneschal.' He paused, his smile bestowed like new morning. 'Until then, be diligent. After the Shadow Master's blatant acts of piracy, the trade guilds must be given a show to mend their shaken faith. I will ask that my newly launched fleet be ready to sail into Avenor with flags flying to commemorate my nuptials.'

'Your Grace,' Cattrick acknowledged, his bow neat and perfunctory. 'You'll have a display worth your confidence.'

He accompanied the prince as far as the doorway, saw him out into rising wind and a night fallen dense as stuck tar.

Cattrick closed the door and reset the bar. For a large man, he moved carefully. The loft's gapped, wooden floor creaked to his tread as he crossed back to the table and began one by one to tidy and roll up the ships' plans. No fool, he judged as Lysaer had, that Mearn s'Brydion enjoyed any chance to pick fights. He chose not to comment. The clan hothead deserved to be ignored for his scathing lack of manners, his interruption, and his irritating effrontery.

Mearn proved unkindly disposed to the silence. He shifted foot to foot through the distant bark of laughter from the garrison sentry who exchanged parting banter and secured the yard gates. Through the clattering hooves of the royal departure, he pushed off from the sill and completed a stalking cat's stride. A stiletto appeared from nowhere. Steel scribed a hot flash as he threw the weapon across the tentative halo of flameglow.

The blade struck and sang quivering, impaled through the scroll which Cattrick had just laid aside.

'I know ships,' Mearn opened through the diminishing whine as stressed metal subsided into stillness.

Cattrick's lips peeled back in the smile that made even Arithon s'Ffalenn take cold stock. 'That's a claim that demands a forfeit, in this place.'

Mearn laughed. His teeth were crisply white as a ferret's. 'If you are speaking to Lysaer's lackey, I believe you. Don't lie. I have a second knife.'

Cattrick straightened, linked his broad hands, and stretched until the joints in his shoulders cracked. 'All right. The knife's a provocation. Remember that. And I won't need to lie. If I am speaking to Lysaer's lackey, he wouldn't leave the yard gates with his life.'

Mearn's eyes lit, cold as balefire with challenge. 'Imagine my joy. I do think perhaps I might like what I hear.'

'Then why not tell me, if you know your ships?' Cattrick yanked out the knife, flicked his wrist, and let the pierced parchment unroll with a scraping hiss until it lay flat on the trestle.

'Well enough. That's fair.' Mearn advanced and chose a stance on the opposite side of the board. 'The irony shouldn't escape you, I made certain. Now we both have knives.'

Cattrick unbent to a rough, booming laugh, then yanked open the drawstrings of his sleeve cuffs and shoved them back to clear his wrists. 'You clansmen have arrogance bred into the bone.' The knife in his hand described fearless threat. 'Let us also see if your landlubber minds can interpret what I know to make ships cleave a course through blue water.'

Mearn returned his most evil grin and snapped a finger into the parchment. 'This brig might have a grace to her lines fit to melt a man's heart at her launching. But the love affair ends at her shakedown. She'll be wayward as a cow under canvas. I'd bank on a nasty lee helm at the stiffening hint of a squall.' He raised his head, treated Lysaer's master shipwright to the frost of an unforgiving glare. 'In a gale, I'd bet silver she'll founder.'

Outside, the harbor bell tolled to mark the full change of the tide. A gust buffeted through gapped boards in the shutters and fluttered the flames in the sconces. Cattrick flipped the knife and, with his own stamp of insolence, used its murderous edge to scrape tar from the rims of his fingernails. His eyes, half-hooded in apparent inattention, shared the same vicious glints as the steel. 'Go on,' he urged the s'Brydion ambassador. 'You passed the unfinished frames on their bedlogs. What else did you see outside?'

'Mayhem.' Mearn slapped the handle of his knife against his gloved palm, tap, tap, tap, like the winding tension on a ratchet. 'The fleet Prince Lysaer has commissioned from you will be lucky to withstand the first coast-hopping run to Avenor.'

'Opinion,' Cattrick fired back. He sidestepped and sat on the chartloft's crude stool. 'If I'm talking to Lysaer's sworn ally, what then?'

'You have a bigger problem on your hands than ships that won't answer their helmsman.' Slap! went the knife handle, then ceased with an emphasis as startling. Mearn qualified into the teeth of raw tension, 'The craftsmen in your yard are scarcely unseasoned. Why haven't they noticed? And if they have, shouldn't you now beware of their temper? Prince Lysaer can move plain stone to adore him. *You know they worship him as an avatar in Avenor.*'

'A warning?' Cattrick unfolded to his massive height, expansive with stifled delight. 'The knife, you say, won't come from up front, but in the back from some planker's self-righteous turn of conscience? Why worry? This yard's been guarded like a pedigree virgin since the Master of Shadow beset us with thievery last winter. I shape my own risks. The men here in position to know me will also have to choose theirs. High time I ask what reason you have to jam your sniping clan nose in my business.'

'Well, first off,' said Mearn, 'I came here to kill you. A matter concerning a letter scribed in your hand that drew Lysaer s'Ilessid from Etarra with armed troops. A lot of clan blood was spilled over that. That's a stirring provocation; only now, your ships' plans give me reason to take pause. If you've turned coat again, I'd like to know why.' His tone curdled to a whiplash of bitterness. 'There's an opportunity to weigh, in light of that gold that's promised from Erdane for Lysaer s'Ilessid's pledged marriage.'

Cattrick hooted. 'It's a woman, after all!' His sarcasm raked. 'Princess Talith *didn't* commit suicide.'

Mearn's first response was a whitening about the lips as the muscles of his jaw sharply tightened. 'On that, *there's my knife*. You can draw your own conclusion.'

'I don't need to. Nor will I fight for a woman whose sorrows are ended.' One sudden, strong move, and Cattrick impaled the fine blade in the tabletop. 'The truth holds no passion. My defection last spring was forced by a Koriani oath of debt, sworn on behalf of my sister. Their hold on me's forfeit, discharged by that letter.' He leaned forward, his shadow looming over the damning designs on the trestle. 'Let's by all means stay forthright. If this is an offer to join Alestron in conspiracy, I accept. If it's not what I think, then hear my sweet warning. You'll leave Riverton by sea, with a load of stone lashed to your ankles.'

Mearn's mercurial laugh intermingled with the chime as he cast his own steel to sliding rest beside the dagger impaled in the trestle. Metal struck metal. The pealing clang reechoed to the wicked bent of his gambler's delight. 'I have a much nicer idea. Why not sit down and stop bristling hackles? Let me extend an invitation: let's both drink beer to the Shadow Master's health over a certain chest of gold in the ducal hall at Alestron.' As an afterthought, he grinned. 'We build ships there, too.'

Cattrick's brows furrowed upward. 'Then you're Prince Arithon's covert ally?'

'Since Vastmark,' Mearn admitted. 'We, too, had our reasons for turning coat.' He hiked up one leg and perched on the edge of the trestle. 'I can write my brother in coded state language and demand his swiftest galley to bear me homeward come the spring. First, I'll need to know what date to ask for, and which port of call will offer the most favorable rendezvous.'

'The outer reefs, northwest of Orlest,' Cattrick said with scarcely a second's hesitation. 'The timing, of course, must depend on the prince as he sets final plans for his wedding.'

# Dispositions

On the snow-dusted moors of Araethura, the herbalist's cottage stands empty and cold, the enchantress who lived there gone north to ply her talents in the stews by the Morvain quay, where street children snatch life by robbery and wits; and knife wounds acquired by randy sailors and the unending afflictions of poor quarter harlots will take her mind far from the betrayal enacted through a black-haired shepherd boy's trust . . .

The day before Prince Lysaer's sealed orders reach Caithwood, the Sorcerer Asandir stands under the frost-turned crown of a great oak, his expression like chisel-cut granite; over his head, the winds of late autumn thrash the leaves to a song of rare fury, and the drumming of twigs and the moaning of pines transmit the tattoo outward through the forest like the ripples cast across a stilled pool . . .

In the teeming port city of Innish, on the southcoast, a fair young man entrusted as merchant's factor sits by the wavering light of a candle, reading a letter in sharp, coded script that describes a specific tavern in Southshire where dispatches are to be left, and closes with the laughing, wishful observation, 'Keep your harpy of a sister well clear of my affairs, or one better, tell her I'll play tasteless ballads for her wedding if she'll find the good grace to exchange feckless seafaring for marriage . . .'

# III. Caithwood

T he sealed orders from Avenor reached the small settlement known as Watercross in the shortened days of late autumn. There, the river route through Ilswater intersected the trade road that spanned Caithwood, linking Valenford to Quarn and the southern seaports of Tysan. Built at the threshold of the ancient stand of forest, the massive old land bridge, with its mossy stone pilings, spanned the river in the elegant arches which bespoke the masterful skill of centaur masons. Since the departure of the Paravians, mankind had made free with the axe. Five inns clustered by the verge, a congested accretion of multiple wings of timber raised three stories high. These were fronted by a commodious barge dock, and boasted between them a post stable and a prosperous smithy. The streetside cluster of shops fanned into a disordered tangle of clapboard cottages, each with a cow and a garden patch. The steadings were inhabited by the families of serving girls who had married rivermen or drovers, and raised sprawling families whose lifeblood was tuned to the movement of commerce.

The summer's campaign to suppress Caithwood's clansmen had spurred wider change. The inns were jammed to screaming capacity, each room and attic housing crown officers and stockpiles of perishable supplies. In response to demand, every Watercross resident had rented out bedrooms and haylofts at extortionist prices, then relocated their displaced and bickering offspring in the crannies of pantries and woodsheds.

Talk of new building abounded, while tents and picket lines crowded the riverbank, and more timber fell to clear acreage. Amid the chewed ends of stumps and the trodden, pocked earth quilted over with flame-bright swatches of fallen leaves, the orderly tents of an Alliance encampment nestled into the river's south bank. Its hub of command was a sagging board building that, in springtime, had served as a pig shack.

The sow and her farrow had long since graced the pot. Under the damp thatch that had been their last shelter, Etarra's Lord Harradene snapped off his gloves and stamped the caked mud from his boots. The day officer delivered the most urgent news through the noise of his jangling impatience, while a gesture saw the wrapped packets of dispatches accepted by his breathless equerry. Harradene stilled as he heard the reports. His cliff-edged frown stayed quarried in place as he learned that the camp north of Caithwood had withdrawn in disorder back to Valenford.

'No, don't repeat that,' he snapped. 'I heard damn all the first time. Puling ninnies, every milk-nosed captain who let his company turn tail. Fact's known well enough. Fellowship conjury never kills.' He slapped the royal writ on the trestle with the maps and glowered at his ring of cringing officers. 'I don't care *horse apples* if some fools have fled from a display of arcane posturing! Your prince wants a fire. Therefore, this stand of wood's going to burn! We're driving clan dogs out of hiding with singed tails, and the crown's bounties won't wait for the hindmost.'

Through a spattering of cheers, someone's raspy question prevailed. 'Is this wise?'

The boldest of the sergeants appended a protest. 'The Sorcerer claimed he would waken the trees.'

Lord Commander Harradene spun back, his spiked brows still furrowed, and the shoulders under his sunwheel surcoat bristled as a bear's before a charge. 'Oh, did he indeed?' His rankling, Etarran sarcasm thundered, sifting fine dust from the thatch. 'And what will that mean, do you think? That hundred-year-old oaks are likely to rise up and *walk*? That greenwood is going to bear steel?' He turned in a tight circle, leaving no officer unwithered by his scathing contempt. 'Is there anyone else present with the brains of a chicken?'

No one spoke or moved. Pent silence expanded like poison, sawn through at a distance by barking dogs and the wailing of some mother's toddler.

'Good!' Lord Harradene slapped the wet ends of his gloves against the dulled mail of his byrnie. 'Now show me you've kept the two bollocks Ath gave a newborn. In one hour, I want ten relays of messengers assembled. They'll bear my orders the length and breadth of Taerlin. By dawn on the day of the new moon, every man marching in the service of the Light will be in position to torch trees. We'll have archers in line to take down the flushed clansmen. Hereafter, these roads will be safe enough for a naked virgin to travel unscathed!'

Ahead of all argument, Lord Harradene snarled his ultimatum. 'Any man who fears trees may turn in his insignia right here, right now, and go home stripped of all honors. Ones who run later, or ones who drag feet will be burned and run through by the sword as no less than Fellowship Sorcerers' collaborators!'

The pig shack emptied to a stampede of boots, and the last couriers streamed away well ahead of the hour allocated for their departure. Some galloped north and east, mounted upon fast horses and given escort by tried veterans in sunwheel surcoats. Others ducked spray from the oars of swift boats, commandeered from trade service by crown authority. These careened downriver into the wilds, their course sped by the winding ribbon of the Ilswater's lower branch in its rush to meet the sea estuary.

The trees dripped and brooded in the mist-heavy air. They exhibited no change as their sovereign territory became invaded by the Alliance couriers, who dispersed the written orders for Lord Commander Harradene's campaign of fire and sword. Their stillness magnified the trepidation of the men, who rode with ears tuned to the wind in the leaves and heard nothing, only autumn's chorus of dying vegetation as the unmoored foliage chattered and danced in the gusts. In the boats, beneath breaking cloud, sweat-drenched oarsmen watched the shadowed deeps on the bank, prodding at waterbound roots with unease as they moored to make camp for the night.

Yet no living tree displayed any sign of an uncanny movement. The fiery pageant of changed maples unveiled at each bend in the river, their outlines punch-cut and serene. The hollows wore carpets of scarlet and gold, turned by the furtive brush of night's frosts presaging the advent of winter.

Whatever the Sorcerer Asandir threatened, no Alliance scout's sharpened vigilance detected anything untoward or amiss. Mice continued to nest in blankets and stores, seeking shelter against the chill; the hunting owls sailed the starry dark, silent and sleek as lapped silk. Days, the hawks circled and called from a blue enameled sky. Geese clamored south in straggling chevrons as they had for time beyond memory. No one saw oak groves tear up roots or talk. If every place a man trod to seek firewood, his steps felt stalked by hidden watchers, that unease more likely stemmed from the clan scouts who shadowed their movements, unseen.

The spate of outrageous speculation peaked and subsided, restored to a general complacency as Lord Harradene's orders reached the far-flung Alliance encampments, and the days waxed and waned without incident. The rank-and-file troops who occupied the deep wilds were experienced and staunch. They curbed all explosions of foolish hysteria lest they draw in the prankish attention of iyats, the invisible fiends that played living havoc with a man's kit and gear. Evenings were spent wrapping fire arrows with cotton, or binding oiled rag to pine billets. The casks of pitch and resin that would fuel their brands were drawn from supply, and tallied in readiness for action.

Across Caithwood, the ordered companies marched into position, unmolested beyond the nipped flush of cold fingers and the paned skins of ice on the bogs. No signs appeared of arcane workings. The only change any troop captain could pinpoint was the scarcity of traps set by the lurking bands of clansmen.

'Well enough, they know when to tuck tail and run,' dismissed Lord Harradene when the duty officer drew the oddity to his attention. 'We already know they were warned by that Sorcerer. Should they stay, do you think, just to burn?'

The eve of new moon arrived in due course. Over the jittering light of night campfires, tucked under cloaks against the wind, the archers waxed longbows and cracked bawdy jokes lest the silence be claimed by the rush of tossed leaves, or the bared scrape of oak twigs find voice. Dawn would see all of Caithwood aflame, by the grace of Prince Lysaer's dispensation. If some men who had families lay awake out of pity for clan children and wives destined to fall in the carnage, Tysan's headhunters celebrated. Other scarred, grizzled veterans recalled the bloody knives that had dispatched their wounded with no mercy given at Tal Quorin.

''Tweren't natural,' those whispered. 'Our wounded all died, throat-cut and choking, done in by the hands of mere boys.'

Two hours before the new moon's pale dawn, at chosen locations across Caithwood, every man not on watch as a sentry sharpened and readied his weapons. The archers checked arrows and quarrels, and positioned the casks of oil and pitch. No one sensed any flare of worked sorcery. Trees loomed dumb as they always had, amid their shed mantles of leaves. Against black, forest stillness and a nagging, keen chill, troops bolstered their courage with whatever cruel memories could fan their passion for vengeance.

The graying east sky brought a scouring north breeze that promised an auspicious campaign. In the posted positions set forth by Lord Harradene, the most hardened veterans wolfed down cold bread. They teased laggards with jokes as they girded on mail and weapons in the steadily strengthening half-light. By horn call and barked order, they formed ranks and fanned out, the forefront to wield torches and fire arrows, and the rest set at strategic points to intercept whatever might flee from the heart of the lethal conflagration.

'On time, and no quarter,' read Harradene's last orders. The fires would be kindled at sunrise, with no reprieve given for clan prisoners, grown man or woman, child or newborn. The Etarran field troops blew on chilled fingers. They eyed the dense trees, their ink-blown branches entangled against the brightening skyline. The gusts smelled of dead leaves, and cookfires, and oiled metal; ordinary, even surreal before the butchering bloodshed to come. Today, fair retribution for the long string of massacres at Tal Quorin, at Minderl Bay, and at Dier Kenton Vale, each one the design of murdering clan war bands in collusion with the Master of Shadow.

Now came the fierce reckoning for so many dead, and a long-overdue salve for the interests of trade. Caithwood was to be cleansed of barbarians by decree of the Prince of the Light.

The Alliance ranks stilled in the mist-laden gloom, prepared with tinder and steel. They fingered the honed edges on their knives and drew swords; tested the grip on halberd and lance and soothed their restive horses, sweating in anticipation. A long-sought, elusive quarry would be theirs to bring down. The sunwheel banners fluttered in the stiffening north breeze, and the leaves spoke, scratching, against the eaves of the forest.

One moment rushed into the next. Under light turned pearlescent, the eastern sky brightened into a sheer, cloudless citrine. The black borders of Caithwood limned in silhouette, the wind-tossed verge of an ocean of linked trees, their collective awareness and their language dumb noise to more limited human ears. On that poised instant, a Fellowship Sorcerer spoke a word: *the Paravian rune that meant* one *and which tied all things in Ath's creation into the prime chord of unity*.

The next second, the reddened edge of the sun sliced above the horizon.

Illumination speared the heavens. At each of two hundred and eighty locations, Alliance horn calls rang out; the cried order clove through the burn of chill wind, to execute Prince Lysaer's sealed order. Men steadied drawn steel. Excited fingers grasped flints, began the decisive move to strike sparks and set pitch-soaked arrows and cressets alight.

There came no connection. On one Sorcerer's word, a wave of awareness crossed time and space, sped fleeting as light on the cognizant tide that passed from one tree to the next. The moment lagged into an unnatural sense of hesitation. The stir of the wind gained a surreal impetus, and the susurrant scratch of dead leaves acquired a magnified roar of wild sound. That nexus of vibration caught the conscious mind and sucked human thought into a whirlpool that overwhelmed all reasoned continuity. No live thing was exempt. The deer ceased their browsing with wide, glassy eyes. Hawks on the branches mantled and blinked, for the moment too muddled for flight. Among the two-legged, whether clansman or soldier, that pause gripped the heart like old roots. Busy purpose made no sense. Logic lost meaning. A peace deep and vast as the slow turn of seasons, the ordered dance of a planet's annual journey round its star grasped and drowned every shred of animal identity.

For that one given instant, the speech of the trees reigned in smothering supremacy. The staunch patience of fixed roots and the wine taste of sun rinsed warp and weft through the weave of all breathing, warm-blooded awareness. Iron prejudice shattered. Those Alliance-sworn men who were townbred and ignorant now learned what the hawk, and the deer, and the insect had always known, and what Caithwood's clans kept alive by tradition. Their unbroken, old ways reaffirmed the immutable truth through words that gave thanks, and through timeworn, small rituals which renewed by expression of gratitude. That trees were *alive*. Their gifts and their bounty might be taken at will. They could be raped and robbed, or they could be acknowledged, a trust of consent sealed in the language of humility, granting each bough and trunk its due recognition for generous sacrifice.

Yet the wisdom of Paravian law had dimmed with the passage of centuries. Men now walked Athera who gave back no such grace. Whether the lapse stemmed from blind carelessness or the vice of acquisitive greed did not matter. The chain-linked communion that was *forest* discerned no gray shade of distinction. Trees grasped no code but the one that acknowledged the grand chord of Ath's primal order. They owned no concept to forsake whole awareness for individual separation.

No second was given; no freed train of thought broke the noose for shock or humanborn fear. The vise grip of the dream on men's minds was unyielding, a crescendo wrought of numbers too massive to deny, each note tuned to urgent communion.

The blow fell, bloodless, in that trampling breadth of vision. Lost in the vast ocean of forbearance that defined the existence of greenwood, the trees' vision reclaimed hate and violence for peace. Townborn minds stilled and sank into an abiding continuity that frayed sensibility, and awoke a remorse without mercy: of wood cut, unblessed; of saplings uprooted. Each thoughtless twig broken in callous disregard framed a cry of acid-etched clarity. The impact stunned beating hearts like a wound. A day's pitiless industry, which sought to turn fire and steel to rend life, ripped a chasm of shame through shocked conscience.

Men screamed without voice as the dream of the wood flooded through them and clamped like the embrace of black earth.

There came no reprieve, no concept for pity. Each hand that had moved with intent to strike spark; each arm, to grasp weapons for slaughter; all dropped, limp. Names and identity and meaningful purpose submerged without trace in the flux. What remained was the everlasting communion that passed between root and leaf and spread branch. The peace of the forest seized the mind like fast ice and held with the endurance of centuries.

Determined experience served none in that hour. The strongest and best of drilled veterans gave way, sapped of will and inclination. Any who ventured near Caithwood unprepared, all those who embraced human purpose beyond the encompassing calm of live trees was undone. To the last rank and file, to the most steadfast captain, the Alliance veterans buckled at the knees. They dropped swords and tinder, crumpled like rags, or slipped reins through slack hands and toppled off startled horses. When the messengers came riding from Watercross to inquire, they found Lord Commander Harradene's troops felled to a man, sprawled comatose on the cold ground.

Flurried searches confirmed: not one Alliance supporter inside Caithwood was left standing. Nor did the camp servants who lurked on the fringes remain in command of their wits. Dazed, even weeping, they forgot their own names, while livestock and woods creatures raided their supplies, and their oxen browsed loose through the brush.

How the clans fared, no city man knew, since no one saw hide nor hair of them.

In the depths of a glen, ankle deep in red oak leaves, Asandir lifted long, lean fingers from the bark of the ancient patriarch that ruled Caithwood. He murmured a run of liquid, sweet syllables, a blessing framed in the tongue of the vanished Paravians.

Clear of eye, his mind and his purpose vised to ruthless alignment, he stepped back from the tree whose compliance had keyed a whole forest's salvation. Subtle as shadow in his featureless leathers, he traversed drifted leaves with a step like a wraith's and retrieved the tied reins of his horse. He tightened the animal's slack girth and remounted. Two hours' ride through the breezy afternoon brought him to a clearing in a glen, where he met the eldest in the circle of clan chieftains who maintained their *caithdein*'s guard over Caithwood.

Cenwaith was a great-grandmother, wizened, but not frail. Tiny hands with the weathered grain of burled walnut clutched a bronze-studded quarterstaff. By the scars crisscrossing her knuckles, she had wielded weapons throughout a hard lifetime. Her jacket of fox fur blended her diminutive form amid the changed leaves of the maples.

'How long?' she asked him, her voice the aged quaver of water-smoothed stone, rinsed by a tumbling brook.

Asandir paused, his gaze turned to flint beneath a fringe of dark lashes. 'Days. Maybe five, before the first caravan from the south can use the road without leaving prone bodies. No man bearing steel will escape, even then.' He brushed a caught leaf from his hair and firmed the reins to stall his inquisitive horse from nipping the sleeve of his shirt. 'No victim will suffer, rest assured of that much. The awareness of trees regards time very differently. Lysaer's troops who fell senseless will lie in stasis until they find release from the dream. Your people must take flight as soon as they may. Abide by my warnings. They'll stay safe as long as none breaks the covenant laid down to appease the roused might of the greenwood.'

'No steel and no fire?' The grandame wheezed out a fluttery laugh. 'Our folk know their place. We've laid in stores to hold us through the next fortnight.' Before then, the last clanfolk would have slipped past Lord Harradene's unstrung cordon. Their fighting strength would regroup in the rugged mountains in Camris. The young who had families would cross Mainmere estuary by boat to claim sanctuary in Havish. The Alliance's campaign of persecution was this day deferred, with Tysan's threatened bloodlines granted reprieve for continuance.

That such survival came at a price, the old woman and the Sorcerer never doubted. Tysan's trade route to the east was now irremediably severed from the moment northern snows closed the passes; and with slave-bearing galleys disbarred from King Eldir's coastline, the crisis would find no relief.

Blame for those woes would only lend impetus to Lysaer s'Ilessid's pitched campaign of intolerance. Asandir foresaw the cost of this day's reprieve written in bleak terms on the future: more armed troops raised for the purpose of war against mage talent and, ultimately, to hunt down and kill by the Mistwraith's fell geas, the Shadow Master, who was Rathain's last living prince. Too aggrieved for speech, he moved to return his borrowed horse.

Cenwaith's firm touch caught his wrist in restraint. 'You'll not be staying, Kingmaker?'

The Sorcerer shook his head, the weariness bearing upon his broad shoulders a yoke he dared not defer for his own needs or comfort. 'I cannot.' He gathered himself, while her kind eyes sought and failed to plumb the extent of his urgency. 'The troubles I forsook in Midhalla to come here have strengthened and grown in my absence.'

Courtesy kept her from pressing with questions. Since he need not seed pointless worry at his back, he answered with direct speech. 'The trees will lapse back into somnolence on their own, once they're left undisturbed, and if the crown rescinds its sealed edict to enact their destruction by fire.'

Caravan masters would eventually learn not to hack down live wood. Nor would Tysan's leagues of armed headhunters fare reiving for scalps with their former impunity. An eerie unrest would settle and linger. In the odd, haunted glen, the oldest stands of forest would cling to isolate pockets of self-awareness. Years would pass, perhaps a century or more, before equilibrium was finally restored.

'The Alliance offenders who are comatose will be carted away and cared for, if not by the crown, then by their own friends and families.' A mote of thin sunlight struck through the chill air, and lent fleeting warmth to farseeing gray eyes as Asandir spoke his conclusion. 'The trained men of war and those minds most firmly committed to violence may linger in trance. But unless they were sickly before this began, no lasting harm will befall them.'

Not so easily solved were the dangers in Mirthlvain left at large in his haste to cross the continent; nor must the stout heart give way before sorrow, that the act which spared Caithwood must force Taerlin's clanborn to forsake their beloved home territory. 'The forest will guard itself well enough. Your people can safely return in due time. Once Sethvir finds his way back from the grimward, he will act to settle what loose ends he can. The trees here will abide by his reassurance and release those lives held in abeyance.'

A gust raked the grove. Leaves fell, gilt and chestnut and flame red, ripped into capricious eddies. Cenwaith pressed thin hands into her fur jacket, the quarterstaff rested against the straight frailty of her stance. Her dark eyes tracked the flight of a jay and returned no reproach for fate's cruelties. Then the locked moment ended. Her regrets stayed sealed into stoic silence. She cocked her head, her sparrow's pert gesture infused with the implacable will to survive the onslaught of bitter storms. 'Keep the horse, Kingmaker. May our gift of him speed you to trouble-free passage.'

Asandir's leashed austerity broke before a smile of revealing warmth. 'My need is far less.' He unwound long fingers from the leather rein and clasped hers in their place with a moth touch that promised the endurance of mountains. 'There will be strayed Alliance war mounts trailing their bridles and hanging themselves up in thickets. There I can borrow without hardship. Let my thanks be the more for your care of me, lady. Carry my blessing with your people, and pass on my regards to your *caithdein*.'

He left her then without fanfare, a reticent figure who fared forth on foot, mantled in forbidding solitude. His presence claimed no grandeur. The formal blue cloak with its loomed silver ribbon stayed bundled inside the rolled blanket he carried slung over his shoulder. His long strides bore him into the deepwood with the unconscious grace of the king stag. Nor did he look back as the grandame waved him on his way in farewell.

Already his restless thoughts bent toward Mainmere. For stark necessity, another word of thanks he owed the reigning clan duchess there must be deferred to blind haste. The spawned horrors of Mirthlvain would wait for no niceties. Shepherds on the Radmoore downs would see their flocks slaughtered if the seasonal migration from the mire was not swiftly curtailed.

Asandir quickened pace. Harried as he measured the hours he had lost in oblivious communion with the trees, he knew he must raise the power of the lane with the utmost dispatch and transfer his presence out of Tysan.

The first winter snows rimed the roads when the Alliance courier bearing word back from Caithwood reached the seat of state government at Avenor. Gace Steward gave the shivering, chilled rider a weasel's darting inspection, asked once, and was shown an authentic set of seals from the supply officer stationed at Watercross.

'Come along.' A discerning intelligence lurked behind the royal house steward's furtive, quick carriage. He snapped narrow fingers for the servants to open the door wider. Against the scream of raw wind and the stream of the wax lights set in the sconces by the entry, he beckoned the tired courier inside. 'Follow me. His Grace of the Light is at light supper with his Lord Commander, Erdane's resident delegate, and eight city ministers of trade, but for news out of Taerlin, I promise you'll have his ear.'

Too weary to have scraped the mud and rime from his boots, even had time been given, the courier directed his stumbling step down the carpet that paved the wide hallway. The chink of his spurs cast thin echoes off the vaulted ceiling, and his cloak slapped, wet, at his ankles. His impression of gilt-trimmed opulence framed too great a contrast, after his weeks of enduring chapping gusts off the river and reeling, long hours ahorse on roads choked in wet snow and darkness. A liveried servant pattered ahead and flung open the door to the banquet hall. The light flooded outward, too bright, and packed with a heat of perfumes and rich sauces. Noise rolled into the corridor, a barrage of argumentative voices fit to stagger the exhausted courier where he stood.

Gace Steward's clever grip set him steady. 'Just wait. I'll have you inside for your audience straightaway.' As if the prospect of injecting disaster into the scene's rampant discord amused him, he plowed like an eel through the close-press of Avenor's shouting dignitaries.

On the sanctuary of the raised dais, only two men held their tempers in check. The Prince of the Light sat with his elegant, ringed fingers lightly curled on the stem of his wineglass. The other hand lay flat on the damask tablecloth, stilled amid a spread of gleaming cutlery and food that had not yet been touched. He wore no diamonds. A doublet roped with gold and white pearls hazed his outline in the glow of soft light, a display of pale magnificence artfully set off by the indigo tapestry hung behind his gilt chair. Beside him, dark panther to his bright grace, the Lord Commander, Sulfin Evend, leaned against a pilaster with his narrow hands hooked through the bronze-studded harness of his baldric.

Once a captain at arms in the Hanshire guard, he had eyes like poured ice water, a square jaw, thin lips, and a ruthless penchant for analysis that posed even the event of light supper as a mapped-out strategy of war. His whetted vigilance encompassed the room. Through the cadence of the servants who refilled carafes and platters, his slitted gaze noted Gace Steward's furtive entry with the infallible assessment of a predator.

He unfolded crossed arms, bent, and spoke a word to the Exalted Prince.

Lysaer showed no change of expression. Intent and possessed of a monumental calm, he continued to listen as the current complainant shot to his feet, jewels sparking to his purpled state of fury.

'. . . there's no recourse and no redress! Every galley sent southward through Havish with slave oarsmen gets struck helpless by Fellowship sorcery!'

Hats jerked, feathers trembled, and vintage wine sloshed in its calyx of crystal as the uneasy company grumbled and muttered, engrossed in remonstrance for recent infamy. Angry sentences broke through the hubbub like the crack of stone shot through a hailstorm.

'We *can't* extradite the prisoners!' The exasperated consonants of

Lord Eilish, Minister of the Royal Treasury, spattered through the grim background of noise. 'Yes, it's the same damned numskull policy men bled to throw down with the uprising. Yes, we already tried. There's no chance for ransom.'

His woolly head snagged in the turmoil like fleece off a peasant's card, Avenor's seneschal stabbed a harried finger and reviewed the core problem yet again to quell a latecomer's uninformed temerity. 'Word came through under High King Eldir's seal just this morning. His Grace has freed the chained slaves from the benches. He won't negotiate. Every officer and captain caught in breach of charter law will his tribunal and be indicted under Havish's Crown Justice.'

'Sail's no help at all!' pealed an importunate voice. 'Every laden vessel to strike out across Mainmere gets waylaid by barbarian *pirates*!'

More caustic, the delegate from Erdane slammed down his fist; cutlery and pastries jumped and resettled to a clashing complaint from fine porcelain. 'Such marauding is done in hulls stolen from us! They've been outfitted with weapons and trained crews by hell's minion! *Arithon s'Ffalenn* is the plaguing curse that's gutting the marrow of our trade!'

Profits were being eaten alive by clan pests crying vengeance for kinfolk, branded and chained at the oar. Sweating in ermine too dense for the heat, the minister of the glass guild at last hurled the gauntlet. *'What is your vaunted Alliance of Light doing to cap the bleeding breach?'*

*'What's being done?* The crown seneschal hurled back, the stringy wattles of his neck creased by his massive chains of office. 'Answer me this! Just why would we have four companies of crack Etarrans maintained at Alliance expense, given arms and standing orders to burn the clan dens out of Caithwood?'

Against that broil of seething, high temper, Gace Steward wormed onto the dais. Lord Commander Sulfin Evend straightened and met him. Tiercel pale eyes glinted like turned steel as he heard the man's breathy, fast message.

'News!' he cracked over the burgeoning noise. 'A courier's brought word back from Watercross.'

The Prince of the Light pushed back his chair. He stood up, his grace like subtle, poured light before his less polished guests and court ministers. At his movement, the baying complainants faltered. Shamed by the calm in his steady blue gaze, they shuffled aside and made way for the courier.

His travel-stained cloak and mud-splashed boots screamed disaster the instant he entered. His stumbling step raised a jolting clangor of roweled spurs through the delicate chink of state jewelry. The last yammering talk crashed to blighted whispers. The scintillant glint of rubies and cut gemstones froze, nailed still within a tableau of choked quiet. Avenor's favored dignitaries turned heads and clasped hands, breasts locked in an epidemic seizure of stopped breath.

The messenger reached the dais stair, caught and braced by Sulfin Evend. Against the gold-trimmed tablecloth, he folded to his knees in a homage that verged upon total collapse. 'Your Grace, Prince Exalted.' Every mile he had ridden rasped through his spare words, a cry of appeal for his sovereign's mercy against the ill news that he carried. He offered up the sealed roll of his dispatch with hands that shook beyond recourse.

'Give the rider my chair,' Prince Lysaer said, his shaft of exasperation for the lapse of humanity exhibited by his own stunned staff. 'See him comfortable at once.'

Caught staring along with everyone else, Gace Steward started, then leaped to obey that ominous, struck tone of command. A brisk snap of fingers summoned a page to bring wine in a crystal goblet.

'Sit,' Lysaer said. 'Since I see that the missive you carry is secure, you may count your mission as accomplished. Please accept your due honor and my praise for the hardships imposed on you by the season.' Nor did he move to accept the dispatch until the man had been settled, and had drained the glass of Carithwyr red to the dregs. The creased parchment changed hands in resignation, not fear. The courier's gratitude for small kindness served as fuel, cranking the onlookers to an unbearable, fever-pitched tension.

All eyes tracked the Prince Exalted, poised on the dais with the scroll case in hand but not yet opened. The seal was genuine, its imprint that of the Etarran commander who captained the campaign to rout the clan enclaves in Tacrlin. Yet the superscription was not in Lord Harradene's bold script; his cipher had been imprinted in haste by the secretary posted with the supply train at Watercross.

The glow on Lysaer's pearls hazed to sudden motion as he ripped through the ribbons and wax. He read, while his courtiers hung, their anxiety unrequited by his majestic demeanor.

He reached the end and looked up, locked in private shock. Then, overcome, he closed his eyes, while the last bloom of color receded from his fair skin. 'We are to mourn,' he announced in a strangled, gruff utterance. Brute strength sustained him. He regained full voice. His announcement sang out with hammering force and rocked the far corners of the room. 'Every brave man who stood ground for the Light in

Caithwood has been struck senseless by conjury set loose by a Fellowship Sorcerer!'

An indrawn gasp swept the company.

'Worse,' Lysaer said, 'there's a haunting by trees that has closed the road to armed caravans.'

An explosion of fiends in Avenor's main market would have created less havoc; this fresh disaster slammed home even as the first blizzards choked the high passes through Camris.

'Grace save us, *now even our land routes are strangled!*' pealed the distressed Minister of the Royal Treasury.

Before wailing pandemonium could upend the whole room, the Prince of the Light met injured rage with a cry of derisive astonishment. 'Did you expect our triumph over tyranny could be simple? Or did you believe the Fellowship of Seven would abdicate its stranglehold of power for this, our first stir of opposition?' Avid as white flame, Lysaer paused. His gaze raked the choleric tangle of courtiers, and his rebuke rolled on like a dousing of pure arctic ice. 'You amaze me, afraid as you are for your gold, when four companies of dedicated Etarrans lie stricken. They have offered their lives on foreign soil for a cause far more grave and far-reaching than a short-term hoarding of wealth.'

'Our coin paid for those troops,' a man in claret velvet dared from the rearmost ranks.

'Are you so faint of heart you can cry for results, but not weather even one setback?' Lysaer's tone shaded into ineffable sorrow. 'I am shamed, then. Count endurance so lightly, then expect to fall short! The course we embark on will not ride on one effort, nor even flourish without a concerted, long-range vision of sacrifice. Upon petty greed and divisive hearts will the Sorcerers and the evil embodied by the Shadow Master achieve our sorry defeat. Men will weep then, and not just for one season's lost profits in trade. No. The suffering price will be written and paid by our children's descendants for all time!'

Tense stillness descended, stirred by the shifting of hats and corpulent weight, and the sweating of bodies discomfited by constraining state clothes and pressed velvets. Only Erdane's man seemed unmoved, as a volatile defensiveness swept through the gathering, the smoldering spark of unease touched against their deep-seated fear of dispossession.

Prince Lysaer gave the guildsmen's sullen quiet no quarter. 'Very well. If the great citizens of Avenor lack the character and dedication to sustain the full course of endeavor, I shall expend every resource I have to remember humanity first of all.'

An eruption of protests rattled the salvers, with the shrill, angered cries of Avenor's guild ministers ringing the loudest of all.

'What's to be done?' snapped the Minister of the Royal Treasury. 'You have no vast funds to wage a winter campaign, and your dowry's been promised to the shipyard.'

A hard, weighty pause; then Prince Lysaer turned his back. His appeal was presented to no one else but his steadfast Lord Commander. 'You have my direct order, and an open note on my possessions. Sell every furnishing, every tapestry, every chest of gold plate in my household and use the proceeds to succor those fallen. Give all in my power to provide for their care. You will make free of Tysan's crown resources, and call the full garrison back into field service. Their immediate muster will lend you the muscle to move every man stricken down into dry quarters and comfort.'

Against the dismayed rustle arisen at his back, his words lashed with stinging reprimand. 'Every captain or soldier who refuses my summons will be turned off without pay! More than that, any city too engrossed in self-interest to supply aid will be cast outside my protection.'

He exhorted no more, spoke of no retribution. In suspense, his courtiers craned forward. They expected the usual smooth flourish of statecraft that would frame the grand plan to build forces and see justice done.

Lysaer gave back the barest, leashed glance of exasperation. His carriage displayed his most acid contempt as he dismissed his Lord Commander to shoulder the duties set upon him.

The impact struck home: outside of all precedent, there would be no fiery speech of inspiration, no brilliant new strategy to banish the perils of high sorcery.

The Prince Exalted awarded the grave majesty of his regard to the mud-splashed courier, who sat dazed with exhaustion in his chair. As though that picked audience was intimately private, he bestowed the magnanimous accolade of his kindness. 'For your care for your fellow Etarrans, please stay. Sit and sup in my place. Enjoy the best food and drink in good health, for in sad fact, my presence is wasted. The truth is a tragedy, as you see. Avenor begs for no guidance beyond the bare need to see its trade and its merchants feather their own nests, *and I was not born, nor gifted with divine powers for the purpose of rich men's protection.'*

A muted flash of his pearls underscored his gesture to summon his page to his side. Then the Prince of the Light stepped down from the dais. Without further ceremony, he swept from the hall, leaving Erdane's delegate struck thoughtful, and Avenor's state ministers gawping like fishes tossed onto shores of dry sand.

# Prime Enchantress

At the private banquet in Avenor's royal palace, two deferent servants sprang to open the doors for the Prince of the Light's precipitous exit.

Stunned silence reigned through the first, dizzy breath of disbelief. Then tumult resurged with a bang of wild noise that rocked echoes off the groined ceiling. On the high dais, seated in the royal chair, the road-muddied messenger who dispatched the bad news blinked over the abandoned spread of fine food. He watched Avenor's state officers and trade ministers recover shocked wits and argue themselves into a fervent volte-face.

Their claims of bare coffers only minutes before suffered a miraculous readjustment. New offers of gold to be pledged for the Light materialized from dim places. Like chain lightning, caches hidden in deeper pockets resurfaced in the spate of high feeling that rolled and rebounded through the room.

Lord Eilish, Avenor's Minister of the Royal Treasury, recovered grizzled eyebrows from the heights of his gray-fringed hairline. No fool, he clapped his hands to recall his scurrying secretaries. Then, shot to his feet, arms beckoning, he rousted pages and wine servers to clear aside platters of roast duck and strip the table near the door to bare boards. There, ensconced like a judge with a row of state witnesses and a brace of Prince Lysaer's guardsmen, he dictated records and set under seal the promises that tumbled like charmed birds into his lap. He did not look up as Erdane's delegate slipped out.

But Gace Steward, who missed nothing, expected a fast courier would ride the north road before midnight. The impact of that evening's masterful play of statecraft would make itself felt far and wide.

Among the first to detect the fresh currents of change, an array of quartz spheres set in stands flashed to life in the stifling, close heat of a private chamber a hundred leagues distant from Avenor.

There, Morriel Prime, Matriarch of the Koriani Order, sat her high chair in the sisterhouse at Capewell. Reduced by age and infirmity to a bundle of thin bones wrapped in a tissue of creased flesh, her robed form was propped upright in pillows. Wax candles burned like pale pillars at both elbows. A violet silk throw bordered with bullion ribbon mantled her lap. Her strengthless hands cupped another sphere of rock crystal, aligned by her trained circle of seeresses to fine-tuned spells of scrying.

In momentous synchronicity, the image of Avenor's disrupted state banquet danced to the sigils and seals their inveigling mastery had stitched through the stone's aligned matrix. Morriel absorbed every nuance of the scene, intent as a cat poised over a glass bowl of goldfish.

Her colorless lips pleated into vexed wrinkles, as, in distanced miniature, Lord Eilish arose and stretched, then closed and locked the boards of the ledger which kept his account of the Alliance treasury.

'Clever man. Clever, clever man,' she rasped on the tail of a stertorous exhale.

Though her attendant page boys and servants knew not to respond to anything but her direct summons, the dewy, blond woman perched on the stool at her knee had yet to be curbed from such frivolous liberties. 'Do you mean Prince Lysaer?' Her fluttery gesture singled out another quartz, the end sphere of the array of eight, cradled in its silver stand, and positioned in a semicircle around the Prime Matriarch's chair. 'But his Grace has apparently abandoned his council.'

While she spoke, the torchlit depths of the quartz showed Avenor's Prince Exalted mounting a handsome cream horse in the taciturn company of his Lord Commander.

Morriel looked up. Her eyes sustained the drilled hardness of obsidian, opaque beside her younger colleague's innocence. 'He has left them, don't you see? Let them know absolutely their money can't buy his complaisant protection. Watch them. They'll stew in his absence. They'll sweat and pace themselves silly, then raise still more coin as a blandishment. Oh yes. Lysaer's read their worth and their secret fears to an exquisite, fine point of accuracy. He'll take his sweet time coming back. When he finally returns, his council and trade guilds will fall over themselves to welcome the policies they would once have argued past death to prevent.'

The woman's youthful features stayed blank, lips parted as she awaited the binding conclusion.

'Lysaer will have to take Sulfin Evend's council, now,' Morriel mused, finger tapping the quartz, and her eggshell brow tucked with speculation. 'He must hire talent to keep track of his enemies, if he's not to find himself continually blindsided by the doings of Fellowship Sorcerers.'

'How can you know this?' the girl said, admiring.

'Study the present,' the Prime Matriarch instructed in dry malice. 'The clues to unlock the future ever and always are written into the patterns of each moment.'

The initiate furrowed her fresh brow and made a dutiful survey of the scenes logged and transmitted by the quartz spheres. Time passed, and the candles burned lower. Morriel Prime closed eyelids the webbed texture of dead leaves, her crabbed hands stilled upon the purple velvet in her lap.

'Cast your net finer,' she suggested, unprompted.

The young woman started. 'Yes, Matriarch.' She deepened her survey, saw a ship with furled sails rock at chilly anchorage at Tideport. She watched torches weaving through the gusty night at the crowded settlement of Watercross, where the fallen from Caithwood were bundled like cordwood in the common rooms of the inns, or sheltered under the gust-slapped canvas of the field tents. She tracked the Prince of the Light, who hastened his column of guardsmen southward, then followed the galloping outriders who raced ahead to secure them a galley passage out of Riverton inlet. She traversed a chain of dockside taverns in Orlest, and tight knots of men at the trader's wharf, where talk ran to raids and losses to the minions of darkness.

'I see widespread fear of the Master of Shadow,' she lisped in uncertain conclusion. 'The moil seems unfounded. He's far at sea, and surely no direct threat to the continent.'

'At sea, yes.' Morriel spoke with shut eyes. 'Yet he has not withdrawn his presence or his interests. Look for connections. Cast your net finer still.'

The girl fidgeted on her footstool, unable to find any relevance in the current view, of three trollops sharing gossip over hot chocolate in gilt cups, while a fourth one penned a letter in overdone script on the back of a secondhand parchment. Squint though she would, the initiate could make no sense of the contents. She raised a tentative hand and sketched a cipher for clarity, and watched the image shift from the prostitutes' boudoir to the taproom of a seaside tavern, where a soap merchant with fat jowls and a marten collar lost a devastating hand of cards to the nerve-wound youngest son of the clanborn Duke of Alestron.

'Nothing fits,' she said, plaintive.

Morriel scarcely stirred, patient as none before ever saw her. 'The trouble with new servants is the tedious time teaching them who should and should not be admitted. Lirenda is here.' Eyes still closed, the Prime added, 'She will demonstrate the thread of reason your inexperience has overlooked.'

The next instant, the latch clicked. The haughty, black-haired initiate swept in, a damp cloak on her arm, and her woolen skirts rimmed in the pale clay wicked up from the trodden-up yard of a countryside posthouse. She sank into obeisance, exuding the frost-keen scent of winter air. 'I return from Araethura with word that the child, Fionn Areth, has been made our oathsworn servant.'

Morriel's pinched face tipped aslant in the candlelight. 'How convenient for you.' Her eyes opened, black glass flecked in spite and the false, warm reflections of flame. 'Forgive me if I don't reward you with credit until your vaunted plan brings a success.'

Lirenda's flare of rage was adroitly masked behind a facade of decorum. 'How may I serve?'

The Prime goaded, relentless. 'Since you've come, you can show Selidie how to draw out the connecting thread for the Shadow Master's interests on the continent. I hedge all my options these days. You'll know that already, since you've assiduously applied all your training to sorting the rumors.' A rim of worn teeth lent an edge to her smile as Morriel watched for the signs her baiting had chafed on a weakness.

The former First Enchantress arose to full height, self-contained as a panther. She chose caution before argument. At the end of a difficult, cold-weather journey, this needling trap the Prime spun presented a mazework of pitfalls. Not least, the scrying would demand a calling rune set through the resonance of Arithon Teir's'Ffalenn's true Name. The ignominy burned, since a near-fatal fascination with that same prince's character had tripped her downfall from the Prime's favor. Her meddling desire for personal revenge had upset the grand construct that had formerly failed to take the wretched man captive.

Lirenda lidded her personal bitterness under a mask of humility. Morriel herself remained a cripple since that day, confined to the Capewell sisterhouse in the months that followed her collapse. Through her tedious convalescence, the most gifted of her healers yet failed to restore her lower limbs. While concern began to be fretted in whispers, that the Prime might never recover her lost strength and walk, Morriel herself was not sanguine. Burdened with the need for additional servants, and pinned between bedridden ennui, or the jostling discomfort of a sedan chair, her eggshell-frail bones and translucent flesh contained the irascible fury of a volcano denied any vent for eruption.

Over that whelming maelstrom of infirmity, the frustration of balked will and spent hope, amid the perilous turn just taken by Tysan's curse-driven politics, the Prime Matriarch still ruled her domain like honed diamond. Nor did she allow fraility to loosen her grasp upon current events.

Lirenda knew better than to misjudge the request as a petty bid for vindication. She stepped forward and accepted the ice weight of the quartz from her Prime, set on notice by the play of cruel ironies that her character stood on trial yet again. She must perform this small office without flaw, or be judged inadequate to win back her lost rank as the Koriani prime successor.

She dared not vent her towering rage, that her competency was being used to tutor the green candidate set up as her replacement. One deep breath, two; she reestablished her calm. Any work done in concert with quartz required absolute emotional control. Lirenda assessed the sphere held in hand, its directive the tuned key for the array of eight ranged in their stands about Morriel's chair. One of the Prime's unobtrusive servants brought her a claw-footed stool.

She sat. Travel-stained clothing could not dim the innate poise of her breeding; she might as well have been offered a throne. The eyes she fixed on the young, blond initiate were antique amber, notched with pupils like primordial night. 'One begins with the rune of relationship,' she explained, her tone detached as struck bronze. 'Such power draws the lane forces into alignment, that one quartz sphere will resonate with the next, letting a live current pass between them.'

Her hand traced the symbol over the crystal, each cross stroke and upright inscribed in etched ribbons of light. 'Bind the energy into unity with the sigil that demarks the joined circle.'

'The rune seal for holding?' the initiate asked, her diffidence emphasized by an affected flounce.

Lirenda's smile turned graven. 'Then you've learned the twenty-eight primary seals? Very good.' Her polished encouragement showed none of her contempt, that an enchantress chosen for Morriel's training should have mastered such basics beforetime. 'Do you know the next step?'

The woman pinched a peony lip between her even, pearl teeth. 'The circle is empty?'

'Yes.' Lirenda stifled an exasperated sigh. 'Every spell needs a vector, an energy, to lend it purpose and direction. In this case, your Prime requests linkages to the affairs of the Master of Shadow. Therefore, the tie must begin with knowledge of the subject's true Name.' Lirenda cupped the master sphere, stared into its depths, and inwardly sealed herself into a calm that admitted no chink for distraction. She could feel the eyes of the Prime upon her like hot probes, testing, observing, awaiting a reaction that might expose any lingering canker of weakness.

But Lirenda had long since shielded her vulnerable core against Arithon's beguiling attraction. Venomed hatred remained. She would see the last scion of s'Ffalenn struck dead before she allowed his compassionate potential to awaken the seed of her dormant passion. Disciplined to perfection, she spoke the invocation to call and to bind. Over that matrix, she added the sigil of self-mastery, then into that waiting vessel of containment, the shaped memory of an unmistakable male face. Three times, she called the name of Arithon Teir's'Ffalenn.

The quartz sphere absorbed her building intent. Its matrix took fire and responded, amplifying the tuned alignment of gifted talent and aimed thought. Lirenda sensed the impacting force of that presence storm her unassailable calm. Prepared, she held firm. Trained will locked her mind into permafrost clarity, until an unexpected influx of outside force wrenched her alignment off course. A sweet, sustained note pierced through, then a chord that melted all armor. The opening measure swelled into an intimate play of glad sound that beguiled beyond will to deny.

Lirenda lost grip on her construct of ciphers. The unbearable purity of a melody she had most diligently expunged out of memory burst through and flanked her shield of defenses.

The quartz in her hand pealed back in kind, and magnified that clear cry of rapture into joy that burst all restraint. Then the wrought spiral of harmony raised raw desire, and whirled her off center into trance . . .

Sucked down, and down again into a well of absolute darkness charged with delights and addictive possibility, Lirenda cried out in furious protest. Her denial just raised a more clamorous, inward betrayal.

The whispered male presence of the musician gave her back his lilting, unbridled laughter. 'But lady enchantress, surely in this case you made the first effort to call me?'

Dragged into a vista of dreaming vision, Lirenda beheld a starlit night where the winds blew mild and warm. Far beyond the winter's fast grip, a ship's masts with its spiderwork of running lines and tarred rigging sliced the sky into graceful geometrics. Nor was the vessel's quarterdeck unoccupied.

Framed against the sturdy, spooled taffrail, and jeweled constellations skewed at unfamiliar angles by an extreme change of latitude, she confronted the brigantine's helmsman: none else but the slim, dark-haired bard whose mastery had loomed the exquisite snare that entrapped her.

The angular, stamped features of s'Ffalenn royalty were unmistakable, cast now into a patent, amused inquiry that tipped up one corner of Arithon's mouth. Across the friable trance which suspended her, his presence ignited her confusion, fed and fueled by a whirlwind of formless emotion.

Lirenda fought to resist the influx of detail that split second of contact engraved on her inner awareness: the fine grace of his carriage offset by commonplace clothing, and the jet strands of hair fallen loose from their tie to tangle and wisp at his temples. If the events of the summer had harrowed his health, in seafaring solitude, Prince Arithon had won back a carefree, if temporary, freedom. His dark breeches were buttoned with engraved silver studs, and his strong, arched feet were bare. His plain linen shirt was a soft, unbleached ivory, and the loose, doeskin laces with their beaded pearl ends were flicked and teased by the winds. The agile fingers which had danced those honeyed measures on fret and string were wound now on the spokes of a ship's wheel.

Apparently he had sensed her intrusion before her shocked moment of recognition. His sharpened gaze was not fixed anymore on the stars or the compass he steered by.

Nor was his face entirely invulnerable, caught as he was in the listening intensity of sounding her presence in return. She received the impression of eyes that were haunted and deep, and disturbingly focused until he captured her individual identity; not by sight, but by some unseen resonance of intuition kept entrained by his prodigious talent.

'Ah, Lirenda.' His voice made disturbing music of her name, while his expression showed dry irony, and his lips widened into the faintest, curved smile of mockery. 'You've reconnected with the gift I left in your quartz crystal, I see.'

Formless in fury, imprisoned in the flux of an involuntary scrying, Lirenda reacted before thought. *'This should not be possible!'*

Arithon's eyebrows arose. 'No?' He brightened. 'Shall we use the occasion to indulge in a philosophical argument on the principles of magecraft? The result might leave you wiser, if no less enlightened.'

She disdained to answer.

'Your thinking is crippled by limitations, dear lady, not to mention your beliefs.' A pause, jammed by the stone-walled strength of her obstinacy. 'What, no riposte in dry wit? No unhappy jabs at the cuticle? Enchantress, you *wouldn't* prefer having me speak for us both?'

Head tilted sidewards, the free wind in his hair, he delighted in choosing the words for her anyhow, teasing and blithe as a swallow. 'Well for argument's sake, let's say you'd affirm the crystal carries a vibration. If fire's your base element, you would understand that water stands as the placeholder for emotion. Is your foot tapping yet? It would be, you know, as you moved on to insist the salt contained in the ocean must obey its coarse nature and negate every trace of transmission.'

A toy to his whim, Lirenda returned nothing. The dream held her fast, while the stars rocked to the gentle roll of a ship's hull. The hand that had recently known trials and illness held her course with relaxed and infuriating competence.

'Then perhaps you need clues to unravel the riddle?' Arithon grinned in provocation. 'Very well. I'll be generous. The sound I created was vibration also, if pitched for the octaves inside the range of hearing. The seed for my music is carried by air, the primal element of inspiration. Dear lady, wind wanders where it will. It knows no boundary, nor heeds human law, nor answers to the earth-grounding virtues of salt.'

'*I reject your rank meddling,*' Lirenda hissed back, slapped by the truth that he had just volunteered the keys to reclaim her self-control. 'One day you'll know sorrow. My hand will break you. I promise you then, no schoolboyish prank played on learned theory will spare your insolent autonomy.'

A gust heeled the brigantine's deck. Arithon glanced at a star to ascertain his heading, then spun his wheel two points to starboard to compensate. His green eyes lit then, alive to his shrug of apology. 'No originality there. You'll be one of a very large crowd falling over themselves to claim the first blood at my capture.' He ended his byplay in corrosive apology. 'There's a curious reverse. I always thought you the type to rule the pack rather than follow.'

'Demon!' she gasped, riled into unwitting defense by his slicing truth of perception.

Shamed to have yielded that morsel of insight, she rallied her scattered self-command and framed the sigil of negation. Once she set the dark seal to command air, the shock of forced severance tumbled her back into vertigo. While she raged in the threadbare shreds of her dignity, her naked mind rang with the contrary echoes of his laughter . . .

The rinse of white static released her hobbled faculties and gave back the closed heat of the Prime Matriarch's chamber. Lirenda shuddered through the moment of transition, whiplashed back to cognizant thought by the rasp of Morriel's reprimand.

'. . . must be a lackwit, girl! Haven't I told you time and again? Keep that spell crystal doused in black silk!'

A snuffling stir of movement, as the young initiate returned a dutifully weepy nod. She fumbled for the remedy bag hung from her girdle, loosened the strings, then shoved tear-drenched fingers inside.

Morriel's chastisement was instant. 'Dry your hands! Never, *never* let salt near a crystal set into a resonant spell pattern!'

Trembling now, the girl blotted her damp knuckles on her skirt; and Lirenda, caught aback, received the demeaning revelation that she had been led to engage the Named resonance of Arithon s'Ffalenn *in the presence of her personal spell crystal. The misfortunate quartz had yet to be cleansed of the melody Arithon had imprinted to lay bare her vulnerable heart.* The girl initiate had been given the task of lifting the impurity from the quartz; and though months had passed under Morriel's direct tutelage, she had not only failed to master so simple a task, but had also neglected the basics of handling an activated focus pendant.

The sheer magnitude of the incompetence rankled. The novice initiate Morriel had chosen to groom had raw talent without the brains of a flea. Lirenda contained her resentment, well aware that the Prime would discern far more than the young woman's stupidity. She dared not invite the parallel comparison, that she herself had strong aptitude and skilled training, but a woeful inability to checkrein her personal feelings.

Eyes closed, wrapped in the evanescent perfume of hot candle wax, Lirenda forced down her inner turmoil. While the girlish initiate restored the crystal to proper wrappings and retied the cords of her remedy bag, the older enchantress slowed the sped beat of her heart. She doused heated nerves and noosed the wild, wakened spate of her anger back into settled calm, then rebalanced the sigils which fused the burst web of the quartz scrying. Left to mark time, she bent her will back to the master sphere in her hand.

Where the sigils of command already in place should have revealed Arithon's image, the crystal hung smoke dark and veiled; no surprise. The effects of sea brine alone would inhibit the virtues of quartz scrying. In addition, the man would have cloaking spells and circles of guard set about him by Dakar the Mad Prophet. Morriel Prime herself had long since established the futility of scrying for the Prince of Rathain. Yet though his immediate presence stayed obscured, his peripheral connections were less ruly. In the marginal spaces, where random event and emotion spun loose ends, the quartz could tag subtle connections to Prince Arithon as the unshielded currents of conscious activity deflected the signature vibrations of the earth's flow of magnetic lane force.

Linked through the darkened rock crystal in her hands, Lirenda changed focus. She searched the bloom of movement and color as vision coalesced in the depths of the slave-linked spheres on their stands.

One showed the stripped trees of a glen in Halwythwood. Under the night's dusting of snowfall, a cluster of clan lodge tents, guarded by a large-boned, rangy man wrapped in a bearskin mantle. By the glint of bronze hair revealed as a woman passed by with a torch, Lirenda recognized the man as Jieret s'Valerient, *caithdein* and steward of the realm in the seafaring absence of its sanctioned crown prince. The trill of infant laughter that brought the smile to his lips would be his daughter, Jeynsa, named his heir by the Fellowship of Seven, and not yet aged one year. A steadfast adherent of the old charter law, the liegeman served as Arithon's voice in Rathain. Like the Koriathain, Earl Jieret could do little else but wait for the day when his oathsworn sovereign chose to return.

In a scene purloined from a fortified tower farther east, another sphere revealed the massive frame of Duke Bransian of Alestron, sprawled at ease in a chair with a hound's muzzle propped on his knee. His war-scarred fingers stroked the dog's ears, while a diminutive old lady with crab-apple features stabbed an ebony stick in ripe argument over his decision to appoint his state galley for a winter voyage down the southcoast.

In another, the clan chieftain who was High Earl of Alland broached a beer cask in a pine glade, while companions sharpened their knives for a cattle raid, and a runner sewed up a holed pair of leggings, his new orders to bear a message to a secret destination in the west.

Yet another sphere reflected a high mountain in Vastmark. There a herder woman with bells tied into her tawny braids regarded the stars, and thought wistfully upon Arithon s'Ffalenn. 'Luck ride your shoulder, wherever you are,' she murmured in dialect, then appended the heartfelt blessing of her tribe.

In the deserts of Sanpashir, an elder dipped a hawk feather in fresh blood and read omens in the scattered droplets. The augury received brought a spark to filmed eyes, and sent a young man to fetch darts and knives on his gruff bark of command.

Arithon's contacts were varied and many, Lirenda was forced to concede; in yet another sphere, three chattering whores in a Sanshevas garret sewed a marked strip of goatskin into a hem of pink silk.

A minstrel playing a tavern in Etarra paused to converse with three dicers wearing the colors of the town guard; farther south, an innkeeper who owned a dingier dive in Ship's Port threw silver to a galleyman, then engaged in whispered talk too faint for the crystal's tuned matrix to capture.

A scribe in King Eldir's service penned a letter by the fluttering light of a candle, while elsewhere a vivacious woman in sailhand's slops and a gaudy scarlet shirt locked horns in ribald language with a stiff-lipped customs clerk in Tideport.

Immersed in close survey of the eclectic array, Lirenda could almost touch the intangible thread that tied each disparate player into a logical web of continuity. She sensed the flow of information and the move-ment of rumor. Yet whenever she grasped any piece of the puzzle and sought to find linear order, the pieces slipped, formless, through the sieve of hard cognizance. The pattern remained stubbornly elusive as water absorbed into felt.

Lirenda released a soundless sigh, too experienced not to realize when outside forces deflected her practiced technique. Arithon had a trained spellbinder for his watchdog. The Mad Prophet had seeded invisible snares that would smother her most determined attempt to link random event with its core of revealing conclusion. She might glean the surface viewpoint of the Shadow Master's correspondents, but never decipher their interrelated connection, nor the guarded cache of their secrets: the links that would yield the site where the brigantine *Khetienn* made landfall to replenish provisions.

Lirenda shivered with starved longing to break through Dakar's web of safeguards. How she ached to smash the flesh-and-blood source of her weakness, which had deprived her of privilege and the fruits of her earned inheritance. Immersed in dire passion, she failed to notice that the Prime's reproval of the young initiate had long since reached final closure. Nor did she hear the crone's scratchy address, or look up, until the yawning, expectant silence intruded, and quenched her rush of hot need.

'Your pardon?' she murmured.

A figure of shriveled ivory and wax in the faltering glow of the candles, the Prime Enchantress regarded her. Morriel's hands were crabbed knots, tucked in smudgeless velvets, and her black eyes light-less wells of malice. 'The sigil of summoning to trace and mark the future?' she prompted, succinct as flung acid. 'I bade you to finish the scrying.'

Lirenda flushed. The request was impossible, as the Prime knew quite well. Set up to fail before a green novice, she stiffened, her heart struck to glass-edged fury, and her thoughts plunged into a quicklime stillness that the Prime's waspish wit could not pierce. Her voice was chilled honey as she made the traditional reply. 'Your will.'

The sigil with its barbed runes and crossed square flowed off her scribing fingernail. Its coiled directive sank into the quartz orb like charged wire, filed to razor-edged light. The energy sank into the stone's matrix, bit through its dimmed depths, and unfurled a riptide of backlash.

Lirenda fell into a flowering burst of color and noise, then a sleeting gray static through which one sensation emerged to rush the blood in her veins: she felt a man's lips on hers, and an eruption of passion to burn every nerve incandescent.

Then Morriel's laughter, like the scrape of dry leaves, hurled Lirenda earthward and grounded her back into shrinking humiliation.

'It would appear your feelings of superiority are unjustified,' the Prime said. While the initiate looked on in vacant confusion, she added, 'Tell me to my face, if you dare, that I should not stake my trust in your replacement.'

Lirenda arose. Self-contained by her desperate desire for vindication, she curtsied in defiant breach of form, that she need not behave as all others in the order, and request formal leave to depart. 'Stake your trust where you please, until the year Fionn Areth grows to maturity. Then I will face the sure test of your reckoning. On the day I deliver Prince Arithon in chains, let any latecoming applicant for your office overmatch my fitness if she dares.'

A pungent, breathy laugh brushed her challenge aside. 'I do see that my years of infirmity won't pass without entertainment. That is well. I have no intention whatsoever of biding my time in blind faith. You must prove your competence to assume the seat of my power.' Small triumph became punishment as Morriel flicked her wrist in derisive finality. 'You are excused.'

While Lirenda swept out to a rustle of splashed mantles, the Prime's fathomless eyes fixed a predator's stare upon the untried face of her current favorite. 'We've seen what we needed,' she rasped in conclusion. 'Those spells Dakar's cast throw off a wide resonance. When Lysaer s'Ilessid binds loyal talent to his cause, that unsubtle touch could become a dangerous liability . . .' As her musing trailed off into stillness, she realized the young woman drooped like a lily kept past its best bloom. 'Rest now, Selidie,' the Prime crooned, almost fondly. 'See yourself off to bed. One of my servants will go to the kitchen to arrange for a bowl of warmed milk.'

# Althain's Warden

The guard spells securing the grimward in Korias were a maze framed in paradox, a blaze of wild power channeled through ciphers that bridged both sides of the veil. Entangling coils wrought through time and space framed both bulwark and bias, a weaving of consummate delicacy that layered chaos through primal order like acid burns struck through taut parchment. The barrier carved an isolate pocket between the fabric of Athera's solidity and the dire peril contained inside. No spells in existence were more deadly; nor did the Fellowship Sorcerers command better means to stay the unbinding currents of flux energies unleashed by the dreams of dead dragons.

The juxtaposition of hours to months always made the last crossing a feat of unparalleled danger, even for a Sorcerer whose hand had renewed the bindings that laced those same ward rings to renewed stability. Flat weary, aching in shoulders and neck from the wear of unswerving concentration, Sethvir bent his head and whispered encouragement to Asandir's long-suffering black horse.

The stallion flicked back an ear; responded. His stride lengthened. He bore his rider through the dusty, stale air locked in stasis within the outer perimeter. Sethvir raised a hand marked red with cinder burns and traced the final string of seals in blue fire. Power surged through him, sure as aimed lightning, the discharge drawn into an exacting harmonic balance. His labor completed, the Sorcerer sensed the shimmering currents lock shut in the windless void. He sighed his relief. The grueling task of sealing the breached grimward had reached completion at long last.

'We're done here, little brother,' he confided to the horse.

The black stud shook his mane, gave a ringing stamp on the white-granite paving, and wheeled. The eerie song of charged forces slipped behind as his step carried through the outermost spell of concealment.

Waiting on the far side was the damp, winter blast of a sleeting snowfall in Korias.

Sethvir drew in a shuddering breath. Early dusk spread a pall over the land. Around him, the low, rolling ground was patched gray and white, rocks and lichens snatched bare where the gusts whined off the weathered hillcrests.

Bone tired as he was, for a half second the Sorcerer sat the ebony stud's back, confused. The sting of the storm on his face, the bite of cold air on bare knuckles seemed discomforts that belonged to another man's body. Althain's Warden blinked as though jostled into a dream. He watched, all but mesmerized, while his breath puffed plumes in the gathering darkness.

Then even that fragmented awareness upended. His senses whirled away in kaleidoscopic chaos as the restored torrent of the earth link hurled his mind through a cataract of impressions.

For a brief, helpless interval he swayed in the saddle, hands locked in black mane to stay upright. Visions rinsed his mind like actinic static, a deluge of disordered, random events spiked by the odd, recognizable fragment . . .

*He saw a royal birth in Havish laced through the mating of whales in the china blue reaches of South Sea. In a cedar-paneled room with red curtains, Duke Bransian of Alestron read a letter penned by his brother Mearn, his iron brows bristled to irritation. Black bears in Strakewood huddled deep in hibernation. An old tree dreamed of rage, and a snarl of stalled trade sent mounted couriers splashing through a rutted ford in Camris, led on by torchlight, and given right of way by their rippling sunwheel banner. A field mouse snatched kernels of corn from a granary, and a shepherd child in Araethura complained of a deep ache in the bones of his face. Southward, where windy rain fell, a brig with a white star carved on her counter cracked out full sail on command of a fair-haired female captain . . .*

For one moment, two, Sethvir's mind pinwheeled, hazed through the gauntlet of images that came on as senseless bundles of color and noise. Then the innate mastery of his gift resurged. He recaptured those uncountable, disparate threads, deftly sorted their origins, and loomed them back into one web of exacting, immaculate order.

Moon phase and tides reset his awareness. The grounding solidity of the earth lent him roots to withstand the vast void of the sky. Then the vista of storm-ridden landscape around him regained continuity and rebalanced his position to the cardinal points of direction. Restored to his venue as Althain's Warden, Sethvir sat with closed eyes. In one snap-frozen second, he mapped the changed patterns of harmony and discord. Another fractional instant let him touch each of his distant colleagues with the informed assurance of his return.

Asandir stood, hip deep in a snowdrift on the Plain of Araithe, retuning a damaged stone marker that smoothed a confluence of earth's lane force; Traithe, on the storm-beaten strands of Lithmere, was completing the final ward in the chain forbidding landfall to slave-bearing galleys. Luhaine, an arrow of liberated joy, rode on a breeze that ranged southward out of Atainia. Kharadmon still stood on watch amid the sealed silence of the void. There, where the distant sun of Athera was reduced to a candleflame glimmer, the star wards raised against the mist-bound wraiths trapped on Marak posted a vigilant guard across arc seconds of darkness. Last, though in pain and peril, never least, Sethvir sensed the presence of Davien the Betrayer, lurking in self-imposed isolation in the caverns beneath the roots of the Mathorn Mountains.

Of Ciladis, as ever, his earth-sense found no sign, though he combed all the planet in vain hope and sorrowful reflex. Then, the raw cold offered welcome distraction from the razor-sharp pain of old grief.

Sethvir stirred from his stupor. Mauled by the teeth of the gusts, he closed slackened hands on the reins. The sleet seeded droplets of melt in his beard, and the horse underneath him blew a loud snort of impatience.

'Brave one, I'm with you.' He stroked the stallion's wet crest, chilled by much more than inclement weather as he measured the days that the grimward's torn wards had engaged him.

Summer's hot winds had changed guard to midwinter. Five months had elapsed since he left Althain Tower, a grievous interval, but necessary. Any overlooked weakness in the complex ring of guard spells could spin final havoc through Athera's stability. For one crisis averted, old problems had acquired vicious new impetus. Foremost among them, Sethvir tracked repercussions from the roused trees in Caithwood, an event that had seeded a canker of strife across the Kingdom of Tysan.

Asandir's stopgap action had jammed travel and trade to a strident halt. Balked merchants bandied damning accusations against sorcery, while their craftsmen hoarded every coin they could squeeze for the purpose of Alliance retaliation. While goods piled up on the barge docks at Watercross, and guild tempers frayed and shortened, tales of armed men falling prey to fell sorceries fretted the towns to hysteria. Quarn's mayor was left indisposed after five hand-wringing weeks of protestation. Valenford's treasury had been emptied in the purging belief that Lysaer's claimed divinity could avert the ruin of prosperity. Each passing day and each fallen victim lent Avenor's crown examiners refreshed cause to denounce the practice of magecraft as a felony. Despite the season, small troops of sunwheel riders scoured the backcountry settlements in search of herb witches and birth-gifted makers of talismans.

Sethvir shivered. Cloakless, hatless, and clad in holed leathers ingrained with a damning reek of cinders and brimstone, he knew he might need more than tact at the door where he stopped to ask shelter. He turned the stud's nose north and westward toward Riverton, then spoke into a back-cocked black ear.

The horse picked sure steps down the ice-crusted slope, the reins looped slack on his neck. He had served as a Sorcerer's mount long enough not to balk at spell-sent directions. Sethvir tucked his fingers under his beard to foil the blasting wind. Lapsed into the half-tranced, dreamy inattention that widened his access to the earth link, he sifted the montage array of new images that knit each moment into the next.

Lysaer's thread of strategy snaked through the weave, steering Alliance interests to bind terrified trade guilds into a strangling dependency. Lord Harradene's Etarrans still languished unconscious. Now lodged at conspicuous expense at Avenor, they were made the graphic incentive to catalyze townborn distrust of sorcery. In disturbing, hard knots, Sethvir saw the cry for redress shift into committed resolve to take action.

All points converged toward an outbreak of war in the spring.

From the public misfortune of the comatose Etarrans, Lysaer s'Ilessid built doctrine in tireless speech and skilled statecraft. His inferences became accepted as certainty, that Fellowship Sorcerers worked in collusion with the Spinner of Darkness. From close talks in town taprooms to the whispers of mothers threatening unruly children, the unrest took root in even the most far-flung farmsteads. Outside Tysan's borders, frozen roads rang to the hooves of fast horses bearing sunwheel couriers. Alarmed city mayors heard the ready advice of crown officers and assumed the bright badge of the Alliance.

The flow of gold and information moved from hand to ringed hand, born out of the festering frustrations that raged behind the closed doors of the guildhalls. Savaged by seaborne attacks from clan pirates, gouty ministers were shown the Alliance hulls under construction at Riverton as firm proof of the crown's promise of protection. Lord Eilish brooded over Avenor's thickened ledgers and notated his fussy entries under a crawling halo of candlelight. Beneath his cramped office, Sethvir could hear the iron strapping the piled chests in Lysaer's treasury sing to the pitch of struck currency tendered from cities across the continent's five kingdoms.

Harried by more than the season's chill winds, the Sorcerer traced the crosscurrents designed to consolidate power. Lady Ellaine's hand-fasting to Lysaer wrought shifts: Erdane's new-fledged ambition wound intrigues that stitched through state policy in clandestine meetings, and in the dunning of farm crofts for tithes in the cause to eradicate sorcery and shadows. The revenues outfitted forays in winter, when campaign was not normally feasible.

In Westwood, hare and sparrows fled the march of armed men, who scoured the forests to slaughter the wild game and starve out a dwindled encampment of clansmen. The earth link unveiled the gaunt faces of children, and the obstinate courage which kept bows and drawn steel in the hands of their driven parents. Death wrote its lines of spilled blood in the snow. In a bare, wind-raked hollow, Maenol s'Gannley's cousin miscarried a seven-month pregnancy.

On the black stud in Korias, Sethvir wept, aggrieved for the loss of an irreplaceable infant who would not live to see daylight. He traversed the storm-swept barrens of Korias, nagged to chills, while Avenor's high council convened in a snug tower chamber. Cosseted in furs and damascened silk, they sipped vintage wine and administered Lysaer's policy with fatal ignorance of the stakes their chosen path courted. While their armorers forged weapons to uphold a wrongful cause, and crown instigators whispered their damning false testimony reviling minions of darkness, Kharadmon kept steadfast watch against a range of perils beyond the pale of mortal politics.

The massive, wrought ward ring that shielded Athera in the vast deeps between stars was never for a moment left unguarded. Should an invasion of free wraiths ever sweep in from Marak, a populace stripped of its natural-born talent would be left defenseless and wide-open to threat of possession. Then would mankind have cause to fear, and women weep, and innocent children suffer horrors.

'I fear the same thing.' Kharadmon's stray response reechoed across an incomprehensible distance as he affirmed the passing concern of Althain's Warden. 'All's quiet here, now. Too peaceful, perhaps. Those wraiths never rest. Through the months when they stalked me, they seethed and hated like a wasp nest stirred up by fiends. My watch *feels oppressive. Sometimes I worry that we're being shown what we wish to see in a mirror.'*

Sethvir winced, brought back to earth as icy runnels of snowmelt snaked down his open collar. His sleeves were soaked through, his leathers grown soggy. Against his back, the undaunted winds scoured down with their barbed burden of ice. He endured the cruel blast without rancor. As ever, the world's broadscale tapestry of events left him small thought to spare for the nuisance of bodily discomfort.

Nor would another poured current of cold, just arrived through the barrage of gusts, allow him to dwell upon Kharadmon's ruffled foreboding.

'You're back, and not one single moment too soon,' Luhaine carped from a backdrop of tenantless landscape. 'Of course the Koriathain used the months of your absence to their unscrupulous benefit.'

'You refer to the shepherd boy set under a change spell last autumn in Araethura?' Sethvir raised eyebrows the ice had grizzled like magnetized clumps of steel filings. His sharpened gaze tracked the invisible wraith flanking him. 'Fionn Areth was beyond our protection from the moment of his ill-fated birth. Since Elaira could do naught to cast off the life debt he owed her, she was most wise to entrust his fate to Prince Arithon's devices.'

Luhaine rattled through a gorse thicket hunched under a leading of sleet. 'Then you've already seen what Lirenda's wrought on the flimsy pretense of his innocent word of consent?'

Sethvir said nothing. The unnatural seals of regeneration which guided the transformation of Fionn Areth were too bitter a subject for talk. 'First tell me how long Asandir was convalescent before he left Althain Tower.'

'Four days.' Luhaine whirled in place. 'You're evading my question.' Presented with Sethvir's obstructive inattention at its worst, he stormed into motion again. 'Asandir asked for his stallion to be—'

'. . . sent on to the master of horse at the Red Water Inn,' Sethvir finished, unperturbed. The hostler there knew the stud's habits, and kept a clean stable with glossy, contented occupants. 'I already saw,' he added, before Luhaine could drone through every mundane detail surrounding Asandir's departure. Mirthlvain had brewed up a new strain of predator, and no colleague's lingering weakness could excuse the dismissal of unpleasant facts. The spellbinder who stood guard as Methisle's warden could never have curbed the late outbreak of aberrants without a Sorcerer's help. 'Just say whether Asandir was fit enough to be on his feet when he left.'

'He blocked your inquiry also?' Luhaine poised, a circle of seized stillness where the downfalling sleet changed course in midair and slashed like white needles straight earthward. 'That's worrisome.'

'But scarcely the first time,' Sethvir pointed out.

The vortex of Luhaine's presence poured headlong through a barrier of blackthorn. 'Stop hedging. I see how you're vexed.'

Althain's warden hunched his shoulders as the experienced stud plowed ahead through the winter-stripped branches. His answer came muffled behind his raised forearm as he rode a rimed gauntlet of storm-burdened sticks. 'Asandir's never been foolish.'

'Well, foolish or not, I couldn't hold him,' Luhaine retorted. 'We stand too shorthanded for any one of us to mismanage the limits of our personal resources.'

Sethvir disguised an untactful snort by wringing the ice melt from the draggled ends of his beard. The earth link exposed the residual glimmer of the warding maze Asandir had set on his back trail. In trying to eavesdrop on his progress through scrying, his discorporate colleague had been spun in blind circles for three days.

Flustered and embarrassed, Luhaine snapped anyway. 'Don't act so smug. Of us all, you know you're the only one who can match him and win.'

'Not always, and never in a contest of straight force.' Sethvir stared back, his blue-green eyes wide in his guileless effort to invite a diversion through trivial argument.

But for the sake of the shapechanged child in Araethura, Luhaine fastened on like a terrier. 'We should curb the plotting. That boy can't be left as a Koriani puppet to lure Arithon s'Ffalenn into jeopardy. *Morriel's meddling nearly drove his Grace to insanity the last time!* How *dare* she presume to risk triggering Desh-thiere's curse again.'

'We cannot interfere.' Sethvir's words were hammered iron. 'Misled or not, Fionn Areth gave his unconditional consent.'

A silence weighted with terrible memories settled between the two Sorcerers. The brutal wind howled, while its freight of barbed ice tapped and bounced off the spears of browned sedge, and the frost-turned canes of wild briar. For a time, the only living sound in the world was the grate of the stallion's shod hooves against the glazed crust frozen over the primordial slabs of scoured limestone.

However the Fellowship mages might be tempted to use power to stop the abuse of a child's innocence, they had no grounds. The Law of the Major Balance disallowed any choice which obstructed the course of free will. Unless Fionn Areth came to ask their assistance, the Sorcerers could not act, could never engage the force of grand conjury against the informed consent of the spirit.

Sethvir regarded the knuckles of his hands as if the streaks of unforgotten, past bloodstains remained branded into wet skin. 'We cannot step
back and resume our old ways. The boy's fate is Arithon's, now.'

Though his agonized whisper seemed masked by the storm that
whined over the barren landscape, Luhaine heard. 'You're shivering.'
The discorporate mage asked a permission of the elements, and shifted
the brunt of the wind. 'Have you given a thought to finding shelter
for the night?'

Sethvir regarded the slow slide of moisture from the crusted rime
on his sleeve cuffs. This time the grain of a desperate weariness let all
his sorrow break through. 'There's a farmwife nearby who hid an herb
witch from crown soldiers. If she knows me for a Sorcerer, she won't
turn me out.'

For her kindness, Sethvir could set wards of concealment on her
cellar. He might lay a blessing over her livestock that would encourage
them to bear twins for the next five years. The small comforts he could
bestow for a night's hospitality chafed against sensibilities left outraged
by other, immovable bounds of restraint. Timeworn wisdom granted
no comfort. Against the entanglement planned for Arithon s'Ffalenn
through the fate of an innocent child, the uncertainties ahead posed too
graphic a peril to dismiss. At least Luhaine chose tact and suppressed his
need to list the appalling facts: that Arithon was no match for Koriani
plots, not since the hour of the atrocities at Tal Quorin, when he had
gone blind to mage-sense in remorse. The Mad Prophet could remain
at his side to protect him only so long as his spellbinder's powers could
be spared by a Fellowship caught critically shorthanded.

'You'll return to Althain Tower to regroup?' Luhaine asked.

'Not yet.' Diminished by the desolate landscape, Sethvir squared his
shoulders against the flaying edge of the wind. 'For the sake of the
Etarran men-at-arms still spellbound by the dreaming of Caithwood's
trees, I intend to demand a state audience at Avenor.'

On that point, the compact gave the Fellowship Sorcerers clear
entitlement to act. Balked as they were on all other fronts, Althain's
Warden resolved to wring merciless advantage from that narrow chink
of opportunity.

# Developments

Just past his seventh birthday, the herder's son, Fionn Areth, returns from a scuffle with a peer, one eye bruised black, and a cut on his lip; and is dispatched to his blankets in the loft without supper while his father snaps to his goodwife, 'Well who wouldn't pick fights with him? No child in this valley, nor even his own brothers can bear the arrogant look that boy's learned to wear on his face . . .'

Far south of Araethura, a wizened desert seer recasts his third augury in bones on the sable sands of Sanpashir, and his reading affirms the arrival of Shadow, and the living future of his tribe; his instructions to his people carry the weight of action as he concludes, 'We go now to the ancient ruins to stand guard . . .'

On the east shore of Melhalla, a galley flying the scarlet bull of Alestron embarks for Avenor, where the duke's brother, Parrien s'Brydion, will attend the wedding of Prince Lysaer s'Ilessid and post an ambassador to relieve Mearn, whose appointed service to the Alliance of Light has kept him from home for eight years . . .

# IV. Reckoning

At Avenor, the victims of the Caithwood campaign were tended in a string of dockside warehouses donated to the cause by the city's disgruntled trade guilds. The arrangement proved far from felicitous. Always before, the rich sea trade through Havish had ensured steady profits through the lull while the passes in Camris lay snowbound. Other years at midwinter, those same buildings were crammed with the fruits of industrious commerce. The fact this season's goods were summarily displaced by a misfortunate company of sick men raised a clamoring chorus of complaint.

Where bribes had once sidestepped Havish's crown rights of enforcement against galleys manned by slave oarsmen, now the wide-ranging deterrent of a Fellowship ward seal put closure to the market's furtive evasions. With eight illegal craft snared outright by spellcraft, and no sign of reprieve in sight, the merchant factions sweated in their lace and brocades, and argued the dearth of alternatives. Their options were choked, they knew well enough. No palliative could salvage high losses. Not with the less direct route to the south closed by hazard, the land passage through Caithwood turned haunted by trees raised to wakened awareness.

In boneheaded fury, the most determined guildsmen attempted to bypass the forest. These dispatched slave galleys up Mainmere Narrows, or outfitted others with free labor at perishing expense to access the trade road beyond Ostermere. Few arrived there unscathed. Barbarian raiders roved the sea-lanes under sail, outfitted in the selfsame hulls the Spinner of Darkness had stolen from Riverton.

The wharfside taverns brewed up angry talk. Seasoned galleymen refused well-paid berths for fear of bloodthirsty predation. Clan crews lately reclaimed from chained slavery were likely to choose vengeance before mercy toward oppressors who had shown them the brand and the whip.

Alliance retribution would stay paralyzed until spring, when the royal marriage with Erdane's daughter brought the dowry to launch the new fleet. In the dockside climate of snarling frustration, and the clatter of the mounted patrols sent out by Avenor's Crown Examiner to redress the complaints against sorcery, one man handled the upsets of fate with ironclad equanimity.

In the wind-raked, cavernous warehouse jammed with stricken invalids, Avenor's royal healer made his daily rounds in shorthanded resignation. He was a gangling man, given to brusque speech and a harried expression of perplexity. One cot to the next, he lugged his worn satchel with its chinking phials of remedies. An emetic prescribed here, and there, a soup of barley gruel and butter where one of his charges had lost flesh; the passing weeks had produced no improvement in the condition of Caithwood's victims.

Their affliction followed no ordinary pattern of malady. Sprawled comatose on straw ticking, the body of the man he currently examined had lost neither tone nor vitality. The suspended state was unnatural. Muscle should atrophy from disuse, and the organs slowly fail in their function. Yet of the ninetyscore Etarrans afflicted that autumn, not one wasted from starvation. Wrapped in an uncanny hibernation, their heart rate and breathing had slowed. Their life signs languished, faint to near nonexistent, as though their animate function stood in abeyance. Somehow, they subsisted on infusions of broth, with most none the worse, while their bodily needs were tended in infantile helplessness.

Winter let in the damp drafts off the harbor, a seeping cold that defeated even the thickest wool stockings and waistcoat. The healer's charges lay oblivious, muffled under blankets in thick quiet. A half dozen volunteer wives and a brace of overworked junior apprentices shuttled to and fro in the gloom, bearing trays of broth and hampers of soiled bedding, with the crown surgeon's authoritative presence marked out by a bobbing circle of lanternlight.

For the twentieth time in an hour, sleeves rolled up and his cowlicks pushed back from his forehead, the royal healer peeled back the blankets and examined the next cot's occupant. This one was a burly troop captain whose scars were by now familiar territory. He counted the man's pulse rate and pinched slackened, papery skin for the first warning sign of dehydration. When the intrusive shadow fell over his shoulder, he barked from reflexive habit. 'Please don't block the lamp, boy! I've said so before. If you've stuffed all the cracks in the sea-side shutters, I need well water drawn and heated. We've got twenty more who need bathing today. No one gets supper till they've been groomed and dried.'

'The wick in your lamp just wants trimming.' That deep velvet tone belonged to no whining apprentice. The light brightened, set right by the same individual's quiet touch. 'The ladies in the factor's office know your needs very well. You'll find the tubs have been filled and heated already.'

The crown healer straightened, both fists knuckled into his aching lower back. He blinked, as if overstressed vision could be made to explain the mischievous old man waiting patiently at his left hand. 'You're here to help? That's a gift and a miracle.' Disbelief yielded to practical authority that would grasp and secure even chance-met opportunity before it slipped through the back postern. 'We have women to manage the washing and towels, but the boys will be needed for the litters.'

'They're still busy stuffing the cracked boards with rags,' the strange elder replied in his whiskey-grained baritone. Spry as a cat, his diminutive frame was doused in a shapeless old coat, cut from what seemed a ragpicker's leavings, and mismatched swatches of worn blankets. Crimped white hair spilled into the riot of beard he contained in the grip of sensitive fingers. 'I can manage one end of a litter well enough.'

The healer's dubious glance met a pixie's bright grin and turquoise eyes folded with laugh lines. 'Did I not haul your water and roll in the washtubs?' Then, in afterthought delivered with irreverent distaste, 'Your magnanimous ruler might have provided something better than vats bought used from the dyer's.'

'They often have terrible splinters, I know,' the healer apologized. 'We're pinched to the bone for expenses.' Too honestly overworked to dismiss his good fortune, he tucked the blankets over the prone hulk of the captain and gestured toward the ramshackle shelving erected against the far wall. 'Litters are stored over there. Our work's laid out. A council delegation's due here this afternoon, and the Prince of the Light won't like their report if his former crack veterans are shabby with a week's stubble.'

The old man retrieved the lantern in mild deference. 'We're trying to impress someone?'

'You didn't catch wind of last month's proclamation?' The crown's master healer snorted his disgust. Granted the boon of unburdened hands, he stowed his loose remedies, hiked up his scuffed satchel, and threaded his way through the rat's maze of invalids installed on their mismatched cots. 'Avenor's recruiting its own talent, these days. You know that snake-tongued Hanshire captain who's been given the post of Lord Commander? Well, he's pushed through a change in policy.'

A pause through a stop to adjust a slipped pillow, then a laugh that stabbed for its sarcasm. 'Sulfin Evend's said, for straight tactics, we need to sign mageborn into Alliance service. Use talent to divide and conquer the ranks, then make the ban against sorcery stick when all disloyal spellcraft's eradicated. Now, every mageborn offender hauled in is offered a blandishment to practice for the Light. The one who can lift these Etarrans from ensorcelment will be awarded a paid crown appointment.'

The healer's lips thinned to harried distaste. 'The trials are held here. Stay and witness the farce, if you've got a fancy for uproarious entertainment.'

'You don't sound appreciative,' the old man observed, his interest engaging, and his dreamer's gaze grown astute.

'I don't like dead men. Or broken bones. Or amputations, or holes carved by arrows, not for any misbegotten cause made in the interest of crown politics.' The healer secured the strap of his satchel and hoisted the pole handles of a litter, still talking. 'Seen too much cautery and too many splints in this campaign to throw down the clanborn.'

The old man secured the lamp in a niche and stooped to bear up his share of the burden. 'You don't fear shadows?'

'I should.' The healer gave back a gruff, barking laugh. 'Maybe I will, if I see any. You ask me, what we have is a crisis in trade that began with the bold-as-brass theft of crown ships by a scoundrel. I don't see any Spinner of Darkness storming the kingdom by sorcery. His clan allies are left as convenient scapegoats, dragged in to vindicate the old hatreds.'

'Strong words,' the elder murmured in peppery provocation.

'Men don't burn in Avenor for opinions. Not yet, anyway.' Arrived at the end of the near row of cots, the healer lapsed in his tirade. His scrutiny turned critical until he observed that the oldster knew how to raise and move a helpless man without causing careless injury. 'Whoever trained you, you're good with your hands.' Then, the ultimate compliment, 'Can I call you by name?'

The request raised a mumble drowned out by the scraping scuffle of footsteps as the litterborne man was conveyed toward the tiny, partitioned room that had formerly served as the warehouse factor's day office. Sudden light knifed the gloom as a woman in a farmwife's loomed skirts threw open the door to admit them.

Steam billowed out, spiked by a ghost taint of apricot brandy, and a drift of female chatter. 'Bring the dearie in here. Aesha's got balsam to sweeten his bath, and Ennlie's cousin's new babe needs a wee syrup for the croup. Could you mix her the dose? We'll see to your work with the razor.'

'Have I ever refused you, love?' said the healer, absorbed as he maneuvered the burdened litter through the constraint of the door-jambs, careful not to scrape the chapped skin off his knuckles. He added in snatched explanation, 'These are widows of the men lost on campaign back in Vastmark. They're all volunteers, and we would be paralyzed without them.'

'I can prepare cough syrup,' the old man offered. His quick smile reassured the redheaded Ennlie; the healer was given his calm list of the herbs in proper proportion for the recipe. 'If you haven't any cailcallow, fresh wintergreen will do.'

'Ath,' said the healer, amazed. He braced the litter on a tabletop, planted his stance, then eased the heavyset occupant into a waiting tub brimmed with suds. 'Wherever you came from, we could use six others just like you.'

'Petition the crown to stop burning herb witches?' the old man quipped.

The healer's solemnity gave way to the first belly laugh he had enjoyed in long weeks. 'Now, that might see me arraigned for collaboration with evil.'

'Surely not,' the old man argued. 'Avenor's palace pages could scarcely fill your shoes as replacement.'

'Well then, definitely don't brag on your skills while you're here. I'd rather be sure this court gets no leeway to decide my sharp tongue's a crown nuisance.' Smiling, the healer offered his satchel and the freely made gift of his trust. 'Everything you'll need for that remedy is inside. Just rummage away. Oh, and shout if you can't read my labels.'

The morning streamed past in camaraderie and hard work, with the harried master healer relying more and more on the old man's competent assistance. If the fellow seemed given to peculiar silences, his lapses of woolgathering seemed not to affect the compassionate skill of his hands. Nor was his remark about arcane connections entirely the lighthearted artifice of humor. He had a gift, or else an empathic touch that wrought an uncanny string of small miracles. Those victims whose vitality had faltered through their prolonged and unnatural sleep seemed to stabilize under his influence. When *yet again* the royal healer felt a man's fluttery pulse rebound and steady for no reason, he glanced up.

The oldster was only washing the unconscious man's hair, his hands wrist deep in dripping lather, and his expression vague as a daft poet's. Except that no mind could decipher his reticent secrets, nor read into eyes that held the innocence of a spring sky.

The healer stared over the rim of the washtub, a swift chill of gooseflesh marring the skin of the fingers still clasped to the guardsman's limp wrist. His attentiveness this time demanded the courtesy of a straight answer as he said softly, 'Who are you?'

The old man in his whimsical coat of sewn rags turned his head. He smiled, disarming, then tipped his chin toward the closed door, a half beat ahead of a disturbance arisen outside of the warehouse. 'You're going to know very shortly.' As the commotion resolved into the scouring rumble of cart wheels, and the clatter of a sumptuous company of outriders, his seamed features kindled into beguiling delight. 'We have company? Your party of councilmen has arrived two and a half hours early.'

'Dharkaron's Black Spear!' The crown's master healer rammed to his feet in flustered annoyance. He pressed through the busy women in the factor's office, cracked the door, and yelled to his youthful assistants, 'Get busy lighting the sconces and candles! Now! Jump on it! His Grace's high officers have no liking at all for musty dim corners and shadows that remind them of darkness.'

Abandoned in the wake of last-minute preparations, the old man retrieved the dropped pitcher. He rinsed the soapy head under his fingers, and without visible hurry, toweled the comatose soldier's streaming hair. Then he left his charge in the care of the women.

'Don't scream if he stirs,' he admonished on parting, his amusement damped back to a madcap twinkle in the artless depths of his eyes.

'Ye're moonstruck,' the grandmother among them replied, laughing, and shooed him back into the warehouse.

There, he might as well have been invisible for all the notice anyone paid him. The frenzied scurry of preparations flowed right and left, banked candles and lanterns set burning at profligate expense. If the Prince of the Light went nowhere without ceremony, his high council officers emulated court style. The old man chose an unobtrusive stance against the sagged boards of old shelving. His ancient, patched coat flapped against his booted ankles as the large double doors that fronted the dockside were unlatched and dragged open.

Two pages entered, their deep blue crown livery adorned with sunwheel sashes. Next followed a herald, his tabard roped with gold, the glittering white silk smirched with a dusting of snowflakes. While the chill swirled and flowed to the farthest-flung crannies, and candleflames streamed with the draft, he bawled out his formal announcement of the imminent presence of crown officers.

Two magistrates stepped in as the echoes died away. They wore their formal robes of judgment and collars of gleaming links. With them came the Lord Crown Examiner, robed in ermine and white silk, and a second figure of impressive presence and seal-colored beard and hair. Diamond studs shot scintillant fire, warmed by a linked chain of dragons masterfully wrought in tooled gold. The inclement weather had not ruffled his fine clothes, which meant that somewhere outside, a stoic pack of servants had borne a closed litter or palanquin.

The argumentative clutch of clerks trailing the first pair did not merit such nicety. They wore snow in their hat brims, and discommoded expressions of forbearance. Last came the lean and predatory form of the Alliance Lord Commander at Arms. That one strode in like a hungry hawk, his black-hilted weapons and alert carriage in sharp contrast to the disdainful court secretary who waddled, self-important as a citybred pigeon. Six sunwheel guardsmen escorted the retinue, their glittering trappings and ceremonial helms buffed to a dazzling polish. These ushered in their turn a trio of curiosities: a tall woman trailing a sequined train and a shoulder yoke of pheasant wings and peacock eyes. Next came a skinny, bald man robed in sable and purple velvet; then a wizened creature of indeterminate sex, with one gouged-out eye socket and a blackthorn walking stick capped with a crow skull and fringed with rattling bone beads. Four liveried footmen brought up the rear, loaded chin high with oddments and bizarre paraphernalia.

The array was eclectic. From his unobtrusive vantage outside the hub of activity, the old man picked out several portable bronze braziers, clay vessels stamped with runes, and two amphorae of ruby glass. Less wholesome than these, stained with the aura of dark usage, was a goblet made from a cranial bone rimmed in tarnished silver. A trailing tangle of embroidery identified the filched mantle from a ransacked hostel of Ath's Brotherhood. Two matched onyx candlesticks wafted a perfume of heavy incense, even through the rampaging wind that rushed in, rank with the salt rime razed off the harbor.

Through a sifting swirl of snow, the rattle of bone beads, and the sonorous flourish of the herald, the page boys wrestled the heavy doors shut. There panoply paused. The crown's master healer hastened forward and bowed under the gimlet regard of the Lord Commander. The high councilmen looked bored, and the clerks stood resigned, while the countrywomen whispered from the inner doorway of the factor's office, their capable hands pink from wash suds.

Their interest was matched by the old man in the rag coat, tucked in his corner with the pert fascination of a house wren. 'You know that's a necromancer's stick?' he commented to no one in particular. 'Very rare. Dangerous, too. I wonder whose unpleasant little sigil lends it power?'

Across the warehouse, the official with the resplendent dress exchanged smooth talk with the healer. His seamless, court bearing set each gesture apart, while the more heavyset Lord Examiner shifted from foot to foot in resentment, and the servants divested their burdens with thinly concealed distaste. The guardsmen and the robed magistrates looked on like cranes, overseeing disposition of the eccentrics, who were named as prisoners under arraignment for the practice of unlawful sorceries.

Their condemned status notwithstanding, they argued. The discord swelled into an arm-waving clamor concerning who held right of precedence. The magistrates deadlocked over whose authority should silence them, while the herald, resigned, waded in and settled their shouting with a peasant's practice of drawing straws. In decorous language, the clerk of the court then assigned each mismatched contestant to a cot with an unconscious occupant.

The bald man jabbed his splayed fingers and demanded that everyone stand back.

'What, for you?' the woman retorted, skirling in spangles to face him. 'Why should we give way one inch for a showman who couldn't draw spells to drop fresh dung from a pig?'

The altercation flared, while the withered oldster caught in between remained single-mindedly oblivious.

'Good people!' the herald called in vexation. 'There will be no specialized treatment between you. The Lord Examiner and Avenor's crown magistrates will judge merit upon equal standing!'

A strained truce prevailed, while the master healer looked irritated, and the contestants who had rudely invaded his domain reclaimed their sundry paraphernalia. Under the frosty regard of the Lord Examiner and the unnamed, dapper high officer, they began setting up with business-like self-importance. The heavyset secretary broke out his lap desk and uncorked his inkwell, while his chilblained apprentice sharpened his quills, and the robed clerks readied the sunwheel seal and gold wax, and snipped lengths from a spool of white ribbon. The magistrates shook melting snow off drooped hats. They peered down long noses to render judgment as the woman unclipped the clasp at her throat, shed her train amid an electrical jitter of reflections, and undertook the first trial.

She began by spreading her sequin train over her assigned victim. She lit tapers. The ancient, carved sconces streamed cloying smoke as she waved long-nailed hands to a chiming descant of silver bracelets. For an interval, the officials coughed and dabbed runny eyes, while she circled the cot and muttered a singsong incantation.

'A farce, indeed,' muttered the old man in the shadows. His eyes became piercing, narrowed to slits as the flashy train was whisked off to unveil the man underneath. His pale face was still, the comatose limbs no more responsive than before.

The magistrates straightened from their whispered consultation. The elder one rapped out his verdict. 'The accused is proved guilty of fraud.'

'Another charlatan!' the Crown Examiner concurred. He pronounced the lighter sentence. 'The objects used for this act of chicanery shall be burned without recompense. The offender will be fined ten silvers and set free with a warning not to repeat her offense.'

'No more have I coin, since your constables ransacked my lodgings!' the woman yelled in defiance.

The magistrates lent her outburst no credence. 'If she has no relations to dun for her fine, give her penury and hard labor with the city's slop crews.'

The secretary scribbled the added amendment, and the woman resorted to curses. Her shouts turned shrill as two burly guardsmen ushered her, struggling, through the door and remanded her into the custody of the garrison men-at-arms posted in the snowfall outside.

Due process ground on, as ribbons and seal were proffered by the clerks, under candles that flagged in the draft as the outer doors were shoved closed. The healer masked his face in weary hands, and the raggedy character with the crow skull stick flashed a triumphant smile celebrating a rival's departure.

'Next defendant,' droned the magistrate. 'Make your case for the court.'

The man in gaudy velvet strode forward. Chin held high, each gesture theatrical, he unwrapped a set of shell rattles, then lit something in his brazier that gave off a reek like singed wool and cat piss. His display opened with patterns chalked in a circle around a row of candles, moved on through a muttered consultation with a smoky quartz scrying ball, then broke into rattling, with a swaying ululation over a brush tied from a hanged man's hair. The act ended in daubing a sticky decoction over the face and the feet of his still unconscious subject.

The fine for his failure was double the woman's.

'Well, at least they recognize a fake when they see one,' the old man said, bemused from the sidelines. His expression now shaded toward genuine concern, as though he perceived something more than straightforward trial and judgment.

Last came the shapeless oldster. The shed hood revealed female gender and a filthy bristle of white hair. She wore a necklace of pig's teeth. The necromancer's stick pinched within her twig fingers seemed to glare blue for an instant as she bent and ignited the twisted black rootstock she had shredded in her brazier.

'No!' The old man flipped up his cowled collar and strode out of the shadows, no longer deferent, but charged to a startling, sharp air of command. 'You will not light that here, madam!' Nor was his authority less than absolute as he entered the circle of candlelight. 'The herb you've chosen will cause harm in this case, and that stick is an unclean implement with which to recall a man's blameless, strayed spirit.'

'The lad will awaken,' rasped the crone, the glint in her single eye sullen.

'Pass the Wheel, more likely,' the old man corrected. The improved illumination fully revealed him, even to the peculiar, detailed thread-work that patterned his coat of drab motley. The boots he wore underneath the long hem were a horseman's, scuffed with hard wear and marred at the toes with small holes that looked punched by cinders. For some reason beyond logic, that oddity lent his presence a fierce credibility.

The royal guardsmen deferred to his onslaught of aimed purpose. The Lord Examiner's bellowed query passed unheeded as the old man burst into the inner circle, quashed the sullen, smoking coal in the brazier with a bare-handed touch, then faced the herb witch head-on.

'My lords, beware!' snapped the Alliance Lord Commander, spurred to an explosive rush forward. 'This newcomer wields true magecraft.'

The old man in his motley turned not a hair, despite the scrambling retreat of crown officers, then the Lord Examiner's outraged order to stand firm, and the subsequent cry for the royal guards to form a defensive cordon.

'The stick,' the stranger demanded. Each word fell distinct through the wail of bared steel. As though disconnected from the surrounding consternation, his attention remained fixed on the woman as he extended his hand. 'I'll dispose of it safely.'

'This is a rank outrage!' Avenor's Lord Examiner elbowed past the dumbstruck secretary and clerks, his slab jowls jerked to a tic. 'Who are you?'

The old man smiled, the turn of his lips beneath beard and hood disarming as new butter. 'Someone you'd dearly enjoy burning, no doubt.' Still focused on the hag, he asked, 'Woman, what do you fear?'

'No fear!' shrilled the crone. 'Not of you! None for him.' Her distraught gesture encompassed the diamond-still presence of the state official who had thus far not deigned to speak. The moment of impasse gained force and momentum, while the crone clutched the stick, and a cold like spun current ran off its incised runes and shaved the air brittle with danger. The court magistrates stopped their clamor; the guards froze to a man. Lord Examiner Vorrice turned his nose sharply, a hound on a scent, then snarled at the Lord Commander at Arms, whose hard restraint trapped his wrist.

'What do you fear?' the old man repeated. His entreaty held a note of compassion that belled through explosive stillness.

The woman's gaze fell. 'I fear to burn. You know this.' The stiff, clawlike hand clasped to the artifact spasmed to trembling frailty. Whatever malevolent force the stick channeled seemed poised, unstable as the suspended cling of a waterdrop.

The old man surveyed her desperate stance and discerned deeper meanings behind her simple admission. 'You're cold. The winter is cruel where folk are made fearful of those who sell the old remedies. You may take my word for your safety and the promise of shelter.' He shed his rag coat in one fluid motion. 'Go to freedom in Havish in exchange for leaving that stick.'

'You have no right to release a crown convict!' pealed the Crown Examiner in flushed rage.

'But I have, in this case.' Underneath the drab motley, in startling transformation, the old man wore wine red robes with edged borders of black interlace that looked newly made from the tailor's.

'Your bond, I can trust,' the crone relented. Her short laugh held an unlooked-for delight as she yielded and curtsied, and let him accept the stick from her unsteady grasp.

The pending sense of danger built and trembled on the air. Though the candles burned straight in the draftless atmosphere, the stone floor seemed to rock without movement.

With no fanfare, no warning, the old man ran his gnarled palm hard down the length of the wood. The staff spoke, a chilling vibration of sound like the wail of a terrified child. In shattering contrast, the light that bloomed under his sure touch was wrought out of limpid clarity. A wash of bound energies whined past and dispersed. The candles streamed then, and the scentless backwash ruffled the feathers and damp hats of the magistrates, and shot queer, starred pulses off the steel of the guards' helms and weaponry. Nor was the staff scatheless.

The carved runes dissolved in a spatter of red sparks, licking scintillant fire through the odd, silent courtier's pale ermines and exquisite linked diamond studs.

What remained in the old man's hand was an oak stick, polished and plain, now innocuous as a countryman's walking cane.

'Thank you, grandmother.' The elder returned the stick to the crone with unstudied, gallant courtesy.

At his back, the Examiner's outrage inflamed the bunched mass of courtiers.

'You've no right to grant a reprieve to crown prisoners!' Lord Vorrice burst out. To Avenor's taciturn Lord Commander at Arms, he ordered, 'Restrain him, at once.'

The guards moved. The metallic notes struck off their mail and edged weapons splashed echoes the full length of the warehouse.

The old man glanced up, droll. 'Are you foolish?' He engaged the masked gaze of Lord Commander Sulfin Evend, even as the royal guards closed and surrounded him.

Amid the official party, the sleek crown councilman seemed the only other man to appreciate the irony of the challenge.

Nor was Sulfin Evend either hot-blooded or rash, to rise to the old man's baiting. His calm called a halt on the guardsmen's aggression, and his speech stopped them cold between strides. 'Sethvir of Althain,' he addressed, his formality reamed through by corrosive sarcasm. 'Why have we the pleasure?'

The named title electrified the gathering to fear. A hairsbreadth from bloodshed, guardsmen gripped their weapons, and the magistrates shrank, feathered hats and jeweled finery shuddering to the beat of sped pulse.

The person revealed as a Fellowship Sorcerer stepped away from the crone, his fingers clasped behind his back like a child caught out stealing sweetmeats. 'Oh, shall we bandy words, now, instead of engaging with weaponry?' He winked at Sulfin Evend. 'For one thing, there will be young wives in Etarra who want living husbands brought safely home to their hearthstones.'

'The crown *would* be grateful,' Sulfin Evend agreed, as cutting as any unsheathed steel in this surprise ambush of courtesies. 'Though your charitable thought is of questionable standing since your colleague was the one who cursed these men to enchanted sleep in the first place.'

Sethvir raised mild eyebrows, offended. 'Asandir did no such thing. He merely allowed Caithwood's live trees to respond to an unfair endangerment. Or did you not make your eloquent case in Lysaer's state council to sue for a decree of burning and destruction?'

'This is rubbish!' broke in Vorrice. 'A *tree* can bind three whole companies of fighting men into a lethal coma? What an asinine flight of fantasy!'

'Actually, no. They prefer not to kill.' Sethvir sidled another half step, disarmingly patient. 'Nor will they, if everyone stays reasonable.' While the crone snatched her chance to melt into the shadows, he coughed politely, craned his neck, then raised his hand to fend off the converging bristle of pole arms. 'How uncivilized we are,' he chided. 'After taking the trouble to travel in winter, I'd rather not step out beforetime.'

Under Sulfin Evend's unflinching regard, the guards stiffened their weapons and held their ground.

Sethvir shrugged. 'Have things your way.' He dismissed the Lord Commander as he might have abandoned an instant's idle survey of a fly. 'You overdressed blunderers make a splendid display, intimidating all the wrong people.' All devilment, he beckoned to the cowering royal secretary. 'Come forward, man. Stop shaking as well. Nobody's going to skewer someone's liver on a pike. Your wooden-faced high councilmen are merely going to set royal seal to an edict that pledges the heartwood of the forests Lysaer's grant of protection, for all time.'

'You won't get the Prince's signature,' the Lord Commander interjected in venomous loyalty. 'I'll kill if you try to use these poor victims' lives for extortion.'

Sethvir actually smiled. 'Impasse. I can leave.' As Sulfin Evend shifted forward to engage the guard, he added, 'Don't make your men party to an embarrassing mistake. No mere unsheathed steel can gainsay me.'

'I will find your weakness. Take that as my warning.' The Lord Commander's burning gaze took weight and measure of Sethvir's timeworn features before he signaled his men to lower their weapons and stand down. 'Go from this place. Make your way back to your tower in Atainia empty-handed. We can afford to lose every man who lies here in the cause of true service to the Light.'

Again Sethvir raised tangled eyebrows. This time his inquiry focused on the smooth countenance of the one crown councilman, whose silence was now striking, and whose masked intelligence bespoke deeper motives behind unobtrusive restraint.

'Every living man's sword counts in this war against shadow,' that glittering personage contradicted. 'Nor will your evil works claim even one who lies stricken for the sake of another's stiff pride. You may dictate your terms,' he said to the Sorcerer. 'Rest assured, I hold the authority to sign documents in the absence of his Grace, the Blessed Prince.' Wholly contained, his hair combed silk under the uncertain flutter of candlelight, he finished in unruffled majesty. 'Make no mistake. This is not capitulation. We are large enough in the strength of our faith to meet your demands and recover.'

'You can't yield,' Lord Examiner Vorrice interrupted, his breath thickened to fury. 'Prince Lysaer would never bow to a threat, nor give this enemy any footing for demand.'

'Peace, Vorrice,' murmured the high councilman, unperturbed, his collar of jewels like pinned points of ice hung on a nerveless wax statue. 'There is no demand our Alliance cannot grow to overcome, given time.' To Sethvir, he assured, 'My writ will be honored. The secretary and the clerks can draw up a document in state language, and the ring on my hand will stand as the seal for Prince Lysaer's personal bond.'

'A parchment inscribed with your signature will do,' Sethvir said, neither set back nor moved by that claim to a regent's high sovereignty. 'True intent of the heart can be read from such things, and a tree has small use for wax-impressed symbols and words penned in noble formality.'

'This is pure outrage!' Crown Examiner Vorrice ground out, hissing loud, whispered protests, even as his rival councilman snapped ringed fingers to a secretary, who responded out of trained habit. 'No Sorcerer should be cozened! Fire and sword would make a fit ending—'

'But not at the cost of six hundred lives,' that glacial personage cut in. His eyes were steel filings snap-frozen in ice, and his voice chilling as he spoke in ultimatum to Sethvir. 'Your hour will come, if not in my lifetime, then in that of my appointed successors. Light will stand firm against sorcery and darkness without making martyrs over principle.'

While the secretary shuffled parchment, then offered the pen for the endorsement, he signed with no trace of regret. His fulsome, flowery cursive spelled out name and title, *Cerebeld, First High Priest to the Prince of the Light, Alliance precinct of Avenor.*

In flawless, cast calm, he stepped forward. His own hand relinquished the document to Sethvir. 'If the forest clan families will ally with the Shadow Master, if they continue to molest honest trade through bloodshed and raiding, rest assured, the Divine Prince and right action will annihilate them. Faith and sheer numbers must tell in the end. Lord Harradene of Etarra will no doubt be pleased to rededicate his city garrison for the purpose.'

Sethvir rolled the new edict into a scroll, his delight rebounded to an unwonted solemnity. 'Dear man, you might hold an office granted by the hand of usurped mortal power. That gives no license to make choices Ath Creator would spurn for the sake of respect. Always ask before you make foolish promises concerning another man's free will.'

The full truth, Prince Lysaer's high priest would discover in due time: that a man who had once dreamed the peace of the trees was unlikely to return to a soldier's life of trained violence. Of the crack Etarran troops imported to clear Caithwood of its meddlesome enclave of barbarians, not a one would arise in fit state to resume the way of the sword. They would garden, or farm, or live disaffected; some few would find their way back to waking contentment in the disciplines of Ath's Brotherhood.

After knowing the tranquil awareness of the trees, Lysaer s'Ilessid's war-bent call to religion would move them to open abhorrence.

Sethvir turned his back on Avenor's delegation. In complete disregard of the magistrates' dismay, the Lord Commander's smoldering fanaticism, and the outrage of Lord Vorrice and the guards, he smiled to the master healer, who waited unforgotten on the sidelines. 'See to your charges,' he instructed, even as the first ripple of movement stirred through the stricken men on the cots. 'They are released now, and waking, and will need human comfort as they find their way back to awareness.'

Someone groaned in the dimness outside the lit circle of candles. Feathers twitched, and fine fabric sighed to the sharp shift in tension as the magistrates craned heads to observe. During that one unguarded moment, the Fellowship Sorcerer slipped away. No one saw his departure. That single, uncanny second of suspension should not have allowed him the time he required to step out.

And yet he was gone. The outer door to the warehouse gaped open. Chill winds bored in, admitting a vindictive blast of snowflakes until a testy official barked for the page boys to shoulder the huge panel closed. Through the yammering complaint of Lord Vorrice's indignation, Commander Sulfin Evend made incisive, dry comment that the old herb witch in her coat of rag motley had apparently disappeared also.

'Sorcery! Evil practice engaged in our very presence!' Vorrice gasped, his face red, and his indignant, ham fists clenched in his sunwheel cloak. He demanded an immediate hue and cry, until High Priest Cerebeld touched him silent.

'Patience,' said the man who was the Voice of the Light in Avenor. 'Evil will not be banished in a day. Nor will our trial against darkness be won through pursuing one Sorcerer prematurely.' His gaze of notched ice raked over his disgruntled officials, then the royal guardsmen, left empty-handed and shamed. 'No one failed here.' His fervor rang, end to end, through the warehouse, fired with faith and invincible conviction. 'I charge you all, *let the timing be Prince Lysaer's*. Tysan needs an heir to ensure the succession. Once the throne is secured, hear my promise.

Our Alliance campaign will carry the Light forward. By the grace of divine calling, the minion of righteousness will see an end to sorcery and oppression. On that blessed hour, every city on the continent will rise under the sunwheel standard!'

By the advent of dusk, Avenor still seethed with the mounted patrols rousted out by the Alliance Lord Examiner. Men-at-arms had spent a long afternoon displacing indignant families. Their search swept street by street, and ranged down every midden-strewn back alleyway, seeking a renegade Sorcerer and an escaped convict named as an herb witch.

Evening closed in, gray under the swirling, thin snowfall that had dusted the city through the day. The west keep watch blew the horn that sounded the closing of the gates; the lamplighter made rounds with his torch. Neither fugitive was found, despite a posted crown reward, and the pointed fact the Fellowship Sorcerer was said to be wearing a conspicuous maroon velvet robe. As darkness deepened, and the keening wind blasted flaying gusts down the streets from the sea quarter, the guardsmen retrod old ground like balked hounds. They endured shrill abuse from shopkeepers and matrons, and dodged the rime thrown off the wheels of drays bearing cord wood, and live chickens caged in tied baskets of withies.

Bedraggled and wet, a mounted patrol slogged across Avenor's central plaza, startling a flock of brown-and-white sparrows. The birds' circling, short flight set them back down. They pecked at the crumbs thrown by a beggar who sat, huddled against the brick buttresses of the council hall, sharing his crust of stale bread.

'Damnfool waste of time,' the patrol sergeant grumbled, spurs gouged to his equally disaffected gelding. 'Sorcerer's long gone, you ask me. Ought to be Lord Vorrice himself out here, freezing his tail in the saddle for rabid love of divine principles.'

'Dharkaron's black bollocks, man!' snapped a companion, brushing off snow that melted against his soaked thighs. 'You'd rather be home warming your ears under your old lady's wasp tongue?'

'I'd rather be settled with a hot meal and beer at the Goose,' another man grumbled. 'Fiends plaguing wind's like to give a man frostbite where the goodwife won't ever need her sick headaches for excuses.'

The deadened clop of hooves passed on by, then faded to the jingle of bit rings and mail. No man on patrol paused over the oddity, that any natural wild bird should have flown to roost before sundown. Nor had a one of them challenged the beggar for loitering. In hindsight, had they shown a half second's thought, even their horses had behaved as though the fellow had been part of the stone-and-brick cranny where he sheltered.

Crouched on his hams in the silting snowfall, the beggar himself seemed strangely contented, his gnarled hands mittened in a pair of cast off stockings with holes poked through for his thumbs. He had no cloak. Only a torn and moth-eaten blanket which should have done little to cut the wind. The incessant gusts skirled and spun, and ruffled the feathers of the birds, who crowded and pecked to snatch handouts.

A woman with a basket of fish passed homeward from the dockside market. Next came a rib-skinny street cur and a thin child in rags. The dog and the boy received the divided last portion of the bread crust. The beggar seemed not to care that his generosity had disposed of his remaining bit of supper. He sat with his arms wrapped around tucked-up knees, and resumed conversation with the wind devil that coiled into slow eddies before his crossed ankles.

'Your suspicion is true, Luhaine,' he mused, while the diamond fall of snowflakes caught light from the streetlamp and spun in lazy spirals that strangely seemed not to disturb the cluster of still hopeful sparrows. 'The s'Ilessid scion's already drawn a born talent into his cause. His high priest, Cerebeld, is no sham, but a natural telepath who has tapped into gifted clairaudience.'

'His inner guidance is Lysaer s'Ilessid?' Luhaine whispered, a voice suspended in shadow. 'If so, the maternal gift of s'Ahelas talent gives rise to an ill turn indeed.'

'I witnessed the transmission,' Sethvir said, bleak. 'Cerebeld can send, and hear in reply the prompt of a master he believes to be god-sent. His presence this afternoon carried more than just chilling conviction. He did not lie when he claimed to speak as the word of true Light on Athera.'

'A misfortune to raise armies and provoke vicious bloodshed, if Cerebeld should acquire a circle of gifted collaborators.' The shade of the Sorcerer concluded that thought with uncharacteristic brevity. 'Then you fear as I do?'

The sparrows took flight, a flurried storm of small wings, and the beggar looked up, his gaze soft as rubbed antique turquoise. 'I fear any landfall, even for provisions, will jeopardize Arithon's safety. Time becomes his deadly enemy, for Cerebeld is no fool. He will certainly go on to appoint his hierarchy and successors by the criterion of his own precedence. He'll have no one admitted to the inner circle of his priesthood who cannot discern the unfailing, true word of the man he has named Blessed Prince.'

The posed possibility of instantaneous communication between the far-flung factions of the Alliance bespoke dire odds for the future. Sethvir's broadscale awareness tracked events well beyond the flight of his game flock of sparrows, who wheeled and alit upon the snow-frosted roof of the cupola set at the center of the circular plaza.

'We're not going to get the reprieve that we'd hoped for, to gain insight against Desh-thiere's curse. Nor will those restless free wraiths left on Marak hold their peace if they bridge themselves passage while we're torn to shreds by the dangerous momentum of a holy war.' The vortex that marked Luhaine's presence surmised, morose, 'You'll return to keep vigil at Althain Tower?'

'That seems for the best. Warning of this new development can be sent most easily from there.' Sethvir arose, dusted crumbs from his sleeves, and adjusted the fall of the blanket that mantled the wind-snagged, white aureole of his hair. His unseen colleague kept pace at his shoulder, and while yet another party of armed searchers plodded by, Sethvir paid them as little heed as the previous ones.

'I'll require a diversion, if you wouldn't mind,' Althain's Warden requested. 'One that won't draw lasting notice.'

Luhaine whisked ahead in derision. 'Be glad it's I, and not Kharadmon, at your side to mask your departure.'

'A pity,' Sethvir disagreed, tracking pigeon-toed prints toward the center of the plaza. His grin came and went like the moon through the cloudy mass of his beard as he stepped over the barrier chain on the stair to the raised platform where the minions of Light dispensed shadowbanes to the poor every noon. 'Cerebeld and his ilk were all raised on sour milk, to have matured with no sense of humor. Kharadmon's style would quite likely bait them to a fatal fit of apoplexy.'

He ducked through the railing rather than trouble to round the staged landing. There, a forlorn figure with the threadbare hem of the blanket trailing, he paused beneath the pillared cupola. The stone underneath the raised dais was far older, laid down in past ages by the great centaur masons. Their work had framed the focus for a power circle neither time nor mortal building could erase.

Standing in the brittle, cold breeze with the blanket slipped to his shoulders, Sethvir heard the imprinted echoes of their song. The notes twined a descant like spun silver through the actinic static that marked the flow of earth's lane force. He clasped stockinged hands, closed his eyes, and lapsed into what looked like innocuous contemplation.

Luhaine, nearby, could sense changing resonance thrum through the focus like a sounding board. He judged his moment with fussy precision, and incited two lurking mongrels to chase someone's cat down an alleyway. A twist of false sound made them appear to turn on each other and engage in a snarling fight.

Shutters clapped open. Outraged citizens cursed the racket and hurled basins of water to quash the yapping disturbance, while the flared pulse of light raised for Sethvir's departure came and went in an eyeblink. Unremarked in the pale swirl of snow, the Warden of Althain tapped the lane-fired energies of a star at the zenith and left Lysaer's royal city of Avenor.

One by one, the sparrows that had comprised the energies of his ward of concealment blurred and faded from the onionskin roof of the cupola. They vanished away into thin air, leaving no trace and no track behind them.

# Twins

While deep winter's blizzards howled in whiteout gusts over the northern passes, the soporific perfume of citrus rode the southland breeze that rustled glossy leaves of the merchant's gardens in the Shandian trade port of Innish. Yet tonight, other scents warred with the fragrance wafted through the cracked window of Fiark's cramped garret office; his twin sister, Feylind, leaned on the sill in her slops. Her presence admitted the distinct bite of ship's tar and a robust, smoky fug carried out of the seedier shoreside taverns.

'That's a ripe crock o' bilge, and you know it.' Arms folded over her breasts in black temper, Feylind bore into her argument. 'To Sithaer you don't know the names of his contacts, and the place he makes landfall also.'

Fiark tallied the last line in the ledger and fastidiously blotted his pen nib. Unfazed by rank language and accusations, he laced his hands above his head and stretched the kinks from his back. Clean fingers and unstained lace cuffs gave sharp contrast to his sister's chapped hands and the sweat-stained string of the turk's-head bracelets worn for luck by most blue-water sailors.

'Whose contacts?' he inquired, his disinterested reference to her nameless subject no less than a jabbing provocation.

'Well, damn you for a spoon-fed liar!' Feylind sprang off the windowsill, her long, yellow braid wisped silver at the ends from overexposure to strong sunlight. 'For that, I should plow a fist through your jaw 'til your teeth greet the nape of your neck! You never kept secrets before this.'

'Before this, there weren't sword-bearing fanatics lining up to swear undying service against Darkness.' Fiark regarded her, his hands clasped at the brass-buckled cuffs of his knee breeches, and his eyes tranquil blue in sincerity. 'I see sunwheel talismans sprouting like mushrooms for each galley lost to a clan raid. The knowledge you ask for holds fatal stakes, and Prince Arithon swore his oath for your safety. You can't reward the gift of his care without staying mindful that danger dogs every rumored move that he makes.'

His sister returned a spectacular, balked scowl, fists cocked on the belt which hung her man-sized cutlass. 'Damn him to slow death on Dharkaron's Black Spear! I was eight years old at the time of that pledge, and besides, his word was given to our mother!'

'He's still in the right.' Fiark laughed in the irresistible way that made shreds of her need to stay angry. 'You're no whit less wild now that you're grown, and anyway, eighteen's not considered your majority. Not by the tenets of old charter law, which Prince Arithon is charged to uphold by crown obligation.'

'You talk like a foppish, mealymouthed lawyer. And dress like one, too,' Feylind grumbled. She paced, her agitation intractable as a caged lioness, while the clomp of her seaboots across the bare floor raised a bellowed complaint from the downstairs tenant.

Fiark closed the boards of the ledger and locked its bronze hasp fastening. 'You know, you're disturbing honest folks' sleep.' When his sister refused to abstain from her racket, he returned her spirited sniping. 'Also, on the subject of clothing, you're nobody's walking example. You'd have trouble courting a draft ox, done up as you are like a sailhand on course for a tavern bash.'

His sister regarded the toes of her boots, her grin wicked, and her laugh deep and rich with enjoyment. 'I need the brass caps to fend *off* randy suitors.' For effect and demonstration, she stamped on the floor, which intimidated the disgruntled downstairs tenant back to meek suffering and silence.

'You won't be excused by changing the subject, forbye.' Feylind cast herself into the battered leather armchair, her boisterous energy riffling the weighted stacks of lading lists piled over her brother's desk. 'Arrange me a cargo for the port where he keeps contact, and let my *Evenstar* carry the dispatches.'

'I can't,' Fiark said, apologetic. Before she could embark on another spate of guttersnipe's language, he handed across a scrap of correspondence written in neat, ciphered script. 'His Grace gave the orders. *Evenstar*'s to be nowhere near the party who's sent to make rendezvous. That's for his own safety, as well as yours. He says the Koriani witches watch everything.'

'But not here?' Feylind snorted her frank disbelief. 'That's an excuse so brainless a baitfish won't buy.' She flicked back the paper, deflated by the fact the handwriting was recognizably genuine. Arithon s'Ffalenn remained the only living spirit she consistently failed to outwit or bully to gain her way.

'Keep your boots off my desk,' said her brother, aware of her intent in the fractional second as intention took form in her mind. Her time spent at sea had not changed the unspoken understanding between them. They still shared thoughts as though loomed from one thread, which made sustained argument difficult.

'The warding was Dakar's?' Feylind asked. The capitulation Fiark had waited for, that had nothing to do with uncouth habits or seaboots, arrived with no fuss appended; Feylind twisted in the chair and unhooked the belt which hung her black-handled weapon. She drew a thick packet of letters from a pouch tucked underneath her man's jerkin.

Fiark accepted the bundle with apology rather than triumph. 'The spellbinder wrought a protection so strong, some days I find just crossing the threshold sets me into a cold sweat.' He settled the packeted documents into a locked drawer, then dealt his twin sister the leveling honesty that kept their inviolate trust. 'There's everything at risk. The Shadow Master all but lost his sanity at Riverton, which is why you'll collect no more unsolicited correspondence in Tysan, and also stop plaguing me with dangerous, prying questions.'

'I'll do that, perhaps.' Feylind poked her cheek, thoughtful. 'But only if you'll shed your fine airs and fop's clothes and share beer at the Gull and Anchor.'

'That dive!' Fiark raked exasperated fingers through his neatly trimmed golden hair. 'You have the bar keeper there in your pocket. He'd spike my drink out of gallantry just to weigh the odds in your favor, and anyway, getting me drunk will damned well not loosen my tongue far enough to spill the secret you're craving.'

'Bet on that?' Feylind's freckled nose crinkled to her wide grin. 'Drink or cards, brother. I'll see you under the table or beggared.'

'Witch.' Fiark laughed, rising. 'You never could.' Grown unfamiliarly fastidious since their beginnings as mackeral shack urchins in Merior, he tipped his crockery jug of goose quills and fished out a candle snuffer. Gone were the days when he would black his fingers pinching out wicks, or cause a careless spatter of wax on his employer's lading lists.

'You're coming?' Feylind prodded, and flung him the mantle he kept on a hook by the doorway.

'Oh, I'll share your shore liberty, you ungrateful wench. But not at a den as notorious as the Anchor. We'll sup at the Halfmoon.' Fiark thumbed through his keys for the one that secured the hasp lock on his office. 'That way, I haven't very far to stagger home, and you can pass out where you won't find yourself tucked in some oily galleyman's bed come the morning.'

'Halfmoon's for milksops who can't hold their liquor,' Feylind retorted, impatiently starting her clumping descent of the stair. 'The landlady there's a damned child's nurse.'

'Oh? Say that to her face, fat Moirey will fell you.' Fiark caught up and matched her long-strided energy with the effortless grace of old habit. 'Two silvers says you don't dare.' On his way past the second-floor tenant's shut door, he paused, then grinned at the abusive threats the matron yelled from inside. He elbowed his sister before she could retort. 'Don't be a pest. The couple have children. Your thoughtless noise could set them crying into the wee hours of the morning.'

With a shrug that reflected no shred of shame, Feylind answered his challenge. 'Two silvers is ant's piss, to brangle with Moirey. Do you want dinner, or a front seat to watch me get drubbed with a meat mallet?' They reached the ground-floor landing; Feylind spun with a flourish and showed off her new trick, a neat, chest-high kick that tripped up the bar on the outside doorway. 'I still have a fiends-plagued dent in my leg from the time the trull hit me with her fire iron.'

'She did that?' Fiark trailed into the narrow, brick-paved alley, rising with pleasure to the lively challenge of an evening in his sister's company. 'What was the offense? You pick a fight with one of her pimps?'

'Drink or cards?' Feylind persisted, a demented enjoyment setting a whetted edge to her grin. 'Choose one or the other. You want every scrap of my sordid gossip? Then you'll earn the right through a winning stake that proves you're not the mim-faced town dandy you seem by the sissified cut of your clothes.'

'Let it be cards,' Fiark settled. 'But if I win, the stake that I claim will be your promise, made on his own name, that you solicit no more news on behalf of his contacts. Nor will you try any other sly tricks that will lead to your knowing his business.'

'I can't give that promise,' Feylind said in a sudden, desperate honesty. 'You've seen for yourself how bad things are turning.' She lowered her voice, lest the echoing sound of their passage carry too well down the alleyway. 'Too many enemies are finding their way to the council tables. The Alliance's cause has been tailor-made to further the townsmen's entrenched hatreds. The hour could all too easily arrive when my role as *Evenstar*'s captain becomes the one cipher that could spare Arithon's life.'

Plain facts, and a truth that cut with razored pain to the heart; Fiark found himself wordless. 'All right,' he agreed, when at last his dark thoughts loosened enough to let him speak. 'No promise, but your given intent that you honor his Grace's wishes where your personal safety is at stake. He lost Caolle to the dark machinations of the curse. If your careless misadventures ever came to break his personal bond to our mother, I don't want to share in his anguish.'

Feylind drew breath, and Fiark interrupted in the same vein of brutal sincerity. 'You didn't see the damage wrought by Caolle's death. Nor will you, if the Shadow Master's fate resolves kindly. Wish for nothing else, Feylind. To do less would not be the act of a friend, but an axe blow to further the frightening cause of his Alliance enemies.'

# Foray

Parrien s'Brydion, next oldest brother to the Duke of Alestron, paced the decks in bad temper. That morning had brought his family's state galley into the overcrowded port city of Southshire. Across the merle chop of the harbor's pale waters, he could already see that the dockside berths were jammed to the point of insanity.

The lighterman he swore at dutifully shouted back. 'We've got moorings still available. But only through making the proper application, with the fee paid in full at the harbormaster's.'

'May Dharkaron's Black Chariot shear a linchpin and drop a wheel foursquare on the heads of the dolts in this city!' Every bit as volatile as his youngest brother Mearn, but built with the shoulders of an axeman, Parrien snarled on in distemper. 'Just what're we expected to do meanwhile? Row in pissing circles while yon simpering, overdressed clutch of officials quibble and suck on their pen nibs?'

With gauntleted fists hooked on his studded sword belt, he glowered askance, and then raised another ranging bellow, this time addressed to his crewmen. 'Damn you all for a pack of mincing laggards! Quit fiddling with whatever part's itching and sway out this gilt tub's excuse for a shore tender!'

The war captain and five mercenaries who strapped on their weapons to go ashore watched, resigned, since the shortage of dock space at this time of year was altogether predictable.

Two months past the solstice, the rag ends of winter still closed off the northshore ports. While howling white blizzards cast snowdrifts like nets over the mountain passes, the wharfside dives on the southcoast of Shand enjoyed their peak season of prosperity. What trade moved at all in the months before thaws must pass by the southern sea routes. Since no man could predict when the ice packs would break, or the high peaks shed their mail of slurry and ice as spring rains sluiced open the roadways, the blue-water captains drove their vessels in a cutthroat race to seize profit. Each year, ships vied to complete one last run east or west before the premium price of their cargoes could be undercut by the first overland caravans.

The month before thaws, every harbor in Shand held a maze of anchored vessels. Having zigzagged an oared course through the crisscrossing traffic of lighters to gain the docks, Parrien clambered onto the sun-bleached boards, steel studs and weapons flashing. Bystanders and longshoremen scattered from his path. With his cadre of mercenaries trailing, he stalked to the sanctum of waterfront authority.

'Wait here until I come out,' he commanded, adding a flicked signal to his captain. Under a graceful, tiled arch and the puckered bliss of a spouting nymph, Parrien rammed through double doors that led into the stuffy, paneled foyer of the harbormaster's office. There, he made his s'Brydion presence felt in blustering language. The three scurrying stewards strove to placate him, then flushed red to the ears and gave in.

A servant swiftly ushered him into the main office in vain hope of keeping him quiet.

Not about to stay mollified, Parrien paced. The sheath of the broadsword he wore at his belt sliced wide arcs that clipped tasseled furnishings. He fumed as he stomped, and disgruntled the robed secretaries by insisting on preferential treatment. When asked to show more seemly decorum, he raised his iron-flecked brows in astonishment. 'Show me why an overdecorated galley from Jaelot should outrank a duke's brother where there's space at the docks to tie up.'

An elderly official in Southshire's silk livery answered in stiff-lipped reproof. 'That vessel's sworn to the Alliance of Light.'

'You say!' Parrien jutted his square chin across the propped ledgers arranged like a barrier on the desk. The foghorn bellow he shared with three brothers rattled the walls as he ranted, 'So *what* if some puffed-up captain from that mayor's prissy galley flies the sunwheel banner? Alestron's in league with that cause as well. You won't see a sniping scrap of white cloth on *my* masthead, just our own family banner. S'Brydion don't claim borrowed loyalty out of need to protect what's ours! Any ignoramus who holds his life cheap can slight our name at his peril. He'll get his head dunted with no cry for help for the Prince of the Light to send in armed might for backing.'

Rawboned and mean as a fidgety tiger, the duke's oldest sibling crashed his forearm into the ordered papers of officialdom. Reed pens and parchments jumped from the blow. The flask burped up a dollop of black ink, to a trilling squeak from a clerk.

For a moment the quiet became thick enough to wring running sweat from cowed servants. The balding harbormaster tapped an attenuated finger into a cheek like boiled leather, while two onlooking captains and several wattled ministers peered with circumspect caution from under their hat brims.

'Sithaer's biting furies, man!' Parrien stormed. 'You know what's good, you'll see me happy. I've a shipload of my brother's best mercenaries manning the oars belowdecks. Once they've drunk a skinful, they like to make sauce out of unsuspecting lightermen with their fists. I suggest you find me a berth at the docks. Let my men stagger back from their whoring on foot, and maybe your bonesetters can keep their chance of getting an honest night's rest.'

The harbormaster blinked, bored. 'Banners aside, we have no berths free at the moment.' His enervated shrug made Parrien's high temper seem overdone to absurdity. 'And if there's a bonesetter anywhere in Southshire's sea quarter who gets an uninterrupted night before equinox, I don't know him. One brawler more or less before thaws isn't likely to matter.'

Which was the plain truth; late winter on the southcoast was no place for a man too refined to withstand the roughneck pursuits of a seafaring neighborhood. Even here, overcrowding made way for no nicety. The raw noise and shouts from the thoroughfare beat through the clay walls, interspersed by the croaks from the rooks nesting in the harbormaster's watch turrets. From that high vantage, each day, sharp-eyed tally boys stood counting ships. They matched their numbers against each entry in the register, and made accurate lists for the constables. Those captains who tied to a mooring without paying were systematically accosted and fined.

The shoreside watch was in fighting trim, with the taverns and brothels packed night and day, and the wharf quarter tuned to the hysterical pitch of a carnival. Street stalls under their sun-faded awnings shook and bulged to capacity crowds. Each morning, men were knifed in hot-tempered arguments. Fights and trade conflicts heated to boiling in minutes, as vendors and landlords elbowed to rake in the easy flow of winter silver.

'What's the price of your extortion, then?' Parrien grumbled, not beaten, but shrewd enough to know when intimidation became wasted enterprise.

The secretary's clerk peered up from his rodent's perch over the cash box. 'Cost for a mooring's six coin weight the night.'

Parrien howled.

The harbormaster shrugged. 'No pay, then no anchorage.'

His bland-faced indifference would not yield to s'Brydion wrath at this season. The slow months would return all too soon. Today's raucous press of patrons would dry up after equinox, until only the high-class establishments could stay open. No responsible captain allowed crewmen on shore leave in summer, when spoiled stores and green flies, and the humid, sick airs hazed the sea quarter, and the brothels, with their louvered galleries, languished in the dense, southcoast heat.

'Six silvers for *mooring*? That's robbery.' Parrien leaned forward; paperwork crackled and ivory marquetry groaned to the press of his weight. 'Find me a berth. I'll pay eight, and my mercenaries will toss no one's taproom.'

'The galley from Jaelot has priority. They carry a half company of new sunwheel soldiers as well.' A last shrug from the harbormaster ended debate. 'Those brutes were recruited from Alland's league of headhunters. Since they're just as likely to hammer my lightermen, your threat of bashed noses is moot.'

Parrien flashed teeth in a barracuda grin. 'Very well, man. Don't say you weren't warned. I don't give any six of your town watchmen a chance against just one of mine when he's pissed.' The duke's brother slapped down the coin for his mooring, then clomped to and fro to vent ripping impatience while the clerk marked the register and the tally boy recited the colored markings on the buoy assigned to his galley.

'Make sure you tie up at the designated mooring,' fussed the hovering clerk. 'Claim another, and you forfeit your legitimate fee and subject yourself to a squatter's fine.'

'Do I look blind or stupid?' Parrien glared. 'I sure as blazes see well enough not to splash my own shoe, which does me credit, looking at you.'

He turned on his heel and shouldered his way out, laughing gales at the whey-faced official, who had swallowed the jibe and now bent like a stork in a worried inspection of his slippers.

Outside in the streets, under sun like fine wine, the reek of human sweat wove through the stench of the midden carts, stale horse urine, and the bouquet of patchouli and lavender worn by the half-silver whores. Parrien collected his captain of mercenaries, a hatchet-faced man with scars on his arms who had no smile to spare for the doxies. Like black steel struck through cloth, the cohesive armed party sauntered off down the docks toward the sailors' quarter.

'Boys,' Parrien flipped back to the swordsmen, who padded like wolves at his heels, 'you've got my leave to tear up this town for the threefold hell handed down by its windbag officials.'

His pantherish stride clove through the press, the otter sleek knot of his clan braid cruising level with the froth of feathers that spilled from the trade factors' hat brims. On either side, between loiterers begging handouts and the clouds of grease smoke from the sausage vendors, his eye caught the gleam of fresh paint.

Parrien's mouth twitched. 'Will you look at that?'

His captain also noted the sunwheel emblems newly blazoned on the doorposts of the houses. His sole comment became the gob of spit he ejected into the gutter.

The frown set in place at the harbormaster's furrowed the ridge of Parrien's nose. 'You saw the sunwheel flying alongside the banners over the guildhalls.'

'I did.' The captain's grin came and went like the cold gleam of quartz in a streambed. 'This town's fawning terrified of piracy, looks to me.'

Parrien curled his lip. 'It's their purses they're protecting, sure enough.' His laughter slapped echoes off the shaded arches of the shop fronts, and turned the heads of three girls buying ribbons.

The raids had become the scourge of seagoing trade. Afloat in armed strength in their contraband ships, Tysan's clans came down like plague on those galleys bearing slave convicts. Despite his family's lip service loyalty to Prince Lysaer, the spreading fashion of Alliance support galled s'Brydion independent sensibilities.

'Best walk softly on our business indeed,' Parrien said in low warning to his captain.

The mercenary gave back a wary, clipped nod. Southshire had declared for the Light with a fervency they had seen repeated with unsettling frequency in their port-hopping voyage down the coast. Just like the guard garrisons at Elssine and Telzen, the uniformed watch here had sewn sunwheel patches beneath the city blazon on their sleeves. At the Fat Pigeon Inn, the recent trend proved entrenched. When Parrien arrived to complete his small errand, the louvered dimness of the taproom was crammed with a large party wearing the white tunics denoting a vow of life service.

'What's this, the new kennel?' Parrien grumbled, but softly. Only his captain overheard.

What seemed a whole troop of Alliance men-at-arms sprawled at ease, dicing and wenching and swilling down beer. Others arm wrestled for coin, companionably mingled with burly deckhands on leave wearing Jaelot's rampant lion livery. Officers in gold braid commandeered all the corner nooks. Their immense, florid captain lounged with his boots propped on the best table, his beefy hands laced over his belly as he hobnobbed with a trio of pouting merchants. Behind their pastel velvets and lace, a ferret-nosed official in a spotless white tabard lounged against the frame of the window sash. He appeared to listen in, but did not participate. His searching glance raked the taproom's noisy patrons with a focused reserve that lifted Parrien's hackles.

'Slinking headhunters,' he mouthed under his breath. 'Never mind those milk-sucking dockside clerks, I'd buy any man a night's pleasure to cripple a few of these ham-brained murderers, and give a life pension for the head of that weasel-faced sunwheel informer.'

A seasoned veteran of Alestron's service, the captain rubbed his old scars. 'Won't stay the night to catch lice for that lot.' He passed a surreptitious signal and closed his men into a wedge, prepared when the familiar wry twist curved the duke's brother's lips.

'Well, you're right on that score.' Parrien laughed. 'Bloodying faces is a sight cleaner fun than the whores would provide at this season.'

Together, he and his companion plowed through the flattering hands of those wenches not engaged by drunken sailhands.

The landlord of the Fat Pigeon held nothing in common with the comfortable name of his establishment. Slender as worn string, he limped on arthritic knees, which had led many to underestimate the hand that could strike with the speed of a cobra. More than one swaggering brawler had found himself flattened, spitting smashed teeth on the floorboards. Given the sight of Parrien's squared jaw and soft tread, the man dropped the damp rag he used for buffing the enameled glaze on his tankards. His black eyes brightened to recognition like a spark chipped off a struck flint. 'Don't give a rat's tail for my customers, I see. That's no excuse. Make trouble, and just like any other scum, you'll land facefirst in the gutter.'

'That's what happens with fleabrains who draw their damned steel in this taproom,' Parrien quoted in an evil imitation of a southcoaster's drawling vowels. He grinned wide as the moon, folded his arms, and leaned across the bar top. The muffled grate of metal beneath his loose sleeves betrayed the fact he wore a mail shirt. 'Don't tempt me. The bodies you'd toss alongside mine in the midden would be for the dogs, stone dead.' He measured the spotless, bleached cloth of his cuff as if weighing the cost of the penalty. 'For that lot, a roll in the garbage might just be worthwhile.'

As a beery new recruit in a sunwheel tunic swiveled to sling return insults, the Fat Pigeon's landlord scowled. 'Fighting armed packs of drunks was beneath your family dignity once. Or has your clan honor gone to mayhem along with the peace in this Ath-forsaken port?'

'So Southshire's been raided, too?' Parrien laughed.

'Three galleys hit, just this past week. Made off with the chained oarsmen and sank every hull without troubling to off-load their cargoes.' The landlord inclined his head toward the merchants wringing lace sleeves in the company of the Alliance captain. 'That lot were just hired on with the gold sent for the cause by the Mayor o' Jaelot's generosity. So now you know why this joint reeks like a barracks.'

'Never mind.' Parrien's grin broadened. 'I like my shirts clean and my steel sticky, right enough. That finicky habit's unlikely to change. Not for as long as I walk on two legs without need of a stick to stop doddering.'

'What's to do then? Do I pour you a beer?' The landlord wiped oversize knuckles on his apron and hefted a crockery mug thick enough to be used for a cudgel.

Parrien folded an elbow, eased the wet rag aside, and leaned close. 'Beer's fine.' His blunt, sword-scarred finger traced a cipher on the dampened wood of the bar, then idly swiped the mark out. 'Along with the drink, I need a wee dispatch slipped to the next courier who happens through.'

The landlord looked up, his shrewd eyes intense.

That instant, the door to the kitchen banged open. Parrien's wary start passed unnoticed amid the leaping commotion as a sweaty, cursing drudge barged into the taproom, hauling a yelping cur by the scruff.

The snapping animal and the woman tussled their way toward the streetside exit, while sailhands caught in her path staggered clear. As she passed, the sunwheel mercenaries hooted and pinched, or called noisy wagers to name which combatant would wind up arse down in the gutter.

'Damned Jaelot thugs have the manners of swine.' A whipcrack snap of Parrien's fingers dispatched one of his mercenaries, who took two fast strides and relieved the girl of her problem. The outer door swung closed on the heels of the cur, to a pounding on tables and derogatory hoots of displeasure. Alestron's swordsman never once turned his head, an astounding display of strong character.

'Those blighty curs take advantage all the time,' the landlord smoothed out by way of wry thanks and apology. 'Though their fracas serves Kats right, since her little daughter steals from my tables to feed them.' Turned reticent since the byplay with the cipher, he blinked, while Parrien waited.

No revealing move was forthcoming from the s'Brydion or his

mercenaries. The one given orders reassumed his post, planted and watchful at his lord's shoulder. The coded request would not be repeated, nor the sketched sign, too dangerous to redraw on the bar top where the sunwheel informer might notice.

The landlord repressed the nervous urge to glance backward over his shoulder. 'The next man who could make your delivery isn't due for six months.'

'No matter.' Parrien jerked loose his cuff lace. 'This news will keep.' He fished a sealed square of parchment from beneath the gambeson under his mail shirt.

Long since, the Fat Pigeon's landlord had given up trying to fathom the recipient: like all such missives, this parchment's wrapping had no mark. Nor did the wax impressions in the seals ever show a device to reveal the point of its origin.

As Parrien pinned him with the same narrow look used to sight down a fresh-sharpened sword blade, the landlord gloved his unease in forced humor. 'Though actually, this could be your day for blind luck. It just happens the carrier who made last month's pickup hasn't left here on schedule.'

That news made Parrien's flesh crawl. Without turning, he knew: someone's eyes watched his back. A flashed glance toward his captain confirmed the suspicion by way of a covert hand signal: the shifty, robed informer billeted with Jaelot's company now took an unwelcome interest.

A silver coin passed across the bar top. 'Get your prettiest wench to sally over to that clerkish type in robes, and trip up, and maybe spill a trayful of beer in his lap,' Parrien suggested. 'His prissy white silk is making me wonder if there's a man with natural parts underneath. Now, say on. Why hasn't this courier taken his bundle and gone?'

The Fat Pigeon's landlord returned the blank, injured gaze of a catfish. 'My girls are never clumsy. The inn's reputation relies on them. With regard to the laggard still camped upstairs, since your mercenaries seem handy at tossing out layabouts, I'd be pleased if you'd lend help with this one.'

Parrien's eyebrows peaked up in startlement. 'The courier's a wastrel?'

'You might say so, yes.' A grin like a twist of sun-faded yarn pulled at the landlord's lean mouth. 'He's been barricaded inside my third-story garret with the best of my whores for three days.'

Parrien went owlishly deadpan. 'He's fat? Has hair in screwed tangles like my wife's wretched lap spaniel?'

'He's a friend?' Surprised, the landlord added, 'You know he carries on as though he's being knifed each time my cleaning drudge tries the door latch.' On a sigh of irritable resignation, he hooked back his rag and grabbed for the next water-spotted tankard. 'Go on. The potboy by the hob will take you. Though by now, the miserable wretch might be prostrate. My Sashka could tumble a spring ox to exhaustion. Three days of her favors would wring most of her partners unconscious.'

Shown the closed panel of a door in a corridor ingrained with stale sweat, closed-in dust, and the musk of randy sailors, Parrien wasted no time. He sent the potboy away with a fistful of coppers. Then he tipped his sleek, braided head toward the strapped pine that had not budged to his opening soft knock and flashed a wild grin at his mercenaries. 'Stove the damned thing in.'

No peep of protest emerged from the threatened sanctum. One ear pressed flat to the door, the captain signed back that the room appeared to be empty.

Parrien frowned. 'Break in, but quietly,' he repeated, too jaundiced to accept the stillness inside at face value. Nor would he credit the landlord's pat theory. 'As I know the scoundrel I think we'll find in there, the whore's more likely the one who's banged senseless. Her client won't have scarpered after the fact, either. Far more likely he's sunk in his cups to the nethermost pit of oblivion.'

The captain at arms straightened, linked elbows with the stoutest of his men, then jammed his steel cap straight, and said, 'Go!'

The pair struck the door shoulder down in neat unison. The latch burst. Torn bits of metal scribed arcs into gloom and skated with a tinny clangor across the floorboards inside. Stray noise ended there; the captain's deft hand hooked the edge of the panel before it slammed into the wall.

Inside, the gloom lay thick as black silt.

The shutters were drawn closed. Fingered by pallid light from the hall sconce, the louvers appeared stuffed with socks, a whore's lace point chemise, and what seemed a rag that closer inspection revealed for the ripped-up remains of a man's pair of button-front breeches. The rumpled-up sheets on the bed were quite empty, and streaked scuffs in the floor wax bespoke a galloping rumpus.

'Ath,' Parrien swore. 'That whore must've fought like a tiger.' His cast shadow loomed inward, obscuring the view as he thrust his head through the doorway.

Something large and dark unfurled with a grunt and swooped like a bat from the rafters.

The knife that Parrien unsheathed to impale it mired to the hilt in a goose-down pillow wrapped in a blanket. On field-trained, fast reflex, Parrien sidestepped. The bundle which plummeted after the pillow missed its broad-shouldered target. It struck the floor with a thud that cracked wood, and a whuff like a challenging walrus. Three mercenaries pounced. They extracted from within its thrashing folds two struggling fists and a pair of larded ankles.

'Hello, Dakar,' greeted Parrien on the congenial note he saved for interrogating spies.

The splayed bundle moaned. One bulky end heaved to expose a beet-round, bearded face and two eyes slewed to rolling rings of white. 'Your men can let up before they dislocate both of my shoulders.'

'Oh?' Parrien folded his arms, unamused. 'You want another chance to slit me in two?'

Annoyance colored Dakar's face. 'I thought you were from Jaelot.' He blanched at a twisting pressure from the captain, and added in patent injury, 'That wasn't meant as an insult, and no, before you ask, I'm not in the least bit drunk.'

Something rustled in the corner and let off a muffled squeal. The two idle mercenaries moved on the sound, found a closet, which they wrenched open. Inside, knees to chin, they found the landlord's famed Sashka bound and gagged with the ripped-off flounces of her petticoat.

'She wouldn't stay quiet,' Dakar explained. 'You must have gathered, I'm caught in an unpleasant bind.'

'The town guard from Jaelot might snip off your head?' Parrien's eyes lit with maniacal delight. 'I'd do the very same, though maybe for different reasons. Whose wife did you jiggle?'

'If that were all, I wouldn't be compromised,' Dakar said with a certain strained dignity. 'I know you dislike me for that dustup in your armory. Try to imagine how Jaelot's men feel. I was with Arithon on the night he aroused the Paravian mysteries through song and leveled a third of their city.'

'My memory's not soft,' said Parrien, tart; yet he relented enough to signal his men to stand down. His glance met his captain's. 'Better take care what the whore overhears.'

'She won't remember. I gave her spelled wine.' Lowered back to the floor, Dakar languished. Gasping his misery like a storm-beached whale, he required a wretched minute before he could muster the will to move. The first thing he did when he pushed to his knees was clasp his thick head between shivering fingers.

'You're a lying, soft wastrel,' said Parrien, offended.

His sword captain's patience snapped also. Hard hands seized the Mad Prophet's collar and dragged him the rest of the way upright.

'I said I'm not drunk,' Dakar mewled. He jerked his chin free of somebody's clamped fist as the mercenary captain brought the sconce candle and spilled the light full in his face. 'Damn you to the agonies of Sithaer's black pit! I won't be handled like one of your recruits picked up on a binge in a tavern.'

'Why not?' Parrien fished for an ear amid chestnut frizz and hauled until Dakar's squinting features were brought under his damning scrutiny. 'I'd ask then, why you haven't used every resource you have to keep to your assigned schedule? Those aren't clanblood swordsmen down there, to notice if you slipped past using some simple spell of illusion.'

'Because,' Dakar gasped with both eyes squeezed shut, 'I'm too busy wrestling the headache I'm given, courtesy of that rat-faced bastard wearing the white robes of the Alliance.'

'The informer?' Parrien curled his upper lip, disgusted. 'You'd better find a more colorful excuse if you want me to think you're not just piss full of gin.'

'He's no informer,' Dakar gasped. Sweat bathed his forehead in sliding drops, until his skin glistened like a burst egg white. 'Lysaer's new policy sees talent burned alive. What sits down there is a trained crown examiner. They're mageborn turned zealot, then unleashed to hunt down anyone born with the gift. Every resource I have has gone into shielding. For three days, I've not dared snatch an hour of sleep. Were I to try spellcraft, be very sure, I wouldn't leave this tavern, except under an Alliance writ of execution, bound hand and foot in steel shackles.'

Parrien forgot his indoor manners and spat. 'This is Shand,' he said, outraged. 'That upstart in Tysan dares a very long arm if he thinks he can impose his false justice inside Lord Erlien's sovereign territory.' As an afterthought, he let go of Dakar's pinched ear. 'See the Mad Prophet comfortable.'

His captain obliged without rancor and lowered the suffering man's weight onto the crumpled bed.

Eyes shut, his pudgy hands pressed to his forehead, Dakar murmured, 'You won't do your brother's reputation any good if you sally downstairs and gut his sworn allies in public.'

'Damn them all!' Parrien spun, kicked the pillow which mired his knife, and snapped up the blade that spun free. Through the whirl of feathers lit like gold filigree in the spill of the candle, he let fly his implacable venom. 'Our two-step charade with Avenor's been a downright strain anyway since the royal writ signed Lord Maenol's captive clansmen into slavery.'

His enterprising glance raked over the room, then lit on the partridge plump whore, gagged and bound, and running her eyepaint to a flood of imploring tears. He regarded her straits with stony practicality, then sorted ideas in the energetic, fast talk he was accustomed to sling at his brothers. 'That squad downstairs haven't got a flea's hindparts for brains. Oh, they know which end of a girl dips their prick, and which orifice to pour in the beer, but I'd bet coin that's their living limit. Shouldn't strain anybody's imagination overmuch to find some way to sneak you out.' He eyed Dakar's limpid posture askance. 'Don't you mind. If you've missed your rendezvous, I've got my brother's state galley in port, packed to the gunwales with mercenaries. All you need do is say where to row. We'll take you to your master offshore.'

Flat with exhaustion, Dakar mumbled through the suffering clasp of his fingers. 'Just so you make a clean job of the foray. I've no wish to revisit Jaelot in chains to burn for the crime of black sorcery.'

Within the half hour, the Fat Pigeon's landlord looked up from his polishing, aroused by a pounding commotion on his stair. Amid the grind of hobnailed boots and a falsetto shriek, came the deeper tones of men's laughter. Next, Parrien s'Brydion arrived on the landing, one thumb cocked in his belt and a smirk on his face. Over his shoulder, clamped by his mailed forearm, a pair of rouged feet thrashed, roped under what looked like the hem of a whore's lace chemise.

Behind clomped his mercenaries, whooping and clattering and clutching their ribs against cramping gales of mirth. The trio of conferencing merchants swiveled to watch, stiffened to prim disapproval. The alert crown examiner peered down his sharp nose, while the Fat Pigeon's landlord slammed down his cleaned tankard with a force that snapped off the handle.

His pealing howl wrecked the taproom's last peace, to no purpose. Parrien s'Brydion held to his course of abducting the corpulent Sashka. He dodged a kick masked in a whirl of petticoats and rounded the newel post of the banister, tossing a spate of cheerful instructions to the saturnine captain behind him.

In response, the mercenary hurled a jingling sack in a flying arc across the taproom. His aim struck the bar dead center. The loose drawstring slipped and let out a trilling, sweet chime of gold coins.

'Ath!' Parrien landed a playful swat on the behind which jounced at his shoulder. 'Your trollop's got spirit, I'll give her that. If she's half as good as you claim in the blankets, she'll be worth what I've paid for her upkeep.' To his captain he added, 'Clear a path to the doorway.'

'What of the layabout?' the landlord yelped back, not entirely reconciled to the receipt of cold coin in exchange for his tavern's best
attraction.

'Left him trussed and locked in the closet, awaiting his trip to the
midden.' Parrien threaded through tables, defending his prize from
the questing grasp of the sailors, and with more gleeful force, the
two-handed clutch of Jaelot's more enterprising mercenaries. 'Quiet,
girl!' His massive forearm swung in alternate rhythm to bludgeon
faces, then to quell the heaving mass of skirts, while the gleam of
white teeth nipped through a beard split in half by a tigerish grin. 'I
trust my coin also settles the three days he's cost you a room?'

Torn, the landlord understood he had only two options: block Parrien's
egress, or rescue the gold spilled over his bar top before his customers
starting pilfering.

'You're a rank clanblood bastard!' he shrieked in frustration.

'Yes to the first, but my dead mother would argue, legitimate down
to the bone.' Parrien ducked a foot, spat out flying lace, and whooped
in triumph as he shouldered his prize through the doorway into the
street. His voice filtered back through the oaths of a carter forced to
jerk his team short of collision: 'If your whore wears me out like she
did her last client, I'll send you back double payment!'

# Exchanges

At the Fat Pigeon, a brief interval after Parrien's departure, the resigned landlord at last finds a moment to attend the wretch left bound in his upstairs closet; except the gagged body he liberates is not the fat layabout, but the opulent Sashka herself, pink and naked and shrieking indignation over the theft of her jewelry and clothing, and queerly unable to recall name or face of the culprit who had first engaged her service . . .

In a closeted room in the city of East Bransing, Prince Lysaer seals a letter, then passes the document to a waiting foreign dignitary with the assurance, 'Avenor has too limited an access during winter, and so cannot remain the operating capital for the armed heart of the Alliance. As my regency of Tysan passes on to my heir, there will be a change. If Etarra would bid to become the permanent seat for the Light, I'll entertain your mayor's offer to host an annual muster . . .'

In the state mansion at Erdane, a lady's maid cossets the daughter pledged to wed the Prince of the Light in the month after spring equinox; the house servants pack the trunks of her trousseau for her journey to Avenor when the thaw reopens the passes; and the captain of the city garrison picks his most reliable men to guard the new princess's dowry . . .

## Late Winter 5654

# V. Dispatches

T he cove, with its wide, protected harbor and barrier islets, was avoided by galleymen because of its entrenched reputation for haunts. A Second Age ruin overlooked the fractured rim of the cliff wall, which reared up in ramparts of basalt and porous gutters of worn lava. The old towers notched the skyline in shattered majesty, brooding and jagged as sheared obsidian against the thin, sheeting clouds which threatened soft drizzle by nightfall. The site was accessed by no inland road. The shifting sands of Sanpashir desert spread like black flint for the waterless leagues lying between Sanshevas and the ports to the west. Yet in the years prior to Desh-thiere's invasion, high kings' sons had been born there. The fortress had prospered in the flourishing, brisk trade that linked its deep harbor with the established sea route to Innish.

Although the ruin still sheltered stone cisterns uncracked by time or weather, the catch water was guarded by wild tribes who hunted outsiders with darts. Captains risked running their store barrels empty rather than suffer the climb, where a Second Age ghost or a shrieking desertman might harry a foraging party to their deaths.

In late winter of Third Age 5654, the barrier isles guarding the harbor still grew their rank tangles of brush. The thin, raked stands of salt-stunted cedar offered poor screening for a small fleet of ships, unless their captains had the wily enterprise to strike yards and topmasts, and festoon hanging moss from the rigging.

When the s'Brydion state galley clove through the gap, shot spray from her oars pebbling the cove's turquoise shallows, her master and captain remained locked in hot argument over the need for a landfall. The steersman's shout silenced them. Turning, still flushed, both master and captain beheld a scrub forest whose roots were not landbound, but set into the raking, clean lines of three brigantines.

'Damn me to Sithaer!' the captain exclaimed, through Parrien's whistled admiration.

Sharp orders from the bosun set the sweeps back. To his master's miffed grunt over usurped authority, the captain snapped, 'Well, why tire good men? The breeze lies astern. Let the ship's drift lay her up alongside.'

When the leadsmen called aft that the waters were shoaling, the captain relinquished the details of anchorage to his mate, and only looked sour as Parrien bellowed through the hatch to roust up his laggard purser. 'There *are* blighted ships here! Three of them, all painted dull gray and flying nests of moss as thick as my grandmother's dress wigs. You can release the fifty silvers I've lost to the Mad Prophet when he's sober enough to ask payment.'

A shout hailed back from a point belowdecks that Dakar was prostrate, courtesy of a cask found broached in the galley. 'Fatemaster's own fury won't wake the sot now. He's bound to stay snoring until a tight bladder drags him back from oblivion.'

Bronzed muscles rippled as, shirtless, Parrien snapped the brass bands of his ship's glass closed. His vexation lifted to raised eyebrows and laughter. 'Dharkaron's own Spear! Dakar found the cook's rotgut brandy? Then we'd better get him bundled back where he belongs before he gets staggering sick.'

'Why not make things easy?' griped the state galley's captain. 'Throw him over the rail and let him recover the senses to swim.'

There followed an hour of coarse comment and jibes, while the duke's red-blazoned longboat was swayed out, and Dakar loaded comatose into sailcloth and lowered in by means of a halyard; then the same process began in reverse as Alestron's tender hailed the brigantine *Khetienn* and asked for her flying jib's shackle to be freed and run over the forecastle.

'We've got you a sluggard to haul bodily aboard!' Parrien boomed across the narrowing span of ruffled water.

An unkempt head nipped over the brigantine's stern rail, with black wire hair swathed in a sun-faded rag. The scowl underneath was creased like shelled walnut, and jet bead eyes viewed the longboat's sprawled cargo with animate, darting suspicion. 'Whoever gave the fat lout the wineskin?' The imprecations screeched on in the volatile accents of the desertman who served aboard the *Khetienn* as both cook and cabin steward. 'I dice his gizzard, that one, for rock-head stupidity!'

'Save the edge on your knives,' Parrien called back. He had donned a clean shirt and a weathered, old field tunic, and still fussed with the hang of his sword belt. 'We've already had to placate our cook. It's his missing brandy that caused all the damage. And anyhow, your Mad Prophet had his good reason for seeking oblivion this time.' The fact the tender's oarsmen closed the gap to mere yards did nothing to dampen the gusto of s'Brydion enthusiasm as Parrien smoothed the last buckle and looked up. 'Five burnings on charges of criminal sorcery happened in Southshire, work of some zealot crown examiner from Tysan. If not for a last-ditch masquerade with a whore's dress, your spellbinder would've been sixth.'

More interested heads appeared at the rail, while someone's barked order sent sailhands to free the line to salvage a carcass.

'No matter.' The desertman evinced the peppery shrug that came ingrained with his breeding. 'We done this before, two dozens of times. I've said, why not end it? Just put the rope round the whale fish's throat. But nobody listens. Not yet.'

Since any euphemism that implied a state of immersion was a Sanpashir desertman's mortal insult, Parrien tactfully changed subject. 'It's your prince I'd like to have words with, anyway. Is his Grace of Rathain with the ship?'

The desertman's dark visage disappeared like a rat that had just ducked a club, and the request for an audience was taken in turn by the cracking impatience of a man with a Westlands clan accent.

'You'll find him up the cliffside, inside the ruins.' The speaker appeared, one of Lord Maenol's surviving cousins to judge by the mink hair braided at his nape. 'If you wait, we'll find you a man whose leathers and boots haven't molded. Stone's rotten sharp from salt weathering and storms. You'll want a guide to lead you topside.'

'Send him on naked, or let him catch up,' Parrien countered, then ripped out an oath for the blighting detail which restrained him: his oarsmen could scarcely row anyplace else before the Mad Prophet was hoisted out of the stern seat.

Atop the seacliffs, the air smelled like flint. Hazed sun sweltered down on pitched dunes of black sand like a hammer sparking shards of light off an anvil. The hot ground burned even through leather-soled boots.

Breathless from his climb up sheer rock, Parrien shaded his eyes with grazed fingers.

In Paravian times, when these ruins stood whole, the fortress had commanded the crest like a setting of filigreed ivory. Centaur masons had raised the ringwalls of white granite, with chains of inner courtyards connected by cloistered arches, most made melodious with fountains. Vast gardens threaded like grottos in the fanned shade of tall date palms or arbors of flowering grape.

Now, an invasion of abrasive basalt sands choked the smashed friezes of sunchildren, and thorn-tipped plants elbowed for survival where runoff from the walls afforded a rare patch of moisture. Here and there, the pale carving of the original arches stood intact. Their cloud-filtered shadows traced the barren soil in elongated, spider-legged grace, while the cloverleaf patterns of their pierced stonework whispered like hollow bones played by the wind.

The two men passed through with sword-trained distaste for the footing. Hobnailed seaboots sank into maws of dry sand, while the breeze fanned behind. Grit tumbled in hissing currents and erased every trace of living presence.

Parrien had no liking for the emptiness. Nor did the heat numb his senses to the point where he missed the fast, furtive movement that slipped through the tumbledown stonework ahead.

'Desertmen,' the youthful clan guide informed him, then grasped his tensed forearm to stop the reflexive draw of his knife. 'Don't rile them. They carry blowpipes and darts, and hit well enough to stick a man through the eye at eighty paces. There's always half a dozen come to guard his Grace's back whenever he makes his way ashore.'

Eyebrows tipped upward in rankling inquiry, Parrien wrenched free, while his instinct for survival took sobering note that these desertmen came and went with disquieting stealth. The insects still clicked and chirred undisturbed from their shaded crannies.

The clan scout rubbed a grazed palm on his leathers, and admitted, 'In truth, the creatures unnerve me as well.'

'You said they guard Arithon.' Parrien scanned the way ahead, but saw nothing else beyond sun-blasted rock, sheeted in mounds of dark sand. 'Why?'

'The tribes here invoke the blessing of their mother goddess, Darkness. Shadows, they say, are her infant sons.' The clan scout shrugged. 'They think Arithon's god-touched. He explained in plain words that his powers were no better than mortal. A mage's birth gift gave him command of the elements. You knew?'

At Parrien's nod, the guide finished, 'Well, none of the desertmen wanted to listen. The local tribe elder just patted his Grace's shoulder and insisted their luck and their goats would increase if the tribesmen give him protection.'

Another shrug; then a kicked bit of gravel that ricocheted through the embittered conclusion. 'No one of us cares if their tribal belief stems from worship or augury. Their vigilance brings no harm, and keeping the Shadow Master's favor won't hurt. My blood for surety,' the scout swore in fierce words that shocked instant respect from any man raised to clan heritage, 'a light-based religion will show these nomads no tolerance. If Lysaer plays the Mistwraith's curse into an excuse for a holy war, his new breed of soldier-priests are likely to pass the wild tribes under Fate's Wheel for heretics.'

'Religion?' Parrien forgot about desertmen and knives. 'What claptrap is this?'

The clansman glanced aside, his uneasy eyes and the lift of his jaw too sharp for the youthful stubble on his chin. 'Hasn't a sunwheel priest chapped on Alestron's postern yet? Well then, as the one Alliance ally who won't wish to spurn the old order, your duke better think what he'll say. The day will come when he's asked to swear faith and string shadowbanes on the stiff necks of your family.'

Parrien laughed. 'I pity the dimwit who dares try!'

'Tomorrow, that might not seem funny.' The guide skirted a ruckle of stones where the sea storms had chewed the foundations. 'High council in Tysan claims Prince Lysaer's the manifestation of righteous good come to save us. They say he won't age, and call him Divine Light. You've been to Southshire. The ports on the coast are buying the lie. The mayor at Innish let that sunwheel examiner dispossess the sea-quarter herb witches as well.'

'More fools, they!' Parrien bristled, his eyes trained ahead and his fingers tapping a nerve-wrought tattoo on his dagger hilts. 'Let five months go by, they'll be tripping over the pregnant whores kicked out in the streets begging charity. If their cities don't like starving babes underfoot, they'll wish they'd left at least one of the old besoms her practice.'

No lighthearted quip came back from the clan scout. 'What will Alestron do when the sunwheel banner becomes a rallying cry for religion?'

'Duke Bransian will probably skewer the first messenger who declares himself Lysaer's priest.' Parrien flashed a wicked, insouciant grin, while the indignant wind lashed the white strands licked through the seal hair at his temples. 'That's if my brother Keldmar didn't seize his chance to handle the idiot first. He's said before that sunwheel tunics make tempting targets for archery. He's been frothing at the mouth to sharpen his aim in case things come to a brangle.'

Through the shade of another etched archway, the scout said, 'Lysaer has a way of bending allegiances.' His shrewd glance measured. 'Once, we counted on Cattrick.'

Parrien scraped sweat from the nape of his neck, bristled to sudden ill temper. 'You imply we'd turn? Or that Mearn would?' His outrage slapped echoes off dusty stonework like the portentous growl of thunder. 'Alestron's not sanguine with Alliance affairs. My brother's no dreamer. He's set new revetments in his battlements and kept the armory forge fires busy for the time this charade of arse-kissing amity breaks open.'

Yet even for a Westlands boy marked with a galley slave's brand from Lysaer's crown policy against clansmen, the ultimate loyalty of the s'Brydion armed forces was too forthright a question to ask.

The moment for more probing inquiry was lost in any case. Past the crumbled shell of a bastion and the miniature tracks stippled by a foraging scarab, a poured avenue of sand shimmered across the gapped portal to what had been a spacious bailey; nor was the space empty, or desolate, or dead.

Out of that sun-fired shell of baked stone poured a shimmering cascade of pure harmony. The tenor and pitch was liquid and minor, wrought of a stark tension to lacerate peace and wring tears from dry eyes to succor the tortured desiccation of the earth.

Parrien stopped before thought. His hand left his weapon hilt without conscious volition and clutched in a fist to his chest. On emotion torn like grained rust from his throat, he whispered, 'Ath show blind mercy!'

The clan guide stopped also. His sympathy was reverent, and no little bit tinged with fear. 'Dakar told us once, if his Grace pours out music, sometimes he won't get the nightmares.'

Parrien swore hot enough to anneal the war temper from cold steel.

If the bard overheard, his sealed concentration never faltered. That wounding progression of notes spiraled on, seamless as ribbon drawn through the silk weave of eternity. Lent poignant echoes by the enclosure of ruined masonry, the inspired mastery of his talent broke reason and loosed passions which purveyed the mind to the borders of madness.

To listen too long was to court sheer despair, cankered too deep to rout out.

Parrien shook himself. He glanced hard at the clan scout, and sweated to ram words through the pain of a need beyond language. 'I think I'd better go forward alone.'

The guide flicked a tear unabashed from his cheek. 'That's wisest. I'll wait at the cliff head.' He departed, secure in the knowledge the distrustful guard of the desertmen would stay true to Arithon's interests.

Alone with that stripping, glass-edged cry of sorrow, Parrien wrestled reluctance. There seemed no more barbaric a desecration than to go forward and disrupt the bard for the sake of a mundane purpose.

Then the lyranthe's rending performance cut off; the furtive footfalls of desertmen, or some musician's instinct had perhaps served a merciful warning. Arithon's voice called out from across the vista of broken rock. 'To your right.'

Parrien clamped down his unstrung nerves. As if bodily exertion could shake off the hurt left strapped like chain through his chest, he moved to lay claim to his audience.

The bard sat on a broken length of wall, clad in dark breeches and a loose, open shirt of plain linen. The unbleached, ivory cloth rippled and snapped in the wind. His black hair streamed also, untrimmed and tangled beside the hands laced white-knuckled over the scroll at the lyranthe's peghead. The instrument was not either flashy or new. A frayed-off end of scarlet silk showed where a past owner had adorned it with tassels.

At first measure, Parrien judged that Prince Arithon was ill. His war-trained eye tested fitness at a glance, and read in that delicate stillness the posture a stricken man used when a sword thrust bled beyond remedy.

Then the musician laid down his instrument, stood up, and turned. His straight stance was too fluidly poised for a man just arisen from sickbed. He acknowledged his visitor with wide, wary eyes; and Parrien measured a face like stamped steel, with a spirit inside that grief had left stranded in a solitude as cruel as imprisonment.

'If that's Parrien of Alestron, you've brought more bad news,' Prince Arithon opened, his inflection vised to indifference.

'Not exactly.' Squinting against the cloud-glare, Parrien played for disarming humor. 'Unless you count your Mad Prophet brought back drunk on brandy a disaster of major proportions.' On the strength of shrewd guesswork, he added an afterthought. 'Your packet of dispatches is safe.'

Arithon closed the last distance between them and stopped. He was unarmed and guileless, clear enough indication that his mood was doubly dangerous. 'Dakar's scrapes are scarcely earthshaking events. Why come here in person?'

'I could ask the same.' More than the harsh light made eye contact difficult. Parrien surveyed those angular, cool features, his skin raked up into gooseflesh. A decade had passed since he and Arithon s'Ffalenn had last parted on a wind-raked Vastmark hillside. And yet, for all the hard years in between, the Master of Shadow showed no mortal sign of aging.

'There's not any mystery,' Arithon said, jolting for the ordinary way he responded to a mannerless interrogation. 'I plan to search offshore until I find where the Paravians took refuge. Unless I would risk leading men into madness, my ships are best sailed by a crew with unbroken clan lineage. They're here for training. I came to secure the integrity of our supply lines. The voyage we embark on could last for years. We aren't rushed, but I admit to worry when Dakar was overdue back from Southshire. No doubt you're owed thanks. If his rescue requires repayment, name the sum. I'll compensate for the bother.'

Gauze bands of cloud scattered the sunlight between them. Despite the heat, Parrien shivered. 'Ath,' he burst out on a stab of unease. *Who in Daelion's name are you?'*

'Lysaer's half brother, and human as you.' Arithon waited, hands clasped to contain his faint exasperation, while the desert winds braided raffish strings of elf locks into his shoulder-length hair. Since the s'Brydion flint stare allowed him no quarter, he sighed. 'You've heard the new claim of s'Ilessid immortality? Don't believe it. Our gift of longevity stems from the same source, and divine cause has no connection.'

'Go on.' Parrien's tongue had gone dry in his mouth, and the palms on his knife handles, drenched. 'I think my family should know, being entangled in the destiny between you.'

Arithon said without rancor, 'Davien the Betrayer once built an enchanted fountain through the West Worldsend Gate, in the Red Desert by the ruins of Mearth. Both of us drank while delirious with thirst. The mistake held high stakes. One swallow inflicted a Sorcerer's burden of five hundred years' added life span.'

'That's scarcely reassuring,' Parrien snapped. 'In the next generation, will you weep to remember? The rest of us have only one life to spend in your service.'

Arithon flinched, a fractional slip of control, but one that unstrung his masking appearance of sangfroid. 'The enchantment is fallible.' He spun, but the refuge of the curtain wall was too far. Clear air could not mask his untenable agony, and for pride, he refused craven use of his shadow. 'A sword thrust might not serve to dispatch the spirit, but death could be sealed by dismemberment.'

'And fire?' pressed Parrien. 'That might work, too?'

'That's why they burn sorcerers,' Arithon lashed back, flat and fierce with impatience. 'Flame is considered unequivocally reliable. If you're going to examine my murky integrity, could I suggest that we continue in privacy?' He inclined his head.

Struck by the passionless edge to the cue, Parrien s'Brydion glanced behind.

Still as sinister shadows, eight gray-robed desertmen fanned in a half circle, hair spiked with resin and blowpipes poised at their lips. They had advanced from their niches in the stonework without even a whisper of scuffed sand.

Parrien faced back to the Shadow Master, the creeping flesh between his shoulder blades a goad to his simmering temper. 'So, are we enemies? If not, I can hope you speak desert dialect well enough to explain.'

'They trust what they see,' Prince Arithon replied. 'Since they hold a touch sacred, any small gesture of amity should suffice. Let us embrace, then retire in comfort to my chart room aboard the *Khetienn*.'

'You know me better.' Parrien laughed, causing the desertmen a tense and unwelcome start. 'We'll talk on my galley or nowhere at all.'

'Just so my packets of dispatches wait there.' Arithon closed the last step between, prepared to evince his personal trust. Glare no longer masked his condition as he exchanged a formal embrace. The s'Brydion brother ached then for the evidence under his hands: the Master of Shadow had indeed suffered illness. Under the deceitful folds of loose clothes, his whipcord-lean strength had worn down to attenuated sinew and bone. Nor did he carry a knife in concealment, even beneath the voluminous drawstring sleeves.

'Forgive me for testing,' Parrien said in husky apology. 'We know well to trust you. But it's no canny matter, these whispered rumors of blood magic, demons, and divinity. On the streets in broad daylight, I've seen merchant's children wearing white prayer cords and shadowbanes.'

Arithon stepped back. His green eyes stayed hooded beneath the peaked browline stamped with the unmistakable heritage of his ancestry. 'I don't like it either,' he admitted with self-haunted honesty.

Whatever he was, whether or not he was begotten by a s'Ffalenn prince upon a mortal woman, none who faced him could deny his human burden of grief.

'What do you say we forsake this scorching cliff top, and see if Dakar left anything liquid in my wine locker?' Parrien fell in stride as Arithon swung back to retrieve his lyranthe from the wall. By the time they retraced their steps toward the cove, the desertmen had melted back into the ruins, leaving only the dimpled smears of footprints.

*　　*　　*

Nightfall brought in a mantling sea mist. A needle-fine drizzle chased droplets like mercury down the amber-tinged glass of the galley's stern windows. The brisk slap of wavelets came interspersed by slow footfalls as the deck officer paced out his watch. Forward, contained behind muffling wood, Alestron's mercenaries worked goose grease salve into the calluses hardened by hours at the oar. The sail crew diced, or bragged over their beer rations of their prowess while on shore leave. Inside the privacy of the stern cabin, behind a companionway guarded by the field troop's scarred captain and two of his steadfast veterans, Parrien leaned across the table to pour wine.

His eyes flashed offense as he found Arithon's goblet untouched in its place on the sill. 'You aren't drinking. From anyone else, that would become a fighting man's grounds to take insult.'

Arithon attacked without looking up from the sheet of reed paper he held poised over the unshielded candle. 'For anyone else, I wouldn't accept the polite burden of guest traditions at all.' The leaflet in his hand betrayed slight unsteadiness as the lines inked in lemon juice smoked and seared brown, revealed like script penned in by a ghost.

The verbal byplay ongoing since sundown suspended while the Shadow Master read.

Neither man had changed clothes since afternoon. Parrien's creased field tunic seemed fit for a rag against the scarlet leather and brass buttons upholstering the benches. The lamps with their cut-crystal panes made Arithon's stark dress seem a rebuttal of state manners and the comforts of civilized opulence.

A flick of long fingers tipped the page to the flame. Paper flared up and blackened, then shriveled to ash in a pot filched without the cook's knowledge from the galley. The saloon with its heraldic carving and scrolled brightwork, and the salt-musty smell of wool tapestry cushions already wore a layered haze of smoke and a nauseating reek of singed parchment.

Parrien dropped nicety and drank from the flask. 'If you keep that up, my brother's going to ask who we tortured with hot irons for a confession.'

Expressionless, Arithon used the sharp knife from the chart desk to snap through another wax seal. 'If you want the details of my sordid affairs, you can hire henchmen to sift through the gossip yourself.'

Yet already, Parrien's prying had plumbed the vulnerability behind the late round of snappish defenses. His ruthless observation had not missed the missive bearing Rathain's formal seal. *Caithdein*, Earl Jieret, had again served his duty as the official royal conscience. His written exoneration for Caolle's death while in s'Ffalenn service lay amid the curled sheets that survived incineration. S'Brydion interests notwithstanding, Parrien respected the loss. He had witnessed the bond between Shadow Master and war captain firsthand at the close of the campaign in Vastmark. The sorrow of his wounding by his own liege's hand sliced unimaginably deep.

Light from the gimbaled lamp on the bulkhead accentuated Arithon's fragile exhaustion: the bright, circled eyes and the precise way that he perused and absorbed the fresh impact of bleak news. The trumped-up charge of black sorcery made by the Alliance against his actions in Vastmark had been used to spawn an insidious unrest. Everywhere but in Havish, Lysaer's minions had been diligent to incite small fears to paranoia. Sunwheel garrisons were being funded by trade guilds exhorted to groundless dread. More than one missive had cited burnings for criminal sorcery. In remote parts of Melhalla where Arithon had never trod, far less called down shadow, misinformed citizens had risen in vociferous declaration against him. Three farmers had slain a traveler with black hair for refusing to tell his identity.

Crown examiners rode out to question remote villagers. Their arraignments passed uncontested. Fellowship Sorcerers were too overextended by their burden of holding the land's law in the absence of the Paravians. Koriani seniors chose not to intervene, proprietary in their disdain for the hedge lore of country goodwives. They held their cold stance, that healing should remain the exclusive provenance of those women oathsworn to the rigid, high vows of their order.

Parrien twirled the flask between hands chapped rough from his habit of armed practice in steel gauntlets. 'You may find the news from my brother in Avenor a bit more to your liking.'

Arithon looked up. The pressure of his undivided attention touched like the bearing threat of a rapier point. 'I'm listening.'

The exchange raised an indefinable challenge, fed on Parrien's side by cold-nerved anticipation. While a dicer on deck quipped to peals of disjointed mirth, and the anchor watch called off the hour, the s'Brydion brother sprawled at false ease with his swordsman's hands tucked round the wine flask. 'We're not your enemy,' he reminded.

'Don't hedge.' The spark of s'Ffalenn temper might have been the green fire spiked through a faceted emerald. 'Whatever your brother's stirred up in Tysan might not be in my best interests.'

Too slit-eyed and ornery to mellow with drink, Parrien prodded, 'He doesn't like Lysaer any better than you do. Not since the cavalier expedience which excused the murder of Princess Talith.'

The item was news; a quick, sharpened breath shot tension through

Arithon's shoulders. Feint and riposte, Parrien added, 'You did know the Prince of the Light was remarrying.'

Arithon flattened emptied hands between his ordered piles of correspondence. The mild pose was a foil for the unsheathed threat of pure rage. 'Dakar said earlier the princess had been lawfully put aside for faithlessness. Tell me the truth.'

Not quite sober, Parrien taunted the teeth of the tiger. 'Officially, she took a suicide leap. My brother Mearn swears by blood honor she died in secret by decree of Avenor's inner cabal for a treasonous liaison with the powers of darkness.'

A lightning move saw Arithon on his feet. Another step turned his back. The knuckles he braced on the stern sill were not visible, but the fickle properties of darkened glass reflected a face ripped into shock. 'She was innocent,' he murmured. '*I never touched her.*'

And Parrien gained insight that the Shadow Master blamed her charge of infidelity on the months he had held her to ransom as a tactic to defer Lysaer's invasion of Vastmark. Shaken by a reaction he could not have foreseen, he broke the rest quickly. 'The public accusation was not false. The lady was pregnant beyond question when she died. State officials bore witness. Their signed testament stands. The adulterer was a servant, as Mearn's own letter corroborates.'

Arithon answered with venom, still facing the window. 'That doesn't exonerate me for destroying the trust between husband and wife in the first place.'

'I don't see you had much choice in the matter.' Disgruntled to find himself blindsided by pity, Parrien took refuge in disgust. 'Unless you'd prefer that Prince Lysaer's war host was left free to decimate a generation of Vastmark herdsmen.'

'And was that my choice?' Unendurable bitterness made Arithon fling back his words like edged weapons. 'Am I, as my half brother, to displace Ath's order and decide who lives and who dies?'

Which was no just comparison in Parrien's opinion, but the prickle at his nape warned him against futile argument. If his retreat to silence was no kind alternative, at least Rathain's prince used the interval to contain the agonized burn of his conscience.

Several fraught seconds passed, ripped by a splash as the cook's boy dumped a slop bucket overboard. A shift in the breeze rocked the galley on her chain and a fringe of disturbed droplets tapped the sill. Parrien weighed the distraction of rising to trim the wicks. Yet Arithon released his death grip on the molding and faced back into the cabin.

He looked like a torn rag doll whose parts had been strung back together with wire. 'Now tell me the news you thought I would like.'

A chill chased the length of Parrien's spine. He wished he had tended the lamps, the better to interpret the wide-lashed, direct stare upon him. 'Your shipwright, Cattrick, was never a traitor.'

'I knew that.' Such mage-trained attentiveness became bruising to withstand, yet Arithon yielded no quarter. 'The man held an oath of debt to the Koriathain. They used that to force him against me. The past doesn't matter. New ships are his passion. He and his family will keep in safe comfort on his pay from the Alliance's coffers.'

'Sound strategy.' Parrien could outlast a rock for tenacity. 'Except that Mearn's letter said Cattrick's pride won't stand for the change in loyalty.'

'That's madness!' Arithon's cheeks flushed to raw streaks from embarrassment. 'Our terms went no deeper than a master laborer's fair wage. Cattrick's no fool! He's lived too close to Avenor not to recognize the dangers of keeping my service.'

Parrien licked his teeth, his smile all devilish insolence. 'He's allied himself with Mearn. The pair of them have plotted to sink the royal fleet and destroy the Riverton shipworks in one stroke as a wedding gift to Prince Lysaer.'

The highbred s'Ffalenn features went brittle as porcelain. 'They can't. I won't sanction this.'

Parrien raised his eyebrows. 'Do you think they are children? My youngest brother won't settle without due redress for Lady Talith, and Cattrick deserves blood in recompense for the stain on his given word. If you're a wise prince, you'll rejoice for the setback given to your enemies, then send two bold heroes the grace of your thanks for embracing an opportunity.'

When Arithon yielded none of his implacable reserve, Parrien slammed down his fists. 'Quit sulking and have done! What choice is there, anyway? You'll have a rough time trying to stop their planned action from Sanpashir.'

'I won't stop them from here,' Arithon agreed.

Fast as he moved, Parrien matched him. His greater bulk shot up from the table and blocked the shut door to the companionway.

'We aren't enemies,' Parrien reminded again. Running hot sweat despite mulish strength and a lifetime spent mastering battle nerves, he throttled the shrill instinct which insisted he ought to draw steel for self-defense. 'The risk to Mearn is not in your sovereignty to refuse, but involves his personal honor.'

'We aren't speaking of Mearn.' Arithon advanced another step in coiled anger. 'Whatever the scale of the damage inflicted, the blame is going to become mine.'

'Oh, and your hands are clean?' Parrien lashed back.

Arithon jerked his head in patent impatience. '*You aren't listening.* I don't attack innocents. What blood has been shed since Vastmark's been confined to men who mishandled justice and broke Tysan's charter against slavery.'

'How righteous,' sneered Parrien. 'After Vastmark, I can't imagine you squeamish.'

'Call Mearn off,' insisted Arithon, unfazed by the slur. 'I'll handle Cattrick. This attack must not happen. The ones who die this time will be uninvolved sail crews. On Alliance home ground, before outraged envoys invited as Avenor's royal guests, that's going to touch off an explosive retribution such as this land has never seen.'

'I won't tuck tail,' said Parrien, obstinate. 'Nor will Prince Lysaer be permitted the free rein to prevail. Did you think my brother Bransian dispatched his state galley to bear letters and take his best troop of mercenaries for a seaside stroll? I've been given my orders to support Mearn's effort. Our family doesn't like losing; nor will we sit still and suffer the risk of a s'Ilessid charge for conspiracy and high treason.'

Arithon strove one last time to instill reason. 'Public opinion has turned hard against me. Any unprovoked criminal act gives my half brother the touchstone to launch another broadscale war. If Mearn's part is noticed, no s'Brydion duke is going to find himself exempt. Alestron would be visited by an army to make Davien the Betrayer's rebellion seem like a tournament by comparison.'

Parrien's lip curled. 'Don't think us cowards to withdraw out of fear.'

'Then withdraw by main force,' said Arithon, and sprang.

He was unarmed. The unbalanced fact lent him a stunning advantage of surprise. Parrien caught a shoulder in the gut that slammed him backward into the bulkhead. Caught breathless by the speed of the wrestler's jab that hooked the hinge of his knee and wrenched in a practiced move to fell him, the duke's brother struck back with locked fists.

One battering return blow snapped the force of the hold. Parrien sidestepped and countered. The leverage against him melted away, and he staggered. A fist grazed his neck. The follow-up hook would have stunned him silly had he not already twisted to retaliate. His left jab sliced air. His right-hand punch skidded, glancing, and tore a screaming rent as he snagged into Arithon's shirtfront.

'Desist,' he gasped. He ducked another fist, then just missed the evil feint and counterblow intended to blacken his left eye. 'I don't need

Earl Jieret's retribution for breaking the head of Rathain's last s'Ffalenn prince.'

Arithon landed a knee and an elbow in brute gouges that eschewed every rule of fair play.

Parrien roared. Roused now to blind fury, he closed in and grappled a body that eeled through his grasp, then came back and battered with the wanton unpredictability of a windstorm. What blows he landed were never square hits. Even in war he had not encountered the whiplash ferocity of the prince who assaulted his stance in the doorway.

'Hold the chart room secure!' he bellowed. The mercenaries posted on guard outside must surely hear the commotion. 'Let nothing through!'

That moment, the lamps snuffed. Out of absolute darkness, Arithon's knuckles struck Parrien's jaw and split skin.

'Devil!' He spat blood, evaded. Something snatched as a weapon hammered the lintel and gouged up a mess of snapped wood. Another second, and the inveterate Prince of Rathain seized the bench to use for a ram. A current of disturbed air; Parrien dodged, hit the gimbaled lamp, and howled as hot oil seared down his back. Wood screeched on the decking. The bench struck its mark, *not the door*, but the stern window. Glass shattered. The invasive, flint dampness of rain-sodden rock whirled through the smoke and the singed stink of skin and wool tunic.

'This is Duke Bransian's state galley you're wrecking!' Parrien shouted in outrage. 'The last time anyone dared scratch her brightwork, he got mad enough to spit balefire.'

For answer, the bench rammed the bulkhead groin high. Parrien caught only splinters as he moved, still blinded. He cracked into the strut left in wait for his shins.

He yelled and went down, while the flyweight body of the Shadow Master crashed on his chest to deal him still more thrashing punishment.

Parrien threw him off, pounced, and caught nothing. Just an eddy of blank air and a ripe bruise on his palms. The bench, thrown from nowhere, bashed into his shoulder, and his cheek slammed into the table leg. While he groaned, stunned and dizzy, his senses tracked a drawn breath, then the busy scrape of brass, which bespoke some fresh plot afoot with the broken lamp.

'Damn you!' Rather than risk fire on his brother's prized vessel, Parrien dived at the source of the noise and howled for reinforcement from his mercenaries.

The door crashed back.

'No swords,' gasped Parrien, barely in time.

His three field-trained veterans barreled into the fray, and the darkness exploded to mayhem.

Wood banged and groaned. Flesh smacked into flesh. Someone cursed, and the oil fumes thickened.

'Don't allow him the striker!' Parrien warned, then skidded headlong to defend the lid of the stores locker.

Someone was down and retching by the bulkhead. Another combatant roared an epithet maligning vicious minds and broken glass. Then Parrien swore as two bodies thrashed into him, one of them fine-boned and murderously quick. The other locked arms and strove to peg down what seemed the kinetic force of a juggernaut.

Parrien snatched at the folds of a half-shredded shirt, twisted, and used his superior weight to contain the body bagged inside. When the linen jerked backward, then burned through his hold, he chose the fast option and banged its struggling contents against the brass edge of the locker.

A grunt; a sharp hiss of expelled air.

'Serve your royal hide right!' He struck again, and received a kick in the ankle that undid the last of his tolerance. 'To Sithaer with niceties. Hit him.'

The mercenary captain used the pommel of his sword as a bludgeon. There came a dull thunk, and the wildcat struggles under Parrien's grasp sagged into jellied deadweight.

Shadow burned away, to reveal one lamp still burning. The other hung skewed and fluttering on bent gimbals. Arithon dangled between Parrien's hands like a puppet entangled in the shreds of his oversize clothing. One elegant, angled cheekbone was bruised. A meaty swelling disfigured his forehead, and one forearm and both hands were gashed bloody.

'Fiends plague the damned glass!' Parrien sucked in a lamed, burning breath, his own toll of damages as bitter. He noticed he had only one man left standing, and to him, demanded, 'Put up your steel. Do whatever you must, just keep his Grace down.'

He unfolded his sore leg, tried a step, winced. 'Good wine never did do a damned thing for pain.' Still muttering imprecations, he wrested a basin from behind the mangled door of a locker. Since movement felt wretched, and the cut on his head made his ugly mood worse, he waved to the mercenary just straightening up from a semiconscious daze in the corner. 'Mind the edges of glass and dip up some seawater.' He proffered the basin. 'Douse the bastard until he wakes up. I want him cursing and conscious.'

To the watch officer, belatedly arrived at the companionway, he added his snarling reprimand. 'Yes, I need you! Grab this uncivilized royal wretch by the ankles. Woe betide you if you slacken your hold, because he'll try to kick you to impotence when he wakens.'

The man at the stern window hobbled back with the basin just as Arithon's eyes flickered open. His senses cleared fast. He measured the three mercenaries whose vengeful hands roped him prostrate. The jerk of his breathing just barely allowed words. 'This isn't finished.'

'I'll break your sword arm,' Parrien snarled. 'Then you won't be fighting fit to meddle with Mearn or anyone else for a long time.'

'Leg,' Arithon gasped, implacably berserk.

'Dharkaron's two-eyed vigilance!' Parrien crouched, grasped black hair with grazed hands, and gave the Shadow Master's head a drubbing shake. 'You're *supposed* to capitulate!'

'No.' Green eyes wide-open and serious, Arithon said, 'But I ask, not my arm. For pity, don't spoil my music.'

'Ath, *that's a plea?*' Parrien felt sickened.

Unable to turn away, Arithon shut his bruised eyelids.

'Speak, damn you!' Parrien would not trust the face, hard-set with agony beneath him. 'Give me your royal word.'

Arithon answered with razor-sharp clarity. 'I already have.'

'Well you'd better change heart! Sithaer, you're knocked down and winded and kicked to a pulp!' Parrien let go. A studied assessment of the defiance held pinned and bleeding by his mercenaries made him vent a more poisonous oath. For Arithon s'Ffalenn, there would be no yielding, no civilized alternative to curb his set will short of actual bodily harm.

'You ravening idiot! Don't say after this you don't deserve all you get.' Disgusted with entreaties, Parrien snapped off a nod to his captain. 'Hold him fast. Fail me there, and I'll see you regret every day you survive before Daelion Fatemaster drags your carcass past the Wheel.'

He set his hands on his knee, pushed heavily erect. A shaken stride carried him to the chart table, where the wine flask stood miraculously upright. He snapped out an arm, grasped the neck, and yanked out the stopper with his teeth.

The ejected cork rolled across blood-smeared boards and bumbled to rest amid the burst cushions and smashed glass.

Parrien spun away from the appalling damage. 'Pry open his Grace's mouth. Brute force isn't the only way to take a stubborn man down.' Eyes sparkling malice, he knelt. His captive's enraged glare struck him full in the face. 'Why not just relax and enjoy your defeat? The wine's a spectacular vintage.'

The Shadow Master's spread-eagled limbs contorted in a wild explosion of protest. Yet for all of the furious struggle left in him, he failed to break from the mercenaries' grasp.

Parrien gave his most evil smile, the wine raised in salutation. Then he tipped up the flask and poured the duke's best Shandian red between teeth forced apart by the merciless fingers of his captain. 'Share your miseries with the Mad Prophet,' he murmured, while an ungentle fist in the ribs compelled his victim to swallow. 'If Dakar's up and walking, no doubt he'll nurse your hangover with the practiced hands of experience.'

# Send-Off

The finesse required to return Arithon to his brigantine became a cold trial of patience.

While the *Khetienn*'s night watch subsided to suspicious mutters, and a bristling crewman moved on the foredeck to stow the flying jib's shackle, Parrien cradled the bundled-up form of Rathain's unconscious prince. The only parts visible outside swathing blankets were a dangling hand and a trailing twist of black hair.

'Everybody drinks with their friends now and then,' he argued, while the pounding discomfort of his own cuts and bruises threatened to ignite his rank temper.

The rest of the crew had outworn their disbelief, except for the *Khetienn*'s belligerent steward. That one never moved from his stance of obstructive, arm-folded mistrust. In desert accents inflected to pure venom, he said, 'Show me.'

Parrien swore, careful to keep the flare of the afterdeck lantern behind him. 'Have some respect for his Grace's dignity.' In trust his two mercenaries would keep station at his heels, he jostled forward, hooded head aimed toward the companionway to the stern cabin. 'Dakar's in there?'

The desertman's teeth flashed in the blood orange glow of the lamp. 'Asleep. I think you speak lies. Except once with Cattrick, his Grace has shunned too much drink since the day the shed blood soaked the shores at the Havens.'

'You don't know that for certain.' Parrien tapped his foot. 'You weren't there to mother him. And anyway, Shandian wine's too smooth and sweet to bring on terrors and nightmares. Do please move aside. Or else go rouse Dakar before I get upset and dump Rathain's prince in an unconscious heap at your feet.'

'You wake up Dakar,' the desertman snapped. 'Let you be the one to clean up the sheets when your drinking guests render their gorge.' Sly in contempt, he sidled ahead and flicked up the latch. As the ship's mild roll swung the door wide, Parrien's party invaded the sanctum of the *Khetienn's* stern cabin.

The interior was black. Dakar had always eschewed light with his hangovers, and, obliging, the vindictive little steward had left the lamps dark at sundown.

'Sithaer's plaguing furies!' Parrien resisted the instinctive urge to shove back the hood masking the bashed state of his own features. 'Can't see a damn thing.' Two steps behind, his mercenaries groped a bumping course past lockers and unfamiliar furnishings. 'Somebody, dig out an Ath-forsaken light.'

They purloined the burned-down stub from the chart desk. A lump of flint from a pocket and the blade of a dagger struck the necessary spark. New flame wavered over the quill pens, the dividers, the leather-stamped covers of the brigantine's logbook, and the scrupulous rolled ends of her charts. A glass-paneled cabinet held the priceless lyranthe inherited at Halliron Masterbard's death. An adjacent empty peg showed where the lesser instrument with the cutoff tassels had hung. The green baize cushions and blankets on the quarterberth were neatly brushed and untenanted.

'Dakar's about somewhere.' Parrien glared at the unhelpful desert-man, then rattled terse orders to his mercenaries. 'Search the port and starboard quarters, by force if need be.' The ache of his bruises and a swelling cut on his lip made even simple speech onerous.

'He's in here,' came the call from the depths of another darkened doorway.

'Take the candle,' Parrien said to the guard captain at his elbow. Still bearing Rathain's prince, he followed the slip of yellow flame into the aft cabin, then slammed the door shut before the inquisitive steward could decide on an afterthought to trail him.

Dakar lay wadded like a kicked hedgehog in a wallow of crumpled blankets. His exhaled air reeked of metabolized alcohol. The lingering, sweetish reek of cheap brandy wafted from the irregular stains soaked into his collar. A ruthless shaking by Parrien's mercenaries eventually rattled a tortured groan out of him. He shot a wild fist at the candle thrust in his face, then growled something obscene a man could try with his bollocks, a basin, and a rock.

'Dakar, you're needed,' Parrien said in succinct and irritable urgency.

The Mad Prophet plowed his head under a pillow. Unintelligible grumbles emerged through the muffling goose down.

'Is there a bucket to douse him?' the mercenary captain asked his subordinate.

That threat caused Dakar to shed bedclothes and sit up. His hair was rubbed into a rat's nest of spikes, and a flustered moment passed as he unsnarled his beard from his shirt buttons. 'No water, I'd lose it,' he said clearly. He had time to register the hatchet visage of Parrien's field captain before vertigo overcame him. Folded in half with his forehead resting on his knees, he said to the laddered socks on his ankles, 'Why are you back here?'

'Not to play nursemaid!' The duke's brother lost patience. 'Damn you, sit up. Your prince has need of your services.'

Dakar rolled his neck. An indignant brown eye turned upward. 'I'll have to use the privy first.'

For answer, Parrien flipped the back the blanket that covered his burden. A quick signal moved his men, who hauled the Mad Prophet bodily erect to confront the gist of the crisis.

The blood, the puffed scrapes, and the slack jaw of unconsciousness swam in the flickering flood of the candle.

A blink, a stark moment of igniting disbelief, then the Mad Prophet slapped off the hands which slung him up by his shirtfront. 'You fought him?' His voice climbed into outraged disbelief. 'Merciful Ath! The last affray in Tysan laid him low for three months. Didn't anybody tell you? He just barely got back on his feet!'

Parrien at least had the grace to look sheepish as he pushed back his covering hood. 'Your royal charge wasn't knocked out from blows. Just an unholy excess of red wine.'

'Lay him on the upper berth.' Dakar jerked down his rucked shirt, scrubbed his face with his sleeves, then ordered the sword captain to fetch a jug of water as though he were a born servant. Then he gouged crusted eyes with his knuckles and wrestled his disjointed dismay into speech. 'Why in fate's name did you have to use violence?'

Parrien shed the slack prince, blotted an oozing scab on his forearm, then faced the interrogation straight on. 'I had to stop him. Unless you wanted him sailing straight back to Avenor to intervene on behalf of Cattrick and Mearn.' In rapid, plain words, he outlined the conspiracy arranged with the master shipwright and the scheming, wild plan set in place by his youngest brother.

'Ath!' Dakar stabbed stiff fingers into the shining, dough folds of his cheeks. 'I hurt too much for this. Your cook's brandy is evil and ought to be banned from civilized consumption for eternity.'

'Well my Shandian wine won't be much more merciful.' Parrien licked his split lip, then added, reluctant, 'We had to dose a second flask with valerian since the first one failed to put your prince's lights out.'

Dakar's hands fell. He flopped back on crushed pillows, the resolve all leached out of him, except for his eyes, which stayed piercingly wide and direct. 'Dharkaron, you're serious. His Grace wouldn't quit, even when he was beaten?'

Parrien was sour. 'My best archer's got a thumb bitten down to the bone as living proof.'

Dakar's worry intensified. 'His Grace only gets that difficult if he's desperate.'

'Or insane.' Parrien winced at the jolt to his balance as the kick of changed tide in the inlet riffled rip currents beneath the *Khetienn*'s keel. 'When I threatened to break his arm to keep him passive, he asked me point-blank to break his leg.'

'To spare his hands for his music? Sweet Ath!' New sweat sprang and dripped down Dakar's temples. He laced sausage fingers into the screwed hair at his nape, his frown pinched to alarm. 'If Arithon said that, he's not going to be reasonable. The only way to be sure he won't act is to follow through with your threat.'

'That's barbaric!' Parrien's square face stood wide open to shock. 'An honorable man couldn't.'

'But this isn't about honor, or decency, or pity,' Dakar blazed back from his agonized prostration. 'This is about keeping the Master of Shadow away from Prince Lysaer's throat. We can't survive another curse-driven bloodbath. Are you hearing me?'

Parrien stopped raging, his blunt hands raised in a gesture of warding disbelief. 'You believe Mearn's predicament provided an excuse? *That the Mistwraith's own curse could have raised this uncontrolled outburst of ferocity?*'

'I don't know that for certain.' Dakar rallied sick nerves and propped himself upright. 'Except we can't risk the possibility. All the future's at stake if we judge this wrong.'

'Dharkaron's fell Chariot, you mean, *break his leg?*' Parrien back-stepped as if the Avenger's Black Spear might fall dipped in fire to torment him. 'We don't do things like townsmen, nor cause wrongful harm to sworn friends for expediency.'

Dakar said with queer dignity, 'I wouldn't call preventing a needless, mad slaughter anything so simple as expedience.'

Flattened to the bulkhead, Parrien weighed that terrible truth, his circling conscience trapped and raging. 'If this happens, before Ath, we'll answer our clan blood debt to the s'Ffalenn prince up front.'

Before Dakar could smooth down the thorns of rankled pride, Parrien beckoned to his brother's prize captain of mercenaries. 'Step forward, Vhand. Dakar needs to know you're no hireling soldier.'

In fact, the taciturn veteran was Duke Bransian's oathsworn commander at arms, bearing clan bloodlines back to the uprising. The spare phrases Parrien chose for introduction gave too little recognition for the man's impressive record on the field. 'Tell me, Vhandon,' Parrien finished, his depth of stark weariness struck through his bearing, and his eyes like the heads of iron nails. 'Is Talvish there your most steadfast man?'

'None finer.' Always grudging with words, Vhandon shot an appraising glance at Talvish, then added, 'He's a man for tight corners with the sword.' His eyes remained calm, the color of rubbed jade under the ash-colored jut of his eyebrows. The wrinkles at the corners looked quarried in granite as he held his fighting stance, feet braced against the ship's roll.

Parrien nodded, satisfied. 'Very well. Hear my orders as if they come from your duke, for his name and family honor are now yours to keep. You and Talvish will break Prince Arithon's right leg. Make a clean job. I don't want him lamed. Then you will stand by him, through convalescence and beyond. For s'Brydion good faith, you will swear this spellbinder a blood oath to serve him. Then defend him, life and limb, for as long as you are fit to bear arms or until the curse of the Mistwraith is broken.'

Dakar jerked erect, mouth opened in protest. 'You can't do this. These men have ties, surely. What of their families left in Alestron?'

But Parrien shouted him down. 'No! Don't speak. Compensation is fitting. Who else could your liege ask to take Caolle's place now?'

Into stunned silence, Vhandon's deep voice added emotionless support. 'My sons are grown, my one daughter married.' He tipped a nod to the tall, blond swordsman in the corner. 'Talvish is unattached, yet, and Earl Jieret's clans have no able lives left to spare, not since their best fell to their liege's defense by Tal Quorin. Someone must stay who has enough muscle to keep your Shadow Master flat until the affray with the Riverton shipyard reaches quittance.'

'Fine, then,' Dakar snarled. 'What if Talvish objects?'

The younger man leaned at ease against the closed doorway, his spidery hands quiet and his air of lithe stillness unruffled. 'For the s'Brydion good name, I'll serve Prince Arithon as if he were my bloodborn charge.'

'And get your thumbs bitten, too?' Dakar countered, too much in pain not to vent his distress. 'A viper's less volatile. Don't weep to me when you discover his needling temper.' Since threats and appeal gained him no satisfaction, he accosted Parrien again. 'Dharkaron wept! We're beleaguered enough by patrols and sunwheel galleys, we risk death each time this vessel takes on provisions, and his Grace himself's a damned killing nuisance, convalescent. If I've got to live through this when he wakes up, one Ath-forsaken leg won't be enough to hold him back.'

When Vhandon looked irate, Dakar explained, his round face a misery of apprehension. 'His crew will act for him. More than half were redeemed from slave labor at the oar by his active intervention. If Arithon asked for Fate's Wheel to be stopped on its axis, his officers would die in the attempt. For the sake of the peace, we might have to bind and gag him for the duration.'

Parrien looked doubtful as a dog about to slip its collar and run amok. 'His crew would support a curse-driven intent to stir up fresh mayhem in Tysan?'

'His crew would see us gutted the moment they found out we'd compromised Arithon's free will.' Dakar cracked back. 'I thought that's the disaster your outright gift of guardsmen were being offered to prevent. You don't want to discover how your innards might look strung over the *Khetienn*'s topsail yardarm? Then blindside that wretched little desertman and shuffle your arse back into your longboat. Pull your duke's galley out with the tide, and don't even think to look back.'

In the black hour before dawn, Prince Arithon began his muddled return to full consciousness. Dakar, poised by the berth on silent vigil, read the first warning sign in the slight, taut flex of his lips. The green eyes were masked behind damp cloths to ease contusions and swelling. But the fingers, once smoothed in relaxation on the blanket, clamped closed in the dawning awareness that the brigantine's hull tossed in motion. No longer did the *Khetienn* ride placid at her anchorage behind the barrier isles at Sanpashir. The thundering draw of full canvas aloft bespoke someone's treasonous order to effect an immediate departure.

Dakar was ready for the first, surging thrust as Arithon pushed himself erect.

'Don't,' he murmured gently, then caught with both hands in support.

A terrible stopped breath, to choke back the scream as the body discovered its wracked agony, and convulsed in an outraged spasm of reaction. Face turned away, Arithon allowed Dakar's careful strength to lower him back against the pillows piled up for a sickbed.

'Your three ships are bound offshore. The worst has been done.' The Mad Prophet plowed on out of mulish need to stamp down his knifing remorse. 'If you lie still, I'll bring something for the pain.'

'My leg?' gasped Arithon, when the shocked breath in his chest unlocked enough to allow him civilized speech. The hand he raised trembled wildly as he explored the poultices which swathed his forehead and eyes. 'For bruises, I trust?'

Dakar swallowed. 'Your sight isn't damaged. There's a cut needed stitching. The herbs are to hold down the swelling.'

No dignified means existed for masking helpless relief. Beneath the soaked cloth, Arithon's mouth thinned to bitterness. 'Don't ever run afoul of the s'Brydion. They keep their clan word like fell vengeance.'

A pause; then, 'We owe them.' The startling break moved beyond plain confession. 'And for more than stopping my fit of insanity this evening. You wouldn't have escaped the grasp of that crown examiner, except for Parrien's intervention. I saw the proof in one of the letters. The man's a sensitive to spellcraft, a true talent, if one without formal training. Lysaer's chosen trackers are growing more dangerous. Worse than my darkest imagining.'

'I know.' Dakar dashed away liquid which welled from his eyes. In dogged, vain hope, he clung to the banal. 'We can't use that tavern to collect dispatches again.' He fumbled, caught the bulkhead in support, then managed to grasp the cup with the elixir he had kept ready and waiting.

'A potion won't mend things,' Arithon murmured. More than pain edged his impotent fury. 'For blood at a wedding and another fleet savaged, what will be the cost this time?'

He believed they were alone. In a tactic of silenced desperation, Dakar used the cup to cut off the flooding spill of words.

But when Arithon finished, sunk back in the pillows with all of his vulnerable core stripped for the eyes of two strangers, he caught the Mad Prophet's wrist with suffering force and added the devastating finish. 'That's three times, now, Dakar.' He referred to the need to use crippling violence to deny him his willful, free choice. 'When will it end? When I'm blinded, or broken, or witless? Caolle need not have died if I could have turned to the knife in the hour before sanity left me. Now I almost made the same misstep again. The Mistwraith's curse is not manageable, not anymore. Tell the Fellowship when you see them, I beg their reprieve. Release their blood oath, and give back my option to abandon this life if I must.'

With one arm held prisoned in Arithon's grasp, and the other hand clenched to the cup, Dakar bit down on his lip to choke back his howl of naked outrage and sympathy. Words forsook him. Nor would he abandon a loyalty grown into a quandary to torture the spirit. Nothing remained except to endure through the terrible wait until the dosed wine took hold and the Shadow Master's hard fingers slackened. Too many minutes elapsed before the ragged, tormented breathing eased into the false tranquillity of drugged sleep.

Blinded in misery, Dakar arose. Oblivious to company, he blundered into the drawn, watching presence of Parrien's two clansmen, bound now into Arithon's service.

Before their stricken quiet, the canker inside of him burst. 'Well, did you think him the immoral criminal Lysaer's Alliance is wasting the countryside to kill? He's Athera's own Masterbard, and he has a true heart. Just like he won Caolle, he'll earn your deep loyalty. Nor can his Grace give you the peace he can't win for himself. You'll find this a desperate, difficult service before Daelion Fatemaster sets final seal on your record.'

# Resignation

Prince Lysaer returned to his fair city of Avenor as the thaws broke, the roads transformed overnight into a grabbing morass of slush. Splashed mud thrown up by the hooves of the royal cavalcade smeared the destriers to the hocks, and spattered the hems of the outriders' surcoats. The Exalted Prince himself was not exempt from the earth's seasonal anointing. His reentry into Avenor's central plaza occurred under standards whose streamers displayed the only unsullied silk in his company.

In reverse irony, the revived field troops from Etarra had turned out in dress ceremony to meet him. Their appointments were flawless, their sunwheel tunics without stain. The flooding, pale brilliance of the late-season sunlight starred reflections off their polished steel helms and buffed quillons.

The Prince of the Light motioned his honor guard to a halt. He let his cream charger advance to the fore; passed his paired standard-bearers, flying the gold star on blue of Tysan, and the sunwheel pennon, each with cloth-of-gold streamers, snapping full length in the day's brisk breeze, to his right and his left. A horse length ahead he drew rein. No smutching of mud could diminish the majestic figure he cut, tall and stately in a saddle wired with bullion trappings.

His eyes were the blue of a summer sky zenith, unclouded. Nor did his countenance admit any shadow as he held his station to receive formal greeting from the troop's commander, Lord Harradene.

'You will have a reason to have supplanted my garrison troops in this mundane duty, old friend.' His tone was grave, his words pitched low, that only those nearest might hear. 'Why this show of a public ceremony? My ear has always been yours for the asking. What event under sky could have altered that trust? Think carefully. I would grant you this audience in private.'

'Your Grace, welcome back.' Etarra's gruff field captain bent his knee to his sovereign, a man irremediably changed. No one who remembered the spiked, iron force of him failed to observe the startling new diffidence in his bearing. The bear's glower once turned on his recruits was no more. Under the tissue of lucid, thin sunlight, his rough-cut features were downturned in a wrenching flush of embarrassment.

The huge, mail-clad arm, which had never shown weakness in the grimmest press of battle, now raised his great sword in salute, marked by unsteady trembling. This occasion would not mark joyful reunion, nor celebrate the recovery of the troops he had led for the glory of the Light into Caithwood.

'My Lord Prince, I speak in the open,' Lord Harradene insisted. Harrowed uncertainty burred his voice as he reversed the grip of huge hands and offered his sword pommel first to his sovereign. 'Let no closed door stand between you and your people of Avenor. In plain words, in honesty, I give my confession: I can no longer serve as the terms of my oath to the Light would demand. I speak as well for the men in my company. All who stand with me today will fight no more against Shadow. Whether our lives were undone by sorcery, the future we face is not arguable. We will cause no more bloodshed. I am unfit to carry out your orders on the field, nor are these men suited to bear arms for your purpose of war against the Spinner of Darkness.'

Prince Lysaer moved no muscle. For the one, sustained instant he seemed a figure spun of glass against the backdrop of Avenor's state buildings. Under clear sky, pinned to formal duty by the unforgiving regard of public accountability, he had no choice but confront the cruel truth as given. Nor could he mediate the inflexible disposition of crown justice for these men, self-confessed to be forsworn in their oath to the Light.

'Your announcement strikes like a blade to the heart,' Lysaer said, his hand taut on the rein in bitter regret for the ironies. The cream charger tossed its head. Fast reflex let him gentle his grip; no such small mercy could relieve the attentive focus he trained on the field commander from Etarra. 'No praise of mine can measure the extent of your loyal courage.'

For Lord Harradene had chosen to make the break clean. His self-respect as a strategist demanded no less; he would have no ground ceded to the blurring ambiguity of friendship. Rather than risk his sworn prince to an exposure of human weakness, he ensured his last victory to the s'Ilessid cause. Here, in Avenor's wide plaza, with the commoners his unforgiving tribunal, prince and field commander faced off in the painful, shared knowledge that the high morals of state dared not bend for the sake of personal amity.

Detached to ice, Prince Lysaer reached out. With a hand that showed the bearing of rock, he accepted the grip of the sword. 'State your case.' He inclined his head toward another of the riders, who spurred forward on command to bear witness. 'The crown seneschal shall make official record.'

Gone, the option to appeal for reprieve; Lord Harradene plowed on through a torn note of heartbreak, 'My liege, keep my steel, to break in dishonor as you choose.' If his voice did not reach the farthest edges of the plaza, his gesture left no shadow for doubt as he fell to his knees, disarmed before Lysaer's stirrup.

Nor would the intrigue of governing politics forgive the humane hesitation, as Lysaer weighed options or words. Hand closed on the sword grip, he must not shrink from the crux, or lessen the gravity of due consequence.

'You have called your oath forfeit.' His magisterial reply carried on the chill quiet, and reached every riveted onlooker. 'I accept your blade in full recognition that your service is ended. But never in shame. Arise. Stand tall before these, the people your actions at arms have defended at Minderl Bay, at Vastmark, in Rathain's fell wilds, and not least, here on crown lands in Tysan.'

A pause, while Lysaer transferred the weapon's cold weight. He extended his hand to the man who knelt at his stirrup. As Lord Harradene was raised to his feet by divine strength, the prince's final disposition reechoed throughout the plaza. 'Let no one in Avenor speak your name in dishonor. Your service to the Light has ever upheld truth and right, and that record shall stand untarnished. Go home. Live in peace until the day you pass the Wheel. For what befell you in Caithwood, cherish my promise: I will one day deliver my revenge upon the Sorcerer who has dared to curtail a career of flawlessly dedicated service. Your sword I will keep, and bestow upon the man who succeeds you. His first charge shall be an undying pledge to break the unholy alliance between the Master of Shadow and the minions who practice the corruption of free minds through spellcraft.'

Lysaer released his gloved grip, saying softly, 'Live well, old friend.' Then he dug in his spurs and wheeled his charger, and addressed the captain of his honor guard. 'Detail someone to collect the arms of these men. Let them gather their kit. Then assemble an escort from the garrison to see them safely on their way through the city gates.'

His cavalcade moved off then, stately in the grime of their travel, with the banners bravely snapping in the wind. They vanished behind the grilled archway of the state palace bailey, while the crowds screamed and cried adulation. Throughout the short distance completing their march, neither the Divine Prince nor his guard accorded a look back at the proud, polished field troops from Etarra, honored, but stripped of trust, and excused from loyal service to the Alliance.

Restored to the comfort of his personal chambers, Lysaer s'Ilessid allowed his valet to remove the yoked weight of his cloth-of-gold tabard. He tossed off silk gloves and cast himself in a chair, while a page rushed to unbuckle the straps of his spurs, and another as eager removed his splashed boots, to be cleaned and buffed with fresh blacking. Stripped to his hose and a tinseled silk shirt, the prince rammed ringed hands through the hair at his temples to contain the fierce throb of a headache.

'Damn the man's stiff-necked pride! What would it have cost to have told me in private?' Still raging at Lord Harradene, the prince let his hands drop limp on the chair arms. Head turned toward the figure who stood, stilled in shadow, outside the ubiquitous bustle of the servants, Lysaer reopened limpid eyes. 'For pity, if he had, I could easily have arranged for an honorable early retirement. He'd the record in service to support that reward. At least then, if he wants to grow old farming earth, he could have collected a pension.'

When no answer, and no sympathy was forthcoming, Lysaer shoved half-upright and sighed. 'You advised Harradene to broach his dismissal, beforehand. The public presentation was yours all along?'

'It was necessary because of the men,' confirmed a voice of fruity, round vowels, and consonants of crisp authority. Cerebeld gestured to the page boys with the boots, and the valet, who hovered uncertain. 'Go. I shall serve your prince with my own hands tonight.'

Lysaer allowed his servants to be chivvied out the door. As the panel closed to the touch of Cerebeld's scrubbed hand, he loosened the braided gold laces at his throat. 'I did ask for a bath.'

But Cerebeld had made the arrangements already. His suave gesture encompassed the archway that led through the tiled foyer. 'The tub and the water are waiting. You object?'

'No.' Lysaer tugged the shirt off over his head. His grimace as he stretched showed all of the weariness he kept masked before all others. 'After thirty leagues in the saddle over damnable, bad roads, I will gracefully let you handle my toilet and towels.' He pushed to his feet, fighting the lassitude which had seeped into his muscles from even that short interval of rest. 'You don't trust a whole troop of men not to talk? That's probably wise. For myself, I doubt I could have found the stone heart to turn them off with no pay and an uncertain future. Most haven't a pedigree family to fall back on, unlike Harradene and his high-ranking officers.'

Cerebeld shut down pity with surgical logic. 'The treasury will fare better without the unnecessary burden.' He held out his palm.

Prince Lysaer removed the regent's ring with its massive, cut-sapphire seal. Cerebeld received the signet, then the diamond-set collar of state, and placed them in the velvet-lined tray the valet kept at hand for the purpose.

'Oh for the days when the flow of cold bullion did not rule our every move.' Lysaer stripped his hose. The lines of firm muscle in his buttocks and thighs as sculpted as the haunch of a lion, he walked unabashed into the next-door chamber, and stepped into the steaming bath. 'You're right, of course.'

The more difficult factions in Erdane would pay generously to kill clansmen. But all the mavens in the trade guilds would shut their purses like oysters before lending even one coin weight to fund pensions. Already, the doubled bounties for headhunters drove Eilish to hand-wringing fits.

'There could be compensation,' Cerebeld allowed.

'When my plan for Etarra reaches fruition?' Lysaer frowned. 'Perhaps.' The Alliance would soon begin its campaign to recruit farmhands for armed service. Harradene's veterans would not lack for work in the fields, as younger sons were called to leave their family steadings. 'Though I warrant the Etarrans' wives will be sharp for the uncharitable change in their station.'

Immersed to the neck in hot, soapy water, Lysaer tipped his head back against the bronze rim of the tub. He closed his eyes, at boneless ease as Cerebeld poured a dipper of water over his golden hair. As his high priest massaged perfumed soap into his scalp, he murmured, 'Give me the news. Were you able to uncover any links into the Shadow Master's correspondence network?'

Cerebeld plucked up a warmed towel from the rail by the hearth and delicately blotted his pink hands. 'Very nearly. The carrier evaded my informant in Shand, but the crown examiner you had billeted with the recruits from Jaelot picked up a strong resonance of spellcraft. Someone needed to shelter their activity from the eyes of Koriani scryers.'

Spurred to sharp impatience, Lysaer ducked his head and immersed, splashing suds over the rim of the basin. He emerged, rinsed and dripping, and fixed his regard upon Cerebeld's inscrutable features. 'There's more.'

'Oh yes.' Cerebeld passed a dry towel. His meticulous, polite pause let the Prince of the Light blot the streaming scented water from his face. 'The trail we followed was muddied by the antics of Parrien s'Brydion. He's been dispatched to sea by his duke to pay Alestron's respects upon the occasion of your forthcoming wedding.'

'No hard proof of collusion with Shadow?' Lysaer lapsed back again with closed eyes, while the heat worked its magic with his kinked muscles.

'None. I suspect, nonetheless. Parrien's flamboyant escapade was unlikely to have innocent origins. Coin smoothed the loose ends much too well. The parties involved shared no talk, and no one else paid much notice. The s'Brydion penchant for colorful mischief was dismissed by the southcoast officials as an embarrassing irritation. Unless you wish tactless pressure brought to bear, they'll stay reluctant to take such routine brawling seriously.' Cerebeld laced his hands over the beautiful worked emblem of the sunwheel gracing his belt buckle. His stance was the only relaxed aspect to him; his eyes on the prince kept the gleam of analytical steel. 'Did you seek this intelligence? You had other plans for that family I thought.'

Lysaer stayed expressionless. Serene as a masterworked sculpture in alabaster, he engaged in a sharp change of subject. 'If news from Shand is running to schedule, we must know by now how each town has responded to the invitation to attend my wedding.'

'Gace Steward has made lists.' Cerebeld's slick complexion showed no frown line, the linked rapport he shared with the Divine Prince enough surety his inquiry had not met with rebuff. Secretive as the trained statesman, Lysaer enjoyed the close privilege shared with his high priest; in Cerebeld's company, he never needed to smooth over small gaps in dialogue with the meaningless honey of diplomacy.

The man knew his royal preferences well. When the Prince of the Light was ready to share confidence, or exert his will to examine the irregularities that flawed the s'Brydion promise of loyalty, he would do so in forthright conversation. In respect for planned timing designed for the greater good of the Light, High Priest Cerebeld steered the discussion toward the arrangements for the Erdani bride and her escort. Her cavalcade would depart for Avenor once the passes through Tornir Peaks were opened and made safe for a wellborn lady to negotiate.

'Expect her arrival just after the equinox.' Cerebeld bowed, prepared with the large towel as his sovereign lord arose to step from the bathtub. 'The girl's mother's no fool. She's overseen every aspect of her daughter's disposition. Expect to trip over a bevy of aunts who are almost as difficult to please. My new acolyte in Erdane sends news every fortnight. You knew the chit had written you in her own hand?'

'I knew.' That subject caused Lysaer a swift, fair-skinned flush, immediately masked into a pallor he buried in the nap of the towel. Through the brisk strokes he used to dry his gold hair, he said, 'Your thinking is noisy. Girlish fancies and sweet talk, I gathered? You'd approve. I had one of my young secretaries answer her in like-minded, flowery language. She won't need intelligence to bear Tysan an heir, and for that saving grace, I expect you and my council will all be suitably thankful.'

'Her strict westland upbringing should hold her in line.' Cerebeld bowed, soothing over the difficult topic with ceremony.

Lady Ellaine of Erdane had been carefully chosen for her retiring, sensible temperament. Hot blood and passion, and the pressures of state politics were unlikely to drive her to the outspoken independence which had bought the late princess Talith her downfall.

Lysaer smiled, reassured, then stretched, and regarded his high priest with disarming humor. 'Now that you've tested my prenuptial nerves and plumbed after the source of my motives, I trust I may summon my valet with fresh clothes?'

Cerebeld laughed. 'My interested adulation was never intended to leave you stranded and naked. I'll call your servant to attend on your Grace as I let myself out.'

**Late Winter-Early Spring 5654**

# Setbacks

Far out to sea, strapped restless in splints, Arithon s'Ffalenn rejects Dakar's latest posset in a testy explosion of anger. 'You can leave off the nursing. I'm not going to order this brigantine about! Whatever war and mayhem Mearn's sparked in Tysan, you'll have worse right here if someone doesn't fetch me my lyranthe . . . !'

On the cresting spring tide, the night after the newly launched Alliance ships were invested and sailed on their maiden voyage down the Riverton inlet, a fire breaks out in the royal shipyard that reduces every stacked plank and rope, and levels the craft sheds to ashes . . .

The following morning, when Cattrick and his senior craftsmen are not found in the city, an Alliance rider is dispatched northward to Hanshire, bearing word of the sabotage and the suspicions cast upon the names of possible arsonists; and en route through the lowlands to the west of Mogg's Fen, the courier falls from his horse, dead as he lands, from an arrow dispatched by a sharpshooter clansman . . .

# VI. Marriage

T he ill news arrived at Prince Lysaer's chambers in Avenor on the
hour the royal valet shook the sweetening herbs from the indigo
tabard his Exalted Grace would wear for the afternoon ceremony.
No sunwheel device, but the star and crown blazon of Tysan would
commemorate the marriage of the Mayor of Erdane's eldest daughter
to Tysan's time-honored s'Ilessid bloodline. By midday, the squalling,
gust-driven clouds had not given way to fair weather. Rain seeped in
tinseled runnels down the casements, steamed gray on the inside from
the close heat of foreign envoys and celebrating courtiers.

The best vintage wine from Carithwyr had been flowing all morning.
Through loud, raunchy jokes and backslapping laughter, the recent
arrival passed unregarded until the discord at the entrance to the royal
apartment turned heads. Hat feathers aligned like grass in high wind;
the pedigree highborn and those few merchants privileged to attend
the prince's robing looked down their noses, perturbed.

'Invitations bedamned,' cried a leather-clad man with a commoner's
middle coast accent. 'I bring urgent news!'

The tussle crescendoed. Lysaer's flustered chamber steward lost the
upper hand, and the intruder barged in, mud spattered, reeking of soaked
wool and lathered horse.

Overdressed courtiers cleared from his path in a breaking flurry of
velvets.

'Where's Sulfin Evend!' The man's shout clove ahead through the bedlam. 'I seek the Alliance Lord Commander!'

Chain mail glinted through the flower petal brilliance of brocades as the taciturn captain who laid claim to that title tossed off his gloves and slid like a ferret through the crush. 'To me! Now!' His hardened fist caught the courier by the shoulder. 'Whatever your news, the whole world shouldn't hear. You're from Hanshire?'

'The north quarter, yes.' The man caught his breath, his face pinched with exhaustion. 'Word will fly, soon enough. Four of the launched vessels from the new Alliance fleet just foundered themselves down the coast.'

'In this weather?' The Lord Commander narrowed winter gray eyes. 'Hasn't been wind fit to drive off the drizzle.'

'No storm,' gasped the courier.

Sulfin Evend did not delay to hear more, but elbowed his way through the jeweled press of courtiers gathered to eavesdrop and gawk. He pulled the stumbling courier along, then propelled him ahead in a no-nonsense rush to the prince's private dressing room.

The courier received a blinding impression of lavish gilt trim, velvet footstools with lion-claw legs, and damascened cushions shot like fire with reflected candlelight. Then he and his forceful escort broke through the fawning coterie around the prince.

'Exalted, we've got trouble!' Without regard for propriety, ignoring the spluttering mayor he displaced, Sulfin Evend fended away the valet who bore the sapphire tabard in a single-minded sally to reach the Prince of the Light.

'Is there news? Let my officer through!' Lysaer s'Ilessid should have appeared ordinary, half-clad as he was, the laces of his finery untied and trailing. Yet his fierce inquiry as he straightened to meet the disheveled messenger and the taut urgency of his Lord Commander snapped his disgruntled sycophants to stillness. In breech hose and a shirt edged with gold, he seemed a figment stamped out of light. The diamonds flared like caught ice in his sleeves as his trim shoulders braced for bad news. 'What's amiss?'

Sulfin Evend pushed the reeling stranger forward. 'Give word to his Grace.'

'Four ships out of Riverton, Lord Exalted.' The muddy man faltered, embarrassed.

'Go on,' Lysaer urged, his patience a branding example of courage, while the tap of sullen rainfall slid uninterrupted through a silence of stopped motion and held breaths.

The courier coughed his reluctance. 'Sunk, your Grace. Burst, dismasted, foundered, lost. The new hulls ran aground on the Hanshire coastline. None could be salvaged. The sea has battered them to wreckage on the reefs.'

'How many drowned?' Lysaer demanded.

'Can't say, your Grace.' A shift foot to foot, and the courier qualified. 'I was gone at a gallop before the rescue boats launched.'

A glance like blued steel passed between the Divine Prince and his coiled and volatile Lord Commander at Arms. Then, with a calm that annealed for its steadiness, Lysaer voiced the brute logic no one else dared to address. 'There's been no weather to run a ship on the cliff rocks, I know that.'

Relieved by the tact which spared him from breaking the first, harsh impact of disaster, the messenger loosened. 'Sabotage. The harbormaster at Hanshire believes the shipyard's master played your Grace false with the designs on his boards down at Riverton.'

'No man in my kingdom stands accused without proof, even a common-born craftsman.' Unmoved from his image of tight-leashed serenity, Lysaer gave rapid orders to his war commander. 'Look into this. Quietly. The high council must convene on my state galley the moment the wedding festivities are over. Have the vessel provisioned. See five of my warships ready to sail south on the midnight change of the tide.'

Sulfin Evend bowed, a falcon unleashed for the hunt, but for Lysaer's touch holding him back. 'Hear the rest.' The royal head lifted. Blue eyes surveyed the avid circle of courtiers. Unflinching, direct, that measuring majesty drove the most hardened sophisticate backward. Jammed in a welter of velvets against the tables spread with warm wine and comfits, the pedigree elite of Avenor received the prince's unequivocal warning.

'Let no one disclose what has passed in this chamber. For the good of this kingdom, my wedding goes on. I'll have no taint of black news, no one's busy secretary, and no messenger in guild pay sent abroad to spread talk and premature rumors. My justice will not fail to address all wrongdoing, but action shall await upon my bride's pleasure. Woe betide the man who dares break his silence beforetime.'

The barest hint of leashed temper flicked through Lysaer's bearing as he released Sulfin Evend in dismissal. 'Be sure the courier's needs are met, and on your oath to serve the Light, let *nothing* upset the celebration arranged to honor Tysan's new princess. Once the marriage has been consummated, I'll attend my sovereign duties at the wharf.'

Sulfin Evend's eyebrows furrowed in drastic surprise. 'Tomorrow?'

'Tonight. By midnight, latest. Be ready.' Lysaer snapped his fingers, startling the valet who hovered at a loss with the royal tabard draped on his forearm.

While Sulfin Evend shouldered toward the doorway, and the servant shrank hesitant on the sidelines, Lysaer softened into a debonair smile. 'Do you think me a bridegroom without tenderness?' White upon gold against the gloom of the casement, his ebullience burned like a torch. 'There's no frightened virgin who can't be made pliant. Carithwyr wine and a posset should ease any girl's skittish nerves.' He dipped his fair head, still talking. 'Gace Steward will instruct the lady's handmaids. Now, please, can we go through the motions of dressing? I've no wish to marry in shirtsleeves and hose, and if you strangle that tabard in a death grip any longer, I'm going to wear fingerprints in the velvet.'

In the peach-and-gold decor of the palace guest suite, the wax candles burned with extravagance. Velvet curtains with white silk fringes masked the drizzling rain, and the chatter of highborn Erdani women fell mellow and warm as the weather denied by Tysan's changeably fickle west coastline.

'Your chin, miss,' murmured the lady's maid. The polite request came with a firm, guiding hand, then a pinch of hair nipped and turned under a pin to crimp a ringlet into her coiffure. Ellaine shut her eyes as the damp, hot towel pressed the confined strand against the flushed skin of her temple.

'I'm sorry,' she whispered. 'My mind feels as scattered as the mist.'

'Ath's glory, who wouldn't be distracted for a bridegroom who fills his hose like the stuff of legends themselves!' The heavyset aunt who had spoken shot out a cheerful, dough fist. She caught the loose toddler who charged past, squealing, in a tangle of untied ribbons and a rosy absence of underthings. 'Love us, we're going to be late, every one, if this gentleman keeps kicking off his breeches.'

The mother of the youngster arrived and scooped him up, breathless in her exasperation. 'Easier to keep clothes on an eel, I'm afraid.' Her apologetic smile dissolved into laughter. 'Come on, wild thing! Let your pipsqueak equipment grow a few years before you show off to the ladies.'

Ellaine closed her eyes, while other hands patted and primped, and tucked ruches and arranged pins and jewelry. She could scarcely share her sister's breathless excitement over the bows and fine laces, or the delicate embroidery of gold worked into satin ribbons. As a comfortable cloud of patchouli arrived and settled in a whisk of silk at her right hand, her mouth turned up at the corners. 'I'm too pale, I know.'

Her mother patted her chill hand. 'Never mind, Ellaine. Your eyes will be dazzling. We'll just brighten your skin with a dusting of rouge powder.' The beautiful, ringed hands which had managed each detail of her father's state palace in Erdane snapped once, and a maidservant jumped in response. 'Mind, not too much, girl! She'll flush with the dancing. We don't want her looking like a hussy, nor leaving streaks on her husband's fine cuffs as he touches!'

Ellaine chewed her lip; caught herself; stopped. A fortnight in residence had shown her how tightly the wheels of efficiency meshed in Avenor's state household. Gace Steward ran everything like a high-strung dictator, until even the pot scullions feared to spread gossip. 'Ath, where will I be needed?' she blurted aloud.

Her mother caught her shoulders in a careful, quick squeeze. 'Women's wisdom, my dear. You'll make your own way. This bastion of male authority will have chinks, and you'll find them, just as I did when I wed your father.'

Ellaine opened velvety, tea-colored eyes. Her answering smile trembled at the edges, but courage shone through, steadfast and determined. 'Are you sure you taught me everything you know?'

Her mother arose from her perch on the chair arm. 'You will bear the royal children. That will make you an influential power in this land, don't you ever for one moment forget. Your worth will come to be measured as Crown Princess. Nor will you fall short. You hold the threads of your prince's dynasty, and in that arena, your place beside him is *equal*. One day, your blood will shape Avenor's policy. Your son will sit the throne that commands Tysan's four principalities, and his deportment as a king will come to be the purposeful achievement of your life.'

The lady's maid slipped the pins, and deployed the little ringlets that softened the line of a face which required little artifice to adorn the clear bloom of youth. Another hand arranged the jeweled pendant at her throat, and the room very suddenly seemed half-empty of life; the squealing of children and the companionable chatter of women relatives rolled into a sudden, poised hush.

Her mother's wise eyes misted over. 'Blessed be, girl, you're lovely. You'll do very well. Come now, the carriages are waiting.'

In twenty brisk minutes, impeccably on time, the Prince of the Light emerged from the privacy of his chamber. He had called for no emergency council. Beyond his first orders to Sulfin Evend, he had done nothing more than let his servants attend to his dress. His stature ensured that their fuss was not wasted. The cloth of gold sash and sapphire tabard finished that precise, frosty poise that could intimidate at twenty paces. By the lighthearted charm annealed through his expression, no doubt clouded his committed intention to grant his new bride her day of carefree celebration.

The talk of the courtiers drifted around him, brittle as beads of blown glass. If none of the pedigree elite could ignore the royal seal of silence, word of the smashed ships would break loose from other sources. The trade guilds had private couriers. The noon post run from Hanshire would reach Avenor by evening, to questions and unrest if the gate watch detained them. Ill news could not bide in close company for long. The ministers' wives in their layered gowns and amethysts, their velvets with silver-tipped ribbons, would hear from the lips of their lackeys.

Like the flocking of sparrows before breaking storm, the guests poured in for the bridegroom's reception, smiling and oblivious. The palace halls jammed with their packed heat and noise; their grooms and their footmen thronged the vestibules. While the bride's procession wound through the city in gilt carriages with outriders tossing flowers, the highborn and the powerful gathered to toast the health of Tysan's prince. In crowded splendor, cloaks and jeweled mantles crushed together in steaming warmth and perfume, and a sibilance of flowery language, they wished him vigor and bliss through his upcoming nuptials.

The secrecy imposed on the master shipwright's defection wove through the opening festivities, a thread of cranked tension as conversations faltered around Avenor's high councilmen, then lurched through a cascade of inane subjects on bursts of determined energy. Stifled intimations of disaster rode through empty compliments and innuendo like the pall of a ghost ship, passing. Strain tugged at the weave of the music and gaiety like the subliminal false note: here the jarring trill of laughter from a lady unaware of the pending call to muster; there the odd gap in mannered pleasantries which a member of the prince's inner cabal jumped to fill.

Prince Lysaer himself was the picture of candor, his stunning good looks and royal bearing a sight to break hearts and wring sighs of envy from every female bosom in the room. Too soon, for them, the reception ended. His Grace owned that charmed manner of listening to each word, his blue eyes trained in riveted attention. And yet, the tongues of the gossips all noticed: his mind was a statesman's. He drew the morning formalities to a close precisely on the hour appointed.

'And not out of ardor for his pale, nervous bride, you ask me,' hissed a dowager matron from under the fringed lace of her hat. 'Something else is afoot, I could bet all my pearls.' A porcelain, ringed finger stabbed home the point. 'The high chancellor's out of words, a first-rate astonishment, and the seneschal goes claptrapped as a rabbit anytime somebody mentions reclaiming the trade down the coast.'

As the horses for the prince's cavalcade arrived in the outer archway, each led by a liveried groom, not a minister or high councilor failed to draw a deep sigh of relief.

For his Erdani bride, Lysaer s'Ilessid had arranged a state ceremony, founded in the tradition of town law. The appointments he made had been lavish enough to overawe even the massive envoy from Etarra. His great hall had been bedecked with spring lilies. Garlands of primroses trailed in strung ropes from the hammer beams, tied up with ribbons of cream silk. By Westlands custom, the bride and her family were given first seating. They and their invited guests sweltered in their rain-dampened finery, while the youngest children ate dried fruits and fidgeted, and the bridegroom's procession wound through Avenor's main avenue, cheered on by merchant admirers and the heaving press of commoners clad in their holiday best.

Decorum reigned, despite dreary weather. The state dignitaries paraded in their wilted panoply, red noses and broad hats clustered like posies under the fringe of swagged awnings. Their ladies tapped through the puddles in pattens, their rich mantles strung with pearls that fogged in the unrelenting drizzle off the sea.

Once, a crofter from Korias broke through the mounted cordon. Through the press and the cheers, he demanded to know why an adept from Ath's Brotherhood had not been invited to officiate.

The Prince of the Light heard that cry and drew rein. In glittering ranks, his honor guard halted. While his snowflake-dappled palfrey sidled and champed at the bit, he answered through an oddly bitter sorrow. 'You didn't know?' Unerring, his gaze singled out the man who had offered complaint. 'The adepts have been cozened by the delusion of Darkness itself. If you ask, they will insist that the Master of Shadow is innocent of his crimes against humanity.'

'Innocent?' A burly cooper shook his fist from a second-story alcove. 'My own brother's bones lie buried under a rockslide in Vastmark, alongside his unblooded sword!'

'Just so.' Gold fillet gleaming, Lysaer tipped his head in salute to the man's tragic loss. 'Our land and people will not be exposed to blind trust in a sorcerer who has torn down a mountain to cause a massacre. The adepts of Ath's Brotherhood are not welcome in my city. For that reason, Erdane's high chancellor is given the honor to preside over my marriage to Lady Ellaine.'

The white horse leaped ahead to a touch of gilt spurs, while the rain misted the prince's collar of white diamonds to dim pearl and streaked tarnish through his unprotected hair. At the looming archway that fronted the great hall, the decorous procession reached its end. The bridegroom dismounted. His jewels spat reflections beneath the ragged flames of the torches. Two pages in white velvet took his palfrey, and liveried servants opened the doors. More light flooded out, scented with incense and primroses. Satin ribbons in Erdane's colors dripped from the wreaths by the entry. Watched by a spellbound populace, Lysaer s'Ilessid stepped inside, between the high pillars of rosewood, and the sagging, plumed hats of his courtiers.

Cheers resounded from the street as the Mayor of Erdane handed his daughter to the prince. She was on that day seventeen years of age, with the brown eyes of a trusting deer and hair like burled walnut, twisted high in wire combs. Lips lush as peaches were flushed where her small, nervous teeth had pinched the blood to the surface. Her royal bridegroom touched her cheek. She smiled back, shyly radiant. The retinue of high officers trailed the couple inside, and the heavy oak panels swung closed. The riveted interest of the onlookers waned, leaving wet, cold people restless in the dusk, and the sheen of chill flagstone dulled from silver to lead under the whispering rainfall.

Inside the dry sanctum, where privilege reigned, the shining perfection of the evening sustained, against odds. The ceremony passed without flaw. The cream of the company retired to the state ballroom. There, the inner circle of Prince Lysaer's guests dined their way through nine courses. Branched candelabra blazed with beeswax lights, and the boards were drawn from the feast. The Exalted Prince swept off the dance floor and returned the Mayor's pigeon-pert wife to the care of her beaming husband. Her blush cheeks glowed through the rice powder the inclement weather had not yet managed to smudge, and her eyelids fluttered from the royal flattery bestowed through the lull in the music.

'Madam, my pleasure,' Lysaer murmured, his glance on his bride, whirled giddily away in the embrace of a middle-aged cousin.

Gace, steward of the royal household, slipped in like a weasel and plucked at his Grace's sleeve. His lashes slitted in sly confidence, he whispered, 'There's been widespread comment, my prince. No delegation from the s'Brydion duke has arrived to honor your nuptials.'

His manners unshakable, Lysaer s'Ilessid bestowed a light kiss on the soft, scented cheek of his mother-in-law. 'Madam, please excuse me.' His engaging smile never shifted, but his eyes were blue as fired enamel as he drew Gace Steward aside. 'Shouldn't your concern lie closer to home? Whatever has caused Alestron to withdraw, unless you speak to the servants about wine, Avenor's hospitality will be faulted.'

'Your Grace.' Gace clicked his heels and bowed, his smug manner stiffened as he realized: the red was indeed running low. No doubt the fact had been pointed out to his prince by the unforgiving, sharp eye of the mayor's wife; the embarrassment galled him beyond his concern for the state of s'Brydion loyalties.

Lysaer masked a smile as his steward scuttled off, primed with frustration and no doubt, stormy reprimand for the servant in charge of the cellar.

Since Gace's failed attempt, more than one courtier with the perspicacity to mention Alestron's lapse discovered the bridegroom escaped to the dance floor. Lysaer's elusive opinion on the subject sparked whispered speculation in dim corners. Behind their sealed silence, Avenor's peer statesmen pondered whether the four foundered ships might in some way be connected.

Outside, unconcerned with the snarls of conspiracy, the rain-dreary twilight melted into a gusty, black night. Stars spiked between shredded clouds. On the knoll above the harbor, Avenor's high towers bloomed with a twinkling garland of lights. Largesse was thrown to the beggars in the square, new-minted shadowbanes interspersed with commemorative coins struck with the princess's profile. When the coffer was emptied, the crowds loitered in the streets and the wineshops. Rich and poor jostled elbows, hoping to glimpse the royal couple, while an uneasy current of movement heaved through them, as men raced to arms from the taverns and barracks, and the ship's chandler loaded his supply drays by torchlight. His long-haired, plucky daughters drove them in thundering haste down the back streets to the docks, where the swearing stevedores packed casks and salt meat onto the galleys appointed to depart.

Lord Commander Sulfin Evend presided over the messengers, coming and going. Still clad in dress finery, his unadorned field sword slung on a belt set with cabochon turquoise, he chewed a lamb pie someone had brought him and raised eyes like gray sleet from the latest list of lading. His tactical survey encompassed a high tower window with rose garlands spilled like clotted shadow over the edge of the sill. A light burned there, the solitary star of a candle.

The time was two hours before the tide's turn at midnight. 'Be ready,' the Lord Commander barked to the state galley's captain, stalled by the rambade to chastise a green sailhand who fumbled to batten the forward hatch. 'Our prince will be timely. If not, you can claim the sunwheel badge off my tunic.'

'For a dozen coin stake, I'll accept.' The captain's flinty laughter entangled with the boom of a rolling wine tun. 'Which makes for a heartless quick bedding of the bride, if you win. Or dare you place gold that the princess isn't a virgin?'

Sulfin Evend flashed a sardonic grin. 'If she's not, then you'll see a mayor elect's head roll to a royal for treason. His Grace can't afford another taint on his wife.'

Shouts swelled from the celebrants who swayed, roistering drunk on the seawall. By the harbor gate, small knots of stragglers had knit into groups of fist-waving craftsmen. Here and there, the plumed hat of a merchant appeared among them like a stray mushroom.

'His exalted self had better not tarry,' the galley captain mused, his critical eye trained on the argument about to flare between his purser and the spitfire minx in charge of the wagon on the dock. 'The lid's coming off the bad news from the south. Angry trade guilds won't wait for our prince to prove out his prowess in the sheets.' Sea routes were open, but the old deadlock held; no goods could pass southward by galley with Havish's ports closed to slavery. Since thaws, the landbound trade through the Camris passes vied to press full advantage. Caravan masters had hiked up their haulage rates to the despair of the incensed merchants. 'Those ruined ships have left a rank mess. Believe it. We've got the entire high council belowdecks, buzzing like a pack o' hazed wasps.'

'The wait won't be long,' Sulfin Evend assured. Upon his next glance, the window in the tower had gone dark.

Lysaer s'Ilessid leaned back against the wall, his ringed hand still clenched on the cord he had jerked to shut the heavy curtain. The candle by his elbow spat driblets of wax. Shouts from the street reached him muffled through velvet, meaningless as the noise of sea breakers. He shut his eyes, opened them, watched the jeweled rings on his fingers flicker like actinic static. He could not stop their trembling, though he gripped the silk drawstring until his knuckles gleamed white to the bone.

Across the narrow landing, the door to the bedchamber cracked open. The Erdani lady's maid appointed to the princess swept into a tactful curtsy. 'She's ready, your Grace, and virgin in truth. Be gentle. Behind the excitement, she's frightened.'

'You may go.' For a miracle, his self-command stayed intact, his voice a cool ribbon of steadiness.

The maid bobbed another curtsy and departed to a proprietary rustle of skirts. Lysaer stood alone in front of a door he would rather have died than step through.

'Merciful Ath,' he whispered before he recalled his forfeited right to beg help from that quarter. The beams overhead and the creamy brick lintels with their lion-bossed rods and tapestried hangings closed him in like a prison. He jammed down a memory: of long hair spilled like tawny satin between his fists; the breath he sucked in smelled of roses and beeswax as he pushed away from the wall. Two steps, three. He marveled the body could follow instructions when the mind cried out for escape. His duty to Tysan set in traitorous conflict against the cry of his heart, he raised the latch whose touch was ice under his filmed, sweaty hand.

The bedchamber beyond held the stuffy perfume of the citrus oil used to polish the massive carved bed, and the cloying, heavy sweetness of roses which trailed from the urns by the casement. Damask curtains closed out the night. One candle burned on the pearl-inlaid table. Alongside lay a basket of oranges, and a tray bearing two cut-glass goblets, a wine carafe, and a stoppered decanter of brandy. Lysaer blinked, stabbed by the recollection of another chamber laid out with chilled wine and fruit, and a floor tiled in a turquoise motif of sea creatures.

Then a runnel of sweat threaded his lashes and dragged him back to the present.

This floor was eggshell marble, its polished shine broken by a patterned carpet from Morvain. He could not look at the girl on the bed, nestled in a drift of white sheets. She would be naked, scented, adorned in the gold bracelets and necklet he had given that morning as a bride-gift. She watched him with huge sloe eyes, and a trusting innocence that left him battered and speechless.

He managed to pour her wine without snapping the fragile, stem goblet. With the brandy he was less successful. The spill ran down his fingers and flecked amber stains on the gold-stitched silk of the coverlet. Ellaine's silent censure seemed to sear his skin through his tabard as he drank, seated on the mattress with his back turned, and his eyes on the pleats of the curtains.

'Lord Exalted,' she whispered. Glass clinked. She set her wine on the table untouched.

He reached sideways, closed his hand over her slender wrist before she could withdraw from the gesture. 'Will you not drink?'

Her trembling increased at the snap in his tone. Hand still locked to her wrist, he knocked back the brandy. The fire of the alcohol blazed down his throat, seared a path through the hollow in his chest, and settled a spark like damnation in his belly. He sat, the girl's delicate limb in his grasp, and waited to welcome the numbness.

'I'm not afraid,' she insisted. Her courage took away the last of his breath, and still, her blithe tenderness misread him. 'I heard that four of the Riverton ships were lost. Your chancellor said you'll leave to hunt down the shipwright who betrayed you, and I'll be left as your last wife was, with your household here at Avenor. Unless you promise to take me along, I prefer to remember this night with clear wits.'

Lysaer let her go. Once more on his feet, he refilled his brandy glass, then drained it. His body felt lined in white flame as he turned and regarded his bride on the bed. His eyes were dark sapphire, the pupils distended. 'Drink the wine. You would be better off.'

Her heart-shaped chin tilted, and her hair, combed free, spilled down her shoulders and breasts. For answer, she grasped the goblet by the stem and emptied it onto the carpet. 'Shame on you,' she said. 'I need no drugged posset.'

'Your choice.' Lysaer set down his glass, reluctant. If he swallowed neat brandy until the pain was burned out of him, he risked becoming incapable. 'The tide goes at midnight. There won't be time to plead my forgiveness, and the wine was the only lame courtesy I could offer.' He jerked off his sash, stripped the gold-blazoned tabard over his head, then kicked off his boots and discarded them on the heaped silk. The points on his trunk hose seemed defeatingly intricate. Since the brandy had robbed his fingers of finesse, he settled for tearing off pearl-studded eyelets and letting them scatter to the floor.

Ellaine managed not to flinch as he whipped back the sheet. The bite of his hands on her shoulders shook her nerve. He could feel her confused uncertainty as he refused the soft lips upturned for his kiss. Her mahogany hair spilled warm over his chilled hands, and her skin, like fine pearl, smelled of rosewater. He felt nothing. Only the calculated drive of necessity, the hardened heat in his loins lit at last by the mindless anesthesia of the brandy. He parted her legs. Then, without apology, he let go of sanity and allowed the animal instinct of his body do its raw work for the kingdom.

Ellaine jerked. She cried out but once, cut to painful betrayal, then strove through her tears to silence a misery no trained deportment could master.

Sickened by grief and self-hatred, Lysaer bore down. As Tysan's Prince Exalted, he must admit no vulnerability; therefore, he heard nothing, saw nothing beyond his ringed fingers, knotted into sweet waves of dark hair as he muffled his wife's tormented gasps in his shirt.

Then release; the act was completed. He arose. While his conquest wept in limp shudders against the pillows, and the small spot of blood marked the sheets with incontrovertible proof of consummation, he flung open the door and shouted. His valet came, bearing clothes and a sea cloak; then the elderly handmaid, her face clamped to anger as she awaited his royal bidding.

'Attend to my princess.' He could wish that the brandy did not slur the command in his voice.

The handmaid stepped to the bed. Lysaer endured, regal in reserve, while she asked her young charge gentle questions. Her competent hands touched and soothed with a tenderness the new bride might never know from her husband. When the girl's ravaged nakedness had been covered over in the impersonal embrace of cool linen, the old matron regarded the prince.

Through a silence as pained as the twist of a knife blade, he spoke. 'She need only give this kingdom an heir to live in comfort for the rest of her life.'

Foolish, stubborn, unmindful of consequences, the handmaid launched from the bedside. 'For shame!' She raised her stout arm and dealt Lysaer an openhanded slap across the face.

While the valet gasped in shock, Prince Lysaer stood motionless. The candle spun glints of gold through his hair. His eyes stayed direct, stark with an unflinching guilt that became a torture to witness. While the welted print of the maidservant's fingers flushed the bloodless plane of his cheekbone, he asked, 'I was so rough?'

'No.' Her woman's glare savaged him, and still found no flaw in the merciless gift of his honesty. 'But who will answer for what Ellaine is to become? The hurts to her female body are nothing beside the wound you have dealt to her spirit.'

Impatient, unspeaking, Lysaer stepped away.

The handmaid moved also. She blocked his path to the doorway, her disapproval immovable stone. 'Your princess has a face,' she accused. 'Look at her! She has a name. Would it unman you to use it?'

Lysaer froze in place, the queer, fragile majesty of him through that drawn-out moment enough to brand sight for eternity. 'Her Grace does have a name,' he agreed, the indelible depths of his suffering ripped at long last to the surface. 'To speak of her would destroy us both, since the one fit to claim that hold on my heart has died, defamed by the hand of the enemy. You want truth for the woman who has married to continue the s'Ilessid royal line? I will have sacrificed everything I ever loved well ahead of the day the Master of Shadow is brought down.'

He brushed past. The valet scrambled after, threw a cloak overtop of his liege's unlaced shirt. 'Your Grace, you'll need clothing.'

Yet the solicitude paid to royal dignity was meaningless. Once over the threshold, Lysaer slammed the bedchamber door. The explosive force of his own temper mocked him. Sealed to a course of desolate justice, he knew that no anger, no violence, no punishment of grief could ever serve to heal the void rent through his spirit.

'Sea boots, and breeches and a white-and-gold tunic,' he said in iron restraint to his valet.

Behind him, Talith's memory burned unspoken on the air while the beautiful, broken creature his royal duty claimed for Tysan swallowed back the drugged wine and slept at last in the loveless sheets of their marriage bed.

By the hour before midnight, news of the wrecked ships was just breaking. If the elite of Avenor still drank to the health of bridegroom and princess, the guild ministers were absent. No one had noticed the moment, but the notable courtiers and all of the city's high officers had left to nose out the scope of disaster.

Beyond the lit hall with its carousing, oblivious sycophants, the last clouds had fled. Stars burned cold pinpricks through the black arc of a sky the wind had finally swept clean. Pennons flapped on the battlements above the western gatehouse, while the city's tiered towers glowed with the light of a thousand celebrating households.

The prince their wine toasted passed in haste through dim streets with three guards, inconspicuous in a mantle of dark wool. Crowds were now gathering in ominous knots by the breakwater. He passed through, unobserved. A word to a sergeant, and the hurried tramp of a late-mustered company parted its ranks to admit him. Lysaer s'Ilessid might have reached his state galley unremarked, except for the ruthless, wary vigilance of Sulfin Evend.

'He's here, and before the change in the tide.' The Lord Commander extended his hand, lips curved in a sardonic smile. 'I win.'

'Damn you,' murmured the royal galley's captain, forced to relinquish ten silvers from the opened strings of his purse.

The Alliance Lord Commander played the coins between his fingers, their chime a melodious cascade through his prince's low word of greeting.

He responded, succinct, 'Your Grace, be on guard. Sharp eyes have noticed Alestron's duke sent no family emissary to honor your wedding. Bold rumors are flying. Hotheads who hate clansmen have already linked Mearn s'Brydion's name with the defection of Riverton's master shipwright.' A piercing, short pause; then Sulfin Evend added, 'Is that what you wanted? If not, we'll need some pat answers to muzzle the trade guilds. Their craftsmen already clamor for a lynching.'

Whatever his opinion on s'Brydion loyalty, Lysaer preferred reticence. 'Has my council assembled?'

Sulfin Evend raised his eyebrows, surprised. 'You can't hear the bickering? Koshlin and the Mayor of Erdane are howling in chorus to rip down Alestron with a siege.'

'If the duke's brother's guilty, we'll face that cold certainty.' Gold embroidery snagged sullen glints as the prince glanced behind, uneasy as his guards with the awareness that informants already raced to spread the alarm through the alleys mazing the shoreline. 'Old distrust of clanblood won't be settled by a hanging, even if the s'Brydion duke would acknowledge Tysan's right to pass sentence for treason.'

Lysaer swung back, impatient. The deck lantern's candle flared in the wind and splashed light underneath his drawn hood.

Sulfin Evend shut his lips. He dared not acknowledge the livid weal a woman's hand had left marked across the face of Tysan's bridegroom. Fixed in that splintering, too worldly royal gaze, he averted his eyes and regarded the black swirl of high water, the lines of slack current just starting to suck at the pilings.

'We're provisioned?' Lysaer asked, as though nothing were amiss.

'Your best company of field officers has already settled in.' Sulfin Evend accepted the lifeline of tact, brisk as he listed details. 'Crewmen are lashing the last of the water casks. The steersman couldn't be sobered. His replacement is due any minute.' Then the calculated afterthought, 'You should hear I took liberties.'

A gust off the sea plucked at Lysaer's cloak. He trapped his errant hood in a death grip, while the dock lines tugged and creaked on the bollards, and someone ashore raged to spill blood for the works of s'Brydion treachery. Like an echo from Sithaer deep inside the galley's hold, a muzzled hound snarled at its handler.

'Skannt's trackers are aboard?' Lysaer smiled, his ebullience fanned by the lift of the brandy. 'That wasn't liberty, but divine inspiration.' He clapped his Lord Commander's shoulder, raw with the need for human warmth.

'Then you did want Alestron's alliance to be suspect?' Sulfin Evend let the touch pass, passionless as a trained falcon. 'Mark their clan for death, I'll tear apart their city and hunt them like rats through the wreckage.'

'Not yet,' Lysaer said, then snapped himself short. Old grief and the maudlin warmth of fine spirits had nearly upset his sensibilities. In darkness, the flare of the lamps on buckles and mail and sword hilt had blurred into a host of older memories. Chills touched him, and a sorrow that all but stopped his breath. Never again could he share long-range plans as he once had confided in Talith's brother.

The pause stretched too long. Sulfin Evend watched, his rapacious instincts already fastened on discrepancy.

Flicked to self-disgust, Lysaer masked his slip of tongue behind the less damning intimation, 'Cattrick or Mearn, the placement of the Riverton yard has hazed the wrong enemy to light.'

'Ah, then you meant the lost ships for bait to lure out the Spinner of Darkness? Your guilds would cry murder.' His devotion set above the frank pull of curiosity, Avenor's Lord Commander surveyed a fresh wave of weaving torches, sure enough sign that a targetless fury was building unchecked in the streets. 'Whoever's responsible, unless you want a war fought on the suspicion of conspiracy, you'll need Cattrick's proven guilt, and Mearn's bleeding corpse as a scapegoat.'

Lysaer quelled a shiver, faintly sickened by the ruthless analysis his own laid plans had encouraged. He knew himself vulnerable. Marriage and brandy bared too many wounds that lay too near to the heart. Besieged by emotions beyond risk to express, he excused himself, then moved on, the unflinching dignity displayed at each step an act of bald-faced bravado.

Tide rocked the galley's keel. Still poised on the rambade to see the dock lines cast off, the sea captain watched the prince mount the gangway. His interest shifted to incredulity as that sovereign figure swayed and caught rope in both hands to keep balance. The wind took advantage, snatched off the dark hood. Pale hair blazed bright gold under the yardarm lanterns.

A cry of acclaim swept the disgruntled masses on the shoreline. 'Look! There's the prince!' Disunified voices merged into a chant, fired by the promise of redemption. 'Defender of the Light! Defender of the Light!'

Lysaer raised an arm. The power of his gift blazed up like a star in acknowledgment. Then his guardsmen closed in. Their deft intervention masked his passage across the deck, and the revealing stumble that sent him through the companionway into the private stern cabin.

'Young bitch must have claws.' The galley captain chuckled in rich appreciation. 'Did ye see? Bedamned if our prince isn't flying three sheets to the wind!'

'So what if he's drunk?' Sulfin Evend spun on his heel, his killer's grace tracked by the petulant chink of his chain mail. 'The lady you slander is Avenor's crowned princess, and we're going to have riots securing that gangway if you don't get this tub under oars right smart!'

## Spring 5654

# Entanglements

The clinging, fine rainfall which had dampened the wedding feast at Avenor still misted in the coastal bluffs that thrust seamed, sandstone ramparts down Tysan's west coastline and broke the hard crash of the sea. The crests grew no trees, only rolling acres of salt-burned grass, tossed and combed by the winds. Scrub willow thicketed the rain-carved hollows, rooted in tough sedge and cattails where the hard, stony soil shed water from the heights and channeled runoff in twisting streamlets. These fed the wider catch basins and small marshes, pooled like dropped silk in the valleys. At the change of the season, the deer came to graze on the pale, tender greenery that seeded the mud on the verges. By night, the horned owl raked the ridges hunting rabbit, its broad-winged, wild majesty undisputed until summer, when the plains drifters drove their horse herds southward for grazing.

Yet tonight, the bleak territory overlooking the sea was not empty of human activity.

A band of men crouched in fugitive silence on the seamed side of a bluff overlooking the broken shoreline, with its straggle of irregular islets.

'No mercy for us if your brother's ship doesn't show.' Ivel the blind splicer leaned forward, his horn-callused hands tucked around bony knees. Unlike other men, the dank darkness shrouding the view on all sides left his observant, snide nature unhampered. 'We've been stew meat for an Alliance patrol since the instant you asked for clan help to take down those northbound couriers.'

'Be glad for that favor.' Mearn s'Brydion's grin held a trace of a sneer as he faced into the wind from the sea. 'Even the deer don't move on these heights, that they can't be seen with a ship's glass.'

'Oh?' Ivel's contradiction came smug. 'Even through night fog and rain?'

'Through fog and rain, and much worse than that, you can depend on clan honor to guard your miserable safety. My kind don't go back on their given word. Ever. Forget that at your peril, old man.' A whisper of damp leathers informed of Mearn's movement as he opened the shutter of the lantern that burned with a reek of hot pitch by his knee. Light flared; died as he slid the aperture closed.

Down the ravine, which dropped in slate steps to the sea, an answering flash of orange blinked twice, snagged in the woolly halo of the fogbank.

'There's Cattrick's signal,' said Mearn, with the particularly evil lilt he used for his winning bets. 'The boat's already put in.' While the renegade band of high-ranking shipwrights moved ahead through the shadows, he added, 'Are you coming? Or were you planning to root your bones on this hill as a monument to sheer spite?'

'Devil,' snapped Ivel, annoyed for the fact the s'Brydion quick tongue made him flush. 'Did you want me to beg for your guidance?'

'Never thought of it.' Mearn stood, passed the closed lantern off to another man, then extended a hand to the splicer. 'Particularly since I see you don't trust your compatriots from the shipyard to render you the same service.'

Ivel accepted the assistance with a grip like a bear and a bark of derisive laughter. 'Trust them? You imply there's a choice? They dosed my tea once with black hellebore for a prank, while you just finished swearing birth and death will bend for the pride of your family honor.'

'Come find out.' Mearn's invitation was just as cat sure as his step on the rain-wet slope, guiding the blind man's descent. 'My brother's hospitality's not the sort of experience a man's very likely to forget.'

The flank of the gully was seamed with runners of vine. Dune grass caught in the clefts where the gannets would nest and lay eggs. Layered slate pushed through vegetation and moss, weathered to a knife-edged fragility that crumbled under each step. Mearn chose the footholds with detached patience, his soft, steady words talking the blind man down after him.

'You're good on the cliffs,' Ivel commented, breathless, in the windy niche where they rested.

Mearn gave back the pause that bespoke his triangular smile. 'Alestron's an eyrie, didn't you know? My blood ancestors all learned to climb almost from the moment they walked.'

'Oh?' Ivel warmed, that gleaned spark all he needed to strike back in disparagement. 'The ones who lacked the agility of a spider didn't survive long enough to breed?'

But Mearn laughed aloud, his humor unshaken. 'There could be some truth to that. Dame Dawr, my maternal grandmother, once scaled the east wall for a tryst with my grandfather. The revetments there are now mortared over and embedded with crushed glass, as much to deny her fool's route to an enemy as for the fact that her love match galled my great-grandfather to fits.'

Mearn sidestepped. His neat touch steered the splicer around a dripping stand of furze. 'My great-grandame had the sense to let the pair marry. Before, as she said, the next generation of s'Brydion dukes wound up smashed like displaced guillemot eggs on the rocks . . . step down, there's a boulder. The footing at the bottom is loose stone. Do you feel it?'

Ivel's trusting stride arrived on the drenched shingle, with Mearn scarcely winded, and his ebullience dimmed not at all. 'For Dame Dawr, crushed glass only sweetened the challenge. She just climbed the facade of the adjacent tower, then used a rope and grapple slung across to the roof gutter. The story goes that she conceived my late father through the hour the new mortar was curing. As proof of her child's paternity, she left handprints. They're still hardened solid in the battlement under my grandfather's window.'

'The lady's still living?' Ivel inquired on that knife-point intuition that so often provided the leverage that fueled his jibes.

'She's chosen the woman I'm promised to wed,' Mearn admitted, while the waves surged and ebbed, and the cluster of master craftsmen already arrived admitted the mismatched pair of latecomers.

'That could be the curse or the blessing of a lifetime,' Mearn finished, this time showing honest trepidation. 'No way to tell which 'til I'm shackled.'

Stiff currents swirled where the tide met the bluffs, the broad swell of the combers chopped up and confused after threading the crooked channels between the jumbled landmass and its reef-ridden train of bare islets. The foam pulled and surged in an unruly boil. Most of the renegade shipwrights waded thigh deep in the flood, steadying the galley's sent tender between them. Now and again one would curse as he slipped on the weed-slick rocks.

Cattrick awaited also, stilled oak where he stood in a cranny in the cliffs, guarding the shuttered lantern just used to signal the galley lying offshore. Made aware of Mearn's presence by Ivel's piquant retorts, he said softly, 'The craft will take six. Do you want to cross first load, or second?'

'We'll go last, you and I,' Mearn replied without forethought. He passed Ivel's bear-paw grip off to another for guidance into the boat. Enveloped by the tingling fog of thin rainfall, no man on the shore could see clearly. The inevitable fumbling as passengers piled into the lighter caused a mild havoc of banged knees and curses, marked by a breathless, cheerful relief after days spent lurking in wet brush. The Alliance patrols had been relentlessly persistent, even through the expert diversions laid down by the clansmen Lord Maenol had sent to escort their flight across country.

In that hour, with deliverance at hand, Cattrick remained marked apart by his reserved silence.

'Regrets?' murmured Mearn, settled beside him. He rested his own covered lamp on a rock ledge.

'Some.' Cattrick turned his head, his powerful, craftsman's build masked in darkness, and his tension deceptively blurred by his mellow southcoast accent. 'Yet I have always believed that life is what a man makes of it.'

From this decision, there would be no return course. He would no longer be free to choose where he lived; from the hour his fleet of flawed vessels launched, and the moment the torches had been set to level the royal yard at Riverton, parts of the continent had forever become closed to him. In the quiet of words unspoken, the most painful facts would not bend before sentiment. Cattrick already knew his own birthplace at Southshire supported an entrenched Alliance presence. He could never return to his native soil, nor grow old in the land of his kin.

'This I promise,' Mearn stated through the ragged, white rush of the surf. 'Whatever passes, believe me, Alestron will give you greater freedom than any you'd know had you kept your contract with Lysaer s'Ilessid.'

A fuzzed flare of orange burst and vanished in the night, over the fog-shrouded waters.

'We'll see, then.' Cattrick pushed his large frame off the rocks. His deliberate hands adjusted the signal lantern to emit a short flash, marking the beachhead for the returning longboat.

Neither man voiced the uncomfortable truth, that the acceptance of s'Brydion hospitality and employment was no longer a matter of choice. For the sake of his pride, and the Koriani oath of debt used to force his betrayal of Arithon's employment, the master shipwright had rebelled against the dictates of his fate. The price for his act to recoup his lost honor had forever thrown his well-being upon the Duke of Alestron's mercy. His life and livelihood rested in s'Brydion hands, with no recourse at all should clan honor fall short of his irrevocably given trust.

Silence reigned between clansman and shipwright, written over by the thrash of the waves and the trickle of rain over rocks. In due course, the longboat sent from the galley reached shore, announced by the grate of an oarshaft fending off of the shoaling stone shingle. Cattrick lifted his lantern. As always, each motion was planted and sure. His step betrayed no uncertainty. Yet to Mearn, wading into the icy shallows beside him to make their escape out of Tysan, the moment held the fragility of a bubble of blown glass, given the trembling promise of form, but no surety of survival through the punitive stresses of cooling.

Nor was Cattrick oblivious to the pitfalls that might await in the unknown. 'I stand on your good word,' he said, as the icy waters swirled over his boot tops. 'Whatever passes, never forget. I knew Tharrick, who once served as a captain in your city guard.' The s'Brydion brothers all knew that name, must acknowledge the implicit message: that the master shipwright had seen that man's *loyalty* to Alestron earn him a scarred back from the whip and the fate of a permanent outcast.

Mearn sucked a breath between his clenched teeth. 'We all make mistakes.' He caught the longboat's thwart, passed his lantern to the coxswain, then leaned into the work of turning the bow face about in the heaving surf. 'Our biggest lapse through that botched affray was misreading Prince Arithon's motives in the first place.' Strain on his muscles was reflected in his voice, as the craft swung seaward, helped by the odd shove from an oarsman. 'In defense for our bad call against Tharrick, I could add that the Teir's'Ffalenn has a mind that's too clever, and worse than a maze to decipher. We s'Brydion have straightforward, warmongering ways.' A pause as a wave rolled under the boat's keel, followed hard by the bitten conclusion. 'It's no secret. The uprising five hundred years ago throttled our gentler nature in bloodshed. I make no apology for that. We've survived with our city still ruled by crown charter through keeping an unbreakable code. We kill first and ask questions later.'

'A warning for me?' Cattrick asked, while the ebb sucked and whorled around his knees.

Mearn laughed. 'Very likely.' He leaped into the boat. 'Are you coming or not? When all's said and done, my brother Parrien has a rabid, quick temper. He isn't the sort who likes pacing his decks while we browbeat a frivolous point of philosophy.'

'Frivolous, is it?' Cattrick boarded as well, the heated bronze lantern still grasped in his hand, and his cloak bunched up in the crook of his elbow to raise the hem clear of the sea. 'You've a damned queer outlook for an intelligent man. I rest my case for uncertainty upon Ivel's observation, that in your duke's town of Alestron, life seems to take second place, after idiot courage and cleverness.'

Mearn grinned, grabbed an oar, and shoved off. 'Well, the foul-mouthed old coot got that much right.' His haste sparked to a devilish wild humor, he snapped, 'Forward, stroke!' Duke Bransian's war-trained oarsmen dug in. The boat cleaved forward into the murk with a lurch that sat Cattrick down with an undignified smack on the stern seat.

The passage was short, sped by the first, riffling pull of turned tide, and guided by the furtive, timed flash of the lanterns. The oarsmen pulled the longboat into the lee of Alestron's state galley, where the deck crew waited with lines slung from turned davits to hoist the tender aboard. While the oarsmen stowed their wet looms and wrestled the pins on chilled shackles, Cattrick climbed the side battens, with Mearn athletic as an otter at his heels. Strong hands caught the shipwright's thick wrists as he reached the high deck and pulled him securely aboard.

By then, fog and rain had thickened the darkness to smoked felt. He could see very little. The air wore the biting scent of tarred cord through its underlying miasma of soaked canvas, and bilge, and the sweat-pungent wool of benched rowers. The men who kept hold on him were armored and callused, and carried their balance like field troops. Chilled by what seemed overzealous security, Cattrick fleetingly wondered why Ivel and the others who had arrived first should be so unnaturally quiet.

Then a voice, more grainy than Mearn's, but bearing a sibling's inflection eased his mind. 'Your men are below, given quarters already.'

'Parrien s'Brydion?' Cattrick said, a touch brusque since his first, testing tug had not prompted the men-at-arms to release him.

Mearn's older brother returned a bitten affirmation of identity, immediately followed by a nerve-wound command to his crew to douse the wick in the helm lantern.

Through the flared glimmer as the shutters were drawn, and the flame was duly snuffed out, Cattrick received the brief, stamped impression of gloss varnish and gilt. Men moved, unspeaking, about unseen tasks. An unsettled creak of leaded beach below decks bespoke a crew with readied oars. By now aware the men-at-arms had no plans to release him before they received direct orders, the master shipwright clamped a stranglehold on his impatience.

This shoreline was under s'Ilessid sovereignty; to be caught here engaged in treasonous activities with none other than Alestron's state galley would carry unimaginably dire consequences. The s'Brydion were well within their rights to be cautious, even to the point of taking unpleasant steps in protection.

Nor was the crew lacking an envious, smooth discipline. The longboat was shackled with almost no noise.

'Heave!' called the bosun from amidships. 'Bring her in smart, boys!'

The capstan crew responded to a clacking of pawls, and the lines in the davits smoked taut and arose, bearing the tender inboard.

A scrape of damp leathers saw Mearn at the rail, flanked by the adept pair of oarsmen.

'You took long enough,' Parrien groused. 'We've been watching the lichens grow on this spit for two days.'

'Liar,' Mearn greeted, white teeth split by a grin. 'At least, Bransian's gilt brightwork isn't spattered to Sithaer with the clam-stinking guano the gulls leave all over the beach. Have we turned out the pretty flags and state trappings to add pomp to the s'Ilessid wedding? If so, no one's awed. You've missed all the fun since the feast and the ceremony were celebrated yesterday.' Fast talk transformed into liquid, light movement, the younger s'Brydion embraced his taller, brawnier sibling.

Distracted by their sparring reunion, Cattrick took one fatal instant too long to react as a kiss of cold steel snapped over his pinioned wrists. He drew breath to bellow; felt a hand clamp his mouth. His shout emerged muffled, and his outrage exploded like magma from a volcano.

Powerful as he was, Parrien's mercenaries were trained fighters. Their hands wrung him helpless before he could do more than jerk up his knee and snap off an impotent kick. The effort missed cleanly. His shackled wrists were dragged to an excruciating angle, while his ankles were lashed and his mouth gagged with a professional speed that drove him to tears of wild fury.

Mearn said in mild inquiry, 'Parrien? What passes?'

'An arrest,' said the older s'Brydion, unperturbed. 'Did you think we could turn traitor before Lysaer's whole council and his pack of foreign dignitaries, and not start another bloodbath against clansmen?'

Through his doomed struggles to strike back at his captors, Cattrick heard the crisp order to the mercenaries that sealed his fate as Parrien s'Brydion's prisoner. 'Set rivets in those chains. Then confine him in the sail hold along with the rest, and make sure the gag stays in place on that blind splicer's insolent mouth!'

'That's scarcely civil,' Mearn interjected, his tone too complacent to be taken for more than small needling. 'You were told these men are my invited guests? Parrien?' While the bruising efficiency of the duke's men-at-arms bundled Cattrick toward the hatch grating, and the deckhands plowed on with the task of raising the galley's set anchor, Mearn's nerveless prodding raised Parrien's exasperated bass.

'I saw Arithon at Sanpashir, damn you! He has a tongue by lengths nastier than yours, but between his rank insolence, he spoke sound sense! Now here is how we're going to play this.'

Cattrick shrieked into the salt-musty cloth. He managed a desperate, jackknifing wrench that bashed one of the mercenaries off-balance. That one jostled an onlooking officer, who dropped something metallic with a belling clang and a splash of broken glass.

'That was the ship's glass I heard hit the deck?' Stark out of patience, Parrien vented his testy annoyance on his mercenaries. 'Keep on like this, and that fool's hobnailed boots will tear more gaping chunks out of Bransian's brightwork. Will you just damned well hit that big wretch and be done!'

'Man, at your pleasure.' Someone in mail with a mace for a fist efficiently reduced Cattrick's ox struggles to a limpid state of unconsciousness.

**Spring 5654**

# Summons for War

The small war fleet from Avenor swept into Hanshire just after daybreak. Adrift amid the opaline tatters of dawn mist, the ancient walled port rode the jut of the coast in forbidding, tiered splendor, its high turrets crowned by the signal fires kindled to mourn the misfortunate lost mariners.

From the decks of the royal flagship, Sulfin Evend swept a riveting survey over the city, from its lofty, swept heights, to the charcoal sketch outlines of the merchant docks and the straggled pilings of the fishermen's wharves. His lean fingers tapped the rail with expressive impatience.

'Fetch his Grace topside,' he demanded in a lightning shift of mood that allowed for no explanation. His scowl tracked the bosun's departure, then raked the length of the vessel's upper deck.

All appeared in regular order, aboard. The royal flag galley nudged shoreward, her stately grace quickened by oar strokes that sheared curling white water from her beaked prow. Her smart lines and clean brightwork reflected sharp discipline, and her heading clove the arrow-straight course through ebb tide that reflected exemplary seamanship.

'What's amiss?' asked her captain, gruff in defense. At his back, the ship's watch officers shared unsettled glances, unable to tag the detail which had snagged the Alliance Lord Commander's impatience.

When Sulfin Evend held to his sulfurous fuming, the sea captain came back, blunt. 'You know something?' He endured the Lord Commander's rebuffing, curt silence with the stoicism that rode his ships through the vagaries of coastal weather.

'I was born here,' Sulfin Evend admitted at length. His eyes were pale smoke as he resumed his scouring survey. At second glance, even a foreign observer must note the peculiar quiet settled over the shoreline. The brothel windows fronting the dockside quarter showed no lights, nor any sign of debauched guests making their late departures.

Sulfin Evend gripped the rail and stretched, wringing the kinks of a long, chilly vigil from his taut-knit shoulders. 'When signal fires burn during daylight, the high council believes there's cause for war in the wind. Also, you'll see the wharf's been cleared of berthed ships.'

Given the sea captain's ungratified patience, Avenor's Lord Commander jabbed stiff fingers through his straw bristle hair. 'We're expected. That shouldn't surprise me. Avenor's flags will have been identified already by the Koriani scryers who reside in the palace. Hanshire's Lord Mayor keeps an enclave of them in city pay to report inbound ships to the harbormaster. His council might have a long-standing aversion to royalty, but every ranking town minister with ambition has learned to respect his wife's habit of ceremony. She'll have sent a state party to welcome the prince, or you wouldn't be seeing a yard of free space to tie this ship up at the landing.'

The galley edged forward, drifting before the reduced beat of her rowers. Ahead, the towers of the upper city loomed from the blurred folds of the bluffs, pricked by the glow of the watch lamps. Ashore, the only sound stirring was the thump of the crab sellers' skiffs, inbound under oars with filled traps. Through rags of pale mist, the layered silhouettes of the rooftrees and notched walls of the trade mansions framed an interlocking puzzle shaded like mother-of-pearl.

Hanshire had launched ships in Paravian times, and the striated basalt of the old city battlements still bore the raked gashes left by the balefire of dragons. Ivy clothed the deepest clefts, and softened the arrowed teeth of crenellations still capped in ancient blue slate. Lower down, the newer walls by the quay had been raised out of block from the local quarries. The soft, red-gold sandstone had worn smooth with weather inside the course of five centuries. Boys and lovesick sailors had carved names of sweethearts, or sigils for luck into the jetty, where the tide slapped green at the ebb, and the barnacles clung like calcified mildew.

But the grand panoply Sulfin Evend expected did not show for the royal arrival. The sea-quarter cove stayed unnaturally subdued, its day-to-day commerce suspended. Knots of loiterers surrounding the fish stalls looked briefly up as Avenor's fleet of warships made fast to outlying moorings, then returned to their huddles and fast talk.

Where the flagship docked, a lone officer in the blazon of Hanshire's elite guard headed a liveried contingent of grooms. Each of these waited with two saddled horses. Ahead and to one side stood another man, of wiry build, his interest too bright to be casual. His hatless, close-cropped head of salt hair riffled to the whispering kiss of the sea breeze. The rest of his lean height was cloaked in black velvet, cut to his boot tops of scarlet-dyed suede with their patterned cuffs beaded with seed pearls. While Avenor's state galley secured lines and fenders, he measured the performance of her crew, his narrowed eyes the verdigris tint of aged bronze.

Sulfin Evend muttered what might have been an obscenity, then added, 'Get his Grace up here, *now*.'

The galley captain stirred his planted frame, and all but collided with a figure in a plain cloak. Lysaer s'Ilessid stood one pace away, wrapped in the dull mantle which had secured his anonymity the night before. While the realm's stick-thin seneschal fidgeted behind, stiff in primped velvets and jeweled hat, the prince said, 'If you know who that is, you'd best tell me.'

When Avenor's Lord Commander did not speak at once, the flag captain smothered a nervous cough. 'Has to be Raiett, the mayor's dour brother. Folks call him Raven, for when he appears, they say that fighting soon follows.'

'Then I haven't misjudged.' Lysaer's satisfaction rang through the squealing grate of wood as four sailhands ran the gangway down to the dock. He flipped back his hood, unsnagged a frogged fastening, and tossed his mantle to the ever-present, hovering page boy. Against shredding mists, the revealed magnificence of his sunwheel tabard shot fire like gilt on white porcelain. Beneath the fragile, stamped pallor that lingered from the previous night's indulgence, his expression was marble, echoed and reinforced by the immaculate set of his shoulders. The sword in his gem-faced scabbard was a field weapon, and the helm tucked under the vambrace on his forearm was forge-hardened steel, without plume or ceremonial visor.

'You expect we'll have bloodshed?' Sulfin Evend laughed, his approval as sharp as the well-kept gleam on his chain mail.

'I expect to serve justice.' Prince Lysaer inclined his head toward the restive party of grooms and blooded horses. Over iron-shod hooves drumming thunder on the planked wharf, he said, 'Stay at my right hand.'

While the displaced seneschal gave way with a sniff for losing his accustomed place, the Prince of the Light debarked, with his war commander fallen in step beside him.

Raiett Raven strode forward. The incised flesh that bracketed his mouth described his rife impatience. 'Forgive our poor welcome. The Mayor of Hanshire is this moment at sea with our war fleet. He asked that I stay to greet you. If you will please mount? Our high council waits in the old city with news. You'll have comfort, with wine and refreshment.'

'War fleet?' Prince Lysaer's bearing was magisterial silk, immune to such chivvying haste. 'My news at Avenor contained no detail. I know that four ships under my standard have foundered. How many good men were lost with them?'

Already half-turned to wave the grooms forward, Raiett stalled in a swirl of dark velvet. 'Eight ships.' His correction came crisp. 'The others struck the rocks farther south. The misfortune was a conspirator's plot. Strategic attacks by barbarians made certain the news was delayed.'

Lysaer endured through a penetrating glance from inquisitive peridot eyes.

Then Raiett said, 'That's a total loss of your newly launched trade fleet, am I right? As to sailhands and officers, we hear there were drownings and injuries. Firm numbers aren't in yet. The council will give you what facts we can verify.'

Lysaer raised his eyebrows, mild before that barrage of obstructive courtesy. 'What else are you keeping unsaid?'

From Raiett Raven, a ferocious stillness to mask his keen-edged shift from managed diplomacy to respect. 'Hear the worst, then.' He, too, could be blunt. 'Your shipyard at Riverton has burned to the ground.'

'Go on,' Lysaer said, his eyes glacial ice, while the leashed rage in him ignited like balefire and the gulls wove oblivious overhead.

'The event happened days ago, but word just arrived in the night. Clan archers took down three messengers. The one who got through came in wounded. We have the man here. He was a laborer, and has sworn before our council as an eyewitness to events.' Raiett gestured again toward the grooms and readied mounts. 'You'll want to question him as soon as may be. He insists Mearn s'Brydion was implicated.'

'And your brother's warships downcoast?' Lysaer interjected with the delicacy of jabbed wire.

'Half went for relief of the seamen cast ashore. The others left not an hour ago to seek the s'Brydion state galley. Her flags were sighted off the Riverton estuary one day ahead of the fire. She'll be detained, once Hanshire's fleet finds her.' Raiett folded his arms. Fingers strong and supple as an owl's talons rested easy on obsidian velvet; his face wore its years of aristocratic power with a seamless and impenetrable reserve. 'Our magistrate believes she'll be lurking in the islets downcoast to pick up the shipyard conspirators.'

'My ships, my men, and my forsworn allies,' Lysaer summed up. Through the calls of the inbound fish trappers, and the cries of street children, begging, which shrilled through the percussion of stamping of horseflesh, he concluded, 'My seneschal can treat with your council in my place. He's qualified to take down the witness's testimony. Please also extend my regrets to your town ministers. For if the s'Brydion clan name is tied in conspiracy with my master shipwright, then more than our cities in Tysan will suffer. A charge of such gravity might see us all hurled into war with the Spinner of Darkness himself.'

Raiett was too much the man of decision to waste breath in useless argument. 'Then you'll sail south directly in support of my mayor's offensive?'

'I can do nothing else.' Already Lysaer's thoughts ranged ahead. His dismissal of his seneschal to act as his envoy was peremptory and final. Since Raiett made no move toward the horses and escort, Avenor's prince flung back his last word in challenge. 'Stay and guard your fine city of Hanshire. Or come along with my ships like the crow, and stay at hand for the bloodshed as you please.'

Raiett laughed. 'Couched in such terms, what else is left but to soothe down hackled feathers and accept?'

Under a gold sky and the diving flocks of gulls who scavenged the rocks at low tide, the livery mounts and grooms sent to dispatch Avenor's royal delegation to the beamed hall in the old city left the wharf with empty saddles. One groom and one gelding trailed after them, bearing the shrewd old seneschal, who would serve as Prince Lysaer's ambassador. The Mayor of Hanshire's full brother, Raiett Raven, boarded the Alliance flag galley. He perched at the rail, sharply watchful as his namesake, while Avenor's fleet of five cast off from the docks and cleaved their smoking-fast course from the harbor.

Beside him, faced inboard with mailed elbows braced upon streaming, wet wood, Sulfin Evend lounged with the settled ease of close kin. Both men observed the unearthly transformation, as Lysaer in his stainless white-and-gold tabard walked among the sweating banks of oarsmen. After a night passed in killing exertion, he asked more: that they raise themselves to the task of overtaking the fleet which had departed from Hanshire ahead of them.

'Impressive,' Raiett murmured, drumming his long fingers against the ruby-and-silver bracelets he wore everywhere as a talisman. 'So tell me, nephew. Since you've deserted your birthright for soldiering, is this Prince of the Light all he claims to be?'

Sulfin Evend returned his enigmatic regard. 'What do you know?'

'What I see.' Still entranced by the sacrificial dedication of the rowers, Raiett smiled. 'His Grace has an impressive style. His handling of men is extraordinary. The shipyard laborer who carried us word of the late conspiracy was drawn to turn informant on a master who trusted him.'

Mail chinked, sullen, to Sulfin Evend's shrug. 'You aren't one given to belabor the quirks of a simple commoner's loyalty.'

'Just as you weren't expected to cast aside the privilege of your family ties.' Raiett's gaze over the silver flash of his bracelet assumed the fixed focus of a cat. 'Your father asks why, since Hanshire has never favored Tysan's return to the outdated mores of a monarchy.'

'What do you know?' Sulfin Evend repeated, while the sea heaved, rocking, under the keel, and spray thrashed and creamed to the redoubled pull of timed oars. The galley's wake streamed behind, white lace against indigo, erased by the indistinct pallor of mist as the fleet drew away from the shoreline.

Raiett straightened, annoyed. He stabbed a closed fist into the rail as if his clasped fingers held steel. 'Very well. Forget social subtlety. We'll play instead for bare facts. Cattrick's a native Southshire craftsman with cousins and kin ties in Merior. The seer who advises your father's council links his betrayal of Arithon s'Ffalenn to the demands of a Koriani oath of debt. Since the shipwright's true loyalty might not ride on crown gold, the question begs asking. *Why didn't Lysaer s'Ilessid prevent his defection?* His Grace had to suspect sabotage before this. Why didn't he catch the flaw in the designs which saw his eight ships hit the rocks?'

One stroke, two; the galley plowed through a stiffening crosswind, flags cracked to the beat of her urgency. Sulfin Evend jerked his dagger from the sheath at his belt and presented the point toward his uncle. 'His Grace does not confide in me, ever. Nor would my counsel be fitting in his affairs.'

'Ath!' Raiett's quicksilver explosion of frustration warred with his close-held restraint. He did not respond to the ritual opening offered by the bared knife. 'You can't believe the man is creation's divine gift to spare all Athera from darkness!'

Hard gray to searching, pale green, the eyes of the two men locked. Still holding out the gleaming, sharp blade, Sulfin Evend looked away first.

Raiett's utter astonishment woke disused lines of humor over his crag-thin features. When he spoke, he was gruff. 'Put up that steel.' He waited until the dagger was sheathed, made tactful at last by a dignity even his striking contempt could not shake. 'Very well. At least we know it wasn't the quarrel with your father that sent you off slumming with the guard into Riverton.'

'I stand here alive,' Sulfin Evend replied, 'because I pursued the Master of Shadow through a grimward, and the Name of the Light and Lysaer s'Ilessid spared me from the horror which killed every man of my company.' His final pronouncement came chill as black ice. 'Every accusation of shadows and fell sorcery the prince charged of the enemy is true. These I have witnessed. The rest you must judge for yourself. Tell my father I have sworn life service to s'Ilessid. I won't be returning to Hanshire.'

Beneath, on the benches, the oarsmen streamed sweat, driving heart and sinew to surpass the limitations of human endurance. Avenor's flag galley cleaved the wavecrests, sheeting spray, while astern, her sister vessels trailed in their frustrated effort to keep pace.

Shown such living proof of the prince's inspired leadership, Raiett chose the grace of retreat. 'If you won't come back, at least lend your family the continued benefit of your judgment. You've always had a fine touch for state intrigue. Don't waste that gift in stubborn silence.'

'You always make the loose stones roll your way.' Sulfin Evend drew breath, the hooked curve of his brows knit through a moment of revealing, self-searching thought. 'Very well. I see a prince with a vision beleaguered by our political ploys and mean bickering. He fears for us all. His mission to defend humanity's cause is made vulnerable through our petty differences. Since you ask, yes. I believe his Grace saw the flawed ships' plans at Riverton for what they were.'

'Damn you, give us particulars,' Raiett snapped.

Again goaded to challenge, Sulfin Evend gripped the rail until his sword-hardened strength scored nail-bitten crescents in the varnish. 'All right. I can speculate. His Grace didn't expose Cattrick, because Mearn very likely noticed the selfsame discrepancies in the drawings. Add on the persistent frustration, that the wild clans won't be suborned from the Shadow Master's influence. Since they die for their causes, Lysaer sought to intimidate them. But his effort to break their heart by enslavement has backlashed, and the Fellowship's intervention with Caithwood's trees surprised and outflanked him. Repercussions from that has mangled his sea trade, an ill turn, *unless* Tysan's prince seeks a grand cause to unify. Then he might let such a friction raise a force of ill will to eradicate the old bloodlines. Bleed the towns into fighting, he'll gain troops and funds. For that, I would say he has gambled his ships. Today, perhaps he has won.'

For if Mearn s'Brydion had been left the temptation to collaborate in treason with Cattrick, and Duke Bransian had dispatched his state galley in support, then a just retaliation must follow. A campaign in the east to lay siege at Alestron could be used to marry Lysaer's support in Tysan with those towns in Melhalla which had not yet suffered a hardship to align them with Alliance interests.

'He needs a clan war to build on, I thought so!' Raiett slapped his knuckled fist into his palm, the unformed suspicions of recent years distilled to a crystalline certainty.

'Aren't we a trifle premature?' said a voice. 'Mearn's guilt isn't proved, but still only hearsay.' While Sulfin Evend faced seaward, flushed and hot with embarrassment, Raiett lifted his head. He turned just in time to see Lysaer s'Ilessid step up from the oar benches onto the raised deck by the rail.

His Grace seemed unoffended, the ingrained reflex of royal bearing unfazed by gossip or criticism. The blue eyes were wide-lashed, clear as the spring sky that brightened like new satin over the misted horizon. 'To convict Mearn s'Brydion of treason, or establish his innocence, he must first be found. Then he must be taken into safe custody to stand trial.' To Raiett, poised as a leaned sword against sea swells that came and went through the late-breaking fogbanks, Lysaer posed the conversational question with the same forthright edge. 'If I could ask an opinion in exchange for the ones volunteered by my Lord Commander, do you think your mayor's fleet lies under the command of reasonable men?'

Raiett shrugged. His dark mantle snapped to a sudden gust. 'What's reasonable?' He elaborated, soft as the first testing tap of a sword point. 'If our slave-driven galleys stay disbarred from King Eldir's ports, and none of your promised sailing vessels survive this disaster to replace them, more than your merchants in Tysan will see ruin. Mearn's head on a pike would salve pride, if naught else.' Sarcasm thinned into velvet-clothed challenge, Hanshire's First Counselor finished. 'If you preferred his skin living, I wonder why you didn't trouble to remand him into secure custody sooner?'

'For trust of his older brother, who gave me true service at Vastmark.' Lysaer settled between the two men, eyes lucent as cut aquamarine, while the oars clove dark waters, ripping up rooster tails of spray. 'Do you think my flag vessel can overtake Hanshire's war fleet?'

'I cannot speak for Hanshire,' Raiett said, his appraisal revised since the wharf. The stark edge of his profile showed hollows like scarped granite in the breaking ale fall of sunlight.

'Then speak for humanity and justice instead.' Lysaer stripped away pretense. 'Even conspirators deserve a fair hearing. If we fail to catch up with your mayor's galleys before Alestron's state vessel is boarded, do you think there will be an accused man left alive to receive the grace of a public trial?'

'No.' Raiett laughed. 'Not a prayer. And you can't overtake, though you burst the hearts of your best string of oarsmen by trying.'

The prince must have known the assessment of Hanshire's counselor was accurate, for as sun razed through the last layers of mist, the wind would stir brisk from the west. Any galley southbound would roll on her keel, to the detriment of her oarstroke. 'You'd have to summon a gale from behind in order to sight their masthead banners by sundown.'

Lysaer s'Ilessid measured the oarsmen, streaming sweat in the extremity of effort. 'I thought so, too.' He straightened, the riffling breeze entangling gold hair with the ruff of his ermine collar. 'Then we'll just have to serve your mayor an unmistakable message to wait for due process and the administration of my royal justice.' He raised his locked hands, faced toward the galley's bow, then straightened his arms over his head.

Sulfin Evend knew enough to mask his face.

Raiett Raven caught the searing, fireball blast full in the eyes, as the power exploded from Prince Lysaer's shut fists. The light bolt sheared a terrible, spitting line of fire across the pale arc of the heavens and vanished away to the south. Its aftermath left a slamming, rumbling crash of concussed air that slapped the galley like a toy, then eddied away into thunder.

'Let that be the portent to inform of my coming,' Lysaer pronounced through the creak of stressed lines and the sullen flap of furled canvas. He left the open deck to the stupefied stare of Hanshire's First Counselor, whose widespread fame had been built and made on his reputation for unflappable decorum.

# Pieces

At Avenor, aching inside and out as she sits before her mirror in the empty opulence of the royal suite, Princess Ellaine regards the hollow-eyed image of herself, then shouts for her maid, the beaten defeat of her pride snapped to rage; spurned once as chattel, she will not stand down before Lysaer's callous handling without giving the spirited protest of a fight . . .

Leagues southward, at Innish, Fiark pores over charts and sorts lists of lading, fingers thrust through his spun gold hair; and the letters he writes in the secrecy of late-night candlelight arrange, like a delicate web, the supply routes of the provisions that will keep Prince Arithon's small fleet safely at sea, beyond reach of Lysaer s'Ilessid and the curse of Desh-thiere's machinations . . .

In a closed, curtained chamber scented by a birch fire, Lirenda of the Koriathain clasps shaking hands around the returned chain of her quartz focus; the first scrying she effects on the lost keys of restored power frames a sleeping herder boy in Araethura, whose round, child's face has begun to firm with the first hint of angularity set in train by her spells of transformation . . .

**Spring 5654**

# VII. Premonition

The spellbinder's call reached Althain Tower just past nightfall on the same day that Lysaer's light beacon flared down the Korias coast. At that hour, Sethvir sat tucked in his breakfast nook mourning the demise of his favorite buskins. After countless years' service, the soles were too thin to last through another season. The fur had rubbed off. Only odd tufts remained, clinging between shiny patches of leather so worn, it dissolved into cobweb under the efforts of needle and thread. The prime black wolf hide had been the gift of a Camris trapper who now lay five decades dead. Sethvir sighed, while the spring drafts teased his bare toes and ankles, and the earth link channeled the events of the world through the limitless vaults of his mind.

Then one fragment snagged.

*. . . a thousand leagues east in the Cildein Ocean, a chip of stone taken from the Khetienn's ballast sank through clean brine, trailing the sultry heat infused by flame, and a distress cipher scribed in fresh blood . . .*

Althain's Warden picked a wisp of shed fur from his beard. He blinked misted eyes. Disgruntled as a roused owl, he narrowed the thundering span of his vision and touched the source of the conflict knotted into the stone's ritual sinking.

Its signature Name speared a chill clear through him.

*Through the torchlit beat of a galley's sped oars in the night spread over Tysan; between the padded steps of a forest cat hunting the wilds of Deshir; across the knifing flight of a bat over Lithmere*, the Warden of Althain retrieved the steel needle which had failed to revive his aged footwear. The sharpened tip served him in place of the chalk left upstairs with his books in the library. He shoved his cold tea mug aside, rammed buskins and spooled thread out of the way to clear open space on the tabletop. An ink flask tipped over. Oddments of paper scribbled with notes flew airborne and scattered about his bare feet.

Sethvir paid no heed. He scribed a swift circle in the wood of the trestle, then summoned to invoke the powers of the elements. Air and water responded to urgency and need. A line of fine energies shimmered through his demarked geometry and bridged him a merciless focus.

'Dakar?'

The pull of that call sent vibrations coursing outward through the drawn span of the circle. An image bloomed over the wood like spilled oil, then transformed into cohesive contact. The Sorcerer gazed through that window across distance and beheld the tight confines of the *Khetienn*'s stern cabin.

There, the Mad Prophet hunched in despair on a berth. His moon face was pressed between his cramped fingers, and his screwed-up hair dripping sweat.

'Damn those blighted, warmongering weasels to the ugliest pit of oblivion!' Through muffling fingers, Dakar's next imprecations changed target. 'And may Dharkaron's Black Horses piss on the obtuse doings of mages! You demented, miserable dreamer! Get your dighty nit-picking nose out of your books and lend me some help when I need it!'

'I'm already here,' Althain's Warden announced with acerbic clarity.

'Sethvir?' Dakar straightened, flushed with disbelieving, wild hope. 'Thank Ath! Have you seen the disaster Parrien and Mearn s'Brydion have stirred up with Cattrick at Avenor?'

'Nit-picking?' Sharpened to a forbidding attentiveness, Sethvir added, '*Dighty?*'

He did not withdraw, though his tart remonstrances raised no sign of embarrassed contrition.

Miserably pale above his rucked doublet, the reprobate prophet displayed every sign of being sunk in a wasting indulgence. Sickness imprinted the dough folds of his skin. His laces were snarled, as if he had been too befuddled to locate the business end of his points. Yet the earth-linked awareness of the Fellowship Sorcerer saw beyond surface dissipation: the damp fingers trembling in the flare of the oil lamp could not have lifted a wine jug.

'Please, will you help?' Dakar whispered.

Sethvir touched his fingertips to the edge of the circle. He probed past the burn of Dakar's nausea and affirmed that its cause was not excess drinking or seasickness. Unthinking as reflex, the Warden's tuned powers singled out the thread of happenstance that had wakened the Mad Prophet's wild talent for prescience. 'You foresaw the citadel at Alestron under siege by Alliance forces.'

'In a dream, yes.' Dakar flopped backward in prostrate relief. 'You must see the scope of my problem.'

Sethvir tracked the converging angles in one vaulting chain of swift thought: *that the two retainers Parrien s'Brydion had left aboard the* Khetienn *to guard Arithon were the duke's sworn men. Their old tie of loyalty might supplant their charge's safety if their lord's domain became threatened; and should the Master of Shadow return headlong to the continent to intercede in Alestron's behalf, nothing could stop an encounter with Prince Lysaer and the wrath of his southbound war fleet. The insidious grip of the Mistwraith's curse worsened with each successive encounter.*

'Dharkaron's Black Spear!' Dakar exclaimed. 'How can you stay calm? The half brothers can't meet, or Arithon will shatter.' At Riverton, even the proximity of a Koriani fetch endowed with Lysaer's auric energy had hurled the Master of Shadow beyond sanity. 'An armed conflict now would destroy your last hope to reunite the Fellowship and keep the s'Ffalenn bloodline alive.'

Sethvir looked away. All of time seemed to hang in the balance while his awareness expanded to plumb the night sky through the arrow slit over his head. 'We cannot intervene, Dakar.' As though something inscribed in the distant stars moved him to nameless sorrow, he added, 'You know this.'

Yet stakes on Athera were no longer malleable. Two accursed princes held the world's fate between them. The risk unleashed by a live confrontation would fling wide the gates to disaster.

'Don't even dare to *suggest* I break his leg.' Dakar winced as the force of his vehemence lanced stabbing pain through his temples. 'And anyway, Parrien's crude tactic just let Rathain's prince learn the notes to fuse shattered bone.'

Sethvir said, mild, 'Arithon knew those already.'

'From Elaira, at Merior, I remember.' Dakar hugged himself through a wretched shiver. '*You* didn't have to listen through his hours of practice until he recaptured the tonalities.'

Sethvir set a knuckle to his lips in forbearance. In cold fact, he had; the earth link was unremitting, its depth of detail as intricate as the patterns inside a revolving kaleidoscope. The melodies wrought by Arithon in convalescence had made more than the new retainers from Alestron blot streaming tears in broad daylight.

The Mad Prophet ground his fists against his closed lids, but the memory remained, embedded like nails through the brain. 'That music could strip a man, spirit from flesh, then remake him in ribbons of light. To hear, you could never believe any suffering could lie past the reach of such mending.' He broke off and sighed for the sorrowful fact that Desh-thiere had worked the exception. 'Your Masterbard was walking without splints in two weeks, yet the hurt in his heart was no less.'

'I know.' At whim, Sethvir could affirm the devastating grief inflicted by Caolle's death. Nor had he missed the scarring sorrows left since Vastmark that still destroyed Arithon's sleep. The accusation told hardest of all, that the Teir's'Ffalenn's peace had been sacrificed for the blood vow sworn at Fellowship behest on the sands at Athir nine years ago.

For Dakar's discomfort, Sethvir scribed a healing glyph into the link that established the span of his circle. 'Granting Rathain's prince permission to die is not an acceptable compromise.'

The gifted relief of his suffering did nothing for Dakar's strangling concern. 'One day your Master of Shadow will go mad, and nothing in anyone's living power will be able to call him back.' The threat carried weight: against the thick gloom, a pale streak at each temple, the hair grown in gray since the hour when Dakar had drawn on his own life force. His sacrifice then had been all that contained Arithon's fit of insanity brought on during crisis at Riverton.

Sethvir caught the unused thread on his needle and wound it in loops on his thumb. 'Go to sleep,' he advised, his turn into vagueness a whim that defied understanding. 'The s'Brydion have always been first-rate strategists. They would scarcely start a war for the sake of an escapade to foul the Riverton shipworks.'

Dakar shoved erect in fish-eyed suspicion. 'That's much too evasive, in particular since Cattrick has already betrayed Arithon's interests before this.'

'No faith without proof?' Sethvir's tufted brows rose. 'Very well.' He slipped the thread off his knuckle and stretched it two-handed, faintly singing and taut on the air. 'Pay close attention. You aren't going to see what you expect.' A deft flick set a slipknot into the end. 'Fetch the lamp, or a candle. Any small flame should serve.'

A flurry of trepidation arose from the circle of spelled wood framing the connection across land and the vaster leg over water. Then a mundane yelp as the brigantine broached a swell and fetched Dakar into a bulkhead. 'Pox on all sailing!' He rummaged a candle and pricket from the locker beneath the *Khetienn*'s chart desk, then peered uneasily over his shoulder. 'Will this scrying stay private?'

Sethvir set another knot into the thread. His eyes were blank sky, at odds with the sly smile which stirred the untrimmed cascade of his beard. 'Arithon won't see. But Ath Creator himself couldn't stop him from hearing the spell's resonance if he has inclination.'

Dakar paused in dismay, the striker left dangling, while the wick flared and glazed his bunched frown and the pale moon curve of one cheek. 'You do have your way of letting me know when I've pried outside of wise limits.'

Althain's Warden said nothing. His seamed, pixie features held strict concentration, while the strand in his fingers came alive. Whipped by unseen spells, it turned in contortion and formed an animate chain of fine ciphers. To these, Sethvir fastened the tail of a thought.

Power surged through the construct. Spell-wrought twine glowed silver and threw off smoking trails of blue light. 'Now hold the flame steady.'

Aboard the *Khetienn*, clammy and chilled by uncanny trepidation, Dakar sensed someone's footsteps emerge from the quarterdeck companionway. As a second presence took station at his shoulder, he had no time to acknowledge that Arithon s'Ffalenn stood motionless in the shadow behind him.

For the Warden of Althain stabbed his steel needle into the circle, straight into the heart of the candleflame. That contact joined an arc across time and space. Earth-linked Sight and elemental heat achieved flash point union, and the scrying that Dakar had begged for intercession flooded in and became manifest inside the brigantine's stern cabin . . .

Five Alliance vessels in command of Lysaer overtook the mayor's war fleet dispatched from Hanshire in the dwindling light after sundown. By full dark, Lysaer's rotund ship's master was immersed in the delicate maneuver of merging the two disparate fleets. Orders were shouted through bullhorns, and the blink of signal lamps rocked over heaving waters when, bearing northward, the inbound s'Brydion raked into the muddle at attack speed. The boom of the drum which timed their crack oarsmen barreled through the breach, dire as the oncoming storm that opened the gates to stark chaos.

Those captains who executed the command to join forces screamed orders for their oarsmen to hold stroke. Steersmen leaned hard on oak whipstaffs and veered. Lysaer's royal galleys and the vessels from Hanshire scattered like schooling fish set to flight by the splash of a boulder. Oarblades entangled. Rowers and captains vented rank tempers, and transformed a calm night off the coastal cliffs to a bedlam of clashed discipline and oaths.

Amid the confusion, one man's enthusiasm overrode the clamor of bellowing irritation and splashed looms. 'Almighty Ath! Did Prince Lysaer engage every seagoing ship inside hailing distance of Avenor? Who in Sithaer has he launched off to fight? Naught's left to be saved. His shipyard at Riverton's already burned. The ashes are cooled for three days.'

'Who speaks?' Lysaer's fleet commander yelled back. He gestured for his officers to withhold hard action, stalling for time as a tactic to allow the other galleys to surround the brash new arrival and close in. 'You're fresh out of port? We're anxious for news from the estuary.'

The voice claimed identity as Parrien s'Brydion, then added, intrigued, 'What, were your scheduled post riders waylaid on the road?'

For the disastrous details should have reached Avenor by courier well before a galley could row the long way around the outthrust reef spurs and chains of jagged islets sprawled off the Korias coast.

Through the ensuing stiff silence, Parrien's commands to his crewmen rang across the inked darkness. Alestron's port rowers backed oars. With a cool that brooked insolence, they spun the duke's galley in a froth of kicked spray, then drew her abreast and matched pace with the sunwheel flagship.

Her flanking course made the royal fleet's flag captain edgy. The close quarters forced him to cease stroke to avoid an entangling collision. Amid the blundering noise made by other ships manned by less polished crews, he hailed back, 'If our dispatch riders were waylaid, then where were yours? The duke's family blazon might have seen the news past the clan raiders who caused the delays.'

Through the slap of the bow wake, and the rumble of wood as oarshafts were raised and run in, the companionway door squealed open. Raiett Raven stepped out, trailed by Avenor's justiciar, who minced no words, but shouted across to the lamplit rogue who commanded the s'Brydion galley. 'Or are you too late for the royal wedding because Alestron has joined in conspiracy with other renegades who favor the Shadow Master's packs of barbarians?'

Against every precedence, Parrien failed to take umbrage. 'I know there were vessels deliberately foundered.' Across the heaving span of light chop, he strode up the rambade and took position beside a slimmer figure, until then unobtrusive as a wraith. Both men were armed. Nicked glints of orange gouged up by the stern lamp played over the chain mail on shoulders devoid of a surcoat.

'You make a grave mistake, if you accuse s'Brydion,' Parrien added, while the man at his side remained silent. 'Arson and sabotage against Tysan's crown interests are not any folly of mine.' While the distance between galleys closed to the jostling nudge of the rip currents, the duke's brother seemed more interested in the faces which inhabited the flagship's decks than in defending the slur just leveled against his family honor. Nor did he mind the predatory circle of vessels which maneuvered to cut off his escape.

The flag galley's captain belatedly realized his autonomy had gone with his elbow room. Raiett stood silent vigil on his quarterdeck, and Avenor's high councilmen now crowded en masse from the companion-way, Lysaer s'Ilessid among them.

The Prince of the Light had small patience with delays. He pursued the charge of s'Brydion disloyalty in the imperious manner he used to freeze his trade ministers in mid-argument. 'Your brother's representative missed my state wedding.'

'I was late,' Parrien amended. While the figure at his side held the queer, lethal stillness of a cobra gauging its distance to strike, he added in silken patience, 'My reasons are forthright. I expect the gift I bear strung from my yardarms will fully exonerate the lapse.' His following gesture to an unseen crewman caused a lantern to be unshuttered and tipped aloft.

From amid the pack of brocade-clad officials, one of the trade ministers gasped. 'Ath's own mercy! Are those corpses strung up there?'

Hats and feathers flurried as necks craned to see.

The Prince of the Light simply raised his right fist and let the brilliance of his gift shatter the obscuring veil of darkness.

Light flared over ships and men with swift and revealing brutality. There were indeed bodies noosed to Alestron's squared yardarm, eight of them dangling, and each of them over a day dead. Rigor had left them. Their slack-limbed remains hung by the neck and flopped to the roll of each swell. The victims had not danced overlong in their agony. Each had been dealt the Wheel's swift passage with a ballast rock lashed to the ankles.

Nor did the evidence stop at execution: each body was encrusted with bruised wounds, the dried blood on slack flesh like rust stains too vividly rendered.

'Mercy, do you see?' Raiett Raven murmured. 'All of their fingers were broken.' Beyond Lysaer's stance, a fainthearted councilman laced his hands on his belly and retched.

'Your wedding gift,' Parrien stated, flat as a whipcrack across the hellish reflections chipped off the waves between hulls. He grasped the shoulder of the figure beside him. 'My brother Mearn has spent a busy winter in behalf of Alliance interests. You might thank his vigilance, since you see before you the cut heart of the Riverton conspiracy.'

In stark truth, for those with the stomach to look, the bloated gray features of the corpses were known. Nearest, the recognizable brown hair and blunt jaw of Cattrick. Beside him, the face with the half-toothless rictus was Ivel the blind splicer. Next in the lineup, the plump joiner who had fitted the ships' brightwork, and after him the master sawyer and the yard's wiry caulker, who would harry his laborers no more with his fits of perfectionist temper.

'They were tortured,' Lysaer said, revolted by the unrecognizably swollen appendages that once had served as human hands. Through the distant, flint scent off the cliffs by the shoreline, wind wafted the clinging miasma of putrefied meat. Murmurs of disquiet ran through the oarsmen stilled on the benches, while on the bunched galleys adrift with the tide, Lysaer's light beat down like the molten flare of poured steel.

'Well yes, they were tortured,' Parrien agreed, his bear-stubborn features surprised. 'How else to be sure we had caught all the ones who were guilty?'

Lysaer's fury broke in a wave that fired his gift to white static. 'How *dare* you take these men's lives and usurp my right to administer royal justice?'

Limned in unbearable, silvery glare, Parrien s'Brydion laughed. 'Why trouble to split hairs? Shouldn't you thank me? Or are you and your councilmen so in love with due process that you'd rather spend your wedding week haring off south to wage an unnecessary war? No need to put all of Riverton to the sword. The bunch swinging here are your criminals.'

The diamond clasp on Lysaer's white cloak spat ice to his indrawn breath. 'I cannot know that for certain.'

'Then you'll just have to trust me.' Parrien's smile turned wicked. 'Or not. I see you have envoys from Erdane and Hanshire on board. They can bear witness if you want to show your *gracious* ingratitude and cast public doubt on the validity of s'Brydion honor.'

'Oh, he's very good,' Raiett Raven observed softly. To the nephew slipped up to stand by his side, locked to hard-breathing frustration, he added, 'How does your prince handle stalemate?'

Lysaer's blue eyes shone with volcanic rage. 'No man in my kingdom should be condemned without trial, or die before my royal seal authorizes his execution.'

'Oh, that's rich!' burst out Mearn. 'As a prince who rules Tysan without legal sanction, take care to recall that we're clanborn. The mores of town law can't constrain us, as allies. On the matter at hand, our own scruples bind us. No man of mercy could keep these conspirators alive once they had delivered their confession.'

'He's right.' The mouse-timid minister of the weaver's guild dabbed at moist lips with his handkerchief. 'To have held these for trial would have prolonged a vile and unnecessary suffering.'

The council delegate from Erdane offered argument. 'That's a glaring assumption. Would men like these have acted in conspiracy without ties to the Master of Shadow?'

'Never so lofty an evil as that,' Parrien rebutted. 'Look closer to home. This lot was disgruntled after two years of scant wages.'

Exclamations from the councilmen, with the trade minister's outcry the loudest. 'But we sent them three hundred coin weight in gold!'

Mearn shrugged in that boneless way which set townborn teeth on edge. 'If your prince sent bullion, the payment you specified never reached its destination at the shipyard.'

Through mutters of consternation concerning mislaid funds, with more blame and imprecations heaped on the heads of Maenol's clansmen, other factions expressed their relieved complaisancy.

'To think all of Tysan could have mobilized for war where no real threat of shadow existed!' sighed the trade minister to the coterie of Avenor's guild councilors. 'Imagine the expense saved, not to mention more losses to revenues for the crown to levy more troops.'

At Sulfin Evend's shoulder, Raiett Raven looked amused. 'His Grace won't shift them now. Threat to profits will keep all his armies at home. I wish I could hire on the duke's younger brother as strategist.'

Mearn was speaking again, his ultimatum to Lysaer hurled over the water in a voice the whole gathering overheard. 'Believe us, or brand the s'Brydion liars, then swallow the consequence of that.'

Still etched under the perilous threat of Lysaer's gift, Parrien signaled to seamen he had kept on station in the mainmast crosstree. 'Cut the carrion down. This vessel has served Avenor's interests as a gibbet long enough.'

'Why are we drifting here arguing, anyway?' Mearn snapped. His mercurial gesture of impatience encompassed the lightless horizon to the north. 'Presumably there's a bride ashore pining for her absent prince. If all of the wine in this kingdom is drunk dry, Avenor serves her allies a muckle-poor welcome.'

On the decks of the flagship, the beribboned city dignitaries subsided, content. Never disposed toward seafaring in the first place, they seemed more than eager to grasp the excuse to fare homeward. Since the captain could not order the fleet to put about without royal authority, they regarded the bejeweled prince in his white-and-gold silk with unified expectation.

Lysaer withstood that nailing regard, his eyes darkened sapphire and his coinface profile expressionless. While the misting night airs riffled his filigree hair, the corpses of eight traitors splashed into the sea, one on the heels of the next. His gaze moved to Parrien and measured; then surveyed Mearn in turn. No more accusations passed between ships. The Prince of the Light kept his right to hold judgment in suspension, while the fires of his gift singed the rigging overhead and wafted the rank taint of carbon.

He had been stood down. Raiett Raven would have laughed for the irony; except something to the quality of Lysaer's bearing stopped the mirth cold in his belly.

Danger walked in that magisterial stillness.

The fire of human pride was a powerful force. Temper, frustration, and hostility must lend fuel to an explosive desire for reprisal. Tension spun out like the pent force of the arrow nocked and held to the drawn bow. The strength of one thought could see Alestron's state galley in flames, as every discomfited councilman realized. Lysaer might seize a mortal ruler's satisfaction. He might ride the moment and indulge in his temper and set off his politically desirable war with Alestron; or he could accept the peace thrust into his hands by s'Brydion intervention.

He could relax his strict point of principle and allow the invigorating campaign he needed to expand his resources for warfare to become disarmed by the spurious lynching of eight disgruntled conspirators.

A drawn second passed, while the moist sea winds collided with raised light and spat ghost trailers of steam at the interface. The swell slopped and heaved against the timbers of stalled hulls; gear creaked aloft to their rolling. Raiett Raven's lips were a sealed, strained seam; the councilmen sweated in abeyance. The Erdani, Lord Koshlin, clamped his jaw in sour fury.

Only Sulfin Evend appeared unaffected as the fair prince he served resumed breathing, deep and even.

Lysaer brought his seething fury in check, the change as effortless as the sheathing of killing steel into silk. His exacting, fair character raised a majesty that burned, and choked throats. As though all of time must bow to his disposal, he bent his bright head and opened the fist held aloft. The spattering, star brilliance of his gift of light dimmed and released its harsh grip on the night. His presence reduced by the glimmer of mere lamp flames, he smiled with the lucent diplomacy that riveted men to allegiance. 'For your services to Tysan, then, let me welcome s'Brydion to the crown's hospitality at Avenor. My new princess shall arrange for your public commendation.' A signaling flick of one finger, and the flagship's captain shouted orders to run the war banners down from the masthead.

While movement returned, and captains received orders to regroup into fleet formation, Raiett Raven watched Lysaer s'Ilessid retire with eyes gone panther wary. 'Never mind whether he's the world's divine savior,' he murmured to the nephew at his elbow. 'He's dangerous beyond compare since no one alive can guess his preferred agenda.'

Sulfin Evend unglued his fingers from his sword hilt, the gesture a running flare of chain links touched orange under the lamplight. 'He'll go on to Riverton. Care to lay coin on it?'

Raiett's chuckle came warm in a darkness that felt inexplicably empty since the Prince of the Light had ceded the deck to his fleet captain. 'I'd ask instead, how much gold would it take to bring you back to your father's service?'

'No coin on this earth could buy that,' said the man sworn heart and spirit to the cause of the sunwheel Alliance.

When Raiett replied, his honesty rang bright as ruled brass. 'As Hanshire's First Counselor, I don't know whether such loyalty will become the world's grace, or if it's the most frightening thing I'll ever witness inside of a lifetime.'

As the scried image delivered by Sethvir's powers tore away, Dakar reeled, unsteady and confused through the shock of restored awareness. He forgot where he was and shot to his feet. Rammed crown first into the unforgiving edge of the *Khetienn's* upper deck beam, and suffering a bitten tongue, he yelped, bent in half to avoid further mishap. Every hatred he bore toward the hazards of seafaring revisited with venom enough to stop thought.

'Fiends plague!' Collapsed on the bench by the chart desk, he agonized to Sethvir, 'Never mind that those meddling brothers averted a war. *How do I tell Arithon that his most loyal shipwrights were tortured and killed by the hand of Parrien s'Brydion?'*

Sethvir's patience seemed to rise from the stones that weighted the unfurled scroll, whose lines described vistas of ocean. 'His Grace knows already. Could you forget? He's still with you.'

Dakar groaned, while the pain danced in whorled black patterns across the shut dark of his eyelids. Since he hurt too much to focus, he extended his mage-sense to measure the motionless presence at his back. For ongoing, dreadful seconds, he listened. Tuned to Arithon's temperament like a brother, he waited, braced for the soft, fractured breath that would reflect deeply buried distress.

'Who were the victims?' Arithon asked instead in a tone that was frightening and ordinary.

The Mad Prophet mouthed a desperate, short prayer, poised for explosion, and foolishly lacking the cowardice to leave without giving an answer. 'Your master shipwright.' His voice bound up on the unwonted memory of Cattrick, filled with feisty life and arguing over beer in a tavern.

Dakar coughed, resumed. 'Ivel. That mule-stubborn caulker with the missing finger you lured on a challenge from the shipworks at Southshire.' No movement yet from Arithon s'Ffalenn, an ominous sign his reaction was going to defy every reasonable prediction. Yet the Mad Prophet dared not flag in his office until he had spoken each name.

The shipyard's master craftsmen who best served the Shadow Master's cause were now rotting in the tide beneath the seacliffs south of Hanshire. Each wore the severed ends of a noose on his neck, sent to the Fatemaster's judgment with his ankles lashed to a ballast stone.

'Even the caulker,' Arithon mused, then broke into wild hilarity. 'Parrien's brilliant! He can break my leg anytime in exchange for a strategy as thoughtful and well timed as that!'

'What!' Dakar recoiled, shot straight, his horrified regard pinned to the Shadow Master's face. 'You *can't* be glad of this!'

'Why not?' Arithon's insane ebullience threatened laughter. 'Lysaer's been hobbled.' He tripped the latch on a locker and tugged out a cloak, the original reason for his untimely appearance at the moment of Sethvir's augury. 'The same body of officials my half brother needed to fund his new war will now insist he stay home. He'll have to suspend his armed interests in Tysan and cut back his bid to extend his martial foothold at Etarra. We're free, Dakar. We can now sail for years, unmolested. Not only that, for the few reputations that Parrien sacrificed, we still have two dozen left outside suspicion. They can safely stay covert and keep us informed of Avenor's upcoming policy.'

Dakar damped back his inimical rage. 'Eight men are *dead,* and you've got no access to mage-sight. You *could not* have read so much into that scrying from Althain.'

'No,' Arithon admitted. Unchastened, still pleased, he flung on the cloak, prepared to slip through the companionway. 'My ability to divine through straight sound still has limits. Why else should I trouble to ask after names?'

To the stones on the chart desk, safely unvolatile, Dakar said in cat-footed care, 'Then you won't be aware those men were tortured by Parrien to buy off the others as innocent?'

'But I heard him admit that.' The Shadow Master set his hand on the latch. His last whoop of laughter rebounded through the cabin as he let in the chill of the night. 'Their bones were bull stubborn to break, that I warrant.'

'Mercy,' Dakar murmured, overtaken by a sorrow to make his years of steadfast effort come to nothing. 'Once, the friend I knew had the mark of humanity on him.'

Sethvir's voice reached back in gentle rebuke. 'For five centuries' study under Asandir, you remain remarkably unobservant.'

Dakar pushed straight, disarranging a stone, which dropped with an indignant clatter on the timbers under his feet. 'Don't say I ought to forgive the expedience. Those were living men, and companions who gave trust.' He strangled an uglier, deeper concern, that the *Khetienn* now sailed with two s'Brydion retainers. They had been sworn over to Arithon s'Ffalenn, but were placed in a chilling position if in fact they were spying for the duke.

'Your suspicions are blinding you to the truth,' Sethvir said, the acuity of his earth-linked perceptions as always a galling embarrassment. 'To distrust the integrity of those two clansmen will set the s'Ffalenn prince in danger.'

Dakar winced. Before the stone wandered to the heave of the sea and wound up battering his ankle, he bent and groped in the darkness. 'Parrien s'Brydion might be a ruthless strategist, but I did expect better of Mearn.'

Althain's Warden said, oblique, 'You might then ask why they had to sink the remains, and the stone you can't find has lodged by the locker a half a pace behind your left heel.'

Dakar rested his forehead against the salt-flocked parchment of the chart. His head hurt too much to pick apart circumstance, and his heart ached too deeply to unwind the next flaw Desh-thiere's curse set in Arithon's character.

'At least take the time to admire the science.' Across distance, Sethvir sounded rueful. 'Arithon's ear for true sound has set a new precedent if he's learned to differentiate the separate bands of animate vibration from the broad scale of the life chord.'

The Mad Prophet retrieved the errant stone. 'I'll leave the riddling nuance of the present in favor of hearing your take on the odds for our future.' Exhaustion made all his bones feel cased in lead. He smoothed down the ruffled edge of the chart, where Merior and the sands of the Scimlade hook interfaced with the unexplored leagues of the Cildein

Ocean; his hand shook as he replaced the weight on the corner. 'How long are we free to seek the Paravians before the next threat on the continent forces the Master of Shadow to react?'

From the Warden at Althain, a measuring silence, while the running swell under the *Khetienn*'s keel kept time to the fair weather course that carried her outside known waters. Amid night and ocean, his sight tracked her hull as a tossed seed of warmth at the driven whim of the elements. In the dimmed stern cabin, shut away from the sailhands who diced at the galley trestle, Dakar caught the secondhand imprint of power as Sethvir engaged his wide vision. He could almost feel the unborn currents of cause and effect as the Sorcerer attuned his will to plumb the forward progression of time.

Still touched in light linkage, the Mad Prophet sensed the tunnel of years, laid out in seasonal rhythms and the coiling cycles of storms. Through Sethvir's gift, he traced Athera's binding webwork of energies, from the living, molten fires of her core to the secrets encrypted in crystalline bedrock. Wrapped warp through weft with the world's breathing aura, her quickened tapestry of flora and fauna unreeled, each tempered strand etched in fine imprints of light. The riddles set into their patterns lay beyond his understanding. Dakar lost the translation as the ranging expanse of overwhelming minutiae frayed away cognitive reason.

A mere spellbinder's training could not plumb that intricate geometry. Nor could Dakar sort the movements of men from the endlessly shifting individuality of wind-scoured sand grains. Sethvir worked under no such limitation. The forces he commanded through vast wisdom and experience let him tap the grand mystery. His mind accessed realms where Athera's law did not rule, and the undying song of Ath's creation expanded beyond the darkened constraints of dense matter.

Power rode on that cusp, at the threshold interstice where the sensory boundaries dissolved into the spectrum of higher vibrations. There, rarified energies linked the light-dance of form, made accessible through disciplined mage-sight. Like a particle swept up in a comet's lit tail, Dakar received glimpses of Sethvir's mastery. In flashes and bursts, he snatched trains of sequence he recognized: the seasonal budding of leaves and the lightning of summer storms, stitched through by the lane currents which guided the birds in migration. Between those he sensed the Naming ceremony for Havish's young princess, hard followed by the birth of a brown-haired royal brother. Through the shuttling passage of uncounted trade ships, and the veils of dust raised by toiling caravans, he heard the marching of men under the sunwheel banner.

His effort to milk that image for more knowledge entangled with the late-autumn belling of stags. Blue-and-gold banners streamed from the towers at Avenor to commemorate the birth of Tysan's next prince. Other visions unreeled, scraps too jumbled to decipher, until Sethvir's artistry winnowed the morass and distilled rampant chaos to a final cascade of clear focus. Dakar caught the echo of what could have been Lirenda's proud form, pacing the floor with rapacious anticipation.

Then, through pearly dusk and a dank, autumn rain, he saw the enchantress Elaira, huddled by a smoking fire under the massive white oaks of Halwythwood. She was alone, face pressed into shivering hands, while wet beaded her collar and masked her distraught, silent tears. Then that sequence cut off.

What remained was the last fated link, a disjointed fragment of latent event that Sethvir had earmarked as a closure. Dakar shared that sight: of a straight-backed young rider on the road leading from Araethura's broad moors toward the lakeshore town of Daenfal.

Sethvir said, crisp, 'You might have fifteen years, but no longer.'

Struck dizzy by transition back into the present, the Mad Prophet returned to himself, hunched over the course log on the chart table. Beneath him, the *Khetienn* rose on a swell. She shouldered through the crest, creaking stout timbers, and rolled through a shattered fall of spray. Brushed by phantom fear, Dakar broke into chill sweat. 'Ath, who was the rider on that moorland pony?'

But Sethvir's steady presence had withdrawn back to Althain, leaving the question unanswered.

Alone in the sea-humid gloom, sight reduced to the tiger-lily flare of the flame through the soot-smoked glass of the sconce, the Mad Prophet could but wonder whose future action would trigger the next round of heartache.

The tangle of posed implication became altogether too vicious.

Dakar slammed his closed fists into the chart desk. 'Howling Sithaer!' Pained by the burden of Sethvir's late forecast, he thrust to his feet. Fool that he was, and tied up in sentiment, he could not sit by and leave the s'Ffalenn prince to his cavalier attitude.

'Cattrick and seven shipwrights have died in true service,' he howled to the echoing darkness. 'That has to mean *something*. Or else you've become the cold, heartless bastard the Alliance has claimed all along.'

On deck, the night was a buffeting scarf of black wind, loomed to wet silk by humidity. This far offshore, no horn lanterns burned. Every drop of oil was hoarded to fuel the flame to light the binnacle, with even that wick set to minimal use on clear nights, when Ath's stars could be used in place of the magnetic compass. That hour, a low cloud cover lidded the sky. The waters beneath were roiled ink, sheared into foam off the bow as the *Khetienn* plowed on her close-hauled course.

Dakar clawed his way from the aft companionway. The wood under his tread was drenched glass, doused by the spray that plumed over the bowsprit. He reached for the rail to steady his way to the quarterdeck, and found his wrist vised immobile by sword-callused fingers.

Then, in tones of warning, 'His Grace of Rathain has specifically asked that you not be allowed to disturb him.'

'Ath's own grace, Talvish!' Dakar tugged, peevish for the fact the s'Brydion retainers had taken s'Ffalenn interests so swiftly to heart. 'I'm not Arithon's enemy!'

The grip did not loosen; in painful fact, was cutting off vital circulation. 'For tonight, his Grace might think otherwise.'

Dakar's foul language fell short of his pitched irritation. 'His Grace would not still be alive to sit sulking if steadfast friends had not broken his door and invaded his damnable privacy. Let go. You won't like the headache you'll have in the morning if I need to use spellcraft to pass you.'

'Then fell me,' said Talvish, his clipped laugh indication he found the contest amusing. 'I haven't drawn steel against you, after all. By rights, you're unarmed. Unlike yours, my service is honorable.'

'This isn't a law court!' Dakar snapped through clenched teeth. Braced for the lash of the Shadow Master's temper, he had no patience left for ridiculous impasse or argument. Yet before he engaged dire forces to win free, he sensed more than felt the presence that stalked upon his exposed flank.

He snap-turned his head, saw the upraised sword pommel in time to dodge under the blow. 'Vhandon! Desist! This goes beyond sanity.' Frightening to watch this pair act together, each move a dance step made in lethal concert; Dakar backstepped in surrender. Already the retainers from Alestron guarded their royal charge like men bloodborn to s'Ffalenn service.

While the brigantine slammed smoking through another black trough, the Mad Prophet pleaded. 'Eight men are dead who served Arithon's cause. As well as he knew them, he's not shown one shred of natural grief for their passing. That behavior is worrisome, in light of the curse. If you knew the man's twisted nature as I do, you'd help plumb the bent of his thinking.'

Vhandon lowered his blade, but did not sheathe the steel. A stalwart presence of masked shrewdness and subtlety, he held his ground with the obstinacy of a siege wall. 'Your prince isn't mourning. He believes that Cattrick and the others still live.'

Dakar swallowed. 'Self-blinded delusion,' he husked. 'I saw the corpses in a scrying sent by Sethvir. Arithon caught the resonance of the vision through his bard's gift. When I gave him the names, he was blithe as a man undone by a surfeit of gin.'

'Delusion or no, he's not so blithe now.' Disdainful of talk, Vhandon snapped a curt gesture toward the quarterdeck.

There, to judge by the uncanny, straight course the brigantine slammed through the cross swell, Arithon manned the helm without the assistance of ship's mate or quartermaster.

'He's alone up there?'

Talvish tapped his fingers in staccato tattoo over the studs of his bracer. 'What, you haven't been listening?'

Dakar harkened. Through a lull in the gusts, amid the white hiss of spray, he belatedly detected a snatched fragment of song. The notes were an exquisite rendition in minor, and the phrases of lyric Paravian.

'That's no one's grief for a fallen comrade,' Vhandon observed, his brute manner sharpened to an astuteness the Mad Prophet found more disturbing.

Talvish said, impatient, 'Man, if your prince is heart torn for any one thing, it's the fact he can't break his self-imposed exile without bringing dire ruin upon everyone that he cares about. If he turns back from here, I'd stake my own neck, his decision won't be made willingly.'

Nor was the assessment of character inaccurate. By then, Dakar had absorbed the raw gist; Arithon bled off his anguish in song, his haunting, sweet tribute for the Koriani enchantress who had irrevocably captured his heart. All the salt sea would not be enough to close the wound of that sorrow. Each mile the *Khetienn* logged widened a separation that remained a living torment to them both.

In a gossamer fabric raised soaring over the complaint of the ship's timbers, his melody described a suffering as lucid as etched glass. Arithon sang, in the absence of choice. His bitterness for the years that must lie ahead, filled with the hard forces of water and wind: the vistas of a ship's lonely passage, far removed from the sweet summer smell of earth's greenery, poured into expression in clean sound. His art became his inadequate solace. The vulnerability, the pain, the sheer longing of spirit that cried out for its exquisite, paired match shaped an agony beyond all wounding.

Dakar's resolve crumbled. He found that he lacked the ice-cold nerve, after all, to invade the quarterdeck and badger the singer's snatched solitude. His sigh commingled with the next risen gust, while spray flung chill runnels down his moon face, and sorrow pressed lead through his heartstrings.

'Ath, but who is she?' Talvish burst out, his throat wrung to tightness. Against his turned face, wind-lashed strands of blond hair wicked the salt tears from his cheeks.

'Her name is Elaira,' the Mad Prophet revealed, equally helpless in sympathy. 'And Vhandon is right, the point's moot. Conjecture or delusion, it scarcely matters whether Cattrick and his men are among the dead or the living. I presume we agree? Arithon s'Ffalenn can never be permitted to risk another entanglement with Desh-thiere's curse.'

Through the shudder as the vessel slapped spume off the next crashing wavecrest, neither one of the s'Brydion retainers delivered a word in agreement. Against that spiraling spell of wrought song, gestures came sooner than speech. The older, more taciturn Vhandon stirred first and snapped his sword back in its sheath. 'His Grace won't go back. Not since we've sworn our oath to protect him.'

But the younger, dancer-slight Talvish delivered the most punishing insight of all. 'If there was ever a crime against nature, it occurred on the hour your Teir's'Ffalenn was compelled to lay hand on a sword.'

'That's what Caolle once said,' the Mad Prophet conceded, struck through by undying grief. He did not add that the *caithdein*'s late war captain had taken hard knocks and hot argument before he ever reached that understanding of the torn thread in Arithon's character. These retainers charged to guard the s'Ffalenn prince's safety possessed a fearfully well honed perception. Through the long years ahead, to the ominous event that would one day match Sethvir's forecast, Dakar could but hope this pair owned wit and strength enough to offset the Shadow Master's fiendish cleverness.

Ath help them all if his first fears were truth, and the two men proved to be the duke's spies, with s'Brydion loyalty turned to murder in support of Lysaer's powerful Alliance.

# Aftermath

The frank fascination which first drew Raiett Raven aboard Avenor's royal galley did not fade, but attached him to the side of his nephew, the Alliance Lord Commander, when Prince Lysaer examined the fire-torn ruin of his shipyard. Rain had fallen since the blaze. The huddle of officials and guarding men-at-arms reviewed the grim scene, while the tang of wet ash and carbon spiked the mud-sour miasma of ebb tide off the flats down the estuary. Of the sheds and the timbers, the steam boxes and sail loft, nothing remained but charred beams, tumbled in heaps, or stuck skyward like arthritic fingers. If the drizzle had stopped, the sky remained clouded. The cobbled entry wore a slippery sheen of condensation that made the most careful step treacherous.

No one who attended that royal delegation need argue over the aftermath. The enterprise was a total loss.

'They must have purloined the pitch barrels from the stores to fuel the fires that swept through the buildings. The whole place went up in a whirlwind of flame, just that fast. Bucket brigades formed by the garrison had no chance from the outset.' Riverton's stoop-shouldered mayor flanked the Blessed Prince, morose in quilted gray velvet. 'The heat and the smoke were too thick. Our siege-trained captains couldn't salvage even the steel tools.' He tugged at the drooping end of his mustache, sad eyed and white muzzled as a tracking hound who had outworn the vigor of the hunt. 'Your Grace, I am grieved that misfortune has struck down the trust you placed in my city.'

Diamonds shimmered in the pallid air as Lysaer broke his long stillness. 'Riverton will not shoulder the blame. Nor would I see the craftsmen suffer, stripped of their livelihood.' He snapped his fingers. A liveried secretary delved into a satchel and extricated a sheaf of documents. 'These are copies,' Lysaer said. 'The first list includes the men I wish to interview. The second is compiled from the shipyard's last payroll. By nightfall, I need the verified names and numbers of each worker's dependent family. For the loyal ones still in residence here, there will be a crown pension to keep them until my shipworks can be refounded. When that time comes, the laborers will be given the option to resume work or remake their own fortunes elsewhere.'

'That's wondrously generous.' The mayor dabbed at his rheumy eyes. 'More than one goodwife will bless your royal name for the children that will not go hungry.'

Lysaer pressed on, brisk, and outlined fair procedure for reimbursements to outside suppliers, for by ruthless design, the ledgers and records in Cattrick's loft had been destroyed along with the incriminating ships' drawings. 'The wreckage was caused by malefactors acting against the crown interests of Tysan. Therefore, on my word, the regency gives full promise the hardship won't fall on the shoulders of innocents.'

Riverton's overcome mayor bent to one stiffened knee and embarked on effusive words of thanks. The Blessed Prince heard him through, his smile gracious. He then took his leave, together with his guard and his coterie of councilmen, who all looked relieved for the chance to ease their sore feet. By the gate, he acknowledged the cloaked figure of Raiett Raven, watching his effortless dance of diplomacy with experienced sophistication.

Lysaer paused. The train of groomed officials tagged his heels with carefully guarded impatience while he held the wily Hanshire statesman under his waiting regard.

After a moment, the comment he expected was offered in stiletto sharp phrases. 'Well-done.' Raiett's thin lips flexed, more smirk than smile. 'A prince who keeps enemies could not hold good craftsmen in service if he left them exposed to predation.'

For a moment, the air seemed to crackle between the two men, the prince white clad and shimmering against the overcast, and Raiett in his black, thin and ascetic, with the piercing gaze of a prophet.

Lysaer spoke at last through a fragile tension. 'Since you can't be the dove and accept my act for the charitable welfare of children, then consider the fact I'll outlive them.'

Raiett raised an eyebrow, no whit overawed by the charismatic impact of his adversary's royal presence. 'They'll grow up in your debt, and become fodder for crows as adults?'

Lysaer accepted that searing riposte with equanimity. 'It was not the crow I wished to court at this time, but the fox underneath his dark feathers. Would you care to come along and witness the next round of interviews?'

Surprise rearranged the shrewd wrinkles pinched at the corners of Raiett's eyes. 'I would,' he admitted, and fell into step. The guardsmen, councilmen, and delegate observers moved reluctantly aside and made space for him.

So passed the afternoon, the whitewashed wing where the harbor-master's copyists penned out duplicate records made to serve as the prince's chamber of audience. Two rows of lancet windows let in the light, a sea-damp spring breeze too sluggish to flush the ingrained smells of charcoal and ink, and a pent-up must of candle smoke and winter woolens. Everything echoed, the floors being wood, and the stone walls devoid of woven tapestries. Rank accorded Lysaer the only leather armchair. The copyist's desks and benches were occupied by his councilmen and city ministers, which left the royal secretary use of the lectern, vacated at need by the fussy old man who recited the ledgers and bills of lading for Riverton's half dozen scribes.

The royal guards were left standing along those walls and corners uncluttered by aumbries and shelves.

Raiett Raven did not sit, but took station behind the prince's left shoulder, arms folded, his short hair peppered silver against the jet ruffle of his collar. He remained statue patient, while the room filled and heated with the close, nervous sweat of the craftsmen called in to be questioned. He followed the tedious nuance of each inquiry; watched the laborers brought in, fidgeting and embarrassed in their plainspun, workaday clothing. Some trembled. At first, most evaded the direct gaze of their prince, though his mien was not harsh or forbidding. Lysaer asked them to speak, to tell what they knew, without first defining the subject.

The young and the brash began with excuses, or hot denials that they knew of any treason. Prince Lysaer listened. He said nothing to alarm, nor did he imply accusation. His manner most subtly failed to fan the flame of fast-spoken, defensive fear. In time, even the most surly men eased and warmed to his presence. The true facts emerged then, the small fragments of happenstance linking into seemingly inconsequential strings of detail that gradually shaded into a wider picture.

The older craftsmen, the most sensible and steadfast, volunteered the least. They likely recalled more, but were experienced enough not to trust openly. Yet when presented with the suggestion that Lysaer regarded them as victims of malice whose misfortune now could be shared between friends, even the most reticent set down their guard and admitted that Mearn had a volatile temperament and an untrustworthy, secretive character.

'Those two traits make damned unlikely bedmates,' one bald-headed fastener observed. He blotted his damp palms on the seat of his breeches, and added in frowning hindsight, ''Twas strange now I think on it. Master Cattrick seemed inwardly tormented by something until this past autumn, when s'Brydion became his nightly companion over beer.'

'No one overheard anything?' Lysaer asked, not for pressure, but to jog loose opinions that by now were six months faded.

The craftsman scraped his profusely stubbled chin. 'Too much noise in any dockside tavern to hear aught, unless it's shouted straight into your ear. Mearn and Cattrick were cronies, that I can swear, but not even rumor sprang up to fathom the reason.'

'You're a good man,' said Lysaer. 'Take my blessing home to your family.' Diamonds flashed at his gesture as he casually granted his royal leave to depart.

The next laborer stepped in, a young apprentice sawyer who could elaborate on the favors of every shanty whore, and who knew which dives brewed the best hops. 'Only saw Cattrick up close on pay day.' His eyes darted sidewards as he shrugged his gangling shoulders. Too plainly, his knowledge of master craftsmen consisted of jocular quips to evade being dressed down for shirking.

The next man came in, and the next after that, until the chamber grew stale with the penned heat of boredom, and the exhaustive list was completed. No conclusive evidence had been mined from those common southshore accents. By close of day, no craftsman revealed any pact to prove or belie Mearn's allegiance. The council members and dignitaries dragged in to bear witness shifted in their hard seats, grown restive in crushed velvets and silks.

In the end, the florid envoy from Erdane voiced the dismal conclusion, his voice tight with frustration. 'The proof we could have examined for veracity was deliberately sunk beyond reach.' Incontestable truth: the executed bodies of the primary culprits now rested fathoms deep in the sea.

A scintillant sparkle of gemstones marked time as Prince Lysaer laced his ringed fingers on the studded arms of his chair. He looked inhumanly fresh. The shimmer of his gold-and-white silk became a disjointed patch of refinement against the lymed stone at his back. 'No man can be justly arraigned on suspicion. Nor can a trial be held without grounds. Therefore, we shall adjourn until tomorrow, and take the necessary steps to make plans for closer security in the future.'

Hot opinions notwithstanding, Lysaer was firm. He fielded the smattering of vehement protest and quashed outright one guildsman's insistent demand to incarcerate both s'Brydion brothers for additional questioning. The predictable clamor arose over slave oarsmen, and the looming prospect of more forfeited profits with King Eldir's ban backed by sorcery.

'I will make disposition through policy,' Lysaer assured, his dismissal inarguably final. 'No guild will lose its prosperity. Enough said. The solution will keep well enough 'til tomorrow.'

The councilmen filed out, grumbling among themselves, the last and most heavyset slowest to go, arising to the creak of overtaxed benches and the sigh of rearranged clothing.

When the doorway finally emptied, Raiett Raven remained, unmoved at the prince's shoulder.

Lysaer turned and regarded him. Legs crossed at the knee, one relaxed elbow hooked over the chairback, he appeared all serene equanimity. His hair gleamed in the light of crude candles like the bias burnished on gold leaf, while his grave glance encompassed the statesman from Hanshire. 'You look like a man with something to say.'

'You want my opinion?' Raiett countered, prying, even jabbing at that lordly veneer to test what sort of man breathed beneath it.

Unblinking, Lysaer said, 'Do you have one?'

The mock insult sparked Raiett to the raised ghost of a smile. 'You could start there. With one.'

Lysaer dispensed with formalities then, linking his elegant, capable fingers and stretching his arms over his head. 'What do you think I should say to my council tomorrow?'

But Raiett ignored that venue. He started to pace, the crisp snap of his footfalls marking the measure of a suddenly private conference. 'I would send a man to the stockyards and slaughter pens asking if s'Brydion silver had been spent on bull's bones, legs of carcasses, even wax.'

'Then you think they hung effigies to shield living men?' Lysaer raised an eyebrow, apparently amused. 'Go on.'

'I think there's conspiracy and deep treason, yes, masked behind effusive clan bluster and arrogance.' Raiett paused by the windows, a stark, faceless outline against the bruised colors of sunset. 'Why else should Cattrick and his close henchmen have removed their families from Riverton last month? If you cast your net wider, you could have that war to key the next stage of your empire.'

Lysaer s'Ilessid laughed outright, his delight the expansive bright edge of reflection thrown off a sliver of crystal. 'You're a treasure. What made you think I want war?'

And Raiett stopped again, poised in stunned reassessment. 'No one knows you,' he demurred.

'That's no viable truth. Everyone knows me.' Lysaer stood up, his silk and his gold and his diamonds a flame of moving distraction. 'I am the land's hope of the light to triumph and banish the darkness.'

'So men say,' Raiett said, calmly neutral. 'I might ask for the truth.'

'You'll settle for the gift of my confidence.' Lysaer did not wait, nor allow further opening to deflect the bent of his offering.

'I will not seek to expose the s'Brydion.' Unemotional as his jewels, he met his Hanshire adversary's pale eyes with his most disconcerting directness. 'They have made a public issue of their honesty, and no definitive fact has arisen to defame their true name. For my part, I shall show royal grace and believe them. They remain my cherished allies until the day someone brings me incontrovertible proof of their perfidy. On that hour, if it comes, my judgment will fall as the spear from the hand of the almighty.'

Raiett said nothing, but stared, cold still, while the indrawn breath of revelation chilled all the restless conjecture from his mind. 'No one knows you,' he repeated as he strove to grasp the fragmented gist: that *if Cattrick were ever to be seen alive, the wave of blind outrage would catalyze an emotional explosion, and unleash fuel for war on a scale to make today's resource seem a pittance.* 'You're saving the stab in the back for much later, Dharkaron pity us. I can't fathom the reason. I'm not sure I wish to know anything else.' Then, struck to a flash insight, the point-blank demand, 'What do you want of me?'

Lysaer never wavered, never lowered his searingly candid blue eyes. 'Your trade contacts in Etarra, your connections in the east, your superb network of informants, and lastly, whatever means the Koriani say you have of hiding your plans from the eyes of arcane scryers.'

Raiett jerked back with unvarnished surprise. 'You know me too well.'

'I attend the ranking subjects in my kingdom,' Lysaer stated, his natural candor enough to knit back a seam cracked into primal bedrock. 'There lies my heart, and my focus of interest until the hour the Spinner of Darkness breaks the peace. You are the Mayor of Hanshire's brother. He has no love for the reinstatement of s'Ilessid monarchy, I know. But as I am the appointed regent for the next crown prince of Tysan, it is my place to ask: will you serve the wider cause of this land, for the Light, and for the sake of continued prosperity?'

The pull was enormous, to give way in trust, to join with the serene power of this prince and win the absolute security of his protection.

Raiett Raven was no green boy. He had the hardened years to resist starstruck awe; should have owned enough grit and world-weary cynicism to avoid being swept off his feet. All the same, the blind fervency ignited him anyway.

'State your needs,' he said, shocked for the slip of giving his outright consent before even a pause for reasonable thought, or a grueling discussion of terms. Then, more surprising, the gush of relief that irresistible instinct had leaped past all sensible constraints. More honest in word than he had been in years, Raiett Raven completed his pledge. 'My resources might not be as deep as you think, but if Hanshire can benefit, you'll have them.'

Two hours later, in circumspect talk with his nephew, Sulfin Evend, Raiett shook his head in bemusement. 'Your Blessed Prince had better have real gifts to back up the divine guidance he's claiming. For if he does not, his powers of persuasion are dauntless enough to set all this world marching in the blood and fire of his designed cause.'

# Inner Cabal

The s'Brydion state galley docked at Avenor under the safe conduct of royal favor and disarmed the tense prospect of war. Fresh dispatches and news followed daily.

Prince Lysaer sent word of his pending return amid a flurry of planning, his bellicose trade guilds and disgruntled craftsmen soothed over by his letter of decision to transfer the royal shipworks from the Riverton estuary to the close-guarded harbor of Hanshire. The crotchety mayor there had changed heart and become his close crony, rumor held.

Princess Ellaine had no better means to gauge the contrary currents of politics. Her mannered requests to share in the contents of crown correspondence had seen swift rebuff by Gace Steward. Quietly persistent, she stood on her rank, until a more forceful refusal from Lysaer's High Priest of the Light, Cerebeld, forbade access to the council hall's secretaries. Too well bred to attempt obstructive argument, Ellaine retired, still determined.

She engaged her woman's resources. Word filtered down from the merchant's servants, through the dressmaker's seamstress, that the crown train from Avenor now moved about in a flock of new advisors, all of whom deferred to the black-cloaked presence of Raiett Raven. Never a wayward spirit, but too intelligent not to chafe at her enforced state of ignorance, Ellaine sought the sage advice of her maid, and eschewed the colors of state that would be no boon to her complexion. She chose to greet her royal husband on his homecoming, gowned in a masterwork of damascened peach silk, a wrap of pearl lace on bare shoulders.

The hour the s'Ilessid state galley reached port, the sun fell like thin honey from a sky of washed blue. The dockside pageantry of bunting and banners was snapped by a capricious westerly. The war fleet hove in, chased by that same brisk tail wind. Ellaine waited inside the lacquered royal carriage while the galleys shipped their flashing, wet oars and dropped anchor. The flag vessel, under command of her stout captain, completed her dashing run to the wharf. Dock lines were secured to a bustle of orders. The heralds stationed on shore for the fanfare battled the fierce tug on the banners draped from their shining brass horns.

Ellaine bided, hands clasped, until the clarion blast from the trumpets announced Lysaer's presence on deck. Her soft voice delivered firm orders to the footman, and the liveried grooms held open the carriage's star and crown blazoned door. They bowed to her as she swept down onto the wharf. Then her guardsmen and entourage closed about her to shield from the buffeting press of the onlookers who crammed the harborfront breakwater. Behind, enclosed in a cordon of men-at-arms, the rowed carriages and the caparisoned horses were held ready for the prince and his high-ranking councilmen.

Ellaine gathered her skirts in cool hands. Given no better recourse for her time than frivolous entertainment, she had arranged those arenas left to her control with meticulous practicality. Her mahogany tresses had been done up in combs, a judicious few ends set in dangling, pert ringlets that the wayward gusts finished to a look that was artfully saucy. Image was the only weapon she had, and, undaunted, she prepared to wring every advantage.

Across the weathered platform of the wharf, men made the galley's lines fast to the bollards. Gulls screamed and wove overhead, while the officials on board gathered in impatience for the deckhands to run out the gangway. Acutely aware that the hats and high plumes showed no fair head among them, Ellaine stayed poised, willing her stilled hands not to fidget and wishing her gloved palms were not damp with anxiety.

The plank with its posts and rope railing thudded home, shivering the wharf underfoot. The crowding officials did not press to disembark, but parted with sudden, obsequious energy as a figure emerged from the deckhouse behind them.

This one wore white satin and ermine, and a presence to dazzle the unwary.

The roar of acclaim from the onlookers rocked the waterfront. The Prince of the Light acknowledged the tribute with raised hands. Then he stepped out, the woven chain clasped at the waist of his doublet shining pale gold in the glancing fall of spring sunlight.

Ellaine swept forward as he moved down the gangway, her curtsy pooling a billow of peach silk across his egress to the shore. 'My Lord Prince,' she addressed, her dulcet syllables thin as scratched crystal against the coarse adulation of the crowds.

Prince Lysaer reached out a ringed hand and raised her. His clasp of embrace scarcely impressed any sensation at all through the thin cloth of her bodice, and his lips missed contact with her upturned cheek by an invisible fraction. His affection pure show, he guided her in step, no doubt intending to pass her off to her attendants with a sparkling flourish of mimed gallantry.

Except that Ellaine had foreseen, and obstructed retreat. Her strategic forethought had positioned the s'Ilessid royal carriage such that her husband must take public leave and abandon her if he wished to go mounted to the palace.

The prince accepted the defeat with equanimity, his smile gracious, and his poise tempered steel. He turned his head, said something to the dignitaries still on the galley that raised a spontaneous burst of laughter. Through the dazzle thrown off his sun-struck diamonds, and the matchless strength of his confidence, Ellaine searched for the object of his concern, no doubt the same circumstance that had his seneschal and his Lord Commander standing shoulder to shoulder in disapproval.

Her gaze caught on a figure in sable whose lean face she did not recognize.

'You will not have met the man who was once the Mayor of Hanshire's First Counselor,' Lysaer said, as though he had read her searching thoughts.

Ellaine flashed him a quick, nervous glance. 'Not Raiett, the one known as Raven?'

Lysaer tipped his head in acknowledgment, then caught her elbow to draw her away. At his heels, the man who claimed that fearfully powerful name remained to oversee the off-loading of an ironbound trunk that appeared to carry something precious, or an item of extreme fragility to judge by the number of men who clustered to nursemaid its arrival.

Ellaine had heard Raiett's reputation linked with sorceries, as well as the darker policies set in place by the Mayor of Hanshire.

Again Lysaer read her, plainly as if her thoughts were inscribed on fresh parchment. 'You have nothing to fear.' He steered her up the carriage stair, quick hands gathering her lavish skirts and bundling them clear of the doorway as she sat on the velvet upholstery. The presence and the beauty of him, in that thoughtless courtesy, could not but sear her woman's heart. Nor could she stop the sped beat of her pulse, or the quick stab of longing that caught her as she observed him at close quarters, his effortless bearing as fluid as light as he settled himself by her side.

No expression, no courtesy, no casual handling betrayed his seemingly chance-met intent to touch her as little as possible.

Nor did he fail to smile at the groom who closed the carriage door, granting Ellaine the fleeting victory of a hard-fought few moments of privacy. She responded, hands folded to keep her humid gloves from imprinting telltale ripples in her silk. 'Do you really believe your fear can be helped by keeping me in total ignorance?'

Lysaer turned from the glass window, eyes wide-open with a candor that held the passionless obstinacy of a glacier. 'I married a Westlands woman for the customs of deportment and propriety, that matters of state will not be broached in my bedchamber.'

Ellaine flushed. Her fists clenched. She forced her gaze rigid, too aware that the least movement of her lashes might spill the hot flood of the tears she refused to shed. 'Then in your presence, I am the broodmare without a mind?'

Lysaer leaned back as the vehicle swayed to the onboarding weight of its grooms. His own hands were stilled, his diamond rings like lit water, sparkling to the jolt as the driver on the box shook up the team and the traces creaked taut to the first rolling grind of the wheels. He cut her no slack. 'You will have no standing in this realm, except the earned grace you'll receive when you have borne this kingdom's next crown prince. Which brings us to the point, does it not? Are you bearing?'

'What?' Ellaine's second, more violent flush chased her tears to anger and confusion.

Lysaer regarded her, cat still. 'I asked, are you carrying a child for the realm?'

Her color ebbed, pink to white on the cusp of her sharply caught breath. With restored composure, she answered, 'Not yet.'

The carriage jolted over the marble curb and into the open street, to a muffled swell of noise from the onlookers. Perhaps for the benefit of those who might catch a glimpse through the carriage window, Lysaer took her hand, touched his lips to her glove, and inclined his head, smiling. 'Then, my fair bride, you will instruct your maids to bring spirits and fresh linens as they did on the night of your wedding. Expect me during the hour before midnight. This time, I suggest you drink enough brandy to be comfortable before I arrive in your bedchamber.'

'I dislike the principle as well as the brandy.' Ellaine's voice shook as she strove to stem ebbing courage.

'Do as you please, then,' Lysaer said, equable. 'For my part, the spirits are necessity.'

If he had hoped to demolish her spirit, the attempt failed. Tears vanquished, Ellaine regarded him with the hurt blazing like a war banner in the depths of her deer-dark eyes. 'That's sheer bad manners, if not straight cowardice, to unload your bitterness on me.'

Half-turned to bestow another smiling salute to his admirers outside the window, Lysaer paused a fractional second, then completed his gesture on the strength of his inborn royal pride. When he faced her again, he was not vindictive. Instead, his face held a vulnerability whose depth of honesty was wounding. 'I will speak my heart to you just this once, Lady Ellaine. You are my wife, and the princess of this realm, and the mother who will bear the next high king. As such, your value is inestimable. Your worth as a weapon to my enemy's hand represents a prize behind reckoning.'

Ellaine challenged. 'We are all no more than pieces upon the board of your war against shadow?'

'This union we have made for the good of the land will not stand firm upon the foundations of your naïveté.' Lysaer shut his eyes, not before a cutting slice of his inner pain showed through. The hand in his lap now was hardened into a fist of sharp rings and white knuckles. 'Lady, I do not hate you. But neither do I dare allow even small affection, for *you must understand*: if I am made vulnerable, my cause must fail. Once, I made that mistake. For my love of Lady Talith, the cost became thirty thousand lives, dead in cold blood in the dust of Dier Kenton Vale. You are the wife who will bear Tysan's heir. My trust in your hands, for the weal of mankind, demands that you never become the crack in the bastion that foes can use to let in the dark.'

He did not turn away as the tears came and spilled silver rivulets down her cheeks. His hands were not cold, or remote, as he flicked out his handkerchief and deftly caught the runoff before it could splash her fine silk. 'You do understand,' he said, gentle enough to brand her forever as a needy, inadequate spirit.

'I'm not so strong,' she admitted, striving to match the demand of his unbending royal stature. She discovered, in all ways, she lacked the unflinching nerve to brazen through the last steps of her game plan.

Chill quiet reigned as Ellaine realized they had arrived. Lysaer's concerned gaze upon her suggested that, somehow, she was expected to recover her wits and stand up. They would need to step from the carriage together.

Then, as a commander on a battlefield gauged the temper of his troops, the prince realized she was overfaced. A saddened, soft smile bent the corners of his mouth. 'It would seem we'll be giving the courtiers a show after all.'

He bent, caught her close, and scooped her limp weight against his chest, then banged the carriage door open with an impatient foot. As if she were featherweight, he lifted her out, with her moist cheek sheltered against his neck. The grooms fell away in astonishment. Smiling guardsmen averted their faces as he bore her across the cobbled apron and up the marble stair to the entry. There he paused, head bent to hers. Through what every onlooker interpreted as the searing passion of his kiss, he whispered, 'Your handmaid is inside and ready to receive you. For both of our sakes, I beg you never to be so foolish as to attempt a repeat performance.'

Another smooth stride saw the prince past the doorway. The firm click as the heavy double panel was pulled shut by the servants set final closure to hope and a dream whose fierce edge had turned inward to wound a girl's tender heart.

Ellaine felt Lysaer's cool hands set her down, then melt back, leaving her supported by the anxious clasp of her handmaid. The tears still fell unchecked down her face, though for pride's sake she withheld from sobbing. In the hours that passed, retired in privacy, she endured the dull ache that burned through the tisanes the solicitous palace healer insisted would bring her ease.

The drugged syrups gave no reprieve from the truth: that it had been her own defenses breached on that foray. If Lysaer s'Ilessid could refuse human feeling in the dedicated cause of the Light, she was made of no such stern stuff. Nor could her young heart be schooled to withstand even the brilliant, enameled facade he granted the tradesman who gawped on the street.

Beyond the sanctum of the princess's apartments, other needs laid claim to the Divine Prince's attention. The council hall at Avenor pulsed to the clamor of deferred politics. The residual public outcry over the burned ships resounded to thorny complaint over losses to trade, while the sea routes through Havish remained inaccessible to galleys bearing slave oarsmen.

Having been too preoccupied to pay heed to the first breathless questions flung from the crowd lining the wharf as he landed, Lysaer s'Ilessid released his public statement, and a crown pledge to make disposition. He greeted the dignitaries still in residence from Erdane, and deflected Ellaine's father with sober confirmation that the dower gold had vanished with the shipyard. Then he dismissed social nicety to honor the demands of his guildsmen.

He called an immediate session with the high officers of the realm, and those council members who had returned with his royal galley. To everyone's astonishment, he acceded to demand. With no war in the offing, excess troops would be disbanded. Funds reserved for new weapons and captain's pay would be reallocated. Hard heads and hot rhetoric would hammer out terms for relief in coin weight sums and lowered tariffs.

Hurled from hand-wringing despair to backslapping euphoria, Tysan's merchants never paused to question Prince Lysaer's stunning volte-face. If one or two among them showed concern for threat of shadow, Lord Commander Sulfin Evend raised no voice to back them. Worry for the uncertain future remained overshadowed by the heat of present crisis.

At sundown, clad in shimmering finery, Prince Lysaer rejoined his princess, her peaked looks made presentable by her maid's skill with powders and paint. The newly wedded couple led the formal entrance to the state dinner held to commemorate the royal homecoming. The s'Brydion brothers Mearn and Parrien were given a prominent position in her train, a definitive indication their loyalty remained in the good grace of Tysan's crown interests. Once the banquet began, the princess departed to eat a light supper in private.

The royal bed was made ready by soft-footed servants. Lady Ellaine endured through her disrobing, then retired, wrapped in new ribbons and a nightrobe of rose velvet scented with costly perfume. His Grace arrived later, his step too carefully firm and his diction precise as a scalpel as he excused her handmaid and servants.

She had chosen the numbness of the brandy after all. Her yielding, limp sweetness granted a release that, very nearly, undid the locked cage on his heart. As Prince Lysaer completed his conjugal duty to the realm, only the aged handmaid who showed him the door afterward ever knew how nearly the lady had come to winning the hand fate had dealt her. She prayed to dame fortune, and to every power she knew, that Lysaer s'Ilessid, Prince of the Light, had not yet conceived the heir he desired for Tysan.

With sorrow the handmaid understood: a hurried moment's work between the sheets might too easily become the last time that husband and wife met as intimates.

The full moon came and went. On Avenor's broad dales, the season warmed toward summer. The hardy foliage of the oaks spun the hills in glossy, new green, and the tiny, peridot knots of new apples took the place of bursting blossoms. The wedding guests who had enjoyed Avenor's bounteous hospitality departed at last on dry roads; trade moved as the thaws opened the high Pass of Orlan. The s'Brydion state galley cast off for home port in the east, and left behind a court representative who was a more distant blood relative to maintain the duke's pledge of alliance. The man was given quarters less lavish than his predecessor; nor was he made privy to the trusted inner circle secretly known to itself as the Cabal of Light.

With the guildsmen and trade factions settled to mollified prosperity, Lysaer s'Ilessid retired to the guarded tower sanctum, where he met with those chosen few. Since the failed schism with s'Brydion had gutted their hopes for a clan war to draw the unpledged eastern cities under the sunwheel standard, talk and rampant speculation had circled like a balked dog pack. Just what the Prince of the Light would do next became the spearhead of every conversation. Until the sabotaged ships were replaced, there could be no expansion. The inexorable bleeding of profits to ease trade deficits would keep the royal treasury hobbled. Trained troops could not be replaced at short notice. Nor would the minions of shadow and sorcery rest through the years of recovery.

The volatile flood of complaint reached full spate on the instant Lysaer s'Ilessid arrived and assumed his too-long-vacant seat.

'Save us all!' The realm's seneschal shoved erect in vociferous objection. 'What is the purpose of the Alliance if not to eradicate clan interference with trade and collusion with the Master of Shadow?'

'What use to pursue practitioners of magecraft if they simply flee over the border to take sanctuary under the High King of Havish?' cried Crown Examiner Vorrice. His full sleeve flapped to his vehement gesture as he shouted down other colleagues. 'Since you've reduced the field companies, all men who are bound to cause evil in the world will simply fly to roost under the protection of Eldir's banner!'

Lysaer did not answer, but let the talk swell and tangle, even to the concern raised by Lord Mayor Skannt, that the headhunters' guilds were going to balk at hard service if purse strings stayed tight and bounties were halved to save bullion.

Lord Koshlin accosted in brutal practicality, 'If the barbarians enslaved by crown policy are put to the block, the trade galleys could recover their unobstructed passage through port towns to the south.'

'Let the scum run to Havish, why care?' Gace Steward dismissed with contentious enjoyment. 'We'll just use the peace to build forces and wealth, then deal with King Eldir through an invasion.'

Silence, while heads turned and tilted, to measure how Lysaer s'Ilessid would react to a statement that, perhaps, might have gone too far.

The Prince of the Light gave them back no reaction. His hands remained stilled. Touched by more light than the fluttering flames in the high candelabra seemed to warrant, his pristine white clothing reflected a fine nimbus against the dimmer wool tapestry, sewn with the blazon of Tysan. A drawn minute passed, while the dagged velvet curtains billowed in the sea breeze through the cracked casement. From the yard far below, the whistle of the kennelman mingled with the rattle of chain and the bay of idle tracking hounds, who leaped at their tethers to be fed.

While the drawn pause extended, and the expectant atmosphere became brittle to cracking with pressure, Prince Lysaer unlaced his fingers to a snapping glitter of rings. His smile was butter as he urged, 'Do go on. Every man present is free to air his opinion.'

The settled strength of his patience made the yap of his councilmen all of a sudden seem foolish. Given no response and no target, the majority subsided in embarrassment. Red to the wattles, the seneschal cleared his throat. Skannt fingered his knives, flushed with speculation, while others repressed the urge to whisper among themselves. The High Priest of the Light, Cerebeld, was the sole one among them who felt no discomfort, and yet, these chosen few were not fools.

'Your Grace we are listening,' noted the Minister of the Royal Treasury, his narrowed, pale eyes most observant. 'If you've already chosen our course for the future, dare I ask what's afoot?'

A sharp tap at the door interrupted. Lysaer's placating neutrality broke into a piquant smile. 'Raise the latch and accept my invitation to find out.'

The Minister of the Royal Treasury deferred, since Gace Steward would leap to the task out of jealous intent to be first.

The door swung wide to reveal Sulfin Evend reversing the pommel of the dagger just used to rap at the panel. Beyond the pebbled gleam of his mail shirt, a silver-haired visitor clad in elegant black: Raiett Raven awaited admittance.

'What's this!' burst out Vorrice.

The others rammed straight, declaiming, as the presence of an unsworn stranger threatened to ignite a fresh round of clamor.

'Protection,' said Lysaer, then bade his Lord Commander and the Mayor of Hanshire's former advisor to make free and enter with his welcome. 'Proceed as we planned,' he added to Raiett, who carried a coffer set with inlay and gold studs tucked into the crook of his elbow.

As though he were not made the target of jealous resentment from men who guarded their predatory ambitions, Raiett advanced. His tread made no sound on the chill flagstone floors. His sable clothing seemed to swallow the candlelight and knit his slender frame into the outlying shadows. Against the soft dark, his lean hands stood out, each motion distinct as he set down his burden and unlocked the top with a key that hung from a chain at his neck. The lid opened with the same oiled ease of precise workmanship. Raiett drew out a padded silk bag and deftly loosened the drawstrings.

All eyes in the chamber stayed fixed upon him, yet his features showed nerveless detachment. He reached inside and drew out a fist-sized item that gleamed with the ocher patina of old bone.

The tower had niches built into the brick walls, inset with high arches for candles. Raiett placed the first object on the brick sill, and the flare of wax flame roused the heart's blood sparkle of a jewel. The artifact was a skull the size of a cat's, but elongated and set with fangs and tearing incisors. The crown was inlaid with a circle of jet, and inside that, crimped in a timeworn copper bezel, glimmered a cabochon ruby.

Vorrice stirred upright in alarm. 'In the Name of the Light, what is that?'

'The skull from an unborn dragon.' Matter-of-fact to the point of cold arrogance, Raiett rounded the table and moved on to the west wall, where he reached into the coffer and removed another silk bag, then a relic as unsettling as the first. The sockets of the eyes slanted, filled with shifting shadow, as though the creature's dead mind still flickered, watching from inner caverns of cold bone.

'Wards?' The Minister of the Royal Treasury chafed bony wrists to mask his creeping rush of gooseflesh.

'Just that.' Raiett's progress had carried him to the north wall. Soon a third skull grinned at its fellow to the east, the jewel in its crown a glittering ember. 'These are very ancient, extracted alive from the egg before hatching imprinted their self-awareness. Taken so, they are tools, their arcane qualities enslaved to the will of humanity.' On the last wall, he laid the fourth in the set. 'They watch. The consciousness of dragons is immortal, and the skulls keep a resonance of their awareness, even long after death.' He added, folding the now empty silk, 'This set was mislaid by a Koriani senior five hundred years ago, when a sisterhouse burned in the uprising.'

'Heresy!' Vorrice snapped. His vulture's profile swung and jutted toward Lysaer. 'What witchery is this? You've reduced the loyal war host. Are you also turned by evil to embrace the very powers of darkness?'

A lingering chill seemed to lace through the room, as if unseen currents of draft played from the locked gazes of four pairs of empty eye sockets; and yet, no such airs winnowed the candles. The flames stood up stark and still from their wicks, while the men in their velvets shrank and startled.

Into that uneasy discomfort, Lysaer s'Ilessid gave measured opinion. 'How else to avert the gaze of a Sorcerer than to use powers of spellcraft against him? A dragon-skull ward bends outside time and space. We'll need such protection. We cannot thwart shadow, or break the absolute tyranny of the Fellowship of Seven without long-range intentions. Henceforward, I would rather the Warden of Althain was not made privy to our talk.' White silk defied the encroachment of night as Lysaer rose to his feet. 'We are gathered here, in strict secrecy, for the purpose of arranging how the word and the light will be made *to span all five kingdoms on this continent . . .'*

**Spring 5654**

# Schism

At Althain Tower, caught in a rare nap, Sethvir springs bolt upright as a numbing, unnatural needle of cold pricks through the fabric of his earth-sense; within the same instant, the broad span of his awareness pinpoints the location of the event to a high tower chamber in Avenor, and the expletive he chooses to vent his annoyance singes nap off his age-worn velvet . . .

As the annihilating thread of drake magic slices into Athera's existence, an adept in the white robes of Ath's Brotherhood cries out in a hostel in Shaddorn; Morriel Prime snaps awake from a dream of fell darkness; a mage in a cavern stands immersed in conjecture; and a centaur guardian lifts his horned head and trembles, eyes liquid and wide with what could be grave sorrow, or a rage to seed fear in the wild heart of the four elements . . .

Unaware of the precedent loosed in Avenor, Lord Maenol, *caithdein* of the realm, briefs a clan messenger bound on to his counterpart in Rathain: 'You will say to Earl Jieret that his liege has fulfilled the debt of alliance he swore on my grandmother Maenalle's death. Our clan bloodlines are safely secured under Havish's sanctuary. In Caithwood, we are guarded by the wakened awareness of trees, and with ships to offset the s'Ilessid threat of slavery, we expect to endure through the next generation . . .

**Spring 5654**

# VIII. Strands

The vortex punched a hole through the world's quickened fabric, a canker of interference inflicted at Avenor by Raiett's use of the dragon-skull wards. Its influence raised a darkness that seared, an aberrant field of chaos that skewed the grand chord of Ath's creation. Sethvir reeled from the shock. Bent double as a stab like hot steel lanced the tuned sensitivity of the earth link, he snatched the desperate presence of mind to engage a spontaneous defense. Still shaken, wrung to wax pallor from the reserves just expended to shut out those deranging vibrations, he gasped a clipped epithet maligning the invention of wraith-cursed s'Ilessid royalty. Then he raked down his snarls of disarranged hair. His next thought sent Luhaine an immediate summons to appear at Althain Tower.

Though darkness had fallen, no candles burned in Sethvir's private quarters. The Sorcerer required none. Each object sang from the velvety gloom, a ribboned chorus of light and sound that underpinned all form and matter. Barefoot since the demise of his buskins, he padded, unerring, through his obstacle course of antiquities; the unending array of worn bridles and waxed twine threaded onto curved needles; the chess table with its carved ivory pieces left set in an ongoing match against Traithe; the candle molds and wicking string, jumbled alongside a Second Age dagger that had once been Cianor Sunlord's. Despite his rank haste, Sethvir took no wrong step. He reached the door running and scaled three flights of stairs to the tower's top-floor library.

His discorporate colleague awaited by then, a pool of dense cold in the corner by an aumbry overburdened with a clutch of smoothed river stones.

'We need a grand scrying,' Sethvir opened without pause. 'Fresh trouble at Avenor. Lysaer's just set a dragon-skull ward to mask a meeting with his high priest and inner cabal.'

Shocked by the dangerous ramifications, Luhaine whirled into motion. 'Where's Arithon?' he demanded point-blank. His unsettled passage riffled the opened books stacked in tipsy piles on the tabletop.

'Far out in the Cildein Ocean, and so far as I know, safe for the foreseeable future.' Sethvir's brow furrowed before the daunting task of clearing a space for his work.

A disturbed sheet of rice paper fluttered to the floor. Luhaine froze, his irritation a palpable tingle as his colleague recovered the scattered leaf, then scooped up an armload of pens and parchments and wedged them beneath the clawed stand of an armillary. 'Really, someone should summon a djinn to attend your housekeeping for you.'

Sethvir glanced up, miffed. 'That's sheerest folly. I'd never be able to find anything.'

Since a discorporate spirit made inefficient help with the physical task of tidying, Luhaine grumbled, 'Save us all, you're a creature born without logic.'

'I need no one's plodding, unnecessary logic! Certainly not to recall what's kept where.' Sethvir sneezed at the dust that puffed from the leather-bound tomes he thumped to rest on a stool seat. 'Bless me.' A touch of one finger and a sigil of stasis anchored the pile as it teetered. 'As if the glorious invention of the natural world could be sorted in record lists anyway.'

He brushed off his hands and plowed into a heap of scrolls. His ink-stained cuffs flapped around wrists chiseled by strain to a framework of bone and laced sinew.

'You're thin,' Luhaine snapped in concerned exasperation. 'Have you run out of butter again?'

'It went rancid because I ran out of time, a problem not likely to roost elsewhere.' Once the table's obsidian surface was swept clean, Sethvir delved into the depths of a store chest and recovered a square of black velvet. This, he spread over the mirror-polished stone to damp out misleading reflections.

'Strands?' Luhaine cried. '*You want to cast strands?* Shouldn't the others be called to stand witness?'

The Warden of Althain hooked a chair with his ankle and sat. 'They should.' His acerbity frayed into worry. 'Except for the problem that Tysan's crown examiners have grown unpleasantly vigilant.'

'You're worried for Traithe?' Luhaine's horrified presence shrank to a fixed point that scribed frost crystals on the fogged casement.

'Traithe,' Sethvir concurred. Sorrow oppressed his cragged features. 'Our hopes since the Mistwraith's defeat have borne bitter fruit, have they not? The affray over Caithwood last autumn has seeded redoubled unease. Lysaer's sunwheel patrols have grown vengefully diligent. Given fresh license by the prevailing fears, they're scouring the villages to rout out the practice of small magecraft.'

Silence, filled by a stark truth as ominous as a circling vulture. Traithe's crippled powers could not shake an armed troop without using the lesser practice of ceremonial magic. That exposure, in crossing Tysan alone, could send him to trial and arraignment; no idle threat with the Fellowship itself too overburdened to effect a reliable rescue.

'A telling victory for Lysaer, if one of our number was found to be mortally vulnerable.' Luhaine's distress snapped static from each bitten consonant. 'How did you break those ugly tidings to Traithe?'

Sethvir sighed. 'I told him point-blank: stay well clear of Tysan. Since Shand and Rathain are becoming as dangerous, I urged that he should avoid them. If he was called to the wilds of Melhalla, he should travel with extreme caution.'

Another lapse, while the two Fellowship colleagues strove not to dwell on the grief of Traithe's impaired freedom. Nor could they find aught but outright discomfort in the projected array of possibility. Lysaer s'Ilessid had begun the unthinkable next step in his Alliance campaign to quell magecraft. The facts were not kindly. If he revived the lapsed practice of drake magic, the warping fields set off by such spells posed a dire threat to those Sorcerers who were stripped of their flesh.

'The quandary sets barbs in every direction,' Sethvir agreed at due length.

Outside the latched casement, the spring constellations rode a sky like carpeted indigo. The library, by contrast, was a well of deep shadow, musked with dry ink and cured leather. That illusory coziness became sliced across by the point of sharp cold that was Luhaine, immersed in agitation far removed from his usual rambling remonstrance.

'If you have a suggestion to make, please speak,' Sethvir prodded. The roving chill discomposed his bare ankles, and the poisonous depth of his colleague's silence rankled him to unease. 'Lysaer's plots unsettle the earth link, and tracking your thought patterns out of clear air can be as bothersome as a Koriani sigil of confusion.'

'Very well.' Luhaine roved to the casement. 'Traithe's still at Water-fork?' Given Sethvir's clipped affirmation, the discorporate spirit rushed his point. 'I suggest we unkey the ruin at Earle and call a convocation of the Fellowship. Since Lysaer's intended muster in the east has been balked outright by the s'Brydion, we can expect he'll engage s'Ahelas farsight. I much doubt the plot hatched under dragon-skull wards will develop with short-term interests.'

'Summer solstice?' Sethvir asked, brows raised as his thoughts leaped ahead. 'Asandir's in East Halla, traveling south.' The timing meshed nicely. The itinerant Sorcerer had enough time to spare to review the methspawn at Mirthlvain. 'He could transfer directly from Methisle without difficulty. But Earle? That's extreme.'

'From Earle we can test the fault line through the Skyshiels,' Luhaine argued. 'That would eliminate the need to survey the state of the wards on the Mistwraith.' The discorporate Sorcerer revolved in place, as though he ticked each listed item off on the fingers he had lacked for centuries. 'As well, we can sound the far future. Better to see what Morriel Prime plans for that herder's son, Fionn Areth.'

'Morriel again?' Sethvir's cheeks dimpled into an expression more grimace than smile. 'If I didn't sense your total sincerity, I'd think you were growing obsessed.'

As Luhaine coalesced with offended fire, the Warden spoke swiftly and quelled him. 'Very well, we shall convene at Earle.' He arose, fingers locked through his beard as his thoughts reached out to his colleagues, then vaulted ahead to particulars. He needed to adjust the guarding wards on Althain Tower, and, of course, he would have to pack tea.

By default, Luhaine must fare on to West Shand. His work would unkey the protections left in force on the ruin that commanded the southern tip of the peninsula.

'Hindsight, of course,' the portly shade grumbled. 'I should've thought first, and suggested that onerous burden should fall to Kharadmon.'

'He wouldn't be weaned from the construct warding the star tracks, not under any circumstance.' Already on course for the stairwell, Sethvir shook off sharp chills. The remnant wraiths still at large on the splinter world of Marak yet posed an incalculable peril. Kharadmon's extreme anxiety would be justified. He alone had observed that decimated civilization firsthand. Nothing else in Athera's unsettled history had hardened his piquant character to such rabid dedication.

Nor had his Fellowship peers dismissed the grave danger he stood vigil to avert. On Kharadmon's warning, Asandir had bound Arithon s'Ffalenn under blood oath to survive. The star construct now standing guard for Athera had taken over a year's labor to dedicate. Even for the purpose of a Fellowship convocation, the wards must not stand unattended; if the wraiths left rootless and moiling on Marak ever crossed over to launch an attack, the odds they might spring the penultimate disaster became unthinkably final.

All living things on a green, breathing world would wither and perish.

'Avert all ill,' Luhaine breathed as he drifted through the casement.

Sethvir had no platitude to ease his departure. He passed from the library and descended the spiral stairwell, arms folded to his chest in vain hope the gesture might wring the cold dread from his heart.

Summer solstice shimmered heat waves on the thin spit of land that extended south of the Salt Fens. Sky lidded the savage, untenanted landscape like sheet-fired enamel, and baked the beleaguered shingle under relentless, diamond-bright sunlight. There, the earth's granite bones broke the dunes like dull knives. Seabirds stitched through the moan of the winds that scoured in off the ocean. Word held that the haunts from Second Age history walked over that damascened ribbon of shingle.

In stark fact, the unrest stamped into the site held origins far older. Sere stone and stripped dunes had endured their uneasy siege with the sea since the Age of Dragons, when past duels between drakes had raged in fell fire that remade the coast's western shoreline. The bay at the mouth of River Shonian in Falwood had been formed when the earth's crust collapsed, riven into a molten caldera by two packs locked in mortal conflict. There also lay the bones of Eckracken Challenger, king among drakes, who had fallen to earth, downed by cinder-burned wings. The tortured landscape itself had been carved as his mighty, scaled hulk writhed in the fatal throes of his agony. Legend held that the Salt Fens were formed on the breath of his death wish, as a balm for his terrible burns.

Although Althain Tower kept no record of myths, the first centaur guardians sent by Ath Creator to walk the land and bring healing had never gainsaid the tales of the peninsula's origins. Certainly Eckracken's bones rested still, wreathed in bog mists, the raging, angry dreams of his haunt surrounded and sealed by the spells of a Paravian grimward.

Nor had time erased the trace remnants of drake magic that resounded and whined through the wracked strata of the headland. The resonance of a wanton destruction lay imprinted in the broken stone. The left residue thrummed a subliminal ache through warm flesh where the silted sands mantled the roadside. Echoes still rang through the bedrock spine of feldspar and quartz-veined granite.

As spirit, less constrained to linear space, Luhaine sensed the burn of past forces as well. The sensation ranged like flaying steel through his etheric awareness. By preference he would have shunned this desolate tract; yet unpleasantly as the site could wear on pure spirit, how much worse for the colleague who had trodden these shores to deny Desh-thiere's access through South Gate. Traithe had survived the affray with his life, but at crippling cost to his mage powers.

Few places in Athera held the bitter brew of history ascribed to the strands of West Shand.

The ruin at Earle proved no exception in the annals of legend and lore. Once the fortress had held the first line of resistance against the Mistwraith's assault. The defenders who had shed blood and lost lives were a sorrow too lengthy to list; nor were their memories forgotten. At solstice dawn in Third Age 5654, the sky lay mantled and weeping.

Arrived to a fine drizzle smudged against louring cloud, Luhaine paused. Ahead stretched a sere landscape, with the ancient causeway a tumbled rut, and the puddles poured glass in the hollows. He surveyed the dark, notched profile of the fortress, its sea-broken walls strung with wild briar, and its landward rampart of shark-toothed crenels still whole between the closed fists of the watch keeps.

Though no Fellowship Sorcerer had witnessed the First Age, when Paravian heroes marched and perished to subdue the ravages of Eckracken's haunt, to mage-sight, those events stayed immediate. The infinite sadness scribed into stone transcended all barriers of time. Within recent memory, these sands had staged the hard-fought conflict begun with the Mistwraith's invasion. Here, five ruling high kings, endowed with the activated powers of their crown jewels, had stood their ground for the weal of the land. Shoulder to shoulder with Paravians, they died, to be replaced by grown heirs, who did likewise.

Luhaine gave homage to the past he had witnessed, his chosen expression a masterbard's requiem, and his voice as one with the wind, that hurled spume in raked sheets shoreward . . .

> *While four seasons turn under moon and sun,*
> *and the unicorns' springtide migration runs;*
> *while dancers leap to the solstice paeans,*
> *remember the names of the fallen sons.*
> *This life, the paid gift of their sacrifice –*
> *our brilliance of days their eternal night,*
> *forevermore. Oh, forever mourn them!*

Nor were all the mighty powers from those times faded, or dead, or silenced. One keep in the ruin remained pristine, unmarred by old wars and wild elements. Its fastness yet guarded a brooding awareness still primed for Athera's defense. Through the power focus at Earle, the centaur guardian, Seannory, had thrice laid his claim, and bound the four elements into service for need of the world's protection. The ritual release had not been enacted since the hour of the Mistwraith's confinement. Desh-thiere's ills were imprisoned, not undone. The threat to sunlight lay subdued, but not conquered; and there rested the reason for a Fellowship presence since Lysaer s'Ilessid's inner cabal had convened under the shadow of a dragon-skull ward.

To Luhaine fell the task of unkeying the locks which held the old fortress inviolate. His, the burden of subtlety and care, that the work he enacted disturb none of the primal seals of stasis that checked and balanced the forces within. Burdened by the gravity of the trials ahead, he descended to Earle Keep.

Where Seannory's guarding wards still reigned, the pale granite blocks wore a glassine finish. No mortar fastened their setting. Each face had been raised by centaur masons, mortise and tenon cut to a precision past the skills of human artisans. True mark of Ilitharis Paravian craftsmen, stone sang to stone in linked balance, each fitted block matched and meshed with its neighbors in harmonic resonance. The rampart arose, each buttress anchored through its aggregate minerals, a bonding fashioned in sound and light beyond range of mortal awareness.

Mage-sight unveiled that ephemeral splendor as a strength tuned to outlast the ages. Amid the grand spectrum that framed Ath's creation, this structure resounded and sang, a signature chord of achievement that perhaps might never be equaled. Luhaine beheld the fortress of Earle and mourned the loss of an artistry vanished with the Paravians.

The entry was a sweeping, half-circular arch, chisel-punched from a slab of gneiss granite. A massive boulder plugged the opening, moss-grown and weathered, and possessed of no visible mechanism. The spirit who sought access must win through by means beyond force. The decorative border carved into the archway itself held the key, endowed by Davien the Betrayer. His piquant ingenuity had patterned the geometry beyond the grasp of reason. Those interlocked spirals could tumble a man's mind into madness, as each loop and line unraveled eyesight into dizzy, ecstatic confusion.

No perception bound by substance could decipher that tangle of paradox.

As pure spirit, Luhaine was spared the first challenge; he need not engage the esoteric discipline to lift his consciousness free of dense flesh. From his vantage of subtle awareness, the opening point shone as a blue spike of light from the high curve of the arch. To cross the ward, the aspirant must send his naked spirit within to thread the riddle of the maze.

This pattern would not yield its mysteries freely. Possessed of a questioning, combative nature, Davien had crafted this maze to test character and wisdom, with no crossing ever the same.

Luhaine drifted upward and flowed through the lit access point, well cognizant of peril as he crossed the initial threshold. The first grand turning presented him with a choice between an object that shimmered with limitless desire and a small, gray pebble of no distinction. Luhaine picked the stone. By experience, he knew the vast secrets of matter were recorded in the structure of minerals. The moment he claimed his unassuming acquisition, the pebble sheared into halves. One portion became a shimmering mirror, and the other, a gateway into darkness.

Luhaine entered the black unknown, too experienced to fall prey to the illusions of manifest self-importance and vanity.

The void enfolded him, an obsidian bubble that threatened to swallow his solitary presence. The Sorcerer cast away that sense of imprisonment. He upstepped his vibration beyond the realms of formed thought, reaffirming himself in the primal chord that resounded, plane to plane, and imbued the unbroken flow of life to Ath's ever-varied creation.

Next turning, Luhaine faced the blinding promise of limitless ecstasy, opposed by the bright glyph of power. He opted for bliss, aware as he was that true power sprang out of unbridled joy. The glittering rune framed the lure for those who would dominate, a clear false step for a Sorcerer schooled to abide by the Law of the Major Balance.

Turning and turning, Luhaine made his way on the tenets of mage wisdom, his surety born of truesight and compassion where the dictates of experience fell short. Should his discipline and training prove unequal to the test, he would suffer an ignominious return, for the puzzle crossed outside of dimension and time, and stitched through the planes beyond substance. Davien's puzzle would winnow the foolish. His spiraling noose of conundrums and traps well defended the keep's inner sanctum. None but the accomplished adept could win through and attempt the command of the elemental forces still raised to awareness within.

Each fork in the maze marked a step toward high mystery, until form and substance fell away into streams of pure energy. Here, where naked will could rearrange manifest reality, the uncontrolled mind might forfeit the whole trial on the chance-slipped force of one thought. The last choice, the final step, was always the same. Luhaine knew his way through the mystery of chaos: he imagined himself back before the arched portal, but outside the patterning of knotwork. From that point of power, he spoke the Name of the boulder and asked a polite permission. The heart of the stone would transmute and grant entry, its staid judgment of compassionate character Davien's penultimate obstacle.

The sentinel stone knew Luhaine well. Hailed by a sonorous bell tone of greeting, the Fellowship shade was given his access to drift through.

Disgorged from the crystallized geometry of solid mineral, he emerged into what a grand weight of history had dubbed the Hall of Gathering. The air held the pungent tang of electricity. A floor of tessellated marble gleamed like rubbed pearl, the watery reflections of white-marble pillars melted into the upside-down image of the high, groined ceiling. Had there been a dais, that structure was gone, replaced by a grotto that seemed sculpted from the unfinished strata of a cliff face. At first glimpse, the edifice appeared as a designer's folly, carved with vines and tiered fountains and niches festooned with shell fluting. In fact, the structure was a shrine given over to the play of elemental forces.

Luhaine drifted, his homage no less for the fact he shared an unfettered existence as spirit. The air where he moved harbored conscious activity and an uncanny, intelligent awareness. Drafts flowed here in capricious disregard that no chink existed to admit them. They spun and braided in on themselves, interlaced with ribbons of intangible light and an endowed grace of sentience. Nor was that awareness sympathetic to the foibles of earthbound humanity.

A man addressed the wild elements at his peril, ever mindful of nuance and intent. The odd word or concept could cross-link like wildfire. This close to the powers that underpinned solid creation, any wayward outcome might precipitate into reality.

'Athera has need,' announced the Sorcerer out of respectful silence.

His fleshless whisper sighed through the incessant song of a fountain raised on a plinth. The splashing fall of the water was self-perpetuating. Mercurial showers of runoff dashed into a pool very like the ones found in the sanctuaries of Ath's adepts. Three massive stones flanked the verge. Their rough-hewn edges were mantled with green moss, and dignity clothed them like royalty. Adjacent to the fountain, fire burned in a niche, whirled and winnowed into firefly spirals by the play of an unseen wind.

'Athera has need,' Luhaine repeated, this time louder. Then, in the rolling cadences of a language long since forgotten by man, he summoned four Names, by vowel and syntax shaping the primal resonance that defined the four elemental spirits.

At first, no change; then fleeting expectancy shot a shimmer of light through the air.

Luhaine waited, stone patient.

Presently the fall of the water sang with melodious laughter. A sprite's face emerged from the ripples in the pool, neither woman nor child, but possessed of bewitching ebullience. 'What need shall we answer?' she trilled in a sweet, girlish treble.

Luhaine responded by providing her with an image. His portly form appeared clothed in a dignitary's robes of gray velvet, his silver beard combed in waves to a waist cinctured in calfskin and fastened with a farmer's wide-tanged brass buckle.

'We know you, Defender,' said the sprite in the pool, teasing or contemptuous; seductive or scornful: her tone as always a fractured illusion of duality the unwary found madness trying to fathom.

'Two boons, for my asking,' the Sorcerer replied, staid in his lack of curiosity. 'The Fellowship desires to hold convocation in this place on the night of the summer solstice. First, I require your assistance to admit Traithe. His powers remain crippled since his stand against Desh-thiere, and he cannot undertake the trial of the maze to win right of passage on his own.'

This time, the voice of the wind sylph answered, skirling echoes from the shadowy recesses. 'His courage was our ally when his act sealed South Gate. Rest assured, we will greet him with welcome.'

Luhaine's image bowed in grave thanks. 'Your forbearance is generous.'

He straightened, unsurprised to see that the sentinel stones by the pool had grown gnarled faces, the elemental earth personified in response to his summons by Name. The speech he received as a belling, subsonic vibration reflecting the deep overtones of an earthquake, and magma congealed into bedrock. 'Has Athera's need sprung from the blight that opens a rift like a sore on the northwestern headland of Paravia?'

'A dragon-skull ward has been raised,' Luhaine answered, respectful of truth, but wishing the archaic tongue he used had gentler words to soften the brunt. 'We know the construct hides the seed of a damaging conspiracy. Sethvir of Althain would cast strands to scry warning. For the sake of that augury, he sends me as emissary. Need I explain?'

'You need not.' Stone's wisdom encompassed all secrets, all conjuries, all manifestations that spellcraft could bind over matter. Earth element knew in detail how Fellowship conjury could sift the future and sound the patterns of multiple probability.

'As the makers of form and substance,' Luhaine petitioned, 'we beg permission to access your mastery through the hour we shape our augury. Guesswork is too dangerous. The Mistwraith's curse has stirred the most powerful human factions on Athera to renewed pacts of hatred and violence. Now, the dragon-skull ward blinds Sethvir to the consequences. For the sake of our duty to uphold the compact, hear our formal appeal. We ask elemental help to bend time. Allow us to view the true course of events as they come to be manifest.'

Fire replied, a crackling sibilance of sparks. 'We cannot assist with an act of intervention that would alter the thread of the world's fate. We serve free will; its ordained limits are not ours to cross.'

'Our Fellowship is bound to the Major Balance, which adheres to the selfsame Law.' Luhaine was too wedded to patience to yield to frustration as he clarified Fellowship intent. 'We do not seek to change destiny, but only to align our dwindled resources to the land we are sworn to guard. Dare we allow the last hope of Paravian survival to fail through some mortal brew of ill fortune? By my sworn word, our defense concerns only the compact, which mankind may transgress at their peril.'

A moment passed, weighted in silence that made the falling water seem a shout against the etched quiet of the air. The fire flared down to sullen embers, and the faces on the stones folded back into moss. When at due length, Luhaine received disposition, the words shimmered with the silvery harmonics of all four of the elements combined. 'Your request is granted, given the grounds of appeal. We will lift the veil of time for the duration of twelve years, but no more. No ward set by man will blind Sethvir's vision, but beware: the foreknowledge you gain must not open temptation to meddle.'

Luhaine bowed, too wise to argue the limitation set on the strands' augury. Elemental power encompassed all worlds, not just the firm earth of Athera; given the broad-ranging scope of their influence, such beings abided by their own codes of conduct. Only one force ever challenged their place on the loom of Ath's creation: the great drakes had spun energy into matter, then endowed their artistry with renegade consciousness through the gateway of true dreams. For that transgression, the dragons had earned an enmity that reached forward and back, unto the dawning of time.

'I thank your indulgence,' Luhaine addressed in closing his audience with the raised minds of the elements. 'Be sure my Fellowship will not waste your gift, nor use what we learn to alter fate's course through prime influence.'

By sundown, the other Fellowship Sorcerers converged at the focus at Earle. Luhaine's wraith presence was joined first by Traithe, whose leggings and boots still wore the pong of black mud and crushed fern gained crossing the Salt Fens. His raven hunched, ruffled with wet, on the shoulder of a sun-faded oilskin cloak, bought used from the hay shearers at Waterfork. The hands that slung off his wayfarer's pack seemed too thin and worn for the season.

'How many street beggars did you feed back in Shandor?' Luhaine accosted, concerned.

'All of them.' Traithe's coffee eyes crinkled to his sudden smile. 'Chide all you like, you won't find me regretful.'

He peeled off his cloak, scattering moisture over the silken sheen of the marble. For that, he tilted his silvered head in apology toward the grotto two flights upstairs, where the fountain cascaded its continuous spray of arpeggios. '*Ama'idan*, Water Sisters, I'm sorry. Forgive the small puddles, and receive instead my sincere thanks for your bounty.'

The weather had closed in with the advent of nightfall. Hard rain rinsed the headlands outside in black torrents, yet the drumming cascade could not be heard in the sealed vaults beneath Earle fortress.

Traithe warmed his stiff fingers over a wax taper scrounged from the dry depths of his pack. His colleague exchanged news. Between small conversation, and sharing a supper of raisins and jerked venison with the raven, the focus circle patterned in the stone floor awakened to crackling life.

Asandir stepped out of the glare. Sun-browned and scratched from some rugged errand pursued amid summer briar, he brought in the aromatic scents of mountain fir and long nights spent next to birch campfires. He spoke a sharp word, dispersing the lane forces, and to Luhaine's voiced greeting, replied, 'Bad hunting indeed.'

Lips turned to distaste, he unburdened himself of a horn bow and a quiver of steel-tipped arrows, then the meticulously kept blade of his hunting knife. 'At least where I came from, the weather was clear.' He folded lean legs and joined Traithe on the marble step that rimmed the focus, then proceeded to pick thorns and burrs from his tunic with unhurried, large-jointed fingers.

Luhaine looked on, grumbling and anxious to begin proceedings.

'We can't start without waiting for Sethvir anyway,' Traithe said, one scarred hand soothing the raven, who grew snappish as the unseen shade riffled cold through its feathers once again. When Luhaine refused answer, he plied Asandir for the latest word out of Shand.

The Sorcerer who shouldered most of the Fellowship's field work glanced up, his eyes the silver of filled rain pools. 'I traveled from the crystal veins in the Tiriacs, and haven't seen a city in six weeks. But the kites believe the autumn storms will be harsh, which could increase the shale slides in Vastmark.'

Luhaine broke in then, destroying the illusion of small talk. 'You were abroad in the *Tiriacs?* Then you certainly weren't bow hunting for deer.'

'No.' Asandir sighed. 'Trouble again, from the mires of Mirthlvain. Last season's frosts caused a break in the second Paravian retaining wall. Eighteen broods of methspawn escaped in the foothills, but they maraud there no longer.' Which explained the grain of weariness in his voice and the bramble rips in his clothing. Before Luhaine could lecture, the Sorcerer qualified, 'The predators chose not to answer to Name. Verrain had already exhausted that chance when I got there. Next time, you can try for yourself, and before you insist we can't continue without Kharadmon's backing, the simple fact is, we must.'

'I was going to ask which strain of methspawn escaped,' Luhaine corrected, miffed.

But his question was left to hang on the air as the concave depression of the focus flared into crackling luminescence again.

A bothered oath arose amid the white sparks. Then the Warden of Althain emerged from the scintillance of roused lane force, arms overburdened with rolls of blank parchment, and pens, and an ink-dark length of plain velvet.

Asandir lunged upright and rescued those items in imminent danger of falling.

'I should've brought a satchel,' Sethvir lamented, his face eclipsed by his teetering load. 'The problem was, all of them were full.'

'If you plan to inscribe a formal record, we're lacking a chair or a table,' informed Luhaine.

'The floor has always served well enough.' Sethvir flashed his pixie's grin to Asandir, whose fast reflex next fielded the horn box with the ink flask before it slithered and smashed underfoot. 'Thank you. At least this time Luhaine won't be the one carping over stiffened joints and sore knees.'

Luhaine returned a windy harrumph, spinning ahead through the newel posts of the balustrade some fanciful mason had carved with stylized dolphins. The raven flew, and Traithe followed, as ever too proud to resort to a staff, though his lame leg dragged on the risers. In sympathy with his silent suffering, Asandir pressed at his heels, prepared to offer his tacit support if the grace of opportunity presented. Sethvir came last, still barefoot, since he had found no spare moment to send a clan trapper to find him another black wolf pelt.

Earle Keep had been built on a grand scale, and two landings passed before the party of Sorcerers reached the Hall of Gathering. While the recent arrivals paid the four elementals their respectful greeting, the raven soared upward, to cavort in the eddies stirred by the sylphs dancing under the groins of the ceiling.

'None of that,' Traithe chided, laughing. 'The hour is late. Were we outside, you'd be roosting.' He held up his wrist.

The raven swooped down and alighted, croaking an avian epithet.

'And the same for the egg that hatched you,' Traithe retorted.

By then, Sethvir had shed his goose quills and parchments. Embedded amid the disorderly bundles were a moth-eaten cushion and collapsible camp stool for Traithe.

The crippled Sorcerer raised surprised eyebrows, then whispered his heartfelt thanks. He claimed the stool and took brisk charge of its assembly until Asandir stopped hovering out of misplaced pity and helped Sethvir spread the square of dark velvet over the marble flooring.

Then the Warden of Althain dug through the scrip at his belt and produced two worn stubs of chalk. One he handed to Asandir. In wordless, paired concert, the two Sorcerers inscribed the grand circles to invoke an elemental conjury.

Traithe sat with a quartz crystal in hand, immersed in communion with his raven. The bird was no stranger to ceremonial spellcraft. It launched and soared spiraling patterns overhead, a living shuttle cast upon the unseen loom of the air. The etheric filaments of its master's will trailed white streamers of light off its obsidian primaries.

Luhaine to all appearance had vanished, his being engaged beyond range of mortal senses. His perfectionist touch set the boundaries and wards for a conjury that would extend across time and space. If he missed Kharadmon's acerbic wit, or the counterbalance of a partnered spirit, like Traithe, he withheld complaint.

By sundown, preparations inside the vault stood complete. Although none of the day's dying light pierced Earle Keep's sealed fastness, every Fellowship Sorcerer in the Hall of Gathering sensed the pending hour of twilight. They assumed their position. Silent, prepared, Sethvir took the north, to invoke the grounding heart of the earth. Asandir ranged southward, and opposite, to call fire. In the absence of Kharadmon, Luhaine held the east, and Traithe, in worn black, stood for west. The raven descended and perched on its master's shoulder, eyes like shiny beads that perceived far more than an avian intelligence. For one tensioned instant, the air waited, mute, imprinted by the melodies of water, falling, and the voracious percussion of burst sparks.

'*Alt*,' Sethvir stated, the rune for beginning.

Unseen but for the stir of wild energies that prickled the hair at the nape, the elemental forces Luhaine had petitioned now joined with the Sorcerers' stilled focus. The workings of invisible powers reknit the veil of the mysteries, and subtly, silently, transcended the boundaries that anchored the root of the world.

An electrical current swept the core of the circles, spiked with the sheered tang of ozone. The water cavorting in the fountain sublimated away into nothing, and the sparks in the fire pan whirled up in a crackling vortex and vanished. Blackness claimed the sealed chamber, more dense than the vacuum between stars.

Against that unwritten scrim of poised force, Sethvir spoke again, a lyric line phrased in ancient Paravian that granted an unconditional consent.

A snap just past the limits of sound grazed through bone, flesh, and sinew. Time broke from the present. The air outside the conjured circles went unutterably still, its essence beyond animate concept of dark: lightless, empty as the void of potential that preceded the solidity of creation. Inside the circles, on an islet of chill stone, the square of dark velvet lost contour and form, until it became a primordial extension of the same formless energy. This conjury was no mere seeing, no illusion or reflection, but a perilous unmaking of all bonds to matter by the primal forces of the four elements. By their dire cooperation, the scrying within would go forward outside the frame that maintained the world's form and function.

'Designate,' Sethvir murmured.

The stiletto point of force that was Luhaine's awareness carved yet another ring of protection around the black template on the floor. A melding of four wills set specific intent for the area within to stand proxy for Athera's place in the cosmos. Two seals were laid over the circled square: one for protection and one to admit the boundless grace of Ath's blessing.

'Triad,' Sethvir whispered. He raised a hand gloved in raw power and inscribed three lines of living light upon the air.

Asandir touched those blank energies and Named them, one for the matter which formed solid existence, one for the spirit which quickened life, and lastly, the word for the stream of consciousness which linked those two poles and governed their spin and direction.

The rods of light imprinted. The prime pattern that first sourced Ath's limitless creation formed against the dark field of the velvet.

The Sorcerers spun more filaments of light, then invited the powers of the elements to imbue them. The pattern branched, an exponential expansion that formed the ciphers that comprised Athera and its intricate, teeming web of life. The construct grew in beauty and complexity, a microcosm reflection of geometry and line whose meaning could be read through the analysis of proportion and numbers. Against the loomed light that reflected the world's tapestry, Sethvir tapped the expanded awareness of the earth link and Named the individuals who now lived, whose myriad choices and acts wove the disparate threads of existence into the etheric links which tied destiny.

Here shone the glimmering arc of possibility, last remnant of Paravian influence; there, laid over the phosphor imprint of a reef in the tropics, the searing, pinpoint tangle of light that was Arithon's fleet in search of the vanished old races. The strands shimmered and settled their display, their tight-woven patterns a formed footprint of the world's landmasses. Their nexuses crossed, convoluted, and burned, complex as the life force which quickened the web of creation. Nor was that analog display all brilliance and straightforward movement: at Rockfell, still Nameless, Desh-thiere's wraiths brooded, their intent unknowable except by the impact recorded on passing events. Then, at Avenor, the ugly new threat: the sinister gap torn by the dragon-skull ward.

Sethvir cleared his throat. Into that ranging hole into *nothing*, he pronounced the Names of Lysaer's inner cabal. Earth-sense had shown who had entered that chamber in secret, and reconfirmed those who had left. As the Sorcerer's designation seeded each individual's imprint, the unraveled pattern regained a spectral suggestion of movement. Bright ripples shot length and breadth through the tapestry as root cause became linked to effect.

'Proceed,' Sethvir requested the poised forces of the elements standing in stilled attendance. 'Show us the progression of the future.'

A shock like unseen lightning ghost-rippled over the senses. Traithe's raven ruffled black feathers and croaked, while Asandir gripped his wrists with taut hands, raked by a frisson of chill. All eyes trained on the configured strands, Sethvir to every outward appearance immersed in the throes of a daydream. To those who knew him, that inattentive, soft gaze was sure mark of his rapt concentration.

The energized pattern shifted balance and flowed forward, reflecting the fixed path of augury.

From the unseen heart of Lysaer's inner circle, decisions churned vortices into hard lines which arced outward into causation. Where they crossed the world's spread design, they touched off cascading change. The strands mapped each sequence, and exposed how the cabal's conspiracy would deflect the analog course of world destiny.

'Galleys, how ingenious,' Luhaine noted, his musing spiked irony as he perused the shifts in power and trade that flowed inland from the seacoast. 'Those vessels with chained slaves will carry state dispatches, but only within Tysan. The ones sent abroad into foreign waters will have sunwheel guardsmen on the benches.' Those, entangled in branches of ramification, would extend a far-reaching net of eyes and ears to the distant ports of the Cildein. 'That's damnable.' A mouse would not raid a state larder in Melhalla, that Avenor would not hear of the shortfall. 'Arithon's line of supply for his fleet will be made increasingly difficult.'

'He's up to the challenge, for the moment, anyway,' Sethvir observed, as contraband from clan raids moved by roundabout routes and found their way through Fiark's ledgers, to be doucely redistributed on trade runs made by Feylind's brig, *Evenstar*.

Against the burgeoning bounty of harvest, a concentrated stir of activity at Alestron recorded the return of the duke's state galley. Among the signature energies presented to Bransian s'Brydion were his two brothers, Mearn and Parrien, the master shipwright, Cattrick, and a blind old splicer whose evil tongue reveled in gossip. After them came others whose faces in wax effigy had been sunk in the Westlands' dark waves. Yet the thread of their destiny was not unsnagged; a faint tie of cognizance still remained, strung to the null void at Avenor.

'Lysaer knows that those shipwrights survived.' Sethvir strung his hands through his tangled white hair. 'If I had to guess, I'd say he'll bide his time to spring the trap and expose them.'

And yet, no war happened. The insidious calm settled into a peace that saw Tysan's merchants recoup their losses. The high council at Avenor maintained the marked change in policy that acceded to all trade demands. No new recruits were levied to replace the Etarran companies. Armed patrols were maintained to safeguard the roads, and to arrest the mage-talented identified by Lysaer's Crown Examiner. A star of white brilliance amid a couched web of guildsmen and fawning, affluent courtiers, the prince who made claim as Ath's chosen avatar stayed suspiciously content to husband the fruits of his kingdom. His charm felled the reserve of the ranking ladies at the celebration feast that honored the conception of his heir, while his young bride looked wan in spangled brocade. Her low spirits and quiet were naturally attributed to the stresses of a first pregnancy. No one took pause as the princess retired early, attended by a train of handmaids who came from cities far distant from Erdane.

'She isn't done fighting yet.' Traithe raised a hand to quell the raven, who perched, rapt and restless, at his shoulder. 'Nor can her staunch spirit win aught but grief for an outcome.'

The strands tracked that relentless, small tragedy as the slight, sullen spark of Lady Ellaine's imprint flickered and faded, then resurged as the passing months brought her confinement.

Her son's birth in spring, then sharp confrontation as Gace Steward's block on her efforts to rule the royal household flushed brightened lines over the more shadowy influence of Raiett Raven's collaboration at court. While Lysaer played the role of indulgent regent, and merchant traders fattened to complacency, his new master statesman engineered politics with the stealth of a man laying bird snares. South Tysan had borne witness to the terrors of sorcery. That impetus became rooted doctrine. A groundswell of distrust was nurtured into tinderbox unease that one spark might ignite into mass conflagration.

'A man to be feared, and closely watched,' Sethvir said of Raiett Raven, while the strained silence deepened with shared foreboding. Asandir had no words, chin set on his fist, and a glint in gray eyes like the filings sheared off smelted steel.

The strands burned out the inexorable course of the future, each sequential pattern more grim than the last as Avenor's Lord Examiner was invited abroad by a contingent of eastshore mayors. In the city of Ship's Port, a herbalist burned, the first healer arraigned for malpractice of sorcery inside Melhalla's borders. Sethvir stuffed his knuckles into his beard, heartsick as the old fear and prejudice embraced an inexorable course of violence. The odd contrast widened between the trade guilds' building prosperity and the deeper current of unease underlying Tysan's burgeoning coffers.

'Such dichotomy troubles me,' Luhaine observed, as Lysaer's congenial pandering levered that state of imbalance still wider. 'I sense a designed effort to foster a false sense of security. Imagine the reaction if events should arise to threaten such hoarded wealth. The s'Ilessid gift of farsight might cause Lysaer to aspire toward that end.'

Asandir looked up, bleak, and tapped a strong finger on the ominous tendril of connection that persistently dogged Cattrick's new life at Alestron. 'The s'Brydion should pay heed. They remain the most likely target to be used as an Alliance catalyst.'

The subtle dance of the strands unveiled the tortuous implications underlying Lysaer s'Ilessid's long-range strategy: years that stitched a congealed course of change, from the obvious intentions of ceremonial delegations sent to Etarra to establish a standing war host, to the more insidious, shadowy rage of a mob, incited to throw stones at the walls of a sanctuary where Ath's adepts had lived in gentle seclusion for over four thousand years.

'At least Asandir's intervention in Caithwood will spare the forests,'

Traithe pointed out to relieve the unremitting grim forecast. Indeed, no town interests inclined toward extreme measures to expunge age-old enmities. A guarded clan presence held out in Taerlin. Eastward, in Rathain, the survivors of Tal Quorin kept one wily step ahead of the Etarran headhunters. Jieret Redbeard looked likely to become the first steward of Rathain to raise sons and daughters to maturity after six less fortunate generations.

Yet even such victories came at high cost. Within five years, the Alliance of Light would consolidate a pre-eminent foothold in the port cities of four kingdoms. Inside of a decade, that ranging influence would insinuate itself everywhere merchants dispatched trade caravans inland.

Havish alone held to stable neutrality. Displaced clan families maintained refuge there, to ensure safe continuance of old bloodlines. Controversy arose as their numbers in exile were joined by herb witches and itinerant healers whose lives became hounded by the zeal of Alliance examiners.

Sethvir chuckled over a quirk of politics that left eight pompous merchants without mansions. 'Well, King Eldir's not going to back down, no matter which damn fool thinks he'll be the first one to bribe him.'

Crown rule in Havish endured, even-handed and firm, while its queen bore two more sons and another daughter. By the shining, clear lines of emerging character, the next youngest would become the heir designate affirmed by the Fellowship Sorcerers.

'Ath,' Traithe said, his eyes crinkled with amused delight by the antics in the royal nursery. 'The young prince could so easily have lied about the tadpoles he dumped in his sister's washbasin.'

By sad contrast, domestic affairs in Lysaer's household in Tysan harbored no such spark of merry devilment. As the decade closed, the strand for Princess Ellaine flared and crossed that of Avenor's confirmed high priest over her right to choose her son's tutors. Cerebeld was a man who held women in contempt, and the wife of his divine master as a nuisance to be suffered in stiff-lipped, watchful distaste. Their contest of wills was short-lived and decisive, with Ellaine left heart-torn in defeat.

'She can't prevail, more's the pity,' Sethvir said in despair as the child's youthful vigor branched away from her side, dimmed to sad, subtle changes. The imprint of the mother glimmered and withdrew into wan spirals of melancholy.

Nor did Luhaine's contribution brighten the morose outlook as he moved on to probe the knotted intrigues stirred up by the Koriani Order. 'I don't trust the stillness, here,' he complained at frustrated length.

'The sequences spin too long and too straight without tangling, and Morriel's obsessions run too obsessively deep to reflect such sweetness and light.'

'She's just letting her plot with that herder boy ripen,' Traithe suggested from the darkness.

Luhaine released a crisp huff of exasperation. 'She'd like us to think so. But her spiteful calculation grows the more twisted with age.' Well versed in the order's convoluted, self-serving policies, the discorporate mage exhorted his colleagues to delve deeper. 'No right-minded matriarch would keep an incompetent apprentice. There's more afoot here than simple malice toward Lirenda in maintaining the charade of Selidie's aptitude for prime candidacy.'

Sethvir bent his falcon's gaze over the strands under question. 'I see nothing else to bear out your suspicion.' The patterns for every Koriani senior in the Prime Circle showed no kinks, no runes to mask plotting; nor did he discern any haze of resonant interference to indicate wards of concealment. Through the two remaining years of the augury sealed into surety by the elementals, every chained link of disharmony led through the gloom of Morriel Prime's chamber.

Had Luhaine owned flesh, he would have gnashed teeth. 'The old witch still broods a damned clutch of nursed rancor. How can we be certain she hasn't shrouded her mad intentions through the powers of the Great Waystone?'

'You think we would miss the impacts of causation?' Sethvir combed the strands again on that premise, but still found nothing suspect.

Luhaine remained dissatisfied. 'Then whatever the witch plans hasn't manifested yet.'

Asandir raised his chin from his clamped fist, his eyes like frost and old tarnish. 'You fear we'll be blindsided? Why wouldn't the Koriani lie low while their plot to lure Arithon ripens?'

'I don't like the smooth way Morriel bides her time.' Despite his stone patience, Luhaine's frustration seethed without tangible outlet. 'Like rats bearing plague, her Senior Circle carries their poison unseen. They're too well aware we can't stay free to watch every scurrying move.'

'Perhaps there's no need.' Sethvir traced the one stable line in the pattern. Throughout every sequence of burst continuity, one flame of hope remained steadfast; changeless; an obdurate gleam that burned like a star against darkening misunderstanding: Arithon's brigantines scoured the seas in their exhaustive search for the Paravians. 'When the storm breaks, the Prince of Rathain will have kept his clear-sighted option to choose.'

The elementals' spun vision had guaranteed stable peace for at least the next dozen years. Arithon could rely on that interval to heal and renew his strength for the next onslaught; Lysaer would not hound him, but preferred to nurture the factions of trade until some triggered disaster opened the floodgates of panic. If broadscale war could be wrung from reaction, the telltale signs were yet hidden.

'We'll have a reprieve to reorder our affairs. May I suggest we don't waste ourselves wishing a conjectured affray could be mitigated?' Sethvir tucked restive hands into his sleeves and released the bright energies arrayed on the velvet. The pattern dispersed to a residue like snow haze that winnowed to spent smoke and faded. Head bent, aggrieved as his colleagues, he listened while Asandir addressed formal thanks to the unseen presence of the elementals.

Active flame reignited in the bowl of the firepan; the fountain's voice resumed liquid verse. Then the pall of spelled darkness thinned and broke away, leaving the Fellowship Sorcerers alone in the Hall of Gathering. Through the testy, soft rustles as the raven fluffed wing feathers, each Sorcerer reflected in bleak silence. The strands' augury bestowed an uneasy reassurance, with hidden factors still pending.

Kharadmon must remain tied down with the wards, posting guard against the free wraiths upon Marak. Nameless, their activity could not figure in strands, except by the impact of effect. The fact that no sign of attack had been manifest did not mean they stayed safely quiescent. Asandir and Traithe would still be hard-pressed. They alone would be left to reaffirm the old seals and mind the boundaries which contained the Paravian sites ceded to Fellowship wardenship.

Luhaine churned in place, stirred to a formless unease too vague for a hunch and too strong to be passed off as fancy. 'No matter our diligence, the day fast approaches when our numbers will be insufficient. Even now, we can scarcely maintain the sworn terms of our binding. Morriel knows this. She'll tailor her plots to strike that disadvantage.'

'Well, she fell short the first time,' Asandir pointed out. 'The Shadow Master has yet to run out of resources; nor has the Paravian presence he seeks disappeared from the world altogether.'

'That's pulling at straws, to believe we'll be saved from disaster by the return of the lost centaur guardians.' Luhaine whirled aloft to erase the chalked wards, hard-set for a tirade of pessimism.

'Straw hope or not,' Sethvir interjected, 'until Morriel or Lysaer makes the first play, our own hands stay tied by the compact.'

**Summer Solstice 5667**

# Court Festival

The feast of summer solstice at Avenor's royal palace had become a women's affair over the thirteen-year course of Princess Ellaine's marriage to Lysaer s'Ilessid. At that season, the ranking captains of the guard were absent on campaign in the field, defending the movement of trade on the roads and suppressing established clan outposts. The Divine Prince himself spent his summers with Raiett Raven and Sulfin Evend at Etarra, there to preside over the Alliance grand council, and to review the green recruits signed in for the annual muster.

Through the long mild days, while deer browsed in the dappled shadows at the verges of the oak forests, and barley ripened in Avenor's tilled fields, the sharp-faced old seneschal sat the regent's raised seat and oversaw petitioners and grievances. Lord Eilish turned the cellars inside out and dulled pens through his strict yearly inventory. The common sinew of the realm bent its back to trade and husbandry, which left High Priest Cerebeld immured like a spider in his tower above Avenor's chambers of state.

From there, he oversaw the brisk traffic of servants bearing ribbons and fine silks from the market. His view of the entry to the grand hall showed him plasterers and painters and gilders, coming and going through the labor of adorning the massive decorations with fripperies. Their industry scarcely pleased him. He held a dim view of the ancient festivals, whose dances took root from Paravian traditions, and whose masks and gaiety were imbued with rune lore and sun symbols disturbingly close to the seals sewn in shining thread on the robes of Ath's adepts. No high-handed fool, to ban an extravagance the Light's core of faithful could not yet suppress, Cerebeld delivered the obligatory blessing to open the gathering and retired to engage in private rites with his devoted new coterie of acolytes.

Lord Eilish's sallow clerks were whisked away, also, since the memorable year Ellaine's ladies had seduced them with fruit spirits that left them flushed and by lengths too talkative on sensitive issues of policy. Other absent factions pleaded boredom as year followed year; the arena of male politics quit the floor in self-defense as the celebration of summer solstice devolved into a dance ball arranged for the young.

Tysan's women now reigned, clad in tissue and finery. Their guest list was first drawn by invitation from the three principalities of the realm. As Avenor gained weightier influence across the continent, solicitations were sent to cities far and wide in the kingdoms to the east. Nor did power and influence stand aside in hiatus; each year, the matrons of high privilege and wealth bedecked their daughters in lace ribbons and jewels, and waged fiercely fought contests of matchmaking.

Princess Ellaine presided from her husband's raised dais, clad in a shimmering gown in Tysan's royal colors. Gold and blue had never set off her fine points. The richest tinseled sapphire brocade turned her dark eyes to sunken pits and made her complexion seem sallow and tired. The few women closest to her recognized that glazed mask, paint and subtle powder applied with the ritual care of steel armor. They knew that the desperation she hammered down under trained deportment was not due to sore feet or exhaustion.

The young prince, Lysaer's heir designate, was to be presented this night. Avenor's princess had not seen her son through the year since Avenor's high council had obstructed her maternal right to arrange his education. The cost of that ruling had abraded her, body and spirit, from the hour of the boy's separation.

A swirl of changed movement stirred the dancers, then a stiffening of attention from those nearest the closed double doors; the musicians muted their instruments. Against abrupt quiet, the tabarded heralds by the rear wall raised their horns. A flurried bustle of silk saw the couples cleared from the floor. Then the flourish of brass announced the young prince's entry. Sharp-eyed ambitious matrons formed two lines on either side, with the youngest and prettiest of their pedigree charges placed to the fore to be noticed. The curious craned their necks. The worldly bored murmured gossip; handfastings would follow, but tonight's groomed display was unlikely to yield the sought-after royal betrothal. The weight of Avenor's title rested as yet on the shoulders of a boy of twelve; until Lysaer s'Ilessid consented to hear formal offers of contract, the heir designate he had sired to rule Tysan would stay a child, enamored of swordplay and horses.

Given the growing tapestry of Alliance power linking cities east to west on the continent, none at Tysan's court could afford to prevaricate. A perilous folly, to regard the legitimate issue of Lysaer s'Ilessid as more than a flesh-and-blood cipher.

Princess Ellaine sat stately and still on the dais. Her expression appeared patient. Only the nearest observers might note the tremulous flicker of the seed diamonds strung in the gold wire lace of her collar. When the liveried footmen at the far end of the hall swung open the sunwheel-bossed doors, her ringed hands tightened, powerless in her lap. The young prince marched through the entry.

He came alone. No nurse attended; the engaging, small pages he had counted his friends through the years he had laughed in the nursery were nowhere in evidence. Nor was he clothed as a child anymore, but bore up, straight shouldered, under the weight of a blazoned tabard. The sword at his waist was ceremonial steel; the knee boots were new and, by the scuff of his heels, very likely still pinched him.

He managed to stride with manly dignity, nonetheless. Only as he mounted the carpeted stair could anyone see that his face was too pale, mouth pinched tight to stop his lower lip from trembling.

'My mother,' he piped in a dutiful treble. He bowed, as her station demanded. His reddish honey hair caught burnished light from the candles. The eyes of dove gray he raised afterward stayed wide with unsettled conflict. His deportment pleaded to be treated as adult, while the child he still was craved a mother's affection.

The impact of his suffering stopped Ellaine's breath.

'My lady, your son,' said Gace Steward, arrived without sound, his weasel interest ever lurking at her shoulder to observe and keep notes and gloat.

Rage flared and restored her poor color as she rose. 'Kevor, my young prince.' She could smile despite Gace, let her son see for himself she still loved him. 'I'm proud of you, beyond words. Your grandmother is here, and your aunt, and three cousins. All of them honor your courage, as do I.'

Kevor's chin jerked. His eyes turned suspiciously bright.

And Ellaine ached for each tear stubborn pride would not let him shed. Words fell too far short. She must find a state gesture that would shake her child from the belief she had abandoned him with complacency. Her smile returned, this time whetted to acid-bright triumph.

As though her son were grown, and crowned king of Tysan, she curtsied to the floor at his feet.

Her gesture raised a breezy rustle of surprised murmurs. Gace lost his unctuous humor before that public slap of effrontery. The implicit message she delivered to Avenor's ranking guests all but shattered the young prince's bearing. He flashed a glare of pure hatred at the steward. Then, in a voice that firmed toward the note of authority he aimed for, and just missed, the heir designate of Tysan asked his mother please to rise and be seated in his presence.

Young as he was, he had inherited his father's sharp instincts. Kevor understood better than to stay beyond the requisite ceremonial appearance. Such a moment of hard-won, prideful victory could last only a handful of seconds. 'Let the solstice festivities resume.'

He kissed his mother's hand with mannered formality. His tears fell then, despite all his care, and traced hot, salty warmth through her jewels. Ellaine turned her wrist. She cupped his chin with utmost tender subtlety and let her silk sleeve dry his cheeks. Grateful for that shielding, the boy collected himself. He gave her a smile to melt snow into sunlight, then arose and turned his back to a punishing squeak of new boot leather. As the heralds sounded the fanfare marking his exit, none but Gace saw how close he had come to breaking down in blind shame at her knee.

'You will say *nothing*,' Ellaine hissed through clamped teeth to the steward, as the musicians struck up, and the couples on the floor flowed back and revolved to the figures of a stately slow-step. 'Or by the name of the powers more ancient than man, I'll see you and Cerebeld's inner circle to Sithaer and the joys of Dharkaron's black vengeance. You are excused from my presence this moment.'

Gace Steward's expression curdled to surprise, hard followed by a stare of dangerous calculation. 'As my lady wishes.' Insolent as gall, he made no move to leave.

Clever beast that he was, he had the effrontery to cut her back. Just barely in time, Ellaine perceived the cruel, subtle trap of innuendo: an authoritative show of muscle to enforce her command would destroy her small gesture to shelter Kevor.

Tired now, heartsore and aching, she stiffened her spine to endure.

'How like a man, to carry his pea brain in his scrotum and not realize when overbearing male company's unwanted.' That waspish, crone's scorn came packaged in clanborn accents that sheared like wire through the soothing harmonies of the strings. Heads turned. Two of the dancers broke step in the line, and a group of plump matrons tittered.

Undaunted, as disdainful of royal propriety as her relatives, the straight little grandmother continued her marching advance up the dais stair. Her hair was short cropped, neat as salt, and unadorned.

A gown of white voile wrapped her, wrist to throat, pinned at her high collar with a teardrop ruby strung on a thin, gold chain. Overtop, she wore a shoulder sash of vivid s'Brydion scarlet. One porcelain fist clenched two goblets of wine; the other, with evident, battle-schooled relish, brandished a black briar stick with a silver knurl hefty enough to knock back a charging bull.

'Go away, foolish man,' she snapped at Gace Steward. 'If you don't, I shall certainly get annoyed.'

The stick spun in her grasp with a speed to whistle air, and just missed the steward's tucked groin.

Gace fled, as any man must when assailed by Grandame Dawr in a temper.

'Duke Bransian's grandmother, if you please,' the peppery old woman introduced herself. Her acid-bright smile flashed and vanished, as clever and genuine as her steel character. 'We met in the receiving line, which doesn't say much. A captain on a battlefront isn't likely to recall names and faces for all the rank and file.'

Despite herself, Ellaine choked back startled laughter.

The grandame, whose name she recalled very well, spurned every pretense of royal prerogative. Her dainty self-assurance could have wrecked mountains as she settled in the carved chair beside Lysaer's titled princess. 'I thought you looked peaked. Will you take wine?'

The goblet was pressed into her hand with a firmness that made refusal a frank breach of manners.

Ellaine drank a sip, overwhelmingly grateful as she realized the parched state of her mouth.

'There, dear, that's better.' Dame Dawr raised her own glass in a salute of grimmest irony, then brushed the rare vintage to her lips in a token gesture of camaraderie. Her deep, brown eyes held amusement for the fact that, alone of any invited guest in the chamber, she could brazen through every stilted rule of protocol and chat woman to woman on the royal dais. Clan law did not recognize the s'Ilessid claim to crown rule; if the s'Brydion granted Avenor a warbond alliance, no one had ever managed to enforce the custom of court manners on any of the duke's outspoken envoys.

Nor had the representative sent from Alestron been anyone closer than a distant second cousin for more then a decade, a lapse the inner circle had noted. The remedy for that slight faced them this night. Tysan's writ of invitation had pointedly requested that a female blood relation of the duke should attend the solstice festivities at Avenor.

Lord Bransian s'Brydion had recast the request at his whim, had in fact ignored the salutation addressed to the name of his eminently marriageable youngest daughter. In the girl's stead, he had dispatched his acid-witted grandame; or perhaps not. Now confounded by the formidable collected presence of the woman, Ellaine wondered if the state voyage to Avenor had been Dawr's idea from the outset.

Which twist of cunning politics did not leave her ungrateful for an outright act of human kindness; the wine accomplished a miracle's work of restoring her. 'Thank you,' she said, earnest. Her hands, for a blessing, had ceased trembling.

'I shan't linger,' Dawr said. 'Your rat-faced little steward seems to have an unpleasantly prying personality. Someone should slap his face for listening at doorways, or at least break his slippered foot. With a limp, he couldn't slink. Take greatest care, my dear. Your predecessor, Talith, found her way to a terrible end.'

Ellaine looked up, met and locked eyes with the old woman's shrewd glance. A charged moment passed. The princess took a fast breath, then gambled upon the earnest spark of challenge shared through that split-second contact. 'A suicide. So sad.'

Dame Dawr regarded her back, her reply a scaled snap of honesty. 'No mere sorrow over that one's death, madam. I believe my grandson Mearn, who spoke fierce words on the matter.' She raised her goblet yet again, her gesture pure sarcasm as she yielded proud principle and delivered her withheld courtesy. 'To your s'Ilessid husband and his oath to serve true justice.'

Ellaine caught back her breath in surprise. S'Brydion had never given deference to royalty throughout all the years they had paid court to Avenor.

Dawr's fingers were fine ivory, and deliberate as she set the flute aside on the massive carved wood of the chair arm. 'My dear, I wish you well. My duke sends respects. You have seen all you need of my company.'

On that abrupt note, the old woman grasped her black stick and arose. She absented herself with no bow, no apology, never asking or receiving word of leave. Her steps down the dais stair were frail, but assured. She reached the marble dance floor on her own before she snapped imperious fingers to summon her retainers to her side. They came, two armed swordsmen clad in s'Brydion scarlet, and faultlessly attentive to her wishes. In respect, they assisted Dame Dawr's measured retreat through the double doors of the grand ballroom.

On the dais, Princess Ellaine did not miss the final irony: *that the wine in the lady's abandoned goblet stayed untouched.* Clan custom, by rigid code of honor, never drank to the name of an enemy. Dame Dawr had exposed the terrifying answer to the question Avenor's princess had dared to broach through a perilous exchange of small talk.

The suspected truth, affirmed, shot fear like black ice through and through Ellaine's guarded heart.

By the word of s'Brydion, Princess Talith's death had been no suicide at all.

Shaken to her core, sadly wiser than the girl she had been on her wedding night thirteen years in the past, Princess Ellaine took the implicit warning to her breast. Whether or not she let the matter bide, or if she chose to resume her doomed struggle to keep a hand in her young son's destiny, she had been clearly told of the possible deadly consequences.

If Dawr's grandson Mearn had discerned the rotten truth, then secret factions existed in Avenor, underneath the Light's glory and Lysaer's banner. Their machinations had not stopped at clandestine murder. Against those unknown faces, alone under the heel of such power, the princess dared not leave the hall, or show any sign of her undermining dismay. She must do her utmost to smooth over appearances, as though Dawr's words had held nothing more than the usual banal court courtesy.

The princess retrieved the old lady's abandoned wine flute before Gace Steward's sharp vigilance should notice and discern its private and sinister meaning. While the dance couples turned to the bright beat of the tambours, and the gold-embossed suns for summer solstice glittered by candlelight, she raised the glass to her lips and drained the contents in admiration for Dawr s'Brydion's astonishing, insolent courage.

# Encounter

Morvain's seaside quarter languished under thick fog as midnight drew nigh, the odd burst of raucous song and snatched laughter stitched through the slap of the riptide's first currents. Solstice revelers staggered home under fuzzed torches, or banged into the taverns demanding more wine, determined in their excessive, high spirits to drink and dance until sunrise. The noisiest quarter fronted the dockside. There, the shanties of the poor who worked Morvain's looms crammed up against the alleys where mariners on shore leave bought grog and solicited entertainment. The mill hands and the wenches who knotted carpet all mingled with tarred topmen, stevedores, and the free galleymen muscled like bulls from paid service at the oar. Misunderstandings abounded, over which women were trollops, and which cherished wives or grown sisters. In these sordid streets, lit by pitch pine brands, even the lighthearted pranks played for solstice might start roughhouse fights, or end with a knife thrust in bloodshed, if a body jostled into a mean drunk, or miscalled the start of an argument.

As the captain responsible for a young deckhand who had broken his watch orders and slipped ashore without leave, Feylind of the *Evenstar* snarled in justifiable bad temper. 'In here?' Her jerked gesture of contempt encompassed the gaping door to a wineshop, which spilled light and screaming laughter into the damp, foggy street.

The strapping first mate at her shoulder returned a clipped nod. 'Aye, Captain. In there.' He stood back and allowed the lady first entry, well warned not to cross her when she wore her capped boots and the belt which hung her black-handled cutlass.

Feylind snapped a rude phrase under her breath, tossed back her flax braid, then squared her trim shoulders and plowed in.

Across the stone threshold, the intense, steamy heat and dense noise, and a churning mass of twined bodies impacted the senses like a wall. The tang of summer sweat pressed the air into felt. Feylind never hesitated. The first goatish lout who fingered her hair found himself spun aside, then crunched facefirst against the oak lintel. The next one, who jeered, received a reviling curse and an elbow that folded him, speechless. The third lecher, who pinched to apprise her willing womanhood, dropped howling to the bricks, felled by a lashed kick to the kneecap.

To judge by his swift faint as he tried to stand up, he might not walk again without the skilled help of a bonesetter.

The florid wine seller behind the bar looked around, harried, as the swirl of recoil jammed the dancers and jostled the blithe singers off-key. He beckoned, warned that trouble had entered his establishment, and two muscled heavies pushed off their stools to attend him. Not to be caught weaponless, he snatched up the wood mallet kept at hand to hammer the bungs into barrels. Then he bore through the press to eject the brawling fool who had dared to assault paying customers.

The miscreant met their affronted charge from a circle of cleared floor, arms folded over a rust red suede brigandine studded with steel that hazed sparked reflections to the stuttering flare of the lanterns. Hair like raw gold set off a tanned face just now scowling with searing impatience. A woman; one taller than most men, and charged to the fury of a lioness just shown the outrage of an injured cub.

Too wise to risk life and limb to her wrath, the wine seller lowered his mallet. He stalled the rush of his henchmen with a word. To the woman who regarded him as though he were a slug that had just crawled from under a carcass, he said, 'You have business here, mistress?'

'Captain, to you, pud-wad.' Eyes blue and hard as the glints on fired porcelain raked the wine seller over and fastened. 'You have my lad here, the *Evenstar*'s deckhand, that one of your potboys laid open?'

The wine seller deflated. 'The trade brig, *Evenstar*, of Innish registry? Then you must be Feylind.' As her foot tapped in dangerous, leashed exasperation, he unburdened fast enough to bite his tongue spitting out consonants. 'Yes, the fellow's back in the stores closet with his hurt palm bound up in cheesecloth. We thought best not to move him before the gash had stopped bleeding.'

Feylind tipped up a silver-blond eyebrow. 'Tide's turning, you liar.

You hoped we'd be sailing, with the lad left beached here and forgotten.'

The wine seller flushed deeper than his finest Carithwyr red. 'Show her to him,' he commanded to his most imposing thug. He prevaricated, squirming, and prayed one of his wenches had the smart sense to dart back and unlock the closet. 'The patron you kicked will bear you no charges.'

Feylind laughed. 'Charges? That's funny. He'll limp in my memory, and maybe think twice before he lets a stiff cock interfere with his civilized manners.' She tipped her chin toward the rear doorway, the plight of her wounded deckhand still stubbornly uppermost in her mind. 'That way?' Her no-nonsense, brisk stride, smoothly matched by her mate, forced the muscle-bound servant appointed as escort to trip over himself to keep up.

The young man with the knife wound sat on an upturned wine tun, rinsed in the light thrown off by a fluttering tallow dip. His face was tinged green, perhaps owing to the ripe reek of waxed cheddar, strung on twine loops from the rafters to discourage the ravage of insects and mice. He looked up, blanched white as Feylind stepped in, her head ducked in time to avoid getting brained by a dusty wheel of cheese.

'Captain, the tide—' he blurted in apology.

Feylind cut off his excuses. 'Evenstar took a mooring. Less ruinous than wharfage. Stay on my crew list, and the costs of delay are going to be docked from your pay share. Are you with me or leaving?'

The boy straightened, unhappy and in pain, but grateful to be dealt such a fair-handed chance at redemption. Morvain was a galleyman's haven. Blue-water skills and experience with sail were unlikely to win him a berth above a paid oar bench; and the wound in his hand would brand him unfit until too near the end of the season. 'With you,' he gasped. 'I'll board Evenstar directly.'

Feylind snapped her head in negation. 'First, let's see that palm. How bad is the gash?' She kept no paid healer on Evenstar's crew list. Bellyaches and coughs, she treated herself. The man who stitched up the small mishaps on board was always the one who patched up torn canvas the neatest.

When the boy stalled, reluctant, she gave him short shrift. 'Yank off that cloth, now, mister. You don't want to see what becomes of a limb that puffs up and turns septic, and goes stinking rotten with gangrene.'

The boy grimaced, then looked sidewards as he peeled the soaked rag. Less squeamish by lengths, Feylind gripped his wrist and raised the palm for inspection. 'Bring that light closer, will you?'

The wine seller's lackey lifted the tallow dip and held the flame steady through Feylind's inventive, fierce oath for the fact the slice ran crosswise, with three tendons severed, and bone laid bare underneath. 'Blocked the thrust with your hand did you? Wise up. If you can't snag the knife in loose cloth, then strike with the bony edge of your forearm, yes?'

To the wine seller's man, she said, 'We're going to need an herb witch who can work major spellcraft. Do you know one whose fees aren't robbery?'

'Not here.' The fellow scraped at his stubbled chin, dubious. 'This town's sworn to Light, and the mayor's advisor is loyal to the Alliance. No herb witches left here. For wounds bad as this one, you'd go to the hospice run by the Koriani sisterhouse.'

'No sisterhouse,' Feylind shot back. Her crisp, efficient touch wound the pressure bandage back over the gash, still sullenly bleeding. 'This lackwit can damned well live as a cripple before I show my face there.' She looped the ends of the cloth in a half hitch, fierce enough to wring a gasp from the boy as she finished in planted vehemence, 'Won't encumber my brig with the binding obligation of any Koriani oath of debt.'

'Can't blame you for that.' Shadows pinwheeled and jerked as the wineshop's man replaced the tallow dip on the shelf. He stepped back to clear the open doorway and paused, belatedly helpful, 'There's one herbalist, Koriani, but she acts independently. Keeps no ties to the Morvain sisterhouse. She'll take plain coin, if it's healing, and not charm craft. The street waif out back who begs for our cheese scraps will show you there for a copper.'

The Koriani herbalist inhabited a bait shack jammed into the alley that fronted the seawall. No lamps burned in the deep maze of the poor quarter. Swathed in close fog, and the offal reek of fish guts heaved into the sump and awaiting the scouring ebb tide, the waves slapped over the weed-tangled rock, a stone's throw away in pitch-darkness. Each footstep disturbed the scuttle of rats, or flushed bone-thin, scavenging cats, prowling for live vermin in the gutters.

*Evenstar's* first mate moved with his hand gripped to his cutlass, sharply watchful of his mistress's back. Glad herself for the comforts of knives and capped boots, Feylind scrounged up a silver and dismissed the pox-scarred mite who had served as her guide from the wineshop. 'We'll follow the waterfront to find our way back.' She passed over the coin. 'Make sure you change that with a shopkeeper who's honest.'

The child grinned and departed, his rapid, light footsteps vanished into the noisome darkness. Left alone with her first mate and the shivering lad with the oozing bandage, Feylind took matters in hand and groped over the gapped, weathered wall of the bait shack until she located its shoddy plank door. She tapped, not lightly, in case the inhabitant was deaf with age or asleep in a stupor of gin.

'Hold on for one moment!' called a female voice from within; not old at all, or one whit bleary, which, oddly, did not inspire confidence.

Feylind glanced to the solid presence of her ship's mate, unable to read the expression on his broad face in the sea misty darkness.

Seconds later, the rickety panel creaked open. A woman in a dark shawl emerged, still dabbing moist eyes, and shedding the cheap scent of a half-silver prostitute, struck through by the more biting undertone of an astringent salve to ease bruises. She gave Feylind's company no second glance, but hurried along on her way.

'Plague take the fists of lust-ridden sailors,' snapped the herbalist in riled temper. Planks scraped as she jammed her door open wider to admit the next client on her threshold. 'If you've brought me the meatbrains who savaged that girl, let me tell you, I'm likely to geld him.'

Feylind's teeth flashed in a wicked, wild grin. 'You find him, I'll hold him down for the knife.'

The blurred face half-glimpsed in the interior gloom returned a gasp of pleased laughter. 'Come in. The festival's kept me much too busy to waste time with trifles of courtesy.'

For no reason under sky she could name, that honesty reassured Feylind. She stepped ahead, unafraid, into an enveloping blackness with a distinct scented character wrought of flower spices and bittersweet herbs, and the gritted tang of burned charcoal. The mate and lad pressed in on her heels, the scrape of their steps stiff with trepidation. No doubt they were as aware as she that the threshold was guarded by some unseen presence that raked bare flesh to chills in the dark.

Nor was the enchantress's mood less than briskly professional as she bent the discerning regard of her sisterhood upon the *Evenstar*'s hesitant company. 'Which one of you is bleeding or sick? I don't give philters to abort unborn babes, so if that's what you're asking, seek elsewhere.'

'Shut the door,' Feylind said to her nerve-jumpy mate. Since enchantresses saw perfectly well in the dark, she matched the challenging test set against her with the unadorned truth. 'The lad has a gashed hand with cut tendons, and I have no patience. My brig's got two hours left for the tide, or she'll cost us another day's mooring.'

'Let's see, then.' The pleasant, mild alto recovered its previous biting frankness. 'But I'll warn you, Captain, my services could cost you ten times your ship's fee, and double as much if you rush me.'

'I'll pay to the letter of your demand for the healing, but understand, before you begin. I'll make no binding promise, nor bow to your sister-hood's practice of swearing an oath of debt.'

'Rest assured, then.' The enchantress snapped a simple flint striker, and the concealing darkness she had worn like a mask splintered into a sudden flare of light. 'The Morvain sisterhouse holds my obedience, not my loyalty. My practice here has no ties to their hospice.'

New flame strengthened behind the panes of a clean lantern, backed with polished reflectors of tin. Dazzled and blinking, Feylind made out a stacked set of willow hampers, then the neatly made cot with a quilt of dyed linen, a weathered stool bought used from the cod market, and a worktable crammed with oddments and jars. Before these stood the Koriani herbalist. She wore no purple skirt and displayed no badge of rank on her person. Her boyish, slim form was clad in a simple, loose blouse and what looked like an apprentice smith's leather leggings with laces that hooked up the sides on bone buttons. A smattering of soot and cinder holes were overlaid by green stains, where a stone knife had been repeatedly wiped clean of the sap juices bled from cut greenery. Her feet on the packed earthen floor were bare, and striped with run dye from a pair of thonged sandals repeatedly soaked through in rain puddles.

A cascade of bronze hair tied up with fish twine tumbled over her shoulder as she reached high and hooked the lit lamp from a spike on the rafter. Her eyes, when she turned, were the rinsed tint of dawn mist, and her features, familiar from childhood on the Scimlade sandspit.

'I knew you in Merior,' Feylind burst out.

The herbalist smiled. 'I thought so, too. You're Feylind, Fiark's twin sister? If so, you'd be master of the merchant brig, *Evenstar*, a stunning accomplishment.' Her memory was flawless. She would last have seen Feylind as a girl of eight, yet needed no word to confirm that her visitor was the same spirit, grown into a strapping maturity.

Like many Koriani, Elaira had not aged, despite the passage of two dozen years. Nor had she lost the sharp-witted perception that, by the unfailing prompt of female instinct, Feylind knew had captured Prince Arithon's affection. Because of that memory, the moment of recognition between the two women carried an impacting weight of close secrets.

Elaira's fierce irony as always dispelled unsafe pitfalls and strangling awkwardness. 'You have mooring fees piling up while we wait?'

Snapped back to the subject of safer concerns, Feylind collared the reluctant lad and shoved his rawboned, shrinking frame forward. 'The knife work's the fault of Skjend wine seller's potboy. *Evenstar* pays your work fee, but I'd be much obliged if you'd charge his shop extra for provocation and nuisance.'

Elaira laughed. 'I can try. But prying coin from that skinflint's coffer is like squeezing a pig's bladder and praying the stream that pours out will smell like southcoast brandy.' Her lightning move caught the deckhand's wrist before he quite realized she intended to touch him.

As he fidgeted in dread apprehension, and the *Evenstar*'s brawny, practical mate sought excuses to direct his glance elsewhere, Elaira pulled a small steel knife from her boot cuff. Both men flinched back, yet she did nothing more than slice through the knots in the cheesecloth. The stained wrapping fell away and bared the gashed palm to the light.

Her prognosis was expert and swift. 'Can't move any fingers but the first and the thumb?'

The young deckhand managed a tongue-tied nod.

'Sit. Stop worrying.' Her no-nonsense touch steered the lad onto the stool. 'You won't feel a thing. In ten minutes, guaranteed, you'll be asleep and dreaming of girls, or better, the sweetcakes your grandame used to bake for the solstice.' From a hamper, she pulled a square of clean, boiled linen, and folded it into a compress. 'There.' She glanced to the mate, and evidently decided he would fare better if he was kept busy. 'Hold this in place and press down firmly. That should slow down the bleeding while I mix up a posset.'

Elaira turned her back, pulled a glazed mug from a shelf, then filled it with water poured from a stoneware jug. She asked Feylind, 'Can your mate heft an unconscious lug to his berth?'

Her guttersnipe dialect set the officer at ease, and he answered the query himself. 'Done that often enough when the drinking's been rough, and for louts twice as beefy as this one.'

'Then you're hired.' Elaira tipped in a dosage of carefully measured droplets from several glass phials, then laid a sigil of binding over the brew to augment and speed the effects. 'Drink this down,' she instructed the injured boy. She received back the emptied mug. The ship's mate assumed position at the deckhand's shoulder and propped him as his posture swayed and slackened into a slump. 'Lay him out on my cot, and then be so kind as to hold the lamp while I'm working.'

While the enchantress gathered her sharp needles and gut thread, her surgical knife, and her remedies, Feylind moved in and removed the deckhand's splashed boots. Then she lent her own muscle to the mate's work by shifting the unconscious man's ankles. 'Sing out as you need things.'

'Thanks. I will.' Elaira laid her selected instruments on a packing crate, tucked up her feet, and settled cross-legged on the bare dirt. She then draped a fresh square of linen on her knees. 'The compress can come off now.' A fine line marred her brow as she took the gashed hand into her lap and splayed the fingers over the cloth. 'The cut's clean. The sewing shouldn't be difficult. If you want something to drink while you're waiting, heat the water in the flask slung from the brazier. There's tea in the crock by the dish shelf.'

Feylind unhooked the flint striker and followed directions, while her mate, set at ease like a bone-lazy dog, settled on the stool with the lamp. If the shack's state of spotless, neat poverty surprised her, respect held her silent as she scrounged up two more chipped mugs, a bent spoon, and a small hoard of honey in a jar with a mended lid. She laid one drink, heavily sweetened, by Elaira's elbow, then sat on the floor with her back propped against the pine trestle, nursing the other herself.

By then, the enchantress had already sewn two of the tendons. Her conjury was impeccable; several neat, glowing sigils damped back the blood flow, and a third, pulsing violet, performed a function beyond Feylind's awareness to fathom.

'Don't stare directly at the spells,' Elaira warned gently. 'They can harm the unshielded eyes.' She knotted her gut thread, snatched a swallow of tea, then resumed work in unbroken concentration.

Outside, a cur barked. Someone stocky wearing hobnailed boots crunched past the shack's closed door. More distant, a drunk couple argued. Inured to disturbances, squarely at home amid the packed, squalling denizens of the poor quarter, the enchantress laid down neat stitches like clockwork. Something more than the labor beneath her sure hands pinched her lip between thoughtful teeth. 'Does your mate serve you closely?'

Feylind picked up the odd drift of the question. 'He knows all my secrets, if that's what you mean.' Her quick grin came and went, and a swift shared glance with the man whose silent company attended her. In fact, he was *Evenstar*'s second-in-command, and her lover, those nights she felt maudlin.

A looped knot, a snip of the knife; Elaira swabbed the wound clean with astringent. With one hand clasped beneath the deckhand's elbow to feel for the sequential flex of the muscles, she tested each finger in turn with a slight bearing tension. 'Well, we've apparently joined the correct piece to its counterpart.' Satisfied, she changed needles and started the less fussy process of closing the torn flap of skin.

Feylind could bear the drawn quiet no longer. 'You have something to say? I have friends, perhaps, who could make certain your thought finds the right destination.'

Elaira's hand lifted, paused, then resumed her task, patient. Her directness, point-blank, displayed courage that humbled. 'He swore your mother his oath that you wouldn't take undue risks.'

That pronoun, between them, held no ambiguity. As fondly attached to the Prince of Rathain, Feylind grinned like a shark in the dimness. 'Well, I don't always follow instructions. Do you?' At once, she regretted her tactless phrasing.

Elaira's mouth jerked to a hardened, thin line. She answered, though words cost her agony. 'Where my Koriani vow of obedience is at stake, I've no choice.' Stern discipline kept her touch steady on the needle. The loose tendrils of bronze hair wisped at her temples were but mildly dampened with sweat. Through a strung pause, she finished and knotted the next stitch. 'I beg you, for his life's sake, take extreme care what you say. Nor should you mention those friends in my hearing. If I know who they are, they could be taken and used against him.'

Feylind returned the small grace of her silence.

At considered length, the enchantress stalked obliquely toward the original bent of her inquiry. 'You were young, but do you recall the healing of the fisherman's son who dismembered his wrist in a squall line?'

Feylind took a shaky, sharp breath, and chose to be first to state the unsafe name outright. 'The one who caused the Master of Shadow to leave us, and you to pack up and flee Merior? I recall.'

Elaira's tension broke into laughter. 'I don't know what's worse, your fearless brashness or your brother's habit of throwing small stones with horrible, stinging accuracy.' She set another stitch, then asked the mate to trim the lamp. A sip of her cooling tea eased the interval while she pondered, or perhaps wet a throat grown too fear parched to speak. Aware of the steel in the depths of her eyes, Feylind could not but admire her trust, as she laid herself bare to a stranger.

'There were spells done that night, supported by the gift of the Masterbard's music.' Elaira set down her drained mug. Her neat movements showed resolve as she rethreaded the curved needle. 'The jointure of my art and his talent came at a price. An empathic link still remains in place between us. Distance and ocean blur the clarity of thought, but not the strength of emotion. He knows I'm concerned for him. Until you crossed my threshold, I had no means at all to safely let Arithon know why.'

That name, on her lips, held a bittersweet sorrow, touched to a tragic note of trapped longing.

Feylind caught back an unexpected rush of tears. Hands pressed to her face, as though bone and flesh could eclipse the relentless pain of his absence, she said softly, 'He sings for you. At sea, alone at his ship's helm, I've heard him. Sky and earth can but weep for the beauty of those melodies. He loves you, Elaira. His heart is still yours as no other's.' The last words came hardest; the only poor token of sympathy she could give to ease a separation as relentless as this one. 'I take comfort in knowing you feel the same way, no matter the distance between you.'

Any two other women could have indulged their paired grief and wept in each other's arms.

Elaira just swallowed. Her eyes shimmered, too bright, but only for a second before a smile like fire lit her elfin features from within. 'Thank you for that, from the core of my spirit.' She had to wait for her fingers to steady before she assayed the last stitches. Poultice paste, then the flash-point-bright sigils of healing and closure, and a clean dressing put the finishing touch on her handiwork.

'Your sailor should rest through tomorrow,' she said, brisk. 'If he rises too soon, that last seal will make him miserable with nausea. The hand will recover, but the closed wound must be kept stringently clean. No swabbing decks, and no labor in the rigging for at least the next fortnight.' Face tipped up to encompass the steady presence of the ship's mate, she finished, 'You can dim back the flame in the lamp.'

The shadows closed in like a flood as she rose. By touch, or long habit, she found her rusted bucket of seawater and rinsed her hands. Her words were grained velvet, fast and low, as she added her message for Arithon.

'Tell my beloved, the unbroken calm at Avenor bodes ill. The merchants grow fat and satisfied, unaware they are part of a masking design. Know this: Lysaer's false priesthood has begun to wield magic. Unclean little spells that link minds and send images. Those powers bend lane force to subtle disharmony, enough that some with the talent of birth-gifted mage-sight take notice.' She paused, deadly careful; by word or gesture, she must not reveal any more secrets than the ordinary hedge witch might glean, from watching the flight patterns of birds or touching the awareness of stones in the stream bottoms. 'The deflections are less likely to be felt at sea since they don't carry well over salt water. For Arithon, the new danger will come to bear on the Mistwraith's curse, and must not surface as a surprise: Avenor will soon be equipped to share communication on an instant with other enclaves sworn to the Light. The network will eventually span the five kingdoms. Once that happens, a single informant could trigger a coordinated muster. His Grace of Rathain must not set foot ashore on the continent.'

In a vehemence of desperate and frightful intensity, Elaira locked glances with the *Evenstar*'s blond-haired captain. 'Hear me clearly. *No matter what happens, regardless of provocation, he should keep to the sea and stay safe.'*

A winter-sharp chill ranged down Feylind's spine. 'There's more you're not saying.'

'Ath, how much, you can't fathom. My senior sisters spin secretive webs.' Even inside the order, few realized a fraction of what transpired when an enchantress put off the gray sleeves of charitable service and donned the robes of high administrative rank with their banded scarlet borders. Bleak as scaled granite, Elaira lifted her shoulders in an oblique shrug. 'Arithon's grandfather was wise, in his way. Politics and spelled conjury don't mix.'

Nor was Feylind a fool. She knew from her brother's brokerage in Shand how the westshore merchants who paid tithe to the Alliance had been lulled into silk-wound complacency. Tysan's cities had received sheltered protection for years, with Avenor's crown garrison defending their trade routes until coffers overflowed from the profits. That trend gave rise to ominous overtones set against this fresh news of a high priesthood versant in magelore. The unpleasant conclusion sat uneasily on her shoulders. 'Enchantress, you've implied there are reasons, beyond practice of sorcery, why the Alliance wants gifted talent driven out of town walls.'

'Talent reads pattern and lines of intent.' Elaira blotted her damp hands on her blouse, not owning a towel for the purpose. 'And small conjury affects lane force, everywhere, for anyone with mage-sight to read.'

'Then the powerful don't want back-alley eyes befouling the works of their covert conspiracies.' Feylind's snapped gesture encompassed the made-over fish shack, with its gapped boards and flimsy construction. 'You don't seem terribly concerned, for yourself.'

'Well, Lysaer's no idiot.' Elaira rummaged after her flask of alcohol. One by one, she wiped clean her specialized array of steel needles. 'The Koriani Order's too massive and too organized to suffer persecution from his cult of amateur priests. Morriel hates hedge witches and necromancers of all stripes. The sisterhood has always regarded their works as an undisciplined nuisance, sometimes with good reason since chicanery too often becomes mixed with dangerous, slipshod practice. As long as the Alliance examiners stay focused on lay talent, our Senior Circle won't be moved to interfere.' Which implied, as well, that Alliance interests and Koriani policy trod the same paths, near enough. 'If there's a succession, the new Prime Matriarch may or may not take a stand against the Crown Examiner's practices.'

Which perilously was more than ought to be said, out of safety for the herbalist who had sworn over the key to her consciousness to bind the order's stern vow of obedience.

Feylind gripped Elaira's forearm in profound understanding and thanks. 'Your word will be sent on through trusted hands. Leave the method for me to arrange.'

Only brisk and impersonal details remained to finish a routine transaction. 'My fee for the healing is ten Morvain silvers or the same weight in another town's coinage,' Elaira said. 'You may discharge the debt to the matron who sells fish by the landing. What I send, she will use to feed beggar children.' In parting, the enchantress caught Feylind's callused hand, her sure touch now undone by trembling. 'Go safely. Give the Prince of Rathain my sweet blessing, but hear me: if Daelion Fatemaster shows us Ath's mercy, *he must not meet me again in this lifetime.*'

'What do you know that's too dreadful to tell me?' Feylind pressured in whispered dread.

But Elaira shook her head. She chivvied the larger frame of the *Evenstar*'s captain firmly on past her worktable and toward the shack's single doorway.

The ship's mate understood well enough the enchantress was desperately compromised; he bent to the cot and hefted the unconscious deckhand over his capable shoulders. 'Feylind, come away. Any more that you say could be dangerous.'

'Go at once. Your mate's sensibilities are most wise. Trust me, I'm content as things are. It's enough that you bear word for Arithon Teir's'Ffalenn.' Elaira unlatched the plank door and stood back, her gut a clenched stone for the inevitable fact, that if her beloved paid heed to her warning, if he steered clear of danger as she pleaded, then the boy, a goatherd's son from Araethura, might be left to die for the sacrifice.

That dichotomy brought torment, two-edged as cut glass. Yet the love she bore the man demanded her honor. News of High Priest Cerebeld's twisted practices must reach Arithon, come what might. He already shared her unquiet apprehension. Through the thrummed cord of tension transmitted across the gulf of an unendurable separation, he must sense her conflicted integrity. The extreme, forceful phrases she had imparted to Feylind would let him extrapolate much more. If he had access to scrying, his own mage-schooled insight might forewarn that Morriel's snare of conspiracy against him had grown to embrace an appalling, dark practice that transgressed every limit of decency.

Given the context of Feylind's message, Arithon would be granted the gift of awareness to assess the grave peril which faced him. He could call upon Dakar's wise counsel to guide him. If he chose not to listen on the hour the trap became sprung, he would come prepared, with guarded knowledge in advance of the danger.

# Forerunners

From his vantage tower eyrie at Avenor, Cerebeld, High Priest of the Light, leans on his windowsill, brooding while the late-night festival brands burn to coals, and Gace Steward brings news of the words too closely guarded to overhear between the grandame s'Brydion and Lysaer s'Ilessid's princess; the meeting prompts his immediate disposition: 'High time Alestron receives an Alliance representative who wears the sunwheel seal of a man sworn and bound to the Light . . .'

In the chill hour before dawn, Princess Ellaine of Avenor sits at the window seat of her private apartment, firm in her resolve to expose the faction that arranged for the murder of her predecessor; and an impulse in forethought prompts her to cast a charitable gold coin to the slop taker's woman, whose wagon pulls up at the curbside below to collect refuse and night soil from the palace . . .

Far east, under the massive vaulted dome of Etarra's council hall, a gathering of officials assembles to hear the first minister of the city, who announces, 'As you all know, our Lord Governor Supreme is failing in health. Therefore, time has come to set seal to his document of succession and approve the candidate he sets forth to defend his seat for the challenge of the public vote . . .'

**Summer 5667**

# IX. Discourse and Documents

D awn the day after the solstice festival saw Dame Dawr s'Brydion out and about before the city lampsmen began their rounds to douse the lights at the watch change. She paid her parting respects to the duke's posted envoy over breakfast. Then she gathered her silver-and-ebony stick and departed with a packet of sealed dispatches bound to destinations south and east. The new-risen sun burned pale gold through the sea mist while her escort of clan guard assembled in the yard. She spurned the envoy's kindly meant offer of a litter in scathing language, and set off on foot for the harbor.

Her six retainers knew better than to smile over her irascible independence. Dame Dawr was tough as old boot leather, and even more stubbornly set in her ways. She traveled nowhere in sedan chairs, not when she could still manage a saddle; and she never rode when brisk walking was more sensible. Here in Tysan, a livery mount cost a coin tax for the Light, which offended her belief in Ath's natural order, as well as her ingrained ancestral respect for dumb beasts.

'No horse I know would become willing party to the backstabbing stupidities of town politics.' The black stick jabbed air to nail home her point, driving an inadvertent trio of bystanders to leap with a splash of dismay into the gutter. Dawr bade them good morning in frosty clan accents, then resumed her diatribe in the same breath. Lysaer s'Ilessid's pretty fortress of Avenor, she insisted, was small enough that an insolent boy could spit from one wall and strike the sunwheel surcoats of the garrison sentries who stood rounds of duty on the other.

The old lady reached the harborside, her prickly high spirits undimmed. The early air warmed, thick and tepid as new milk, as the mist thinned and broke off the waterfront. Sweating, bare-chested stevedores ferried the piled boxes and bales to the docked trade galleys before the burgeoning heat steamed the last dew off the cobbles. Dying embers from the festival fires painted the smoky scent of ash and carbon through the seaside taints of drying fishnets and tide wrack. The crushed garlands dropped by the dancers and celebrants wilted, the perfume of bruised blossoms mingled with the damp oak miasma of salt barrels bound for the stockyards.

Dame Dawr waded into the bustle, undaunted. She thumped her stick on the boards of the dock as though testing for rot or unsoundness. Her shrewd glance took note of the quantity and quality of the trade goods and provisions awaiting transport. Only her guard respected her whetted acumen enough to realize her mental survey missed nothing. She might learn more on a short, morning stroll than Avenor's ranking guildsmen could glean from their closeted ledgers. Men respected Grandame Dawr, as wary in her presence as unarmed boys who faced a berserker gone amok with naked steel. Experience branded that caution into them. Duke Bransian's grandmother saw like a hawk, and played deaf as a post anytime she saw fit to indulge in her scathing, inimical temperament.

That her vicious moods marched hand in glove with keen wits gave the s'Brydion retainers sharp reason to humor her.

Another five strides, and the petulant twist to her lips warned them of pending trouble.

'Dharkaron's immortal bollocks!' Dawr snapped under her breath. A virulent rap of her stick punctuated her abrupt stop. 'Will you look at that fool, yapping lapdog?'

Several yards down the wharf, where the deepwater ships berthed, half-hitched to the gray, weathered bollards, the target of her insult stood unsuspecting, his sunwheel robe a scream of bright white against the sun-faded red tunics of two stolid s'Brydion men-at-arms. These had planted themselves in determination across the gangway to the Duke of Alestron's state galley.

Dame Dawr straightened frail shoulders. 'We'll just see what sort of mannerless numskull seeks to board our decks uninvited.'

'That's an ally,' the hard-bitten captain of her escort reminded in a low voice.

'Aye, an ally, you insist.' A brimstone glint of joy lit Dawr's dark eyes. 'Then we agree. We'll have to leave weapons out of this.' She tipped up her chin and bored in with a swirl of silk skirts straight down the throat of the argument.

Arrived like a pestering black gnat, she placed a hand on the arm of the sunwheel acolyte. 'Young man,' she announced in grandmotherly sympathy, 'you must be misguided or lost. This galley takes no paying passengers.'

The victim spun and glared. His jaw clenched tight with renewed irritation as he realized he could not dismiss the mistress of the duke's ship or brush off her senseless nattering.

Dawr smiled. 'I see you're distressed.' She patted his hand, all pearl teeth and daft kindness. 'Will you accept my assistance? One of the duke's men would be pleased to take you to the harbormaster's, where a list will be kept of those vessels prepared to sell transport.'

The man flushed to his eyebrows. His combed, satin hair wisped in the breeze as he curbed bursting temper and mastered his first impulse to snatch back his arm. 'I seek no paid passage, madam.' All icy civility, he made introductions. 'I'm Acolyte Cowill, sent here by appointment of Cerebeld, High Priest of the Light, to return as ambassador to your duke.'

Dawr's pity melted into concern. 'No coin, did you say? How misfortunate.' She turned, craned her neck, then beckoned to the closest man of her guard and told him to empty her purse of small silver. 'Clan custom,' she piped, cheerful as she returned her bright, sparrow's gaze to her victim. 'We refuse no one alms. Brings in ill luck if beggars are slighted, and the needy are left to go hungry.'

The acolyte glanced in flustered appeal to Dawr's escort. 'Tell your mistress her silver's not asked. Please explain. Avenor has appointed me to serve the Light's glory in the duke's court at Alestron.'

Dame Dawr observed this exchange, eyebrows raised in obstructive epiphany. 'You want guest passage to appeal to my grandson, Bransian Teir's'Brydion?' A doddering step marched her into the acolyte's face, where, nonplussed, she reached out and gave his biceps a testing, firm pinch. 'Scrawny, I'd say. Definitely too weak, if you're asking to train for the field troops. That's nothing a few shifts at the oar won't set right. But I'd advise you, throw out that doublet. We're bound south through Havish. King Eldir's officials have no love of priests. White-and-gold cloth with that upstart blazon will certainly set you on the wrong foot with the locals.'

While the grandame regarded him with benign expectation, the acolyte shrugged, then drew breath to restate his request to her guardsmen.

He managed no words.

Dame Dawr banged her stick on the wharf timbers with a thunderous
report that startled every uninvolved party within earshot. 'Well, what
under sky are you waiting for, young man? Do you ask for guest passage
to Alestron, or not?' Not content with waspish railing, Dawr prodded
him square in the chest with her stick. 'If you're coming along, then by
Dharkaron's Black Chariot and Spear, I'm too frail to carry you aboard!
March yourself onto the galley at once. Ath's tide won't wait while we
stand here.'

Dealt the unceremonious choice of being left flat-footed on the dock,
the acolyte fled up the gangway.

The s'Brydion matriarch and her escort crowded onto the deck at his
heels. The last pair of men-at-arms hauled in the gangway with a speed
that suggested they forestalled his last means of escape.

Dawr snapped the ship's master a curt nod of greeting. 'Cast off.
Then see the new recruit settled.'

When the old woman departed for the privacy of her cabin, the young
priest addressed the nearest captain at arms. 'Is the lady always this
difficult?'

The man's bearded face split into a grin. 'Oh, aye. There's times
when you humor her, no questions asked.'

A horn blast cut off further chance for conversation. Given cracking
strings of orders to see the galley under way, Duke Bransian's crews
reacted with war-tuned efficiency. Every man, including the ones who
had served as Dawr's escort, appeared to have something important to
do. In breathtakingly short order, Alestron's sleek vessel was set under
oars and beating a steady, swift stroke from the harbor.

As the work seemed to slacken, no crewman fell idle. The sunwheel
acolyte politely awaited his moment to request a guest envoy's accom-
modation. To his dumbfounded outrage, the chance never came to seek
civilized words with the captain. The galley's bare-chested, mountain
of a mate stepped up and collared him first. 'Ye're to be assigned a
shift at the oar, and a berth in forward quarters with the crew.' He
laughed at the acolyte's steamed spate of protest. 'Old lady's orders.
Nobody crosses her, it's that or swim. And she says that white tunic's
to go also.'

The priest spat scalded outrage.

The mate folded his massive arms and just shrugged, the puckered
white scars inscribed by past wars glistening sweat in the sunlight.
'Small difference, whether the old bat's gone daft or not. She's dead

set on the notion you want a place in the guard. You'd risk both of your bollocks and even your life trying to change her mind. If you were dismissed from her presence alive and ungelded, Duke Bransian still won't allow us to haul deadweight. His policy forbids paying passengers, since our enemies would likely use such an opening to saddle us with spies. Envoy or recruit, you'll row, or you'll swim. Your choice. Which is it to be?'

A glance right and left showed a gathered ring of deckhands, every one of them muscled and welted with the calluses of a veteran field mercenary. Since Cerebeld's acolyte was an indifferent swimmer, and the tide in the channel ran full ebb, he yielded to sense. The white tunic, perforce, was surrendered. The fine fabric was no sooner snatched from his grasp, when some whooping barbarian appeared with a ballast rock. To jokes and rough laughter, the sunwheel emblem of Lysaer's brave order was bundled and knotted, then cast off to sink under the thrashed froth of the wake.

A credit to his staunch determination to carry out his mission for the Light, the priest acolyte blistered his hands at the bench, rowing down Tysan's west coastline. He shared meals with the crew, suffered their ribald chaffing of greenhorns, and fell into dreamless, exhausted sleep in the salt-musty twine of a hammock. The work in the slow, turgid air of high summer could wear even a seasoned man surly. When the galley's beet-faced quartermaster insisted that he also turn out for weapon drill, none were surprised when Alestron's guest acolyte jumped ship in the sailor's stews of Tideport. His desertion was timely, since the docks there offered the last port of call before the duke's ship left the crown territory of Tysan.

No man to bemoan the loss of a whiner, the ship's captain ordered the vessel's oar ports sealed off. On experienced guesswork and instinct, he judged his best run of weather and cast off for a risky, offshore passage to Cheivalt.

Dame Dawr was informed of the acolyte's defection over the brown bread, butter, and jam she preferred for her breakfasts at sea. By then, the men had lashed the stowed oars inboard. A following wind rammed the galley through the swell, to smoking bursts of spray off the prow beak.

'No loss,' she admitted to the mate who delivered the report. Her pursed lips unpleated to a cackle of delight as she invited him to strip off his baldric and cutlass and eat. 'We gave Cerebeld's whelp his brief taste of the fate the s'Ilessid pretender decreed for the clanborn forced captive in Tysan. He can now run home to his kennel and yap. Whatever amends are demanded through state recourse, I say the fool's gotten off kindly with a sore back and a healthy few blisters. Suppose he'd survived the course of this voyage and arrived to set foot in Alestron? One canting spiel on the Light of true justice, and Bransian would likely have lopped off his misguided head.'

While the sunwheel acolyte made his disgruntled way back to complain to his high priest at Avenor, and the s'Brydion galley sped downcoast to exchange courtesy with King's Eldir's court at Telmandir, the dust kicked up by the Alliance summer muster cast ocher haze over the encampments spread beneath the squat towers of Etarra. There, each year, boys just sprouting beards and young men of ambition and prowess gathered to enter their names as candidates for service to the Light. As equals, they stripped to the skin. Those found in sound health, without flaw or deformity, were issued saffron-dyed hose, a hemp sash, and a coarse linen tunic. Sorted by age, they were assigned to a drill sergeant and given a cot in a stifling barracks tent.

Through the long, hot days, under blazing sun, they would train and be tested for fitness: trials of strength, of coordination and fast reflex, of endurance; other exercises challenged them for mental acuity. The contests were unforgiving. Some applicants shattered bones, others broke nerves; a few misfortunates lost their lives, and so earned their place on the Light's list of fallen, with a stipend sent to placate their grieving families. By season's end, no longer equal, but ranked according to merit, the candidates might swear their oath to the Light and sign for a term of Alliance service.

No applicant who completed the month's screening was turned away. The brawny but dull could drive carts or cook bread, and do menial tasks in a war camp. The bright who were clumsy could keep tallies and scribe. The middle-rank competent trained at arms for two years and wore the badge of the Alliance garrison, assigned by company to bolster the ranks in those towns who paid tribute for the privilege of Lysaer s'Ilessid's defense.

The better, the brighter, were offered choice training as officers. They enrolled in the school for tactical warfare Lysaer had endowed at Etarra. Graduates served three years on campaign in the field with the Northern League of Headhunters, then entered paid service for tours of duty renewed by choice every decade.

Only the cream of each summer's muster earned the chance to swear for life service. Enrolled for seven demanding years of advance training, then seasoned in arduous field trials, these alone might vie for the right to wear the white surcoat and gold sunwheel of the Divine Prince's elite guard. Those who succeeded in winning that accolade were the bone and sinew of champions. They became the very mainstay of the Light, sworn by oath to fight and to die until the last shadow of sorcery was expunged from the land. Nor would their ranks be disbanded until the hour the Spinner of Darkness was cast down in final defeat.

The families of such chosen men were listed among the most fortunate. Their aging mothers, their fathers, their wives and young children became eligible for an Alliance pension; if misfortune struck, and their kin passed the Wheel, coin from Lysaer's coffers ensured that they never saw want.

While the raw blaze of sunrise dissolved the night mist off the broad plain spread under the high walls of Etarra, the sons of farmers and poor tradesmen flocked in from all quarters of the land to vie for the honor of armed service. Their earnest endeavors were not delegated to second-rate officers or lame veterans retired from the field. Lord Commander Sulfin Evend handpicked each year's roster of captains, and the Blessed Prince personally oversaw every facet of testing. While the morning fog thinned over the practice fields, he might be seen astride his cream war-horse. His white surcoat and diamonds shone, pure frost and light, through the trammeling haze of stirred grit as young candidates sparred and cracked through their drills with wooden weapons. Noontide, in the close, panting labor of tearing down field tents, while a company of archers pelted an assault with blunted shafts, a man might glance sidewards and discover the comrade who sweated at his shoulder was none else than Divinity Incarnate.

Whether silted in dust, or mud-splashed from a squall line, or stripped of his surcoat and shirt, Lysaer's presence could not be mistaken. His pale, gold-shot hair and candid blue eyes were as distinctive as his sunwheel banner; the attentiveness he granted to each man's small needs uplifted morale and engendered spellbinding awe. His inherent majesty was not cast off with fine clothes or an absence of jeweled trappings. He had a quick laugh, and an incandescent smile, and a kindness through hardship that welded men's hearts in devotion. Where he passed, humor flourished. Though the hazards of each exercise were difficult enough to break hearts and strip tempers, even fell the stoutest man, body and spirit, no rough circumstance seemed to outstrip his ability to inspire hopeful applicants to renewed effort and dedication.

That gift of exalted leadership made Lysaer s'Ilessid a trial to locate on those days when he surrendered to impulse and joined ranks with his green recruits. His fine horse, his sunwheel banner, and his liveried retinue might often be found idle and dozing under some shade oak, or else soaked and morose in the rain. They might have left their divine charge with the scullions in the field kitchen or with some wagoneer hauling new spear shafts. A search of the quarter where his train was dismissed infallibly ended in failure. His Divine Grace's previous choice of close company would regretfully relate he had left and gone visiting someplace else.

'Sulfin Evend dogs his heels,' offered the white charger's groom. The latest balked messenger had been dispatched in full panoply from Etarra by the Lord Governor's house steward. Overheated himself in the clogged, humid air, he took pity on the man's sweat-ringed livery and fresh flush. 'Look for the crow's nephew. He'll be the one bearing sheathed steel, grimly watchful, while everyone else grunts and swears.'

Like others before him, this latest messenger must run the dusty gamut of the practice fields in a goose chase that might well exhaust the whole morning.

The Lord Governor's pampered servant trudged off, resigned. He edged past the boys set sparring with quarterstaves, and narrowly missed getting brained. He peered at each face on the archers' lines, inciting oaths and a rash of wild volleys. The lance captain cursed him for getting underfoot. When he paused to scrape manure from his quilted velvet shoe, someone's loose mount all but kicked him. Smeared with grass stains from crossing a drain ditch where other men assembled footbridges out of twine and hacked branches, he collided with a hurrying lackey, who thrust a tray of new-risen dough into his unwilling hands.

'Hold this.' The bald cook turned his rump and bent over a field oven. Words emerged, muffled, haranguing the brainless recruit who had forgotten to remove the preceding batch of baked bread. The spoiled loaves were dragged out, black and smoking as bricks, to some outspoken bystander's hoots of laughter.

Relieved of the tray, the disgruntled messenger picked his way across the packed, dusty ground where boys sparred with oak sticks to a swordmaster's bellowed instruction. He ran the gamut unscathed and reached the far side. Paused, panting, in the shadow of a siege engine, he had scarcely recovered his wind when a yelling, half-naked troop of men sprang out of the grass. Brandishing billets wound with lint soaked in oil, they commenced a determined exercise in demolition by fire.

Where the ground sloped into a dry gully, the servant blundered into an armed ambush of shouting men who wore camouflage paint like barbarians. These carried javelins and short bows, and through rank, tangled beards, smelled as though they had not seen a bath for a sevenday.

Prince Lysaer was beyond the next rise, immersed to the chest in a trout basin where a stream splashed out of the high peaks of the Mathorns and swirled on its mad, jagged course toward the river bottom. He was soaked. Dripping hair fronded his magnificent build, while he called helpful advice to a boy who chased a flip-flopping fish through the lush summer weeds on the bank.

'Grit your fingers with sand, or else pounce with a shirt. That one? Very well, *there's* my man. That way the slick devil can't slide through your grasp.' His amiable encouragement dissolved to laughter for the fact that the garment snatched up for netting was his own. 'Never mind. A few scales won't matter. The embroidery should acquire a fascinating glitter. The sensation might become the new rage in fashion for the pedigree rakes in the city.'

Too timid to intervene, the city messenger neglected to recall Sulfin Evend's guarding presence until a hand grasped his shoulder from behind, the bite of mailed fingers demanding. 'You came bearing word for his Divine Grace?'

The house servant startled half out of his skin. 'My Lord Governor begs leave for an audience,' he blurted, as intimidated by the Alliance Lord Commander's ice eyes as by the sight of the Blessed Prince, who emerged dripping from the stream, his poised self-command lent intimidating force by his state of unabashed nakedness.

While Sulfin Evend's snapped questions probed the nature of the errand, Lysaer's seamless good nature just as meticulously attended loose ends. The panting trout in his shirt was released back to freedom, then the boy recruit dispatched at a run to his drill sergeant. The gold-sewn linen shirt saw further abuse as a towel, then lay discarded over the flat muscle of the Divine Prince's shoulder.

'Something's wanted?' He bent and retrieved his immaculate white tunic and trunk hose from the grass.

'Etarra's Lord Governor Supreme has asked to receive you,' Sulfin Evend filled in. His restless hands stayed too well married to weapon hilts for him to volunteer for service as dresser, even when haste might be called for: Etarra's aged despot was failing. 'Something to do with a sealed city document.'

'I presume Morfett wants to announce the ratified agreement concerning his imminent succession.' Lysaer tied off his points, tossed his head to clear the running beads of water from his hair, then bent his grave gaze on the red-faced palace servant. 'I'll seek audience directly. Make sure the water boy gives you a dipper. Then ask at the cook's camp for a ride in the next wagon sent inbound through the town walls.'

Morfett, Mayor of Etarra, Defender of Trade, and Lord Governor

Supreme of the Northern Reaches languished, dying, in silk sheets, a heavyset man of short stature and liver-spotted skin, and a complexion tinged jonquil with jaundice. The daytime bedchamber where he conducted the affairs of his last will and testament was built of marble and lozenged glass tile. Noon sunlight strained through the awnings shading the wide-open casements. What minimal breeze wafted through wore the flint-earth smell of baked brick.

The sluggish air inside reeked of medicine and stale sweat, embedded in the costly musk of incense and attar of roses. A servant with a peacock tail mounted in ebony, lapis lazuli, and gold fanned the supine figure on the bed. To one side, a plate of nibbled melon rinds drew flies, and a tattooed half-breed physician from Atchaz mixed philters in a row of blown glass vials.

His desert tribe parentage had instilled the rites of Mother Dark along with rare knowledge of herb lore, for the tiny man grabbed his ring of bone amulets and fled, muttering dialect, as Lysaer s'Ilessid crossed the threshold.

Strong sun had dried the stream water from his hair. Through the steep ride to reach the pass commanded by the city's stolid watch keeps, the blond ends had curled in wind-combed tangles over the superb carriage of his shoulders. If he had taken no pause for grooming, a servant had rushed him into fresh hose and a fine, pleated shirt, with yoked collar and cuffs worked in gold wire and faceted beadwork. At each move, the ornamentation caught light; the needle-fine scatter of reflections danced and flitted across the heavy, oiled gloom of the state palace's furnishings.

'How may my gifts serve your city?' Lysaer asked as he stopped at the foot of the bed.

The Lord Governor opened pouched eyes, the corneas milk hazed and unfocused. 'Blessed Prince.' His cracked lips parted, more grimace than smile. 'You came.'

Knowledge of imminent death weighed his tone. He bore no resentment, but took settled comfort in the miraculous proof of divine intervention: Prince Lysaer had not aged throughout the twenty-eight years he had known him. Still vital, still strong, here stood the same man who had reknit the backbone of Etarra's defense through the mangling losses meted out by the Shadow Master on the banks of Tal Quorin.

'I have two last bequests,' wheezed Morfett. 'The city council has already set their seal of approval to one of them.' He gave an impatient jerk of the chin, the gesture all but buried in folds of flaccid flesh. 'Come nearer. Examine the writ for yourself.'

Small points of illumination flitted like ghost mayflies as Lysaer stepped forward and opened the hasp of the document chest at the bedside.

'The scroll has black cord and ribbons of silver and scarlet,' said Morfett. 'You should find it resting on top.'

Lysaer drew out the weighty parchment, sealed with the nine sigils of Etarra's city guilds and the massive wax imprint of the Lord Governor's blazon, its knotted closure unbroken. 'My Lord Governor? I hold the document.'

'Break it open. Read. It concerns you.' The dying man on the bed sank back in stained pillows, the dome of his forehead dewed shiny with overripe sweat. 'I spent my last breath and will overriding the arguments against a ratification.'

Lysaer cracked the seal. A faint nimbus seemed to emanate from the wisped gold of his hair as the parchment unrolled. At the top, the twined cipher of Etarra's city council was handpainted in vermilion and gilt; beneath that, the heavy, ornamental script framed two brief lines, appended by rank upon rank of sprawled signatures. Its grant appointed Lysaer s'Ilessid, old blood prince of Tysan, the sanctioned right to be named as a candidate for election to Etarra's ruling office of lord governor supreme.

'You don't ask why,' the aged incumbent wheezed, his suffering eyes shut amid the propped morass of pillows.

The flicked light off exquisite bead embroidery stirred and stilled as Lysaer raised his head. His resonant voice filled the lofty chamber with assurance through the whispered rhythm of the peacock fan in the hands of the servant. 'I would leave you your dignity.' His sure, sun-browned hands stayed unhurried as he rolled up the parchment and looped its dangling ribbons over the split seams of the seals.

'Shrewd man.' The Lord Governor repeated his death's-head smile. 'I see I won't need to remind you that the office lasts for life. But first you have to manage to win the common vote. Fail me in that, and the curse of my last breath will lie on you.'

Not to be drawn by barbs masked in banter, Lysaer placed the scroll on the bed.

'You'd wait for my liver to fail, first? Very well.' The Lord Governor reopened irascible eyes. 'I am afraid. The Master of Shadow has made himself scarce, and your guilds at Avenor have lost their edge in pursuit of their trade. Too few of your guard there survived Dier Kenton Vale to remind them of the perils still at large. Here at Etarra, we haven't forgotten Tal Quorin, but those who witnessed the devastations there and at Minderl Bay are aging. I'm a suspicious man. I believe the Spinner of Darkness will return to sow evil on an unsuspecting, new generation. If so, the next decades are critical. Preventive measures must be sealed into place before my peer councilmen step down for their retirement.'

'You mentioned two bequests,' Lysaer replied. 'Go on.'

The Lord Governor barked a wheezing laugh that bled off into gasps and a pallor that left his jaundiced face runneled like half-melted butter. 'I want new walls, prince. Rings of strong defenses that can be manned twenty-four hours a day. A siege here would be an ugly affair, soon over. The stone slopes of the mountains cannot sustain our large populace. We have no rain cisterns and no secure inner citadel.' The pale, sausage fingers plucked and wandered on the coverlet, too palsied for vehement gestures. 'I'd have defenses erected on the Plain of Araithe, where livestock and grain could be held secure to provide my city with sustenance. We have mountain caverns that could be set up for storage and granaries. I ask you to build Etarra into a stronghold for the Light, lest weak hearts and short memories fail your cause at Avenor. Will you do this? As my dying wish, I would leave the city's interests in dependable hands. Yours, if you will accept.'

Lysaer arose. Flecks of light arrowed and spun from his cuffs as he reached out and captured the Lord Governor's hands inside his sword-callused fingers. 'Consider your wish granted. Etarra shall have walls, each stone of them pledged to stand in the fight against shadow. A side benefit of thriving trade at Avenor, the crown treasury can find funds to pay stonemasons. Which keep do you wish to be named in your memory?'

'The one overlooking the north, and Tal Quorin,' whispered Lord Governor Morfett. His eyes flagged and closed, his vitality drained by the minimal effort of speaking. 'Go in the Light's grace, Blessed Prince, and ask a servant to send in my daughters.'

'I'll take the word to your family in person,' Lysaer s'Ilessid said gently. He reached left-handed, pulled up a stool, and sat down. 'But after you've heard what else the Light plans to secure your great city of Etarra.'

He started to speak. Throughout, he held the Lord Governor's ice-cold, moist hands firmly clasped in his generous strength. By the hour he finished, late afternoon cast tea-colored light through the sun-faded canvas of the awnings, and grateful tears seeped down the seamed chasms in the Lord Governor's aged cheeks.

'I can die unafraid of the darkness.' Morfett settled, replete on his pillows. His bleared eyesight encompassed the man by his bed, but saw only stars set into a gold haze of brightness. 'In the Light, may you win the election as my successor. Deny the s'Ffalenn bastard his crown at Ithamon, and rule long and ably after me.'

Two months past the hour the death bells tolled for Etarra's Lord Governor Supreme, Alestron's state galley blew into her home port ahead of a black squall line that stitched the dark harbor with lightning. An adept from Ath's Brotherhood had just finished blessing the shorn barley, and the last straw sheaves were bundled and dry in the East Halla lofts. As sun-browned as his field hands, Duke Bransian strode into the lower hall of his citadel. His servants knew all of his habits. Before he could bellow, a kitchen boy brought him a tankard of ale. The duke praised him for his foresight, then opened his mouth to slurp at the foaming head which spilled over the fist wrapped around the crockery tankard. Two deerhounds and a mastiff dropped in panting heaps at his feet, ears turned back to screen out the energetic noise of the household's two-legged offspring. Children tumbled and laughed, or toddled sucking fingers, the dozens of nieces, nephews, cousins, and bastards indiscriminately mixed with the get of dairymaids, craftsmen, and servants.

Clanblood held the concept of birthright in contempt; even five centuries after the uprising, a stablehand's son could grow up to captain the guard, based on his mettle and merit.

A girl runner dispatched from the harbor found the duke wiping ale from his beard, one boy of three years wrapped around his dusty boot. An apple-cheeked daughter, just able to walk, shared her bread crust with the deerhounds, and a third child, missing breeches, screamed with laughter and let the mastiff lick the jam off his face.

'State galley's back, uncle,' yelled the messenger through the clamor. 'Dame Dawr's halfway up to the citadel.'

Duke Bransian choked. Beer suds flew from his beard as he howled. 'These weans are more muddy than the hounds in my kennels!' He waved a huge hand at the oblivious sprawl of Alestron's next generation. 'Dawr finds them like this, she's likely to nail all our skins to the gatehouse. Somebody better drag at least half of them out for clean clothes and dunk the rest in the horse trough.'

As Mearn's sharp-tongued wife took charge like a sergeant, the duke drained his beer at a gulp, glanced down, and found the girl still breathless at his shirttails. 'What else?' Lightning flickered; rising wind shook the glass in the stained-glass arches of the casements while the duke glared down at the child, one of Parrien's, or Keldmar's, to judge by her mulish, square chin. 'Isn't the old besom's arrival quite enough to ruin my day?'

A barrage of close thunder shivered the thick stone. 'The brig

*Evenstar*'s also inbound from the north,' the girl resumed in a rush. 'Lookout at Great Rock saw her masts in the channel before the squall line closed in. He sent a horseman. That man says she flies Keldmar's banner and the pennant of the Fellowship of Seven.'

'Dawr *and* an interfering Sorcerer, both on the same misbegotten day?' Duke Bransian wiped the back of his hand on his sun-faded red surcoat; he was wont to wear his mail shirt, even in the barley fields, and his great sword never left his side. 'Daelion's cock and bollocks!' He thumped his drained mug on the nearest trestle, raked loose straw from the shorn ends of his hair, and loosed a laugh that lit his gray eyes to a battle-crazed spark of delight. 'Well, things just woke up and got interesting.'

Then, belatedly aware of his own muddy boots and the sweat rings and stains on his shirtsleeves, he snapped new orders to the girl runner. 'Find my wife or her maidservant and have one of them toss out a clean shirt.'

While the child took to her heels and the dogs yapped and howled at the inbound storm, he stripped. Stained cloth and mail flew into a heap. His worn, quilted gambeson sailed onto the top. He kicked off his boots and strode through the side door unclad except for his hose. The deerhounds balked at going out. Forlorn and whining, they watched the lightning flare and crack. Then the squall broke. Rain hammered the cobbled yard to a froth of wind-driven current and puddles. The mastiff crouched on its haunches and endured in the open, sneezing mournfully. Grinning at the mayhem, since the weather matched his mood, Bransian sluiced his head and torso in the raging gouts of runoff that spewed from a gargoyle downspout.

Alestron's inner citadel had a high, slender tower with a top chamber secluded as an eyrie. The embrasure was punched through with arrow slits. Their vantage overlooked the upper-fortress walls, and a view which encompassed the descending steps of town rooftops and the outer bastion that rimmed the canyon-steep cliffs of the estuary. Bransian s'Brydion favored the room for close councils. The site provided an effective deterrent against eavesdroppers. As an added advantage, it held too few chairs, a tactical point that gave graceful avoidance to the opinionated presence of family wives.

The bullish bastion of male authority would have stayed uncontested, in any case. Given the duke's openhanded invitation, the s'Brydion women would have kept their wise distance. Whenever the duke and his brothers met in parley, no firm decisions resulted. Accusations inevitably led to contentions that became spectacular, fur-ripping arguments.

Experience had taught the ladies that each point of dispute would be repeated in exhaustive detail when their husbands descended to salve their wounds. They would hear the whole list of rife insults exchanged, the items at issue larded through with opinion on the mutton-headed faults of each sibling. Accustomed to the blustering nature of their men, the wives gathered in private to sort out the tangle with cool heads. Duke Bransian's high-handed stubbornness had prevailed but a handful of times, and only if the women failed to reach a consensus or arrive at a sensible compromise.

Those notable occasions when the Fellowship sent a Sorcerer to arbitrate, the four brothers' wives shared tea and cake, and gratefully left the role of wise counsel and adroit restraint to the powers of higher authority.

Grandame Dawr, at her whim, proved the indefatigable exception. Her hand latched on the silver head of her stick, she thumped up the difficult turnpike stair, crossed the landing, and perched like a sparrow in the massive oak chair appointed with the ducal blazon.

Bransian deferred to her. Arrived at her heels, with his beard blotting moisture into his clean shirt and dry doublet, he kissed her cheek in greeting. His massive bulk always made the round chamber feel close as a closet as he unbuckled his broadsword and laid its russet leather sheath on the round oak table. Then, discomfited as a parade horse yanked back from a roll in the mud, he spun one of the smaller chairs backwards and straddled the seat to a squeaking complaint of glued struts.

Outside, the storm snapped and thundered. Gusts winnowed fine dousings of rain through the arrow slits and licked trickles of damp down the walls, where a thin, channeled drain released the overflow through the bared fangs of a gargoyle crouched on the vertical stonework outside.

Parrien stamped in next, his clan braid dripping, and the tops of his breeches plastered against the bunched muscle of his thighs. Word of the arrival must have caught him at the boards, since he still gnawed at the early apple impaled on the point of his dagger. Mearn dogged his heels, his narrower face contentiously thoughtful. A soaked raven flapped in from the stairwell, lit on a chairback, and beat the wet from its wings with a rusty croak of reproach.

'Traithe's here?' Bransian bellowed through the opened doorway.

'Aye,' came Keldmar's reply, spiraled through with the echoes that arose from the lightless depths one flight down.

Moments later, the Sorcerer entered, black-clad and composed despite the lamed step he had wrestled through the ascent. His broad-brimmed felt hat had prevented the storm's sheeting rain from streaming down his high collar.

Keldmar, behind, had disdained all protections. Parrien's near twin, and unrivaled for recklessness, he entered, skin wet, his boisterous, scuffed strides muffled by the squelching slosh of a salt-musty pair of holed seaboots. He unslung a waxed leather map case from his shoulder. The bronze ends clashed on wood as he banged it onto the table next to Bransian's sheathed broadsword. 'Who's got oiled rags?' he demanded point-blank. 'Old storm's damn well going to set rust stains on my favorite steel.'

Mearn passed him the oil lamp from the hook by the doorway, 'What,' he said, mocking, 'did you do to the *Evenstar*'s captain to keep her sniping nose on her brig?'

'Feylind?' Keldmar's laugh boomed through his bristled wire beard. 'Nobody forces that busy wench to do anything.' He yanked out his knife and pried open the lamp's reservoir, sloshed oil on the unkempt hem of his doublet, then drew his sword from the scabbard and commenced rubbing down the cold, blued length of the blade. 'She booted ourselves off her decks at the quayside. Made sail back to sea straightaway, storm or no. Apparently she had a message to move southward, the contents of which wouldn't keep.'

As Parrien drew breath for some snide provocation, Dame Dawr rapped her knuckles on the tabletop. 'Have you louts lost your ancestral ties to obligation along with your civilized manners?'

Effortlessly strong, Parrien gave up the most comfortable chair and placed it for Traithe's convenience.

'Welcome to Alestron,' Bransian said in sheepishly belated greeting. 'How may we serve the land?'

The Sorcerer sat and arranged his game leg to ease the sharp ache of old scars. The actinic play of lightning through the arrow slits deepened the lines on his face and lit the silver band on his hat to white fire. 'Let Keldmar deliver his tidings first. Most of what I came to say bears on the news he brings from Etarra.'

Dame Dawr bared her teeth. 'What's the mim-faced false godling done this time?'

'You didn't hear yet?' Parrien leaned back, folded his arms, and crossed his spurred boots on the table. Clever as a weasel underneath his bluff brawn, he smiled in Keldmar's face as he diverted everyone's riveted attention. 'Lysaer got himself legally elected as Etarra's new lord governor the instant fat Morfett expired.'

Keldmar howled, banged the table, and snatched back the stolen thread of conversation. 'The funeral rites had barely ended when six chests of bullion were sent downcoast by fast galley. You won't like the bent of the s'Ilessid pretender's first act in office.' He set aside his bare weapon, flipped the cap off the document case, and disgorged its contents overtop of the duke's sheathed broadsword. Sheaves of rolled parchment unfurled with a hiss and revealed the penned plans for a massive, triple-tiered bulwark.

Against sudden, stunned quiet, Keldmar retrieved his blade and resumed his unhurried polishing. 'Lysaer wants to hire the best family of stonemasons working the Elssine quarries.'

'The ones who practice the fragmented secrets gleaned from the old centaur lore book?' Oak creaked as Bransian sat forward, his iron brows snarled to a frown. 'That is bad news.' While Traithe's raven launched off the chairback and hopped onto the tabletop, head cocked in a purposeful survey of each inked notation for the proposed keeps, the duke added, 'Ath's angel of vengeance, is this massive array of new fortifications to be built on the foothills surrounding *Etarra*? Whom did you knife to make off with these drawings?'

Keldmar shrugged, the salt stains on his jerkin glinting in the leaden gray light that shone through the storm-besieged arrow slits. 'We don't all share your bloodletting temperament.' He released the wad of hem he had used for a rag and bent a considering squint down the cleaned edge of his sword blade. 'A mutual friend drank beer with a guardsman and purloined his whole set of keys. These drawings are copies. The originals had to be found and recovered, though we made certain the blame would fall where it caused the devil's own mayhem.'

'Confusion to the enemy,' Bransian allowed, unconcerned as the raven hopped over his wrist and pecked at an ink splotch on the outer edge of the parchment. 'Whose silken feathers did you ruffle?'

A wicked, hot gleam fired Keldmar's gray eyes. 'The rat-faced clerk in the treasury who pays out the bounties for the headhunters, who else? He's now being tried for a turncoat.'

'Well, you'd better have covered your tracks,' Mearn cut in, his tone all acidic clarity. 'Lysaer's inquisitors are thorough. If the one posted at Etarra discovers your man's honest, he'll run down the list of his enemies until they have a confession and somebody guilty to roast.'

'That slinker? Honest?' Parrien laughed, slit eyed and restless under Traithe's discerning regard. 'The creep's the same clerk who sells captive clan children to horse knackers. He's also lined his pockets for years taking bribes to dispatch assassins for trade guilds. He's made enough enemies to mince him to dog meat, and anyway, Keldmar's only bone stupid when he wagers his best horses on one of Mearn's swindling card games.'

The sword struck the table with an outraged clang as Keldmar banged erect in raw temper.

'Enough!' snapped Dame Dawr. The wise raven took flight and settled on a cornice, as, snake fast, the old woman brandished her stick. She thumped the one brother who lunged to recoup his maligned character by thrashing Parrien senseless and quelled Mearn with the withering force of her glare even as he drew breath to liven the conflict with a choice round of baiting insults.

While Keldmar recovered his blade and subsided, nursing a smacked wrist and grumbling, the grandame s'Brydion shifted her attentive glance to the duke and vented her acrid opinion. 'I don't like what I saw in Tysan one bit. The merchants there have grown fat on their greed. They stockpile gold with no fear for tomorrow, apparently too busy to question the talk that makes policy in their prince's closed councils. I don't trust the quiet, or such honeyed prosperity. There are intrigues running so deep in that city, even the whispers are silent.'

'Althain's Warden agrees with you.' Traithe snapped his fingers and recalled his bird, who unfurled jet wings and dropped into a glide downward to reclaim a perch on top of his hat. 'Sethvir sent me to ask you to consider sending three children of your bloodline to be fostered in the Kingdom of Havish.'

Duke Bransian lifted offended eyes from the sprawl of plans in front of him. 'These keeps at Etarra aren't even built yet, and to my knowledge, our walls and defenses are solid. We held our own through the Betrayer's last uprising, and watched Lysaer's whole war host get tail whipped at Vastmark. Except for his sword-rattling musters at Etarra, he's stayed in retreat at Avenor. Merchant trade is now running the heart of his policy. What under Ath's sky makes Sethvir think us weaklings, that we should fear threats from such enemies now?'

Traithe regarded him, level and unblinking as the harbinger bird perched on his hat. 'Because the very strength of your citadel here makes your family a sitting target.'

'What's changed then?' Mearn was first to demand, his thin, vibrant frame outlined in lightning as the storm cracked and slammed at his back. 'When I left Avenor, the lies were paraded in full daylight, the most glaring of them the false claim that Lady Talith's fatal fall was a suicide.'

'The summer muster's all you've been shown in the open.' Pegged oak struts squeaked as Traithe shifted, perhaps to ease the pull of old scars. A snap of his fingers, and the raven hopped down and resettled on his raised forearm. An undefined tension pulled at his mouth, as though he chose words with reluctance. 'Other developments are afoot, more threatening than these plans for new battlements. Lysaer's Alliance has been busy recruiting what gifted talent the Crown Examiner doesn't burn. Etarra will be gathering the library to train them, at first to hunt down their own kind. But a tool in the hand will come to be used. Such is the way of human nature.' His keen glance at Bransian showed earnest concern as he finished his threadbare conclusion. 'Your walls will hold against arrows and steel. What of an attack launched in fire and light, and backed by the powers of dark spellcraft?'

Across a prickling, uncomfortable silence, rain thrummed in tantrums against stone and slate. Dame Dawr sat, bright eyed as a small, ruffled hawk. Mearn shoved back his chair and paced outright, while Bransian rubbed his wire beard with a thumb, his expression bearish and disgruntled. Parrien, in absently thoughtful unease, traced an intricate old watermark left on the oak table by a past visit from Asandir.

Singled out by the raven's unfathomable stare, Keldmar relieved his discomfort through speech. 'We are clanblood, still.' He slammed his oiled sword back home in its sheath. 'We uphold this town's charter in name for a high king whose ancestor swore your Fellowship a blood oath of service to rule under strict terms of the compact. Could we not ask you Sorcerers for help if an assault threatened to overwhelm our defenses with conjury?'

'You could ask,' Traithe admitted. 'Against misuse of power, our assistance is entitled. But a promise is worthless without resource to back it. The extended range of the Fellowship's responsibilities has left our diminished number sorely strained. If the Alliance moved with intent to forestall us, we might have no hand free to send. Sethvir was plain. His earth-sense reads patterns. He sees the hoarded wealth gathering at Avenor, laid against the new template for a fortress that will reforge Etarra into the dedicated sword of the Light. Spark and dry tinder, was his precise phrasing.'

No need to reiterate, that Alestron might become the struck flint to ignite that volatile fuel to burning, not with Cattrick's craftsmen alive and busy building ships in the citadel's inner harbor.

Bransian spoke over the hammering roll as thunder rebounded from the hills. 'Did Sethvir foresee trouble?'

Traithe matched his grim honesty, a shadow stamped out in silver and black against the rough play of the elements. 'Not yet. He saw possibility, coupled with ominous warning.' The laugh lines at his eyes seemed expunged from his flesh, and the raven a more somber extension of his forthright concern. 'Sethvir bade me remind you that Lysaer s'Ilessid bears the s'Ahelas gift of farsight through his maternal lineage. *Never discount what hidden seeds that man might hold in his hand.* The Mistwraith's curse drives him. If he suspects you are Arithon's friend, he would hold that knowledge in close calculation. He might bide for years if he thought he could wring best advantage from arranging your moment of downfall.'

'S'Ilessid already knows we've changed loyalty, I've no doubt left on that point.' Seated stark straight, her features sharpened with testy autocracy, Dame Dawr clasped neat hands over the ferrule on her stick. 'At Avenor, I caught too many prying eyes at my back. The sunwheel initiate we put off at Tideport was young, but no fool. More than a spy, I would wager my last pearls that he was a natural-born talent sent to act as Cerebeld's informant.'

The raven swiveled its jet bill toward the inimitable old matron, its eyes as sharp as sheared gimlets. Before Bransian could inject a scoffing remark, or Mearn stab back to defend her, Traithe said, 'That's a most astute guess. What made you draw that conclusion?'

Dawr expelled a derisive breath through her nose. 'Raised the hair at my nape, that young man did. The woman's a born simpleton, who mistrusts her instincts where the safety of her family's concerned.'

Traithe's startling, bright smile came and went through the flare of the storm through the arrow slits. To Duke Bransian, he concluded, 'You would do very well to pay heed to your grandmother's hunches.' As though aware the audience had drawn to a close, the raven launched off and flew, then vanished on spread wings down the stairwell. The Sorcerer arose, the grace of each movement undone by the unkind ache of old injuries. He braced one palm on the table, leaned over, and swept the flat of his hand across the copied lines inscribed on the unrolled parchments. 'The masons from Elssine know fragments of old lore?'

Bransian rested his massive forearms on the chairback he straddled like a camp stool. 'Judge that for yourself. This tower was built by the master craftsmen's great-grandfather.'

'Then Sethvir was not wrong.' Traithe gathered himself, well aware he faced a difficult night after a long, slow descent of steep stairs. 'These new walls at Etarra are going to skew the free flow of the fifth lane, if our Fellowship doesn't walk over the ground there and give the earth her fair warning. At least one of us must go to reaffirm the lines that channel the subtle magnetics.' He tipped a nod to Dame Dawr, then clasped wrists with the duke. 'Forgive my rushed parting. This round of ill news means I must send word back to Althain Tower and ask for a summons to Asandir.'

# Grudge

The Mayor of Jaelot had gout, which pained him to distraction at the first onset of cold weather. Each autumn, when the sea air off Eltair Bay raked its damp chill through his city, he muffled himself in flannel and took to his bed, his puffed ankles braced like bloated red sausages in the lace-bordered pillows his wife favored. His face above the pleats of his nightshirt bore a scowl; his pouched, bulldog jowls and narrow-set eyes became indelibly lined with distemper.

If the experienced servants knew well to stay clear, the new clerk standing in for the municipal secretary droned away in pedantic oblivion.

'Our treasury is still grossly in debt from the last annuity granted to the Alliance. Two raids at sea caused setbacks to trade. We can't tax the merchants' lost profits.' His lecture lagged as he fussed with his parchments, ticked a mark with his pen, and wagged a vague finger toward the bundled invalid on the bed. 'With our city finances on the verge of collapse, the cost of sending state funds to Etarra in support of Prince Lysaer's proposed war host would seem an imprudent extravagance.'

The mayor lost his last shred of equilibrium. He rammed his fists in the quilts, tore a seam in the lining, and shouted through the resultant explosion of goose down. 'Damn your advice past the Wheel to Sithaer! And damn the expense to perdition! I've waited fifteen years for the Divine Prince to tire of pandering to the whiners on his council back in Tysan. His heir's all but grown. Do you think a black sorcerer who bends darkness itself will wait while we bemoan the theft of a few cargoes? Jaelot will pay this new tithe to raise arms! Our delegates will endorse Lysaer's call for better fortifications against shadow if we have to beggar every last one of our craft guilds.'

The clerk looked up, blinking. While the Lord Mayor still glowered, hair raked up in tufts, the young man under scrutiny tipped the feather on his quill and made casual effort to scratch an itch underneath his wool collar. 'Surely, your lordship, other cities than ours could underwrite the burden of routing such evil from society.'

The mayor choked, rendered speechlessly purple. Through his stertorous rasp as he struggled to recover, the door to his chamber flew open. The panel rebounded from the wainscoted wall and trembled every silken tassel on his bedhangings.

A wire-thin woman in pearl ropes and ruffled taffeta sailed through, spouting distressed imprecations.

'Oh dear,' sighed the mayor, defensively mollified.

His wife, her ladyship of Jaelot, stalked up to his bedside, her dark hair rammed up like a ship's prow with combs, and her pointed chin cocked for a tirade. The first victim became the guileless clerk.

'What have you said to upset my lord? He's ill, can't you see?' Wafting a breeze of patchouli, she thrust her beaky nose in the shrinking man's face and snatched his ordered parchments from his hand. 'Get out! Take these and your nattering back to the countinghouse and use them to balance the ledgers.' She slapped the sheaves of parchment against the man's chest, driving her point home as he frantically snatched to save his notes from cascading onto the carpet.

'Where the capture of the Shadow Master's cohorts are concerned, no man questions the mayor's will.' Her ladyship sniffed. 'Jaelot's depleted revenue will scarcely come to matter if the s'Ffalenn bastard returns and levels half our walls by means of fell powers and sorcery.'

Through the clerk's rankled mewl of protest, the mayor howled back. 'Where the enemies of this city pose a threat, I can speak for my own affairs, woman!'

His wife ignored him. 'You're ill and in pain.' Her brisk, jeweled hands tugged and prodded at bedclothes, oblivious to his winces as her efforts jostled the tender flesh of his ankles. 'You ought to be sleeping, dear, and not driving yourself to a lather over the treasury's state of debt.' A decisive last slap plumped the pillow beneath the Lord Mayor's tufted head. 'I'll send one of the maids with a posset.'

Pearls clicked and spattered muted points of light as she flounced the elaborate, trimmed layers of her skirts, then pinned bird-beady eyes on the clerk, who still cowered behind the clutched leaves of his tally sheets. 'You had better be gone when the medicine arrives.' She gave a chirp of exasperation and marched out.

Perfume gusted back and rippled the lion-bossed hems of the hangings as she snatched the door closed behind her.

The mayor crushed down the pillow, which poked him in the groin, and shot a whipped-dog glance sideward. 'Nobody ever crosses her without spoiling their day.'

At least wise enough not to answer, the rattled public servant bent his storkish frame into an upholstered chair. Leather squeaked and horsehair stuffing rustled as he evened up the corners of his notes. 'The way you carry on, a man might believe the Master of Shadow was demonkind.'

The Mayor of Jaelot blinked his couched eyes. 'You must be quite new to your post here.'

'Yes, actually.' The clerk dared a smile. 'I trained with a country scribe on the grass downs north of Daenfal, but herders don't require written records. I came east to make my start in the world. The ways of a port city are wonderfully diverse. Beats the plodding bore of counting out bales of shorn wool and verifying ownership on spring kids pastured out in the bogs.'

A grunt issued from the mounded ruckle of silk bedclothes; the mayor slapped down another offending pillow, his irritable mood turned expansive. 'Well, the first time your cronies become garrulous with wine, they'll share what they know of past gossip. The name of the Shadow Master is forever accursed here in Jaelot.'

'I don't like drinking,' the clerk prompted, his fresh features politely expectant.

The entrenched glimmer of ire returned, fanned to warning brilliance as the mayor crossed his arms over the gold-frogged closure of his nightrobe. 'The ugliness happened twenty-five years ago.' He steamed with the memory of the event he had nursed to a virulent grudge. 'The black-hearted mountebank they call Spinner of Darkness came to our city disguised as a masterbard's apprentice. He stayed here six months. No one suspected. His innocent manner could have duped Ath Creator himself. Then on midsummer's eve, as a guest in my hall, the fell creature called down a whirlwind. His sorcery dismembered half the roofs and walls in the district to cover his tracks as he hid. Four days later, he escaped. Disappeared through the heart of a thunderclap. You can still see the marks in the palace hall, where the floor tiles had to be replaced.'

The rest, of course, had to be hyperbole. The clerk folded his arms, and admitted disbelief, that the tower by the east postern gate still showed cracks in the bedrock foundation.

The mayor drew breath, riled back to indignation. 'That's a truth attested by witnesses, man! We still have a half dozen battlements bricked up where the walls are considered unstable. Not even the farmers in the countryside were spared. Their cottages and barns were shaken down in a swath that extends all the way to the Skyshiel Mountains. The destruction struck terror into every honest heart. Let me say, there's no one here in Jaelot who will *ever* forget the event. My council will not rest the case until this shadow-bending sorcerer and his barbarian cohorts lie dead. For myself, I'd stake all my fortune to bring the Light-accursed meddler to the faggots.'

'I see.' The clerk cleared his throat, reshuffled his notes, and fastidiously crossed out the offending tick mark. 'We'll borrow again from the tinsmith's guild. That should raise funds to meet the Light's tithe to refortify Etarra.'

Rapid footfalls sounded outside the door. The mayor flopped back, eyes shut in forbearance as the latch tripped and a maid whisked in, burdened with a tray containing a cup and several bottles of dubious liquid. 'Your medicines, milord.'

The clerk received a gruff wave of dismissal. 'Jaelot won't stay the worse for our effort, be assured. His Grace, the Blessed Prince has kept every binding promise ever made since our fleet went down in flames against the Shadow Master's spells at Minderl Bay.'

The clerk withheld comment, eager not to seem ignorant as he stowed his documents into his bulging satchel.

Jaelot's Lord Mayor gave the vials on the tray his jaundiced inspection, signal enough that the morning audience had reached a precipitous end. The clerk snatched his moment and nipped through the doorway as his eminence burst into another bellowing tirade.

'I'll not touch that repulsive concoction again! Tell my wife! Yes! Say her wretched, bootlicking healer's an ass. Any more tisanes that taste like burned turds, and I'll risk oath of debt and call in a Koriani herb witch!'

## Autumn 5669

# Byplay

Cloaked like a queen leopardess in a throw of white ermine, Morriel Prime extended an ivory finger. 'See for yourself.' Her scrying basin of silver-veined marble stood braced in a copper tripod at the center of her rented room in Highscarp. 'The hour draws nigh. The trap you have planned must soon be set into motion.'

Lirenda arose from her deep curtsy, each movement embedded in the feathery rustle of silk skirts. If she had not yet recovered the honorary eight bands which denoted the First Senior's high office, the passage of years had eased the worst stigma of her disgrace. She no longer dressed unobtrusively or shrank from the summons to present herself for Prime audience. For that day's encounter, she wore royal purple. Her trim bodice and full hemline sparkled with gold thread, laced in patterns of songbirds and vines. Mantled in her air of well-bred self-command, she scarcely nodded her acknowledgment as the upstart initiate who still usurped her place at the Prime's right hand stepped out in response to Morriel's flicked gesture of dismissal. The silent, matched page boys stationed at the door latched the panels for privacy.

The disaffection between the young woman and her displaced predecessor had deepened to mutual antipathy. The new candidate had the gift of raw power, but no brilliance. Though she had grown to three decades of maturity, her lack of imagination made her clumsy and slow, which faults she buried in stiff self-importance when her rival's keener wit left her threatened.

Had the reversal in roles been one whit less devastating, Lirenda might have been amused by the woman's baffled efforts to grasp the nuance of power and authority.

Quite soon, the issue would become a moot point. From the moment Arithon Teir's'Ffalenn was taken captive, the onus of old mistakes would be rectified. Lirenda arose to the occasion with unassailable confidence. Skirts neatly raised, she crossed the inn's wooden floor, scarred by the hobnailed boots of the Etarran troops who now routinely patrolled Rathain's coast.

She knelt on the throw rug beside the filled basin. Since water was not her favored element, she cupped the quartz crystal on the chain at her neck as the focus to access her powers.

For all her pretension, the past still left scars. A wretched sense of gratitude still dogged her each time she accessed her heightened awareness. Her memory of shame and helplessness seemed entrenched since the miserable interval when the crystal had passed from her possession. The branding awareness of just what she stood to lose gnawed at her yet, until the succession to prime power obsessed her, waking and sleeping.

Left with Arithon's freedom as the obstacle to surmount, Lirenda bent her will to the task of arranging his downfall.

She settled her five senses, tuned out the distant, slanging argument between the drudges who swept out the downstairs common room. The swirl of cool drafts and the creak of the inn's cedar shutters faded and dissolved before the strictures of discipline. Immersed within a core of pent stillness, Lirenda laid her hands on either side of the basin. She let her unfocused gaze diffuse into the depths. Slowly, gradually, her passive mind assumed alignment with the subtle energies that coiled through the volatile template of the water.

The liquid clouded, darkened, resolved: she beheld the vast, auburn sweep of the moorlands at the heart of Araethura. Under the bowl of a clear, autumn sky, two men sparred with the longsword. Lunge and parry entangled in thin scrolls of sound. Lirenda first recognized the grizzled old garrison soldier with the lightning hands and the unforgiving jaw as the man hired from Backwater to train young Fionn Areth.

The student he opposed circled over the rough ground in steady, sinuous confidence. His body was shirtless despite the brisk chill, his boy's frame fleshed out into a young man's tigerish fitness. The rhythmic response of parry and riposte bespoke a flawless concentration. Paired shadows flowed over ocher grass, while testing blades snicked and clamored, dipped gilt and cerulean in sky-caught reflection. The dance-step exchange of attack and defense cast shivering, metallic echoes across the swept crests of the downs.

Then the culmination, a blinding fast disengage followed through by a bind. The herder's son whooped and wrenched. His mentor's blade flew through a pinwheeling arc and thumped in the grass, a shimmer of stilled steel in the crisp clarity of the afternoon sunlight.

'That's the fifth time in a sevenday you've disarmed me.' The older man rubbed his chafed palm, measuring his charge with rueful satisfaction. 'Well-done.' His gruff clap on the shoulder was earnestly meant. An aging soldier could not but take pride in a youngster who mastered the skills he had gained in the course of a lifetime. 'Not another trick I can teach you, boy. What learning's left will be found in experience. No man of the sword's fully made until he's blooded his blade and survived. Or else roistered with wenches. There lies another test that'll bring you to maturity. Sure's deep frost, no sparring can match a lively tumble in the hay.'

A smile turned the lips of the victor, who saluted his teacher.

'Don't let my oldster's maundering mess up your head.' The veteran laughed. 'Lasses round these hills have brothers with fleecing shears. You'd get yourself well blooded all right if you sport with a skirt in the bracken.'

'It's the skirts who invite me I worry about.' The young man retrieved the forfeited sword. He straightened, flushed with exertion and praise, and the wind whipped black hair away from a face whose clean angles had no place amid families who raised goats on the moors of Araethura.

Lirenda caught her breath. The impact of *just what* she had made slammed through her and raced the staid beat of her heart. Nor could she tear her hungry gaze free.

Framed in the depths of the scrying bowl, Fionn Areth returned the sword to his master. He exchanged laughing comment with a mouth never made for humility. The bright irony of an innocence never seen in the man whose face had been copied made her gasp.

'That's uncanny!' Indeed, those features lacked for nothing but the stamp of Arithon's experience. Except for that one, trifling detail, Daelion Fatemaster himself might be taxed to distinguish that boy from the prince whose face had provided the model. 'He's perfect.'

'He's now twenty-one years of age, and itching to seek his promised destiny,' Morriel rasped. 'No discipline of his parents can hold him in obscurity for much longer.'

'Then my hour is come.' Lirenda straightened up. Excitement flushed her cheeks like sunrise on snow. 'Why wait? The season is fortunate. Autumn storms will hamper the swift passage of news.'

In fact, like the neat mesh of gears in a winepress, the events of the moment aligned remarkably in her favor. Lysaer s'Ilessid was at

Erdane, lately returned from minding his affairs at Etarra. He would soon ride the last leg of his journey to Avenor, with his court unlikely to gain word of the disturbance she planned before the onset of winter closed the passes.

'Snow and ice in the Skyshiels will forestall any deployment of Etarrans to the eastshore well enough. How could we choose a better hour?' Lirenda crossed the narrow chamber to Morriel's chair, hands clasped to contain her raw eagerness. 'The only difficult hurdle we face is a decoy to divert the Fellowship Sorcerers.'

Ensconced in white fur, Morriel blinked eyelids thin and naked as a songbird's halved eggshells. The sultry spark which lit her black eyes seemed to feed off the fluttering candles. 'You have something in mind?'

The answering smile on Lirenda's lips could have been carved from rose coral. 'A magnetic disturbance of the sixth lane would cast a veil of static over Sethvir's earth-sense. If we placed a circle of twelve seniors wielding one of the order's major crystals in the Skyshiels, they could spin resonance into a quartz vein. That would be enough to excite the lane's energy into a random flux.'

'You'll have what you ask, and by my own hand.' Rare satisfaction thrummed through the reedy timbre of the Prime Matriarch's reply. 'Through me, the powers of twelve sisters will be raised through the Great Waystone's focus to shield you. Also send summons through the scryer on lane watch and recall Elaira from Morvain. The Mayor of Jaelot suffers from gout. She'll do very well assigned to his household as healer.'

Lirenda's instinctive jerk of resistance hitched a whisper through rich layers of silk.

Morriel raised porcelain fingers to her lips to forestall a dry snort of laughter. 'Dare you forget? Through Elaira, you possess the sure key to bring Rathain's prince to his knees. He'd empty the very blood from his veins before he saw her take harm. Keep her close, by my orders. If aught goes amiss, her Koriani vow of obedience will provide you with sure means to force his Grace of Rathain back to heel.'

'Your will.' Lirenda curtsied to the floor, her displeasure offset by an uncontained, dangerous joy. The slow years of waiting had ended. Concerning Elaira, the Prime's logic was flawless. Lirenda would not let the Matriarch's interference cloud her moment of overdue retribution. The clarity of mind left unbalanced by the Shadow Master's influence would be reclaimed in sweet vengeance on the hour he knelt at her mercy.

*   *   *

The heavy, paneled door clicked closed on the heels of Lirenda's departure. Morriel Prime sank back in her chair, one finger crooked in summons to her pages. The boys were well trained. They came in response to even so subtle a signal.

'Move the scrying bowl to my right hand,' the Prime demanded in her scratchy whisper. While the boys did her bidding, she fumbled beneath her furs. Her wasted, claw hands shook with alarming palsy. The breath rasped in her throat, grown labored of late, through even such minimal exertion. Moment to moment, she lived in raw pain, held to life through indomitable will.

She located the box she kept for her remedies, gasping for air as one of the pages assisted with unfastening the latch. The other boy uncorked the syrup-based tonic she used to ameliorate her most alarming onslaughts of weakness. She sucked greedily at the bottle, then lay back, hands flaccid, while the drugs and strong spells took effect.

The room seemed to take far too long to stop spinning. Fretful, impatient, she gasped a command for her pages to leave her in private.

The boys bowed, too intimidated to offer an argument. All but stumbling over their slippered feet, they hastened out of her chamber.

Left utterly alone, Morriel clutched the inlaid cedar box to her breast. Words whispered over her personal spell crystal unkeyed a hidden lock. She slid open a secret compartment in the lid and removed four bundles, cloth-wrapped and tied with dark thread that seemed spun from the mapless void between stars.

'Rue, wormwood, salt,' she whispered under her breath as she unwound the ritual wrappings. 'Tienelle to loosen the bindings of time and space, and lend force and spin to my banespell.'

She turned next to the scrying bowl and tapped on the stone edge with a long, trembling nail. 'Araethura, Fionn Areth,' she rasped. Bound by the rune of subservience to her will, the stilled water inside obliged her by re-forming the image of the herder's son, who currently perched on a sun-warmed boulder, working with an oiled rag and a whetstone to clean nicks and rust from his practice sword.

Fionn's brow was untroubled. Jacket sleeves unlaced to reveal sturdy wrists, he smiled often, and whistled snatches of a jig tune, a quarter tone out of key. Nor did his carefree manner show change as Morriel Prime raised her spell crystal and traced the first rune of discord above the dark crown of his head.

She cast a pinch of salt over the image in the water, then formed the sigil that would strip the boy's aura of any natural protection afforded by blessings or amulets. The incantation passed her lips in a near-soundless stream of syllables as she sprinkled the three herbs on the water in the timeworn, ritual patterns. The language she used was no tongue native to Athera. The crystal responded and took focus through resonant sound, its properties linked to the finespun character of the plants to sow argument, discontent, and restlessness.

The seal of closure that knit the Prime's intent into form also robbed her last vestige of strength. Morriel rested, flesh and bone nested in her throw of white ermine, and her eyes like chipped beads of jet. A faint smile of victory quirked her lips. Her spell of disharmony would not be stopped now, joined as it was with its victim.

Lent that added spin of dark impetus, Fionn Areth would take leave of his family in Araethura two fortnights before Lirenda could possibly set her more restrained plan in motion. With the boy gone abroad on his own initiative, the disgraced First Senior must scramble and rush to enact the array of detail that would close her net over Arithon s'Ffalenn. Lirenda would be given no moment to spare to examine Morriel's own interests.

The Prime Matriarch clapped her hands to recall her pages from their post outside of her chamber. Once the boys had burned the wrappings and the stray leaves of spilled herbs, telltale evidence would be eradicated. No one in the order would be likely to notice that a temporary bane-ward had been cast over young Fionn Areth.

Morriel snuggled deep into her furs, confident as a spider in a web. The diversion that arose when the boy left Araethura would allow her full license to complete the personal plot she had prepared in secret through the course of long, lonely years.

**Autumn 5669**

# Overlook

Seething inside for the fact she must importune help from a seer, Lirenda carries out the order set on her by Morriel Prime: 'I require a message sent to the sisterhouse at Morvain. By the Matriarch's will, the initiate Elaira is to be recalled from her independent practice and given direct assignment to serve as the Mayor of Jaelot's personal healer . . .'

Far out in blue waters on the Cildein Ocean, untroubled, the brigantine *Khetienn* and her companion fleet change course to sail back to the verge of known waters; despite the completion of seventeen voyages that have crisscrossed the seas of Athera, she and her clanborn complement of crewmen have encountered no trace of the vanished Paravians . . .

The Sorcerer Kharadmon sends word to Althain Tower from his posted watch amid the ward circles set against wraiths, and his message is received by Sethvir to a grim repercussion of echoes. 'I know we've seen nothing to cause an alarm in the quarter of a century I've stood sentinel. That's the problem. I don't trust the peace in the silence . . .'

# X. Chain of Destiny

D usk veiled the windswept moorlands of Araethura, seeding stars across an indigo sky. Fionn Areth gritted his teeth, splashed the filled bucket over his head, and, shivering, groped for the lye soap his mother had left on the stone lip of the well. To shed the hateful, oily reek of the goats, he scrubbed and scoured until his skin flamed. Two more icy dousings rinsed off the suds. He snatched up the towel, snagged it over the soaked skin on his shoulders, then raked up the filthy pile of shirt, breeks, and boots. He juggled the load, dodging the puddles of runoff, and padded barefoot through the croft door.

Wind banged the panel shut on his heels. The noise raised a sharp glare from the younger brother braiding goat collars but left no impression on the shrilling quarrel in progress between his two older sisters.

Aching, still bruised from his sparring that morning, Fionn Areth basked in the smell of lamb soup. While the fire-heated air burnished the chill from his skin and dried off the last clinging droplets, his mother called from the hearth.

'Fionn? Breta forgot to throw corn to the hens.' She gathered her cleaver, cutting board, and wooden ladle, her hair stuck in rings to her temples. 'Can you do that?'

'Like this?' Fionn Areth dropped his soiled clothing on the floor, while his sisters burst into a peal of giggles at his nakedness. 'Why not ask Lachonn? He hasn't yet washed.'

'Because I asked you.' His mother shed implements with a clatter and scooped up the youngest of his nephews, who had tripped on the poker and skinned a knee. 'Hush, child, there.' Through the toddler's rising wails, she scolded, 'Stop carrying on and dress yourself, Fionn! Those hens don't thrive, we won't have an egg to be seen come the spring.'

Which was too much, for a son come into his manhood. 'Eggs?' Fionn Areth exploded. 'Let them go to Dharkaron! I won a bout with my swordmaster today. Why should I stay to see spring?'

'I heard that,' interjected a gravelly voice.

Fionn Areth shut his jaw, cheeks flaming. He had been a rank fool not to notice his father come in from sharpening the scythe in the shed.

'You'll feed the hens as you are, young man, and stay stripped after that for a strapping. No son of mine treats his mother with disrespect under the roof of her house.'

Nor did the misery end with the sting of the weals his mother brought herb grease to soothe come the evening.

'I couldn't see to you any sooner than this.' The candle lamp mapped her thin, careworn face in planes of ink and gold as she knelt to tend his striped back. 'Your father took a long time to sleep soundly.'

Fionn Areth lay prone on the loft's bare wood floor, chilled speechless. The rough wool blankets and ticking were abrasively harsh on raw flesh, and his pride, too tender to seek a child's solace, burrowed amid the huddled warmth of his brothers.

A rustle of skirts, then the chink of crimped tin as his mother pried the lid off the ointment. 'Your swordmaster's dismissed, boy.'

Her son said nothing. His head remained tucked into the crook of one elbow, the hair like black silk looped in tangles over young flesh.

His mother's deft fingers begin salving his hurts. She could not help but feel the coiling tension sweep through him, though he tried to lie slack and unfeeling. He would not ask, so she told him. ''Twas not for punishment, Fionn. The swordmaster came in after supper to be sure we heard you weren't boasting. He's taught all he knows. Your father said, let him go, since your learning would seem complete. No need, now, to act as though life here was less than what you were born to.'

Her ministrations grazed over a raw patch. Fionn Areth sucked air between his locked teeth.

'Ah, boy,' his mother murmured. 'The thrashings seem ever to go worse for you.' Whatever blessed ancestor had bequeathed him his face, the least glance always hackled his father's quick temper. Her Fionn had a set to his cheekbones and brows that gave even his most honest apologies an air of deliberate insult.

'There's virtue in humility, one day you'll see,' she lied, as aware as he that her sensible counsel fell short. Her sigh brushed his shoulder as she pressed the lid back on the salve tin. 'Try not to cross your father, Fionn. He's gruffer most times than he means to be, and life on these moorlands is bitter enough without flaunting the fate that must part you in time from the family.'

A last squeeze on the wrist; she hooked up her candle lamp and quietly left him, thinking and chilled in the darkness.

Old enough to act with adult patience, Fionn Areth waited until his back healed enough to bear the chafe of the heavy fleece jacket he needed to break the raw winds. Then he caught a pony from the band on the moors and left her tied in the scrub behind the orchard. After dark, while the moon snagged the mist and silver-lit rims of the clouds, he bridled the mare with a twine hackamore. Since the family owned but one saddle, he fashioned a buckle surcingle, to which he tied a leather pack filled with snares and what provender could be spared from the larder – cold waybread, hard cheese, and sausage. His snug herder's cloak would have to serve him as bedding and shelter from the elements. Nor did he worry about bandits or barbarians, his felt boots being his only worthwhile possession. Since the swords used for practice had all gone with the arms master, he purloined his father's skinning knife to gut coneys and shave kindling. Resolved to go forward and claim his own destiny, Fionn Areth turned his back on the steading he had known since his birth. He vaulted astride and nudged the mare east, toward the River Arwent and the trail that wound south toward Daenfal.

A hundred leagues westward, the Koriani seer dispatched with the message from the lane-watcher picked her way through the waterfront stews of Morvain to the bait shack where Elaira had established her stillroom. The woman's abrupt entry came with no warning, was graced by no courteous knock. She did not consider herself a visitor, she snapped, as she perched her ample behind on the only available stool.

Elaira wiped sweat from her brow with the back of her wrist, one palm and three fingers being blackened with charcoal. Damp hair clung in whorls to her temples and neck. Of all possible days, she had chosen this morning to render the fat to mix her emollients. Her quarters were stifling. The cauldron hissed and spat, belching a noisome stench of hog suet. The kettle of steeped rose petals could not compete. Despite the fresh air let in by the roof leaks, and neglected gaps in warped planking, the waste from the knacker's prevailed.

Since the nearest public well was a brisk walk away, Elaira rinsed her hands in the rusted bucket she kept dipped full of fresh seawater. 'Is this a summons?' she demanded point-blank.

The seer broke off her staring survey of the shack, and replied through the sleeve pressed against her disdainful nose. 'How do you bear this?' A flap of her elbow encompassed the rude table, its paraphernalia of the herbalist's trade spread over boards sliced and stained by the knives a past generation of fishwives had used to gut cod and split mussels. The damp off the wharves never tired of resurrecting the stink.

Elaira laughed, her gray eyes direct. 'Perhaps I've never liked the sort of company who insisted on a neat house.'

The seeress stiffened to instant formality. 'I have brought a summons. You're to leave inside the hour, dressed to ride. Pack only what you will need for the road. A novice will come for your things here.'

Her hands foolishly dripping in chapping air, Elaira sighed. 'And my destination? Do you know?'

A faint shrug lifted the seeress's shoulders, rustling lavender silk. 'Daenfal, at all speed, and then on to Jaelot. The mayor there suffers from crippling gout. By the Prime's will, you've been appointed to serve as his personal healer.'

Elaira shut her eyes, the fear like a leaden yoke on her shoulders. Unbidden, she sensed the dire change in the wind. The city of Jaelot was Prince Arithon's implacable enemy; her forced change of residence could only mean Lirenda's cruel plan to use Fionn Areth's destiny could not but hang in the balance. She had cast all her trust upon the Shadow Master's cleverness; now the hour approached for the payoff. Either Arithon s'Ffalenn could prevail against fate, or Fionn Areth would be played as the pawn to draw him into a Koriani snare.

'You must make haste,' the seeress insisted. 'The Prime's command requires you to reach Daenfal inside the next fortnight.'

'But that's a hundred leagues distant!' In despair, Elaira daubed her hands on her skirts. 'To reach there will cost me a fortune in post mounts.' Her sarcasm bit as she gestured. The dilapidated walls of her current abode could scarcely safeguard any treasure from the beggars and desperate, crippled seamen who wandered these squalid back alleys. 'What coppers the whores can pay for my emollients scarcely see me through a day's bread.'

'We live to serve. If snow closes the Skyshiel passes, the mayor's suffering will extend through the winter, untreated.' The seeress arose. 'Coin from the order's coffers will cover the additional expenses to speed your journey. A saddled horse awaits you at the Morvain sisterhouse. You may pick up the purse when you claim him.'

Denied choice or argument, and unable to share her suspicion that her assignment entailed more than the routine charity of dispensing trained herb lore, Elaira watched the Koriani seeress depart in an immaculate sweep of crisp silk. The door slammed on a gusting breeze off the bay, rude closure to a forced ending.

She fought the lump that arose in her throat as she surveyed her still and her herb jars, now to become part of the common stores under charge of the Morvain sisterhouse. Her life, her home, the mean livelihood she had carved for herself, in trade for a traveling purse and a nondescript gelding to be exchanged for a fresh horse at the first inn on the edge of Halwythwood. She ought to have known, when she met the s'Ffalenn prince, he would come to cost all her peace.

Elaira shook off self-pity, then laughed aloud at her maundering, to be sniveling like some cantankerous grandmother before her hair had turned gray. Only one route led to Daenfal from the coast, and that, the old towpath which laced high and dry along the granite slabs channeling the thrashing flow of the River Arwent. The season was brisk. Maples and oaks would be frost touched to a tangling riot of color. She had two hundred leagues of open-air travel to enjoy before she reported for duty at the mayor's palace in Jaelot.

As Elaira rummaged in her chest after her thick cloak and riding leathers, she embraced the bare truth. She was tired of city crowding and the mud reek of tideflats. A headlong gallop through the brambles of Halwythwood would serve to clear out her head, before the jaws of the trap started closing.

All ways to Daenfal eventually converged to parallel the great river. From the moorlands of Araethura, the undulating hills converged into a high plateau. Here, the winds swept like waves through a sea of high grass and black scrub. The bared, burled granite of the earth scuffed through where the weathering of ages had winnowed away its thin covering of loam. Thirsty, hungry, and blistered across the fingers from resisting his pony's persistent efforts to graze, Fionn Areth followed a path cut by the meandering tracks of wild goats. Fifteen days after leaving his father's steading, he reached the Rim, where the snaking torrent of the Arwent smoked down the gorge at the border of Daon Ramon Barrens. The land fell away into a series of stepped bluffs capped by rustling yellow grass, or else dropped sheer from granite escarpments, into ledges with trees clinging at desperate angles, their roots like exposed, gnarled hands. Sixty spans down, the river roared and muttered, tossing silvery coils of spume.

On the Araethurian side, a trail continued south, slotted with the confused prints of livestock driven to the lakeshore markets. On the river's far bank, the gentle crests rolled away toward the great basin once drained by the south-flowing Severnir, until townsmen had dammed and diverted its course to empty into Eltair Bay. Late-autumn sun burnished the famed hills, which in these times bore little resemblance to the silver-tipped grassland of legend. Fionn Areth regarded the swept, mottled scrub, cross-laced with briar, and burned from the frosts etched by the whistling north winds. The trail on the north bank wore the scarred ruts of the wagons that rolled the goods upland from the barge docks, where the towpath through Halwythwood ended.

Poised on the brink with the chill kiss of winter ruffling through his dark hair, his first freedom sweeter than wild honey, Fionn Areth could encompass nothing but the grand vista of the view. His herder's background gave him no letters, no education, and no knowledge of lore to encompass the ages gone before. He heard the cry of hawks and the scream of the winds, and did not mourn the deep notes of past centaur horn calls. Nor did he guess that the ledges notched over the tumbling waters had once held the rookeries of predatory wyverns.

All the young man felt he lacked in the world was a sword of Elssine steel.

'No need to camp early to snare rabbit tonight,' he said to his pony's backturned ears. 'We'll be inside town walls and begging for charity to find ourselves shelter by evening.' He tugged the rope hackamore and veered southward, eager to encounter the destiny he had left his family to claim.

Daenfal's old city clung to the cliff wall overlooking the Arwent gorge. North and east, a crumbling battlement marked the bounds of what had first been a Paravian watchtower. Through the centuries of the Third Age, that edifice had been enlarged, new walls lapping outward like concentric ripples cast out of gravel and clay. To the south, a graceful revetment of red sandstone fronted the waters of an upland lake. To the west, the town required no defense. There, the outflow thundered over the rim in a mighty falls, and the spume thrown into the air with raw fury settled and streamed like spilled varnish over a precipice of scoured granite.

To gain entrance to the city from the Araethurian side, a traveler must first bypass the gorge. A broad, dusty track scored by ponies and livestock wound through grass hummocks and switched-back curves to the lakeshore. There, a ferry drawn on rope cables breasted the mighty roil of the outflow, propelled by the naked, sweating muscle of chained convicts and the whip of a sharp-nosed overseer.

Crammed between the fragrant backs of three cows, and a farmer's bushels of squash, Fionn Areth clutched his cloak over his nervous pony's head, anxious himself, but determined to stand fast as the barge slammed and jerked in the plowing rush of the current. He fretted, while the sun dappled the western hills with lowering, purple shadow. In a town, he could not nestle in a bed of fallen leaves when the knifing, thin cold came at nightfall. His only copper had been spent for passage. Nor was he fit company to seek work in exchange for a meal at an inn. Not with his hair lying lank and unwashed on his neck. The thick gray felt of his herder's boots was sorrowfully wicking up muck from the cattle, who had all dropped manure and urine in bawling terror as the barge lurched through the first spinning eddies.

The sky had drained to a lucent, pale cobalt when at last the ferry nestled into the stone jetty by the water gate. Put ashore and still fighting the pony, which rolled eyes and flagged its thick tail at the clatter of its own milling hooves on the cobbles, Fionn Areth stared upward. The last sun washed the wall to rose gold. Above fretted crenellations, the sky was diminished; herringbone jumbles of rooftrees and gables arose, fitted in stone or massive, carved beams, and flying the mayor's turquoise pennons. Raised on the open, rolling moors, the young man had never imagined so many buildings compressed into such a tight space.

'Move on, yokel,' cracked the overseer, impatient. 'This was the last ferry. Can't unchain these convicts 'til all the civilians are clear, and the watch won't be pleased if some dawdler keeps them waiting to close the gates. They'll be just as anxious as I am to go for their off-duty beer.'

The pony clattered into a jerking shy, in no mood to fare anywhere but backward. Fionn Areth could not hope to forestall her tantrums with a mere length of knotted rope. He followed, rather than allow her to drag him and skin open his scarcely scabbed blisters.

'You a fool, boy?' called one of the guardsmen from the shadowy depths of the gate arch. 'Move that nag out!'

The mare crow-hopped and reared, threatening to slip Fionn's grasp altogether. Over the hammering beat of his heart and the rampaging clatter of hooves, he saw no choice but to turn the mare's setback into an opportunity.

'You there, who's shouting!' he hollered in defiance. 'I'll have you think better of my horse before I respect any order from you.'

The guardsman bristled and stepped into the open, a bald, broad-shouldered brute with a jingling byrnie and a longsword with a swept hilt. 'Do you say, lad? Not mind my order, and you but a snip with naught but a knife that's never done much but stick goats?'

Fionn Areth gave the rope an almighty yank, and the mare for a mercy came down. She stood, spraddle-legged and blowing, while he spun. Arrogant green eyes flicked the guardsman up and down. 'Had I more than a knife, be most sure, I could fight and disarm you.'

The guardsman roared, laughing, while his peers in the gatehouse poked their heads from the embrasures in amusement. 'Now that's worth a wager,' one shouted, egging on the guardsman whose pride had been challenged.

'I'll bet this pony,' Fionn said, cool as new snow despite his back-country accent. 'If I win, let me keep your week's beer coin. If I lose, then this mare will be left to defend her own pigheaded honor. I'll watch while *you* drag her off of the dock.'

The huge guardsman was incensed, but scarcely a bully. 'Get out of here, goatherd. Use the good sense Ath gave your father's herd billy! Touch a blade, you'd most likely lop off your own leg.'

Fionn Areth swiped fallen hair from his brow. 'If I shear off a limb, it won't be my own.'

'Well, fight him, Uray,' a fellow guard heckled. 'Why not win some horse meat to fatten your new hound? Fool jackanapes can use my sword if he wants to murder himself for a boast.'

'Give him some bruises,' another guard chimed in. 'Teach him a lesson to manner his ripe grasslands insolence.'

'I accept!' Fionn shouted, before the bald guard could back down. He tossed the reins of the pony's headstall to the dumbfounded overseer and strode down the jetty toward the gatehouse. 'Bet on my victory,' he said, and laughed outright as the guard, Uray, bristled with a frown that promised bloodshed for being cornered into dancing the steps of a farce.

The man at the gate windlass emerged to make good the loan of his sword. He was older, tough, and wiry, with an extravagant mustache. His surcoat was sun faded over the shoulders, and his helm showed the dents of two decades of service and etched spots left by rust that had outpaced his diligence with a polishing rag. The weapon he offered was just as hard used, and honed to an evil, glittering edge. Its balance in the hand proved fine enough to lend impetus to the cleaving stroke that would part tendon and bone.

'Mind now,' warned the owner, 'if you blood this, you'll be the one cleaning her.' His assessment turned suddenly slit eyed and critical as Fionn Areth tested the grip. 'Mess up your form and parry with the edge, I'll tear me a strip of your hide for each nick the armorer files out.'

Fionn Areth just nodded, couched the blade on his toe and his opposite thigh as he freed his hands to yank the lace from his shirt cuff. He tied back sable hair, wiped his palms on his jerkin, then took up the sword and stepped forward. 'I'm ready.'

He did not sound anxious. Excitement woke a gemstone glitter in green eyes, but his tanned forearm was steady as he confronted Uray at guard point.

The man was not so sunk in contempt that the herder's assured poise did not touch him. He resorted to bluster in the uneasy hope he could lay bare some sign of cowed nerves. 'Think twice, stripling. You could end up a cripple, and for what? The silver I carry is only as much as a man might toss to a beggar.'

'But I don't beg,' Fionn Areth said loudly. 'And that's silver I haven't got to pay for safe lodging and supper.' Since Uray still hesitated, he seized the initiative and launched off the first, testing lunge.

Uray snapped his blade in a bruising, hard parry, uncaring whether his weight and man's strength were too much for an unseasoned amateur. Steel rang and slid and gave way like a lover, teasing him into a lunge.

Fionn Areth sidestepped like a soft breath of air, shed the force of the thrust just enough to allow the blade to pass over his shoulder. Like a typical garrison soldier accustomed to sparring with the same partners over and over, Uray was that split second slow to recover his overplayed balance. The boy gave way, backwards. He let his blade scissor against his opponent's, then rotated his wrist and effected a bind. Steel snarled on steel. Uray swore, surprised, as his thumb turned and wrenched in the loop of his sword guard. The weapon left his hand with a singing, stressed clang. The clamor as it struck the stone of the jetty belled into a dumbfounded silence.

Fionn Areth flipped back the few strands of hair that had tugged free of the thong. While the guardsmen, the overseer, and the barge convicts gawped, he pressed the loaned sword back into the hand of its owner, and demanded of Uray, 'Pass over the silver you owe me.'

He stepped across the fallen sword, accepted the washed leather wallet that Uray fumbled and gave him. While a chattering throng of blackbirds winged overhead, he retrieved his pony from the overseer. Her tantrums by then had played out. She followed, demure, as he collectedly resumed his interrupted course toward the gatehouse.

'Daelion's cock!' swore the owner of the sword as the pony's sorrel tail vanished into the gloom of the archway. 'A goatboy who's a prodigy, who would have guessed?' He reached out and clapped a mollified Uray on the shoulder, then bent and retrieved the man's dispossessed sword from the causeway. 'I'll buy you beer, man. I owe you that much. After all, it was I who browbeat you into that contest.'

Uray shook his head, still looking bemused as he rubbed the wrenched tendons of his wrist. 'D'you know,' he said, thoughtful, 'if we played things just right, we could win my week's beer coin right back using that boy's talent.'

The mustached guard whistled. 'Why in Sithaer not? He wouldn't have to disarm an opponent. Just hold his own for long enough to outlast expectations.' Teeth flashed in a grin of pure devilment. 'I know *just* the man to finagle into taking the challenge. Do you suppose that boy would agree to the match if I offered him his pick of the second-rate swords in the armory?'

'Captain Jussey?' Uray lit into wicked conspiracy. 'Himself against a grass-seedy moorlands goatherd? By Ath, that *would* be a glorious comeuppance for the bruises we've suffered in the practice yard!'

Edged in step by step to join the conversation, the overseer laughed. 'Ask the herder, why not? And if he accepts, tell him I'll pay his night's lodging along with the stabling costs for that ornery witch of a pony.'

Day spilled like molten gold across Eltair Bay, the long, slanting rays of early sunlight nicked through racing bands of wind-torn, low-bellied clouds. Yet Morriel Prime had no care for the magnificence of the view outside the open curtains of her palanquin. Still laced with the damp of yesterday's driving storm, the cold bit like a flayer's knife. Yet anger, more than the frost in the air, flushed the ancient Prime's nose a brilliant pink. Her black eyes narrowed, couched amid rice-paper wrinkles of displeasure as she snapped a command for her bearers to halt on the verge.

The column of her escort bunched into a racketing snarl as wagons, sumpter mules, and her mounted escort came to a disorderly stop on the steep, rutted track leading into the mountains from Highscarp.

Morriel's querulous demand sliced through the jingle of bits, and creaking axles, and the thin, lonely cries of the marsh birds flocking the misted flats at the bayside. 'Send a circle of six seniors to my side, now!'

A towheaded page boy darted from the shade of the palanquin to gather the peers she required.

Morriel waited, her delicate, claw hands clenched to an obsidian scrying ball. The stone's glassy surface imprinted no natural reflections. Instead of plain sky, or the brightening light sequined over the shifting, gray waters to the east, its black depths showed a scene like an etching stippled in silvered shadows and moving smoke.

In colorless mime between the Prime's palms, a black-haired boy and a surly-faced captain at arms circled, feinted, and crossed swords in a match fight. Above the ghostly and flickering ranks of agitated spectators reared the queer, gabled roofs with stone carvings and talisman dragons that distinguished the city of Daenfal.

'Imbecile boy!' Morriel muttered. Although she had provoked his departure from Araethura as a ploy to unbalance Lirenda, *this* prank outpaced expectations. She fumed in searing, helpless impatience, while her summons traveled the length of her train and brought robed seniors indecorously scurrying from the comfort of their enclosed wagons. Ill at ease in the wilds, they stumbled in soft shoes over the loose stones and snagged their red-bordered hems in dead burdock.

'I want a ward and a trance melding!' Morriel snapped, while the last of them spoke her breathless obeisance. 'Has Elaira passed through Daenfal yet?'

'She's been and gone, Matriarch,' reported the enchantress who served as the train's ranking seeress. 'Your order for haste was taken to heart. At lane watch this sunrise, she was a full day's journey down the lakeshore east of the river gate.'

Morriel stifled a burst of ill temper. 'Then I have words I want sent to our sisters in residence at Daenfal, and without a second to lose.' Between eggshell knuckles with their blued tracks of veins, the scrying ball enacted its shadow dance reflection of parry and riposte.

'Your will,' said the seeress, too experienced for surprise. She relayed her Prime's decree. A second shuffling scramble erupted as the enchantresses fanned into a circle on the broken, weedy ground. The Prime's bearers scrambled nervously clear, wisely unwilling to stay near the palanquin while the Matriarch raised her powers in conjury. Spell crystals flashed through the clear, morning air, as each enchantress engaged her personal focus and performed the requisite sigils to enact a primary warding. Then, in a dedicated obedience which transcended the rough, roadside setting and showed no dismay for the snags in loomed silk, each sat on her haunches, bent her head, and released her will and awareness. The ritual trance melded their separate talents into a seamless vessel of joined intent.

The breeze caught in that vortex. Bent from its blustering, north-westerly course, it whiplashed into a spiral, crackling the cloth of the enchantresses' cloaks, and snarling the ties of the lead-weighted curtains that flanked the chair in the palanquin. Morriel Prime endured the raw blast. Her back poker straight and her skeletal hands welded to the flickering scrying ball, she weathered the first plunge into bone-hurting chill. Electrical tingles razed her thin skin. As the spell forces built and blazed active, more strayed charges snicked flares of static over her rings and her hair. The Prime poised, as though listening to an unseen litany, while the power raised by her circle of six seniors leveled into a unified force.

The flux reached its peak in one burning, bright moment. Morriel Prime released one hand from the sphere of obsidian. She extended a finger and traced the Prime Matriarch's symbol and seal, then added the paired ciphers which granted her unilateral command. The engaged imperative of her personal seal laid claim to the heart of the vortex. A shock ripped the silence, without sound, without source. Morriel closed the iron fist of her mastery around that raw core of energy. She turned the inner fire of her will to bridge her message across the distance to Daenfal.

The demand she imprinted on the peeress stationed there was succinct, and direct as a brand to the skin: *to search through the records of Koriani oaths of service and find one attached to a merchant who could mount an eastbound caravan at short notice.*

'Charge the man to send a packtrain across the Pass of Sards with all speed,' Morriel snapped through the contact. 'He'll transport goods belonging to the order. Include my imperative that they reach the coast for consignment before the feast of winter solstice. Most important of all, I want a young swordsman named Fionn Areth to serve the train as a road guard as far as the city of Jaelot.' She followed up with his concise description, then the name of the tavern where her chosen hired sword could be found. 'By your Koriani vow of service, do not fail me in this. Expect I will contact the lane watch at sundown to be certain you've followed my instructions.'

Lirenda detested the rigors of travel as much as she disdained manual labor, uncouth manners, and poverty. Huddled in a wagon under scratchy wool blankets while the wind whined and tore through the shelter of a north-facing spruce thicket, she cursed the inconvenience of the Eltair Bay trade road in chilled white clouds of spent breath. The guttering wick in the glass-paned lantern scarcely kept the darkness at bay. The flame was an inadequate light source for scrying. That shortfall became added salt in the sore of her bitter frustration. Lirenda shifted her chilled grasp on the quartz sphere. She smoothed the black velvet cloth spread over her knees, then closed her eyes to reframe her disturbed equilibrium.

When at last she laid claim to the seat of prime power, she swore to avoid this forsaken route under the knees of the mountains. The land was too stony and rough to grow barley. The ferocity of the storms that swept in off the ocean discouraged the building of inns, and no galleys rowed up this harborless coastline except in the calms of high summer.

Another screaming gust rocked the wagon. Outside, in distracting, snatched fragments, Lirenda overheard the carefree remarks shared between the low-ranking initiates who journeyed in her close company. Their foolery rankled her nerves like stray thorns and fueled her building annoyance.

Four times, she had sounded Araethura for Fionn Areth. Each effort had drawn a blank. The quartz sphere had garnered no answers at all, no solid reflection of his presence, but only the moorland acres of grasses, wind-bent by frost, and tipped silver-white under moonlight.

The worry could fester inside like a canker. The setback was unthinkable, that on the cusp of her bid to claim victory, something untoward could have happened to the boy who formed the very linchpin of her plans. No choice remained but to repeat her effort to seek him all over again.

He was a young man, hot-blooded enough to be tumbling some wench in a hay barn. Engrossed in lust, his animal preference for privacy would raise instinctive barriers against prying spellcraft. Lirenda forced down her building irritation, then calmed herself back into trance. She cast the refocused net of her awareness into the dimmed lattice of the quartz sphere.

This time her effort snagged an immediate live contact. The sheer strength and force of the encounter rocked her balance, as though a set of steel grapples dragged her down through the heart of a whirlpool. Hazed to startled fear, Lirenda flinched in avoidance; yet her bid to tear free only bound her more strongly.

For one instant of mindless, blinding panic, she held the nightmare-bleak thought that she had tagged, not Fionn Areth, but Prince Arithon of Rathain, with the full range of his trained mage talents revitalized.

'This is your Prime Matriarch speaking, you ninny!' The whiplash command of Morriel's voice shattered the web of illusion. Lirenda startled bolt upright. By desperate reflex, she caught the quartz sphere before it tumbled from her slackened grasp. Her flood of relief as she recognized the Prime's sigil came poisoned by shame, to be caught in a moment of outright incompetence.

Blinking, discomposed, Lirenda snatched to recover her wrecked poise. 'Your summons arrived on the moment I had initiated a scrying to find Fionn Areth.'

'I know that.' Morriel's pinched features regarded her reprovingly from the cleared depths of the quartz. 'Four times, you called him. By now you should realize he's no longer in Araethura.'

Lirenda's breath stopped. Somehow, she managed to push back her shock and cling to the semblance of calm. 'He's left his family?'

'And must I repeat myself four times over also?' the Prime rasped back in tart anger. Through the buffeting wind, and the thrashing of fir branches, her venomous tirade resumed. 'That boy parted from his mother a fortnight ago! The lane-watcher picked him up, alone in Daenfal, fighting a match wager at swords with a veteran man-at-arms!'

Too haughty to cringe, Lirenda felt her face warm into a violent flush. Through the leap of her pulse, she framed the unthinkable question. 'Has he taken any harm?'

'No thanks to your vigilance,' Morriel conceded.

Lirenda drew breath to promise amends, but her words were cut off without mercy.

'You'll do nothing at all, but resume making your way south into Jaelot.' The Prime Matriarch permitted no protest and no compromise. 'When you arrive, find quarters at an inn and draw the Lord Mayor into your exclusive confidence.'

'Fionn Areth—'

'Has been taken care of,' the Prime said, her displeasure a crackle of live force. 'I've engaged oath of debt with a reliable merchant. Your boy will cross the Skyshiel passes in his safe employ as a caravan guard. He'll arrive none the worse for your inept grasp of priorities. Mind me well, Lirenda, and take warning from this. I will not act to spare him should you fumble again. Your whole future hangs in the balance, *and mine, and the order's, and woe unto you should you fail us!*'

The quartz sphere went black. Shaking, enraged, and half-sick with reaction, Lirenda closed bloodless lips. *She was not going to fail.* That possibility had never for a moment crossed her mind; nor had she lapsed into carelessness. Fionn Areth's precipitous departure had been nothing more than the extraordinary bad luck of coincidence.

Far more likely this reprimand had been meted out as another of Morriel's cruel tests. Lirenda sucked icy air through clenched teeth. There were limits to pride, to honor and obedience. She would not buckle under petty intimidation. No matter whose blood and whose fate must be sacrificed, she would take Arithon captive and recover her rightful inheritance as First Senior.

Left the richer from his escapade by a purse of town-minted coin and the gift of a second-rate sword, Fionn Areth idled away the evening in the racketing crush of a lakeshore tavern. He learned to quaff his beer with due caution lest the next round of congratulatory backslaps catch him in the process of swallowing. If the morning's bout at swordplay with the garrison's rough captain had earned him a reputation, inopportune fits of choking were unlikely to impress the soldiers who had welcomed him into their circle.

He had not won the fight. A bound slice on his wrist and a chorus of bruises made him wince over every small movement. His defeat had not displeased his benefactors. They had wagered their silver that he could withstand the older man's prowess through a slow count of one hundred. His defense had outlasted his detractors' expectations, that no yokel goatherder could match blows with a seasoned professional. Now, in a spree of uproarious celebration, the winners seemed determined to spend their hoard of coin carousing at the Cockatrice Tavern.

Uray clomped by to refill drained tankards and noticed him frowning again. 'Drink up, boy!' he roared in boisterous good spirits. 'We've taken a belting from Hamhand Jussey for years. Hurts sore to lose, but few men I know could stand up to him past the third parry.'

The beer overflowed under Uray's enthusiasm. Fionn Areth licked sour foam off his thumb. He returned what he hoped was a confident smile, while around him the taproom's raw noise crescendoed off the beamed ceiling. A man two trestles down had offended a doxy, with every hooting, drunken onlooker hurling good-natured slangs or offering disastrous advice. The air hung thick as moist cotton. The reek of boiled leather armor and oiled steel underhung the greasy fug thrown off by the fluttering tallow wicks burning in pinched clay pots. Under a kaleidoscopic jumble of thrown shadow, past the shrieking gyrations of a whore who danced on a tabletop, the dart game in the corner had dissipated into an off-key chorus of song. Amid that glorious tapestry of bedlam, men clashed emptied tankards to flag down the overworked barmaid.

Fionn Areth looked on, enchanted. Born and bred in the austere isolation of the moorlands, he drank in the noise and the novelty of sharing the company of worldly men. He nursed his beer and his aches and listened while the soldiers traded boasts of past exploits at arms. From a derelict veteran with cataracts he heard an eyewitness account of the infamous slaughter in Vastmark, when Prince Lysaer of the Light had advanced on the Shadow Master with a war host thirty-five thousand strong.

'I served in the ranks of Jaelot's field troop, signed on to bolster their numbers. Firsthand, on the flanks of a Vastmark mountain, I saw the sorcerer weave his unnatural darkness. Cold enough to freeze a man's hand to his weapon and deadly to those in our vanguard. Mowed them all down like wheat through a scythe. Not one man left standing, and not one blow struck.' The veteran rolled eyes like rheumy, filmed egg whites. 'Terrible sight, one I've never forgot though my vision's gone dim as my memory.'

Another veteran chimed in, eager to elaborate. 'I had an uncle who died at Dier Kenton Vale.' Hunched over his beer, he recited the story, heard as a boy from a retired guardsman, of how the mountains themselves were pulled down in malice to destroy the proud ranks of Prince Lysaer's war host. 'Twenty thousand men, slaughtered in one hour. The earth was made to shift by black sorcery; there's a fact to strike fear in the strongest. That evil crime was made public knowledge under the sunwheel seal at Avenor. The documents attest that the Spinner of Darkness wove his dire spells on the blood of five hundred innocents. All of them were gutted while still alive. Hear tell their hearts were cut out and burned in some filthy, secret ritual carried out on the shores of the Havens.'

The accounts maundered on, the original events well colored by hearsay and rumor. Some men insisted the Master of Shadow came and went in the night as a whirlwind. Another, whose older cousin had served with Alestron's field mercenaries, attested the fell criminal commanded the reins of Dharkaron's dark Chariot itself.

Talk meandered through long exhaustive, drunken speculation over the demon bastard's current whereabouts.

Uray laughed and waved the matter away, then bawled for the barmaid to bring the next round. 'Why worry? No one's seen hide nor hair of the bastard for over a decade. Daenfal's not troubled. Who gives a damn what the slinking black sorcerer's doing so long's we've got beer and ladies?'

A soldier with cropped ash hair and chain bracers did not share his shrug of complacency. 'One thing's certain as the whang on a bull, the murdering creature will return. When that happens, you'll know. Children will vanish from their cradles and be found with slit throats from his evil rites. The land's last hope will rely on the men who follow the Prince of the Light.' He tippled his tankard in one draining gulp, then pounded the emptied vessel on the boards.

'Hey, wench!' he howled. 'I'm dry as a harridan's crotch!'

'Where would one go to find this great champion?' Fionn Areth ventured, intrigued.

The soldier swayed and fixed bleary eyes upon the young, eager face turned toward him. 'You, boy. You'd swear for the Light? Talent like yours could support that grand cause. The Alliance guard always needs recruits.'

He said something else that Fionn Areth missed in the risen welter of racket. At the front of the room, a minstrel in peacock blue silk bawled the opening to a lewd ballad. Voices joined in, with stamping and hand clapping. Through the barrage, in pealing frustration, Fionn Areth repeated his question.

The soldier heard nothing. His attention had been snagged by the bosom of a wench in flame red, who heaved through the press at the beckoned invitation of a dandy who brandished a fringed purse.

Through a roar of laughter at somebody's joke, Fionn Areth leaned over the trestle, and shouted, 'Where may I find this Prince of the Light and the troops who train for the Alliance?'

A hand grasped his scruff and jerked him back like an overeager puppy. 'It's a fool who risks fanning a drunken man's temper.'

Dropped back on his bench, green eyes lit to blazing, Fionn Areth spun in challenge. His glower was met, and matched, by a stranger who wore a brown cloak fastened with a battered garnet ring brooch. He had a broad, patient face and his sobriety cut a distinctly sharp note amid the brawling, raucous company of the taproom. 'You're the young swordsman who fought Captain Jussey in the square?'

Fionn Areth nodded, distrustful. He managed the astuteness to hold back his anger while the man's mild eyes swept him up and down, measuring all of him without comment.

The man heaved a resigned sigh. His expression suggested he wished to be elsewhere as he finished his opening thought. 'If you truly want honest work for your sword, you need not look to Avenor to find it.'

Fionn Areth said, cautious, 'What are you offering?'

'A post as a guard on a caravan bound over the Skyshiel passes. We'll want good swordsmen at this time of year. The roads are less traveled before winter.'

Across the trestle, one of the garrison guards called out in knowing derision, 'You're Reysald's road captain? Since when has that miserly, pink sack of lard risked his goods to bad weather and barbarians?'

The man gave a shrug. 'No care of mine, but between all the hand-wringing, he complained he had promised the delivery of a consignment for the Koriathain.'

The guard raised knowing eyebrows. 'Oath of debt to the witches?'

'Seems so.' The road captain grimaced, displeased himself, but too steady a man for histrionics. 'Damned details are none of my business.'

'That's the trick, accepting the sisterhood's favors.' The guardsman glanced over his shoulder, then guffawed, a shrill note straining his humor. 'They're women, and don't they *always* choose the most pesky time to collect?'

'Are the passes that dangerous?' Fionn Areth broke in.

'Captain Coreyn, to you, boy.' Introduction complete, he gave his blunt answer. 'We charge risk pay for crossings made after equinox. That's as much due to storms as the increased chance we'll be raided. The work's not all swordplay. I've no use for a laggard who won't bend his back to free a mired wagon from a snowdrift.' Tired of shouting over the noise, he tipped his head toward the tavern doorway. 'You want the details? Then why don't we both step outside?'

Without pause to see whether the moorland swordsman would abandon his company and follow, Coreyn displaced a cooper who pushed for a seat, and elbowed through the press toward the doorway.

Outside under moonlight, shivering from raw excitement and chill air, Fionn Areth heard through the terms of the hire. He accepted for a fee of five silvers, daily, with an eighth portion added for every fortnight the caravan traveled through dangerous territory.

'No extra pay for armed engagements, mind. But if you kill a barbarian defending the goods, you can claim posted bounty for headhunting.' Coreyn extended a hand, his grip banded wire over the untried flesh of Fionn Areth's offered palm.

'Be at the eastside land gate by sunrise,' he finished, and disengaged his brisk handshake. 'No excuses for lateness. The season's too chancy to waste even an hour stalling for damn fools and laggards.'

'I'll be there,' Fionn Areth promised, his green eyes grave. Under the spill of the torches stubbed into the iron brackets by the doorway, he seemed suddenly young, and too vulnerable.

Coreyn masked his disgust in stiff silence and strode off into the darkness.

Long after the caravan captain departed, the hired sword whose face held another man's bane never thought to wonder if his gift of good fortune held the thread of a wider design. He lingered in the stone entry of the Cockatrice, marveling at his incredible luck, and whispering endearments to the ancient, chipped carvings that gave the old tavern its name. The fretwork on the facings and the interlaced coils of the serpents themselves bespoke work too refined for human artisans.

The world was a wide place, now his to explore. Excitement bubbled up and burst out in a whoop that slammed echoes off the gabled roofs, with their queer, rampant guardians crouched in their scales of shagged lichen. The cry rang over the icy gray cobbles and bounced through the arched columns that supported the massive, hewn beams of the balconies. More than one shutter slammed open, the rudely wakened sleepers inside howling outraged obscenities.

Fionn Areth did not care. Hand clenched in pride on the hilt of his sword, he yelled again for pure joy. A herder no longer, he was free, and at last on sure course for his destiny.

## Autumn 5669

# Stymie

By the hour that young Fionn Areth pledged his sword with Coreyn's road guards in the predawn shadow of Daenfal's eastern land gate, leagues distant, in Atainia, the night's reign had not faded. Against the swept hills of the Bittern Desert, the west-facing casement of Althain Tower's library still showed stars and a setting white sliver of moon. Its Warden was not caught napping through the moment when his earth-sense captured the caravan's daybreak departure. The rhythmic scrape of the pen nib he used to scribe records on sheets of fine vellum broke off. Sethvir peered over his shoulder, his mild eyes piercing, and his eyebrows bristled with sorrow.

'Luhaine?' he whispered. 'Stay with Verrain at Methisle. I've already checked. Nothing more can be done.'

Through the span of one heartbeat, the tower chamber remained quiet. No candles burned. The shadowy, carved dragons supporting the slab table stayed etched into gloom, stone frozen to snarls and bared fangs. Only the restive air shared the charge of a terrible, mounting urgency.

Sethvir elbowed his vellum and ink flask aside, warned by a cascading rush of disturbed wind that his plea had been disregarded.

The next moment, the discorporate spirit wheeled in uninvited, riffling a small tempest of papers across the table and clapping shut the board covers of Sethvir's opened books. 'May those witches suffer Sithaer's seven fires of perdition for their incessant, unconscionable meddling!'

Luhaine's presence focused into a tempest that rocked the crock of spare quills into rustling agitation. Sethvir clapped out a cobra-fast hand and pinned them before they winnowed willy-nilly in the storm.

'I've not become boisterous as Kharadmon,' Luhaine retorted in miffed response to the Warden's raised eyebrows. 'When I throw a tantrum, at least there's a well-founded cause! The Koriani Prime has no morals, no compassion, and no shred of mercy!' Without need for a pause to recover his breath, his tirade rolled seamlessly onward. 'May her black heart char for eternity, and her spirit twist in the lightless pits at the negative pole of creation. If I had to pass judgment, I would suggest the longevity spells that preserve her unnatural life have finally driven her insane!'

'She's frightened,' Sethvir said quietly.

'Well she should be!' Luhaine retorted, his fury transmuted to righteous indignation. 'That dumpling she's chosen to train for her office won't survive the first trial of succession. She has to know. Lirenda's not fooled. But even a frustrating setback of that magnitude can't excuse her scheming manipulation of an innocent.'

'You speak of Fionn Areth?' Sethvir sounded weary, the slope of his shoulders almost beaten as he released the quills battened under his hand. He retrieved the one still dipped wet for writing and blotted the ink against the marked edge of his sleeve.

Luhaine's uncontained angst wafted on past the aumbries, circling the chamber's perimeter. 'They've set that boy up as a road guard, did you know, for a caravan bound into *Jaelot*!'

'I saw.' The mapwork of lines on Sethvir's drawn face revealed all his agonized empathy.

Luhaine whuffed past the casement. The weathered board shutters swung and banged in complaint, dropping rust flakes from tired hinges. 'Save us,' he whispered. 'Don't say the boy's lost. We're craven if we don't lend him help to escape. The more so since this backhanded byplay of Morriel's was conceived to restore her unprincipled use of the Great Waystone.'

Sethvir shot to his feet in a driven burst that flapped a week's dust from his robes. 'Who could be spared? Traithe hasn't been well. I dispatched him to Vastmark to map the new shale faults, since anything more taxing might kill him.'

'Then Asandir's gone to Camris?' Luhaine stated, disturbed into mollified quiet.

'He's rededicating the wards on the Sorcerer's Preserve, yes.' Sethvir sat back down, his chin propped on gnarled fists. 'There were instabilities in the bulwarks about to become holes, and this time, a cursory patch won't suffice. He can't leave prematurely. Not unless we want packs of Khadrim flaming caravans to cinders and marauding the crown territory of Tysan.'

Luhaine grumbled with predictable pessimism, 'No one of us should handle those forces alone.' The powers involved were enormous and intricate, and utterly unforgiving of mistakes. Still worse, the barriers would require five arduous weeks to lay down and seal to stability.

'The crisis couldn't be made to wait.' Sethvir sighed, pressed into silence by desperate tact, while Luhaine fumed in a mute fit of thwarted distress.

He, too, was hamstrung. Ever since Morriel Prime had recovered the strength to command the matrix of the Great Waystone, she had wasted no time schooling a circle of senior initiates to meld their talents through its focus. She now had twelve, with as many more in training. Each initiate added meant an exponential increase in the scope and strength of her power. Pitched alone against such a force, no disembodied Sorcerer dared attempt even subtle intervention. Lacking a dense matter body as anchor, the refined energies of spirit could become fenced and trapped, spellbound to the matrix of the Koriani master crystal and set under a chained seal of binding.

Only one other discorporate Fellowship mage remained at large with the cunning ingenuity to guard a colleague against the dangerous, drawing powers of a trance circle fused through the amethyst.

'I already tried the last avenue of resort.' Sethvir shook his head, sorrowful. 'Davien's shade still won't answer my summons.'

'Serve the Betrayer right if we fall, then,' Luhaine groused in black pique. 'He'll poke his nose out of Kewar Tunnel one day and wonder why sunlight's been swallowed by wraiths and Koriani are running the planet.'

'You'd quit so easily? That's not your style.' Sethvir stroked his beard. A sly spark kindled deep in his eyes. 'The season's our ally. Do you think an early blizzard in the Skyshiel passes could delay that caravan's arrival?'

'I'm already gone,' Luhaine grumbled. His acerbic rejoinder shimmered through the static that marked his hasty departure. 'Though I'll ask you to recall that bedeviling kinks in the weather is more Kharadmon's preference than my own.'

'Trade places with him, then,' Sethvir suggested to the air.

A snort of disdain wafted back across a widening veil of distance. 'Oh no! Let him stay in the vacuum communing with stars. An indefinite stint of boredom attending cold wards might lend him a refreshed perspective on the fine points of civilized behavior.'

Alone once again, Sethvir arose and reset the slipped stay on the shutter. He tucked his unfinished page under a vase filled with the sunflower seeds, acorns, and beechnuts he saved for the birds and small creatures who visited his windowsill. Then he leaned on his elbows and gazed out, while the winds nipped and tangled the ends of his beard, and the gray well of daybreak erased the night's constellations.

The telling facts he had not shared with Luhaine left their pain like thorns in the heart. For *if* a diverted storm in the Skyshiels might stall Morriel's plot through the five crucial weeks to let Asandir try an intervention, other forces remained still at play, every one of which set a dangerous spin on an unpredictable future. The earth link presented every deadly and volatile nuance for review.

Even as the sun rose over the frost-powdered moors of Araethura, Sethvir tracked a courier westbound on a barge flying downriver toward Halwythwood. His dispatch satchel held a letter from one of Raiett Raven's agents, addressed to the nearest officer of Lysaer's Sunwheel Alliance. That missive would reach Morvain inside the next fortnight. A fast galley to Dyshent would bear word into Tysan that a man bearing the Master of Shadow's description had been seen plying swordplay for wagers in the public market of Daenfal.

Sethvir stirred at last as the first brown sparrows chirped from their roosts and took wing. Touched gold by dawnlight, he left to make tea in vain effort to quiet his ominous dread. For naught could halt fate, even if Asandir could effect a last-minute deflection. Fionn Areth's carefree innocence now led him into dire straits, with no surety set on the outcome.

Only one consolation could be wrung from the earth link's converging train of bad news: Arithon s'Ffalenn and his crew aboard the *Khetienn* were far removed from the center of conflict. Three thousand leagues of chartless ocean lay between their logged position and the disastrous affray now setting up on the continent.

# Fulcrum

The snarl of cold winds over stripped stone kept Morriel Prime from her sleep. The frame of the palanquin where she lay wrapped in furs shuddered to each veer in the gusts, and the incessant pain which gnawed at her joints twinged to each tiny movement. Of all possible sites where she might need to winter, the mountain citadel of Eastwall ranked among the most miserable of choices. Yet there, as nowhere else along the sixth lane, the spine of the earth thrust upward, the great slabs of dark granite veined in white quartz. The stone of the Skyshiels formed a natural amplifier for Athera's magnetic currents. In Eastwall, Morriel could lay her thumb on that pulsebeat, and fuse the all but limitless wellspring of raw power into chains and seals of her making.

If the site served her ends, the journey into high altitude was a curse.

No matter how many coverings she piled on, her hands stiffened, each knuckle a cold knob of glass. Imprisoned by frailty, tormented by her circling thoughts, she endured. The burden of the proscribed knowledge she safeguarded for the future benefit of humanity pressed on her shoulders like lead. Nor did companionship bring her relief. The obsequious lisp of the young woman she trained wore at her fragile, strung nerves. Solitude stung her with the trickling passage of seconds that chafed her like separate sand grains. She suffered each day, eaten raw by the unending cycle of hope and despair.

Sleep brought her nothing but nightmares and frustration. While

Lirenda sought to redeem her past flaws and draw Arithon s'Ffalenn to captivity, the Koriani Order looked to a threatened future.

Morriel responded in pathetic relief when the seeress tapped for admittance.

'Enter.' The word was a reedy, thin whisper, scarcely audible through the thrash of the gusts as the curtains were pushed aside.

Morriel tightened her grip on the fur quilts, wincing as the high, thin chime of star energies grazed through her sensitized consciousness. She had lived too long. The more her bodily senses failed her, the stronger grew the inner awareness, until even plain stone seemed to gibber impressions that spoke of the past flights of dragons. Moment to moment, the ancient Prime Matriarch had to fight for the focus to strain real sound from the untrustworthy chorus of phantoms unleashed in her mind.

The seeress announced on a bright edge of triumph, 'Dakar's made landfall, just as you'd hoped.'

'Oh, well-done!' Morriel propped upright and snapped her thin fingers.

A page groped from the shadows at the foot of her pallet. Blinking to shed the confusion of torn sleep, he stifled a yawn, then adjusted the pillows to settle the crone into a seated position.

'I'll need the Great Waystone,' the old Prime directed. 'Also the small coffer that's locked in the cupboard beneath the sedan chair.'

The seeress fetched and carried as the Prime requested, while the page followed orders and kindled the lamp. The shadows danced back as the flame caught. Lavender hangings sewn with silver seals of guard sparkled like frozen rain. The edges of cushions and the laced shine of braid framed Morriel's erect form like a kiosk.

'I'll want the silk cloth that carries the seals for summons and dispatch.' Morriel accepted the covered burden of the Waystone and cradled it between her raised knees. 'Set a circle of guard. Then light the tienelle tapers at the four directions and place the coffer in my lap.'

The loose, wispy fall of her unbound hair made her face seem a dry, wrinkled skull caught in a must of old cobweb. But her hooded, jet eyes gleamed with burning, mad joy as she bade servant and seeress, 'Now leave me. This night's work will be mine alone to complete.'

Left in the flickering spill of the lamp, and crossed in crawling shadow thrown by the sullen gleam of the tapers, Morriel drew a key from a chain clasped to her skeletal wrist. She opened the coffer, then sorted through the silk-wrapped packets inside until she found the one bearing Dakar's name.

'Ah, well, my blundering beauty,' she crooned to herself, while the

winds slapped and moaned through the pennons on the finials outside.
'Your time is well come, is it not?'

White, spidery fingers untied the covering. Inside lay a tied wisp of
curled, chestnut hair, purloined years ago by a harlot. The doxy had
snipped her little keepsake while Dakar lay oblivious in one of his
drunken stupors. No slave to sentiment, she had sensibly traded the
trophy to the sisterhood for a potion to purge a malady caught from
a sailor.

Morriel Prime laid out the deep black square of silk with its embroi-
dered silver circles. Then she unwound the faded ribbon which tied
Dakar's lock of hair. One strand, she placed on the stitched runes
of the summoning seal. A second, laid crosswise, bridged the seal of
dispatch. Then she unveiled the facets of the amethyst Waystone and
positioned its chill weight inside the circle that joined the two points
in opposition.

The wind muttered off the peaks, stirring and stretching the flames
in the drafts. Morriel Prime no longer felt the bite of the cold stabbing
through her aged joints. Immersed in the throes of dire art and high
spellcraft, she mastered the focal matrix of the Great Waystone for
the unprincipled purpose of playing Dakar's power of prophecy as her
personal puppet string . . .

Many leagues over the Cildein's waters to the southeast, the risen sun
blazed high over the sands of an atoll lapped in the aquamarine shallows
of the tropics. The small string of islets capped a volcanic ridge uncharted
by previous mariners. If Paravians had ever set foot there, or if dragons
had alighted to rest in their flights on the thermals as they crossed the
vast waters between continents, none knew. The islets were too sparse
to sustain any settlement. Even the records at Althain Tower held no
vellum with an inked position for the cove where Arithon's brigantine,
the *Khetienn*, currently nestled at anchor.

Sethvir's earth-sense linked the site with the flight of nesting petrels,
or touched on the dry land through the chambered veins of magma
flowing underneath the deep sea floor.

The volcanic cone held a rainwater lake. The outflowing stream
offered one of nine springs where Arithon's fleet put in to replenish
its water casks. Here, also, it took on stores shipped from the mainland.
Such stops for provisions never observed a fixed schedule. The inbound
vessels to restock the brigantine's hold came and went by the whims
of winds and weather. Sometimes the seagoing crews matched their
landfall. Other times, rimed with the salt crust of unbroken passage, the
*Khetienn* and one or more companion vessels might ghost in through

the reefs to find the idyllic cove empty. Their spare lines and nails, their sailcloth and barrels of salt meat and ale would be left, stashed in a dry cave near the shoreline. Over the years, routine became set.

Each hull would be careened and inspected. Between hours of hard labor and needed repairs, the crews would ply the rank jungle to snare birds, then spit them and feast on the beaches. Some years they brewed palm wine. Shipboard discipline dissolved to a bedlam of celebration, while children born to the clan wives at sea would scream and race through the shallows. Replete with fresh meat or a meal of purloined eggs, men would argue and wrestle, content to snatch reprieve as they could, while Arithon riffled through his sealed packets of correspondence. At need, he would open his affairs to discussion, penning out cryptic replies to be left in the cave for the next ship to dispatch to his contacts back on the mainland.

Dakar's requirements were simpler. Resigned from his years of privation at sea, he curled in the sheltered shade of a palm tree and drank himself senseless on spirits. He would dream of women and silk sheets. When he awakened, he kissed the dry ground that stayed warm and solid, with no prank, heaving waves set to trip him. His hatred of seafaring had not lessened with time. The miracle left him dumbfounded, that his heart had not yet shirked its weary task of pumping his bored blood through his brain.

This morning's nap started more pleasantly than most, with a gentle west breeze wafting off the biting flies who viewed Dakar's sprawled flesh as a banquet. He slept with his hands laced over his belly, while the fruits of the tropics gave painless relief to three months' steady diet of jerky, squeezed limes, and hardtack.

The first whisper of danger broke in a dream, arrived without fanfare or warning.

His undisturbed sleep became wrenched out of peace. Dakar was consumed by a sickening sensation of falling through bottomless darkness. His senses were locked. As though his awareness was throttled by wound thread, he could not break free or wrest back the will to awaken. The whirling, downward spiral into vertigo presaged no ordinary nightmare. Dakar battled the gripping pejorative of his unchained gift of prescience.

'No,' he whispered, even as his futile fabric of protest became dashed into fragments of light. Power flamed through him like volatile oil, and he saw past the veil that sealed Ath's creation to the constraints of linear time . . .

*Against the wind-ruffled waves of a lakeshore, a rider sat laughing on a moorland pony. He wore a plain longsword strapped to his waist and the cross-laced felt boots of a goatherd. Yet when the wind tossed the black hair off his cheek, the profile stamped in the morning's raw light had the bone structure of a blood s'Ffalenn prince . . .*

The scene snapped like a cobweb rent through by a gale. Sprawled in trance on the black lava sands of the atoll, the Mad Prophet stirred and moaned. A chill breeze of destiny blew straight through him, and beyond any question he *knew*. That rider signified the break in the peace Althain's Warden had foreseen fifteen years ago. Dakar fought the dream. His hands spasmed to fists, and his paunchy flesh shuddered, yet waking perception eluded him. The reeling onslaught of visions resumed, pinwheeling in wild and vivid disorder across his inner awareness . . .

*Before the magistrate at the prisoner's dock in Jaelot, the same boy stood in chains, pleading innocence. His back moorlands accent quavered with tears, but none heard. The wheels of due process ground on unchecked, until a struck look of terror transfixed his green eyes, and an arraignment for black sorcery was read out by a nasal secretary. Then that scene ripped away, replaced by another: of the accused, chained to a scaffold, stripped for a ritual execution. The sharpened sword waited, and the bundled, oiled faggots. Nearby, a cowled headsman mounted the stair, while a mob shook raised fists and clamored for redress in blood against the Master of Shadow. The vision rippled. Townborn faces contorted and screaming with hate condensed and dissolved into one: that of a bronze-haired enchantress who wept . . .*

Dakar snapped awake, gasping and soaked in runnels of terrified sweat. He could not reorient. The palm fronds and blue sky over his head seemed a jumble of meaningless color. For an interval he squeezed his eyes shut and trembled, raw dread like the tang of flaked rust on his tongue. Something had just gone terribly amiss. His spurious gift of prescience never touched him like this, nor left him with the hollow, used feeling of a discarded old boot. The nausea that racked him carried a taint, as if the violating fingers of a spell had just tickled the length of his aura.

Another chill swept him. An instinct, chased by fear, let him suspect that someone powerful had meddled with his gifted prescience. The unnatural, acidic fragments of his dream stayed lodged in his memory like impressions stamped in smoke and sulfur. A spell seal based on forced mastery would impose such unpleasantness, not a working drawn from the Fellowship's craft, laid down in harmony with the Major Balance. The rare intervention sent by Ath's adepts would be gentle, a feather touch channeled from the prime source that anchored the weave of the firmament.

'Lie under a palm tree, annoyed as all that, and you're sure to get whacked by a coconut.'

Dakar flinched and looked up to find Arithon s'Ffalenn standing over him.

'Go away,' he said in a gritted, forced croak.

Arithon's teeth flashed in a perverse, airy smile. 'Poor man. Has the fruit left you griped?'

He sat down. Clad in dark breeches and a loose shirt with laces left open at the neck, he was enviably vibrant. The effects of seafaring had always agreed with him; his presence held a stunning, charged vitality gained back through his years of free sailing. Sun and wind had reduced the deep shadows in his eyes. The nightmares came less and less in sleep, robbed of their venom by the distance in leagues from Desh-thiere's curse-driven urge to seek bloodshed.

Dakar clamped his jaw through another wretched spasm. He racked his churned thoughts for some telling rejoinder that would send the s'Ffalenn prince safely packing.

Too late; the green eyes now fixed on his face. In a tone very changed, the Shadow Master said, 'Dakar, *for mercy, what's wrong?*'

The Mad Prophet turned away. Even slight movement upset his equilibrium. The spasm returned, steel claws in his belly, and he curled in whimpering misery with his cheek pressed into the sand.

Hands gripped him, found his head, and raked his loose hair away from his gasping lips. He was raised up, supported through the ugly, sick spasms that emptied his last meal in raw violence.

'Hang on,' said Arithon. The whipcut awareness of just what was happening had already dissolved his carefree note of light banter.

Dakar felt swift fingers loosen his belt. He was laid back, gasping, against something soft: Arithon's shirt, folded into a pillow to ease his spinning head. A shadow raked over him, then returned. Cloth soaked in seawater streamed over his forehead, damping the pounding, fierce pangs of a headache.

The Mad Prophet blinked through a salt stream of runoff. 'Too bad I'm not female. You'd have me swooning.' He swallowed the lingering burn of heaved bile and forced the charade a step further. 'Such fuss, for a commonplace hangover.'

Arithon knelt in his smallclothes, still arranging the compress made at need from his breeches. 'Don't speak.' The lame effort at deflection had left him unfooled, the opposite in fact. Dakar sensed the fearful effort in his calm as his exquisite schooled voice tore past the veneer of pretense. 'Whatever string of prescience your talent has uncovered, the news can wait. Lie still. Just breathe 'til you're steady.'

A child shouted inquiry from somewhere down the beach. Through the whisper of palm fronds and the curling lisp of the waves over sable sands, the treble cry jarred the air like tapped glass.

The Mad Prophet held on to his reeling senses, saw Arithon turn his head and call answer. 'I need the simples chest from the brigantine. Now! Also, find the watch officer. Tell him I want a man sent back with a litter.'

Dakar felt a firm hand on his wrist. Then darkness enfolded him like soundless felt and swallowed his flickering consciousness.

Full awareness returned in the lucent chill of twilight. Dakar opened his eyes to the softened gloom of the stern cabin. The ship's wake unreeled like mother-of-pearl through the casement's salt-splashed roundels. The board that worked and squealed in the bulkhead and the taint of salt-fusty sailcloth informed him that Arithon had the *Khetienn* set under way and driving to sea once again. Through the hollow, dull repletion of illness, Dakar kicked his mental processes back into shambling order. Through mage sense, he picked out the ship's course, due northwest, affirmed by the gravitational draw of the new moon and the faint, distant pull of the planets.

From strength he did not believe he possessed, he dredged up a breath and tried the first lie his befuddled brain could assemble. 'You're not going back to the continent for the sake of a rockslide that maimed a few sheep and some unlucky shepherds.'

The soft voice he expected gave answer from the shadows somewhere to the left of his berth. 'Drop pretense.' Arithon dipped a tin cup in a basin and trickled a stream of cool water to wet the Mad Prophet's lips. 'Your raving already told me the truth.'

Dakar rammed up straight to the everlasting zeal of the demons still spiking his temples. He crashed into the cup. The contents splashed over his neck and tickled in runnels down his chest. 'A nightmare. Don't believe it.'

A towel settled over the spill, backed by Arithon's hands, which rammed him inexorably flat. 'No nightmare could possibly be that macabre.'

Defeat took the punch out of Dakar's struggle. 'Then would you mind telling me what you heard?'

Hard fingers softened, then blotted, and whisked the soaked towel away. On deck, the bosun called the change in the watch. Bare feet drummed on wood as the sailhands responded. Forward, a young mother crooned a lullaby to her child, while the ocean, ever restless, wove in splashing refrain as the bow clove like smoke through the wavecrests.

Arithon stirred finally, retrieved the cup from the berth, and hooked its handle to the basin with a clink. He had not lit the lamp. His hair was ink upon shadow against the varnished interior of the cabin. Lapped in failing light, his expression was blurred, unreadable as a blank slate.

'What did you hear,' Dakar insisted. 'At least let's make sure we're drawing presumptions from the same list of unpleasant facts.'

The lean, ringless hands clasped taut on one knee, no doubt to lock down their shaking. Arithon said, ice laid over snow, 'You saw the same future my lord Jieret dreamed and journeyed to Corith to give warning. My death on a scaffold, by sword and by fire. Except the vision foretold by my *caithdein* wasn't accurate. The victim isn't going to be me.'

Brooding stillness ensued, through which the Master of Shadow pondered, and Dakar glowered back with distilled rancor.

'Your blurted prophecy wasn't pretty,' Arithon relented at length. 'You said at winter solstice that an innocent boy will be sentenced for the crimes of black sorcery townsmen claim I committed over twenty-five years ago.'

Dakar swallowed, his throat gone sandpaper dry. 'You can't imagine you're going to save him.'

Arithon arose, moved one step, and braced his palm on the sill of the stern window. He had found a fresh shirt. He wore another pair of dark breeches knotted at the waist with a scarlet sash sent him by Feylind. Wind plucked the loose cloth and feathered the sable hair silhouetted against the coiling foam of the wake. 'Who is he, this boy?'

'Who knows? Who cares?' Dakar shoved up on one elbow. 'He could be the throwback of some ancestor's byblow. He had the accent of a moorland goatherd.' Hating the strangled desperation in his plea, the Mad Prophet tried reason. 'Believe me, if he were close enough kin to carry the virtues of the s'Ffalenn bloodline, *the Fellowship Sorcerers would know him!*'

Arithon spun, a coiled spring of bleak fury. 'Never mind who he is! If this fate overtakes him, he'll be frightened and alone, and condemned to a terrible death for an act even I never stooped to commit.'

'He could be anywhere,' Dakar argued, horrified. 'How will you know where to start looking?'

Arithon's quick breath sliced the night like a knife cut. 'But I do know. Your mimicry was plain. You repeated the arraignment in the voice of the official who will come to pen the mayor's writ of execution.

I know him, as you must. He's the Mayor of Jaelot's judiciary secretary, and that's twice now you've sought to obstruct me. What else are you trying to mask from my notice?'

'You can't do this,' Dakar insisted in an obstinate change of subject. 'To meddle with a chained prisoner in Jaelot—'

Arithon cut him off. 'Then stop me with something more substantial than lies!'

A disastrous pause, while Dakar slumped back, each labored effort to breathe like suctioning liquid lead. He mustered his nerves, prayed that bare bones good sense could prevail against volatile s'Ffalenn temper. 'All right. That dream didn't come through my channels of natural-born talent. The prescience was tagged onto my aura by someone's act of forced spellcraft. Which means that boy won't land in Jaelot through blind luck. He's being set up as bait for a trap.'

He had Arithon's attention now, the unpleasant, ruthless focus of a mage-trained observer measuring an undesired obstacle. A small rustle of cloth as the hand not on the sill came to rest on the edge of a locker. 'Lysaer wouldn't make use of children or innocents.'

'You can't know that!' Dakar swore for the lack of a light. He needed to determine whether Arithon braced in shock, or if he was pitched for combative, hot argument. Left no tool but blind trust, he probed softly. 'In the course of three decades, the curse could have changed the half brother you knew past all scruple.'

'No.' Arithon shoved away from the stern window, his admission touched by an odd, heavy weariness. 'By now, I recognize Desh-thiere's workings firsthand.' His clipped speech wove through his fidgeting steps. 'Lysaer was claimed into thrall through his true gift of justice. Change that, and the Mistwraith's hold on him weakens.'

Dakar argued with bloodless honesty. 'He slew children well enough on the banks of Tal Quorin.'

'For a principle, yes.' Pain shot through, expected and sharp, as Arithon crossed through the diced patch of lamplight let in through the grating. His face contorted in recoil from that particularly harrowing memory, he explained, 'Lysaer caught them killing. This execution you've forecast to take place in Jaelot isn't anywhere near the same thing.'

'There aren't many factions who wouldn't choose mayhem, or consort with Sithaer itself to see you dead.' Dakar swore through the splash as the *Khetienn* knifed through a trough. 'Don't forget, Lysaer's high priests now dabble in spellcraft.'

All the signs pointed toward disaster. Nor could Arithon hedge in denial. The warning delivered from Elaira had been unequivocally plain. Despite her concern, and her strong exhortation, the wise option of retreat had already seen the Shadow Master's emphatic rejection. Abovedecks, the bosun shouted to a thundering flog of canvas. Hands were aloft bending on topsails, sure promise of a drenching, fast passage that battered Dakar's brain and turned his gut inside out with seasickness.

Dakar tried futile argument anyway. 'The boy will burn, no matter how blameless, and no matter how mismatched the evidence. You trod on the pride of the city dignitaries too hard. The Mayor of Jaelot keeps a grudge like a champion, and whoever's behind the meddling this time is sure to have Koriani backing.'

'Then they'll discover the consequence of manipulating me by using the fate of an innocent.' Wound into implacable rage, Arithon grasped the knob to the companionway. 'The *Khetienn* makes landfall on the continent with all speed. Stop her, or me, at your peril.'

## Late Autumn 5669

# Appeals

Unsettled by events outside Althain Tower, Sethvir turns the broad-ranging span of his earth-sense to gauge the uncertainties of time and distance that separate parties whose interests converge upon Fionn Areth's free movements: Asandir, still immersed in repair of the wards over the Sorcerer's Preserve in Tysan; Prince Lysaer, at Erdane, arranging a frantic fast passage to substantiate rumors from Daenfal; and Arithon s'Ffalenn, whose fleet has turned about under full sail for the mainland . . .

Amid worried speculation over breaking word concerning the Spinner of Darkness, Lord Koshlin, posted envoy to the Light, is handed a letter in Princess Ellaine's handwriting, with the contents addressed to her father outlining her careful inquiries into Lady Talith's death: 'On return to Avenor, lend my daughter your assistance to dispel this spurious falsehood,' says Erdane's mayor, more anxious to satisfy Prince Lysaer and his handpicked captains who seek passage to the east with all speed . . .

Elaira draws rein on the verge of the road flanking Daenfal's lakeshore, overcome as she senses the compassion in the man who steers his brigantine in a driving run northwestward across the Cildein Ocean; and tears fill her eyes, for a warning, unheeded, that brings desperate fear for Prince Arithon's endangerment, and renews the wild, outside hope of salvation for young Fionn Areth . . .

# XI. Decoy

L ate in the season, the caravans bound over the Pass of Sards exchanged their wheeled drays for sumpter mules at the Standing Rock on the southern border of Rathain. The site had been a crossroads since ancient times, when the lean, painted boats of the sunchildren plied north and south through the golden hill country of Daon Ramon. A crumbling stone bridge still spanned the dry chasm where the sheet silver waters of the Severnir had once thundered into the east narrows of Daenfal Lake. Now the winds howled unpartnered through that corridor of sheer rock, fluted into dissonance where the tireless frosts chiseled fresh outcrops and cracks.

If the river was silenced by the industry of townsmen who maintained their dam at the headwater, a snug inn still prospered where the road crossed the dry and boulder-strewn gulch. Legend yet brooded over the cliff walls, folded in frown lines where rains had carved gullies in the rims. Dragons had once winged aloft here for mating. In a later age, Riathan Paravians had danced to heighten lane force when the yearly sun cycle crossed the stations of balance and change. The lyrical traces remained on the land where the rituals had enabled those mysteries to be tapped and drawn to span latitude.

Where the road left the shore and snaked into the foothills, centaur guardians had erected a quartz standing stone. The marker was incised with spiraling knots and still overlooked the high bluffs. Travelers who stayed through an equinox or solstice might hear the stone speak as its mighty axis captured the magnetic pulse of the fifth lane and channeled its peak current to resonance.

'Site's haunted,' insisted the inn's lanky horseboy as he hefted a packframe onto the last mule to outfit Reysald's caravan. 'If you stand there from sundown to sunrise, you'll see unicorns passing, all ghostly gray in the moonlight. Some men go mad. Some see past the veil. For certain, they say, if you wish on that stone, every shadow in your heart will come true.'

Huddled in the brisk dawn air of the stable yard, Fionn Areth watched the clouds scud like dirty ice above the brown flank of the hill. The stone was a slender, milk obelisk at the crest, mottled with shag moss and lichen.

The horseboy adjusted the crupper, then slapped begrimed knuckles on his breeches. 'Still, you'll wish you were staying. Snow could be flying by midday, and the caves where you'll camp don't offer wenches and ale.'

'I don't mind the cold,' Fionn Areth said, neutral, lest his imagination on the subject of women embarrass him into a blush. He grasped the mule's reins and led it into line to be loaded under the expert eye of the head drover.

The goods bound for Jaelot required twenty mules, with another ten to pack food and fodder for the train's master, three hired muleteers, and six outriders. The horsemen went armed, ostensibly to guard, but in fact each one carried a stiff leather prod to drive balky animals at need. This turned out to be most of the time on a trail that snagged like shorn thread through vicious black crags of sheer rock. The scarps in between were not steep in these foothills, but strewn with the tumbled debris of old slides and spiked by the stripped limbs of deadfalls.

Accustomed to goats, Fionn Areth did not balk at handling animals. The destination was agreeable. From talk at the inns, he had learned that the Mayor of Jaelot kept a field troop of mercenaries oathsworn to Prince Lysaer's Alliance. The force was committed to guard against Shadow, wherever such conflict might call them. Stirred by the accounts of the earlier wars against sorcery fought at Tal Quorin and Vastmark, Fionn Areth resolved to enlist.

The trail switched back and climbed from the Severnir valley, flanked to the right by the forbidding summits of the spur that gave rise to Rockfell Vale. The rugged knife ridges and dark, fanged peaks were perpetually snarled in cloud. Mornings shook the ground with the distant rumble of avalanche as the slopes shrugged off the night's snowfall. Those few stands of fir which clawed leaning hold against southbound winds off the barrens wore jagged scars from the onslaught of each winter's storms. Steep-sided valleys arrowed from the crests, zigzagged and forked as the imprint of frozen lightning.

'Men die in this pass at this time of year,' the road master cautioned after Fionn Areth strayed beyond sight while foraging wood for the cookfire. 'Storms can whip in off of Eltair Bay with terrible force and no warning. Just a mess of black cloud will come howling down the notch. These peaks trap their fury like a witch's funnel. Never be more than ten steps from your horse. Your life could depend on her instincts.'

The onslaught of two such blizzards delayed them. The first one they weathered in a string of small caves, one of the uncounted fissures that branched from the caverns of Skelseng's Gate. The second storm caught them at the end of their supplies, with no choice but to batter ahead. They made punishing progress against shrieking winds and blundered through chest-high drifts. One mule was lost, and two men suffered frostbite before the caravan struggled to shelter in a wayside posthouse jammed into the oblique cleft of a valley.

There, they waited the fell weather out. The road master grew short-tempered on beer as the days wore past one by one. 'Bedamned to Koriani and their idiot priorities.' He glared at the mule packs piled in the corner, and cursed in complaint of the chimney smoke wafted back down a flue in neglected need of a sweeping.

Fionn Areth tried dicing. He lost a week's silver and his father's skinning knife before he learned not to play fast with the men in the taproom. Holed up in the loft with the horseboys, he fared better. They staked only copper, or broom straws for sport. There, his shy smile won him the attention of a freckle-faced potgirl. Dicing lost favor before the sheer fascination of her teasing, warm kisses and hot eagerness. The hours melted into a swift passage of nights, while the high drifts subsided to glaze ice. Surefooted mules could be trusted to compensate, but horses required caulked shoes.

Fionn Areth spent his last coin in the smithy, then mounted his newly shod pony as the caravan rousted to resume delayed passage to Jaelot.

The trail climbed like a stair through a narrowing gap. The Pass of Sards tucked like a fold in the vast, forbidding fault line, where the continent had buckled in an age-old cataclysm and raised up the Arwent plateau. The spur of the Skyshiels ranged to the north, hammer to anvil against the glittering southern summits. Peaks jumbled one on another against the washed blue of the sky like a giant's clutch of dropped knives.

'Whole of Sards Pass was a dragon's eyrie, once,' the head drover confided in a dawn that splashed the upper snowfields to a riot of carmine and gilt. He squinted, skin creased like old leather, and pointed out the inky, glass scars where the balefires of drakes had melted the granite to slag. 'The creatures had claws big around as your leg, if you can swallow the tales the herb woman told in my village.'

'Light holds they tell lies,' an outrider groused as he mounted his horse.

The old drover slapped the dusty rump of the mule he had just hitched into the traces. 'Light or Shadow, who cares? Old dragons are three Ages dead.' He winked at Fionn Areth, then whistled through his teeth to signal the wagoneer to start his vehicle rolling.

For eight days, the mules skidded and scrambled and made back-breaking work for the drovers. Nights passed to the moaning misery of the gusts, rampaging down from the heights to box and batter the tent canvas, and flutter the cookfires ragged. The caravan suffered no attack beyond boredom. Men-at-arms pinched their frost-numbed fingers sanding rust from their chain mail and passed the slow hours in complaint.

'Nothing alive could be worth this accursed unseasonal delivery,' the master despaired. His second-string horse had shied into a gulch and gone lame when an iyat infested its pack straps. 'Winter's no time to be crossing these mountains. Whatever Reysald did to invoke a Koriani oath of debt, remind me next time to brain him. He'll never again foist a late trip like this one on a fool old enough to know better!'

He returned a solid laugh to Fionn Areth's question. 'Oh, aye, trouble like this is usual enough near the solstice. Accursed fiends always travel in packs, besides. You'll see more, or mark me for a dead man.'

For two nights running, the predicted plague of iyats turned the camps inside out and bedeviled the livestock to bedlam. A storm moved them on, with horizontal snow that yowled like a chorus of hags. Progress through the passes slowed to a crawl. Along the valley floor, the pack train inched forward, each day made perilous by potholes and chancy footing where hot springs leached under the sheeting, white blanket of drifts. The men drew scalding water to launder their clothes. One of their rough company, Fionn Areth combed ice from the bristles on his chin and exalted in his newfound sense of accomplishment.

Eighty grueling leagues, and two months from Daenfal, the cara-van wound downward from the heights. Along the narrow strip of lowlands against the Eltair coast, the footsore mules were prodded northward on the trade road, squelching through wheel ruts paned over with ice and splashed by galloping relays of post riders. Slowed down by the traffic of lumbering wagons, they closed the last miles onto the head of land and arrived to stand shivering before Jaelot's front gate.

The caravan's captain doled out final portions in silver and dismissed the men hired as road guards. Fionn Areth could scarcely contain his wild joy. Granted his coin and his freedom under the sky-rimmed shadow of another great city's black walls, he stood with his collar muffled up to his ears, and said his farewell to Reysald's drovers. The outriders clapped his back in goodwill and accepted his wish to part company. They, too, had been young, and remembered the yearning for adult independence.

Fionn Areth sat his moorlands pony, alone and felt as if the whole world turned in his grasp.

Here, in a momentous past hour of conflict, the Master of Shadow had revealed his black heart and called down a barrage of dark sorcery. The event had shaken down solid stone walls. In the intervening years, the signs of that havoc had been bricked over, the rubble long since cleared away. The trappings of old wealth and grandeur remained. This town was larger, more prosperous than Daenfal, set as it was at the junction of two land routes and served by the sea trade as well. Under a sheeted ceiling of low cloud, Jaelot's slate roofs and octagonal guard towers commanded a hook in the shoreline. The setting was favored by a generous harbor, loud with the unraveling thunder of spume hammering seawalls of granite. Beyond, the rough waters of Eltair Bay heaved lead and pewter, sliced by the oars of an inbound galley with bright streamers flying from her masthead.

Commerce came and went through the gates, even in the late day. Couriers on fast horses spurred past, bearing dispatches. Ox wains rumbled in from the quarries and sawmills, interspersed by the wagons that rolled north and south, hauling cloth goods and barrels, and sacks of ground meal lashed under oiled canvas. Trappers and farmhands plodded on foot. The gilt-trimmed carriages of aristocrats rumbled by, attended by liveried grooms. Under the feet of the Skyshiel Mountains, the gloaming of twilight fell early. A lampsman bundled in fur made his rounds. Torches set burning in steel baskets on the revetments hissed and snapped, harried by a thin snowfall.

Shivering with cold and excess excitement, Fionn Areth steered his shaggy pony from the verge. He wended his way through the city gates behind three chattering servants who returned with cut greens for the solstice feast. The keeps on both sides were Second Age remnants, laid of quartz granite and emblazoned with a gaudy escutcheon of embossed, snake-bearing lions. Tin talismans for fiend bane jangled and chimed. No less than ten sentries stood guard by the windlass, sure enough sign the Mayor of Jaelot maintained a vigilant garrison.

With pay in his pocket and dreams of enlistment against the fell forces of Shadow, Fionn Areth loitered in the cobbled gloom of a side lane. When the horn blew for the sundown change in the watch, he trailed the knots of soldiers released from their posts, trusting their lead to locate the wineshops preferred by the off-duty garrison.

The onset of full darkness found him stabling his pony under care of the Gold Lion's hostler. 'Two pence a night, he won't eat like a war-horse. One if you groom and muck the stall for yourself.'

Fionn Areth paid for full care, weary as he was, and starved for hot food and new company. He handed the pony off to a horseboy, gripped his cloak against the wind, and crossed the rutted snow of the coach yard. Inside the iron-studded doors, the taproom of the Lion was packed. The heavy air held a redolence of fish stew, oiled pine, and wet wool, underslung with the heated aroma of humanity. A man who wished lodging must brave the crush of patrons clumped in camaraderie beneath the sooty lamps slung from the ceiling beams.

In Jaelot, by stiff custom, the wealthy dined apart. The commons of the tavern served those off the street, from women dressed in motley who sold cakes in the market to tradesmen with stained leather aprons. Shopkeepers in neat broadcloth contended with dockside fishsellers for seats at packed benches and trestles. Mule drovers rubbed sweating elbows with couriers still wearing their emptied, mud-splashed satchels slung on shoulder straps.

The space between the brick hearth and the racked phalanx of tapped beer kegs was staked out by soldiers, mail-clad and imposing in dark surcoats. The ones finished eating shot dice or threw darts, or made laughing wagers with coin scattered over scarred trestles. The planks were marked with scratched targets for knives, or lines drawn for bouts of arm wrestling. On other occasions, the same rearranged boards served as the arena for cockfights.

The boisterous crowd at the Lion thrived on blood sport, and the inn's florid landlord turned no one away who carried the requisite coinage. A half silver secured Fionn Areth a tiny room in the attic, with a milk-faced maid to lug him a bath basin and soap. For a copper and a kiss, she brought him a knife from the kitchen. The favor included her chattering interest as she watched him scrape off a two-month rime of black stubble.

'You'll want me back later?' she asked, and then laughed as he flushed ardent crimson with his bare knees poking from his bathwater.

'Later,' Fionn gasped past the fire in his groin.

''Twill cost you another three coppers, then,' said the unabashed girl, then clattered out, leaving him deflated.

The towel was coarse as the nap on new burlap and smelled like wet dog from hard use. Fionn tossed it aside in disgust. He settled for tying the wet tangles of his hair in a thong stripped out of his sleeve cuff. Clad in his spare shirt, a fresh tunic, and the brushed-down wool of his breeches, he strapped on his sword and retraced his steps down a maze of tight stairways to the common room.

The soldiers still congregated, joined now by others with beards like filed iron and the scars of twenty-year veterans. Their rough, tight-knit company discouraged outsiders. The trestle adjacent stayed empty. Fionn Areth settled into the space and smiled, until a fair-headed bar girl brought him a plate of hot bread and cod stew. He topped off the meal with a tankard of mulled wine. Relaxed with fatigue and the comfort of clean clothes, he soaked in the welcome heat off the hearth, content for the present to listen.

Barracks gossip informed him the city pay was on time, but too low, and that overseeing convicts during seawall repairs was the unpopular duty on the roster. Loose comment ranged the gamut from the favors of wenches to the irregularities of the aging mayor's effete secretary.

'Etarra's new tithe put the pinchfist in a howling bad mood,' a man with a sergeant's badge grumbled. He sighted into his near-emptied tankard. 'A stroke of the pen, and there went the allotment for upkeep. We'll live with that leak in the barracks until spring, and watch bats fly and roost in the rafters.'

'Fatemaster's bollocks,' the guard with the sausage red nose chimed in. 'Just let the tenderfoot recruits sleep there. First week they come in, they're too pissing scared to notice the slosh in the bedding.'

A veteran's dice throw clattered across the crammed trestle. The winner hooted his ecstatic victory and pounded the boards, jouncing the litter of tin spoons and crockery and all but upsetting the picked bones.

'By the Wheel, you cheat,' the loser groused back. 'Bedamned if you didn't jink the plank on that throw, and tumble a six down to one. Didn't survive Vastmark just to be felled by your flippity, swindling fingers.'

Fionn Areth leaned forward, his awed anticipation taking the lead from good sense. 'You did battle against the Master of Shadow?'

The broad-shouldered mercenary opposite the war veteran twisted around on the bench. 'Why should you care, boy?'

'If a man can fight sorcery with weapons of steel, I'd like to hear how it's done.' Lent confidence from his stint as a road guard, Fionn Areth raised his chin. 'Is it true that you marched in the Vastmark campaign?'

Preoccupied by his game, the burly veteran snapped his fingers for the dice. 'That I did.' He spun another throw, showed his teeth in satisfaction. 'Can't top two sixes,' he gloated.

'Could match them,' the dicing partner shot back. The pieces were passed and sent clattering again.

'Did you ever see the Shadow Master?' Fionn Areth asked.

'Just once.' Still engrossed, the veteran held out a palm for the coin won back from his fellow. 'I served in the mayor's personal guard on the night the fell sorcerer smashed all the glass in the feast hall. 'Twas uncanny. And Vastmark? Like most wars, a drawn-out, miserable stint in the mud. The shadows froze bone something cruel. Cousin of mine lost half his fingers.' He glanced up at due length. One eye cast into a squint, he stared down his nose at Fionn Areth.

His mouth opened. For an eyeblink of time, he froze in stark horror. 'There! That's him!' The stupefied surge as he shot to his feet sent the bench flying over behind him. 'Save us all! *There's the Master of Shadow himself!*'

'Man, are you crazed?' cried his dicing companion.

A metallic scream answered. The veteran hauled killing steel from its sheath and surged ahead, bent on murder. Two startled guardsmen sought to restrain him. Their belated grab missed. He charged, clambered headlong over the trestle top to skewer the source of his outrage.

Fionn Areth flung sidewards, barely in time. Crockery and bones and tankards pelted airborne as the sword impaled in the struts of the trestle and overturned both by raw force.

'He's just a fool boy!' cried an incensed bystander. 'One packing a grasslands accent thick as the hair on a goat.'

'It's the Shadow Master, I tell you!' The veteran pursued as his target rammed backward, unraveling chaos through the tavern's packed company like parted thread in a knit. 'Might look like a boy. Illusion's his specialty.' The longsword tracked his quarry's terrified retreat, steady and waiting for opening.

'You came into Jaelot before to make mischief,' the veteran accused in low fury. 'That time you looked like a minstrel's apprentice, with quiet ways and brown hair.'

'I didn't,' gasped Fionn. He ducked scything steel. Once, twice, again, he skipped backward. His hip rammed something hard, and a caroling chime of refined metal splashed at his back. The cardplayers his mishap had disturbed reviled his idiot clumsiness. He had nowhere to turn. The murdering attack of the veteran came on, before his numbed fingers remembered the sword and the reflexive training to use it.

'Ath's mercy, please listen!' He ducked under the trestle, came up with drawn steel, somehow prepared for the stabbing downstroke he had been rigorously schooled to anticipate. Through the tangling brunt of a parry, he pleaded, 'That man wasn't me.'

Blade drawn and guarding, he evaded entanglement in the upset table and stools. Displaced patrons cursed him. Coins and cards jostled to each hampered move as joined swordplay erupted in licking, fast strokes across obstacles. Around him he sensed the undermining panic as other onlookers saw he was armed. They shouted and gave way, shoving themselves clear of chance injury.

The gamblers cut losses and swooped to claim their threatened cache as the duel snaked through their midst. A barmaid dropped her tray of filled tankards, screaming outrage. More heads turned. Fionn Areth's protestation became swallowed in bedlam as the Lion's jammed patrons avoided the clangor of bare steel that scythed and snarled in damaging proximity.

A clashing tight parry and a shallow slice splashed blood down Fionn's exposed wrist. His wrenching, taut cry rang through the noise, convincing in petrified innocence. 'This is my first journey from Araethura's moorlands!'

'Put up that fool steel!' The Lion's swarthy landlord cupped his chapped hands and bellowed gruff warning from the bar. 'The city justiciar gives stiff fines for brawling! You brutes fight here, you'll sting for it later when my fee for damages reaches the purser at the barracks.'

'Let be, fellow!' called a concerned comrade. 'Make peace and come back to your beer.'

Others hooted in derision for what seemed the disorderly conduct of a drunk baited into a harebrained attack. 'Why draw blood for a pittance? The boy just wants to sit himself down and go back to scratching his nits!'

From the dimness between lamps, bare sword clanged on sword. The deep, throaty boom as a wine tun tipped over ground into a soprano shatter of smashed glass.

'Soldier, listen up!' A resigned officer on the sidelines muscled forward to intervene. 'Don't make me take you down for a stint of forced labor.' He flipped a hand signal to his off-watch guardsmen. 'Close in. Make an end to this folly before there's a public embarrassment.'

But this scrap was no mismatch between rage and innocence. The glitter of poised blades wove and feinted in deadly, incongruous control. While the mailed guardsmen formed a baffled circle and sought in vain for an opening, crossed steel belled again. Like a hiccup in a torrent, their sympathy canceled to the clanging crescendo of a strikingly expert train of blows.

'But you know swordplay, don't you?' Breathing in gasps, the veteran spoke through that indrawn, poisonous hesitation. 'Did the goats teach you that?' He matched a stunning, well-executed riposte in smooth stride and lunged back. Steel wailed across defending steel, and a wave of freezing consternation swept the onlookers.

'Come on, *show them!*' the veteran taunted. Gut-shaken to fear, he ducked a low-hanging lamp. Hot candleflame burnished his taut, sweating face. 'You fight *astoundingly* well for a yokel raised up in the grasslands.'

'He's telling the truth,' one of his dicing companions exhorted. 'Black sorcerer or boy, that's no fumbling greenhorn.'

Another bench toppled. The veteran caromed through a stew of spilled food and recovered. 'I *know* him, I tell you!' His next cut snatched whining through air yet again. The boy's style matched his skill with a chilling display of confident, practiced experience. 'He's the very same felon our mayor wants dead! Dharkaron avenge us all for blind fools if we let him escape justice this time!'

'You're mistaken.' Shaky and strained into white disbelief, Fionn Areth shook back the hair fallen free of the thong tie. 'I'm no sorcerer.'

'We'll let the mayor's aldermen decide that.' The veteran pressed in, now flanked by two guardsmen. Their combined efforts hazed their beleaguered quarry backward into the vestibule where the aristocracy engaged private rooms.

Cornered, now desperate, Fionn Areth deflected a lethal cut to the head. He countered another lunge with a close-pressed parry, then blazed back, focused by rage. His following stroke whined past blocking metal and broke through.

One of the attackers took a slice in the shoulder of his surcoat. His mail shirt spared bloodshed, a useless distinction. The doubters saw only further evidence of culpability in a stripling who could best a seasoned fighter.

'Save us all, it *is* him, the Master of Shadow!' Panic erupted. Alarmed citizens bolted to escape, their pandemonium sliced by jangling steel and a salvo of hysterical shouting. 'Take him alive! There's a bounty on his head!'

Fat to the fire, an alderman added, 'Don't trust his youth. They say he won't age, the sorcerer who brought the massacre at Dier Kenton Vale.'

'Are you mad?' Pressed at bay as a dozen men-at-arms shoved through to harry his stance in the hallway, Fionn Areth despaired. 'I wasn't even born when the war host marched into Vastmark!'

The hampered fight thumped against the closed doorways. Fionn Areth grasped the first latch within reach and flung wide its gilt-trimmed panel.

A wailing scrape of disrupted melody informed him the room was in use. He turned anyway. Cornered now beyond hope of redemption, he plunged in pounding flight through the heart of a discreet social staged for gentlemen who kept fancy courtesans.

Two steps, and he collided headlong with a vielle. The instrument shattered to a jangle of burst strings and a squawk of dismay from the musician. The bass fiddle crashed to a boom of split wood. Guests peeled away in a flutter of ribboned silk as the fugitive burst into their midst. Bloodied and exhausted and stripped of finesse, he elbowed his way through a cloying maelstrom of perfume and gold-braided velvet. A froth of feathered hats batted his face. He battered, rammed with the flat of his blade, and wrenched clear of the ringed hands which snatched at him. Breathless, bewildered, he shouldered by main force between dandified bluebloods, groomed and prinked and screaming imprecations under a dazzling brilliance of candles.

Fionn Areth tripped on the fringe of the carpet. He skidded on waxed wood, hit the wall, and despaired. The room had no windows and no rear exit. He spun, sword raised and eyes wild, braced for the smashing attack that must come from the guardsmen who pounded behind him.

'Bedamned!' cried a cultured, baritone voice. 'I know that man! He's a criminal!'

Exposed to the fluttering light of the sconces, the severe angled features and sable hair of s'Ffalenn drew a storm of aghast recognition. The effete society of Jaelot hoarded their grudges like heirloom jewels. No infamy in memory was more venomously nursed than the Shadow Master's ploy, enacted one past summer solstice. Under the guise of fine music, his tricks of low sorcery had shamed the city's best families. The diversion he spun to mask his escape had shattered the glass in the mayor's mansion, then razed buildings, gutted roofs, and flattened stone walls in an unhinged surge of wild conjury.

'Dharkaron avenge!' screamed a city councilman, roused from bemoaning his torn lace. 'The Spinner of Darkness has come back! That man's none other than Arithon s'Ffalenn!'

A vase crashed from a niche, torn down by the rush as vengeful guardsmen piled in from the vestibule. Their advance was coordinated. A ranked captain screamed orders. Men-at-arms fanned out and formed an unbroken line of advance. Still brandishing bared swords, they tore the cloth from the feast table. Crystal toppled and shattered. Flung food and dishes smashed to the floor, to the yammering dismay of a servant.

'Stand clear!' yelled the guard captain, out of patience with fools. 'You want that wretch alive and in chains? Then move your mincing, soft arses aside and let us attend to our business!'

He signaled. His guardsmen edged forward, each step crunching glass and mashing stewed quail into the priceless carpet. Mailed hands grasped the table legs. The furnishing was overturned and raised for a shield, then run forward in a ramming charge that pinned Fionn Areth to the wall. His sword arm was seized. Rough hands wrested his weapon away. Still shouting protest, he was caught and bent with his torso jackknifed over the rim of the table. A fist smashed him silent. Someone's forearm clubbed his neck. While his senses spun dark, another guard gripped his hair and slammed him, half-comatose, back upright against the wall. Gilt and plaster chipped down in a pattering rain.

Fionn Areth moaned, dissociated by pain. 'Mercy, please. I don't know you.'

'Do you not?' The veteran laughed. 'Then pray, let us help your lapsed memory.'

Slammed to jelly by the barrage of hard blows, Fionn Areth let his senses go numb. He rode the storm of brutality, helpless, while men vented their fear and their hatred. Their punches and kicks first hammered him flat, then tumbled him, crushed and bleeding, amid the spilled sauces and wrecked porcelain sprayed on the hardwood floor.

Voices pitched high with excitement churned into a vertigo that racked him to paralyzing nausea. Through spinning pain and a sick taste of blood, a command funneled down, blurred into nightmare unreality. 'Go! Yes, waken the Lord Mayor. To Dharkaron with his gout! We've taken the Master of Shadow alive, and our city's tribunal's waited lifelong for this moment.'

When the shouting broke out on the mayor's front doorstep, the enchantress Elaira had just finished her duties as healer in the perfumed warmth of the grand lord's bedsuite. Appraised by the critical eye of his wife, she knelt, repacking her satchel of remedies. Two candles still burned on the nightstand. Their mellow, thin light dusted costly silk tassels and furnishings inlaid with gold wire. Her ornery charge was made comfortable at last, reclining with half-closed eyes in a fortress of down pillows and bed quilts. Wealthy clients invariably tested her patience, and this one had proved worse than most. Nor was the wife one whit less demanding.

When the thunderous clang of the knocker resounded, the woman raised her pinched chin, annoyed to be drawn from her role as active overseer. Her pleated mouth twitched as a bellow from outside demanded immediate entrance. 'Dharkaron's Spear take them! If that's a detail from the watch captain's men, they're probably drunk and disorderly.'

She propelled herself out of the upholstered wing chair. 'Close the door after me, if you please. I would not have my husband disturbed.' Stiff with bossy, self-righteous command, she bustled out to intercept any plaintive servants who had the temerity to waken her lord with bad news.

Elaira shut her teeth in outright irritation and continued bundling her remedies. Belowstairs, the outside door panel crashed open. The shouting intensified, cut by the butler's agitated tenor. 'Begone! His lordship is resting, and in no mood to receive your raw noise.'

While somebody protested in a bullish bass voice, a third party cut in, defending another prong of what seemed a three-way impasse. 'I don't care blazes how the miserable wretch dies! We took all the risk, brought him down alive in the Lion as a service done in good faith. Alliance has posted a bounty on his head. That's a round sum of a thousand gold royals.'

Up the winding stair with its flanged marble risers, the racket shot echoes in crescendo. 'None of us goes till it's paid, or we hold a signed writ in promise of funds from the treasury.'

'If you think the mayor's justiciar will give this case up to Avenor for the sake of Alliance satisfaction, you're mad!' a field veteran cracked. 'My money says he dies right here, tonight.' Then, to the butler's yapping objections, 'Move on aside, or I'll puncture your custard paunch where you stand.'

A finger of draft stirred through the gaped door, while the butler huffed, 'You'll do no such thing! Be off, you drunk fools, or I'll send a footman to summon the guard.'

'We *are* the guard!' bellowed the exasperated bass. The impasse crashed into a snarl of yelling, with the fatuous butler too obstinate to move, and the balked party of armed men set to plow in with cold steel and force their way into the palace foyer.

Elaira swore softly under her breath as a heave of movement ruckled the bedclothes.

'There's some trouble?' The mayor blinked, muzzy from the possets just taken to ease his tender swelling and pain, and bring him the surcease of sleep. 'If my guard captain's soused, he'll live to be sorry. Here, help me up.' His peremptory gesture called for the enchantress to arise at once and assist him. 'I'd better go down.'

'Your wife went already,' Elaira pointed out. 'Please rest. She's able enough to manage the problem, or at least let it keep until morning.'

The demanding, fat fingers continued to beckon.

Elaira omitted the tie strings, slung her satchel to her shoulder, and moved in resignation to comply. Early on she had learned not to try the mayor's temper. If she allowed his presumption that she was a housemaid, her task was reduced from impossible to simply onerous.

'I'll need my robe of state from the armoire,' the mayor snapped, as she raised him. 'Be sure to include my gold chain of office.'

'I'm not your dresser,' Elaira responded. Once her charge was perched upright, she stepped to the chamber door and asked the footman who waited outside to fetch his lordship's valet.

'No, no!' The mayor thumped a balked fist in the bed sheets. 'No sense in waiting. The footman can dress me well enough.'

Elaira and the servant exchanged places without comment, he to set his master to rights through a nerve storm of abusive impatience and she to grip her satchel of remedies and make swift escape down the stairwell. She should have succeeded. The risers were white marble, clothed in a thick runner loomed with Jaelot's gold lions. Her descending step made no sound. But the mayor's interfering wife still occupied the first landing, locked in shrill argument with an official-looking stranger wearing livery of unfamiliar colors. However he had managed to slip past the butler, he was less successful with the house mistress.

'Whatever's amiss, let the town chancellor handle it. My darling's in pain, and suffering, and should be asleep, had he taken his posset without argument.'

While the men-at-arms crowding the entry rolled their eyes, their acting captain braced the door at the downstairs threshold. He tipped up his chin and accosted the irate woman on the landing. 'My lady, the chancellor has no authority to speak for a prisoner too dangerous to keep.'

'I don't care!' From her crow's vantage between newel posts, the mayor's wife stabbed an accusatory finger toward the outside street. 'Send the wretch back wherever he came from. My husband's unwell, and the night is no time to be hazing him out of his rest.'

The frustrated messenger made a last valiant effort to complete his designated errand. 'Surely that's for his lord eminence to decide.' He managed no more, his next line overwhelmed by someone's declaiming remark from below.

The mayor's wife stiffened. 'Oh no!' Leaned over the railing, she tongue-lashed the beleaguered butler. 'Don't you *dare* let those brutes bring any felon under my lord's very roof!'

Elaira snatched her furtive opening to slip past, while the messenger beat a backwards retreat, and the wife's imprecations expanded to include the captain at arms, who refused to give way.

The mayor's wife joined the butler, pushing the door panel against the offending wedged boot. 'You great lummox! Where's good sense? Keep your filth off my floor! Servants these days are too lazy and slow to shine silver, far less scrub up after trampling fools who won't wipe the mud off their boots!'

The Mayor of Jaelot chose that moment to descend in gout-ridden, limping distemper. 'Silence, woman!'

Everyone present ceased their movement and noise. Caught in a scene that had suddenly crystallized, Elaira found herself trapped. She could not make her exit. Half the armed watch were jammed like sheep in the disputed entry. Determined at all costs to escape from entanglement, she stole behind the statue of a nymph.

While snow swirled through the double-paneled doorway, and the drafts sucked and pulled at the candles lighting the ornate, lozenged tiles of the hallway, the Mayor of Jaelot stumped down the curved staircase, leaning on a stick, and huffing like a bull walrus. He crossed the lower landing in plush velvet slippers, his wine-colored stockings crimped over his grotesquely swollen ankles.

The footman trailed him, bearing a hurricane candle. Shadows chased intaglio patterns over his master's velvet robe of office and gold chain of state, bundled in haste overtop the tails of his nightshirt.

Red-faced and furious, the mayor rocked to a stop at ground level. 'What nonsense is this? If my guard captain's soused, he'll live to be sorry.'

The butler shoved forward, tripping over himself to proffer explanation ahead of the liveried messenger.

The raw gist read like madness, with the strange servant's interruptions shouted down, until the beset mayor yanked at his thinning hair, already pushed into spikes from his pillow. 'Merciful maker!' He singled out his butler, then bellowed, 'If you deny my watch captain entrance to my house, why is *he* here in the first place? He doesn't need my authority to break up a drunken brawl in the ranks!'

The butler sniffed and clasped his pink hands. 'My Lord Mayor, the men-at-arms hold a bound criminal in custody.' He edged out the messenger and peered down his nose, as though fussy posture could somehow allay the indignity of the problem. 'His uncivilized blood need not mar your furnishings. Nor should a pack of soldiers in hobnailed boots be let in. They would gouge dreadful pocks in your floor tiles.'

'Criminal?' The mayor elbowed the agitated messenger aside and gimped another stride forward. While his unctuous butler scuttled clear, still apologizing, the door in dispute was flung wide by the party outside. Windborne snow hazed into the vestibule, and an influx of draft doused the candles.

'I'll hear an explanation!' The mayor peered through the fallen gloom, and demanded of his commanding officer, 'You've lugged a common rogue to my doorstep? What for? Do we not have a dungeon to keep him in chains until court is convened in the morning?'

'A cell isn't safe for a rogue of his stripe.' A towering brute in a spike-crested helm, the watch captain stared down his nasal. 'The man we've brought in is the Master of Shadow.'

'Himself!' screeched the wife. 'I'll gouge out his eyes.' Propriety forgotten, she plowed back into the dispute, skirts raised like a galley set to ram.

Unseen in her niche behind the stone statue, the Koriani healer felt as though her heart slammed to a stop between beats.

At the forefront, the Mayor of Jaelot simply gaped, jowls sagging like wattles from his receded chin. 'The sorcerer? Is this true?'

The captain said, steady, 'Your Vastmark veterans are convinced.'

The discomfort of slippers and gout fell aside as the mayor banged out of doors and elbowed through the closed ranks of guardsmen. Their fellows on the outer stair stepped aside, silent before authority, as his Lordship of Jaelot bent to inspect their bagged quarry.

In snowfall and night, the prisoner was an indecipherable bundle, slung inert in the grip of two bearers.

'Where's my Sithaer-forsaken light?' cracked the mayor.

The shrinking footman on the fringes hopped forward, but too slowly. The mayor whirled like a mastiff, and snarled at the circle of stalled men-at-arms, 'If that creature you've brought is the Master of Shadow, bring him inside straightaway.'

'Are you mad?' cried the wife.

But consensus opinion brushed off her protest. The men-at-arms crowded inside on hobnailed boots, despite her nattering, shrill outburst. 'Remember the drunken sot who was prisoner on the labor gang? He freed that one from a scaffold and fetters. Unlocked cold iron without any key, just used the fell powers of magecraft.'

'Well he can't break steel wire!' the sergeant barked back. 'For the rest, it's your mayor who'll make disposition for the scoundrel's immediate death.'

Elaira fought back her paralyzing horror, loosed her sweating grip on the statue's carved marble wingtip. Shaking, near fumbling, she clawed out her quartz crystal. She whispered a swift, guarding cantrip and set a glamour of concealment. Then she waited, on fire with impatience, for the spell to bend light and air. She dared make no move before her cast sigil blurred sound and sight of her presence. The moment crawled while she suffered, agonized in suspension. Her unruly mind played a thousand scenarios of Arithon's maiming and death, while time slowed, and the spell sealed around her. The sensation felt as though the air of itself fractured light. The brief delay lasted a handful of heartbeats, yet spun out in her mind like the Fatemaster's thread, which wove the black cloth of eternity.

She slipped out of hiding. One step into the open, she just missed being bowled over by the butler, who fled before the clumping invasion of snow-drenched men-at-arms. What seemed half the watch crammed into the foyer to a rattle of mail and cold steel. Elaira stole among them, unseen and unheard.

The fear half consumed her, that what she found might undermine her will to keep breathing. One step, two; and she saw the prisoner's streaked hands, bound and cruelly torn with the grazes of manic struggle. Sprawled facedown in the fine-tiled hallway, he stayed limp, as the watch captain and the off-duty guard sergeant tripped over themselves to relate his spurious appearance and the particulars of his capture at the Lion.

Amid their raised voices, the veteran spoke loudest. 'Came in bold as brass, played the innocent as though he could dupe us all over again.'

Elaira edged nearer. Under the glow of the footman's hand lamp, the culprit lay unmoving. Black hair clung damp to the nape of his neck. He seemed an unremarkable boy, sorrowfully battered and bloody. His plain country shirt and laced breeches were ripped. The bare length of the forearm, shoved free of his cuff, showed the sturdy, muscled build of a laborer.

*Not Arithon s'Ffalenn*, Elaira knew with queer certainty, the remembrance of his fine bones and wiry strength a stamped and indelible part of her. That reassurance afforded her little relief. Any victim of happenstance caught by the guardsmen would fare ill if his case of mistaken identity was not rectified.

Ringed by his armed men, Jaelot's porcine mayor prodded the slack torso with the toe of his slipper. 'Roll the wretch over. I want a clear look.'

The guard captain bent, still vehement. 'I've known the criminal in two guises, as well. For me, the feud's personal. I've hunted his scarce hide when he vanished into thin air, then survived his assault by shadows and sorcery in the barren mountains of Vastmark. Don't take any chances now that he's caught.' His mailed hands snagged a shoulder and tumbled the prone body front to back like a fish. 'Kill him at once and be quit of him.'

The prisoner groaned. Black hair slipped back from his angled, fox features. The light of the candle exposed to plain view the sharp, defined chin, and raked browline which marked s'Ffalenn royal blood.

'Ath preserve, Fionn Areth!' Elaira gasped. Rage took her by storm. The absolute, bottomless depth of her order's ruthlessness surpassed her most ugly imagining.

Of all cities, Jaelot's hatred of the Shadow Master was the most viciously entrenched. After the disaster wreaked on their solstice feast, their trade galleys had burned at Minderl Bay, and their garrison had left four thousand dead on the back slopes of Dier Kenton Vale. Long memory and deep grudges would not pause to question the guilt of a look-alike victim.

'That's him, before Ath!' Through the swelling, dark bruises, the Mayor of Jaelot beheld no boy innocent, but the sorcerer who had posed as a masterbard's apprentice twenty-five years in the past. Feature for feature, he saw the face of the man that had emerged from masking illusion when spellcraft had stampeded his guests, and torn stone from indiscriminate stone from city warehouses, mansions, and battlements.

He shuffled an unnerved step back, hands clasped to his paunch for protection. 'Don't anyone believe this appearance of green youth. The Master of Shadow's a crafty illusionist. Our Prince of the Light has cautioned us for years the unnatural creature wouldn't age.'

'We should drag him outside and gut him at once.' The captain at arms enforced his opinion by drawing his steel from his scabbard.

'What about our claim on the Alliance bounty?' a gruff voice cut in from the sidelines.

'We'll settle that issue once he's safely dead.' Steel flashed as the captain angled his sword blade. 'If spellcraft can dismantle steel locks and bars, no dungeon is safe to contain him.'

The mayor was too terrified not to agree. The next instant would see life's blood spilled on the floor, unless some fool dared intervention.

Elaira found her voice. 'No! You'll do no such thing.' She dropped the glamour, burst through the enclosing men-at-arms, and fell on her knees beside the prone captive to shield him. 'You've taken a prisoner on criminal charges. No trial has established his guilt. As a Koriani sent on an errand of mercy, I protest the injustice. By whose law do you order the summary execution of a man given no chance to speak for his freedom?'

'Freedom! Are you mad?' snapped the mayor. 'It's the Master of Shadow they've taken!' Incensed as though a pet lapdog had bitten him, he added, 'The man's a sorcerer, and criminal, and identified before witnesses. There will be no farce of due process in this case. This wretch deserves nothing but a fast sword through the heart and a fire to consume his remains.'

Elaira swallowed, pulse pounding. In desperate effort to defer the inevitable, she traced the sigil for confusion over the tuned matrix of her personal quartz. *For mercy*, she pleaded on an inner cry of anguish. *Let this seed of wild spellcraft win someone to rally in Fionn's support to stall the immediate crisis.*

For a split-second interval, the tableau held unchanged.

Then the mayor's wife shrieked and shoved in from the sidelines. She seized the guard captain's sword arm before the blade could descend.

'You can't think to dispatch this unprincipled killer without first making him suffer! Not after the monstrous damage he's caused us.' She rounded on her husband, white faced and furious. 'This man reviled the best blood in Jaelot! He threw down stone buildings with spellcraft! Let him die in slow agony. Every living person who was shamed or lost property deserves the chance to bear witness.'

'Milady, that's folly! His arcane resources are by lengths too dangerous.' The captain at arms tugged, but failed to dislodge the woman's maniacal grip. 'A corpse can't work spellcraft. Cut in pieces and burned on hot faggots is safest.'

While the argument raged back and forth over her head, Elaira ran her trained hands over the prisoner's slack body. He was shockingly cold, but no bones were broken. Beyond shallow cuts and purpling contusions, he had torn his knee, but sustained no irreparable damage.

Despite gentle care, her touch roused response. Fionn Areth's bruised eyelids fluttered. Preternaturally alert to additional peril, Elaira gripped her quartz. She slipped a swift spell of binding upon him, that her familiar face not be recognized here, with so many hostile eyes watching.

Her ministration came none too soon.

One bound arm flexed. The grasslands boy stirred, then opened green eyes in confusion.

'Save us, he's awakened!' The mayor leaped back, shirttails flapping, while around him, his guardsmen drew their weapons in alarm.

Surrounded by bare steel, the source of their fear blinked in puzzled discomfort. His gaze flickered over the ceiling vaults, with their carved nymphs, and vine and flower motifs painted in gilt. He squeezed his eyes closed, opened them again in patent disorientation. His survey encompassed the ring of armed guards, passed Elaira without seeing, then rested at last on the mayor's fat legs, stuffed into crumpled silk hose and expensive, glass-beaded slippers. 'Why am I here?'

In this ornate setting, within the same walls where Arithon s'Ffalenn had once been constrained through the course of Halliron Masterbard's grueling satire, the rolling vowels of that grasslands accent fell with the effrontery of a slap.

'Fiends, he's not human,' a stout guardsman murmured. 'Battered as all this, he shouldn't be able to manage a clear thought, far less play the guise of hurt innocence.'

'What guise?' Fionn Areth said, stronger.

The mayor's wife tapped her foot, incensed. 'You're quite the rogue to believe we could forget your wiles and your sorceries, even so many years later.'

Fionn Areth shivered, flinching with pain as he unwisely tugged at his bonds. 'What wiles? What sorceries? There's no magecraft in me. I was raised up herding goats.'

'Dharkaron's own vengeance!' snapped the bearded veteran. 'Don't try to playact under my charge. I knew you too well to be taken.'

In clear grasslands dialect, Fionn Areth insisted, 'I've never seen you before in my life.'

'Sweet liar.' The mayor laughed from wound nerves, slapped to fresh reminder of the sincerity and skill of the singer who had blinded his guests to stunned pity during the performance that preceded their ruin. 'We've all seen you spin deceit with plain words. Don't think to escape justice this time.'

'Of what am I accused?' Fionn Areth demanded, then cringed away from the boot that bashed into his side. Left winded by the guard captain's harsh prompt, he gasped the required honorific with no shred of sophisticate sarcasm. 'Please tell me, Lord Mayor. What harm does your town claim against me?'

'My lights, you act as smoothly as you sing. A pity that sorcery corrupted you.' The rage flaming through him with frightening force, the mayor clapped his hands to summon his hovering footman. 'Go fetch the town justiciar! He's needed as witness.' To Elaira, he added, 'You demand a fair trial? There's only one way to be sure of a sorcerer, and that's to set bane seals to hold him. Promise to bind him in Koriani wards, and he might live to be given a hearing. Are you willing to swear surety against his defection? Let him escape, and your life will be asked in his place.'

'I'll swear for him freely,' Elaira retorted. 'Since he is what he seems, just a grasslands herder who bears a misfortunate likeness. His innocence can be proved. Let's start with the fact that his right hand and forearm bear no trace of the burn where Arithon s'Ffalenn deflected Prince Lysaer's light bolt thirty years ago at Etarra. The wound left him disfigured.'

The mayor's wife sniffed. 'The Master of Shadow had no scar at all. His hands were unmarked when he played for the guests at my feast.'

'Nor did the man I sparred with in the guise of Medlir show any sign of blemished sword hand,' snapped the veteran.

The mayor's cracked oath rocked off the domed ceiling. In whispered, vast echoes, the reverberations ranged through the feast hall beyond the vaulted doors. The nightmare memory from the past seemed hauntingly sharp, when the sorcerer had seeded wholesale terror and havoc, and sent panicked guests into flight.

'Let the criminal suffer,' said the wife. 'We ought to hear him scream.'

'My lady is right.' Jaelot's ruling despot blinked drug-glazed eyes from the possets just mixed to ease his pain-ridden sleep. 'How amusing this fell creature will be for us all, standing trial in chains for my magistrates.' He smiled at the prisoner bound helpless at his feet. 'I wouldn't miss the performance for gold as the high officials you've shamed cross-examine you. Let's watch you squirm to deny your black nature. That should salve the pride of our city's first blood for the wicked satire visited upon us. We'll have our revenge for the conniving tongue of your dead master. By the hour we finally put you to death, you'll plead on your knees for release.'

'Plead?' cried Fionn Areth, desperate now, the fear shaking through him in tremors. 'Spare me, I don't know what you're talking about!'

'Take him off,' snapped the mayor. 'I'll waste no more sleep. Lock him in the deep dungeon. The enchantress stays with him to set spells of guard, with my order of slow death if her incompetence lends the prisoner any chance to break free.'

# Midnight

The night was a misery of weather and chill on the hour Asandir reached the Great Circle at Isaer. Sleet fell, driven horizontal by the vicious, stinging gusts. The Sorcerer rode into the rampaging wind, his dark hood pulled low over his crusted eyebrows. He had been traveling at speed for twenty-three days. Upon the hour he finished sealing the wards that closed the Sorcerer's Preserve, he had set off across the barren wilds of Camris, his sleep snatched in thorn brakes through those brief intervals when need for rest overcame him. Across the scoured heights of the Thaldein passes, he shared crannies of rock with consenting wild animals. Spells of air and of earth kept his horse fresh long after the point where the animal should have flagged and foundered.

The relentless concentration he required to keep his works aligned with the Law of the Major Balance took its due toll, over distance. Asandir held on through grim determination, the last leagues an agony of endurance. In swaying exhaustion, he crossed the crumbled wall marking the outer edge of the power focus. The black stud beneath him dripped suds of rank sweat. Its lowered neck steamed. Matted tangles of forelock and mane wore glazed ice at the crest where the melt had run off and refrozen. The sigils of power which sustained the animal's long stride were played out. Asandir had small resource left to continue to stand proxy for his mount's remorseless exertion. The final hours of thrashing through trackless brush had plundered the last of his strength.

In the cruel, biting cold, he dismounted. Around him, the night was a maelstrom of sleet that rattled like glass through bare branches. Sight-blind in the storm, by mage-sense alone he knew he stood inside the cleared circle of the Isaer focus. His booted feet slid on the icy black agate. The Paravian runes that marked each ring of power lay buried in leaves, storm glazed to a crust like old varnish. Braced against his horse's shoulder to stay upright, Asandir reached the focal point at the center by touch. There he stopped, breathing hard, his face like pinched clay as he murmured a cantrip of appeal to the earth.

Soil and stone received his request. Asandir bent his head, patient in gratitude, while the ringing vibration of the lane force played through him and rinsed the fierce ache of travel from nerve and muscle and bone.

In time, he stirred, stroked sure hands over the stallion's shivering flesh. Healing moved with his touch. The creature's laboring flanks eased and settled, and the fevered heat left its sinews. Asandir blew on his hands and loosened the girth, then removed bit and bridle. He looped the tack securely through the leather of a run-up stirrup iron.

The contact he expected from Sethvir came then, soundless and subtle as a shaft of new moonlight. '*Asandir? There's still hope. Fionn Areth's held prisoner in Jaelot's dungeon, pending trial and due process. The enchantress Elaira is with him.*'

Exposed to the flaying chill of the gale, Asandir shut his eyes. 'Thank Ath for that blessing. The woman at least will fight to the last to thwart the mayor's injustice.'

When a flood of sent warmth from Sethvir replaced words, Asandir flexed tired shoulders and straightened under the wet weight of his mantle. 'There's bad news as well. What aren't you telling me?'

A sigh from Sethvir, so slight the sound played like the breath of a ghost through the mind. '*Lysaer's left Erdane early. One of Raiett's agents sighted Arithon's double in Daenfal, and sent word into Tysan by fast post.*'

Alone with the impact of that ugly news, Asandir flicked packed ice from his collar. 'You feel that's worrisome?' Without using his aggressive command of deep sorceries, he himself could not have crossed Orlan Pass once the blizzards set in for the winter.

Leagues distant, Sethvir tracked the query without effort. '*Lysaer didn't try the way through the mountains. He went north by land on fast horses with only ten officers in attendance. Another messenger took the road across the flats to Miralt Head. He carried royal orders to dispatch a galley in swift passage along the northcoast. The vessel will make rendezvous with the Prince of the Light in four nights and bear his party across the cove narrows to Atainia.*'

Asandir frowned, while the wind flicked loose hair against his numbed cheek. 'That's still three hundred leagues distant from Jaelot.' Given unseasonal fine weather and luck, the prince's train could not reach Rathain's shores earlier than the next fortnight; whereas, plying lane forces and the power focus sited in the feast hall of the mayor's palace, Asandir expected to reach that far city within the hour of midnight. 'You can't think I'll need more than a day to spirit a captive boy from a dungeon.'

Again, that shattering, fractional pause. Asandir's mouth thinned to a taut line. He waited, bone still with the certainty he had not yet been told the worst. 'Where's Arithon?' he asked suddenly, his question bladed steel through the frigid, pelting darkness. 'He can't have returned to the continent for this.'

'*He'll put ashore at Sanpashir by morning, likewise a long way from Jaelot,*' Sethvir shot back in rife exasperation. A thoughtful exchange showed how Morriel Prime had manipulated Dakar to a dream of prescient clairvoyance. '*As you see, there's no threat. As long as the mayor's prisoner can be rescued inside of the next twelve hours.*'

The stud chose that moment to shake out its mane. Doused by loose ice and a spray of chill water, Asandir wiped streaming eyes. Acerbic now with concern and impatience, he fired point-blank at the source of his colleague's evasion. 'What ill under sky could defer me?'

'*Morriel Prime and a circle of enchantresses.*' When cornered, Sethvir could deliver bad news like a hammerblow into bedrock. '*She's sitting in the Skyshiels, poised over a quartz vein with her Waystone and twelve trained seniors.*'

'Dharkaron's bleak vengeance!' Asandir burst out, blistered to rare exasperation. 'If she raises such powers to thwart me, she must know she risks tearing a rift of disharmony clear through the aura of the planet.'

'*She's frail and she's desperate,*' Sethvir allowed. '*Are you certain you wish to attempt this?*'

A motionless imprint in the rank, sleeting darkness, Asandir gave back an unbending, dire silence. No need to set words to uncomfortable facts. With Arithon drawn back to the coast at Sanpashir, no doubt remained that Fionn Areth's imprisonment had been planned as the bait for a trap.

'*Take extreme care in your transfer from Isaer into Jaelot,*' Sethvir returned, and no more.

Chills changed to a grue that chased down Asandir's spine like a prickling spill of loose needles. 'Be very certain I will.'

\*　　\*　　\*

In the peaks of the Skyshiels far to the east, winter stars shone like strung ice chips above summit ridges of stone. Thin cloud rode the heights, feathered to ribbons where the teeth of the scarps combed the frigid track of the winds. The gold finials capping the corner posts of Morriel Prime's palanquin speared upright like an adept's staves set as sentinel to the four directions. Despite the bitter cold of high altitude, the frame stood stripped of its layered velvet hangings. The order's twelve most disciplined seniors sat arrayed in a surrounding circle.

Attended by two high-ranking seers, Morriel Prime watched the turn of the stars as the hour to the west approached midnight.

In her papery quaver, she stated, 'Not long to wait now.'

Folded cross-legged, the seeress to her left replied from the dreamy depths of schooled trance. 'Lane-watcher at Deal sends you word that the flux of the third lane is shifted. The signature chord is a Fellowship working. As you guessed, Asandir draws on magnetic forces to arrange for a northbound transfer.'

'He has circled his horse,' the right-hand seeress chimed in, hands cupped to the sphere of clear quartz she employed to capture clairvoyant vision. 'I see the veil as the power's engaged. He's sent his black stud on to Althain Tower to receive Sethvir's care in his absence.'

A rustle of silk in the glass-edged cold, then a tinge of lavender breathed through the pitch scent of spruce; Morriel thrust a hand from her quilts and stroked the faceted sphere cradled upon the silver tripod before her. The three legs extended through an opened trapdoor in the palanquin's floor, the spikes of each foot grounded into the stone of the mountain by gold wire, and chains of ciphers and forced spells. Their imprint had scarred the face of the stone, rune and seal branded inside a slagged ring of obsidian.

Alive to the summoning touch of the Prime, the Great Waystone threw off a flared spark of violet in response to her signal of readiness. 'As I thought,' Morriel said. 'The fool will not balk in the face of adversity. He'll use the change in the magnetic tides at midnight to effect his own transfer across latitude. He will dare to meddle in Jaelot, despite Sethvir's warning that we stand prepared to obstruct him.'

She snapped bone-thin fingers. 'At Isaer, the hour of opportunity draws nigh. Enchantresses, assume trance and make ready.'

Bared to the elemental dark of the night, the poised circle of seniors stirred beneath their wool cloaks. They joined hands like linked wax in the pallid half-light of the moon's late-rising quarter. Strong discipline blinded. Not one of their number sensed Morriel's masked smile of elated anticipation. In oathbound subservience, each woman surrendered her power and awareness into the Waystone's glittering dark heart.

Alone amid silvery needles of sleet, Asandir mopped sweating temples. The risks he would shoulder within the next seconds were grave enough to cause even a mage of his stature second thoughts. Not the sure grounding of earth beneath his feet, nor the steady well of possibility scribed in the dance of elemental air could lend him the boon of reassurance. The steps he must tread crossed a field of rank thorn, barbed and coiled with unseen peril.

He blew out a plume of white breath in trepidation, aware as he stood that the hour had arrived to act or stand down in defeat. High above the disruptions of sleet and tempest, the winter stars turned untroubled in their slow-spinning arc. Sun crossed the meridian a hemisphere away, engaging the lane flux at midnight. Feet spanning the central focus at Isaer, Asandir linked his hands at his breast. He pulled another breath of ice-ridden air and held, while the life energies inside his quickened flesh coursed into harmonic equilibrium. Eyes closed, he stilled thought, listening with mage-sight. He engaged the pent strictures of discipline until his active awareness encompassed the outermost edge of his aura. The closed rune of stasis appeared as a flame in his mind, to seal a ward of protection around body and spirit through the chaotic forces of transit.

Next he called on the infinite, streaming chord of prime power to transmute the vibration of matter. His physical being shimmered and dissolved, raised upward into a patterned resonance of pure energy. That polarized state held peril incarnate. Danger stalked in malevolent forms, shadows born of thought and hatred given spin by the mass consciousness of humanity. Here also lurked temptations to tear unmoored spirit from flesh. Poised at the crux of duality, where the veil demarked the soaring edge of high mystery, awareness could become swept away on the spiraling dance of forces strung in laddered waves between polarities. Here, in the shimmering rainbow of energies, all possibilities existed: the full gamut beckoned the unfettered mind, from the dance of lost unicorns to the white fires of dragons, which in Athera's distant past had remolded the face of creation.

For a spirit whose service extended through Ages, with no end yet in sight, the call tugged weary nerves like sweet ecstasy. Ever the desire lured like a siren, to unfold in joy into light and abjure forever the trials and pains borne in the burdensome guise of dense flesh.

Asandir resisted, obdurate; the binding laid down with the gift of his wisdom could not be so lightly cast off. Steadfastly grim as a scarp of seamed granite, he held, while the midnight change in the lane field swept its cascading current, north to south. Fixed iron in pursuit of his dedicated purpose, the Sorcerer mastered that essence. He launched through its charge, at one with the spiraling tide of the earth flux that clothed the night face of Athera. One fractional second, that surge of suspension threaded the arc of creation. Asandir retuned the harmonic vibrations of his essence in one deft leap of trained vision. Upstepped to merge with the planet's magnetic field, he passed in a contained band of static from third lane to fourth, and thence, to the fifth lane, which devolved through the vortex at the great power focus at Ithamon.

There, the Sorcerer paused a split second. A ghost frame of intent became all that preserved the imprinted signature of his body. Spirit and awareness remained immersed in the tingling, raw band of the lane flux. Prepared for trouble as he crossed into the sixth lane, he would venture no farther without safeguards.

The ruin where past s'Ffalenn high kings had ruled hung still and deserted under starlight. Hoarfrost limned a sheen like dulled quicksilver off broken facings of rock, except where the four standing towers still rose, pristine and whole against sky. The Paravian-wrought wards which knit their disparate stone into one seamless defense fanned like a cry of pure light through the weave of solid creation. Aware of that strength as an undying harmony touched through the ephemeral fabric of his being, Asandir cast an anchor of binding deep into earth at the site. Should aught go amiss, he could link with that cipher and access those powers still active in the heart of Ithamon's shattered citadel.

One final time, he retuned his vibration, this stage to match the great power circle inset in the feast hall of Jaelot's palace of state. Even as his essence shifted alignment to close the last leg of his journey, he sensed a disharmony impelled through the lane's magnetic flux.

Asandir pinpointed the source instantaneously.

He had handled the Koriani Great Waystone in the past. One encounter was enough to instill lasting memory of its matrix, the wise energies of amethyst warped by long usage into a trammeled, mad tangle of trapped malice. Though the Koriani Order preserved those ancient imprints as an irreplaceable repository of knowledge, to Fellowship sensibilities the gemstone's enthralled pain framed a cry of cruel offense. Yet the Law of the Major Balance forbade his intervention. Since all the talisman crystals in Koriani service had been brought to Athera from offworld, the compact claimed no jurisdiction.

Poised in vexation, Asandir measured the lane's imbalance. Although earth herself had embraced Sethvir's offered permission to reject any seal of forced mastery imposed through the amethyst's tainted focus, no wakened power of discrimination could deflect an influx of distortion struck through an unshielded quartz vein. Morriel's Waystone had been denied all empowerment to inflict direct conjury upon the land; but as an act of self-will, the old Prime could engage the gemstone and wield her own malice in assault against nature. She and her circle of trained seniors raised a cone of raw force to haze Athera's aura and malign its field of magnetics.

The disruption threatened Asandir's safe passage into the great focus at Jaelot; no surprise. While Koriani magics wrung the lane to random chaos, the Fellowship Sorcerer was stonewalled, unable to rematerialize at the portal inside the mayor's palace.

Exhaustively versed in the harmonic skein of the earth's diversified energies, Asandir picked out the dissonant strand in a second's reflexive survey. The inherited trust of the centaur guardians fell under Fellowship auspices; against willful destruction to Athera herself, the Major Balance demanded no grace of permissions. Free rein was his to unshield dire will and hurl the Waystone's channeled current of interference to harmless dissipation in the salt waves of Eltair Bay.

Few beings might stand in defiance against a Fellowship Sorcerer. On the breath of a whim, whole mountains might walk, or seas flatten to glass sheets of ice. Asandir could rule wind and tide as he chose, or divert the earth's molten core to burst through her crust in white magma. Like the force of blind cataclysm refined to a feather touch, he extended a whisper of power and flicked. The ranging mesh of static sustained through the Waystone spun into recoil, its polarity reforged into an arrow of combed force.

The instant of contact touched off an explosion.

That split second too late, Asandir realized the sixth lane's distortion had been a smoke screen. He could not evade. The torrent of force the Koriani loosed against him snapped closed like the jaws of a trap.

He knew blinding pain, a burning, corrosive attack of disharmony as the conjury lashed his defenses. His long centuries of experience became as driven reflex, to distance the fright and emotion. Torment could be ruled as mere sensory information, cut away from its link to mortality. Asandir was a master mage versed in all keys to the spectrum of existence. From the negative pole of dense-form matter to the exalted realms of pure spirit, his command was absolute, if governed by wisdom into a steel-clad restraint. Against him, the buffet of Koriani conjury should have been as fog and thread before bonfire.

Except that his natural form was in lane flux, translated above the threshold of matter. He dared not close with heavy energies while immersed in a transformed state of higher frequency. The smallest, most subtle attempt to engage adverse forces would open the floodgates to disaster. In unbodied form, the altered vibration of his physical being and the unbinding spells of attack would combine in one shattering burst of annihilation.

Asandir met the reeling onslaught on the knife-edged awareness that his peril was unforgiving of mistakes. Hurled with the focused impetus of the Waystone, strung runes leached his being like flung acid. Sigils of unbinding deranged his perimeter of defenses and threatened his state of pure energy. Each countermove he engaged unleashed more force against him. Spells tied in chains seemed to magnify and splinter into thousands of needling echoes. Nor was the momentum behind them intelligent. The quartz vein in the Skyshiels thrummed like a sounding board, magnifying Morriel's attack to exponential proportions.

Against outright dissolution, Asandir knit veils of intent like bright mirrors to spin distorting energies back on themselves. While static and vertigo sapped his stability, he traced circles to carve small pockets in time. Given a fractional second, as he pinned those vortices stable, he must effect intervention and freeze the catalyzing cascade of events.

Through that heartbeat of bought time, he engaged his full resources. Senses refined far beyond mortal limits let him parcel the impact of each energy sent in assault against him. From his years spent with sly, temperamental old drakes, he identified the forms of dissolution that cast ordered wisdom into void. Other seals recombined in dark resonance to unbalance and bind. Here, he isolated the sigils to seed terror, and there, a spinning entropy which destroyed human will. Other seals played on the fires of addiction, invoked twisted passions and abject despair. Others engendered a spiraling distortion which led to inexorable decay. To spells of leaching ruin, Morriel had linked gyroscopic spirals of diversion. Cantrips to stall thought, and narcotic procrastination; seals of blight to rot flesh into putrefied liquid. Through these, she had knotted tangling mazes to steal reason and shackle the mind into nightmare.

Speed of reflex held the Sorcerer's only salvation, and also his greatest peril should he slip, or miss even one turning through the morass.

Beleaguered as he was, Asandir admired the Prime's ingenuity. The spells cast against him ranged the gamut of spite, a thousand small shards pitched to wound on the chance he could be overwhelmed and outflanked. Almost, he fell prey to the snares in the mesh, cloaked in false trappings to imprison him. Destroy, or maim, or take captive; Morriel had laid ambush for whatever end she could snatch out of reeling confusion.

Asandir played her net of self-contained fury. Disadvantaged since the moment he had excised and secured the dissident powers in the lane force, he dared not seize the safe route and translate his body back to tangible form. The change would release those disruptive currents. Ripples of shock would thrash through the world's aura; too many vital wardings wrought by the centaur guardians would resound into damage and disintegrate. Khadrim might fly free, released from sealed boundaries, and drake spawn long chained beneath Mirthlvain's dark mire could resurge and rend lives in bloody slaughter.

Quandary remained. Asandir could not sustain that influx of disharmony, safely split into isolate channels, without wreaking havoc on his auric defenses.

His dangers were myriad, and aligned on all fronts, which disallowed a clean strike to negate them. Responsibility to his art of itself stymied action, a twist Morriel had exploited. She sought to entangle his fierce competence through complexity, her weapon the intricate strictures of a code which demanded that every nuance of cause and effect be aligned with due care for the Major Balance. While he served the necessary steps, the spells on his flank chafed and tore at his reserves. Their threat dogged his balance, nipped at his masterful deliberation, and clamored to deflect him to wasting anxiety.

No matter the extent of his personal danger, his first sworn charge was the land. Those damaging energies swept up from the lane must be contained inside a rim of impermeable seals, an intricate conjury with no tools at hand but the bare frames of will and intent. Asandir faced the daunting task without flinching, though to close a clean ward on a field of disharmony while suffering corrosive attack posed dire problems for a spirit in flux amid the volatile currents of live lane force.

His call to prime power ignited a flare of white light. Like cracks crazed through glass, the stacked planes of existence recoiled and discharged a rainbow corona of wild energies. Asandir haltered that force in clear purpose and rewove, asking a swift permission of air. The element responded in joy for his need, his appeal to fire the runes of command given voice by the cry of the wind.

Above the snowy summits of the Skyshiels, a vast gust arose, scooped inward, and carved out a howling whirlwind. The cyclone encased the parcel of warped frequencies Asandir had unraveled from the lane flux. Aligned to that spiral, he spun static charge and wove a barrier that Koriani meddling could not cross. His refrain became the barrage of bass thunder as the ward circles became manifest, each ring a bright arc of chained light. Air cracked into a glassine shield, welded to solid, impenetrable continuity. His construct took form but lacked in finesse. The crisis invoked by Morriel Prime's meddling disallowed a swift closure. Under stress, Asandir could not fashion a safe conduit to quench those warped fields of flux into the brine of Eltair Bay.

He had no alternative. His best effort reset the wardings for change, allowing the imbalance to disperse in gradual, safe increments and ground in the core of the earth. His search for a suitable mountain gave rise to a dangerous delay. Twice, sore beset, he fought off incursions created by entropic attack. Morriel's conjury pressed in, relentless, to wear and weaken and distract. Through her gnawing swarms of hostile spell seals, Asandir reamed a clear channel. His awareness touched rock, and was recognized. Steadied in patience, he braced through the retentive, slow interval that stone demanded to ponder the scope of his request.

Seconds dragged into minutes, all the more fraught with tension. The fractional trickle of time was his enemy. Let Morriel's assault engage him too long, her dark workings would seek out the breaches. Let one destructive sigil inside, its pattern could shred his foundations to ribbons and drain off his personal strength. In the riptide of weakened control, he risked disclosing every damaging detail of his origins to Morriel's grasping interest.

That above anything, he must not allow. Those ancient blood debts had been fully redeemed. Events carried through on distant soil and other worlds served no place here and now on Athera. Set in the wrong hands, or whispered in the ears of Lysaer's fledgling priests, the damning history of Fellowship affairs might be used as an arsenal to damage the future.

At length, in a bell tone resonance that rang agelessly massive, the iron-dark summit of Quaire Peak responded and offered itself as receptacle.

Asandir paused only to return heartfelt gratitude. Then he snaked a tangling chain of new ciphers into his warded circles. Power flowed through in precise increments.

The backwash of shed forces shot off fierce jags of lightning that grounded themselves in black ore. The leakage to ionized air became minimal. Only a small static discharge bled down the sixth lane, a dance of loosed energies no more harmful than the flares of a northern aurora. Until they played out, they would draw nothing worse than the appetites of stray iyats.

Unyoked at last from encumbering duty, Asandir rallied against Morriel's invasion. He seized on the anchor left rooted in earth amid the old towers of Ithamon. Light pealed, then a rattling slam of deep thunder as he engaged his raised will and downstepped his vibration back into the physical spectrum.

Solidly himself, now standing on frost-silvered grass amid the crumbled foundation of the King's Tower, he tipped up his face. Winter wind flung back his hood and lashed silver hair to his cheek. He screened out knifing cold and the sting of the elements as he linked his right and left hands. Then, eyes closed, he gathered his trained awareness and cast his sharp focus inward.

Morriel's construct buzzed and whined through his aura, shrill as a swarm of roused bees. His skin tingled and burned, hazed by conflicted forces. Asandir safely ignored the discomfort. For him, minor ills of the flesh held small consequence. So long as the provenance of his spirit stayed whole, he could mend any bodily dysfunction. Free at last to respond to Morriel's assault, Asandir admitted the energies into his being *and claimed them*.

All the horror, all the hate, all the disruptive, chaotic destruction wrought through cramped seals and sigils, he welcomed, then Named as wholly his. On the catalytic crux of annihilation, at the bitter edge of total sacrifice, he reached out with an acid-etched core of intent and engaged every last wasting sigil. Self-will and mastery matched dark force with light. He did not seek to reverse, or control, or manipulate. Instead, he melded the unbinding force of destruction with his own creative exuberance. The gush of that wellspring arose from the core of his individuality. His invention was bottomless. Through an awareness honed into relentless refinement, through the reach of his limitless compassion, he diluted the ruinous barrage set against him into cascading change.

What remained of each warped patterning at the last was its original core of emotion: the impetus behind the enmity that founded the need for Morriel's vindication. Her fear, her dread shame, and her outright worry for the proscribed knowledge she held in trust for her order were as surface ripples over a shattering void of bleak loneliness. No family or friend remembered her girlhood. Her glory days of idealism were spent, leaving only the unbearable burden of an office grown onerously heavy. Her days, her acts, her purpose had grown hollow, until, each hour, she battled her withering, frail flesh, tormented by uncertainty and a burning self-righteous indignation. No consolation might ease her cruel strait. The fate she was sworn to accomplish before death could not be impelled to fruition.

Against a despair beyond tears to encompass, Asandir held his dispassionate balance. His long-suffering strength had known worse and survived. Poised in tender care, with a gentleness that could have cupped a cobweb against a gale, he wrapped that anguished residue in compassion, shored up by his sorrowful understanding. Once he, too, had lost hope to despairing grief and stark hatred. His recovery had come at the bitter end of hope, through the gift of Athera's Paravians.

The channel to prime power their wisdom had opened had reforged his Fellowship in redemption. That source was inexhaustible as tide, limitless as the flight of an imagination set free of shadow and doubt. Asandir engaged the higher octaves of resonance. He let the life dance of celebration that strung all existence shift the misaligned strands of Morriel's hostility. For a mage of his stature, converting barbed spite into transforming joy was an act as unthinking as reflex.

No discharge of fey power marked the event, no display of dazzling sorcery. The last sigil subsided as a whisper into the abiding stasis of true peace.

Asandir opened his eyes to the white blaze of stars over the dark hills of Daon Ramon. Around him, the four Paravian towers speared skyward. The ethereal harmonies of their pristine wards intertwined with the unquiet lament of the breezes. Ithamon yet sheltered the cries of its ghosts. Air still voiced the imprint of past betrayal through tumbled stone walls and the rims of shattered foundations.

Under his feet, where the transmuted forces of Morriel's malice had been grounded, the frost had melted away. Earth had responded to the influx of grand mystery to raise up a circle of green grasses. Amid their feathered stalks, a briar sprig bloomed, a flawless primrose fresh as new morning. The Sorcerer bent, the weariness in him an ache etched down to the bone. He sketched a blessing over the site, then asked for leave and plucked the bloom before the icy night wind could shrivel its fragile petals. He pressed the flower's sweet fragrance to his face. Burdened of heart, he sighed for the plight of a Koriani Matriarch whose hope and humanity had grown twisted, her altruism warped under too many years of prime rule.

He had been where she sat. For him and his colleagues, how terrible had been the final step into wisdom. Compassionate tolerance had been bought in blood, that ends did not ever justify the means, and that help for the world's sorrows could never be won through the exigencies of power or control.

Tonight's reckoning would bring no succor for Fionn Areth, languishing under threat of an unjust execution.

Asandir faced the larger defeat inside his personal victory, while the cold set him shivering, and Ithamon's sad spirits moaned their perpetual refrain of lament. Morriel Prime had succeeded in cutting off his swift access to Jaelot. Whether or not she dared use her Waystone to mount another assault against him, for prudence, he knew he must not stress the flow of the sixth lane with another transfer. Not until his stopgap spell of warding expended the pooled reservoir of dissident energies into the summit of Quaire Peak. The elapsed time would delay him until past the day of winter solstice, more if he fared eastward on foot.

Until then, he must hope Elaira's good sense could withstand the mayor's vindictive fury and the pressure of Jaelot's town council.

# Fell Signs

The Mayor of Jaelot's dungeon had not changed for the better since the Mad Prophet's fateful incarceration twenty-five years in the past. Seepage from the limestone strata of the headland still beaded and dripped, clouded by the ancient layers of soot the pitch cressets left on the ceiling. The erratic tick of moisture into rank, moldered straw stitched through Fionn Areth's dazed thoughts. His last lucent memory was of the posset given by a Koriani enchantress he could not see in blank darkness. Through a fogging numbness which dulled the worst pain, the touch of her hands came and went, sure in skill, mapping the list of his injuries. He had her assurance that no bones were broken. More pressing worries remained unassuaged, while the herbs in her remedy spiraled his mind between fitful sleep and nightmare.

Time returned him, unwilling, to the splashing plink of water and the revolting, acidic reek of rat. Thirst left him unmoored. He had no sense of the hour. Around him lay darkness fretted by the sultry, spent flicker of a pine knot torch. Someone's lent cloak, steeped in sage and lavender, muffled the worst of the cold. Under the cloth, bound in the heat of strong poultices, the ache of uncountable cuts and bruises throbbed in lockstep with his pulse. His sides seemed a mass of outraged flesh. The guardsmen had kicked him with hobnailed boots, and his bed of damp straw and sweat-clammy clothing combined to knot cramps in his sinews.

'Keep still,' urged a female voice, one he recognized. 'I have seals of mending at work on your knee. Should you move, you'll unstring the fine energies.'

Fionn Areth shut his eyes. The splintering pound of blood through his swellings did little to refresh his memory. 'I know you, I think.'

No answer came; only the icy breath of the draft across the exposed skin of his cheek. The competent restraint of the woman's hands as she bound the stitched cut on his forearm suffered no break in steadiness. Her face was obscured. Fionn Areth made out little more than a lit curve of cheek, sliced by a dark fall of hair. The tight-focused glare of the spell crystal she engaged cast an actinic halo too fierce for his unshielded eyesight.

Fionn Areth battled an overpowering urge to give way to leaden drowsiness. Through muddied thoughts and the torpor of drugged dizziness, he managed, 'You're the healer who once lived in the cottage on the moor.'

Her hands paused, then resumed in delicate firmness. 'Yes. That's how I knew for certain you couldn't be Arithon s'Ffalenn.' She tucked in the ends of the bandage and settled back onto her heels.

'I look so much like him?' Fionn Areth asked, bitter. 'No one seems willing to believe me.'

'Hate has no ears.' Elaira pushed back the stray hair slipped over her brow. A small tuck of worry pinched the line of the forehead he remembered, as she added, 'Nor are grudges in Jaelot ever too old to pursue.' She let the light in her quartz flicker out, then did something to his knee by the blood weak spill of the cresset. 'I'll help you in every way that I can, and as far as the vows to my order will allow. Believe this, your predicament is serious.'

Fionn Areth caught in a wincing breath, then another as a flare of sharp warmth hazed through his stiffening tissues. 'What's wrong?'

'With your knee? Torn cartilage and a puncture.' She raised a hand, her wristbone chiseled in unsubtle shadow, and captured the lick of auburn hair which stubbornly troubled her eyesight. 'I'm sorry for the sting. I'd rather be thorough than risk complications.' Her neat, narrow fingers flicked the stray lock into a braid and secured it behind her left ear. 'You'd lose the joint if the wound became septic.'

Fionn Areth let his head loll back, unable to think while his innards twitched in sickly protest. When next he spoke, the worst of his fear grated through. 'The leg won't much matter if the mayor has his way, and I find myself on the scaffold.'

'The leg matters,' snapped the enchantress, as though a raw nerve had been scraped. 'As for the scaffold, don't hold any doubts. The Lord

Mayor's misdirected justice landed Jaelot its trouble with the Master of Shadow in the first place.'

Fionn Areth shut his eyes against another surge of healing force, this one a sweeping rain like fine silver needles down his spine and into his leg. 'You know him?'

'Very well, thank you.' Another queasy pause, while the enchantress traced a seal and sigil over his flaming, sore skin. 'Arithon of Rathain has a rife quarrel with anyone who trifles with his personal affairs or his loyalties. Now be still. The energies should soon settle into a closer alignment.'

Beyond the particulars of healing his damaged knee, the ramifications of her statement about the Shadow Master took a tangled minute to sort out. Fionn Areth pondered, while the cresset flared and spat dying sparks over the noisome stone wall.

'I didn't come here to meddle in any sorcerer's private feud,' he protested at length.

The enchantress ran light, testing fingers over the traumatized tissues of the knee, cross-checking her meticulous work. The little braid of hair slid undone and escaped the constraint of her ear. She raked back the persistent strands with an unnerving, jangled impatience. 'No. It's the mayor the Master of Shadow will target, once he hears what's afoot. Don't despair. He's lifted prisoners out of locked chains before.'

Which presumption was too much; Fionn Areth vented his flood of unease in outright disbelief. 'He's also slaughtered thirty thousand at a stroke, on the field at Dier Kenton Vale. I came *here*,' the herder's son clarified in acid affront, 'to sign on my sword with the ranks of Avenor's Alliance. A bloodletting criminal is as unlikely to stir a hand to spare me from his own laid fire as I am to run steel through his unmerciful heart.'

'Do you think so?' Ill-tempered at last, Elaira sat down on her satchel. She fixed Fionn Areth with a stare bleak gray as the winter-frozen puddles on the moor. 'Well, think first, and carefully. Because you may get your chance. Just like the mayor, you can strike out of prejudice before letting your victim speak in his own defense.'

'That's unfair!' Fionn Areth chose argument, more than desperate to stave off the fear that whiplashed him toward an abyss of unutterable terror. 'No question exists over Arithon's guilt. Against the sealed record of evidence against him, his death would be named as a boon to society.'

But the enchantress appeared to reject his assured view. 'Be quiet.'

Fionn Areth insisted, 'Why hasn't your sisterhood stepped forward to proclaim his innocence?'

'Be quiet, I said,' Elaira snapped, sharper. Head raised, chin turned toward the rusted steel grille at the doorway, she had gone rigid with tension.

Brushed to sudden chills, Fionn Areth subsided. 'What is it?'

Elaira shook her head, frowning. She closed her grasp over the spell crystal chained to her neck, her sudden uncertainty palpable even in near-total darkness. 'Something's gone wrong.'

'Perhaps the Shadow Master's sorcery,' Fionn Areth suggested, still bitter.

'No.' Inarguably certain, the enchantress clasped her quartz and stilled into concentration. Whatever the probing nature of her inquiry, the crystal flared into sudden, bloodred sparks of light. As though their touch stung, Elaira cried out, and her hands jerked away in recoil.

'What was that, lady, if not some fell working of darkness?'

'Not Arithon's,' the enchantress rebuffed. 'The trace signature I caught was warped light, born of fire. And the charges of dark sorcery against Arithon are false, whoever claims otherwise. It's a little-known fact, but the Prince of Rathain lost his access to mage talent thirty years ago.' She held back the rest, that the event just picked up through the staid calm of earth had more likely been the caught resonance of a Koriani sigil. 'I don't like what I feel.'

No time was given to survey the source of her qualms.

A wave of wild shouting filtered in from the street, hard followed by the crash of splintering wood. Excited voices echoed down from the upstairs guardroom, no dispute between bored sentries in disagreement over a dice throw, but a shouted confrontation between armed men bent on forcing their way into the dungeons.

One voice clashed and rose above the duty captain's protests. 'Man, you haven't looked outside. There's unnatural lights all over the night sky! That sorcerer in your dungeon has been stirring dire portents. This time, we won't wait for sound walls and roofs to come clapping down in fell heaps. If you have the brains of an egg-laying goose, let us through. We'll slit the spell-winding criminal like a herring and string out his tripes for the ravens.'

The captain's reply came fragmented between fist-shaking threats and the hot-blooded jangle of weaponry. Reference to the mayor's decree of due process became mown down in midsentence. 'What need for a trial? Already the whole sky's alive with fell conjury! The wretch is as good as proved guilty with every man's eyes as my witness.'

Steadfast, the captain shouted back. 'Then show me a sealed writ from his lordship granting you lawful right to dispose of the prisoner.'

There followed a slamming exchange of armed blows. The raw din of steel flung ugly reverberations off the stone walls and bare ceilings. A man's choked-off scream signaled somebody fallen. More swordplay followed. Then a stampede of feet in hobnailed boots thundered from the wardroom down the steep, lower stairwell.

'Mercy, they're through.' Elaira shoved to her feet, her hand clenched to her spell crystal. A short step saw her to the locked and barred door, the studded, strapped steel marred like old blood with streaked rust stains. 'Whatever happens, lie still. Say nothing. Wisest if we can make them believe you're drugged beyond reach of your senses.'

Light speared down the stairwell, felted with the distorted shadows of angry men brandishing mismatched weapons. A straight silhouette against that juddering spill, Elaira held her stance by the doorway, her quartz pendant tucked in her right palm. She raised her free hand to frame sigils of protection in the air. Conjured light spilled like ribbon from her moving fingertip. Seal paired with counterforce and locked the raised energy in stasis. A chained mesh of spellcraft laced like thread foil across the threshold of the cell. Before the insane paranoia of mob panic, her concentration stayed clear as stilled water. Through sheer force of will and her order's stern discipline, she would not admit fear in distraction. Her arm remained steady. Though the effort stippled sweat on forehead and temple, her quartz burned hot and bright as glass set above open flame.

'If you pray,' she said through clenched teeth to Fionn Areth, 'better hope there's an ally in this town who has enough power to uphold your right to fair judgment. For if I should fall defending your innocence, believe this. Your vaunted Alliance fanatics will see us both dead without even one second's thought.'

Fionn Areth said nothing, too paralyzed with dread to do aught but feign limpid unconsciousness.

Elaira had no words of encouragement to spare him. The first wave of the mob surged down the staircase in a battering press of torches, bristled with bared swords and cudgels. The front ranks encountered her chain of defense wards and slammed to a stupefied stop.

'Go home!' cried the enchantress in the face of their wrath. 'You'll do no more murder in cold blood this night. Not as long as I stand to oppose you!'

Far north of the disturbance in Jaelot, light snowfall and a knifing, cruel wind raked over the Skyshiel Mountains. Snug in the privacy of her palanquin, the Prime Enchantress of the Koriani Order sat awake by gold lamplight, tatting a band of spelled lace. Aged hands etched down to tendon and cartilage picked and rearranged the ebony pins stuck on her frame of dark velvet. Her bundled spools of metallic thread dangled. Glints caught like thin drizzle in the flare of the wick as they swung to the twist and turn of her weaving. Her lace was not fashioned from ribbon or linen. The patterns she knotted were strung into chains of sigils and seals, their filaments drawn steel and copper.

The bobbins were carved bone, stained dark with age. The drafts which rippled through the curtains of the palanquin clicked them like primitive amulets, causing the dutiful apprentice successor to blink with unease at her post.

'Selidie,' Morriel rasped. Her frailty grown disturbingly pronounced, she raised a peremptory hand, as if the young woman had never grown to maturity since the hour of her selection. 'I'll need the canister of tobacco infused with tienelle. You may pack the stone pipe with the snakeroot stem and have the striker ready. Then fetch me another opium taper from the lacquered box in the herb chest.'

'Your will, Matriarch,' Selidie replied, her voice sweet with childish sibilance. She attended the first chore, then crossed the cramped quarters as though balanced on eggshells, each movement infused with awed reverence.

The senior seeress crouched beside Morriel's pallet remained absorbed over the quartz sphere she used for clear scrying. Her murmur cut through the shriek of the gusts that clawed through the black spruce outside. 'Your moment is nigh. The Mayor of Jaelot has been roused from his bed to quell the vigilantes storming his dungeon. As you wished, Lirenda has convinced the town magistrates of the need to place spells of protection over the walls of the city.'

Bone spools clacked as Morriel plucked a pin and preset the next stage of the pattern. Her fingers looped threads like a spider's legs, spinning webs to net hapless prey. 'Well-done. The timing's immaculate.' An interval passed as she tied off a thread, one knot in the ritual rune of ending. 'Selidie!' she snapped. 'Quickly now! Light the taper. Then drink the posset in the corked flask on the stand by my pallet. The herbs I've prepared will allow you to sleep undisturbed throughout this night's work.'

The seeress looked up then, inquiry written into her wrinkled face.

Morriel returned a quelling gesture. 'You'll stay. Your skills are yet needed.'

'Matriarch, your leave,' lisped the young initiate. She placed the lighted taper on its stand, then curtsied and uncapped the squat wooden flask. The contents smelled bitter. She wrinkled her nose, then dutifully drank, while the restless drafts toyed with the curtains. Morriel watched, eyes half-lidded. As a sated cat might follow the movements of a mouse, she surveyed each detail of the girl's smooth limbs as she stripped to her shift and snuggled into her cot by the corner post. Morriel sat without speech or movement. Limned in the unstable flicker of flame light, she appeared as a death's-head amid a catafalque of pillows and quilts.

In time, the girl's breathing steadied and slowed into the rhythm of deep sleep.

'Do you know how to call in and tie the life energies to a proxy?' Morriel husked to the seeress.

The enchantress set down her crystal in the dense, scented gloom of the palanquin. 'Of course, I'm familiar with the steps.' Unsure of what service her Prime might demand, she resisted the urge to direct unsettled glances at the motionless young woman on the pallet.

Nor was the Koriani Matriarch forthcoming. She gave no explanation for the drugged posset as the minutes dragged by in suspension. Bone clicked on bone as she tied in her last knots. One by one, she removed the pins which nailed her worked pattern in place. The meshed chain of ciphers swung free. Light caught like sparks of live fire amid the tied threads, twined in a contorted, array of interlocked sigils and seals. Their sequence framed chaos, each meticulous cipher a spun spell to unilaterally foul order and balance.

Sunk in her mood of poisonous amusement, Morriel watched the seeress's expression vacillate between dread and unwholesome curiosity. 'A lovely recipe for ruin, I agree. How better to divert the Fellowship of Seven as Lirenda sets seals of ward over the walled battlements of Jaelot?' She folded the lace ribbon aside with due care. Her hands threw insectile shadows on the counterpane as she picked up the demon-stemmed pipe. 'For that purpose, earth itself will be made to act as my sounding board.'

She snapped a thin, yellowed thumbnail. Flame bloomed at its tip, fanned to life by a breath through her withered lips. The infused leaves caught and burned red in the whorled stone pipe bowl. A lingering reek of sulfur clogged the air, aftershock of the sigil to rule fire. The acrid odor persisted through the rich, blooming fragrance of tobacco smoke, and the narcotic spice of the tienelle.

Through the first twining streamers, Morriel's eyes were chipped jet. 'You will stand ready to send my signal to all senior initiates in the order who are not on active duty in Jaelot. At my word of need, each one of them must engage in trance and give over their powers to me. By the grace of their discipline, our will shall prevail. On this night, Sethvir of Althain will learn better than to align natural forces against the might of the Koriathain.'

The seeress's tired eyes flicked toward the silk-covered tripod supporting the faceted Waystone.

'No,' Morriel answered her unspoken thought. An unholy pleasure warmed the scrape of her voice. 'Not the Waystone just yet. For this work, I'll engage the Skyron aquamarine first. That and the items I will need for the opening ritual are in the small coffer by my feet.'

Long used to the Matriarch's autocracy, the seeress fetched and carried without rancor. She was also wise enough not to badger her Prime with unwanted questions. Her patience was rewarded. Once the perimeter circles were sketched out, Morriel unkeyed the spell seals securing the lid of the coffer. She picked through the raw silk wrappings inside and laid out the contents in age-old, arcane configurations.

First came the traditional axis aligned with the cardinal directions. In the feeble glow of the draft-torn flame, the seeress identified the dulled, iron gleam of polished hematite for grounding; the rods of black tourmaline for protection and shielding; the false gold flash of the cubed pyrite Morriel would use to strain interfering energies from the four quadrants of her construct. Next, the icicle rods of six quartz wands, each one unique in its chiseled aura of energies.

Although Koriani practice disdained the use of animal talismans, tonight Morriel rejected tradition. She rifled the depths of a soft linen bag with string-tied bundles of bird feathers. These were not windfalls, shed during molt, but the glossy, crisp quills taken from birds killed in summer. The Prime's plundered hoard included the barred plumage of hawks, owls, and wrens, the fierce blue of jays, and the black quills of ravens, delicate beside the razor-edged primaries plucked from an ocean shearwater. Their presence threw off thin auras like smoke, affirming the sacrificial deaths had been done on a dark moon, in painstaking ritual with stone knives.

The Prime Matriarch arranged her feathers in a circle inside the warding ring of laid minerals. She used cantrips to stitch their hazed magnetism into a focused cone of tiered power. Later, those energies would be used to command the element of air, which cradled every wavelength of energy instilled in the earth's subtle aura.

The construct to stand as Athera's proxy had been fashioned from a globe of raw clay. It, too, had been ritually prepared in advance, with layers of fine spellcraft invoked. The two missing elements, water and flame, would have gone into its making. Nor would any vessel or implement of iron have been used in the course of its shaping. Morriel cupped its dry weight in seamed palms and intoned the lines of summoning. Her words drew ephemeral geometrics in the dark, lacing will through the trifold forms of intent: wrought of thought and scribed rune and incantation. Where the signature of earth's imprint had been bound into clay, she secured those significating energies from attrition with lightless seals of stasis. Each sigil was incised with a fingernail stylus, and a brow crimped with concentration.

The seeress observed. Half-forgotten in her corner, she watched the bound forces swell, a nexus of stitched light noosed coil by coil in the fist of Morriel's will. Step by slow step, the alignment was stabilized. The Prime placed the enabled proxy at the center of the crystal array, surrounded by its aureole of feathers. Another invocation, and a second renewal of the perimeter circles of protection; inside the palanquin, the atmosphere stilled, made stifling with the pent-back force of an oncoming major event. The whine of the winter-chill winds outside became lost and distanced by shifting curtains of raised power.

Morriel Prime delved into her silk-lined coffer and unveiled the Skyron aquamarine. The gem's star-cut eye gleamed like a fissure in ice. Its aroused presence suffused the palanquin with a radius of cold far beyond any chill engendered by seasonal elements. The steps to engage and master its focus aged the Prime's taut-laced features, each crease underscored by her arduous effort. As her will engaged with the prime axis of the crystal, the flame-cast shadows themselves seemed to shrink, and the drafts move softly in her presence.

The last linkage remained. Morriel retrieved her length of spelled ribbon, a meshed weave of sigils imprinted with the directives of her desire. She wound the fine wires of one end around the enabled aquamarine. The tail, with its convoluted knots of closure, she swathed about the clay proxy.

All preparations now stood complete. The Skyron crystal with its winding of filaments rested in Morriel's stilled hands. Focal point of the feather array, centered in the raised circle of power, the formed clay construct linked to Athera's Name awaited the impact of change.

Morriel delivered her final instructions in a stress-cracked whisper. 'First, engage your powers as seer to frame a link with Lirenda. I'll need affirmation of her success as she sways Jaelot's mayor to our purpose.'

'Your will becomes mine.' The seeress bowed her head. Eyes closed, she cleared her mind of distractions. The quartz sphere in her hands clouded to haze, then darkened as the blurred flicker of an image took slow shape in its depths. The shadow resolved to the texture of dank stone, and the slot in a barred cell door . . .

*Before that small gap, Senior Enchantress Lirenda was addressing an unseen party inside. 'You'll never establish his innocence now. One* look outside will show why, and the next hour will just bring you another lynch mob of citizens howling murder. They've taken to arms because there's a run of static charges bleeding down the sixth lane. The whole sky flamed red, result of a Fellowship intervention.' An arrogant pause, then Lirenda resumed, disdainful in her contempt. 'Of course, the display is quite harmless. But a man accused of sorcery is incarcerated here. The panic in the streets has pinned blame on his presence. There can't be a trial. Jaelot's citizens would riot. The mayor has been forced to rearrange his priorities. The public execution will now take place as part of the solstice festivities.'

'The day after tomorrow?' A rustle of sharp movement through the slot inflected Elaira's retort. 'Never mind you know better! The scapegoat you're letting these people revile is barely more than a boy! Don't try to claim the Fellowship Sorcerers ever act without provocation. My hunches are screaming. Something's gone unspeakably rotten at our core, or why would our order stoop to involvement in petty deceits and town politics?'

Lirenda responded in freezing displeasure. 'More's at stake than you know.' Rushed by the clump of a guardsman's tread descending the upper stair, she added, 'This place is not private. I can't stay any longer. The mayor's been assured my work on the walls will guard against further sorcery.'

'We're lying now, also?' Elaira scrapped back. 'Or have you learned some new stayspell to achieve what both of us know is impossible?'

'Be still!' Lirenda glanced over her shoulder, annoyed, since the echoes made voices carry. 'And be grateful. The deception was necessary to spare you and the boy from another attack by men bent on bloody revenge.'

'We were holding our own down here well enough.' Elaira gripped the barred steel with blanched knuckles. 'Why don't you do the right thing and rescue us.'

Lirenda stepped back, half turned to depart. 'Don't test my tolerance, and don't build a mission on false hope. Tonight, Morriel has arranged a diversion to sidetrack Sethvir and the Fellowship. Her instructions to me were explicit. Fionn Areth's the set bait for a spring trap to flush out Arithon s'Ffalenn. If the Shadow Master comes to prevent the execution, we'll have him the moment he crosses my wards on the city walls.'

Within the freezing enclosure of her palanquin, Morriel Prime savored her moment of deep satisfaction. Every pawn in the play she had arranged for years awaited in place for her end game.

'All lies in readiness.' With her left hand splayed over the Skyron crystal, she lifted her right and whisked the silk veil off the Waystone. Violet glints spiked her jet eyes as she flicked a peremptory finger at the seeress. 'Once I have aligned the focus of the amethyst, you will disperse my set signal. As the initiate enchantresses in our order assume deep trance and align their powers to my cause, you must bide. Maintain the protective circles I have set. For as long as you are consciously aware, *let nothing and no one intervene.*'

'Your will,' said the seeress, sobered to reticence and stripped of desire to question Morriel's grand conjury. If the clandestine whispers of rumor were true, and time had driven the Matriarch insane, the sigils of prime power made her position unassailable. No ranking senior dared gainsay her will. The individual who confronted the issue with inquiry would court a sure course of destruction.

Too late, now, to foment a rebellion. Morriel woke the Great Waystone.

Minutes crawled by, measured by the throaty rasp of Selidie's sleeping breaths. Outside, the wind moaned over bare rocks and tossed the limbs of the conifers. Snow settled soundlessly into the hollows, winnowed into ribbed drifts. If there were owls, they hunted in silence.

Denser stillness gripped the close quarters of the palanquin, where Morriel poised, her right hand capping the faceted sphere of the amethyst Waystone. Strain dragged the pleats at the corners of her mouth. Sweat stippled the bone polish of her brow. The sinews of her neck tautened to the drag of each exhalation, and her fingers were clenched, rigid claws. Her invisible battle of will with the jewel stretched the stillness like a mute scream of agony.

Then the threshold was past. The spat flare of fires in the depths of the amethyst subsided and burned into a malevolent spark. Morriel opened lightless, dark eyes. She spoke, monotoned as a dreamer. 'Now. Call the names of our initiates, one by one. Through the channel of the Waystone, the strength of our order shall be forged into a single, honed instrument.'

The seeress gripped her scrying sphere in hands that would not stop shaking. She began the lengthy, arduous task of unreeling her talents again and again through the hammered lens of her discipline. When the roll call was done, dawn leaked gray light through the flaps of the palanquin's tied curtains. The taper had burned to a rufous glint, and the stale scents of mandrake mingled with the musk of spent tienelle and tobacco smoke.

Morriel Prime sat in her nest of piled cushions, eyes unseeing and open. Right and left hands rested yet on the focal channels of two crystals, with her frail body in linkage between them. The Great Waystone twined the given talents of thousands of enchantresses into one. Upon that cold flux, the Prime imposed her given will. She had no sentimental attachment to Athera; on the contrary, the viability of any one planet became an expendable resource. Break the compact and the covenant of Paravian preservation, and mankind could reclaim its interdicted knowledge and remanifest the technologies of star travel.

Taut as a crouched predator, Morriel framed the rune of beginning. Given impulse and direction, the surge of held power pulsed into the Skyron aquamarine. From there, impetus carried the flow onward into the corded meshes of the lace tied in seal after seal of configured chaos. Light bloomed and blazed down each knotted binding, the feathers recaptured the energies in resonance. Their thin, silvered auras pulsed a dull, heavy red. The power channeled on, conducted through spelled wire, to garrote the clay construct ritually created to stand proxy for the world of Athera.

'Now,' Morriel whispered. 'Now, now, *now!*' Her voice broke on a cracked note of triumph. 'Let Sethvir of Althain know the cost of his meddling and suffer ruination for all time!'

Each ongoing second, power charged the array, hissing into a flash point of stained light. Heat washed back, wrapped in a stressed note of sound that climbed outside the limits of hearing. As forced witness on the sidelines, the seeress cried out, sweat commingled with her salt tears. Bound by the order's oath of obedience, she could not intervene as the Prime Matriarch's construct seized the flux of the planet's magnetics and drove their staid frequencies into a raging explosion of chaos.

The small upsets struck first: birds and fish and great turtles in the seas lost their homing instinct and the inborn knowledge of their spawning grounds. Climate recoiled into aberrated cyclones of weather. Worse things cascaded into ruin as the vortex fanned through Athera's aura. The sharp, static burst disrupted harmonic balance. The frequency shift smashed every delicate tie in those wards held in stasis by Fellowship guardians.

In the seeress's lap, the quartz sphere she had forgotten recorded the first toll of damages. In Tysan, black Khadrim took flight in a gusty storm of wing leather and flew free of the Sorcerers' Preserve. Other fell creatures in Mirthlvain's dark mire stirred and blinked, awake for the first time in centuries.

The last image the crystal imprinted showed Sethvir before the cluttered table in Althain Tower's library, his bare feet inundated by a cascade of books, tossed pens, and torn papers. Across the space just swept clean with indiscriminate haste, the Sorcerer chalked row after row of swift ciphers. If his hand was not steady, his art was infallible. The spells he commanded bloomed and burned in straight lines, their withering light raised to hold eighteen grimwards secure through Morriel's firestorm of deranged lane force.

Then the scrying sphere shattered. Shards of quartz flew like daggers. Flung fragments ripped with lethal force, and killed the seeress where she sat at her post.

# Backlash

Shaken awake by a drastic shift in the tuned awareness of his mage-sight, Asandir leaves the safe shelter of Kieling Tower and sprints through the spirit-haunted ruin of Ithamon to engage the power focus; by the ranging imbalance sensed through his feet, he knows he has scarcely minutes to bind the fifth lane energies back to harmony before their magnetic alignment becomes snarled beyond hope of recovery . . .

On guarded watch in the airless deeps of interstellar space, Kharadmon answers the flaring damage which blooms over the continent of Paravia; he leaves at once, his destination Methisle, where the spellbinder Verrain sends his beleaguered distress cry, warning of hordes of roused drake spawn; while Luhaine descends into the deep rift beneath South Sea to prevent a destabilized fault line from collapsing . . .

Within a hostel of Ath's Brotherhood, under trees whose soaring heights extend across the veil of the mysteries, the adept who keeps watch cries out in blind pain as the water in the sacred pool darkens to tarnish, and while the animals and birds who inhabit the glade flee and vanish to a rustle of foliage, she sees images: of fissures that blast gaping holes through the innate balance of the world . . .

# XII. Dire Portents

S tatic discharge set off by the imbalanced lane flux hurled white chains of lightning across the night sky the length and breadth of the continent. In the absence of overcast, the forks spat and flared against the jewel-strung brilliance of Athera's winter constellations. Sleepers awakened by the actinic bursts responded with fear and dismay. Where storms masked the view, or sifting snowfall sheeted the hollows in trackless mantles of white, the jagged flares threw an eerie, diffused light over the snow-clad landscape.

Nor did those ranging, skewed crests of vibration escape notice, even beneath Athera's surface. Under the knife peaks at the heart of the Mathorn Mountains, far removed from the smoking, white veils of the blizzards that mantled the swept granite cornices, Kewar Tunnel spiraled downward into the bewildering maze of deep caverns cut by the refined forces of spellcraft and a genius command of grand conjury. There, the unquiet spirit of Davien the Betrayer had withdrawn in adamant solitude. Nor had he emerged throughout the ongoing span of his self-imposed exile from the Fellowship.

No living spirit had broken his isolation for over five hundred years. Sethvir's intermittent, polite messages went unanswered. Davien himself made no overtures. He refused all outside company. His presence walked lightly on the face of creation, a trace resonance so slight, Athera herself scarcely carried the imprinted signature of his presence.

Whether the Sorcerer had built etheric walls out of seals and wards of his making, or whether he had turned his awareness inward, or let himself fade through attrition, none knew. His nature had never been quiet or retiring, nor his work, which had fomented the rebellion that overthrew the old order and dethroned the five chosen high kings. For that act of violence, made against the will of the other six Fellowship sorcerers, he had received his due hour of censure. In recognition of the damages caused by his hand, he had been rendered discorporate through a ceremonial destruction of the flesh. Since then, his colleagues had granted their strict respect to his right to private withdrawal.

His retirement was made by the dictates of free choice, which the Law of the Major Balance held sacrosanct.

None knew if the Betrayer retained any interest at all in the passage of events on the continent. His presence had been neither seen nor felt. The four seasons turned one into the next, and became years; passing years piled up into decades, which became centuries, without sign of remission or change. Davien made no effort to mend long-standing differences. He asked for no reconciliation. On the hour Morriel's meddling cast Athera's lane forces into imbalance, the Black Rose Prophecy, which offered the sole promise of hope, lay entangled in the knot of the Teir's'Ffalenn's life thread. The fated resolution of the Fellowship's schism still hinged upon Arithon's free acceptance of a royal birthright he rejected with every fiber of conscious awareness.

Whether or not Davien knew such an augury existed, or whether he cared to reconnect with outside events, the bursting chaos wrought by Morriel's banespell rocked the black depths of his refuge. Kewar's chains of caverns lay in alignment with the natural flux of the fourth lane. Earth and stone resounded to the snarl of torn energies, until the glassy, still stands of underground water shivered into rebounding ripples of stress. Stalagmites cracked and fell, exploding to fragments of limestone and calcite. Stones rolled into fissures; in the geothermal vents, the mud in the hot springs boiled and spat brine and sulfurous fumes.

Far beneath the bedrock strata of the mountains, under the layers of petrified sediment where Davien had fashioned Kewar Tunnel and its range of reactive mazes, not every secretive, subterranean hollow had been formed by natural forces.

In a sealed, round chamber seven furlongs underground, a branching spring welled up and fed into the roaring spate of the watercourse that emerged into daylight at the mouth of the River Aiyenne. Here, where the structural language of minerals had reigned supreme since the dawn of Athera's existence, that trickling flow had been reforged by grand conjury into a pool rimmed with engraved stone knotwork and minuscule chains of linked ciphers. No artistry with hammer and chisel had fashioned such intricate patterns. Complex, interwoven lines of geometry ran like song and light through the carving. The dynamic resonance instilled through their presence was direct, and material, and yet, like the untamed flow of primal energy, the currents had no definitive beginning and no end. The self-sustained emanation of radiance crossed the veil into mystery: a chord that climbed the scale of vibration and ranged beyond the upper limits of hearing, then reemerged in the octaves of visible light, only to vanish into the refined frequencies past all reach of mortal senses.

The chamber had been created in the painful years after Davien was first rendered discorporate. Existence as pure spirit galled him to bitter frustration. The intricate artistry set into grained stone, the puzzles of interlocked ciphers that had once been the delight of his handiwork were no longer so facile to produce. Balked by the loss of his physical form, Davien had not been thwarted by inconvenience. His penchant for cleverness was in fact the product of wild-card genius; he owned determination, but not patience, and though to the eye of an outside observer, such a fine point might seem insignificant, the masterful innovation that had rechanneled the spring into a construct of grand conjury represented decades of brute labor and a monumental pinnacle of achievement.

No torch burned within that cylindrical structure. The walls were mirror-polished granite, and the ceiling, a mathematically perfect parabola that refigured sound into a needle's point focus. Built without entry or exit, the space was not lightless. Soft illumination rippled over the walls, bearing the imprint and signature of water. The chill, clear flow welled up and spilled in soft, sheeting melodies over the wrought framework of ciphers which, in turn, flared and burned with electromagnetic discharge. Nor was the trapped pocket of air stale or stagnant. A tight, contained draft spindled and swirled an invisible course of agitation. Now and again, a white spark would arc from an unseen origin and snap out above the tireless cascade of clear water.

Then the soft light that rinsed the stone walls would shift into mazed colors, rainbow hues split into irregular patterns like jostled shards of stained glass. An image would bloom on the surface of the pool, recaptured in simultaneity from an event that occurred on the surface world outside . . .

Night winds moaned over the wilds of Camris, battering man and beast, and lashing through bundled mantles and gloves to sear naked skin without mercy. The men chosen to accompany Lysaer s'Ilessid had spared no time to gather field tents and equipment when the travel-stained horseman first clattered into Erdane, bringing breathless word that a man bearing the Shadow Master's description had been seen abroad in Daenfal.

With minimal provisions and a skilled headhunter's scout to guide them cross-country, they made hasty arrangement to meet an oared boat at a remote cove on the northcoast. Now en route to that rendezvous, the Blessed Prince and his handpicked cadre of officers camped as they could in the open. The glacier-scarred plain of Camris fell under interdict by the compact, preserved without habitation or footpaths. Shallow dales and scrub-clothed downslands offered browsing for wild deer, but no feature of natural cover. Except for the field tent pitched to shelter the Divine Prince, men lay wrapped in their cloaks, snatching sleep in the hollow carved through an old moraine by the flow of a frozen watercourse. When the sharp, bursting discharge of stressed lane forces spat branch lightning across the starry arc of the sky, the Alliance Lord Commander, who was the blood son of Hanshire's mayor, stood his assigned turn keeping watch. No man to panic in the face of dire spellcraft, Sulfin Evend clenched his jaw. He cursed in his precise, patrician accent, his sculptured fist clamped on his sword. Townborn though he was, eight summers spent with Etarra's league of headhunters had changed him. His brisk stride back toward the banked coals of the fire fell almost without sound in the brush. When his cautious word at the flap of Prince Lysaer's tent raised no answer, he snapped back the canvas and ducked inside. The bedding that should have sheltered the Divine Prince lay unused, the thick blankets still rolled and lashed to the rings on the saddle pack.

Sulfin Evend slapped his thigh, irritated, and abandoned the empty tent. Overhead, another actinic flare traced the heavens, sharp as snagged wire, but unpartnered by the expected percussion of thunder. The sky was black crystal, unmarred by mist or cloud. The stars burned unsullied, though the bitter, north gusts hissed and snagged in queer eddies, thrashing the bared twigs in drumming bursts that unmoored the last paper-dry leaves. The unsettled horses stamped on their picket lines and blew in high, nervous snorts. Braced against the buffeting elements, the Alliance Lord Commander reached the fireside, found the officer appointed as his second-in-command, and jabbed his toe into the man's mounded blankets. The officer shot awake, barraged with his superior's fast-paced instructions to rouse the camp and stand steadfast. 'Once Lysaer's found, we'll have orders.'

'Do you think—' began the captain, broken off through an uneasy glance skyward at the etched flare of turquoise that sheeted the stars overhead. The display was too hard-edged to be mistaken for a seasonal display of aurora borealis.

'Don't think,' Sulfin Evend corrected him, brisk. 'Just act. Roust everyone else and get them busy. I want the horses saddled and ready.' He straightened, each movement spiked to volatile impatience. 'If the portents we see are signals of threat or some other work of dark sorcery, the Blessed Prince will be saying where he expects us to march.'

Too disciplined to argue, the captain groped in the dark for his weapons and strapped on his studded sword belt. 'The guide out of Erdane might bolt when he sees this.'

'Well, tie him down here and now if you're worried! I don't want mistakes or unnecessary fuss.' Sulfin Evend spun away from the warmth of the coals. Despite the rough ground, he moved with oiled speed. The light set to his carriage reflected the instinctive, neat balance of a man who wore steel with killing experience. He paused only once to assess his surroundings. Spinning wind devils kicked through the brush. Deep in the night, a wolf howled. Shown no obvious visual sign to provide his search with direction, he bent and read the frost-silvered grass for traces of Lysaer's footsteps.

A tentative touch on his forearm made him start. He whirled, sword half-drawn, every muscle tensed to fight.

'Peace,' lisped a whisper-thin voice from the dark.

Caught back just in time from striking on reflex, Sulfin Evend confronted the shadowy form of the sunwheel priest attached with the officers of the company. Faint starlight drizzled thin glints of reflection over the six chains of rank yoking his high, cowled collar. 'I know where to look for his Blessed Grace.'

'Damn you, man!' Sulfin Evend shook off the priest's womanish clasp, his aggression clipped back to disgust. 'Creep up from behind, quiet as all that, and you're lucky not to get skewered.' As another flare of blue streaked the sky overhead, he tightened his mailed fist at his sword hilt. 'I hate riddles, as well. You say you know where to look, then get moving.'

The initiate priest laced bony hands over the woven gold cincture at his waist. He bowed without word. On uncanny, soft footsteps, he then led the way, his expression recessed in the voluminous cloth of the hood that obscured his gaunt features. Sulfin Evend disliked that habit of dress. Always, he distrusted a man who would not look him squarely in the eye.

Thin and gangling as a stick puppet beneath his lush robe, the priest picked a fussy path through clawing thorns and wind-stunted furze toward the rise of the neighboring hillock. A birch copse crowned the crest. Spindly trunks slashed the gloom like blotched bones snagged in a grave shroud of shadow. Beneath the black spokes of winter-stripped branches, Lysaer s'Ilessid stood alone.

Clad all in white, he seemed an ephemeral form stamped on the stark face of darkness. Whatever odd whim had made him withdraw from the circle of human company, he was not averse to interruption. As the sound of oncoming footsteps broke his solitude, he turned his head, and Light bloomed around him in welcome.

He greeted both arrivals by name. 'Sulfin Evend, Jeriayish.' Above his golden, haloed presence, another sheeting flare of static branched and faded into an eerie, cobalt violet. The discharge subsided back to starry night, cloaked in disarming tranquillity. A stray gust rattled the bare tree limbs and shivered through the frost-spangled underbrush, there and gone as Lysaer's gesture encompassed the settled arch of clear sky. 'The hour brings us fell portents.'

Sulfin Evend raised his eyebrows, taken aback by the explosive anger he sensed dammed behind the Divine Prince's disarming civility. 'You're surprised? How often you've said the works of true evil never carry the stamp of convenience. I have men back in camp awaiting your orders.'

'Would that I had definite orders to give them.' Lysaer's masked rage burned the more fiercely for the fact he was caught at odds in an untenanted wilderness. With no target at hand, and no other distraction of state crisis, he could not ease his hard-driving urge to eradicate sorcery and destroy the Master of Shadow. The current balked state became as raw salt on an open sore of frustration. 'The rotten truth,' Lysaer said, bitter. 'Fell powers are afoot without any doubt, and at the one moment I've gone beyond reach of town messengers. The minion of Darkness himself could not choose a better moment to disadvantage me. One cursed stroke of timing has just undone the painstaking work of two decades!'

'We're still bound for Daenfal?' Sulfin Evend pressed, his stalker's instinct aroused by the implied upset to long-range, secretive plans. Left uninformed, denied the sure insight to lend strategic backing and guidance, he waited in coiled stillness, his question dangling unanswered.

'Suppose Arithon s'Ffalenn chose this hour to unleash his sorceries on the continent?' This once oblivious to his Lord Commander's razor scrutiny, the Divine Prince almost lost to the tormented urge to pace the ground in obsessive agitation. 'Such a man would scarcely allow himself to be seen, except by intended design. At first, I expected the reported sighting at Daenfal would resolve as a case of mistaken identity. Now, I'm not sure. The event may have been set up as a blind to draw me away from Avenor.' A tight gesture of defiance encompassed the heavens, lit now by the adamantine glitter of winter constellations. 'The fact major sorcery has reared up in portents drastically rearranges priorities. If Arithon s'Ffalenn has returned, he'd bid to make use of our weaknesses.' In the rapt intensity of the instant's blind passion, Lysaer's veneer of majesty cracked through. Voice and bearing this once revealed his vibrant base feeling: not fear, not concern born of righteous distress, but the focused rage born out of pride and a stinging, personal defeat. 'Avenor will panic without my protection, and *I'm not there to capture the plum as the tree shakes.*'

Struck to deep insight that prickled his nape, Sulfin Evend stared at the prince before him. His keen glance read a frustrated anguish few men alive ever witnessed. He said, cool and neutral through a shocked leap of epiphany, 'You meant all along to use the s'Brydion clan as your game piece to trigger the selfsame reaction?'

That turned Lysaer's head and earned a considered, sharp stare from the cowled priest who stood in dispassionate quiet on the sidelines.

By faint starlight, Lysaer's face held a chiseled, ice sculpture symmetry that momentarily eschewed every trace of human emotion. 'Dame Dawr's affray with the priesthood was pardoned after Duke Bransian wrote us a formal apology.'

Sulfin Evend said nothing.

The chill darkness became weighted by his charged expectation, and something more sinister, a thread of deep and dangerous concealment, treacherous as the current that sucked through the weir of an unruffled millpond. Prince Lysaer brazened out that nailing regard, silent, while the wind snarled and whistled through the scrub in the gully, and the blossoming star of a firebrand traced the movements of the men who broke camp.

Since Sulfin Evend had never backed down from a challenge, Jeriayish finally relented. 'Given firm-handed guidance, and the right crisis as inspiration, Tysan's rich guilds would have emptied their treasuries. We'd hoped to fund a fortress and garrison as ambitious as the one now under construction at Etarra.'

The Alliance Lord Commander sucked back a snort of amazement. He regarded the white-clad avatar before him, his perception jarred to cynical reassessment. 'Then you've been outflanked by surprise? Of course, in hindsight, an upset of this magnitude would convince a guild with no fighting arm to pledge every resource to stand on the side of the Light.' The censure that followed was delivered with the same, distanced ring of soft irony. 'Still, that can't excuse the hard facts. In pandering to guild greed for a future gamble, you've left a whole kingdom exposed and all but defenseless.'

The glance Lysaer s'Ilessid fixed on his Lord Commander revealed a grim depth of honesty. 'Fear has its uses. As the powers of darkness exploit our vulnerabilities, shall we foolishly spurn the same tools? Too much lies at stake. We face an enemy who threatens the stability of the world.' His acute, inward conflict spurred his fury as he added his bald-faced endorsement to the priest's veiled hint of conspiracy. 'Naturally, I would have preferred to arrange a safe means to rock the proverbial boat.'

Level steel in adherence to the letter of sworn duty, Sulfin Evend asked again for his orders.

Yet Lysaer clamped tortured fists to his temples, still agonized by indecision. Whatever fell power had crafted this setback, its immediate impact would outpace his most careful expectations.

'I dare not return to reap the rewards I have ripened through years of patience and planning,' the Blessed Prince confessed. His cry for vindication flawed his conviction as he added, 'Nor can I fail to rise to the gauntlet thrown down by tonight's fell round of portents.' As the world's given gift to cleanse darkness and sorcery, he could not disregard the real chance that now, innocent lives stood at risk. Wrung by a passion that raged to shed blood, Lysaer finished, '*I dare not miscall how the Master of Shadow will use his power to unbalance us.*'

The choice of which coast to guard had passed beyond compromise already, with snowfall choking the high passes. Winter storms would allow them no second alternative. Sulfin Evend could assess the logistics well enough. Either their handpicked strike force of officers turned tail now and took the river route through Korias to reach Avenor the long way. Or they committed to go on and cross Instrell Bay and make landfall in Rathain before ice locked the northern strait that would give them swift access to Atainia.

The thin priest skirted the issue of lapsed morals with delicacy, 'If tonight's events are connected with the reported sighting in Daenfal, your Grace fears the worse threat will arise in the east?'

Lysaer tipped his face skyward. His posture strung taut by a need that poisoned the very marrow of his commitment, he admitted, 'I fear so, but what if I'm wrong? Avenor and all of Tysan must stand or fall upon the wisdom of an aging crown seneschal and the word of High Priest Cerebeld. As Athera's given power to defend against Shadow, *I cannot afford to miscalculate the site where the Spinner of Darkness will strike.*'

While Sulfin Evend looked on with veiled eyes and masked thoughts,

Jeriayish bowed again. The sunwheel priest's tone raised a silken whisper against the tireless whine of the gusts. 'Blessed Prince, I have been trained to serve. The way exists to find out . . .'

Within the sealed chamber fashioned by conjury beneath the stone mazes of Kewar, a spark of light scalded down and poised in the air above the image reflected in the pool. An answering flicker played through the rune patterns incised into rock underneath. Through a queer, tensioned second, the tall, ascetic figure of a man appeared to lean over the burgeoning ripple of springwater. He wore a leather doublet the burnt orange color of autumn leaves, and a shirt with crisp, pleated sleeves tied at the wrist with braided sable laces. His hair fell shoulder length, a tumble of frost-streaked russet. The planes of his face were ascetic, shaped flint, and his foxy chin was clean-shaven.

His hand rested wrist deep in the pool. The narrow fingers were an artist's, long and flexibly capable. Ripples flowed over a cast, silver ring inset with a citrine, and carved with three interlocked crescents that framed the sign of the moon.

Dark, shrewd eyes surveyed the image still held in suspended reflection: of a blond prince caught in the crux of duplicity as the geas of the Mistwraith's curse collided with the dictates of conscience, and again, deflected Athera's future. On the cusp of resolve, before Lysaer s'Ilessid sealed his consent to his priest in the hinterlands of north Camris, the enigmatic figure by the pool far under the Mathorn Mountains straightened up from absorbed contemplation. He raised a wet hand. Droplets scattered to the brisk snap of his fingers. The bright spark of intent poised over the pool flickered out. The scrying erased, and took with it the imprinted form of the watcher.

The softened play of the light that arose in formation as the water rippled over the channeling course of the rune patterns did not stay unpartnered for long; another spark descended. The next summoned image formed in the pool. This one reflected another incident within the closed walls of Avenor . . .

Couched alone in silk sheets in the royal apartments, Princess Ellaine stirred to the sliding rustle of bed curtains. Urgent hands prodded her. She was forced awake despite the unconscious need to remain lost in oblivious dreaming. 'My lady? Your Grace? You'll want to arise.'

Ellaine opened her eyes, aware all at once that the handmaid's determination held fear. She pushed erect amid a silken slither of comforters and hooked tangled hair from her face. The room was still dark. No candles burned but the one in the pricket gripped in her handmaid's trembling fingers. 'What's amiss?'

A ghostly presence in the wan flicker of flame light, the woman's generous features were pinched into terrified pallor. 'Dread sorcery, madam.' Her jerked, distraught gesture encompassed the night window, cracked across by an unseasonal flare of lightning. The bright discharge burst and died without sound; no report of shocked air reechoed and pealed into a barrage of natural thunder.

'Light's mercy upon us!' The maid shuddered and wailed. 'Folk say the Spinner of Darkness is returned!'

'Hush,' Ellaine snapped. 'You don't know that for certain.' She kicked free of her blankets and stood up. Winter's drafts bit through the fine lace of her night rail, and the icy tiles underfoot set her shivering. 'I'll need to dress. Then send for Gace Steward. If we're being visited by some harbinger of disaster, my son must be seen at my side.'

When the maid wrung her hands in paralyzed dread, Ellaine lost her poise to impatience. 'Attend me, at once!' She padded to her wardrobe, too distressed to observe the everyday grace of courtly propriety. 'Avenor has need of its ruling family before panic sets in on the streets.'

Yet as fast as she donned formal clothes and state mantle, Avenor's High Priest had acted in step to forestall her. One of his obsequious sunwheel acolytes barged into her apartment as she swept from her darkened bedchamber.

His bow to acknowledge her station was grudging and brutishly rushed. 'Lady Ellaine, his eminence, High Priest Cerebeld, has called for an assembly of the council. He requires your presence for form's sake and reassurance, but Avenor's seneschal will preside.'

'Where's my son?' Ellaine demanded, her tense hands folded into the shimmering silk of the skirt she reserved for ceremonial appearances. Her firm bearing suggested she would let no one's plans disrupt her immediate priority. 'I'll go nowhere and do nothing until I'm assured Prince Kevor will sit at my side.'

The sunwheel acolyte assumed the role of royal escort unasked and clasped her elbow above her caped sleeve. 'The young prince's servants are dressing him now. His attendance will be necessary to assuage the false rumor that Prince Lysaer has abandoned the regency.'

At fourteen, young Kevor had grown beyond such limited use as a figurehead, but Ellaine saw little point to be gained in bandying words on that issue. She let the acolyte's curt tug usher her down the corridor, while the tall, lancet windows on either side flickered to another show of uncanny lightning. The wax candles lit at dusk had been left to burn low, their blown glass sconces shaded to umber with soot. The feeble flicker of the last, spent wicks became overwhelmed by the discharge that sparked in blue forks overhead. Dawn would not break for another three hours, and the moonless night showed no threatening wall of cloud or the combed cirrus of an approaching squall line.

'What's happened?' Ellaine demanded. 'Does Cerebeld know? Or will we be maintaining a brave front at Avenor in the absence of my royal husband?'

Turned down the gleaming marble corridor that led to the vaulted state chambers, the priest's glance held harried exasperation. 'His eminence, the High Priest, says there's been an attack of fell sorcery. What we see are the discharged effects of that imbalance.'

'Lysaer's at Erdane,' Princess Ellaine pointed out, determined to outface the man's patronizing attitude. She could not remedy the fact that Gace Steward cut off her best links to those informants who were versed on state interests and politics. 'His royal Grace could intercede.'

'No longer.' The sunwheel servant paused, while two guardsmen in royal colors flung open the arched door to the council hall's anteroom. 'The sky's a fell portent, forewarning a change. Cerebeld has received divine word that the Spinner of Darkness intends a return to the continent. The Blessed Prince has already gathered his best officers. They've pressed east with all speed to cross Instrell Bay and call a muster of arms to challenge the enemy.'

A stunned, hollow feeling slammed through Ellaine's gut. She quashed her instinctive response to ask questions, less successful with the small lines of worry that pleated her forehead. 'Then Lysaer won't return to stand guard at Avenor?' The rejection stung yet, that the blood ties of family never bound the man to his marriage. Cut off from her Erdani kinfolk, Ellaine could but mourn and strive for adult understanding. If moral zeal had sealed Lysaer's heart from affection, other loyalties should not be disregarded. His son was here, as well as the guildsmen and merchants who had been first to swear fealty to Tysan's restored monarchy.

Yet matters of Shadow were Lysaer's born cause to pursue. As the mother of his heir, Ellaine tried to eschew sentiment in favor of hard practicality. 'Our winter garrison scarcely offers us an adequate defense if our people believe these queer signs in the sky foretell an assault wrought of sorcery.'

'Then our faith must sustain us. Or was the Blessed Prince not sent to Athera to oppose such unclean practice?' Cerebeld's priest produced keys to unlock the royal entry, which allowed direct access to the high dais with its gilt-and-white chairs of state.

Ellaine had no chance to wonder how he had come to acquire such privilege. The common floor of the hall was already packed with the realm's ranking dignitaries, showing the disheveled signs of being rousted from bed. No doubt some had been called untimely from the arms of the courtesans they kept in cosseted luxury. Plumed hats slid askew, and aiglets dangled from half-laced points. Clamorous voices locked in shrill argument and rocked echoes off the hall's vaulted ceiling. The court herald blasted a quavering fanfare to announce the princess's arrival. His trumpet passed unheard. Everyone appeared to be shouting at once. The thin voice of the realm's aged seneschal was disregarded as the buzz of a bothersome gnat.

Ellaine gave the scene a raking, fast glance. The observant few courtiers who noticed her presence dismissed her with preoccupied contempt. Fired to rare annoyance, the princess ripped off her gold crown. She raked the rim in clattering dissonance over the gold-embossed arm of the regent's chair. As heads turned, she cried out, 'I'm ashamed! Are we frightened schoolboys masquerading as men when the realm stands in need of strong counsel?'

The harsh edge to the tumult subsided, as much from surprise and embarrassment. Ellaine granted that reprieve little quarter. 'We have sound walls! I hear no armed enemy battering our gates, nor do I see a war host outside equipped with rams and siege engines. I have seen lightning, but where is the sorcerer? Our prince has marched east to raise arms against Shadow. Is our courage pinned to his shirttails to the point where Avenor's high officials can do nothing else but cower and wail over threats that have yet to be manifest!'

A cosseted merchant with a Northerly accent puffed up and took spluttering umbrage. 'But my Lady, the portents—'

The princess cut him short. 'The portents are a warning! Wise men would not waste themselves arguing, but use what time we are given to prepare. Where is Lord Eilish? Has anyone sent for the captain of the watch? Let those two come forward and start with an accurate list of Avenor's trained men and resources.'

A gruff voice arose from the rear of the chamber. 'Garrison captain's already here.'

Ellaine took charge before the crown seneschal could seize opening to force her aside. 'Let him pass!'

Sweating guild ministers and agitated merchants made way for the heavyset officer who answered the princess's summons. He carried a field helm tucked under his elbow; his ceremonial sash with its sunwheel insignia had been left aside in a rush that left time for only his daggers and baldric. Hemmed in by the fretful packs of courtiers who still jammed the dais stair, he squared his shoulders and delivered his report from floor level. 'Princess, an unruly throng jams the square, chanting for Lysaer of the Light. Every guardsman we have who's fit to bear arms has turned out to form cordons at the gate. They carry standing orders to hold their ground in the event sweeping panic should cause an assault on the palace.'

'Has a company been detailed to barricade the guildhalls?' The crown seneschal elbowed his way to the fore, his leathery, hound's jowls livid pink.

'If iron locks won't stop trouble, armed men can't either.' Ellaine faced down the wiry old man, this once determined to wield the prerogative of her rank. 'I will not authorize our city garrison to draw steel against our own terrified people!'

The incredulous yelp of a trade minister cut her off. 'You'd risk the realm's wealth to riot and looters?'

Scarcely aware of the door that opened and closed at her back, Ellaine drew breath, without words. She clenched dampened hands, shamed for the fact she had no shining gift for inspired leadership. The despair became suffocating, that she saw no foothold to grapple rank greed. All the years Lysaer's policy had catered to self-interest had defined Avenor's solidarity. Confronted by courtiers decked out in the ostentatious, jeweled trappings of their arrogance, she sensed their dog pack readiness to tear down any obstacle between them and their threatened security. Ellaine tensed, made aware she lacked the authoritative stance to checkrein such ruthless hostility. As the disgruntled mutters from the chamber gathered force, she realized how gravely she had miscalculated the potential for uprising inside Avenor's headstrong royal court. One move, one word wrong, and two decades of crown rule could be torn down in a flash-fire outburst of mass hysteria.

Yet before the moment's impetus crossed the line into violence, someone interceded in a steady baritone that struck a clear note of reassurance. 'Honest folk don't panic unless they are given no direction, and are left with nothing to do.'

Ellaine turned her head, astonished at how closely that tone matched the gifted, state poise of Lysaer s'Ilessid himself.

Yet the one who had spoken was not the Blessed Prince. Reed slender, clad in the crown and star blazon of Tysan, and a mantle with a sunwheel emblem, the newcomer assumed position at Ellaine's right hand. His hair was red-gold, not shining blond. The ringless fingers that clasped hers were awkward and large, like the paws of a tiger cub not yet come into the power and grace of maturity. Set against the polished gleam of long-stemmed candelabra, white wainscoted walls, and the rich tinseled backdrop of tapestries, he was raw youth bearing the unmistakable stamp of generations of royal ancestry.

Before the gaping city counselors and high realm officials stupefied to amazement, Ellaine was first to recover herself. 'Prince Kevor.' She swept into a curtsy that forced even the most stiff-necked state ministers to recall their lapsed form and propriety. They bowed before the royal heir who would one day assume crown rule over them.

Child no longer, Lysaer's son at fourteen had taken a leap toward his manhood seemingly overnight. His smile acknowledged his mother's support and melted her heart for its depth of adult sincerity. Then, restored to formality, he released her hand and addressed Avenor's belligerent courtiers. 'Our princess speaks sound sense. Force of arms is no use when the people are frightened. Too likely the first fool who lost his head would incite them to needless bloodshed.'

'How else to avert mayhem?' The cantankerous seneschal stabbed a bony finger toward the massive, closed doors of the council hall. 'The rabble out there isn't rational or calm. In case you hadn't noticed on your way from your bed, there are mounted guardsmen with lances keeping a pack of enraged tradesmen from storming in here for protection. They fear they'll be slaughtered by Fellowship Sorcerers. Right or wrong, they won't pause to hear pretty speeches before they start hurling bricks! If we don't use the armed guard to hold them in line, how would you propose to subdue them?'

Prince Kevor crossed the dais with that startling majesty inherent in Tysan's crown lineage. He took the grand chair of state reserved for his father, as Lord Regent, and with perfect aplomb, sat down. 'First of all, that rabble as you call them, are not faceless invaders. They're the same master craftsmen and shopkeepers who form the foundation of Avenor. Let one of them die at the hands of the guard, and I promise, they will become your enemy and mine. Would you risk our prosperity for the sake of a warehouse, or one season's stockpiled profits?'

Amid shouting detractors, one shrill voice prevailed. 'What else can we do but show force when there are maddened men howling murder and rattling our gates?'

Unruffled as though the diadem of high kingship already circled his head, Kevor said, 'I was going to offer to go out to the cupola in the square and ask the faithful to stand forth and light candles. The more flames they show in support of the Blessed Prince, the better the chance their prayers for deliverance will be answered. If the portents continue, we can encourage the belief that their faith is insufficient to enact a divine intervention.'

'Such tactics might work.' The garrison captain rubbed his stubbled chin, thoughtful, and overrode the seneschal's objections. 'Lighting candles will give the folk focus and calm. The organized presence of any group action would pull in the attention of those on the fringes who otherwise might turn to violence.'

Yet the fractious, ribboned ministers adhered to their divisive factions and rejected the strategy out of hand. 'What about safeguarding our guildhalls? If you detail the garrison to look after the young prince—'

'Enough!' Kevor cut them off. His eyes bored into them, arctic blue, and his inborn drive to seek justice charged him to lordly contempt. While the yammering courtiers bridled at his authority, he said, scathing, 'If some of your gold had been turned to the greater good, we would have had more trained men defending our walls! Why should Avenor's populace not fear for their safety? They're not the fools who brought us to this pass.' He went on to use names. 'You, Odrey, that emerald in your thumb ring would have outfitted ten men. Mennis, the gold and ruby buttons on your doublet would have kept our town armorers busy for a year!' Above pealing shouts, Kevor's leveling invective prevailed. 'I dare to suggest that the jewels and bullion adorning your persons could have bridged all our shortfalls long before we found ourselves face-to-face with a crisis!'

While the subjects of his scorn flushed purple and bristled with self-righteous, humiliated outrage, the young prince pressed home his rebuke. 'As for protection, I never asked for armed backing from the city garrison! Princess Ellaine has forbidden force of arms in our streets. Show her due respect and give thanks for her foresight. The word of the Light must prevail over Shadow without the bullying threat of bare steel. I say Avenor's people will honor my lineage. As heir to s'Ilessid, I'll go to the square and take only the two men on duty as honor guards outside the door of my chamber.'

Ellaine choked back fear, that Kevor was young yet to be wearing the mantle of royal authority. Despite his inspired instinct for self-command, he was painfully young. Caught up in heady, adolescent heroics, he might not yet grasp the full impact of possible consequences. If events went amiss and touched off mass panic, he would be offering himself up as a target to assuage the mob's unleashed fury.

Yet to speak even a well-meant warning in public would undercut the firm hand with which he had taken first charge of the authority due him by birthright.

As though he understood his mother's paralyzing worry, Kevor gave her a swift glance and a smile. 'I am Lysaer's son.' His confidence refreshed like new sunshine. 'Who better to send?' The sapphire brooch at his throat shot blue sparks as his raised arm encompassed the press of Avenor's courtiers, still shamed into a seething, flushed stillness. 'I might not have his Grace's powers to wield the blessed Light, but given the choice, our people would prefer to believe his gift will defend them.'

All unwitting, he had lifted the courtiers out of their narrow self-interest. His shining honesty had displaced in one moment the rancors of trade gain and politics. Under the gilt-washed glow of the candles, grown men and elders responded to the rallying cry of Tysan's untried young prince. 'I am the promise of my father's intercession! Let this town see our strength, not our fears of failure. Nor will I be misrepresenting the truth. The Divine Prince's pledge to fight Shadow has called him away to the east. He would not choose his course without solid evidence. Others must stand in far greater danger than we. Let us rise to his trust, that we are equal to the task he has left us! Defense of Avenor is our charge and our duty. Let us stand strong and uphold the Light, as he would, and protect the weak and the helpless!'

Stunned to sudden tears for her pride in Kevor's courage, Princess Ellaine recovered the nerve to wrest back bold initiative. 'Send a man for Gace Steward,' she commanded the seneschal. 'The palace will be providing the candles to encourage the vigil in the square . . .'

Within the sealed chamber deep under the Mathorn Mountains, the spark sustaining the keyhole view of Avenor's council hall flickered out. The water drops spilled in continuous cascade from the blank face of the pool, tinged to softened, hazy light by the ephemeral play of forces that ranged through the interlocked rune patterns. For a handful of seconds, the sheer granite walls mirrored their burnished reflections. Then the quiescent draft flicked to life out of nowhere. More sparks lit and blazed, whirled into flurried, frenetic existence like a madcap swarm of summer fireflies. They fell, a rain of slow-motion fire that excited the pool through a rapid-fire sequence of glimpses: of Cerebeld in his tower, opening a locked chest; of mounted crown messengers dispatched from Erdane to points south; of beacon fires lit to signal unrest at Isaer and Castle Point; of a galley flying a sunwheel banner cleaving a course at war speed through the frigid waves off the coast north of Camris. A return pass showed Prince Lysaer, emerged from his tent slightly pale, but restored to brisk confidence after a private consultation with the priest, Jeriayish. Then the view that did not fit in sequence: of a pack of Khadrim in wheeling flight against a backdrop of stars and forked lightning.

A pause ensued, dense silence filled by the unending ripple of water and the rinsed imprint of light across seamless walls.

The next spark, descending, wore a diamantine scintillance, born out of relentless, hard focus. Its word of command woke an aerial view, high over the volcanic ledges surrounding the mud pots at Teal's Gap. Fir stands and bare rock scabbed the snowy flanks of the foothills, the scarred gulches engraved by solidified lava softened under weak starlight. Against that vast tract of proscribed territory, configured in geometrics like folded lines starched in translucent ribbon, the ring wards demarking the Sorcerers' Preserve glimmered over the landscape. Yet where Asandir's recent work had lately framed a flawless, bright barrier, the erratic lane flux that ranged over Athera wore and stressed the locked seals of his handiwork. As a fresh static discharge ripped across the night sky, the spell boundary threw off a resonant flare of dull red. Wide, snagging gaps were already torn where the damaging range of low-frequency bursts had disrupted the integrity of the spellcraft.

The image was not permitted to fade, but became blasted aside by an arcing explosion of light, this one a hard, electrical blue, and dazzlingly stellar in brilliance. Its call seeded a view of the crumbling Paravian ruin crowning the hill beside Mainmere. Yet even through the imbalance unleashed by a radical deflection of lane force, the stones of the ancient foundation sung to ward by the centaur, Imaury Riddler, remained silent under a velvet tarnish of frost. The rime of thin ice flicked to lit spangles as another discharge of white static raked the darkened sky overhead.

The vision in the pool slowly faded, rubbed to attrition by the flow of cold water until it became thinned to a gossamer cobweb that erased back into the void. The ponderous stillness settled deeper, the unmarked refuge of earth-enclosed darkness braided through by the tremulous trickle of droplets. The dustless space held the tang of wet rock and dissolved limestone; mirror-polished walls abided in the vast patience that endowed ancient granite its strength. Amid the drawn pause, the power of an unseen presence thrashed through a turmoil of conflicted debate.

Then another spark fell, this one a whispered imprint less seen than felt as a tracing of air onto a blank template of existence. Its directive unfolded the vantage of two bubbles of void space, written and defined by the secretive, bound power enchained by Koriani ciphers; one, very small, was sited over the quartz veins in the Skyshiels near the mountain settlement of Eastwall. Larger, more sinister in meddling implication, the other encompassed the entire walled city of Jaelot.

A snap of brisk breeze fanned over the pool, marring the water's limpid surface into a puckered lens of distortion. The lightless maw of the spell-circled town shattered like black glass, then relit to display the spider's web pattern of impact on the course of outside event. Fragmented imagery captured details. A thousand incandescent threads of connection unreeled over the night landscape. The will of the presence that dwelled beneath Kewar selected but three to trace back to their living sources.

The first captured impression showed a bonfire lit in the dockside shanties at Southshire. While white lightning portents snapped across the night sky, a chanting crowd of zealots led by guardsmen wearing sunwheel badges surrounded a ceremonial pyre. The victim for execution was no herb witch, this time, but the demonic straw effigy of a black-haired sorcerer, run through the heart by a rusty billhook and pelted by the screaming onlookers with salvoes of offal and garbage.

The next sequence to be mirrored in the rock pool revealed a desertman elder, crouched muttering on the black sands of Sanpashir. His thrown bones of augury blazed white as another blinding burst sheared through the heavens above him. Yet his voice as he cited his reading was steady. 'Behold the truth! The son of Mother Dark will make landfall at the ruin and go on to try to avert an ill deed and a wrongful shedding of blood on the solstice.'

Last, a lone brigantine flying the leopard blazon of s'Ffalenn heeled on a close-hauled course, bearing due north across the ink waters of South Sea.

Then the pool stilled, singing its trickling melody of droplets within the underground deeps. The rune patterns ceased their manic flare of light. Within that womb of utter blackness, the draft whirled and whispered, restless. Through a taut span of minutes, nothing changed. The presence sealed in the isolate cavern whisked to and fro in unquiet cogitation. Nor could the surrounding earth offer help, or the nurture of grounding comfort. The needling burn of lane imbalance transferred through layered bedrock and caused the water to shiver and rebound through the fissure. The splash of runoff surged and dwindled, erratic, still distressed, but no longer abandoned to the forces of freewheeling chaos.

In the far-distant south, above a rimwall of Vastmark shale, a Sorcerer's raven soared through an intricate pavane of circles. A brilliance of energy trailed from its feathers, and its croaking call resounded through all four of the elements and begged help to renew Athera's upset stability.

The presence in Kewar heard, but did not bestir in response. One last time, the rock pool flared into a shimmer of rainbow light. Yet the final image showed nothing more than the momentary view of a large golden eagle unfurling broad wings and launching into steep, upward flight.

# Resolve

Under the massive, bare oaks of Halwythwood, Earl Jieret, *caithdein* of Rathain, broke out of his sprint and snatched a moment to recover his breath. The deep, hidden glen he chose for the pause was stitched through by a shallow streamlet, laced in glass panes of ice. The young scout who had partnered the extended patrol flashed him a glance of limp gratitude and folded, head down and panting, on the glazed-over bark of a deadfall.

'How much farther?' he gasped to his chieftain.

Jieret glanced sidewards, no less exhausted. Each heaving breath he drew into his lungs knifed through his chest like cold fire. 'Three leagues, maybe.' He leaned on the gnarled trunk standing nearest, his forearm compressed against his left side to ease the nagging, first knot of a cramp. Each second of delay chafed at his overtaut nerves. He adjusted the hang of his deer bow and quiver to free his right arm for his dagger.

Another queer burst of lightning snapped across the dark bowl of the zenith. The discharge affected more than the high atmosphere. With each flaring bolt, Earl Jieret sensed a recoil jolt through the staid earth beneath the hide soles of his boots. The same disturbed current traced an answering prickle up the full length of his spine.

'You don't think that's the sign of a Fellowship working,' stated the scout, perhaps touched to concern by the marked wariness he observed on his chieftain's weathered face, or else moved by the deep-seated instincts inherent in most of the old clan bloodlines.

'No.' Jieret's certainty rang unequivocal. 'Something's amiss. If the Sorcerers are involved, they'll be working to clear the source of imbalance.' He surveyed the frozen wood, locked in a bitter, windless silence, the blown ink tracery of limbs overhead crusted in a thin rime of snow fall. No natural feature appeared out of place. Aside from the marks of their own running footsteps crushed through the crusted ground, yesterday's game trails showed as dimpled imprints where the noon sun had melted the edges. Yet the deep, biting cold that had followed the storm front now and again showed disturbance. A sharp, fitful breeze stirred the high branches. Sudden and oddly contrary in nature, the spinning gyre of air was there and gone before his forest-honed senses could tag its direction. 'We'd best move along.'

The scout arose from his perch on the log. He was duty bound to withhold his complaint, though the snatched interval of rest had scarcely relieved his wrung-out state of fatigue.

'You'll be all right?' Jieret asked, as tired himself, but hagridden by pressing instinct. He could not shake off the overriding sense of some nameless, looming disaster. Though the chain-lightning portents that cracked the night sky had not gained in force or frequency, and the Companion he had chosen to take charge in his absence had well proved his cool head through a crisis, Jieret's mood stayed unsettled. The persistent, gut-deep conviction hung over him, that he stood at the crux of a cataclysm, as though the firmament around him had gone subtly unstable and subject to change without notice. Urgency drove him to near-reckless haste. He burned to rejoin the central encampment that sheltered the clan's elders and young children.

'My wife and daughter are back in camp, too.' The scout slapped clumps of granular snow off his leathers and tightened the looped thong that secured the loose arrows in his quiver. 'I'm ready.'

Yet as Jieret led into his first running step, he cried out, overset and bewildered. The foot that should have struck solid ground seemed to plunge into an abyss of *nothing*. Hurled into sudden, violent vertigo, he heard the scout call his name. Firm hands caught his arm, and still, he was falling. Earth and sky upended and cast him headlong into drowning disorientation. The scout's dismayed cries thickened like felt in his ears, until words became lost into noise that choked out cognitive meaning. Then all his five senses let go into darkness; *he was not in Halwythwood*, but hurled through the heart of a maelstrom and into his gift of Sighted dreaming . . .

As though he looked down from a dizzying height, Jieret beheld the weathered barrens of Daon Ramon, the rocky leagues of deserted scrubland lit dismal gray under a scud of storm clouds. Bitter winds raked over the desolate dales. Driven snow mantled the ice-glazed heads of dead grasses and deepened the mounded drifts already snagged on the twigs of thorn brakes and thickets. Despite the cruel weather, the vista was not empty.

Touched by a prickling surge of foreboding, Earl Jieret beheld ragged companies of armed men braving the unkindly terrain and the freezing barrage of the elements. He could make out no banners. A harsh edge of fear scraped down his nerves, warning of pending danger. The cruel cold of deep winter bit into his lungs, as though his watching presence carried back to the detached awareness of his body. From the eagle's eye vantage lent by the dream, he searched the harsh land, but encountered no sign of opposing forces. Whatever quarry the troops harried in pursuit remained elusively invisible. Lacerated by concern for his people's safety, Jieret swept the thorn brakes and gullies. He combed every secretive cranny where a helpless band of fugitives might seek cover to escape the swords of an enemy war host.

Yet he found nothing hunted. Only more bands of headhunters armed with town steel, relentlessly tracking *something or someone*. The fir-clad mountains on the horizon could have been the rugged, high spur of Skyshiels, or perhaps the white teeth of the Mathorns, which rimmed Daon Ramon to the north. No feature of landscape affirmed the location. The flat murk of the overcast foretold of a blizzard and obscured the subtle, directional clues that might have been gleaned from a sunny day's cast shadows. Every other detail bespoke a massive Alliance invasion. Here, a swarm of support troops dragged laden supply sledges over a snow-covered watercourse. The flat, windswept channel could have been the dry bed of the Severnir, or else the ice-sheeted span of the shallower River Aiyenne, which snaked southward in meandering loops from the verge of the Mathorn Road. Whichever site the augury disclosed, a sunwheel troop captain ordered a lame horse killed to ease the privation of depleted provisions.

The vision forecast a multipronged Alliance campaign, yet yielded no key to unveil its directive.

Tormented by a stabbing, sharp wave of premonition, Earl Jieret cried aloud for the boon of Fellowship guidance. *Someone, somewhere*, would soon be riding a suicidal course toward disaster. Clanblood, or close kindred, he had to know whom. No townborn war host would venture the barrens in winter. Not without threat of dire proportion, or an extreme source of provocation.

Then a sheet of light bloomed; a radiance like a honed blade cut through the dull steel of the overcast. Bearing due eastward another small force of headhunters rode out of Narms, led by Lysaer s'Ilessid himself and a train of specialized officers.

Dreadful certainty jabbed Jieret's vitals. He tasted futility bitter as wormwood. As Rathain's sworn *caithdein*, he understood that innocent blood would stain the snow red unless he gave orders and dispatched steadfast clansmen to stand in the breach.

Against townborn numbers, such defense would cost lives.

His torment tore an animal scream from his throat. 'How do I know the grief of such losses will match the cost of the sacrifice?'

The cry of his heart ripped the dream's continuity. The image of Daon Ramon ran like spilled dye, churned to a whirling blur that burst into a flare of white light. Dazzled blind, struck deaf, Jieret lost all ties to the earth. Shoved through the eye of chaos itself, he sensed the pull of the sorcerer's blood bond he held with Prince Arithon of Rathain. Paradox ripped him, cruel as a jerked wire, *and he knew*: the liege lord who had won his trust like a brother walked into lethal danger . . .

The roaring noise in his ears became the splash of salt spume, sheeted off the bow of a hard-driven brigantine. Wind shrieked in gusts through tarred stays and taut rigging. Yardarms overburdened with close-sheeted canvas transferred the element's raw burden of violence into timbers that bucked and groaned in complaint. The craft's lean hull heeled, shining like foil with runoff. Defiantly flying the royal banner stitched with her leopard namesake, the *Khetienn* sliced northward at reckless speed, the clean lines of her strakes masked in smoking spray at each battering joust with the wavecrests.

The sodden, wrapped figure who manned the rank helm was no less than Arithon, Prince of Rathain. Where two men might have lent him assistance at the wheel, he muscled the pull of the wet spokes alone, drenched to the skin through his oilskins. The tormented flicker of the lamp in the compass seemed a match for his mood as the wind whipped the streaming, rag ends of black hair from the drenched planes of his face.

He turned his head. Something he saw changed his harried expression to a mask of reviling mockery. 'Don't say you came out to get soaked for sheer fun, or are you earnestly expecting to stop me?'

The larger of the two men who approached responded in challenge, his clanborn accent infused with the mild vowels of country East Halla origins. Whether his ancestral background was farming, the hand lightly grasped to his scabbarded sword bespoke a chilling competence.

Arithon hauled the wheel two points to starboard against a pounding gust. 'How touching. Why not use bare fists? As you see, I'm not armed.' He laughed in the teeth of the man's blond companion, who had dared threaten force if he failed to reverse the brigantine's troublesome heading. 'Why trifle with talk? The hour won't wait. If you're going to try bloodshed, you'll need to draw swords. Best finish this well before we make landfall at Sanpashir.' A showering backfall of spray razed the deck. Arithon held his braced stance through the dousing, then resumed his razor-sharp sarcasm. 'On my first step ashore, a half dozen desertmen are sure to be shadowing my back. They'd make my close friends into dart-riddled pincushions, if they ever once thought I was threatened.'

'Your life's not at issue,' said the tall, slender blond man. 'And Vhandon backs up his promises. You should know, since he once broke your leg.'

Arithon's reply came fast as a slap. 'Do the same this time, and an innocent dies screaming.'

'That could be an excuse,' said the gruff, older clansman. 'How can you be certain Desh-thiere's curse hasn't inveigled you onto a path to suicidal destruction?'

'On that point, there's no outside surety,' the Shadow Master agreed. 'I would plead, if you stop me – and there's no doubt you can – that what you would shatter is the backbone of my integrity. Break that, and who am I? Deny my free choice, tear down the last foundation of my character, and what will I have left to withstand the pull of Desh-thiere's curse?' A pause, while his steep eyebrows angled up in derisive amazement. 'You think I don't battle the ugly directive of that geas *with every breath and throughout each waking moment?*'

The younger, blond swordsman looked away, shamed. The older one held to his obdurate stance. 'Dakar said as much. He begged us both not to trust you.'

'Then don't!' Arithon corrected the brigantine's strayed course with a vicious pitched effort that demanded the last fiber of his strength. The anger that shielded his vulnerable desperation acquired fresh edge as the wind screamed and rampaged through the thundering, stressed gear aloft. Twice, he had refused the mate's advice to reduce sail. Single-mindedly determined, he wrung the last ounce of speed from a vessel that quivered and slammed over the rough havoc of the night ocean. 'Take me down. I've said I'm unarmed. You could use rope, or forged chain and shackles. Whatever you decide, however you choose to hobble me for the sake of Dakar's shrinking cowardice, you already have my given word I won't raise hand or steel against you.'

'However you plead, we were charged not to listen.' The more stolid, older clansman set his footing, prepared to follow through in pitiless devotion.

Warned of his peril by that small move, Arithon braced the ship's wheel and faced forward, all the terrible, bright anger gone out of him.

He said in clear and unflinching surrender, 'I won't resist. That's the measure and sum of my trust in your judgment.' Through another veiling shower of spray, pinned in the sputtering flare of the deck lantern, he met the well-meant opposition of his protectors with an honesty that laid open his defenses. 'Faith in my character should argue my case. Surely, if the Mistwraith's geas held sway, I'd fight to kill anyone who sought to gainsay me.' Horror and old pain snapped his tone of surgical logic as he added the unthinkable, last weapon he had to forestall his loss of autonomy. 'Think, Vhandon, I ask you! Don't cross my will, Talvish! Give Caolle's memory due grace to stand as my inadequate testimony . . .'

The vision of the brigantine's deck vanished back into darkness, leaving Earl Jieret cast adrift. The helpless, aching conviction stayed with him, that s'Ffalenn compassion would vanquish sound sense and keep Arithon on course for the mainland. Whatever the problem his Grace vowed to set right, whatever the implied threat hanging over an innocent life, his adamant choice to effect intervention would trigger a chain of untold consequences. Unless Vhandon and Talvish stayed firm and rejected his cause by main force, at daybreak, far southward, the *Khetienn* would set her anchor into the shallows of the harbor at Sanpashir.

Still lost in the void where Sight crossed the veil, Jieret tried to cry warning that the last living prince of Rathain should turn back to sea and protect the irreplaceable legacy of his lineage. The survival of Rathain's clans dangled on the slender thread of his life. Whether or not Arithon escaped Desh-thiere's curse, he jeopardized the unfulfilled promise of blood descendants who could uphold charter law and restore crown rule at Ithamon.

Yet trapped in the vise grip of prescient dream, Rathain's *caithdein* had no voice. His burdened awareness of future disaster unfolded a fresh wave of precognition.

The blank dark burned away to a stripping, fierce clarity that seared into branding vision: of a portal carved into the face of a mountain, the blank gloom of the entry guarded by gryphons and gargoyles, and framed with intricate knot patterns. Power moved through the stone, a ranging vibration beyond eyesight or hearing that answered a warding presence. The place seemed to radiate uncanny peril, with even the sere, winter runners of briar broken out here and there in curling green leaves and exotic cascades of summer blossom.

Nor was the stairwell that led to that archway deserted, despite ice and snow and the ripping, thin winds of high altitude. In dream, Jieret heard a pounding flurry of rushed footsteps, ascending.

Arithon s'Ffalenn breasted the high landing, turned at bay with his clothing ripped ragged. He bore the Paravian-wrought longsword, Alithiel, unsheathed and at guard point, *left-handed*. The reversed grip was not whim, but unequivocal necessity: his quilloned dagger was held in the opposite fist, hampered by a bandage wrapped over a seeping, raw wound. Arrested in midflight, the Prince of Rathain poised and shot a swift glance behind.

Whether or not enemies were closing on his back trail, in the distance, spread across the throat of the vale, a war host advanced in phalanx array. Sheer numbers cut off his chance of retreat into the sheltered dells of the low country. He had no cloak, no saving store of supplies, and the sky above threatened snowfall. From the valley below, the flare of a light bolt bit through the low-hanging gray overcast. Earl Jieret required no other proof that Lysaer s'Ilessid spearheaded a curse-driven pursuit.

The bared sword flickered warning. Arithon agonized over his predicament. By his taut expression, he was already pressed near his limit by the forces of Desh-thiere's geas. If he refused to give way to insane, vengeful hatred, his last option left was to hazard the arched entry imbued with a Sorcerer's wardspells.

The place was not dead. Movement flickered and stirred in the shadows across that forbidding stone threshold. Perils would lurk in the darkness within. Yet Arithon would be faced with the untenable choice of crossing inside or allowing Desh-thiere's curse its free rein to drive him to madness.

'Save us all!' cried Earl Jieret, from the throes of his dreaming unable to divert the course of that unwritten future. 'Where are my feal clansmen, that my s'Ffalenn liege should be faced by straits such as this?'

Yet no answer came to him. His view into prescience faded and bled into nothing. Again he was falling, a slow, prolonged spiral that ended with a slamming, harsh impact. Unyielding earth drove the last gasp of breath from his lungs as he measured his length, facedown in the chill of a snowdrift. Shocked back to a semblance of waking awareness, he rolled onto his back, spitting ice chips. Overhead, tangled ink against the night sky, the tall oaks of Halwythwood whirled in a stately spin, in step with his lingering dizziness. Poised on the cusp between the world's time, and the hidden veil of deep mystery, he struggled and tried to reorient his upended senses. His effort brought only limited success. The young scout who knelt and steadied his shoulder mouthed words that imprinted no sound.

Earl Jieret felt his gaze drawn upward as though tugged by intuitive compulsion. He made out the hulking silhouette of an eagle, perched in the tree over his head. For an uncanny instant, the bird's flat, golden eyes met and locked with his own.

Then all the world seemed to shatter into a sleeting rain of bright sparks. At due length, the conflagration rearranged back into firm form and substance. This time, the aching cold in his joints left no doubt the power of Sighted dream had ebbed and left him unstrung.

In harsh fact, he lay full length in crusted snow, his fall no stray figment of nightmare. The young scout still knelt at his shoulder, voicing his distraught concern.

Jieret found no answer for words that sliced sound into meaningless increments. If his hearing seemed blurred, the air in his lungs held a surreal, sharpened clarity, and his vision, too remorseless a focus. He inhaled a mouthful of snowflakes, coughed, and turned his whirling head. Sundered from prescience, not yet firmly anchored to the confines of his flesh, he forced a careful survey of the ice-scabbed branches overhead.

No more flaring portents ripped the night sky. The limb looming over him was bare as stripped bone against the night glitter of stars. If an eagle had perched there, or any large owl mistakenly identified by his swimming, untrustworthy eyesight, no sign remained of its presence.

Nor could Jieret recall the details of the last augury that had shown Rathain's prince in flight through the split-second span of an instant. Only the elusive impression remained, and the bedrock conviction that his liege would enact his free choice to court danger and return from sea voyaging.

Why Arithon elected to tempt fate made no difference. Jieret had heard through Fiark at Innish that Cerebeld's new circle of acolytes dabbled in unsavory practices. Seers and diviners would be tracking the Shadow Master from the instant he set foot back on land. If the earlier sequence of augury held truth, that opening would set his armed enemies marching amid the fierce storms of deep winter.

Earl Jieret pushed away the scout's grasp and sat up. The overriding urge harrowed him, that he must rally the clans in response.

The phrases he blurted as he came back to himself shocked his younger companion to outspoken dismay. 'You would call up the war band? Has a bash on the head left you daft? If our clans ride to arms, who will be left here to defend the clan families who shelter from headhunters in Halwythwood?'

'Our women use bows just as well as our men.' Jieret grimaced as a finger of snowmelt ran under the snugged collar of his hood. Disgruntled as a bear kicked untimely from sleep, he checked only to assure that his sword was still with him, then clawed himself upright. Back on his feet, still weak at the knees, he shook clods of ice from his leathers. 'I don't care if it's winter! Or that Daon Ramon Barrens is no sane place to set watch for an Alliance invasion! My Sight has cried warning. Arithon s'Ffalenn has set the *Khetienn* on a return course for the continent. Whatever ill twist of fate's brought him back, unless we stand ready to effect intervention, Desh-thiere's curse will draw Lysaer s'Ilessid into the crown territory of Rathain.'

# Winter 5669

# Vigil

Still flushed from hot argument over the dispensation of the palace store of wax candles, Gace Steward bristled like a belligerent rooster before the outer gate that accessed the main square. A watch captain with a set, bulldog jaw crowded the postern behind him, in command of the row of sunwheel guards posted outside the entry. Beyond their armed ranks, the unruly crowd milled and shouted. Catcalls and the intermittent crack of thrown gravel signaled the temper abroad in the streets. Neither steward nor captain seemed inclined to open the iron grille for the determined, small party just emerged from the secure hall of state.

Prince Kevor led, clad in the deep blue mantle sewn with the gold star blazon of Tysan. At his heels marched the pair of honor guards royal protocol assigned to his presence. Princess Ellaine came after their staid, martial tread, firm courtesy leashing her motherly instincts. An exasperating interval spent coercing stout servants to carry the requisitioned crates to the square had worn her self-command. Just barely bound to civilized manners, she paused in stiff silence as Kevor confronted the impasse that blocked the outer gate. Love and pride for her son all but burst her last semblance of dignity. Yet her role as a parent demanded restraint. She understood she must defer the oncoming confrontation to her son, who had startlingly seized his sovereign power of command. Let the boy achieve his success without adult help in his proud bid to lay claim to a ruler's autonomy.

The bitter, hard fact that Ellaine herself had failed to win the same

due respect through all the years of her marriage must not be permitted
to hobble Kevor's fledgling effort. Her protective unease seemed shared
by the honor guards, who marched in matched step the requisite two
strides behind. If the young prince had claimed their heart's loyalty,
the watch officer beside Gace outranked them. His direct order to stand
down and return to the palace would force them to break Kevor's trust,
or else bring a charge of insubordination.

Chin up, head encircled by the fillet of his princely rank, Kevor
retained the born statesman's instinct to offer his challenge first.
'You will stand aside.' The resonant baritone of his matured voice
rang through the bleak, icy air. He did not slow his pace until he
confronted Gace Steward face-to-face. Taller than the weasel-quick
steward, he waited.

The presence of the man he would grow to become shone from him
in that moment, a burst of transcendence that stopped Ellaine's breath
and caused the honor guard to stand straight with squared shoulders.

Gace Steward was caught short, evidently expecting a boyish outburst
of justification for outrageous behavior. Kevor said nothing, but gave a
clipped nod to the captain, demanding deferent obedience.

'There are rioters, young master,' Gace interjected, his rushed words
glibly patronizing. 'Your safety must not be compromised.'

Kevor turned his head. In the light of the torch that burned in the
gate sconce, his hair wore glints of carnelian. His eyes, freezing blue,
swept the steward up and down in magisterial dismissal. 'The realm's
security is at issue. I will not have innocent lives set at risk. My place
is to act, or I was not born royal, and the circlet I wear is a mockery.'
His regard framed the watch captain, his focus a chiseled imperative.
'You will open the gate.'

A gruff man, but honest, the officer folded mailed arms in planted
obstinacy. 'Two honor guards are insufficient protection from—'

Kevor interrupted, his impatience no child's balked pique, but a rage
founded by his righteous concern for Avenor's threatened people. 'How
many guards were assigned to my father on the days he gave alms in
the square?'

'Ten.' The watch captain shook his head, his admiration no match
for his stolid good sense. 'But we already had a half company outside,
formed into a protective cordon around the cupola before the Divine
Prince made his public appearance.'

'There's no time for that.' Above Kevor's head, more lightning flared;
distant shouts broke over the booming din of the populace converged in
the palace square. 'Get me ten, or answer for every drop of shed blood
if a riot breaks out in my absence.'

As Gace Steward drew wind to cry protest, Kevor rounded on him with stunning speed and a shaming, collected dignity. *'How dare you set my safety above my born charge!* Crown law in Avenor is at risk! If you have no courage to do right by her people, then I will invoke Tysan's royal justice and take your life here and now as a traitor who acted against the well-being of the realm.'

The captain glanced in frenzied despair through the jostled ranks of his cordon. 'But the riots—'

And again, Prince Kevor cut him short. 'If Avenor's people embrace bloodshed and violence, they will do so over the dead meat of my corpse, and that of the ten you pick as my escort! Choose them well. Send no cowards who might break and run. Nor will you, or any others who lack heart hinder my duty as the son and sole heir of the Blessed Prince who is your sworn regent.'

Young Kevor drew his sword. In astonishing, inspired loyalty, his bared steel was joined by the unsheathed blades of the two honor guards.

The watch captain dropped his jaw. 'You men! End this foolishness! Put up your steel. You must know you risk your careers.' When the guards remained steadfast, he straightened, shook his head with stunned amazement, and delivered his ultimatum to Gace Steward. 'I cannot raise steel against the Blessed Prince's born son! Nor can I dishonor two stout men for offering themselves as his bodyguard. Tysan's young heir is not wrong, besides. This crisis demands his immediate attention. For the sake of Avenor, he must be permitted to pass. The encouragement of his presence is the best chance we have to keep peace, may the divine Light grant him the grace of protection.'

'Choose my guard, Captain,' Kevor s'Ilessid insisted before the palace steward could muster an argument. Then he smiled. The scintillant power of his bloodline shone through the unfinished gawkiness of youth. The direct, steady warmth of his gratitude was no spoiled boy's exultation, but a force that branded the heart of each man-at-arms with its brave and boundless sincerity.

Watching, Princess Ellaine lost her composure to a flood of pride and tears. Despite strain, faced by the overwhelming conviction that the forthcoming venture into Avenor's packed square would be unimaginably dangerous, the moment also lifted her to an exalted recognition: that her son was more than the fruit of her loins, but endowed as well with the gift of s'Ilessid royal justice. He was born and bred for the seat of high kingship, a spirit who had unexpectedly revealed the true cloth of his heritage. That leap had vaulted him far beyond her claim to maternal love and ties of kinship and family.

Nor were the onlookers oblivious to the change. The watch captain drew himself up, then gave a bow. 'Your Grace, it's my pleasure to serve for the well-being of Avenor and the higher good of the realm.'

Yet before he could address the issue at hand, one of the hard-bitten veterans from the gate guard cried out over the tumult, 'I'll go, your Grace.'

'And I!' called another.

Then, swept along by a wave of inspired feeling, the whole line of men who stood within earshot volunteered to escort the young prince. Their number fast swelled beyond ten.

Flushed red with embarrassed pleasure, Kevor found his poise and once again rose to the occasion. 'My mother is with me. As princess, she would be entitled to guardsmen to attend her in her own right. Therefore, we shall take an escort of twenty.' He nodded to the watch captain. 'Make your selection from those who are willing, but have them understand. We will march disarmed! The people must be shown living proof that we rest our faith in our belief of the Divine Prince's protection. Instead of weapons, each man who accompanies shall bear a lit candle for the Light.'

Past the first, gripping instant of dismayed consternation, the grizzled veteran set down his halberd. He unfastened his baldric and handed his sword to a hesitant companion. 'Hail Kevor, son of the Prince of the Light!' Head high, he stepped up to the closed gate to affirm his place with his young liege.

Ellaine shook off the torpor of nerves. Spun to marshal the stunned servants behind her, she snapped, 'Open one of the store chests. Quickly! We'll need to break out the candles.'

As though mollified by the brave display of the gate guard, the palace lackeys obeyed. The man in the lead laid down his strapped chest, flung open the lid, and passed a tied bundle to his princess.

Ellaine ripped off the binding string. She wielded the flint striker, resolute despite the flooding terror that palsied her hands. Somehow, she found the grit to ignore Gace Steward's glowering rancor. She stepped forward and passed the lit candle through the wrought-iron bars of the gate and into the bold hand of the veteran. 'Bless you for courage and generosity. By the good grace of men such as yourself, Avenor will be redeemed from mindless panic.'

The royal escort became assembled in short order. Twenty volunteer guards stripped of their weapons and formed up wearing only their blazoned surcoats. Their mailed hands shielded the flames of their candles against the fitful north gusts as the gate was unlocked and cracked open. Princess Ellaine stepped out with the heir to the realm, flanked by his honor guard of two, wearing the royal colors. The procession of crate-bearing servants followed after, wide-eyed and grumbling their apprehension. The watch captain took personal command of the small company, his first sergeant left in charge with Gace Steward. His emphatic instructions said no man was to leave his post in defense of the palace, even if Kevor's effort in the square met disaster.

'If violence breaks out, you will hold this gate shut! The young prince won't be pulled down, so long as I live. Your task is to preserve the sanctuary at our backs and keep loyal service to Lysaer s'Ilessid.'

The chosen ranks re-formed around Princess Ellaine and her laden train of servants, with Prince Kevor firmly insistent that he should march at the fore with the watch captain. 'I'm not here for protection, but to let our people bear witness to the promise their danger will be met by higher powers.' More false lightning flicked over his head. The flaring burst illuminated no exalted son of incarnate divinity, but a boy in the glory of his human courage, his hair a dull russet beneath a gold circlet and the mantle emblazoned with Tysan's crown and star too massive for the unfinished breadth of his shoulders.

He assumed his place spearheading the advance despite his apparent frailty and took the candle from his mother's hand with the awkwardness of a child stepped into a frightening burden of adult responsibility. Yet his grip did not shake. His step as he faced the seething wrath of the crowd remained resolute, a shining example of triumph as inner spirit took charge over the shrinking shortfalls of the flesh.

The mob surged and bellowed under the manic flash as more portents crazed the night sky. Lit by the merciless white crack of each discharge, the expressions on that wall of howling humanity ran the emotional gamut, from rage, through resentment, to ungoverned terror. Kevor never flinched. Candle held shielded by his ungloved hand, he marched forward into the press.

'Where is your faith?' he demanded of the stout craftsmen who shook workworn fists in his face. 'Or does fear loom so large, you believe the Divine Prince will abandon his promise of protection?'

'He's not here!' a matron in threadbare woolens howled back. 'Or why does he not show his face?'

Kevor handed her his candle, then accepted the replacement touched alight by the watch captain without a half second's glance sidewards. 'The illumination of my father's blessed gift opposes the darkness, even as we must. Carry your share, madam, as I carry mine.'

He pressed past her, stopped again as a crying girl child crossed in front of him. Too small to be alone, she had probably been torn away from her mother in the press. Driven by instinctive kindness, Kevor bent and scooped the mite into his arms. 'Here, it's all right.' The fact she was filthy and sloppily clothed did not take him aback. 'We'll find your family. Trust me, they haven't abandoned you.' He passed the candle into her tear-streaked hands, saying, 'Hold the light high. Your mother will see your face, or you will find hers. Someone who loves you will come forward and take you home to your bed.'

The tear-stained girl hiccuped, one wet fist clamped in his mantle. Ragged as she was, and redolent of the fire smoke that pervaded the homes of the poor, Kevor's smile was genuine as he hoisted her onto his shoulder. 'Lift that candle. Yes! Just like that. I'll bear you over there, to the dais. Do you see? At the top of the steps, we'll stand taller than everyone.'

The child forced a brave nod, her smudged chin puckered, and her wide, round eyes still brimming. She lifted the candle.

'Let's go, tiger.' Prince Kevor stepped ahead, swallowed into the tossing maelstrom of packed flesh. Here and there, bared steel skittered in hard-edged reflection. Other malcontents wielded bricks, or billets of wood purloined from a forester's wagon. Before the threats screamed into his teeth, Tysan's royal heir carried forward. His youthful, brave innocence, paired with the fear of the toddler he carried formed an incandescent presence of humanity. Rage melted before him. The breeding fires of panic took pause. Shouting women stood back, abashed, and men lost their will to vent the helpless terror raised by portents they did not understand.

Into that swirling shock zone of calm, Ellaine handed out candles. 'For the Light. Show your faith. The Blessed Prince will not fail you.'

Flames blossomed in the hands of the people, small, tentative flickers of carnelian and yellow yet outmatched by the dazzling bolts that snapped and seared overhead. Families drew together. Fathers set down their heirloom weapons, their oak staves, and their makeshift bludgeons. United by the focus of purposeful prayer, the crowd surged and pressed, an uneasy current breasted by the steadfast progress of the watch captain's wedge of guardsmen.

Ellaine passed out candles. Hands shaking, her heart pounding, she scarcely dared glance aside to see how her son fared. Kevor moved unprotected. Nothing else shielded him but the resolve of his bearing, a caring commitment to Avenor's well-being that would not back down before danger. He carried a wax light and a commoner's child and pressed forward, into the very maw of unrest, as the town's citizens vented their rage and hysteria. He showed no dread of sorcery, no shrinking nerves, only the steadfast truth of his being, as the bloodborn heir of his ancestors.

'There. My lady Princess,' a man encouraged, 'we've arrived. You'll need to mount the stair to the dais.'

Ellaine looked up, saw the blue surcoat of one of the young prince's honor guard. He held his fluttering wick in one hand, with the other outstretched to assist her. 'Never mind.' Touched out of nowhere by an unlooked-for courage, she declined the false trappings of safety. 'I'll stay here.' She passed another candle to the next reaching hand, then accepted its replacement from the servants. 'I beg you, watch Kevor. Stay at his back.'

On the dais, rinsed now by strong light as the guardsmen kindled the pine torches on the cupola, Avenor's young prince stood in the very footsteps of his father. He lacked Lysaer's finespun fair hair, nor would he ever own the sculptured masculinity of his sire's feature and form. No glow of divine presence washed him in gossamer haloes. Yet the human clay that comprised him held no lesser majesty as he raised his voice, and called, 'Will the mother of this strayed child please present herself!'

Spellbound by the force of unassuming compassion, the crowd near at hand stilled and quieted.

'Her name is Teis!' Kevor shouted. 'Will one of her family step forward and claim her?'

An answering cry resounded from a shop front across the square. A woman called out, and the child screamed, overjoyed. Heads turned, then more heads, as one, then another person became caught up by the manageable drama of a mother's reunion with her daughter. The temper of the crowd softened while the matron was let through, and the toddler passed from the prince's hands into her tearful embrace.

Through that hard-won interval of calm, Ellaine distributed candles one after another. She reached, sensed the lag as the servant with the striker pushed an emptied crate aside, and asked his fellows to pry the lid off another. The supply was not limitless. Spurred to fresh dread as she realized the palace stores coerced from Gace Steward were going to fall short, Ellaine asked breathless questions.

She heard the bad news, that the chests brought by the cook's boys were all exhausted but the last, and the bundles in that one barely minutes from being depleted.

Beyond the shoulders of the guardsmen who cordoned the dais stair, the watch captain caught her frantic signal. Field trained, he foresaw the looming disaster. He spoke to Kevor, his quick gestures suggesting time had come to effect a prudent retreat. The prince shook his head in emphatic rejection, raised his arms and his voice, and shouted across the packed square. 'Who here owns a chandlery? Unlock your doors, now! Let every citizen bear a flame for the Light!'

'The crown will grant recompense!' Princess Ellaine reassured. 'Any goods given out in donation will be paid from the treasury by Lord Eilish!'

'Here then!' a goodwife called back from the crowd. 'My husband's a chandler. I'll open his shop, but the apprentices are all scattered.'

'Never mind.' The watch captain cut four dependable men from the cordon. 'My guards will be dispatched to help you.'

Princess Ellaine dispensed the last candle. Shivering in sudden awareness of the cold, she straightened. Her back was a bar of welded tension. From the dais above, Kevor smiled back at her, his triumph a glow that reforged the adolescent shape of his face. For the miracle had happened. The ravening noise, the shouts, the raw tumult had all calmed. Around her, under a night sky scintillant with stars, the square of Avenor held a sea of rapt faces, bejeweled with a thousand small flames.

The moment of Kevor's victory proved short-lived. Aware of a murmuring disturbance at her back, Princess Ellaine glanced over her shoulder. Against the hulking mass of the watch tower, revealed in the full glory of white vestments and gold, High Priest Cerebeld advanced through the square. He was attended by seven priest-acolytes. They carried a sunwheel standard and a brilliance of oiled rag firebrands. The swath of illumination washed their ceremonial garments into etched and glittering clarity.

As the Voice of the Light, the High Priest's entrance was untimely. The peak moment of crisis had passed. Avenor's gathered populace had refounded their confidence in the presence of the young s'Ilessid heir. He was all that his exalted father was not: gawky, unfinished, a crude replica of the luminous personage Lysaer presented through maturity. Yet, in the boy, the fallible honesty of his youth gave rise to the possibility of something more. His birthright as the scion of generations of high kings inspired a glimpse of the gifted ruler he would someday become. On that fated hour, Kevor displayed the untarnished potential of his s'Ilessid ancestry, bright as the flame in his hand. Humanity had supplanted the presence of divine promise. Salvation had come through the example of a boy's steel-clad courage and the ordinary kindness he had shown to a craftsman's tearful strayed child.

Thrown into inadvertent eclipse, High Priest Cerebeld reached the line of guards surrounding the dais. When they did not immediately stand aside, he demanded his right of admittance. The look of resentful fury he directed toward the young prince cast a chill through Ellaine's raced blood.

The love and respect fairly earned from the hearts of Avenor's people had made Cerebeld the boy's implacable, lifelong enemy. Overcome by a mother's instinct to cry warning, the princess gathered her mantle. She whirled to mount the dais stair, caught back as she turned by restraining hands. A self-important young priest made overzealous use of his orders to clear the way for his master's grand entrance. Ellaine yanked free of untoward interference, but too late. Cerebeld had already swept past her.

In an overwhelming show of ceremonial majesty, he stepped under the high dome of the cupola. Kevor's stance became lost in the influx of white mantles, the glitter of citrine and diamond and gold foil all but dazzling as the High Priest assumed charge in his place. There, framed in center stage by the glaring flood of torches born by his coterie of acolytes, Cerebeld opened his arms to be heard.

His orator's voice boomed over the throng, boundless in reassurance. 'Behold! The portents have ceased! I am come before you to announce the given Word of the Light! The Blessed Prince bids me tell you that he travels eastward with his finest troop of officers to encounter the Master of Shadow. By our faith in his gifts, the land will be spared from the depredations brought by the Spinner of Darkness. Let us pray in this hour for victory! Let Lysaer of the Light deliver the weak from the power and deceptions of true evil!'

# New Day

Far south, in the cliff-walled harbor beneath the Second Age ruin at Sanpashir, the brigantine *Khetienn* furls sail under the hands of her crewmen; her dropped anchor splashes into the shallows while her mate gives command for her longboat to be unlashed for the party bound ashore with the Master of Shadow . . .

Clad in his ruby crown and fur-trimmed scarlet mantle, High King Eldir of Havish sits his throne at Telmandir in stern judgment, before him a triumvirate of firebrand mayors who had attempted a rebellion during the night's portents; their spurious, false charges of dark spellcraft done by the mage-gifted refugees, and their frightened conspiracy to overturn charter law and the kingdom's set policy of sanctuary earns them a sorrowful arraignment for treason and a lifelong sentence of banishment . . .

At dawn in the Skyshiels, inside the curtained palanquin next to the dead seeress, the ancient Prime's corpse slumps over the incinerated ash of her construct; both spell jewels lie quiescent, recontained, and in an unprecedented change, the initiate successor still asleep on the pallet is no longer one and the same spirit consigned to drugged rest the night before . . .

# XIII. Passage

Aboard the brigantine *Khetienn*, rocking gently at anchor in the cove beneath the grim cliffs of Sanpashir, Dakar watched like a cobra, the creases at his eyes tightened in concert with a grave collection of frown lines. He had to use mage-sight, since the lamps were unlit. Across a thickened, premature gloom cast by the battened-down hatch of the stern cabin, Arithon picked through his chest of bard's clothing and chose the black velvet jacket trimmed at the shoulders with fur from the elusive northern leopard.

Like a man under threat of a fight on slick footing, Dakar assayed questions cautiously. 'Isn't rare fur a shade overdressed for a visit to share small talk with tribesmen? I never yet saw the desertman who valued a pearl ahead of a spool of spun goat hair.'

Arithon tipped up his eyebrows. 'I have a point that needs making.'

Vague suspicion firmed into dreadful, ripe certainty. 'Not with the tribesmen.'

'No.' On that casual syllable, Arithon slipped on the jacket. He threaded the eyelets and adjusted the looped waistline over his belted, plain hose and a baldric already hung with his sword, and a main gauche that carried an unbearable history.

'Not that blade,' Dakar whispered under his breath. 'Any other sharpened length of steel under sky, but for Ath's blessed pity, that one should be thrown in the ocean.'

His entreaty ignored, he added, 'Damn you!' as the Master of Shadow flicked up the latch on the hanging locker and picked out the one cloak inside that was dyed a true emerald green. 'Step out wearing that, and every loon who sees color will be handed the gift of your bloodline.'

'A prize observation.' Arithon tossed the garment over the too-elegant jacket, then tucked back the hood until the dove gray silk lining became less blatantly visible. His hose and ankle-high boots for a mercy were plain enough to be any man's. The cut of the cloak included no ornament, a choice orchestrated to blur the distinctions of class. In maddening character, Arithon prefaced the outrageous with a smile to wear the edged facets off diamond. 'Some things won't change. The mayor's upper-crust cronies in Jaelot still measure a man by the worth of his clothing.'

The last trace of color blanched from Dakar's curved cheeks.

'Weak nerves?' quipped the Shadow Master. 'I'm surprised.' Ripe sarcasm warned of his shortening temper, and the futility of further argument. 'Given such an elaborate invitation, we already know I'm expected. Since the Koriani took this much trouble to draw me, they might as well get what they've bargained for.'

Dakar swallowed, raked by the unpleasant, sweaty awareness that only one method existed by which he and Arithon could reach Jaelot before the execution preordained to occur on the solstice. 'Well, you've grossly underestimated my part in your plan. I can't harness lane flux. Nor have I even the flimsiest hope of raising the power to enable a transfer across distance. The operant works of a Paravian circle lie far outside the scope of my experience as a Fellowship spellbinder.'

Arithon paused. The directness that marked his most volatile mood lit sparks like filed iron in his glance. 'But you do know the runes and ciphers and permissions the Sorcerers use to harness the raw force once it crests.'

The Mad Prophet let fly, his exasperation masking sharp fear. 'Don't *think* to try meddling on that scale of magnitude. For one thing, the Warden of Althain would take umbrage.' Touched by the ice-cold remembrance that Asandir had taken elaborate care never to let Arithon witness such mysteries, Dakar stood up too fast. His crown thumped the jut of the overhead deck beam hard enough to jelly his brainpan.

Swearing only added to the vicious burst of pain. One hand clamped on a goose egg bruise, the Mad Prophet railed on with his list of sensible remonstrances. 'We're both past our depth. Last night, the entire *lane* went unstable. The pulse patterns might appear to have settled, but planetary magnetics deranged by main force have been known to recoil in backlash. Static interference has upset my contact with Althain Tower. That speaks volumes for the packet of trouble that's afoot. If you think the root cause isn't Morriel's doing, nothing else in five kingdoms has even the basic, brute resource!'

'I agree.' No whit less obstinate, Arithon opened the glass-fronted cabinet and unlashed his lyranthe, then hooked up a dark bundle of cloth already set waiting against the aft boards of his berth. 'That's why we're going to raise power in that circle and ride the solstice surge north into Jaelot.'

Eyes squeezed shut against tears of frustration, Dakar sifted through his last statement for the ill-fated word which had opened the loophole to allow contradiction.

'Dakar, it's because of Morriel's extraordinary effort.' Arithon freed a kink from the strap that hung his fine instrument at his shoulder. As he scooped up the sealed pages of orders he had penned for the *Khetienn*'s mate in his absence, he volunteered, 'Why else would she frame her opening move as an outright attack on Athera? Her feud's not with me. She's more likely just presented her demand that the restraint on the Waystone be lifted and reversed by the Fellowship.'

'Not entirely,' the Mad Prophet shot back before thought.

The pause afterward shredded a handful of seconds.

Poised against the light-filtered square of the companionway, his cloth bundle at rest against the wrapped neck of his lyranthe, the s'Ffalenn prince no longer smiled. *'Then what else do you know?* In what way could my doings leave the Fellowship Sorcerers vulnerable?'

'The idea is nonsense,' Dakar agreed, a transparent lie that would surely come back to haunt him. His own vision of prophecy had cast Arithon s'Ffalenn as the indispensable linchpin; on his life and sanity turned the Sorcerers' hopes for their restoration back to seven.

Arithon knew only that he had jabbed and blindly encountered a weakness. 'Then for *nonsense* you'll help me achieve a lane transfer to Jaelot. At the Fellowship's insistence, I vowed to stay alive. But my blood oath to them gave no sanction for my name to be used to lead innocents to slaughter as the pawns of political byplay. While the Koriani Prime stoops to setting such traps, I shall disarm them, with or without your assistance.'

Inexpressibly angry, Dakar flared back. 'Well, whatever you do, I won't parade into Jaelot prinked and jeweled like an effete townsman! Not for the sake of your arrogant pride, which could spring an unbridled disaster.'

Arithon already strode toward the main deck. A blurred outline against the molten gold of a midwinter southland sunset, he said in brass calm, 'Lysaer's in Tysan, smugly counting his assets. If you won't join the party in feathers and brocade, you'll just have to pass as my servant.'

Dakar bit back retort, canny enough to cut losses before he became mauled beyond recourse. Lysaer in Tysan was sheer supposition; and Arithon's comeuppance would be served soon enough by the hand of a Fellowship Sorcerer.

'Just waken that circle, and see what you get,' the Mad Prophet warned as he trailed his charge out of the stern cabin. His own memories of chastisement under Asandir's authority still made him cringe and sweat. A puffing bear to the prince's cat grace, he heaved his bulk down the ship's side battens and into the *Khetienn*'s poised longboat. 'I swear on my dead mother's virtue, you'll be sorry as the fool who pissed on a flagstaff in a thunderstorm.'

No man who dared trifle with the flux of the earth escaped censure from Sethvir himself.

The wind blew cutting and thin from the north, sifting through the ruin on the cliff top. Hunched like a turtle under three layers of cloaks, Dakar blew a sigh of resignation. The chalk in his hand seemed a sliver of ice. Where drifts of blown sand had not buried the old rune lines, dry stalks of weeds taken root in cracked stone clawed at his shins through each stride. Nor did his gut-deep uneasiness abate with the choice to let Arithon's willful nature run the course of inevitable consequence.

Fellowship reproach at its mildest form was an experience no sane man repeated.

Nor did Parrien's two liegemen fare better in their effort to divert Rathain's prince from disaster. The blistering argument which kept them aboard the *Khetienn* could have hazed solid bedrock to give way. The reasons Arithon used to ram home his point made sound enough sense, until one recalled he intended to spring a Koriani trap with only an apprentice spellbinder's backing.

The sole avenue left was complaint, and the bloodletting sting of rife insult.

'I can configure old ciphers until we both freeze,' Dakar snapped as he jammed his toe on yet another fragment of loose rock. 'That still won't raise enough lane force to shift the arse end of a gnat.'

'We'll see,' rebutted Arithon, bent over his lyranthe with his ear laid against the ebony and pearl inlaid soundboard. He tweaked the peg of a bass string, then tested its pitch by striking a glass-clean harmonic. 'I won't ask for miracles. Just have the last figure in place before midnight.'

'Ask or not, you expect the impossible all the same.' Dakar set down his foot, fed up with wrenched tendons. 'When you come to suffer the sorry results, don't say I didn't warn you.'

He shifted the offending stone out of his path and scuffed at the detritus of lichens. The fragment of inlaid white agate he laid bare framed a curve that raised the small hairs on his nape. Excitement coursed through him, despite his misgivings. He had found the grand axis of the pattern.

Dakar faced the east, his next steps taken softly as he sensed the fine current which married the live lane force into the pattern's tuned spiral. 'I doubt these old runes have spun power for centuries. You're fully aware that just one broken line could hurl us both to perdition?'

Arithon stifled a sharp crow of laughter. 'Asandir's right. Your memory's as holed as a sieve.'

Dakar flushed, embarrassed. The reminder of the late Masterbard's death hurt far too much. The roots of that tragedy led back to Jaelot, a sorrow he would have paid blood to erase. Nor was Arithon's jabbing, cruel humor aught else but an effort to mask the same lingering grief.

'You're forgiven, for that,' the Mad Prophet said. 'I just don't want to die with another grand blunder on my already overworked conscience.' Under stems of dry sage, his questing fingers had found the east interstice. He knelt, swept a clean space over black agate, and wielded the chalk to scribe the rune for the element of air. 'Damn you, Teir's'Ffalenn, are you *sure* you have to go through with this?'

No reply from the bard, perched on a broken drum tower's foundation; westward, the day-old sliver of new moon dusted the black landscape of dunes in weak silver. Six hours remained until midnight. Dakar would need every minute to complete an array that Asandir could invoke with precision inside a half dozen heartbeats. Mounded sand on the pattern would have posed no impediment; for a Fellowship presence, the bedrock underneath would volunteer its deep secrets in homage.

Ripped on the hand by a runner of thorn, Dakar swore aloud. He glared at the prince, whose trained background included all the constraints of wise conjury about to be broken. 'You know that boy has small odds of being saved. You'll risk everything anyway, and not one damned thing I can say will shake you out of this folly.'

'There are limits.' Arithon struck a fierce minor triplet into the teeth of the wind. 'Find another way to bring my double out of Jaelot before he gets torched on false charges.'

None existed. Dakar licked the seeped blood from his knuckle and grimly set to with the chalk.

Night deepened. Winter stars replaced the low moon. The wind keened over the clifftop ruin, sweetened by the lyric, plucked strains of Arithon's lyranthe. Dakar sat huddled in the lee of the foundation, his work with the ciphers completed. Amid the sparkling runs and snatched crotchets of grace notes, he picked out isolate fragments of the melody Arithon had once captured by intuition to waken the old circle in Jaelot. Knees hugged to his chest, the Mad Prophet cherished the mean consolation that perhaps Sethvir's intervention would not fall on their heads after all.

Carefully, quietly, he masked smug relief, that the music sung by Paravian dancers to channel the life chord across latitude had not been accomplished by means of a single composition. To raise lane force to peak magnitude, the orchestrated balance of vibration and tone must be tailored to match each disparate location. The keys sung for Jaelot would not waken Sanpashir. No matter how perfectly Arithon played, his rescue was foredoomed to failure.

Complaisant that sunrise would find them still on the cliff top, Dakar settled into his cranny of stone. He tucked his bearded chin on his forearm and snored himself into sound sleep.

His rest proved short-lived.

Mild dreams of warm women and hot taprooms with beer tore away to the unmistakable raw thrum of potentized lane force.

Dakar shoved erect, skinning both elbows on the rock supporting his back. 'Merciful Ath, I don't believe this!'

Just past his feet, the Sanpashir focus gleamed active, lines of old inlay rewritten in phosphor and smoke. The north to south axis lay darkened in places where banked sand still obscured the design. Three major interstices were choked in crabbed briar, but those buried fragments would scarcely impede the coiling flow of raised lane force. Dakar had seen Asandir come and go from Paravian circles sunk beneath tons of smashed masonry.

The Sanpashir pattern was proved intact, its ring wards and runes unimpaired. It would draw the earth's magnetic forces into focus in answer to the will that commanded the burgeoning scale of its resonance. Since Arithon's powers of mastery were blocked, he had to have accessed the gateway to deep mystery through his trained sensitivity to sound.

Dakar stumbled forward, bent on reaching the bard, who still played within the rim of the focus. The soft, seeking notes he recalled between catnaps were now wholly changed, re-formed and melded into a breathtaking fire of unity. This was no longer the known composition Arithon had used to waken the circle at Jaelot.

A fresh theme had been added, the original phrasing reduced to a fragile, high counterpoint, exquisitely rearranged to partner a counter-melody refigured in a new signature. This one rang grander, darker, with notes that spoke of burning black sands and bladed rays of fierce sunlight. Set in starkly ranged measures and acid-bright chords that shifted in majesty through the major keys and grand sevenths, Arithon had reforged the original dance the Paravians had celebrated at Sanpashir.

No time left to wonder how that daunting feat was accomplished. If bardic sensitivity could cross the barrier of time, Dakar beheld its dangerous consequence as the pattern flared up into sheeting, hard light and rocked the still night with leashed power. By his flustered measure, the stars turned a minute away from the inaugural solstice flux at midnight.

Sethvir, with his earth-sense, *should have responded*. No exceptions were granted, no stays of tolerance. The compact's law was unequivo-cally stern when Athera's mysteries were channeled for use without sanction.

Yet no Sorcerer arrived to put down the lane's rising. Dakar watched in horrified consternation as the casually chalked ciphers implicating him as Arithon's consenting accomplice flared also, branding the dark-ness into an actinic brilliance.

'No!' he shouted. 'Arithon, desist!'

His protest availed nothing. Mere words passed unheard. Around him, the circle responded in wild light, well beyond mortal power to subdue. Arithon's playing had successfully tapped the high mysteries. The upshifting vibration that portended a transfer already resounded through the energetic linkages of matter. The solidity of lines and forms lost their stasis, until the surrounding drifts of sand and the tumbled stone foundations appeared distorted by roiling heat waves.

The guiding tones from the lyranthe were no longer necessary. Athera herself now impelled the stepped measures of the song to a peal of meshed resonance and vibration. The confluence of roused energies interlocked with the ciphers that lent them guidance and intent.

Arithon sensed the instant his work stood complete. Alone at the cross of the central axis, he arose. Through the fountaining brilliance as the lane's flux thundered toward its inevitable crescendo, the Mad Prophet heard his hailing shout. Then he bent and laid down the heirloom lyranthe inherited from his past master. At least, Dakar saw, Rathain's prince retained enough presence of mind to place her beyond the radius of the grand arc. Since every grudge-holding citi-zen in Jaelot would surely recall the exquisite workmanship adorning

Halliron's instrument, she would be left safely outside the coruscating threshold where raw power would lift into transfer.

Then, whipped by the uncanny forces he had raised, Arithon beckoned to Dakar. 'Are you coming or staying?'

The Mad Prophet, worried fool that he was, stepped forward rather than back.

Asandir returned to Althain Tower past the hour of midnight that led into the morn of winter solstice. Ragged, exhausted, drawn hollow with worry, he materialized at the grand junction inside the focus circle. While the powers of the lane flickered and flared back to uneasy quiescence, he winced for chilled feet still numbed from exposure on Daon Ramon Barrens. When he glanced up at last, he found candles lit in the gargoyle sconces and Luhaine there to receive him.

'You look pale as a marsh wisp,' Asandir greeted in caustic sympathy, well aware of whose dogged, meticulous touch had restrung the continuity of the third lane energies. That boon alone had allowed his prompt transfer from the ruins of Ithamon. As workworn himself, he stumbled a step, recaptured his balance, then brushed the lapse off with a question, 'How is he?'

The reference was to Sethvir, who, amid breaking crisis, had shielded with spells of raw power to bridge space and time and protect the stability of the grimwards.

'He's resting.' Luhaine's presence drifted at the edge of the focus pattern, too distressed to try even the pretense of his usual fatuous dignity. 'You should be warned. When the lanes went unstable, his earth-sense was marred. He said he could see and feel nothing across the entire breadth of the continent. That set him back to plain augury and scrying. He had no choice but to use his personal resources to buffer every one of those wards from the backlash of magnetic turbulence.'

'He did all that *earthblind*?' Asandir understood that disaster had struck. He had not imagined an impact of such broad scope and depth. 'Then all seven lanes on the continent deranged? *Even the ones in the west*?' Given Luhaine's whispered affirmative, he balked to imagine what the effort had cost Althain's Warden in sacrifice.

Asandir pushed back his cuffs, the frayed hems scorched ragged from bare-handed encounter with forces inimical to flesh-and-blood contact. 'How many lanes are still left to reconfigure?'

'Three.' Luhaine said, his maddening habit of lectured detail this once cut away to terse urgency. 'Ath's adepts are helping. They set anchors into the first lane on the hour of Morriel's intervention. The second and third lanes are now retuned and stable.' Not modesty, but embarrassment caused the discorporate Sorcerer to pass over his prodigious accomplishment. Perfectionist to the core, and resentful his work came too late to prevent the Khadrim from escaping into free flight, Luhaine rushed on with particulars. 'As we speak, Traithe sits on a peak in the Cascains. He says he can hold the wobble in the fourth lane in check until one of us can be spared to assist.'

The fifth, Asandir had set stable himself; quelling those wildfires of rampaging energies had left him drained to a husk. His own stopgap spells of balance set over the sixth *should* have lasted. Although his rough seals had not been tempered for a cataclysm, the warding rings held safeguards enough to contain the worst of the damage.

Luhaine dispelled that niggling doubt. 'Your construct over the Skyshiels endures.' Kharadmon, he affirmed, yet labored at Athir to reset the frequencies of the seventh, with Ath's adepts on the Scimlade peninsula standing anchor to keep the fields of leaked energy stable.

'Damn the interfering witches and their bothersome urge to manipulate.' Asandir flexed his hands and winced at the sting as the movement pulled at his blisters.

'They intended much more. We were lucky,' Luhaine amended.

'Now there's a pessimist's warped sense of logic.' Asandir glanced up, bemused, then laughed aloud at his colleague's convoluted opinions. 'If perversity matters, then on one count at least, you've scored a telling point.'

The Koriani powers were based in spells of forced mastery, enacted through direct transmission and contained inside the boundary of linear time. By remorseless intent, Morriel had designed to cut into the planet's magnetics. On one count, she miscalculated. The seals she configured into steel-bearing thread could not span the breadth of the oceans. Not while whales and dolphins ranged free to intercept and realign those warped frequencies into harmony by resonance. Their songs could compensate for destructive shifts in vibration, and salt waters by their nature absorbed and dispelled the energetic ties which drove conjuries whose powers were amplified through the spiral of quartz crystal matrices.

Asandir shook his head, by turns grieved and grateful. The Prime never shifted her adamant stance, that human interests reigned supreme. Her prejudice rendered the study of elements and fish an insignificant afterthought, and for that oversight, the lanes whose channels ran outside the continent had escaped her debilitating mischief.

On thrifty, past habit, Luhaine moved from sconce to sconce, neatly snuffing out wicks. Darkness followed on cat feet. For each flame that died, the cold, steady light of the Paravian circle hazed a glow like rinsed silver on the satin-veined marble of the walls.

The matching reflection in Asandir's eyes was unforgiving, gray steel. Braced for a fresh onslaught of rapid-fire bad news, he tackled his colleague's delicate omission with all of his sledgehammer bluntness. 'Tell me what else has gone wrong with the sixth? I know well enough the wards I left there were not shaped to withstand an assault of this magnitude.'

They had reached the open stairwell. Luhaine's presence ascended the narrow turnpike with the whipping agitation of a dust devil. 'You won't like this one bit.' He paused, moved to powerful, knowing compassion.

Asandir stopped. With one hand braced against fitted stone, he took painstaking care and again reviewed the brutal array of stark facts. His dread ran the gamut of encroaching possibilities, since two Ages of experience with natural forces had taught him the flux of Athera's magnetics could never be a dissociated phenomenon.

Life formed a vast tapestry, with each myriad thread of consciousness interconnected. Birds in their seasonal migration moved the fine energies of creation here and there in the deep, knowing harmony of their existence. To a Sorcerer's sight, their flight paths traced glowing lines through the element of air, and spun subliminal links of harmony from treetop to treetop. The land's disparate mantle of quickened awareness was not an unstructured chaos of live forms, but a whole cloth meshed into a fine, lockstepped balance, and tied by vibrations of light.

Plants, trees, and fungi interfaced air and earth in a blanketing tapestry of tuned energy. Nor were minerals inert. Their frozen imprint of individual signatures could be mapped through refined mage-sight. Even in their most humble manifestation, stones and sand acted as placeholders, keeping in timeless, faithful trust the calibrated tones which anchored the chord of world life force. Rivers, rain, the oceans themselves moved the grand currents of elemental power. Weather cycles cleansed the world's firmament and refreshed the planetary aura.

By wracking the frequencies of lane force out of true, the Koriani had wrought a cascade of damage past the range of mortal perception. Led by Morriel's spiteful pride and a vengeful bid for supremacy, their spellwork this night had bled chaos into all things under sky and rocked the root of the Major Balance.

Asandir reviewed each unraveled loop in creation. The implied enormity of one possible slipped thread made even his iron nerve falter.

'Don't hold back. I can guess well enough where the trouble lies.'

He let his grazed knuckles fall loose to his side, grateful nonetheless for the one thoughtful moment of reprieve.

Luhaine broke the news gently. 'Arithon used music to reawaken the Sanpashir focus. Dakar provided the sigils of passage in rash certainty that Sethvir would be free to intervene.'

'Of course, Morriel timed her ploy with that end in mind. Then prince and prophet will reach Jaelot before daybreak?' Asandir resumed his interrupted ascent, to all outside appearance restored to equanimity. 'Best say where Lysaer is, and quickly.' His stride lengthened. Worn features seemed lined in lead by the daylight filtering down from above.

Luhaine grappled for means to lighten the ominous portents. 'Sethvir says the s'Ilessid will be crossing the strait to Atainia.'

'Bound on to the Kingdom of Rathain?' Asandir's words spiraled away into echoes as he emerged through the narrow trapdoor.

'He'd expressed his intent to seek passage to Narms before the lanes misaligned,' Luhaine huffed, spinning over the polished floor between statues.

'Then count on his landing inside the next fortnight. He won't stay ignorant of Arithon's return. The witches will make sure of that.' Already Asandir's thoughts leaped ahead. 'Which brings us to Arithon's untimely choice to wake the Paravian mysteries. I suppose we're left to gauge the measure of his prowess if he reaches Jaelot without mishap?'

'We can't access that knowledge,' Luhaine contradicted. 'Lirenda's on-site with a circle of senior initiates, and they've set the whole city under seal.'

Under the stone gaze of carved centaur guardians, the two colleagues shared the silenced, sharp anguish, that spellbinder and prince would spring Morriel's trap with no hope of outside assistance.

'Mercy on us,' Asandir said at last. 'The fall of Dharkaron's aimed Spear surely would have been kinder.'

Athera was in crisis. By the terms of the compact, the Fellowship's first charge remained clear: the needs of the land must come first. Bound to that priority, the Sorcerers were already too pressured to divert every critical disaster. Losses were happening, moment to moment, each one a small sorrow with far worse pending if immediate steps were not taken. The smashed links of the containment spells the vanished Paravians had left to hold drake spawn would require the most desperate attention.

Luhaine retained his terrier's trait for pursuing detail without flinching. 'If Arithon's successful, the second and third solstice tides are going to pose thorny problems.'

'I already see that.' Still raw from the punishment of Morriel's assault, Asandir pondered the impacting turn of fresh damage, as the roused chord of world life force rolled down the sixth lane, in concert with the seasonal energies. The primary channel was sorely distressed, still patched in chains of remedial spellcraft. The vortex of wild forces contained in the night had already sustained an increase to the thin edge of tolerance; then that fragile stasis was bombarded again by the powerful harmonics unleashed by Arithon's re-creation of the ritual tones Paravians once used to seed rebirth and renewal across latitude. The noon surge would seed the first resonance of attrition.

'My construct can't hold beyond midnight,' Asandir assessed in foregone conclusion. Fresh crisis would break within twenty-four hours, when his stopgap protections would crumble. Because of Arithon's awakening, each tied seal of stasis must be abraded away by the absolute purity of healing forces, pitched to set right the imbalance of every disharmony that stood in their path.

Amid Luhaine's dense silence, Asandir read the unremarked danger that waited, concealed, as the release of shed chaos sought to flow to safe ground in the earth. 'Don't say *the damned mountains* were plunged out of alignment from Morriel's meddling also!'

'Oh yes.' Luhaine's response rang bitter with offense. 'We'll pay all the grim price of her warped crystal resonance striking over a quartz vein. The whole southern spur of the Skyshiels was affected where her transmission ran out of mineral carrier and recoiled into sedimentary bedrock.'

Unfailing in his ability to target the root of a problem, Asandir cut in ahead of Luhaine's involved expostulation. 'Spare us all, we have trouble if Rockfell is stressed!' When the peal of the Paravian mysteries unreeled through their ancient, lateral courses, the damage could cost the world dearly. 'The wards on the Mistwraith might very well sunder deeply enough to be breached.'

'Sethvir will know,' Luhaine finished in shared agony as he flanked Asandir's lengthened stride.

The grievous truth tore the heart for sheer pity: Fellowship resources were going to fall short. Nor could their help unburden Althain's Warden soon enough. Until Sethvir resumed full command of his earth-sense, their moment-to-moment grasp of affairs would stay irrepairably crippled. No one could spare either time or energy for the ritual augury of cast strands.

Asandir reached the upper stairwell at last. He found the oak door bound and locked in stiff spells, a desperate precaution made on the hour Sethvir felt his faculties failing.

He rapped out the cantrip to unbind the latch, while the following draft that was Luhaine flapped the tapestried caparisons of centaurs and flicked points of disturbed light over the jewels of sunchildren. 'Go on ahead,' he snapped in explosive exasperation. 'I'll meet you just as fast as this body can be hurried to mount three more flights of stairs.'

A lone candle burned in Sethvir's quarters. Disordered light capered over the plush red carpet. The shadows danced in grotesque reverse image, thrown off the collection of sculpture and gear mounded on chairs and in corners. Horse harness with burst stitching lay draped over porcelain, and the lion's head bosses of a table. An overturned turtle's shell cupped the diminutive bones from an owl pellet and the wing feathers of a male kestrel. Sewing awls huddled with goose quill pens, poked in the necks of clay jars. Floor and tables became the repository of precarious towers of stacked books. River stones filled a sea-pitted bottle. The cellophane husks of three snake skins were twined overtop a spool of silk ribbon.

Within the confines of his personal domain, the Warden of Althain shirked his housekeeping as much as he disdained to sleep.

The first, shocking sight of Sethvir prone as a wax doll stopped Asandir cold on the threshold. The field Sorcerer caught his breath, reined back sharp alarm, and shut the oak door with a feather touch.

'Why didn't you tell me?' He glowered toward the circle of air the dust motes disdained out of Luhaine's strict penchant for cleanliness.

For Sethvir lay in an untidy sprawl across the cot by the clothes chest. He still wore his robes. His ink-stained cuffs and unraveled hem seemed more ragged and threadbare in prostration. One fragile, veined hand was entangled in his beard, while the other, fingertips pallid with chalk dust, trailed in slack abandon on the floor.

'In fact he collapsed first on his library table.' The discorporate Sorcerer breezed an acerbic sigh. 'I managed to rouse him. He stayed on his feet just long enough to find his way here and lie down. What more could you have done before now, except tear yourself raw with blind worry?'

Metal chimed as Asandir shifted a chair hung with bridles to open a path to the Warden's bedside.

'He's not sleeping,' Luhaine cautioned.

Asandir's gray eyes flicked a wide glance of startlement over his weather-stained shoulder. Sethvir awake, but with senses closed down, it meant he had engaged every trained faculty past the wise limits of self-preservation.

Warned to fresh caution, Asandir knelt. His attentive, bright survey recorded the eggshell complexion, the saucy nose, and jutted cheek that looked somehow diminished with the blue-green eyes pinched closed. At due length, he extended his callused, lean grip and tucked the Warden's chalk-marked hand back on top of the antique counterpane. Last, his butterfly touch rested over one temple, that his words not require the effort of hearing to be understood. 'Do you wish me to help?'

A sigh fluttered through the rumpled-up wisps of white beard. 'Asandir.'

'I came as soon as—'

'. . . possible.' Sethvir's lips flexed in a fractional curve of dry irony. 'Two trips in one night through an unbalanced lane flux must have been mightily trying.'

'Well, I'm going to make three,' Asandir rebutted. The rage coiled in him, entangled in bleak pity, for the cost of Morriel's intrigues. On every level of energetic vibration, his mage-sight revealed the currents of ephemeral light bleeding out of his colleague's aura. Wherever the earth lanes remained spun to chaos, Althain's Warden had no choice but to bridge past their weakness with the controlled stamina of his personal reserves. The stability of whole grimwards relied now on endurance, meted out from moment to moment with no hour in sight for reprieve.

Careful lest an inadvertent movement of his own should stir eddies in that chain of intent, Asandir stroked unruly tangles of hair away from Sethvir's nose and face. 'I will lift the most critically damaged of the grimwards from your shoulders, but first, brace up. I'm going to make you more comfortable.'

Sethvir gave the tiniest flick of a finger to signal his moment of readiness. Still, the skin around his closed eyes pinched taut as strong and capable hands straightened his sprawled form, then folded him into soft blankets.

Through a grief that struck him down to the heart, Asandir kept his voice steady. 'Are you thirsty?'

A thready whisper dredged up from the depths of pillows that propped Sethvir's head. 'No.'

Asandir turned aside, his fists clamped white knuckled as he posed the thornier question. 'Can you muster command of your earth-sense enough to say which grimward stands in the most critical jeopardy?'

'If I can bear to open the scope of the vision.' Those few breathless words spun off into a turmoil of painful impressions: of Khadrim flying free, setting forests and farmsteads in Tysan alight; of a pod of whales in the southern ocean beaching themselves on the diamond-bright shards of the ice cap covering the pole. Sethvir's lids flickered open. No longer dreaming, or fogged by wide thought, his eyes were turquoise enamel. 'You're aware, the axis of Rockfell Peak has been hurled out of alignment?'

Asandir's fingers tightened. 'Worse. I know Arithon broke the Paravian seals and raised the resonance of a confluent grand harmony.' When solstice midnight arrived, and the culminating force of that ritual pealed across latitude, the currents would inevitably touch Rockfell, most carefully situated between lanes to assure that magnetic disturbance would be minimized. 'Kharadmon could check on the Mistwraith's prison and sound the extent of the damage.'

'Attrition,' Sethvir breathed, labored and faint as the scrape of a scribe's nib on vellum. His resources were taxed over an appallingly widespread range of problems. Still, he managed a bridged half second of contact that encompassed the concept for Asandir.

The images framed a fleeting, grainy impression of future event, as the energies rocked from their sure, channeled track, and skewed off into disordered eddies. The residue would not die, but turn and pool, and sink at last into stagnation where the flawed transmission through the mountain failed in its natural function. Since the wards over Rockfell were calibrated to mesh with the stable emission of stone, even an infinitesimal change would admit a dangerous, weakening influence.

'We could have days, or a month, or a year before the damage becomes threatening.' Sethvir shut his eyes, worn threadbare from even that minimal effort. 'Or we could have only hours. I dare make no forecast. Not since the Mistwraith revealed that it knew how to act on those spells from within. Your choice, whether clearing the seals on the grimwards ought to be shouldered first.'

'No choice at all,' Asandir said, his calm forced. In truth, an abyss yawned at their feet.

Should the seals that contained the boundaries of even one grimward let go, the very template of creation would shift. The unbinding ruin to land and life would see destruction beyond all repair. Desh-thiere's ills, with their long-range potential to choke sunlight, could not touch the coiled power of the drake shades spelled and bound in their sealed-off pockets of warped time.

'Eckracken's haunt, then,' Sethvir gave out after a labored silence. 'His spite is most vengeful. When the mate interred on Kathtairr dreams of coupling during the full moon, his ghost always bids to escape.'

'That's less than a fortnight away,' Luhaine despaired from his hovering roost in the doorway.

The grimward which prisoned the skull of Eckracken lay in the Salt Fens of West Shand, far down the southern peninsula. Asandir faced a transfer down the third lane to the ruins at Earle, followed by a desolate ride up the wind-raked winter coastline. No hostels, habitations, or inns graced that broken stretch of roadway, with its towered, gray pinnacles of limestone. Trade gave wide berth to that abandoned expanse. The last bastion of a more civilized age had gone also, the old enclave built by Ath's adepts left roofless for centuries, drained of its powers during the Third Age defense to stem the Mistwraith's incursion.

'My black stud is well fed and rested, at least.' Asandir tugged a crimp in the coverlet straight. Unwilling to be first to broach the necessity, that all of Athera's seventeen grimwards would have to be tested to guarantee their stability, he reached out with spread hands to clasp Sethvir's temples.

His gesture was arrested by a snapped flick of air and a sensible admonishment from Luhaine. 'Enough. You'll need every bit of your strength. I'll attend to Sethvir. Kharadmon will be called if need warrants.'

Not trusting that tone of dismissal one bit, Asandir pushed to his feet. 'Remember this,' he said in grave parting. 'Of the pair of us, Sethvir's not expendable.'

'Well he can't hold the compact without help in the field!' A moment of impasse, while the dust motes streamed in chiaroscuro eddies from Luhaine's agitated presence.

Asandir said nothing, did nothing, but stood with his hands hanging empty.

'You've always had the stubborn set of old granite.' The discorporate Sorcerer gave way at grim length. 'Watch your back. Stay inside safe limits, or be sure, I'll kick the four chambers of Eckracken's thick skull to bedevil the unstrung wisps of your consciousness.'

Asandir tipped his head, his mouth lifted into a half smile of truce. He spoke his last words from the doorway. 'Sethvir, keep you safe. If anything good can be wrung from disaster, at least, by clear terms of the compact, we have reason at last to put an end to Morriel's reign of self-righteous power.' On one lingering, last glance, he raised the latch and swiftly let himself out.

For a stark, silent interval, dust motes settled their stealthy patina over statues and books and the oddments of stray hardware stashed in their haphazard corners. Even the candleflame burned straight and still, as if time had paused in reflection.

'I couldn't tell him,' Sethvir admitted to Luhaine after a tormented interval. 'Not now. Not about Morriel's unconscionable possession of that misfortunate young initiate.'

That one stark truth canceled comfort. The Prime Matriarch's willful acts of damage against lands held in trust by the terms of Paravian generosity had been crowned by a last, diabolical masterstroke. Morriel had arranged her web too well. Fellowship authority now could not touch her. No redress could be claimed for as long as her spirit seized sanctuary inside the body of the victimized girl.

When the Fellowship Sorcerers tapped into lane force for travel, the effects were instantaneous and disorienting to a wrenching degree that always left Dakar blinded and dizzy with nausea. The effect when the power was charged active by music from the ancient Paravian ritual was different, a slow, turning, lazy spin that felt like a fabric of dream whose meaning had melted and gone formless. Through a fuzz of intense color, and a descant of clear song, Dakar was aware of the anchoring pull of the night constellations, their high, ephemeral range of vibration ringing in the advent of winter solstice. He felt beneath him the spin of Athera, her iron core driving her magnetic engine and re-creating from second to second, the mighty flux of the currents which buoyed him.

Drawn like syrup through that queer keyhole through time, the Mad Prophet sensed that the transit from Sanpashir's focus had spanned the course of three hours.

He felt no urgency as the kaleidoscopic net of suspension gradually dissolved. On the cusp of that moment, as he recrossed the threshold of material continuity, he felt only calm and the peaceful, sweet union that welded the natural elements.

Then awareness of his body resurged with a crash of hard impact that snapped his jaw shut on the trapped meat of his tongue.

He yelped, tasting blood. In stunned reflex and cross-eyed, reflexive bewilderment, he flopped like a beached fish off the shards of smashed porcelain that threatened to impale his backside. The bewitching last strains of Paravian melody ripped away with his oath as he slid headlong off a table.

The linen cloth ruckled and dragged with his weight, its contents disgorged in a clattering rain over his importunate head. Battered by spoons and almond paste comfits, silver plates and soiled napkins, and, finally, the limpid flutter of lace doilies, Dakar swore. A finger bowl sloshing with rose petals doused him. He blinked through the runoff, spluttering. Insult to rank injury, the tureen which had broken the brunt of his landing glopped gravy into his hair and down the skewed nape of his collar.

'Dharkaron's black vengeance!' He had neglected fact, on departure from Sanpashir. In Jaelot, the mayor's palace of state was built over the old site of the lane focus. Arrival had hurled him, undignified and bruised, amid the uncleared leavings of the feast to honor the eve of winter solstice.

Dakar threw off the stained tablecloth and stood up to a cascading jangle of flatware jostled loose from his cloak hem. He groped through black gloom, found an upright table, and all but impaled himself on a centerpiece of gilt paper lilies in his quest for a napkin to sop congealed sauce from his clothing.

Hard fingers caught his arm, faced him around, and impelled him in another direction.

'Sithaer's raving furies, let me alone!' he snarled to his scatheless companion. 'Damn you for luck, you didn't fall backside first into a cold dish of pudding.'

'No.' Neat as a cat, Arithon flitted between the fake archway of a kiosk, swagged with gilt ivy and plaster-cast doves flocked together with wire. 'Be grateful. We unleashed a shock that just shook the foundations. Once the house staff stops quaking, your noisy crash landing will bring servants running with candles to see if the ceiling has fallen.'

In passing, Arithon snagged up a decanter. The scanty slosh of liquid inside proved to be lees of stale wine. 'We'll find you dry clothes.' With no more word of apology than that, he upended the dregs over Dakar's redolent head.

The Mad Prophet's yell of fury was silenced by the same hand that launched the outrageous offense. Struggling, snarling insults into the fingers clamped in the bristled stubble of his beard, he landed just one vengeful kick on a shin before being dragged through a corridor. He identified the smells of the kitchen and pantry before a sharp sidewards turn pitched him through a narrow side doorway.

The closet room had pallets for scullions who shared turns at the spits through the night. Dakar knew the place. One fateful evening a quarter century past, Halliron Masterbard had been laid here unconscious from the head blow that had finally killed him.

This time the pallets held children. The filtered gleam of a lamp through the window revealed their sprawled forms, soundly asleep from long hours of labor under a short-tempered kitchen staff.

Dakar assayed another vicious kick, cut short by the Shadow Master's frantic whisper at his ear. 'Act like you mean this, or else we're both going to burn.'

The bard's fingers maintained their punishing grip on his mouth. Dakar howled anyway. Never more tempted to bite in his life, he wrestled, as Arithon's other arm clamped him by force into a lover's embrace.

Then the Shadow Master's taunt, shot through with a manic hilarity, 'How exciting. Moan again. In fact, you can scream all you like.'

Dakar felt himself pressed backward into the mimed pose of a blindingly passionate tryst between a wealthy young blueblood and a servant. His howl of protest broke into a squeal as light flickered, then poured through the opened doorway.

The liveried footman who carried the pricket gasped in embarrassed surprise.

'Stayed on from the feast, did you?' A boy's voice, probably coach staff to judge by the surly accent. He was thankfully too young to remember the connection between a short, rotund convict with ginger hair and the Sorcerer blamed for the infamous ruin of a solstice feast twenty-five years ago.

A sniff of disgust, then the dry admonition, no doubt inspired by the wine fumes that wafted off Dakar's sticky head, 'Got inns in this city where beds can be found. Take the heat of your passion off elsewhere.'

Arithon straightened, the hood of his cloak skewed over his eyes. He affected the extravagance of a rich, wellborn rake caught slumming in a dim corner. Over his shoulder, Dakar's furious, bright blush lent his slurred protest full credence. 'Oh, but my dear, we're *much* too drunk to find our way through the streets.'

'Well, that's no problem of mine, now is it?' The servant held his candle in sour impatience for the amorous pair to move on.

Arithon smiled, willing to oblige, and in disarming conspiracy asking to be let out the back. 'One of the late watch is my uncle, you know. He could cause merry hell with my father, if we're seen. They both think I'm visiting a courtesan quartered on Threadneedle Street.'

'Forget the niceties,' the serving boy grumbled. 'I'd need the porter's keys to do that.'

A discreetly palmed silver sweetened the request. 'Oh come, now. You must have some way to slip out for the wenches.'

Arithon laid his other arm across the boy's shoulder, good-naturedly encouraging mayhem, while Dakar strove to rein in rankled temper and smile through his thunderous frown.

A footman was kicked awake to pick the lock at the rear of the pantry. An older, bald man with a throaty, wet cough and the bloodshot eyes of a head cold, he shared Jaelot's relish for gossip. 'You heard the town alderman's daughter got herself a big belly? Slept with the lad who cares for the carriage teams.'

'Our grooms knew that two weeks ago,' said the boy, masking a yawn with the back of his hand.

The footman warmed to the challenge. 'Well, you won't know the town executioner just quit his post. Thirty years of unbroken service, and he chooses now to retire. It's stinking bad timing, for all of that.

Got a wager laid on with the cousin in the shoe trade, setting odds on how long a Master Sorcerer takes to die.'

'Headsman's cold frightened,' scoffed the coach boy.

'Likely so, likely so.' The footman shrugged. 'Would you put a Sorcerer to the fire and the sword, and risk his death curse on your family?' He twirled his bent wire against the last, stubborn tumblers. 'Off you go, now, young sirs.' Leering in salacious conspiracy, he swung open the strapped door used by the cook to admit butchered carcasses from the stockyards. The scrubbed stone floor harbored a death reek beneath the taints of lye and old blood. Mixed with fresh gravy and clammy lees of red wine, the odors drove Dakar to nausea.

He was in no mood for wild pranks and exhilaration and said so, in pungent, choice phrases, the instant the door thudded shut. In afterthought, he added to his errant companion, 'I do hope you used a kind twist of shadows to lend me the glamour of a maid.'

'Of course not,' Arithon quipped in barbed malice. 'After all, this is Jaelot. Or do you think styles have changed?'

Poised on the rickety wooden stair with the steam from the midden spiraling past his dark hood, the Shadow Master laughed, a full-throated peal of extravagance that set the coursing hounds yapping in their kennels. 'Dharkaron's sure vengeance, the sheer irony's priceless!'

'What irony?' Dakar grumped, still nursing bruised dignity and blackly unwilling to share humor at his own expense.

'But it's glorious, don't you see?' Arithon swiped brimming moisture from his eyes. 'I've developed a reputation so bleak, a professional's terrified to kill me.' He strode forward, determined, past the flare of the torch left burning as a deterrent to rats and other two-legged scavengers wont to lurk in dark alleys.

The Mad Prophet followed, disgruntled yet, and altogether too rattled from the unlikely success of the lane transfer. Never, even in nightmare, had he planned to abet Arithon s'Ffalenn in his choice to run riot in Jaelot. The unresponsive silence from Althain's Warden chafed his thoughts to disturbing unease. Too worried to field manic ebullience concerning the superstitious whims of hired killers, Dakar hunched up his gravy-stained shoulders. 'If you're not surprised, you must have a plan to use that grim fact to advantage.'

'But of course.' From out of the dark, Arithon's teeth came and went in a ripping, tight smile of invitation. 'Come along and see how. That's if you don't want to stay under that torch and get clapped in irons as a beggar caught scrounging for chicken bones.'

'You're enjoying this,' Dakar accused, wincing as the first blast of winter air kissed the wet patches soaked through his clothing.

'And why not?' Arithon ducked down a side street. Evidently he remembered the convoluted shortcut the street waifs used to reach the wharves from the rich quarter. Through the ramshackle maze of the fishmonger's sheds with their salt barrels and stacked wicker baskets, his rapid-fire patter floated back. 'Koriani presumably know that I'm here. Why tire ourselves out over subtleties?'

Yet Dakar noticed: Arithon had remorselessly quickened his pace. The flaring pine knot by a sailor's brothel revealed a fanciful enthusiasm turned hard, even angry, as the adamantine glitter of sheared diamond. 'We might as well be *disruptive* and give the interfering bitches their due share of cheap entertainment.'

# Third Upset

The first blush of solstice dawn brightened the sky over Jaelot, a streaking of gold through stringers of dove gray cloud. For the aftermath of a night torn by terrifying portents, the new daybreak brought in a queer, almost deadlocked quiet.

Moored galleys rocked on the ribboned steel breast of the harbor, or tugged at fixed bollards by the quayside, fretted lines squealing against the pull of the ebb tide. In that stilled, half-lit hour, while the curs yapped underneath the lamps by the fishmongers' wicket gates, and the earliest slopman's cart rattled over the cobbles collecting nightsoil, the damp, heavy stir of the sea breeze ruffled the collars and cloaks of the servants who waited in the dim lanes, their buckets and basins clenched in raw hands, waste sewage being under the strict control of common rights law and city ordinance. The workaday acts of necessity seemed oddly disjointed, a tapestry backdrop changed overnight, as if a vital, but significant thread had jerked free, casting an unsettled pall over the established patterns of normality.

Peat smoke coiled over rooftops leaded in gleaming winter ice, but the air was empty of flocking gulls.

No birds flew or cried. The anomaly lay outside the long memories of the cod fishermen who ranged along the stone verge of the breakwater to launch their cockleshell dories. Nor had the seagoing trade captains known such an unnerving silence. Up and down the blustery expanse of the seawall, men spat over their shoulders to ward off the following train of ill luck. The name of the Master of Shadow was whispered with sidewards glances and choked fear, and the rumors kindled like wildfire up and down Jaelot's wakened streets.

The Gold Lion retained its nightlong reputation as a hotbed of news and conjecture. Rich and poor shared salacious speculation, while servants sent out on morning errands spread the details of the Shadow Master's capture. The event had acquired striking embellishment. Sleepers who had missed the commotion when the sky had flared with red portents heard the troublesome news over breakfast, as strings of agitated messengers dispatched sealed orders from the mayor to the ranking city dignitaries, and conscripted lackeys were sent scrambling to the woodsellers to bundle the faggots for a burning.

By the hour the sky lightened, the first idling onlookers clustered in the city square. A group of inspired zealots chanted litanies for Lysaer of the Light and demanded death for the Spinner of Darkness. Tradesmen gossiped on their way to open shops, their discourse overheard by the countryfolk bearing crated geese to the market. Everyone defended their vehement opinion, that Jaelot had escaped the ugliest fate by only the narrowest margin. Always the uncanny silence of the gulls was blamed on the work of meddling spellcraft.

The fine point no one seemed able to settle was argued with passionate conviction: whether the mute birds were provoked by the criminal Sorcerer in the dungeons or the protective result of the Koriani bindings laid over the city walls through the night. Safe or threatened, Jaelot's rattled citizens churned up talk with a turmoil that upended routine.

Full daybreak flushed the sky the luminous gray of poured mercury over the square rims of the battlements. High on the curtain walls, ruffled by wind, six Koriani enchantresses in violet robes lit the air with the flare of sealed sigils. Their work spun a thousand invisible threads. The bold weave of uncanny forces skittered in bursts through thought and mind, until the lamplighters who trimmed the spent wicks in the streets made their rounds in anxious, mute haste. Strange, pent-back stillness gripped earth and sky, a queer sense of suspension like pause, but not, as if some massive, unseen force waited to freeze the incoming breakers on the cusp of each crest and ebb.

Nor did that tension lift as the bell tolled to signal the opening of the roadside gates. The night watch came in, cheeks burnished raw from the winds and blowing on their numbed fingers. They ordered hot mead and sweetrolls in the taverns, and suffered the onslaught of sharp questions concerning the enchantresses who laid wardspells over their wall walks and posterns.

The sanctified quiet of the mayor's grand palace itself housed the eye of the tempest, as the hard-bitten captain of Jaelot's guard burst into the tiled foyer. He had not slept. His eyes were red-rimmed, and his mood clipped short as the gray rime of yesterday's stubble.

'Conniving damned witches are here in strange force,' he concurred with the mayor's mousy valet. He stamped caked ice off his boots, impervious to indignant censure from the house staff until after he delivered his report to the mayor. 'Queer, that so many should be here all at once, given the onset of winter.' He peeled off his wool cloak, then shed his steel helm; the fleece-lined rim had printed a red, transverse groove across his weathered forehead. 'You ask me, we're fools to keep a liaison with their kind at all. Man wasn't born that could figure their ways, and their bitch tangle of political interests.'

'They'll want something for certain,' the aged footman agreed, arrived to hang the captain's cloak. His disdainful grasp filled with rust-smelling wool, he jerked his sallow chin toward the shut door to the parlor. 'Mind you don't speak your opinion too boldly. His lordship's inside, sharing counsel over breakfast with the order's ranking enchantress. No telling how long you'll be made to wait. I'll send a boy with a chair, unless you want to stay standing.'

'A hot mug and something to eat would be better.' The guard captain flicked the servant a coin to speed his request to the kitchen. Then he settled with his elbow hooked around the landing newel post and chewed his lower lip in calculation.

Behind the closed doorway, not thoughtful at all, the Mayor of Jaelot sat with his wife and one guest at the lacquer-and-pearl table imported at great cost from Vhalzein. He had just demolished his third plate of sausage, with a basket of warmed honey cakes to sop up the grease. Conversation that had run the gamut of innuendo grew animate in the friction of impasse. Crumbs cascaded down the velvet-frogged front of his dressing robe as he gestured, pink-tipped fingers still sticky with jam. 'Well, our part certainly hasn't progressed without snags. You can thank the Light for one favor at least. We've found an executioner who's unafraid to practice his trade on a Sorcerer.'

The mayor repeated his peremptory beckon, and the servant just arrived with basin and towel bent to the task of dabbing his fleshy hands with their encrustation of carbuncle rings.

'I didn't know you'd had problems.' Her eyes the wide gold of a languid tigress, the enchantress sat in her high-backed chair, stirring sugarless tea with an elegance that suggested she had used silver spoons all her life.

'Oh yes.' The mayor heaved a replete sigh, chin nested in the crimped flesh of his neck. 'Our own headsman refused. The work falls by default to the garrison commander, but even he had second thoughts since last night. Swore he'd be cursed, should he take a Sorcerer's blood on his hands.'

'Spare me,' Lirenda murmured.

'I don't need to.' The mayor belched into the back of the plump wrist just freed from the servant's ministrations. 'We posted a notice offering triple pay. The brute who took the job can surely wield a sword and a torch well as any.'

Lirenda said, impartial as ice, 'Well, if he's an amateur and bungles a clean stroke, no one's likely to protest.' She set her cup in its crested porcelain saucer, the tilt of her chin dismissing the servant who moved in, deferent, with his basin. 'Be sure I'm told when you're planning the execution. When the Sorcerer's moved, my enchantresses must take sure and proper steps to seal your town in protection.'

'But the disposition was made yesterday evening.' A wren before the Koriani peer's inbred elegance, the mayor's wife dabbled at dissatisfied lips with a fold of her brocade napkin. Pearls winked through the lace at her sleeves and fur collar as she settled flighty hands in her lap. 'The spectacle will open our winter's night festival.' Having decided the event was a social occasion, she chirped through her list of preparations. 'The men-at-arms on parade guard will wear their dress surcoats. We've timed the event for just before dusk. The bonfire will be left to blaze until dawn. All Jaelot shall celebrate as the Master of Shadow receives his due punishment for the cavalier wreckage of our city.'

That moment, a peal of raw thunder rattled the glass in the casement.

The mayor's wife screamed. The servant dropped his basin with a crash. Water spewed everywhere. Porcelain cups jounced and juddered in their saucers and slopped tea on the linen tablecloth, while from the foyer outside, the shout of the watch captain brought the house guard running to barricade the palace. Then the service door burst open. Four red-cheeked linen girls fled through from the laundry, trailing steam and rose-scented suds, and shrieking like geese in blind panic.

'That's enough!' shrieked the Mayor of Jaelot, as their pandemonium destroyed the sanctum of his parlor. Flushed to his wattles, he banged a ham fist onto the table. Silverware, salvers, and honey crock went flying. 'No more! That damnable Sorcerer is going to die now, and to Sithaer with the flourish of a festival!'

He shot from his seat. The heavy, upholstered chair flew back and upset with a splashy thud on sopped carpet. 'You!' He singled out the cowering footman. 'Fetch my steward! Tell him I want that executioner ready at once with his tinder and sword.'

An outraged squeal interrupted.

'No,' he cracked at his rankled wife. 'Not this time. That's final! I won't risk my city to distress and discord for the niceties of your social pomp and ceremony.' His vitriolic tirade transferred to include the Koriani senior, arranged in her seat as if sealed in place by her veneer of poise. 'And so much for relying on a woman's promise and your order's spells of protection!'

Lirenda disdained to acknowledge the insult. She righted her tipped cup, her composure loomed silk in the face of disruptive setback. Inside, she seethed. *Something had disturbed the set wards on the walls. She knew by the sweeping ache through her bones, as the roil of snapped sigils cast eddies of disharmony through her tuned link with her quartz crystal.*

While the mayor stormed out in limping agitation, Lirenda excused herself with sugared almond courtesy. Avoiding smashed glass and the stains of spilled tea, she followed his lead through the doorway.

The fanned breeze of her departure flicked out the candles and caused an elaborate, pinned lock of the wife's coiffure to tumble like a loop of dropped knitting.

That final indignity lit the firestorm of temper she could not indulge as a hostess. 'Damn the shadow-bending rogue to the torments of Dharkaron's vengeance!' she shrieked at the gawping footman. 'May he burn for eternity beside Sithaer's scaled demons for the nuisance he foists upon guests and genteel entertainment!'

Cast clear of state policy, free at last to pursue her private mission in the face of an unknown crisis, Lirenda smoothed her immediate, base impulse to bolt from the mayor's state mansion. The elegant expanse of the tiled marble foyer echoed with agitated voices. She cut through the traffic of running servants and strode in a brisk swish of silk past the armed captain from the garrison, who convened with the partridge-plump mayor and was barraged with shrill instructions.

Throughout, she extended her awareness, each faculty pitched to trained height. Like a prick of hostility, she sensed the sharpened regard of the watch captain swing to follow her back. She did not look around. Her business at hand concerned nothing else but the directive of her Prime Matriarch: first to right the current upset, and then to pin down the elusive person of Arithon Teir's'Ffalenn. The raking concussion that had unbalanced the wards still shocked static through her aura. An upset of such magnitude surely meant her thrown gauntlet had been accepted; the snare she had crafted on the fate of Fionn Areth had hooked its desired bait. Inwardly thrilled by the prospect of bringing her personal demon to heel, Lirenda quickened her pace. The magisterial, driving joy in her bearing caused drudges and footmen to backstep and shrink from her path.

Ahead, the justiciar's blustering arrival set the doorman into cowering apologies. While a blast of gray glare and wintery cold invaded the untended threshold, Lirenda quietly slipped out.

Above the notched roofs of the mansions and domed hall of state, a low cloud cover sheeted the early sunlight. The air bore the glass-sharp taint that presaged a snowfall. The enchantress shrugged off the chill, unwilling to delay for a servant to send for her cloak. She pushed through the flustered press of officials flocking the outer terrace. Frost rimmed the stone. Without her pattens, Lirenda picked her way on slippered feet down the marble stair, past the ornamental pots quilled with the dead stems of summer peonies and seized in a crystallized armor of ice.

Before she reached the gritted rime of the street, a middle-aged seeress from the order rushed to meet her. Hood torn back, her crystal worn under a band of silk at her brow, she offered the brunt of bad news. 'Every ward we wove through the night is cast down! Your lane-watcher confirms. The quarry we seek did not breach by way of the walls.'

Lirenda's fists clenched in convulsive irritation. 'You're certain?'

Panting, her short-cropped gray hair wisped floss in the wind, the initiate skidded to a stop by the lower step. 'Thrice over. We checked. Nor did the bastard gain entry to Jaelot through a gate or rear postern. Save us all! Cadgia, Third Senior, insists the disturbance that plagues us was unleashed from *inside* the city.'

'Don't look so surprised. The prince we would trap is Torbrand's true lineage and thinks with the mind of a fiend.' Lirenda considered, her shelved coral lips thrilled to a faint smile as Arithon's challenge rose to meet her. 'Our fish has swallowed the lure, don't you see? We have only to close and take him on the hour he steps in to spare Fionn Areth.'

That moment, a hand sheathed in chain mail snatched the Koriani senior by the shoulder.

Lirenda spun around, eyes narrowed. 'Your pardon, sir?'

The watch captain jerked back his offending grasp as if his gloved flesh had been scalded. His bristled chin jutted in uncowed determination, he just managed to hold his own ground. 'What lure? What quarry? You've played Jaelot's moves for your order's own ends, and I demand to be told the truth.'

'There's been duplicity,' Lirenda admitted. Calculation buried in preening distaste, she twitched her crumpled silk straight and flicked the wrinkling twist from her red-banded sleeve. 'One of our own first suspected the ruse.' Her obstructive suggestion came silken smooth. 'Like initiate Elaira, I urge you to watch your prisoner most closely, and ask if he's not a decoy.'

'*What?*' The watch captain clapped a chapped fist to his sword hilt. 'You'll clarify, now, witch. By the orders I bear, I'm to see that wretch up from the dungeon. He's to be bound over for immediate execution, and you dare raise the question that *he's not the Master of Shadow?*'

Lirenda looked arch. 'I claim nothing with certainty. My task, by Morriel's direct order, is to hold Jaelot under Koriani protection. The man you would kill wears the face of a Sorcerer, with no other sure proof to condemn him. None have seen him work spellcraft. I would be negligent if I didn't weigh that issue from every possible angle. If your town was singled out for another attack, how better to throw up a smoke screen? Distract you with a victim held harmless in chains, and the actual Spinner of Darkness might keep complete freedom to cause harm as he will.'

The guard captain shot back an oath, shocked to stark disbelief.

Flat amber in color, Lirenda's eyes on him held a knife-point spark of impatience. 'Detain me at your peril. Our guard spells have collapsed. If Arithon s'Ffalenn is at large within Jaelot, my sisters alone can engage the necessary action to save you.'

'You can't ask a stay on the prisoner's death sentence,' the guard captain said through locked teeth. 'The mayor's hard-set, and the city will riot.'

'Why should I trifle with changing your orders?' Lirenda's quick laugh of dismissal came barbed. 'You'll want your additional men mustered anyway, to see that command carried through.' She slipped a hand under her cloak, gripped her quartz crystal, and cast in mental image the first rune of power against the recalcitrant officer's forehead. 'You need do nothing more than redouble armed vigilance, since it's possible our sister initiate was right.' Hazed now with a glamour of spell-brightened sincerity, she touched the man's bracer and drew him ahead, into the ice-crusted street. 'Don't press your luck. If the boy is in fact not the Shadow Master, but a foil, the true fox might slip out the rear postern.'

'True fox?' The watch captain's iron conviction wavered. 'Then you honestly think we've caught the Sorcerer's double in our dungeon?'

'The pair could indeed be collaborators.' In diabolical timing, the freshened breeze purled over the cornice of the roof, bringing the sheared taint of ozone.

Another lace-worked mesh of false lightning cracked the sky. Lirenda raised her free hand to secure her pinned hair, while the slamming, thunderous report shook slates and rattled the iron spires on the rooftrees. A street child who had been begging flitted past, someone's purse in his filthy fist. No one gave chase. The merchants who fared on their errands in the street poured in panic for the shelter of doorways and arches fronting the verge of Broadwalk Way.

Buffeted by wind, determined to turn the spread of wild fear to advantage, Lirenda tightened urgent fingers and tugged the watch captain's reluctant step into the thoroughfare. 'Would you waste your time doubting? Blameless lives in your city could well be at stake.'

Through the damning roll of echoes, the Koriani seeress shouted back in support. 'Who else would divert us with mayhem and portents, except the true Master of Shadow?'

Lirenda turned right at the first crossroads, the officer of the guard steered like a shambling bear toward the barracks. 'Levin bolts aren't the work of the boy you hold in your dungeon, I can swear to that much. Since last night, we've had him laced into wards against magecraft not even a fly could slip through. Even if you won't take my word without proof, dare you risk being caught in the wrong?'

One hand half-raised to scratch his chin with incredulity, the watch captain shook his head. He squinted, though the thick scud of cloud threw no glare. Before thought, for no reason, he found his mood charged to a queerly exhilarant capitulation. 'All right. Suppose for the sake of brevity your unlikely theory holds weight. If the real Sorcerer's still running free, what remedy do you suggest?'

'A cordon, and swiftly! Seal off the main square. Have guardsmen posted at the mouth of each street, each alley, and in the doorways of all the shop fronts.' Lirenda turned aside from the roiling blast of another gust, then sidestepped the buffeting elbows of four merchants racing to secure locks on their warehouses. 'To safeguard your men from acts of foul sorcery, I'll have my enchantresses back them with watch seals and powerful talismans of banishment.'

Upon the captain's clipped word of agreement, she released her set rune and left him beneath the looming eave of the barracks. While the sky split and snapped through a third discharge of spelled lightning, she resumed the interrupted course of her business and snatched at the seeress's sleeve. 'Send my summons! Except for the circle who stands guard on the walls, and the sisters Cadgia's got scrying, every other initiate we have is to gather in the main square.'

The concussive shock wave of thunder rolled on, slamming echoes through the deep strata of bedrock beneath the justiciar's chamber. The bowels of the mayor's dungeon shook also. Rust flakes pattered off the stained iron hinges, and rumbling vibration shocked ripples across the puddles on the floor. Roused from foul dreams, his senses still sluggish from a drugged sleep, Fionn Areth rolled painfully onto one elbow and blinked the crusts from his swollen eyes.

'What's happening?' The grate to his voice clamped his throat in a cough, half-masking the nearby rustle of skirts dragged across musty, damp straw.

'I can't say for certain,' Elaira replied from the darkness. 'But if I had to guess, I'd lay odds that someone unleashed the quadrangle runes of wild power. The result has raised the free elements into a vortex of chaotic force. Dangerous magic,' she added in afterthought. Despite the warning implied by her words, the lilt to her voice sounded pleased.

'Never mind,' said Fionn Areth, too sore and bleary to decipher the jargon of magecraft. 'My head is mush anyway.'

'Since you're aware enough to talk, how do you feel?' The enchantress stepped closer, a formless shape against the filtered blush of torchlight fallen through the steel grate. Above, someone's boots scraped a volte-face and banged across the planked floor of the guard's room.

'How do I feel?' Fionn Areth lapsed back into his noisome nest of straw. 'All pocked and hammered as if six dozen goats stamped their rutting hooves over my carcass.' More thumps from above, broken through by hysterical shouting and the singing chime of long-bladed weapons being unracked. 'Why are you cheerful? The noise from upstairs seems unfriendly.'

'If I'm pleased,' said Elaira in low, tensioned caution, 'it's because I believe we've been granted an upset in someone's unsavory plans.'

Her supposition gained force with whirlwind expediency as the bullroaring surprise of the mayor's warden racketed down the stone stairway. 'Fetch the prisoner *now*? But his dance with the sword's not supposed to take place until sundown!'

A reply, modulated by jagged hysteria, yammered something clipped too short to hear. Then the warden, through another floor-shaking stampede, howled for his roster of guardsmen. 'You cud-chewing cattle! Roust up from your dice. We're going to need manacles and chain, the good steel ones. That's orders. Can't have the fire melt down the rivets.'

'Not friendly,' Elaira whispered, her flare of exuberance unraveled to threadbare worry. She groped in the straw for her satchel of remedies, then latched boyish fingers around Fionn Areth's left elbow. 'Let's not test their mood. I think you'll do better if you're up on your feet when they come.'

Through the horrible, sweaty interval while the boy fought stiff muscles and the constraint of tight bandages to rise, the warden's henchmen descended the stairwell. They were armed. The pair in the lead bore a chiming length of forged chain between them. Grotesque shadows flittered over the walls, tossed by the flare of pine torches.

Arrived at the cell, the rough, bearded warden pressed his chin to the bars and hailed the Koriani enchantress. 'This be no lynch mob, lady. Requisite orders are sent from the mayor. Can't be a stay now, for trial or argument. Stand down, move aside. We're taking the Sorcerer for his due reckoning with the steel and the fire of retribution.'

Elaira squeezed the trembling flesh of Fionn Areth's forearm, by her touch urging him to bear up. 'I'll walk by his side. He's not steady.'

Keys jangled. The door clashed open and boomed flat against the damp wall. Two burly guards shouldered through, ducking under the five-foot lintel. Both were armored in field helms and mail, and two others at their heels brought the chains.

'Those irons are not necessary,' Elaira protested. 'This boy can't run anywhere. He's injured, you blind dolts! To bind wrists that are bandaged over stitched gashes is an inexcusable cruelty!'

'Won't matter, lady,' snapped the warden, a safe distance removed outside the barred grille of the cell. 'He'll be ash inside the hour, and all your fussy needlework gone to Dharkaron along with him. Cry shame, or cry tears, you won't do a damn thing to stop the sword the mayor wants run through his heart.'

Soiled from the straw, the deep auburn hair she had braided that morning hung straight as oiled bronze between her shoulders, Elaira held her ground. 'By the principles of mercy my Koriani Order was founded to uphold, beware. I will protest every act of undue harsh treatment. By your own mayor's word, my life stands as surety for this prisoner's untimely escape. Leave off the chains! He can go well enough in my custody.'

Fionn Areth, from behind, could not see her features. Small as she was, and weaponless beyond the two little daggers sheathed in her satchel of remedies, something about her determination raised fear. The men-at-arms who carried the chains stalled outright, while two in the lead cringed and found cause to stare elsewhere.

The mayor's warden lost patience. 'Carry on, and no shirking! The orders we have are to bind him.'

'Then use a nice, soft rope.' Sweet reason etched in acid, Elaira tapped her foot. 'We can all smile and wait while you fetch one.' When nobody moved to fulfill her demand, she let fly with the scorn of the streets. 'What do you fear, you cringing, limp daisies? That this poor wretch will walk and haunt you in flames, *after* the sword's let his heartsblood?'

Fionn Areth gasped. Reeling faint, with his gut clenched with nerves and his head split by the pain of a crashing headache, he swayed. A savage rush of vertigo seemed to upend the floor. The enchantress's cool hands and unyielding support were all that held him upright while a shambling sergeant with bad breath and chipped teeth stepped in with a rope and bound him.

'Mind you don't tie too tightly,' Elaira snapped. 'Chafe those dressings in your clumsiness, you'll tear open his wounds.'

The man hawked and spat. 'Who's to care on the matter, when he's bled like a pig on the faggots?'

Elaira bristled. 'Leave that work to your mayor's paid butcher. Do you understand threats? For every small drop of his blood shed beforetime, I'll lay your bollocks under curse as repayment.'

The knots were made firm, but without undue pressure. Elaira insisted on checking. Through a sucking ebb tide of dizziness and fear, Fionn Areth felt an unsettling tremble invade her touch. The change close to unmanned him. She was not one to quail. Through the difficult hours spent stitching and setting the spell seals to heal his gashed knee, she had been unflinching as rock.

'Buck up,' she whispered. Her hand pressed his shoulder, guiding, before his impatient escort could tug at his bonds and drag him out.

Fionn Areth completed the first steps without stumbling. When he faltered, the enchantress held to his side, her grip firm and sure as she braced his failing weight upright. Through his swimming, drunk effort to manage the stair, she railed like a virago, haranguing the guards for their goatish mismanagement and threatening to leave them in a state unfit to breed children.

Had Fionn Areth not been so wretchedly frightened, he might have measured his length from sheer laughter.

Too soon, the stink of rat urine fell behind. Dank, dripping stone gave way to linenfold paneling, and the close jangle of mail opened up into the loftier reverberations off varnished wood floors, gouged white from the hobnailed tread of authority dragging prisoners to the upper hall for trial. Today, no candles burned on the justiciar's dais. The caryatids trapped in suffering support of the massive table seemed a stamped huddle of frozen souls in the gloom. The stagnant air wore the fusted reek of citrus peel and rose petals, and under these, the miasma of degraded humanity, forced down the worn path from incarceration to impersonal judgment.

Fionn Areth battled his panic-struck weakness and a terror that drained his last wits. His senses reeled as the blood left his head. In his state of near collapse, the massive, black pillars seemed to dance on square pedestals, and the high, groined ceiling became insubstantial and prickled with light. Despite his pride, he fainted, jerked short of a fall by the guard who had charge of the rope.

He bled then, despite Elaira's kind heart. Her shouted imprecations thinned and grew distant, then frayed away altogether as he sank in a rising torrent of darkness.

He woke to the splash of ice water on his face. A keening east wind razed his skin. Ugly, shuddering chills danced after the runneled wet, which streamed on and soaked down his spine. Pink droplets fell, rinsed through torn bandages, where his hands were lashed to a crossbar. The pain seemed detached. He blinked water from his eyes and saw he was fastened to a post set upright in an open cart. Four guardsmen were stationed at his shoulders, all fully armed. Their helms shone a dingy, pebbled gray against the graphite gloom of low cloud cover.

'He's awake,' the gruff bass of the warden pronounced.

Fionn Areth surveyed his surroundings through a plastered swath of hair. The enchantress Elaira was no longer beside him. Only the guards in their gold lion surcoats, frowning and jumpy with tension.

'Move him out, then!' cracked the warden.

A drover's whip snapped. The rough-coated horse in the traces shouldered into its collar, and the cart used in Jaelot to bear the condemned to the gibbet creaked and rocked into motion.

The jerk on the ropes reawakened the burning sting of torn sutures. Buckled at the knees, Fionn Areth received the kaleidoscopic, spinning impression of the prison yard, the gapped board sheds used as barracks for convicts frowned over by three turreted towers. Two warders brushed past, running, to fling wide the heavy, barred gate.

Nothing of herding wild goats on the moors could prepare for the noise as the panels swung open.

A mob rampaged outside, a weaving mass of fists and faces, thrashing and screaming and seething in an explosive, bleak fury of hatred. The cordon of mailed soldiers who held them back seemed inadequate, a loose dike thrown down to dam a rank flood. Mounted lancers in field trappings reinforced the line. Eight more in double file escorted the jolting, slow progress of the cart. Death beckoned on all sides, in the shining crescent edges of honed steel, and in the reviling mouths of men, women, and children, contorted with passion beyond even nightmare imagining.

Fionn Areth swallowed. Shivering violently in the rasping, cold wind, he glanced to either side, appeal and desperation on his face.

The guardsman behind him guffawed. 'No hope for you, laddie. Can't shelter behind any damned witch's skirts now. Yon small, mouthy bitch got ordered off elsewhere by direct demand of her senior.'

Spurred beyond fear, Fionn Areth ripped back a grasslands phrase which meant skat of a loose-boweled goat.

A mailed fist split his mouth in punitive fury. He spat blood and glowered, his fury cast in the same mold as the royal heirs descended of Torbrand s'Ffalenn. The guardsman stepped back toward the safety of his fellows, muttering, 'Devil's eyes, that one has. The born spawn of a demon. We'll be better off when he's ashes.'

The adrenaline surge brought on by the pain served to clear Fionn Areth's head. He planted his legs against the sway of the cart, while the horse passed the gates, and the vile imprecations of the crowd closed about him, a battering, dense mass of savagery and noise that built to a force that was deafening.

The populace chanted, as the wagon bore him under the spooled galleries of Spicer's Row. 'Death to the Sorcerer! Death to the Sorcerer!'

Their thousands of voices welded into a barrage of vitriolic spite. The horse sidled, shying. Two guardsmen now walked at its bridle to keep it square in the traces. Every small, accustomed sound became overwhelmed, until all movement near at hand seemed an act done in pantomime, the booming grind of the cart wheels erased, and the oaths of the beleaguered driver. Trapped in that strange, suspended tableau, the mayor's lancers cantered up and down the cordoned verges, the iron-shod clatter of their destriers' hooves drowned utterly in that dinning mill of noise.

Over the spiked helms of his escort, Fionn Areth glimpsed the purple cloaks of Koriani enchantresses embedded here and there amid the tossing motley of the crowd. Their eyes, ever bright, surveyed their surroundings, as if they cataloged each individual nuance of the bystanders on either side of them. None of them glanced in the condemned man's direction, and none of them proved to be Elaira.

Fionn Areth endured, wretched as any of the struggling goats he had led to his father's knife in the slaughter shed. The crowd showed less mercy than he had for dumb beasts. Here, a ham-fisted butcher shook a bloodied cleaver; there, four ragged children who darted on the fringes threw missiles of manure and mud. He managed to duck, at the cost of torn skin where the ropes at his wrists gouged his bandages.

Though the wind snapped his hair, the chill ceased to matter. Sweat rolled down the knotted muscles of his back. The cart turned again, rattling into the narrower lanes of the trade quarter. The jut of the shop fronts, with balconies above, were crammed to capacity with screaming people. Garbage and kitchen peelings rained on his head. Once, the warm slop of a jakes splashed and missed him, splattering the near ranks of guardsmen.

Two broke away, shouting. They pounded in vengeance up the wooden stair from the street, and found themselves beset at the landing by the shrieked imprecations from a trio of toothless grandames. Someone else capped their outrage with another hurled offering, this time the offal steaming and fresh from gutting a slaughtered pig.

The cart lurched ahead, its progress inexorable. The curses of the soldiers and the jeers from the beldames fell into the growl of the crowd. Fionn Areth never knew how the altercation ended. The thinned ranks of his short-tempered escort rounded the smithy and the harness maker's and waded into the choked throng of the eastside markets. There, the cavalcade ground to a halt, blocked by packed knots of onlookers and the ramshackle maze of tinker's stalls and used-wares booths that ringed the public cisterns of Dagrien Court.

Froth flew from the bit as the officer in charge reined his mount down from a half rear. 'Fiends plague! Will you look? The whole town seems possessed!' He jabbed in both spurs, sent his bucketing mount ahead to flag down a lancer. 'Close in the cordon! Then get a dozen men up here with bows. They're needed to cover the prisoner.' He loosed a hand from the rein and shook his fist at the crowd who plunged and howled against the men-at-arms striving to stay them. 'We'll have to back into a side street just to hold our position. Find me two lancers with reliable mounts and send them back to the garrison. We'll need reinforcements to win clear of this impasse without tripping off a damned riot.'

The troop sergeant sounded his brass horn to deliver the urgent command for retreat. Wheeled back to rejoin the mounted escort with the wagon, the captain swore in between his spate of rapid-fire orders. Through bedlam, screamed epithets, and a dauntless assault of bone-hurting noise, he fought to regroup his inadequate band of foot to the task of forming a shield wall to hold off the murderous press. 'Never seen anything like this, not in my born days of soldiering! We'll be lucky to reach the town gibbet before dark, bearing a live prisoner between us.'

# Fourth Upset

The old vintner's shed off Wheelwright's Lane in Jaelot had ceased being inhabited by tradesmen since deeded ownership had been claimed in recompense for a Koriani oath of debt. The mullioned window overlooking the street remained black, but the interior was not empty. On the hour that Fionn Areth was delivered to his fate, an initiate's cloak blocked the incoming light filtered through the latched boards of the casement. One lit candle burned on the sill, the hazed edge of the flame upright in the dust-laden air. Its halo fell like dipped brass on the heads of the three women stationed over the rim of the vat once used to pulp grapes.

Each enchantress held her spell crystal in hand. As one, their gazes stayed trained on the water filling the wooden vessel to the brim. The surface was ironed to rippleless stillness under the influence of their spellcraft. Across that sheened mirror, in animated miniature, the choked confrontation in Dagrien Court played itself out in reflection. The crowd clamoring to witness the blood and fire of execution rolled and surged like stirred cloth scraps, while the cart which bore the condemned to his doom wedged the mouth of the spindler's alley, circled by beleaguered guardsmen.

One of the lancers lost hold on his horse. The creature reared and struck out with its forehooves. Hecklers caught too close scrambled back. An opening gaped through the thronging mob behind, ragged as a snag in torn knit.

'Spell seal has weakened,' the seniormost seeress murmured in a tranced monotone.

480

The sister initiate to her right closed her eyes, and intoned a rhythmic binding to sharpen her flagging will. The resonance of intent carried through her quartz matrix, amplified and heightened into focus. The fingertip she raised to renew the sigils of confusion glowed faintly scarlet in the dimness. Her scribing moved over the scene of obstruction, trailing faint, sifting streamers of energy over the spelled vat of water.

In Beckburn Market, the lancer cajoled his charger back down on four legs. The crowd flooded behind like a breaker against a dam, and his shouted oath reechoed, whisper faint, through the dust-filtered stillness of the shed. 'Fiends alive, it's as though the whole town's been possessed to go mad and run riot!'

The conjuring enchantress sealed her dire work, face sheened with a fine dew of sweat. 'I can't keep your victim exposed for much longer without risking a serious mishap.'

As the senior in charge, Lirenda looked on, her skin like old pearl inlaid into gloom, and her oval face loftily dispassionate. 'Hold firm for as long as possible.'

The wispy, thin elder who stitched sigil after sigil of seek-and-find over and through the gaudy surge of onlookers remained unimpressed by such staunchness. 'If our quarry hasn't taken the bait by now, chances are he's not going to.'

'Keep searching.'

Under Lirenda's iron command, the three enchantresses bent back to their scrying. They wove spells of stay and of manipulation, courting the thinnest edge of raw danger. No one of them harbored undue expectations. The fine, wrought line of spells they maintained skirted the brittle edge of peril. If an accident happened and caused the least bloodshed, the balance would irrevocably tip. An incensed, frustrated, volatile mob would outrun all their careful constraints. Fear and anger would spark an explosion of violence. The lancers trapped in that spelled pocket of entropy might not understand why the populace hazed their position. Yet professional instinct grasped pending danger. They gathered in a roiling, nerve-jumpy mass, their pennoned weapons leveled to stand down a crowd who pressed in like riptide, screaming insult and imprecations.

Lirenda uttered a breathless epithet, resisting her need to pace out her frustration. Backed by the honeycomb rows of wine shelving that now harbored cobwebs in place of corked bottles, she fumed, 'Damn the man for irrational stubbornness! He's lurking inside the city walls, somewhere, or why mock us by tweaking our ward spells!'

'He's Torbrand's descendant,' said the stout, gray-haired seeress. 'His inborn nature as Teir's'Ffalenn won't hold to the straightforward course.'

'Don't harp on the obvious!' Lirenda turned her profile, backed by the cloth pinned over the shutters. Faint light leaked through, curling like silver smoke amid the raised dust stirred by her agitation. 'Tell me how long we have before the reinforcements come through from the garrison.'

'They've already crossed into the north side of the square,' the seeress advised, softly neutral before her senior's simmering temper.

'They've sent in armored horse. Heavy cavalry from the field division.' The one initiate with the nerve to interrupt stated fact, fearlessly cold as etched carbon. 'If you maze these poor people to hamper their war destriers, innocents are going to be trampled.'

Perched on an overturned barrel in the corner, all but overlooked in the tension, Elaira awarded the exchange her own stamp of acidic practicality. 'If Arithon tries his attempt at a rescue against a quarter company of lancers, he's far more likely to get himself skewered than we are to pull him out whole.'

'Spare us your impertinent opinion, if you please.' Lirenda spun in pettish irritation and stepped to the side of the vat. 'Let the seals go,' she commanded. 'Release the confusion and allow the garrison escort to get the prisoner's cart moving again.'

Elaira tucked her hands under her elbows, held them clamped to her side to stop shaking. This one tiny victory signified little. At some point, she knew Prince Arithon must launch his attempt to wrest Fionn Areth from the armed cavalcade. Force or weapons would not deter him, nor numbers, nor the riled crowd in the streets. If those factors did not offer obstacle enough, in each small alley and lane along the cart's labored course, Koriani initiates lay waiting in ambush. If Arithon escaped a lance thrust through the heart, he must find himself pulled down from behind by spring traps and spells of constriction.

At the vat, the bent, wizened elder shifted her incantation to effect the cantrip of dispersal. Old fingers that had once worn delicate jade rings began the arcs of the six primal runes of unbinding. She completed the one to strike down by intent, then the second, for stasis. The third, with its spikes, for clearing tied energies, and the fourth, for stability and balance; the flash and flare of configured power streamed down like dropped tinsel, scattering ripples over the image clinging like film to the water. Next to last came the fifth, for containment of chaos, and the sixth, for grounding out backlash. A heat of freed energy cleared from the water as a burst of ephemeral steam.

The spelled impasse set over the market square gradually came unsnarled. In trembling, distorted reflection, the wagon unwedged from the alley where it had been sidetracked for shelter. Bearing its

toy figure prisoner, and flanked by the pennoned lances in the hands
of its mounted escort, the cavalcade re-formed itself into a wedge and
sheared on toward its appointed destination. That labored passage tacked
an erratic course through the ragtag jumble of shanty stalls that sold
used clothing to poor folk.

Lirenda scrutinized each step and detail with a vulture's fixated
intensity. She waited, hands clenched, as the strayed vortices of spent
spellcraft were wound in by the deft old enchantress. Those withered
fingers knew their work well. Cadgia, Third Senior, had strung arcane
power like knitting throughout her four centuries of life. Meticulous and
neat, she grounded and tied off each loose end into harmless, entropic
knots. Their residual force would gradually spin off and fade without
raising accidental disharmony.

The scene in the vat returned to stability, the cart horse settled,
and the lancers moving in front and behind to clear the way for its
passage.

Lirenda straightened in tight-reined irritation. 'Inform me at once of
any changes.' She transferred her survey from the vat to Elaira, her hair
the immaculate sheen of black wing feathers, and her eyes the intent,
unblinking pale brown of a polished tiger's eye cabochon. 'You will go
nowhere without my permission.'

'Your will,' Elaira replied in street sarcasm, her own gaze wide gray
and unflinching.

Her senior would read past her pretense of indifference; yet the sword
cut both ways. Neither was Lirenda herself immune to the slight slips
that tension laid bare to the trained lens of peer observation. Her carriage
was perhaps too fashionably flawless, her chin just a fraction high-set.
She might have been a glass statue dressed out in silk, except for the
fingers wound over both wrists.

'Don't bend your bracelets,' Elaira said sweetly, heels drumming an
insolent tattoo on the barrel. 'Am I not safely muzzled by my initiate's
oath? Or Ath forbid, do you fear I might snap? What are the odds I
might tip off the end play of your double-sided game of butchery in
the square?'

'Try.' Lirenda smiled daggers. 'Nothing would please me more than
to see our Prime Senior strip your mind. I should find entertainment,
watching you live out your days as a slavering idiot.'

'If you want your boots licked, why not get a puppy?' Elaira shot
back, attacking words all she had to vent the unbearable pain strangled
inside her. 'Dogs never cavil at nosing through muck, but whimper and
grovel for the privilege.'

'You've a mind crude as cat dirt,' Lirenda said. 'A grave pity you didn't lose your tongue as just punishment for begging before the Koriani Order took you in.' She glanced toward the vat, snapped her curt order to carry on, then glided in aristocratic superiority through the doorway, where a second circle of seeresses labored to coordinate the movements of the enchantresses keeping vigil outside in the streets.

Confined to her barrel, Elaira endured. Feelings warred in her, ferocious and hot. Too real, the prospect that temptation would lead to disloyalty and see her consigned to the order's supreme penalty. Eyes closed, she took a deep breath and wound fired nerves back to patience. No question now, how her heart would respond. If the opening came to abet Arithon's intervention to save Fionn Areth, she would act in sacrifice with no second thought.

To ensure their escape from Morriel Prime's trap would be worth any cost under sky.

The minutes crawled by in spring-wound suspense, with the reflection in the vat standing witness. The prisoner's cart crept and rocked through the press. Elaira could snatch only glimpses of the scried image that measured its progress. More often, someone else's hand or face obscured the critical viewpoint. Those moments, she was left to interpret events from the nuances garnered from the expressions of firsthand watchers. The vital details that destroyed peace of mind remained elusively past her reach: such as how Fionn Areth fared under the strain. Was he still weak and dizzy, or had the sigil to lend him strength as she left allowed him to regain his balance? Had his guardsmen vented their tempers and been cruel through the nerve-wracking delays imposed by Lirenda's meddling? From her limited vantage on the barrel, Elaira caught only the occasional glimpse of bowed shoulders and a face resting in what appeared sheer despair upon the support of tied wrists.

Two crossroads passed. No ambush happened. The order's seeker found no sign of Arithon.

Lirenda breezed back from her conference with the seniors who readied the spring traps and bindings. The serenity fixed on her cameo features implied a vexed mood for the kink in her plans.

Yet the cart and its prisoner rolled inexorably onward without reprieve or intervention.

The sky capped the scene in clouds like sheet lead, with a tireless north wind snagging at hats and ribbons and crackling the streamers of the lance pennons.

'We'll see a blizzard by nightfall,' the seeress forecast. She touched another sigil to track the image more closely as the cavalcade wheeled around a constricted corner.

Cart and horse reached the sharp, jutted angle where the justiciar's house overlooked a three-way convergence of streets. A horse trough paned over with ice sat beneath a bronze statue of the galleyman whose vessel had marshaled the harbor blockade long years ago in the uprising. Gulls had used the figure's hat for a roost, and decades of dropped guano streaked the shoulders and face, etching the verdigris patina. Past a brick-walled flower bed crusted with snow, the thoroughfare widened into the sloped descent of Broadwalk Way.

The avenue extended like a wheel spoke from the mayor's palace on the rise to the stone-cobbled square beneath the old harbor gate, where fleets of high-prowed Paravian ships had once docked. The stone platform that now staged Jaelot's public executions, in another century and under a clanborn earl, had served as the dais for visiting dignitaries. The sockets that had originally stepped awnings and banners were now inset with iron rings. Two stout posts of oak had been erected in mortar for tying the condemned for the sword thrust. Around these, in tiered piles, lay the bundled pine faggots drenched in seal oil, which would rise into flames and black smoke at a spark's touch.

On a windless day, the fortunate victim might asphyxiate from the fumes before the cruel heat crisped the flesh from his bones, and he screamed his throat raw from blind agony.

Elaira sat on the barrel and watched in the vat as the cart was reined to a halt. She saw soldiers, like toys, dismount from toy horses and ram back the overeager crowd. Men in black surcoats with Jaelot's gold lions unlashed Fionn Areth's wrists. He stumbled once as they dragged him out of the cart, and again, as his forced step caught on the slick granite stair. Half-carried, half-dragged, he was hauled to his fate at the posts.

Welded into a sealed silence of tension, Elaira scarcely noted Lirenda's rapid speech. The slipstream of words reached her in snipped fragments, broken down by the ugly, defeated apprehension that her faith had been founded on vain hopes. Arithon had come, but had seen no opening to act; and Fionn Areth would die as the pawn whose crowning play might never happen.

More than a Koriani conspiracy would fall in the ashes of this day's defeat.

'. . . can't believe he's not acted,' Lirenda said, furious. 'Of all the contingencies we worked and planned for, this one is the most inexplicable. If the boy's death takes place uncontested, all of our theories are wrong. Every effort we make to find and take the Shadow Master henceforward must be done in deep cover and subterfuge.'

The seeress at the vat turned her head to reply. The opening between her elbow and the seeker to her left let Elaira see clearly as Fionn Areth was lashed spread-eagled between the oak posts. Tears blurred her eyes. She blinked them away, unwilling to separate herself from even one second of his agony. The guilt tore her open, stopped her thought and her breath, that she had been part and party to the atrocity which brought him at last to the stake.

The men-at-arms tore off his thin shirt. As the seeress steadied the image in tight focus, the remorseless detail showed that Fionn Areth was shaking.

Elaira bit her lip, the pain shared, and the relentless strain of dreading the inhumane spectacle yet to come.

A soldier arrived with a pine pitch torch propped upright in a bucket of sand. He set the cresset down alongside posts and faggots, then glanced over his shoulder in unsettled deference and made way for someone beyond him.

Behind the miserable, bared back of the condemned, the executioner mounted the block, cloaked head to foot in coal black.

He was not a large man, but the escorting men-at-arms gave his arrival wide berth. Nor would the stoutest of them meet his glance or acknowledge his human presence. Tinnily faint in the etched stillness and dust, the crowd screamed their crude appreciation. The executioner strode into his place in the tableau, the hood of his trade riffled against his cheek by the sea wind, and the face underneath obscured by a mask of cut silk. Wrapped in dark cloth, Jaelot's paid killer carried the longsword that would pierce the condemned Sorcerer through the heart.

Elaira's stunned gaze fixed on that weapon, morbidly unable to tear free of the horror that must follow when its silver length was drawn and laid bare. The gloved hand on the hilt seemed too easy, too slight, for the rending act of its office.

That instant, time stopped. *Something* caught at Elaira's attention and slapped all the air from her lungs.

Those fine, supple fingers, surely she knew them? A tug of wild hope, in the carriage of those black-clad shoulders, and perhaps, the listening tilt of the head. Though he was cloaked and masked, she felt the shock of stunned recognition pass between the executioner and herself.

Then Lirenda's voice, imperative, shattered through her raced thoughts. 'I'm speaking to you!'

Elaira flinched and looked up, the inescapable truth betrayed beyond any hope of concealment by the love and desperation in her face.

Koriani trained in the arts of observation, Lirenda seized on that opportune exposure. 'Ath's deliverance, he's *there*!' She spun toward the vat in an agitated whirl of rich silk. 'Which one? *Which one is he?*'

But in the end, she need not ask after all. Given the sure cue of the Shadow Master's presence, his assumed identity became obvious.

Lirenda's shout pealed through the dead air and touched off an explosion of movement. 'By the power invested by Morriel Prime, we must act fast to confine him! Send word to every initiate we have. Direct them to raise banners of guard across every door, every lane, every shop front and alley that leads away from the main square!'

# Trace Magic

Far south, worn by a bone-stripping ride in cold winds up the West Shand peninsula from Earle, Asandir leads his blown horse through the salt pools of West Fen, then enters the grimward which guards the remains of the great drake, Eckracken; and for the hours, the weeks, or the months he will need to refigure the seals of protection, neither man nor mage might reach him . . .

In a gabled mansion off Spinster's Alley in Jaelot, an aged woman sits in darkness, attentive to the ranging, dissonant tones that run through her home's stone foundations; in disturbed concern, she addresses the servant who waits, deferent, at her right hand: 'Jasque, I suspect Koriathain have set wards to cause harm. Go out, will you please? Find out if someone's in trouble . . .'

Upon solstice noon, the power of a Paravian mystery released by a masterbard's melody peals down Athera's sixth lane; tuned tracks across latitude become reawakened, vibration singing down lateral channels, to skew off the damaged axis of Rockfell Peak, then to peal frustrated, through bedrock, and bare trees; a whisper of that balked resonance doubles into itself, and spills into faint imprint over the ghost track of another spell, the left remnant of a construct that once recalled a Sorcerer from a perilous quest between stars . . .

# XIV. Bait

S tripped for the sword thrust to claim his young life, Fionn Areth resisted the fear that battered him toward mewling degradation and weakness. Bitter winds off the bay lashed his hair and reddened the bare skin of his torso. The scent of volatile resins and pine intermingled with the thick, oily smoke from the torch. The fumes clogged his lungs and laced his gut into nausea. Never in his life had he felt so alone, nor so crushed down by despair. No mauling pain left from bruising and cuts could compare with the agonized terror that spurred the raced beat of his pulse.

Around him, the people of Jaelot screamed revilement. They heaved and pressed, a pack of wild animals ravening to tear at live flesh. Their passion to see bloodshed beat the cold air with an almost palpable force. From the cordon of soldiers set around the stone dais, to the craftshops and mansions which fronted the square, fury held him surrounded, an inimical mass of strangers' faces stamped into all range of expression. Those not engrossed with their sick fascination were chillingly ugly with spite. Man or woman, nowhere could the condemned on the block see one who showed sorrow or pity.

In that absence of mercy, all hope drained away. Fionn Areth coughed smoke from a paper-dry throat. Youth and adventure and the lure of a prophecy had brought him to this. He would leave life as the hapless target of hatred, damned for the crimes of the Shadow Master he had once cherished dreams of pledging his sword to suppress. Nothing remained of his bright fabric of ideals. His shared union with the girl at the inn in the Skyshiels seemed the fragmented wisp of a dream. He owned no goatherd's identity and no fate. Only the cruel, hard certainty of death a handful of minutes away.

The four men-at-arms posted around the piled faggots were all gray-haired veterans, survivors of the legendary defeat arranged by the Sorcerer at Vastmark. Their creased eyes beheld the condemned with etched purpose and the granite satisfaction of a vengeance too long delayed. Nearer to hand, the executioner's enigmatic, wound patience seemed aberrant as forged steel given the breath of life in human form.

Fionn Areth clenched his jaw, unable to quiet his chattering teeth. He endured through the drawn-out, thoughtless delay, while the mayor's wife and entourage pulled up in a black-and-gold-lacquered carriage. Assisted by swarms of liveried footmen, she and her guests were whisked off the street and settled in comfort behind the ornate iron railings of an open-air gallery across the square. Musicians arrived. After them, two more gilded carriages plowed through the press and disgorged their peacock array of wellborn passengers.

While Fionn Areth suffered in tormented suspension, the select inner circle of the mayor's acquaintances flocked in polite company to share the event of his death. Their servants dispensed wine and refreshments. Ladies in fashionable hats and fur muffs exchanged small talk behind the stolid backs of their house guard, brought along to quell rowdy antics or the unplanned small mishaps that might arise in a crowd of mannerless commoners.

From the railed second stories of the merchant's mansions, parties rollicked in similar gaiety. The highborn of Jaelot would enjoy their sensation at safe remove, where velvets were not likely to be spattered with splashed blood, nor the ladies be troubled by noisome stinks and rank smoke.

A herald's horn blared. The state carriage bearing the mayor made its ponderous way through the press. Black plumes on the horses' headstalls nodded in lockstep with the ribboned helms of the city's elite guard. To a second blast of trumpets, his Lordship of Jaelot emerged and ascended the block, attired in his court robes and jeweled ermine hat, his chains of office and emblazoned state finery. He was followed by the city aldermen and the high court magistrate, then a double-file procession of footmen, who spread a carpet over the cleared end of the dais. More servants arrived with upholstered chairs to accommodate the titled circle of state witnesses.

The magistrate stayed standing, and read out the long list of charges. While the wind snapped his parchment and rouged his mournful nose, the howls of the crowd swelled into a clamor. Barely one word in ten reached Fionn Areth, who scarcely knew which malfeasance had caused his arraignment.

Assaulted by the thunderous wall of raw noise, by the fumes of oiled smoke, and by the sick, sweating nerves of a bottomless terror, Fionn Areth fought to keep loose knees from buckling while the warrant recording his death for city archives was rolled, tied in ribbons, and sealed by a black-robed secretary. Second to second, he forced back the screams of outraged self-pity that beat to escape from his throat.

His last, sorry vestige of pride would be lost if the semblance of dignity escaped him.

Soon the horn shrilled again. The herald and the city justice retired in highbred sangfroid. The men-at-arms in their heraldic lion tabards dressed weapons and signaled an end to the forms of due process.

A hand wave from the mayor, then the herald's ritual pronouncement of execution. 'Arithon s'Ffalenn, called Master of Shadow! For the sake of your crimes against our fair city of Jaelot, your spirit shall be delivered by sword and fire to your rightful hour of death. Your case now passes to Daelion Fatemaster's judgment, and thence, to Dharkaron's hand for redress. May the powers past the Wheel show you mercy for the aforesaid burdens of guilt.'

The bursting, wild cheers seemed to batter the air and shake the chalk clouds overhead. Despite the barrage against overwhelmed senses, Fionn Areth knew the executioner's step at his back. His chilled skin recorded each dread stir of movement, and his breath went shallow with panic. Through blinding tears, he beheld the dark shape of the hooded man who came forward and stopped before him. Black-gloved hands grasped a black-hilted sword. The masked face met and measured his shrinking misery, then the wretched sum of his fear.

'Mercy on me,' Fionn Areth gasped out, the words mouthed without strength for voice. He wanted to beg the act done with dispatch, but the last scrap of courage deserted him. At the end, he loved life too much.

The hired butcher stepped close, reached out, and grasped his victim's bared shoulder. The move appeared natural. As though he would steady his victim's frail, shivering body and ensure the lethal first sword thrust pierced cleanly.

Fionn Areth shut his eyes. Bravado failed him. A whimper escaped his locked teeth.

He felt the ephemeral brush of cloth near his face. Through the ugly, undisciplined clamor of humanity, someone spoke into his ear. The voice was cut crystal, each word stamped separate from that debacle of chaos as a filament spun from a dream. 'Boy! Hear me, boy.' Then the insane promise, fired with compassion and backed by a rage to break rock. 'You shall see death and fire on this day. But by the decree of your crown prince's justice, none of the blood will be yours.'

A shake, as though to awaken a sleeper; Fionn Areth opened his eyes. Devoid of hope, emotionally pummeled past logic or even disjointed thought, he watched in uncomprehending numbness as his killer's gloved fingers slipped the ties of the mask. Alone amid a multitude of ravening humanity, he beheld the naked face of the man Jaelot had hired to claim his life by the sword.

Eyes met his, level green, shelved under an upswept browline. The thin, high-set cheekbones slanted into a tapered, neat chin: line for line, as though some mad facet of perception had warped vision into waking delirium, Fionn Areth beheld his own image in the features of Jaelot's executioner.

'Just so you'll know me,' his double said in dry humor that seared like a struck spark on ice.

The grip on Fionn Areth's shoulder clamped down; the other gloved hand cast away the silk mask. In one driving move, the apparition unsheathed his black weapon.

Light burst, and burned. A white fire of explosion ripped sky and earth into a flash-point flare of primal energy. Amid coruscation to stun breathing life, a sound like no other unfurled, arisen into one burgeoning chord wrought of notes pitched to shatter the very foundations of sanity.

Fionn Areth cried out. He felt as if all his flesh came unraveled, jerked loose and restrung into that ringing cascade of raw power. Overhead, the executioner's drawn blade parted the air, its edge of spelled steel a cry to tear darkness and spin mind and heart into soaring and bridleless joy. Then that same sword descended, still howling its unearthly, keyed splendor.

Fionn Areth cringed, jerked short by tied wrists. Yet no stroke of bared steel rammed home through his breast. Instead, the ropes parted with a jerk that should have dropped him to a limp heap in collapse.

The man's hold braced him upright. 'Hang on,' the encouragement a torn rag through that fabric of fearful, wild harmony.

Dizzied and dazzled, rendered witless by that kaleidoscopic maelstrom of tuned sound, Fionn Areth stumbled. By his side, the voice of his rescuer shouted in a pitch that recaptured one facet of the sword's uncanny resonance. Through screams, between the tearing, rending howl of burst metal as the cordon of armed guards were hurled bodily from their feet, his phrasing seemed sheared from forged light.

The forceful words pealed through that cry of celebration, honed and edged by a masterbard's diction. 'This is a city that dismembers justice and makes murdering sport of the innocent! Stand clear, or stand warned! As your sovereign prince under old kingdom charter, my judgment holds no appeal. As of this moment, by crown law of Rathain, there will be no mercy given to those among you who show none!'

Light and sound reached their hammering, toned peak of crescendo. Weeping on his knees, Fionn Areth felt as if his very flesh would refigure into winged form and take flight.

'Lie flat! Now!' The swordsman dealt him an urgent shove.

But the warning became meaningless noise to his ears. Fionn Areth found no response. His body seemed substanceless baggage, even when a buffeting push pitched him headlong against the swept stone of the dais. Sprawled gasping, stunned breathless by chill and ripped into helpless, whimpering tears by the peal of wild power from the sword, he scarcely cared as the same ruthless hand pinned him facedown, unrelenting.

All at once, like a gap ripped through the continuity of creation, the tones of primal harmony snuffed out. The black sword fell mute. The wrenching, immediate cessation of song rocked air like a blow. Despair followed after, fit to whirl the stunned mind to insanity. Whipped mindless with panic, the bystanders screamed. Their cries held true terror and a riven, cruel sorrow, as if all the world had been darkened. Cheated of the glorious, exalted step into grand mystery, they found themselves vised back into the ordinary, drab colors of earthly substance.

A heartbeat passed in bludgeoned suspension. Then the sky overhead ripped asunder.

An elemental bolt of lightning jagged down. The impact tore apart the oak posts set upright amid the piled faggots. Splinters flew airborne and burst into comet tails of shot sparks. In wan, bloody light, the upset on the dais seemed awash in the fires of armageddon. The mayor and his ministers were sprawled prostrate in terror amid their toppled cordon of men-at-arms. Swords, helms, and mail had been warped out of true, as if cast in refraction through water. Except the links of burst mail left exposed flesh scored and bleeding, and the bent sword blades were no nightmare illusion.

Thunder rolled in a slamming shock wave of concussion. Blazing knots of burst wood rained down in clumps and ignited the pitch-soaked faggots.

In orchestrated step, a second explosion whirled the debris like blown chaff. Burning sticks flew airborne. Flaming debris whirled into the screaming, packed crowd like a vengeful storm out of Sithaer.

'Up now. Can you walk?' The insistent grip tugged.

Fionn Areth coughed out a ratcheting breath. 'I don't know.'

That instant, the whole world went black.

'Ath!' he shrilled. 'I'm blind. I've gone blind! I can't see!'

'No,' said the benefactor now veiled in blank darkness. 'You suffer no worse than a shadow.' His assurance became all the more terrifying for its matter-of-fact dismissal. 'Now, on your feet! Quickly. Things might be tied in a muddle for the moment. But the second these people pull themselves back to rights, the descent of Dharkaron's Black Chariot itself couldn't turn them from shredding us to mincemeat.'

Hauled shakily erect, Fionn Areth sensed movement, then flinched as a warmed fall of wool flicked his icy skin and unfurled over his naked shoulders. Understanding shot home, foolishly late: that the cloth would be black. His look-alike rescuer would be none other than the Master of Shadow himself.

He must have exclaimed his discovery aloud.

'Oh, very good.' Through rising screams, a wafted stink of charred hair, and the clashing bellows of two armed officers who shouted for torches and buckets, the criminal Sorcerer paused. He tacked sharply, then lunged to the right. His sword sheared and clanged against something metallic. Another parry, a darted thrust, then a whine as bared steel ripped into something less solid.

'Come on.' Through a ripe reek of blood, the guiding hand on Fionn Areth's arm pressed leftward. As if no one screamed, or no guardsmen crashed in blundering, blind pain at his heels, the Shadow Master recaptured his dropped conversation. 'There's an elegance, don't you think? The fires meant for you are being rained down on the mayor's guard and most of your front row bystanders.' He pursued his unlikely, talkative bent of humor. 'Fair is fair, after all. The explosion which arranged such a neat twist of justice was our mad spellbinder's champion touch. *Now, come on!* You can praise Dakar's genius as much as you like, but after we've survived to rejoin him.'

Then in breathless afterthought, while Fionn Areth was hauled into a staggering semblance of flight, the running lines of monologue resumed. 'Be careful. That lump to your right is an unconscious guard. You may step on his hands, just watch out for the sword. Also, don't spit in the eye of sweet fortune. The darkness you curse just happens to be all that's spared your skin and mine from the burning. Now, here, mind the staircase.'

Fionn Areth's fumbling efforts incited a spectacular oath, hard followed by a snatch of rhymed proverb to the effect that bad actions begat yet worse consequences.

As though drunk on daft wit and exhilaration, the Master of Shadow added, 'My apologies in advance. We've got enemies waking up. There won't be any time to claim the day's prize for grace.' With small care for torn flesh and battered limbs, those taut, busy fingers shifted grip on Fionn Areth's wrist.

His bruised arm was braced across a wiry muscled shoulder, and the bunched hood of another mantle, likely worn underneath the voluminous black cloak just shed from necessity to clothe him. In a downward, swift rush, the condemned goatherd was dragged free of the block, past the tangled, prone bodies of men-at-arms from the cordon, and plunged headlong into the seething crush of the crowd.

The dark was black felt. Blinded and mazed, every person packed into the grand square of Jaelot took to their heels in mass terror. The buffeting press of them bashed the wind from Fionn Areth's chest. His feet slipped and caught on the cobbles. A battering, unseen force in the darkness, the mob elbowed and surged like a beast. Voices shouted and screamed. Hands snatched and clawed. Terror choked reason, while the palpable nightmare of Arithon's shadow ignited a trampling panic.

'You should be aware,' resumed that remarkable, silken voice in his ear. 'Far more than bluebloods from Jaelot are in full cry after our hides.' Through an unrelenting dark as absolute as poured pitch, the Sorcerer steered a definite course through the struggling, obstructive bodies. 'The Koriathain are much worse than unfriendly. There's a sizable pack of them shuffling spells to see our free movement cut short. Are you willing to fight? We'll need more than luck to escape them.'

The closely bunched bodies made swordplay impossible. If the spelled blade was still drawn, Fionn Areth could not see. Forced to stumbling flight, he noticed the Shadow Master's mellifluous voice now addressed the maddened hysteria, words and tone pitched to settle and calm. A man with a cudgel was cajoled into helping a crying woman seek her lost child. The shoving torrent of humanity eased a fraction, as bystanders were urged to assist. But if Arithon managed to blunt the irrational edge from the hysteria nearest to hand, throughout the square, crazed upset still reigned.

Shouts commingled with the clangor of weapons as men-at-arms regrouped under orders to seek the Shadow Master, then resorted to steel to suppress the rampaging ferocity of the crowd. Torches flared. Their light shone queerly battened in murk, as if fog stained with ink roiled and clung against the facades of the buildings. An officer's bugle blared a shrill call to rally, and the hammering clatter of shod hooves warned where mounted lancers shouldered their destriers through the press, hunting the renegade criminal.

More torches bloomed, one startlingly near at hand. Propelled head-long by the torrent and by the relentless grip on his arm, Fionn Areth snatched the chance to look closely. He saw, not black hair, but blond, and snub-nosed features that were fair-skinned and rosy.

His cry of confusion turned nearby heads. One heartbeat, he caught the swift flash of a grin; then blanketing shadow clamped down to forestall any further scrutiny.

'Don't mind the change,' said Arithon s'Ffalenn from inside that knot of smothered flamelight. 'The face you saw first is my real one.'

He found unseen egress between what smelled like a mule drover and someone unwashed and sweaty who worked in a bakehouse. Fionn Areth sneezed out a breath of inhaled flour. Someone else broke an impasse by stepping on some woman's toes. The shrieks of the offended matron fell behind, with Arithon's low comment slipped undaunted through bedlam. 'The odd guard or townsman will be fooled in dim light. Koriathain are another matter.'

Long overdue, Fionn Areth found his voice. 'What makes you think I'll stay with you? I nearly burned for your list of dire crimes. If I win free, I won't take your murdering cause out of gratitude. Just the opposite. I support the Alliance. For justice, why not give your name to the first guardsman I find wearing Jaelot's gold lion?'

'Well that could be difficult, wearing my likeness,' said Arithon s'Ffalenn in quick irony. 'Pull on your hood.'

When Fionn Areth made no effort, he yanked the cloth up himself. Then he released his cloaking of shadows.

Daylight resumed, gray and matter-of-fact, over a scene stirred to roiling motion. The bolting, terrified press of humanity seemed the worse for that stripping exposure. Arithon had swathed his face in his mantle, a green wool broadcloth without embroidery. His head turned away, as if he took bearings, while his supporting hold on Fionn Areth's arm stayed fixed and firm as a shackle. 'You're my drunken brother, if anyone asks.'

The noise and confusion effectively deferred any argument. Blinking at the sudden transition from darkness, Fionn Areth glanced behind.

Smoke spired upward from the raised block, where faggots still flamed and streamed cinders. The rucked carpet burned also, and one upset state chair. The space in between teemed black with clumped guardsmen, fallen over themselves to extricate Jaelot's hysterical mayor. The city magistrate crouched down as though faint, while below, where the cordon of lancers had stood, the belated wedge of heavy cavalry shouted and waved lances, exhorting the pikemen to rally from witless confusion. War destriers plunged and battled their bits as a heedless populace continued to stream past their haunches.

Ahead, more guardsmen breasted the choking press to set a blockade on the side streets. An upset carriage spun random wheels, while its team plunged and kicked, entangled in traces. The rich had fled from the open galleries. Their departed wake left tables of spilled food, upset goblets, and cut-glass decanters. Upper stories showed a wall of barred shutters, while rioters stormed the doors of the street-level craftshops in search of tools that might serve them as weapons. Not every owner was set back by the looting.

Fionn Areth saw a red-cheeked butcher and his family handing out knives and cleavers to all comers with blustering encouragement to hunt down and kill the escaped Sorcerer.

Next step, he tripped over something ragged and wet. Arithon's hold kept him from sprawling headlong into a body left pulped by the mindless stampede of humanity.

Sickened again, and reeling with horror, Fionn Areth lagged back in distress. His nemesis ruthlessly braced him back upright. Someone slammed into him. A matron pointed and screamed. 'Look! there's the Spinner of Darkness himself!'

While Fionn Areth's gut upended in pure terror, he saw a dirk flash off to his right. A black-haired man fell screaming to his knees, with a pale girl bent over him, wailing; *not Arithon s'Ffalenn, but a stranger.*

Yet the blood which gushed through the victim's clamped fingers was no less mortal for the tragedy of mistaken identity. The girl wept and clung, while the bystanders cheered, and the killer flourished his dripping blade in whooping, ignorant triumph.

'Seen enough?' said the trueborn scion of Rathain, now whetted to rage. His shadow clapped down, unmercifully blank, and lidded the carnage in darkness. 'If you're dead set against the small talent that shields you, go *far* out of Jaelot before you try steps that might bring down drastic consequences.'

Fionn Areth said nothing, but forced knotted muscles to carry a more even share of his weight. Movement had loosened the worst of his stiffness. His bruises pulled less. He found he could limp without stumbling, then bear up to the shoves when hapless folk blundered into him. Arithon's hand lent more guidance than support, which was well, for ahead, where Cobbler's Lane met the square, the first Koriathain stood in ambush.

'You see her, too?' said Arithon s'Ffalenn.

In chill fact, even the casual eye could not miss her. She waited before the stone archway that fronted a fashionable dress shop, her violet mantle furled against the raw chill, and her alertness keen as a ferret's. The quartz crystal raised in her hand blazed white light, a beacon whetted in unpleasant, sharp spells that burned a bright star through the uncanny blanket of shadow. Nor did the crowd set to flight in crazed fear wish to pass through that flared burst of spellcraft. The mindless egress slowed and swirled like a river current jammed by a rock. Trapped in the eddy, unable to turn, Arithon sought to stop dead.

The enchantress was not the only threat present. Under the covered roof built to shelter the rich as they stepped from their carriages, four uniformed guardsmen with nervous, drawn swords kept an uneasy vigil.

'More guards in town clothes wait by that pastry shop just across the street,' Fionn Areth observed, apprehensive. 'Two of them were with the dog pack that dragged me into the dungeons.'

'They know your appearance? Then we have trouble.' Arithon need not elaborate.

Jostled and buffeted as the crowd broke and ripped past them, both fugitives saw how the witch surveyed each face that crossed through her net of silvery light. The distinctive s'Ffalenn features would not escape notice on the instant the Koriani seals razed through the shadowed illusion masking his natural appearance.

The time to plan strategy for evasion was lost as a ham-handed blacksmith barged into the fugitives from the rear. 'Mind yerself! Move! Make way for the mayor's guard.'

A squad of mounted lancers pressed for the same side street, with no way to turn or deflect them. Their impetus from behind pressed the logjammed masses inexorably forward into that ring of spelled light.

'I hope you prefer hot tarts over witches,' said Arithon in rife desperation.

He turned his cloaked face aside as the fired glare of the ward fell upon him. Masking cloth availed nothing. The set spell had been tuned to comb auras, infallibly more reliable than the shortfalls of visual identity. Preset rings of ciphers and keys triggered off the instant the flare touched Arithon's person. A sound like a rip tore across the charged air. The baleful burst brightened, rinsing the street into sudden, actinic brilliance.

'There!' cried the enchantress. Unerringly, she pointed. 'Both the Master of Shadow and his look-alike henchman! Take them in hand.'

Still hooded, and brazen enough to react, Arithon raised his master-bard's voice in persuasion. 'Indeed! *There they are!*' He gestured farther down the street. 'Hurry! Clap them in irons! Move quickly, before they escape!'

Blind instinct turned heads and swerved the first steps of the guards' headlong rush. The following cohort of lancers reined back, reflexively searching the press to locate the flight of the fugitives. For a fateful split second, the crowd swirled to an indecisive standstill.

Arithon plunged ahead, an eel through turbid flotsam, towing Fionn Areth behind him.

The first guard by the bakeshop died on his sword. The next, he rammed into a signpost. The last pair entangled in the recoil of bodies as hapless bystanders flinched back from the outbreak of bloodshed.

'Down!' Arithon shouted. He jerked Fionn Areth with him, just as a bolt of uncanny energy sheared like swarming wasps overhead. 'Stayspell,' he gasped, then whistled an odd triplet that rang out in harsh, cringing dissonance.

Across the street, the Koriani enchantress screamed. She dropped her quartz focus, clapped her hands to her ears, then screamed again as the crystal changed resonance and nearly shattered.

The spell the stone matrix had amplified came unraveled. Its skewed impact smashed the shutter. Frame and glass, the bakeshop window imploded to a cloud of hot ash and ripped slivers.

'Go through,' cried Arithon, unwarrantedly jubilant as he yanked off his mantle. He unfurled the cloth like a blanket over the one intrepid guardsman who burst through cowed citizens to seize him. 'Lights out for you as a damned witch's bloodhound.' He skewered the guard mired in the wrack. While Fionn Areth hurtled on and slithered over the smoking, curdled varnish on the sill, he bent, cleared his sword, and snatched back his holed cloak. When he straightened, the guardsman's purloined weapon claimed as salvage, he ducked through the window on the heels of his double.

Innocuously fair haired once again, he looked harmless, except for the bared blades he brandished in right and left hands. In baleful, wild humor, he breathed in the thick, yeasty smells of fresh bread. His green eyes missed nothing as he sized up the tradesfolk who stared openmouthed over their dropped utensils. He measured the journeymen, bedecked in floured aprons and bare arms, rolling out pastries and packing them with fragrant gobs of jam; then the women, muscled like fishwives, who kneaded and braided the dough. Lastly, the red-faced apprentices, caught aback tending the ovens, and behind them, the master baker, a wizened elder with muttonchop whiskers, ensconced like an owl on a stool. The old man brandished a bone-handled cane, his toothless lips puckered with outrage. 'Come here for looting, have you?'

Arithon ignored him. 'Fetch some hot trays!' he snapped to the apprentice who gawped over his shovel by the coal fire. 'Use them to barricade this smashed window, at once. There's a Sorcerer outside, very dangerous.'

With his head tipped in deference to the spitfire patriarch, Arithon spoke fast, 'We are certainly not thieves, but citizens come to protect you.' Credentials established, he tossed the spare sword into Fionn Areth's surprised hand. Then he asked after the wooden stair which connected every street-level craftshop in Jaelot to living quarters upstairs. 'Someone needs to stand guard on the dormers, lest banespells set fire to your roof.'

'My daughter will show you along,' said a woman, against the proprietor's bristling objection. 'Stay quiet, you goose. Nobody needs your dose of hot air while there's a crisis afoot.'

Arithon flashed her his best taproom smile, the universal brand of insouciant charm that won bards past furious wives whose goodmen had misjudged their capacity to hold beer and stay upright. 'We'll go to defend the upper balcony, then. Don't let anybody in or we're done for.'

Fionn Areth, astonished, followed the daughter's lead, with Arithon, still talking, behind him. He scarcely heard what the Masterbard said. No sooner were they pounding up the twisty, narrow stair, when the downstairs door thundered and gave way with a splintering crash. The mayor's mounted lancers had apparently mustered a charge and rammed down the flimsy panel. A hiss and a squeal marked the fate of another man-at-arms, come to grief in a joust with a pastry tray at the window.

The comely daughter glanced behind in uncertainty, while the two fugitives raced on ahead. Arrived on the third-floor landing, Arithon loosed a maniacal whoop of soft laughter. 'Score one for the hounds, but two points for us foxes. They can't chase with horses on the roof.' His critical gaze gauged the limp in Fionn Areth's stride, then the sword and the young hand that held it. 'Good. You know how to use that. We'll see about finding something better forged than Jaelot's garrison issue.'

Two more light steps saw him through an open door. The bedroom beyond had thin dormer windows, and no other egress. Fresh out of safe options, Fionn Areth carried forward. He found the glass casement swung open, and Arithon's shod feet dangling from the roofpeak outside. The shoes vanished, replaced by a down-reaching hand. The fingers were sea tanned, longer and slimmer than Fionn Areth's, yet ringless in their refinement.

'Grab hold, and be quick,' came Arithon's encouragement. 'Those troops are the mayor's elite guard. They've infested the downstairs like ants.'

Fionn Areth felt the floor vibrate to the pounding of boots up the stairway. He clasped Arithon's wrist, cleared the sill with the sword, and swung out on faith, just as another fall of shadow clapped down, impenetrable and dense as a corpse shroud.

'They've got marksmen with crossbows,' the s'Ffalenn prince apologized.

Fionn Areth snapped a crude word through locked teeth. Suspended over thin air, scrabbling for firm purchase against unpainted clapboards sun and weather had raised to an uncouth morass of splinters, he skinned his good knee and wrenched his bruised tendons in his upward clamber onto the bare slate above.

The roof proved no haven. Runneled ice cased the peak. Sea wind lashed his hair and flapped the long cloak like a sail around his wrenched shoulders. Hugged to the soot-tinged brick of the chimney, Fionn Areth coughed out a breath fouled with coal smoke. 'What do you plan to do now?'

'In simplest terms? Run.' Over the yammering shouts from the street, a furtive slither of boot soles and cloth marked where Arithon tested the way down the sloped eaves. 'The Koriani have scryers. If they pin us down before we reach Dakar, we'll have much worse than city guardsmen howling murder.'

Below and to one side came a clang and a clashing scream of smashed glass. Someone had hammered a weapon through the panes of the adjacent casement. Armed men were pursuing onto the roof, with nothing but darkness to slow them. Since a sliding fall into the cobbles below seemed a kindlier death than facing a sword on the faggots, Fionn Areth followed the touch on his wrist that pressed for a speedy departure.

'Mind the loose slate,' said Arithon, breathless. 'How bad is that knee? Can you jump?'

Rushed by adrenaline beyond reach of the pain, Fionn Areth replied, 'There's a choice?'

'Always. It's the outcome that sadly limits things.' The Shadow Master paused, his other hand busy with some unseen task in the dark. He moved on momentarily, tacking what seemed an erratic course down the pitch of the roof.

From above came more shouts, then a belling clash as steel collided with stonework. The cry of abused metal interlaced with ripe language, and an officer's bellow of disgust.

'I left my cloak draped over a chimney pot,' Arithon confessed through the clangor and din of redoubled pursuit on their back trail.

'Should have blunted the edge of one weapon against us, what the Shandians call a one-penny advantage. Come on. We're doubling back.'

Fionn Areth balked. 'Going *up?*'

'No,' came the snatched and hasty reply. 'Sidewards. There's a lady I knew who kept chickens in her attic. Hope and pray that her daughter still does.'

The gap between buildings proved mercifully narrow, where upper stories overhung the back alley that paralleled the main thoroughfare. With the roaring noise of the square to the left, Arithon crossed, waiting only for Fionn Areth's arrival before he used his dagger to slip the locking bar on another dormer casement. He cracked the hinged window open a handswidth. Against the warm sigh of air past his cheek, and the reassuring, ammonia reek of guano, he sang a soft, low note into the loft where an unseen flock of fowl were still roosting.

'That should keep them sleeping,' Arithon said. 'Try to go softly, nonetheless.' His hands grasped Fionn Areth's shoulder and assisted the tight squeeze through the dormer.

Behind, clustered atop the adjacent roof, men-at-arms ranged in noisy descent. Astraddle the sill, Arithon paused again, head bent a fraction to one side. As though exhorting a laggard companion, he raised a distinct admonition. 'Ath's sake, man, move! Can't you go any faster?'

An answering bass shout of recognition, then a scramble among the pursuit. The rush of booted feet lost distinction, turned into a sliding scream of metal, then a pattering of fall of loose slate. More cries, a thrashing scrabble, then a suggestive set of thuds as several bodies lost their purchase on the roof and hurtled to the cobbled street below.

'Loose shingles,' Arithon said, apologetic, as he darted into the close-pressed heat of the attic and assayed a neat path between the railed perches that held rows of slumbering chickens.

'You made those slates give,' Fionn Areth accused, prudent enough to keep his rage contained to a frantic whisper. 'That roof was sound when we passed down the pitch.'

'But of course.' Agreeable, Arithon cat-footed ahead, still speaking between his odd, soothing croon to the hens. 'Bad acts, worse consequences. This is Rathain, where I am crown justice, and you are an innocent fugitive.' A hesitation, while he conducted a tactile search of the floorboards. 'I'm never heartless. A stay of mercy is offered for every man who gives up the chase to succor the injured.'

He had found the trapdoor. The fastening yielded beneath his quick fingers, and the squeal of the hinge roused a sleepy cackle from a hen who expected the imminent arrival of her grain ration. '*Isheal,*' murmured Arithon, which meant peace in the ancient Paravian. Then in prosaic king's tongue, 'There's a ladder. Go down. Just watch where you're pointing that weapon.'

'I should be concerned?' the herder snapped back in his rough grass-lands dialect.

The sole reply his outburst received was a crash of glass and wood as a mail-clad pursuer burst through the attic dormer. The chickens exploded in racketing alarm, wings blundering hither and yon in the blackness. They crashed willy-nilly into steel helms, wrists, and faces; they dropped guano in cackling panic. Fionn Areth, looking up from his vantage on the ladder, realized that all of the shadows had lifted. Nor was Arithon s'Ffalenn still behind him.

He reached the lower floor, wrenched sick with understanding, as a spray of shot scarlet fanned through the trapdoor above him. Using chickens for cover, the Prince of Rathain was indulging his own style of butchery. Inside of seconds, only birds held the violated loft, the crow of a triumphant rooster on the sill undercut by the drum of a dying man's heels in the straw.

Unmoored feathers drifted through the gapped-open trapdoor. Arithon presently emerged and slid through them, slightly winded, one wrist scraped, and the black longsword he carried rinsed bloody. His white face held a look like the locked gates of Sithaer, and he trembled with electrified anger. 'Damn you, *run!* Four lives have bought us no more than minutes. It might not seem natural, given my reputation, *but I don't like killing for necessity.*'

Stunned silent, Fionn Areth took advice. He raced down the hallway, his herder's boots slapping the board floor, striped with the thin, leaden light that seeped in through the second-story casements. The neat chambers on either side were empty, matron or daughter absent since breakfast to judge by the stale smell of grease sausage that lingered in the kitchen stairway.

'Find the back door,' said Arithon, succinct in descent. 'There's an alley, probably jammed with a midden cart. Go under the axles and turn right.'

'You know where we're going?' Fionn Areth cast back, his look-alike profile lined in the glow of the coals left unbanked in the grate.

'To join Dakar.' The uncanny green eyes and black hair were unnerving, attached to another man's body. The voice, more incisive, with accents of chipped flint, 'We need him. The Koriani Order can't be faced down by sword tricks with shadows and flapped chickens.'

The back door, unbarred, let into the alley, complete with the attend-ant slop cart. Fionn Areth crouched low, feeling all of his bruises, and the ice bite of wind through his borrowed cloak. Through the struts of the wagon, he saw flurrying movement and realized: the alley Arithon had chosen was occupied with people still fleeing the square. Apprehensive, he pulled his hood close to his face, just as the man who looked *too much* like himself ducked through the unsprung carriage of the wagon.

'Don't you think we should separate?' Fionn Areth suggested.

'No.' The dark head turned, green eyes piercing clear in a concern that itself was unsettling. 'What are you, suicidal?'

Fionn Areth shook his head, outside of his depth and confused. 'Koriani aren't evil.'

'For me, they are lethal, and without my protection, the citizens of Jaelot would tear you apart on first sight. It's an ugly choice to risk. The witches might pause to spare you from a lynch mob, or they might decide they wanted my capture much more.'

Given Fionn Areth's continued stiff silence, the Teir's'Ffalenn returned his soft, worldly laughter. 'You don't like my trust? Then answer this question. Is it you wearing my face, or me wearing yours? Ask yourself which one of us is the more likely bait in the trap?' He had wiped his fouled weapon. The blade angled up in a competent, gloved grip, he faced forward again, measuring the clumped knots of citizens who streamed down the mouth of the alley. 'Just don't carry the debate for too long. Dakar's at the jam seller's. If we get there late, he'll have eaten so much he'll be sleeping.'

The crowd in the alley were goodwives and tradesmen, intermixed with brown-cloaked apprentices. Since they were rabbit frightened and largely unarmed, Arithon chose to push on. He masked his bared blade against his body, and in one fluid move when no one was looking, cut through the moving stream of passersby. Unwilling to remain shivering under the midden cart, Fionn Areth cloaked his own weapon and followed.

'There's a potter's shop perhaps a midrange bowshot away,' Arithon gave low voiced instruction. 'If anything happens, wait for me there. You'll know the place by its red door.'

They moved out, their presence immediately conspicuous as they passed against the common flow of traffic. If most folk seemed too absorbed to take notice, the more observant onlooker would be sure to view the anomaly with suspicion. The pair of fugitives kept to the shadows where they could. Yet the outdoor back stairs and crannies between craftshops offered inadequate bolt-holes, should intelligent pursuit overtake them. Limping again, feeling the pain of his disparate aches and bruises, Fionn Areth scarcely cared whether the Sorcerer beside him used unclean spells to mask their presence. He had found

Arithon's view of the Koriathain disturbing, and the impact of his truth too entangled to refute; *or why else should he and the Prince of Rathain share identical features?*

A touch on his arm snapped his reverie short.

'Koriani, there.' The Shadow Master pointed.

Fionn Areth tracked the surreptitious gesture, glimpsed the woman bundled in walnut-stained homespun who waited at the next corner. She had a shawl tightly tucked beneath her trim chin. Her bearing seemed mousy, nervous, and strained, not extraordinary. As the hurrying forms of five dyer's apprentices eclipsed the view of her watchful presence, Fionn Areth said, 'How do you know she's one of them?'

'Hear it,' said Arithon, thinking at speed. 'She has a ranging ward running. The harmonics can be felt coursing through wood, if you're sensitive.' He made a decision, his mouth turned tight and grim. 'We're not going by way of the potter's anymore. Come on.'

They passed instead through the wheelwright's back door, into forge-heated gloom alive with the clangor of hammers. Like the bakeshop and the fishmonger's, this craftshop remained too busy to close for the sake of a Sorcerer's execution. Fionn Areth looked about, his hesitant step crunching over shaved scrolls of hard oak, his lungs filled with the steam from the boxes where the wheels were bent and spoked, and fitted with forged iron rims. If he thought to slip through in quiet anonymity, Prince Arithon's intent ran contrary.

Three bold-as-brass steps saw him poised by the scrap bin, where the bent and worn iron of those wheels beyond repair was saved as salvage for smelting. Possessed, stressed-out, or insanely inspired, Arithon began a racketing search through the jumble of broken metal. Two men at the forges looked up, incensed by the jangling noise. The apprentice they dispatched from his post at the bellows implored in nice manners, but failed utterly to convince the small, wayward customer to cease and desist his disruptive industry.

Fionn Areth watched, dumbfounded, from the shadows, as a glib spate of oaths from the Shadow Master seeded a fist-waving argument. Smiths threw down hammers. The wood joiners left the steamboxes, sweaty arms wielding their hammers and pry bars, and their faces maroon with ill temper.

'Everything, these,' Arithon exhorted, his broken language styled in a desertman's accent and his mood expansively unappeased. 'Too little, like fry fish!' His gyrating gesture almost bloodied a man's nose as he flung wide his arm to explain. 'Big! Big! I need a big round! Not these, no better than chick's nests.'

'You want to buy a wheel?' asked the gray-haired proprietor, a horse-faced man with a squint, and huge, gnarled fists that wore scars like white scale from the forges.

Arithon returned a look of exasperation. 'No wheel, me.' When one of the smiths grasped his arm to eject him, he exploded in furious dialect, each word of which carried the ferocity of a curse. 'I am silver, me! Everybody gets paid.' He emphasized his assurance by kicking the scrap bin. The resulting clash of distressed metal made even the deafest smith cringe.

No one was left with the least shred of doubt, the customer demanded a wheel rim. 'One with dents in,' Arithon said with effect, his eyes rolled in baleful impatience.

'He wants the biggest piece of scrap iron we've got?' the apprentice hopefully translated.

'Round! Round!' Arithon corrected, bobbing his chin. The corners of his mouth turned up in a blinding smile. He burrowed a grubby hand under his jerkin and produced three gold coins, the mere sight of which rousted the wheelwrights to boot-kissing agreeability.

As though in love with conspicuous display, Arithon assisted their search for a suitable rim. The proprietor allowed him the liberty, well aware that the worth of his coins could have bought his shop clean of stock. No matter how often the nosy customer got underfoot, or insinuated curious hands into cupboards, his antics were tolerated, then abetted for the sheer fun of watching him comb through every spider-infested cranny. Arithon made rounds with startling noise and coarse epithets. His sparkling, odd turn of humor finally had the most dour master craftsman folded over a stool, convulsed with laughter and blotting his streaming eyes with the back of his work-begrimed wrists.

Three gold pieces the lighter, Fionn Areth and the Shadow Master emerged, the bent rim of an enormous dray wheel borne on their shoulders. A third apprentice was sent along to assist with the load, which was awkward for two men to handle. Yoked in cold iron, the trio passed the length of the avenue beyond, where the mayor's guard now conducted an earnest search, and two Koriani stood vigil. Apparently the properties of the hoop frayed their spells, for as Arithon passed, whistling an odd, catchy melody in threnodies, neither one of the initiate enchantresses glanced once in his direction.

In the alley behind the armorer's, Arithon paid off the apprentice wheelwright. For another two silvers, the fellow was induced to part with his tunic and jacket. Fionn Areth dressed in the armorer's privy, while, in a rapid transaction without show or argument, the Master of Shadow bargained away his scrap iron. The bent wheel and an untold price in hard coin bought him a light, balanced sword and eight bone-handled throwing knives, and yet another craftsman's hard-used cloak as a bonus.

Back into the poured lead gray of the street, bundled into forge-scented clothing cut generously wide across sleeves and shoulders, Fionn Areth accepted the light sword and spare cloak. He arranged the new garment overtop the black mantle, too conspicuous for its color to be ordinary.

While a little girl chivvied by a nursemaid paused to stare, and two roisterers roared past with a wineskin, Arithon s'Ffalenn raked his young double from head to foot with that disturbing regard that seemed to glean the most intimate detail.

'You'll do.' Then he startled the goatherd near out of his skin by answering the unspoken question. 'I gave up the wheel rim because the initiates we fooled were too inexperienced to realize its significance. What worked twice, the third time might just bring bad luck. The sword seems the wiser option. Does it suit you for weight and balance?'

It did, to another unsettling degree. Too honest to be ungrateful for the gift of what he knew was a first-class weapon, Fionn Areth delivered his thanks by way of a breathless warning. 'Guardsmen, four of them, moving our way.'

'Mounted?' On Fionn Areth's nod, Arithon showed himself wily enough, or else by far too unnervingly trusting, by not glancing back to affirm. 'They'll be too arrogant to vacate their nice, warm saddles and manhandle what appears innocent. You look like a smith,' he said in swift reassurance. 'Just don't limp. The jam seller's shop is close by. When we get there, if you're hungry, I'll buy you a muffin. You'll have time to eat it, I promise.'

At Fionn Areth's oath of outright trepidation, Arithon flashed a quick smile. 'Don't worry. When Dakar doesn't want to be seen by town guardsmen, they're more than likely to trip over their own feet and fall flat on their noses than find him.'

'You don't look like a smith,' Fionn Areth pointed out.

The smile vanished. 'Then I'll improvise.'

They moved on, the pace too brisk for Fionn Areth's slashed knee. He could feel the wound bleeding underneath its torn bandage, as the limp he could not successfully hide carried him careening from one side of the street to the other. This quarter of Jaelot had once held rich mansions, degraded now into honeycomb tenements with sagging galleries and rows of ramshackle stalls. The wares seemed a jumble of two-penny merchandise, moldering old scrolls, and the resharpened stubs of worn quills. Smells of cod warred with the grease stink of sausage, stitched through by the cries of the hawkers. While the guardsmen clattered past, Arithon haggled with a basket seller, then bought a white pullet from a goose girl. The basket and its squawking occupant explained Fionn Areth's unbalanced stride well enough to buy them a few minutes' grace.

They ducked into a close. Rats fled, chittering, into the gloom. The wind creaked a shutter overhead. Two steps later, Fionn Areth slammed square on into Arithon, who had jerked to an unannounced stop. The pullet let fly with a deafening cackle. Her wing-flapping tantrum fluttered loose feathers out of the osier basket. The down drifted, unmoored, with the first sifted snowflakes disgorged by the lowering clouds. 'What's the matter?'

Arithon tipped his head, his silence like death.

Ahead, a violet-robed enchantress blocked their egress, ringed about by a purple aura of raised spellcraft.

'Dakar won't be at the jam seller's, not anymore,' said the Master of Shadow, expressionless.

Fear slid like chill steel between Fionn Areth's ribs. 'Is he taken, then?'

'If he's not, I know where to look.' Arithon reversed course, his urgency lending a palpable rush to his stride. 'He'll follow old habits. We'll find him puking drunk at the tavern by Beckburn Lane, or else holed up at the bawdy house over the dressmakers' lofts on Threadneedle Street.'

## Winter Solstice Afternoon 5670

# Cats and Mice

In the fusty, closed dimness of the vintner's shed, Lirenda reacted to Prince Arithon's evasion with a nerve storm of targetless fury.

'A *wheel rim*?' She whirled and berated the seer turned informant, her expensive mantle and purple silk hems whipping drifts of eddied dust from the floorboards. 'How painfully asinine! How obvious!' Her scorn as vicious as the charge one fractional instant before lightning, she stabbed a perfect, manicured nail at the inept enchantresses who mishandled the scrying spells in the vat. 'A bumpkin babe still in swaddling might have known to beware of that street urchin's trick!'

'These were first-year initiates,' Third Senior Cadgia pointed out, her practical nature acerbic. Rawboned and capable, and immured to setbacks after centuries of critical service, she leaned on crossed arms, her straight silver hair rinsed to false bronze by the spill of the flickering candle. 'Done is done. You can rail and cast blame, or let us regroup, mop up the spilled milk, and recover what leads still remain. Or don't we have two wanted fugitives at large, and strict orders from our Prime Matriarch to contain them?'

'Only one of the pair need concern you,' Lirenda snapped. The shocked silence that followed turned even her aristocratic head. The startled disapproval on the faces of her subordinates drew unwanted attention to her state of riled agitation. The rage that ripped through her in searing waves had always been strictly personal. If she failed to regain Koriani decorum, every sister initiate assigned to track Arithon s'Ffalenn would share proof she had lost objectivity.

Yet her private stake in this contest of wills held the linchpin to restore her future; Morriel had set that penance to reclaim her forfeited rank. Lirenda smoothed down her ruffled composure, cat cool as she weighed her array of remaining resources. Only a fool would let underling colleagues know her reinstatement as Prime Senior hinged upon the Shadow Master's capture. Nor should they realize Fionn Areth was her pawn, his life a mere cipher to discard or expend for the cause of the Matriarch's directive.

Lirenda flicked a stuck strand of cobweb from her skirts, her moment's fussy attention to grooming a diversion to mask rapid thought. 'The Koriani Order has interests that loom far larger than surface appearances. We are more than the keepers of mercy and charity. Our policy spans generations. If I admit I am not in the Prime's inner confidence, I can reliably promise this much. If Arithon s'Ffalenn is not found and brought in, two decades of work go for naught. Resume scrying. Use every expedient. We know the boy with him is distrustful and frightened. He is the weak link. Reel them both in on the imprint in quartz that sealed his birth debt to our order.'

Cadgia's excoriating quiet held over, the ebony pins that fastened her hair stilled as flicked pen strokes against shadow. 'Your will,' she said finally. But her broad back remained disapprovingly stiff as she knelt and reframed a new construct of sigils over the water-filled vat.

Too prideful to suffer the cobwebs and grime of a seat on a derelict wine tun, Lirenda herself remained standing. The bone buttons that looped the stays on her bodice seemed to nail in each self-controlled breath. Passing seconds fed her acid impatience. While the scryers' wrought spells combed the town for available portents, she stifled her rampant vexation behind her enamel polish of deportment.

For Elaira, stressed to the same private agonies of suppressed tension, soiled cloth came second to comfort. Still confined by strict orders to the barrel beside a winepress cobwebbed by the industry of brown spiders, she perched cross-legged upon the wadded folds of the mantle last used to blanket Fionn Areth. Its dungeon scent of rat and moldered straw set small pleats in Lirenda's forehead. That petty vindication gave small satisfaction through a wait that leached at Elaira's trapped spirit like slow torture. Elbows on knees, chin braced on clamped fists, she matched her senior peer's masked dismay with deadpan humor. The opinion she held, but dared not express, was that Dakar had abandoned the jam seller's because of unwarranted provocation. Some bungling enchantress had set nine amplified sigils of ward in overzealous effort to cordon the building.

Lirenda's obsessed drive was itself the disharmony that tipped the scales in Prince Arithon's favor.

'Don't look so smug.' Lirenda resettled her amethyst bracelets with a chiming, thin clash of wrapped gold. 'You'll play your due part before the day's over. Or why should Morriel Prime have detailed your assignment to Jaelot in the first place?'

'His lordship's gout continues untreated, the longer you stay my release,' Elaira agreed in testing provocation. 'Or was the man's suffering made the excuse for someone's political expedience? How far have we drifted from the charitable concerns of our order's founding purpose?'

But Lirenda had all her exposed nerves back in hand. 'You're in no position to fathom Morriel's long-range intent.' Her glance slid away in permafrost indifference. 'Nor can your limited vision encompass the danger this Shadow Master poses to civilized society.'

'Well, that's no dark secret,' Elaira needled back. 'His Grace might one day succeed in his search for the Paravians. Their living return would throw marvelous kinks in the order's ambition to upstage the Fellowship Sorcerers.' The old races' presence would reaffirm the compact, with no human faction ever likely to regain the standing to challenge the sanctuary of the free wilds.

But this time the baited innuendo of argument failed to upset Lirenda's obsessive concentration. She stalked to the vat. Intently absorbed by some nuance within, she jabbed an imperious finger. 'There! Go back. Show me a clear view of that side street.'

Cadgia's exhaustive competence picked up the two fugitives on the downhill slope above the quayside breakwater. Her assessment came sharp. 'If they reach salt water, we're done.' Every sigil under the Senior Circle's command would become ineffective against them.

'Bar their way.' Lirenda rejected all second opinion, but drew her next strategy with staccato self-confidence. 'A timely appearance by one of our initiates should haze our quarry away from the docks. Don't show our hand strongly. They must not be flushed into flight prematurely. Take them back into custody too soon, we'll have Arithon's extradition hampered by the magistrates on Jaelot's high council. The mayor and his cronies must now be cut out. Let them believe the Master of Shadow won his escape by dark sorcery.' Eyes narrowed, her expression ruthless as picked bone, Lirenda patted the jeweled combs that secured her coiled jet hair. 'Henceforward, each step that the Shadow Master takes must be orchestrated to our Koriani design. My hand will personally close the last trap. Fionn Areth and Prince Arithon will fall into my sole custody to seal our final success.'

'By our Prime's will.' Senior Cadgia signaled the seer, then bent to the scrying vat and began the cat-and-mouse chase, with the fourfold sigils for domination chained into ranged force and pitched against the Shadow Master's astute cleverness.

A harsh flash of purple splintered the gloom as the construct unleashed, then crossed into the volatile ether that bounded the second grand division of the veil. The vintner's shed stilled, sealed into a tension chisel-cut to the dictates of spelled ciphers. No one exchanged speech. Like ghosts set into that frozen tableau, each enchantress shouldered her part. On a flicked signal from the seer, the initiate in charge of telepathic communication clasped thin hands to her amethyst-and-silver circlet and dispatched urgent instructions. Her sending was picked up by a peer senior in the street, who wove a spell of confusion to cut off the fugitives' course. Then power filmed the vat, a rainbow chaos like an oil slick, as Cadgia reengaged the mighty array of tuned tracking spells. The image in the water spun and reoriented to reveal Arithon and Fionn Areth turned downhill, framed by the sepia boards and wet cobbles of the narrow back lanes behind the fishmonger's. A bone-skinny cat fled yowling from a crate. Unstartled, the exposed figure of Arithon s'Ffalenn grasped his double's wrist and slowed their precipitous flight.

From her perch on the wine tun, Elaira just caught Arithon's half-breathless admonition. 'No, they're driving us on, can't you see?'

'Does it matter?' The disheartened herder crumpled against the hacked post of a lamp, while the prince swiftly sorted their options.

'To the fox? I would say so. If we don't lead the chase, then we've wasted an advantage without putting up any fight.' Arithon's expression did not look taxed, but instead, showed the intent focus of a man mage-trained, who engaged every facet of his faculties.

Elaira stifled untoward elation. From her seat on the barrel, she recognized the fleeting, bright smile that emerged, then the inquiring, sharp lift of his chin.

Lirenda's muttered oath affirmed the fresh setback, that the tight maze of alleys lent prime ground for invention, with their piles of cod baskets, their staved barrels of salt, and their refuse carts laden with fish guts garnered for compost. The enchantress entrusted with orders to pursue found her tracking spells fouled by strewn flurries of rock salt. Her running effort to give chase was confounded by six guardsmen, raised by someone's untimely shout. They drew swords. Charged in blind haste from a side street, they skidded into a clashing knot of stopped force against a dray filled with cod heads their quarry had left wedged broadside across the alley's arched egress.

Lirenda's fuming silence grew brittle as the fugitives scuttled into a weed-grown courtyard, dark heads masked under the weathered mesh of two purloined fish baskets. The pullet in the crate was abandoned in the dim close, where it tripped the one agile swordsman who managed to claw past the wedged slop cart. His mailed coif threw back a scaled gleam of light as he turned his head right and left in baffled annoyance.

A matron whose careless servant left an unlocked back door gave the Teir's'Ffalenn and his double passage through a washhouse, and clear of the belated hue and cry.

Arithon's breathless comment carried clearly from the spelled maw of the dye vat. 'If anything good came from six months in Jaelot, it's the fact I know the poor quarters of the city as well as my milk tongue.' A sly sidewards glance caught Fionn Areth's wrinkled nose. 'Don't balk at the cod stink. If someone sends tracking dogs, the scent will do nicely to throw them off of our back trail.'

Fionn Areth's rejoinder was lost, or ignored, as Arithon vanished into the hemp-scented gloom of the ship's chandler's and reemerged with a firkin of lamp oil. The next lancer who spurred his charger upslope came to grief, his mount skated into a shoulder-down sprawl on the cobbles. Mail and slicked stone collided, screaming. Then the fallen man added shrill cries to the bedlam as he tried to rise on a snapped ankle.

'Save your sympathies for the horse,' said the Shadow Master, well aware Fionn Areth choked back nausea. 'In an hour you might wish I was the wicked brigand you imagine. If we find ourselves taken, remember, I didn't commit the sensible cruelty and fire the destrier's tail for distraction – oh, Dharkaron's bloody vengeance!'

That oath ripped out through a snatched pause, as another Koriani crossed their path and deflected them again from their preferred down-hill course toward the harborside.

'This way. Fast!' Arithon ducked left, then slipped through the trailing, dead canes of a rose trellis. Fionn Areth clawed after him, tearing his bloodstained bandages on the briar and sliding on icy rocks. The pair tacked a desperate, erratic passage through a garden of cast-plaster statues, winged swans and naked nymphs bearing birdbaths stuffed with rotted caches of oak leaves. A side stair at last let them up through a pigeon loft, where Dakar once held assignations.

Relentless, the scrying spells in the vat continued to track their least movement. Arithon's snatched reminiscence of a humorous escapade frayed into static as the thin, flurrying of snow interfered with the sigils that sealed the connection.

'Does that building have an exit other than the front entrance?' Lirenda demanded in glacial objectivity.

The seeress's reply emerged through the whiffle of startled pigeons, set flying across image in the vat. 'The downstairs passage leads into the brewer's. The doorway's kept barred with an iron hasp and lock.' But she sounded unsure such ordinary measures could pin down their volatile quarry.

The next instant, the waterborne scrying went blank. 'We're cut off by earth element,' Cadgia informed.

A subtle change in the quality of Elaira's leashed quiet prompted Lirenda to straighten and take notice. Eyes the flat gold of the hunting tigress surveyed the adversary perched with insouciant obedience on the wine tun. 'What do you know?'

Elaira's pale features remained a closed book, unwritten with sign of dismay. Through the chill, dusty gloom, her regard in return held the same steely gleam as the finished gloss on a sword blade. 'About rearing squabs? Very little. The ones I stole from the dovecotes in Morvain, we ate to get rid of the evidence.'

Lirenda returned a cameo smile, her voice like poison gloved in honey. 'Don't waste my time. Believe this, for the effort, I'm going to see you pay dearly.'

Elaira shrugged, world-weary and indifferent. 'What coin do I have that's not spent already?' But nonetheless, her hands stayed locked tight throughout her unflinching reply. 'The brewer has unsavory habits in bed, and a wife who keeps ironclad books. To pay for his pleasures outside of the till, he takes silver from husbands and dallying wives and lets them keep trysts in his cousin's dovecote. Beyond Dakar's hearsay, Arithon once said folk went in for a jar and came out looking much too exhilarated to account for the watered-down beer the mayor's bailiffs were paid bribes to ignore.'

'A good thing the order has the benefit of your council. No other initiate has the low cast of mind for such sordid snippets of gossip.' The slide of layered silk skirts a poured swish of sound, Lirenda turned her back and resumed her vulture's survey of the scrying vat. While Cadgia and her handpicked circle of talent cast a fresh augury riddled with barbed sigils of seeking, the former first senior maintained her clipped interrogation. 'Do you know how the brewer arranged for covert exits?'

'I don't.' The bare bones of Elaira's honesty rang just as chill off the musty board walls of the shed. 'Arithon was discreet for good reason. Dakar could have been flensed by any number of cuckolded husbands if the love nest became common knowledge.'

'Cast a search ward over the brewer's,' Lirenda commanded. 'We'll tag them as they come out.'

'Who do we have posted in the neighborhood?' Cadgia asked, her rounded cheeks flushed with affront that her quarry had slipped her spelled shackles yet again.

A pause followed, filled by the sigh of tense breathing. Crystal chimed softly to crystal as the seeress dangled her personal stone within the etheric field of the main quartz focus. She then murmured a list of names set amid the arrhythmic verses of advanced incantation. Under Cadgia's painstaking, efficient instruction, a new net of sigils was woven. Through a sending unfurled through the core matrix of the amethyst, other directions were dispatched to the enchantresses stationed outside.

Elaira's short nails mined small crescents in her palms as the drawing spells sealed and, on Cadgia's release, deployed outward.

'I still smell earth,' the scryer announced. 'They've gone underground? A tunnel stair might be angled below the boards of the cellar.' Little else would account for the darkened, featureless surface reflected in the vat; only a specialized few sigils could carry binding influence through earth, and even those were uncertain, unless their powers were channeled through a quartz focus tapped to a flux line.

'Patience,' urged Cadgia. 'Hold strong. The snowfall's still thin, yet. We'll have our quarry nailed down the instant they cross back under the biddable influence of air.'

'Wait,' whispered the seeress. 'Wait. There's something. I sense the boy. Yes, that *is* him. He's broadcasting fear.' Eyes closed, her consciousness sealed into trance, she rocked to a rhythm of perceptions tuned far beyond range of ordinary hearing. 'Look for a dray filled with fuller's earth, I think. The mare in the traces won't settle. She's unnerved by the tension she picks up through the hands of an anxious carter.'

'Fuller's earth? The devil!' Lirenda stalked to the vat, her immaculate grooming cobwebbed in sickly light as Cadgia's swift adjustments to the spell seals charged the water, and resurged to a glow of pallid phosphor to keep pace with the seeress's shifted perception.

A new image unfurled, steady and clear, the moving chaos of street traffic marred by a scrim of flurrying snow. An unpainted wagon centered the scene, heaped with a tarp-covered load of dry clay. The gray horse in the shafts moved head high and snorting, her flanks crowded by a troupe of rollicking gallants wearing gaudy cloaks sewn with ribbons. Their party was trailed by two trollops, equally blithe under billowing mantles of peach silk and daffodil yellow.

The unwieldy cart made balked progress in the press. Ahead, a merchant's lacquered coach tacked a lumbering course down a thoroughfare clogged with confused throngs of foot traffic. In due course, a farm wagon bearing crated pigs jostled alongside in a hub-to-hub jockey for position.

'What street? Give me bearings!' Lirenda brooded over the image in the vat, nails rapping an impatient tattoo on the aged wood of the rim.

'That's the back wall of the exciseman's yard. No place else has iron spikes and gold finials set into capstones of mortar.' In unruffled precision, Cadgia deciphered other details half-masked by the turmoil and the murky, gray weather. 'Our party is northbound.'

The seeress sent precise word of that bearing to her counterparts stationed on watch in the streets. 'The fugitives will soon be picked up by a search point. The garrison guard has posted lancers and pikemen screening traffic at each major crossroad.'

'Very good.' Cadgia raised a glance lit to triumph. 'Unless your two renegades want that clay for their grave shrouds, we'll have them exposed and back on the run.'

'Let the guard flush them,' Lirenda decreed, confident the carter who transported live contraband would turn aside rather than submit to a thorough inspection by nerve-jumpy garrison forces.

The wagon inched forward. On the wine tun, fists jammed to shut lips, Elaira all but stopped breathing. Her insane, almost suicidal plea to let the worst happen, and make an end to her harrowing dread won no pity from Ath Creator. The scene in the vat spun itself out with an agonized, detailed caprice that might have spurred humor had the prize stakes not been flesh and blood.

Nor was reprieve likely. If the dray bearing fuller's earth sought to turn down a side street, the farm vehicle and its bawling cargo of pigs cut off that small chance of escape. Ahead, the broad, satin bulk of the carriage blocked sight of the approaching checkpoint, where a rising altercation unraveled to shrill shouts as the reveling young men in their ribbons and exuberance picked an argument with the mayor's guardsmen. The footmen who attended the coach proved more biddable. When challenged, they stepped off the running board in long-faced resignation and opened the gleaming door on command of the burly sergeant. A broad-shouldered guard with a scar on his chin jammed his torso into the compartment and began a belabored search under cushions and lap robes, to the bilious contempt of the occupants.

The two whores amused themselves as they could. One flirted with the grizzled drover of the pig cart. The other, in her frothy cascade of peach skirts, grew bored poking straw at the snout of the sow in the crates. With her mantle bundled up to her ears in disdain, she sailed on ahead, determined to insinuate herself among the uproarious pack of drunk dandies.

The sergeant, meantime, disengaged from the coach and seized the bridle of the gray draft mare. 'Gotta be searched, no exceptions. Mayor's orders.' He beckoned on his compatriots to attend to the drover, who nodded rather than risk his quaking liver to somebody's excitable pike.

The rabble-rousing dandies flowed aside in a whirl of wild color, divided by the departing coach and a liveried driver who held no compunction against laying the whip on his team in close quarters. Through the grind of iron wheels, and a plowed swirl of snow, two surcoated lancers broke past. They swarmed over the dray, their drawn knives slashing the cords securing the sun-faded tarpaulins. They then grasped their pole arms and used the bladed ends to stab and stir through the load of dry clay underneath.

Cadgia's black curse entangled with Elaira's choked-back snort of wild laughter. 'Ath, they're not in there, of course. For Arithon, the ploy would be much too obvious.'

'Where then?' snapped Lirenda, lips tight with fury. 'How were we misled?'

The young seeress shook her head, the odd, bloodied light thrown off the fired sigils sparking her circlet of amethysts deep red. 'They *are* there. I sense the boy's presence quite strongly.'

In confounded frustration, Cadgia's circle watched the enspelled waters in the vat. Its reflected turmoil quickly brewed into the overblown style of farce only Jaelot's entrenched snobbery could produce as one of the dandies refused to be searched. He waved eloquent hands and howled until all within earshot understood that men-at-arms were known to filch jewelry.

'You can never be certain,' he warned his companions. 'These men might seize our coin on the extortionist pretense of keeping the mayor's law and order.'

Moneyed and reckless, and surrounded by friends, the young rake well knew he could heckle without suffering dangerous consequences. His spate of histrionics should have stayed harmless, except that the trollop in her ruffled peach silk pointed out that one of the young men seemed the lighter of his purse already.

The gentleman she collared slapped a hand to his belt, found cut thongs where his scrip had been moments before, and raised a cry fit to damage the hearing of everyone in the district. Heads turned on all quarters. The circle of Koriani scryers at the vat enjoyed an untrammeled view as the yellow-clad prostitute simpered, then passed off a squealing piglet to the lancer who had just finished searching the wagon. He accepted her offering, too flustered to shed his tongue-tied male leer over curves draped in feminine clothes. Then the farmer screamed also, for the glaring discovery someone had unlatched his sow's crate.

Her four-legged instincts unimpaired by armed might, or confounding human fracas, she spun toward the distressed cries of her young and lowered her snout in a charge.

The lancer holding the piglet went down, his legs scythed from under his mail-clad weight by three hundredweight of enraged porcine motherhood. At first no one heeded his bloodied shoulder, where the yellow-clad prostitute's lightning sword had crippled the arm that wielded the pole weapon.

'That tart's wearing a black petticoat,' Cadgia observed, her surprise distinct over the babble of noise from the vat. Through a blur of commotion, the dandies set to and began battering guardsmen, fist and dirk. Their sergeant gave no curt order to restore peace, hung up as he was like a cod in a net by billows of peach silk fringed with tassels.

That strumpet also wielded cold steel like a veteran. Her victim fell, stabbed through and twitching, while blood blossomed in arterial gouts through the lace-and-silk shroud that muffled his screams.

'That's no petticoat, imbecile!' Lirenda elbowed herself into the closed circle by the vat, steaming with fury and blame. 'That's the boy, Fionn Areth, under that silk! He's still wearing the executioner's cloak, with a thread in the lining interwoven with the elemental signature of the earth.'

'Dakar's work, surely,' Cadgia extrapolated, too professionally engrossed to take umbrage. 'What a fiendish turn of genius, to drag along a cart full of clay to mislay our searching attention.'

A growl underneath their flurried conversation, the street scene exploded into full-blown pandemonium. While bystanders scattered from the wrath of the loose sow, and the farmer barged in fist-waving pursuit, two lancers confronted the Master of Shadow. He poised on light feet, a knife gripped in each hand, the cart of fuller's earth parked between like a hillock of disputed territory.

'Blink,' said Arithon s'Ffalenn in crisp courtesy. Due warning given, he hooked the ripped tarp on one blade and gave the slack folds a swift snap. Clay burst and flew, fanned on by a gust. The guards jerked back, blinded. Then they sat down, folded on the cobbles like dropped marionettes, each with a thrown knife impaled in the neck exposed above his steel gorget.

Their killer retreated, slick as sleight-of-hand flimflam, under the muddied wheels of the farm cart. Two lancers dived after. They emerged, craning confused heads, then barreled headlong through the scried image cast in the vintner's vat. The quarry they mowed down all comers to pursue was a jonquil yellow hem, fast vanishing under a door stoop. They pounced, skinned elbows, and reeled in the kicking contents. The hood strings proved attached to the hind legs of another pig, which squealed in soprano chorus with those crated brethren still penned in the bed of the farm cart.

Elaira collapsed on crossed arms by the wine tun, choking on laughter and tears.

'We've lost them again,' said Cadgia, too humorless to care as she stated the painfully obvious.

Lirenda whirled about and discovered that her thoughtless, tense hands had mangled three heirloom bracelets. She exploded with an oath to redden the ears of Jaelot's most execrable fishwife, then detailed the punishment everyone would suffer if Arithon's location could not be recovered immediately.

A first combing sweep, a second, then a third, exhaustive examination of the neighborhood failed to turn up the two fugitives. When Cadgia tasked the seer to scan the whole quarter for unusual signs of disturbance, all she found was a half troop of the mayor's men-at-arms splashed with horse glue, casting circles of sticky footprints in and out of the furniture maker's. Their noisy persistence touched off a second-floor journeyman, who vented his temper by cascading the contents of three sacks of down stuffing over the heads of his persecutors.

The captain of the guard arrived on the scene and arrested the heckler in an explosive show of armed force.

'Daelion preserve!' Elaira exclaimed, from her recovered vantage on the barrel top. 'Pray they just fine that poor citizen for nuisance. He's much too young to know Arithon s'Ffalenn, far less to have acted in collaboration.'

'Why ever should you care what becomes of that nobody?' Lirenda gasped, vexed. She stabbed a finger at the vat with imperious orders to keep dogging the soldiers' activities.

The mayor's men swarmed in a house-to-house search, leaking purposeful dust storms of feathers and leaving handprints in glue upon door handles, chest keys, and closets. Their disgruntled efforts yielded no fugitives. Only threats from irate servants, and torn boot cuffs from the teeth of a matron's snarling lapdog.

'Stymied,' Cadgia admitted at length. Her announcement held wry admiration as she raked bony fingers through her fallen-down wisps of cream hair. 'Whatever bolt-hole our quarry has found, someone's offered him powerful protection. The sigils we cast all spiral downward. Until something changes, we're hopelessly grounded into a vortex of darkness.'

Lirenda jerked her chin in negation, her exhale hissed through locked teeth. 'No. This isn't the end. Whatever obscuring darkness you find, *keep on trying to track through it*. If our quarry has help, he's still hemmed in Jaelot. The mayor won't allow his arch nemesis to win free. Nor will I do less. Be very sure no one here will find rest until we've untied the knot that is binding our spell weave to find the Master of Shadow.'

# Bolt-holes

The oak-paneled door shut to a well-oiled click of the latchkey. Arithon surveyed the candlelit foyer, with its carved agate cats, waist high, and an ebony side table inlaid with patterned birds of paradise cut from mother-of-pearl. The carpets were Narms dyed, and worn dim with age. The floor beneath, just as old, was maple parquet, merled with the raised grain that bespoke generations of beeswax and silk-slippered footsteps.

Still breathless from a sharp uphill run, one hand gripped to a gashed wrist to keep bloodstains from marring his unknown patron's moneyed elegance, Prince Arithon fought steadiness into the requisite words of courtesy. 'Thank you. We would have been gored on some halberdier's weapon if you had not stepped in and sheltered us. Have I the pleasure of knowing the name of the benefactor who sent you?'

The servant who slid the iron key from the lock was well dressed, but not in house livery. His quality mantle of gray loomed wool more befitted a patronized scholar. Aged, but not frail, he had long-jointed hands and clear, oakbark eyes; the trimmed white hair at his temples curled like the fringe on an egg. His smile was formal, and his hand on Fionn Areth's shoulder too firm to be mistaken for tact. 'You will meet my mistress directly. Please follow?'

Eyebrows tipped upward in inquiry, Arithon trailed the man's gentled tread down a hallway lined with antique serpentine vases. Each one overflowed with dried flowers, bunched and tied years ago with faded lengths of starched ribbon. The candles in their glass sconces were wax.

The air trapped their musk scent and the crisp tang of citrus oil used to polish precious wood furniture. From a drawing room to one side, Arithon picked up the genteel perfume of lavender and spikenard the wealthy in Jaelot used to anoint the heavy tasseled pulls on their curtains.

The lady was well set, whoever she was.

A glance sidewards established that Fionn Areth was still trembling, his limp grown pronounced since a misstep in flight had worsened his damaged knee. Before the boy's mood of stifled desperation could raise argument with the old man, Arithon said, 'Relax. This household is not under sway of the Koriathain.'

The old man's stiff protest, 'I should say not!' collided with Fionn Areth's clashing glare of distrust.

Arithon smiled, head tipped in deference to the disgruntled servant. 'I have a bard's ear,' he explained in swift effort to quell the riled nerves of both parties. 'Since the stones on the threshold asked for my Name, I surmise the lady in residence is no friend to a faction who treat their crystals as tools without consciousness.'

'I'm not one to speak of such things out of turn.' The old man paused before another closed door. 'The mistress will share her confidence as she chooses.' He raised the bronze latch, pushed the panel inward, and gestured toward a room left in stygian darkness. 'Go in.'

At Fionn Areth's balking, flat pallor, Arithon spoke in that steel-gloved gentleness that best masked his own trepidation. 'I'd far rather face this than die on a pike in the streets. Shall I lead?' He did not wait for the herder's answer, but shouldered the price fate's favors had dealt him and strode boldly over the threshold.

His first footfall tapped the same wax-polished wood. The next sank into rich, piled carpet. Incense rode the air, too faint to be cloying. By the deadened lack of echo, he determined the walls were probably hung with wool tapestries. When no voice addressed him, or offered direction, he opened with wary courtesy. 'May I trust the invitation of your servant gave us your sanctioned leave to enter?'

A thin rustle of silk carved sound from the darkness. The reply held an old woman's quaver. 'There is truth to the rumor you were mage-trained, I see. Your careful choice of language would mark you, had the stones at my door not already given their own fair endorsement in your favor.'

'Sweet lady,' said Arithon, enchanted by her phrasing, 'not all things are as they appear, in my case. Is the shadow for your sake, or mine?'

She laughed, her gaiety vivacious as a girl's. 'Oh, you are priceless for nice manners alone. The darkness is for my vanity, as well as your comfort.' The admission bald-faced, 'I am fire scarred.'

'I would ask light, then,' said Arithon at once. 'There is no ugliness about you.'

The melodious laugh this time held a caught edge of grief. 'Suit yourself. If you're shocked, I won't see the offense.'

'You are blind?' The question matter-of-fact, delivered in between a flow of deft movement as Arithon felt his way to a side table.

'Since the fire, yes. I was a young girl.' No pity, but acceptance framed that placid statement. 'There's a striker in the lacquer box to your right, and a candle a handspan farther on.' A pause, while a citrine feather of light bloomed to her guest's ministrations. 'Ah, I am sorry. You're not left-handed by choice, is that so?' Reclined on a settee, the diminutive old lady raised a porcelain, fey wrist draped in lace-worked shawls. She jingled a little brass handbell.

The door cracked, admitting a grudging spear of illumination. The old man, who must have been waiting without, poked his balding head through the jambs.

'Jasque, if you please, a basin and clean linen for bandages.'

'Mistress.' The servant's deference held earnest concern as he left on the requested errand.

The woman who owned such selfless loyalty was tiny, erect, every inch of her frame endowed with a graceful air of self-command. Yet no dignity could erase the cruel marks of deformity. The fingers she tucked in her lap were pink stumps. Her exquisite, fine bonnet of starched lace could not soften a face cruelly wasted to scar tissue; nor the unearthly, high timbre of voice, sadly due to the drawn flesh left by fire inhaled in her trial of agony.

'Sit,' she invited, courageous despite Fionn Areth's inadvertent hissed breath. 'I'm a friend of the Fellowship Sorcerers. My welcome extends for as long as my house can safely provide you with sanctuary.'

'Lady, in gratitude, we owe you our lives.' Arithon restored the striker to the box, but stayed standing, where the free-fallen blood from his wrist would drop without harm on the tabletop. 'You were told we had need?'

Again, the lucent laugh of amusement. 'I dislike the Koriathain, as you guessed. What they want, I would deny them.' Old bitterness colored her sigh as she qualified. 'They asked for me, you see, as one of their initiates. I refused, and the Fellowship enforced my born right to stay free. No one ever proved that the charges for dark witchcraft which saw me to the faggots were made by the order's arrangement. But my mother believed so 'til her hour of death. This house was my sister's, though she has passed also. I live here with Jasque, who first served my father as a message boy.'

'Then who wakened the stones?' asked Arithon, conversational. He caught a stuffed chair and sat as the servant returned with a steaming basin on a tray, an aromatic tin of salve brought along with the requested linen for bandaging.

'I was blind, scarred, and talented.' Pert under her shawls, the old lady tracked each sound as her guest declined Jasque's attentions and took charge of his hurt on his own. 'Sightlessness came to resharpen those senses. What friends I have made over these long years have exceedingly subtle voices.' Her natural warmth and gratitude shone through like fine light as she finished her explanation. 'The stones woke on their own, I think to ease my loneliness after the fire.'

'A tribute and an honor,' Arithon allowed. He paused on a locked hitch of breath, the linen pressed tight to dam the fresh flood from the gash he had just given rigorous cleaning. To Fionn Areth, who looked ready to bolt from the queer turn the conversation was taking, he said, 'Stones recognize honesty. They never speak false, and their loyalty, once given, is held sacrosanct. Trust me. You are protected and safe.'

The old lady concurred. 'Young man, the granite foundation underneath us would shatter before even one Koriani sigil should gain entry and bring harm to your person.'

'That won't be necessary,' Arithon said, arisen with the tinned salve in hand to inspect his companion's torn dressings. 'We won't stay one moment longer than necessary.' He quelled the lady's instantaneous protest, his phrase to Fionn Areth just as brilliantly pitched with assurance. 'I am healer trained. In fact, it was Elaira's own wisdom that taught me.'

'You know her?' Fionn Areth blurted, the question jerked through his wall of distrust by surprise.

Arithon smiled. The expression was haunting – the features struck from the same mold as Fionn's own, but inescapably *not*. The sharp planes of bone beneath sea-tanned skin seemed too sensitive, too fragile, too inescapably human and vulnerable in the light of the candle he lifted from the side table. Eyes and mouth held a fleeting, poignant exposure, doused like the flash on a fast-sheathed blade as he answered the query on Elaira. 'I know her well enough to guess how angry she'd be if she saw how you'd treated her efforts to mend the wound on that forearm.'

Then Arithon subjected his double to the lingering inspection their straits had not allowed previously. He added in hasty apology to his hostess, 'Lady, I'm sorry. Conversation must wait. This boy needs a meal, a bed, and a rest before he'll be fit company.'

The brass bell summoned Jasque, who received clear instructions to see their every need met.

'How can we repay you?' Arithon said, a strange desolation struck through the firm weave of his voice.

The lady's scarred face tilted in its veils, the unassuming human beauty of her smile erased by her puckered scars. 'Sing for me.' This time pleading, she added, 'I heard your music just once, through the stones, when you chastised Jaelot twenty-five years ago. The memory has all but destroyed my sound sleep. No harmony since seems complete.'

Arithon arose from Fionn Areth's side. He stepped forward through the foil-thin glow of the candle, and bent, and lifted her malformed hand. The kiss he placed on her crumpled red palm was a reverence that seared eyesight to witness. 'I will play you the stars and the moon, sweet lady, anytime that you ask.'

Two hours later, the lady awaited, still motionless in her chair. Immersed in deep thought, her lace veils lit to amber, she was like another stitched scene in the tapestries hung on the wainscoted walls. As if, after fire, her life had stopped in place, like the lover's idylls depicted in age-faded thread.

Quietly as Prince Arithon could move, she still sensed his presence at the doorway. 'Come in. You're expected. Your tread on the stair is more springy than Jasque's.' She had not asked her servant to snuff out the candle. Under the friable glow of gold light, she seemed ephemeral, traced out in white and bullion-thread lace, and ethereal as the legendary cutter of life threads who enacted the Fatemaster's judgment. 'Better sense says you should have settled for bed rest. Is the boy made comfortable?'

Arithon moved on cat feet to her side, found a low stool, and sat down. 'He's sleeping, though in truth, an herbal tisane was needful to settle him.' With long, supple fingers, he massaged his temples, sun-browned from his years of sea voyaging. The trimmed ends of his hair licked his high linen collar as he described Fionn Areth's condition. 'The left arm's been restitched. His knee is a problem that will have to be tended once the ice packs have drawn the swelling.'

'You could do more for him.' That insight came piercing, through blinded eyes.

Caught off his usual guard by fatigue, Arithon flinched into recoil. 'Ath, are you Dharkaron's own Spear, or the voice of my deathless conscience? Yes. I can do more.' Green eyes too steady, he regarded the diminutive figure of his hostess with a startled, even wary respect.

'If you see that much, you'll also know the price of intervention could be punishing.'

Her silence held no judgment, but only generosity. 'You came to ask something?'

His smile rewarded, sunlight through storm. For her gift of tact, he chose to answer the question she had carefully left unspoken. 'I'll do all I can for the boy, come what may. He won't walk lame for life. The song for his healing will cost me a painful exposure. I'll support that, if you can, but there's an errand I need to run first.'

'Outside?' The word reflected her sole apprehension, the tragic bounds of a courage that humbled all the more for the fact it had limits.

'You'll keep the boy safe, here?' Arithon asked. 'I give my sworn word, I'll be back.'

'Sworn words are small use if you're dead, or taken captive. The Prime Matriarch's minions won't rest your case until they've garnered one or the other.' The old woman pushed straight, painfully slowed by the binding pull of her scars. She pawed aside shawls, then sorted through one of several silk pouches tied to her waist with wool cords. The belongings inside were well-known by touch. She found what she sought, drew it out with all the reverent care her malformed hands could still muster. 'Take this as a keep safe.'

Candlelight danced like fey gold through the veils of a beautiful, polished quartz sphere. Touched deep by the radiant, soft peace of its presence, Arithon sucked in a fast breath. 'That's no talisman, to be handed by whim to a stranger.'

Indeed, the crystal was wakened, a living awareness whose being shone fair in a room choked with confining shadow.

The woman extended her offering, and waited.

Pained to impatience, Arithon stood. 'You know that bright being would shatter with overload if a Koriani sigil should cross me.'

'I trust you not to try foolish risks.' The woman caressed the smooth surface of the sphere. The stubbed-off remnant of her thumb sensed beyond the seared nerves that stole away tactile awareness. 'Listen. Stone has character as well. Given the freedom to exercise preferences, this one speaks for you by choice. If you reject the honor of that, you must phrase the discourtesy yourself.'

Arithon laughed. 'I haven't the sheer arrogance.' He accepted the sphere, held it cupped between reverent hands, then whistled a clean phrase of melody.

The sound drew an ecstatic, white flash of light from the heart of the stone in his fingers. The old woman cried out. She clapped deformed hands to her cheeks, stunned by wonder as her talent sensed the resonance of the crystal's reply to him. 'Oh, you are blessed, to be gifted with a language to stone that mortal ears can perceive! Why should you question the gift of their protection of you, in return?'

Arithon looked away. In the draftless, close air sealed in by wool tapestries, the clasp of his hands on the quartz sphere became a ghost's grip that threatened to tremble. He did not have the words, then or ever, to explain that for him, Vastmark shale had done murder. For this reclusive old woman, whose gentle nature had brought needed respite in his cause to spare Fionn Areth, the impact of too many truths would become a consummate act of unkindness.

'You both know me too well, and not well enough,' Arithon said finally, subtle in his effort to warn her against the perils of incautious confidence. Humbled by the simpler majesty of quartz, he tucked the crystal sphere into a pocket under his jerkin. 'Expect my return before sundown, on my word as Rathain's sanctioned crown prince.'

The lady tilted her head in acknowledgment, amused by the perspicacious awareness of an oath given rarely, and never without weight and thought. She made light response in an effort to ease the burden she sensed on his heart. 'My liege, the boy will be safe until your return. My Jasque will have hot soup waiting.'

'No liege,' quipped Arithon. 'Just a mountebank gallant who took sad advantage of the retiring primrose. For a keepsake, I'll bring you yellow ribbons from the market.'

The last thing she felt of his presence on departure was a tender, dry kiss on a cheek that had known no such sweetened touch throughout the lonely, long years of a lifetime.

Outside, the winter cold sliced down to the bone. Arithon tugged the mantle borrowed from Jasque around his shivering shoulders. Poised on the stair of the kitchen exit, he knew where he stood. The grand, high house with its queer, wakened stones crowned a crest, and below him, the hillside fell away, snow dusted in the crazy-quilt jumble of cobbled gutters and skewed, slate stairs. Local tradesmen called the byway Spinster's Alley; now, to his sorrow, he knew why. The anger spurred on by that thoughtless cruelty amazed him. He refused the distraction. Above anything he needed clear focus.

He was a hunted fugitive in a city that had condemned an innocent to sate its vindication. The soured fury of its citizens cast an ephemeral aura of disharmony that clouded his mood to uneasiness. Over the distant barking of dogs, he picked out the hobnailed march of men-at-arms; the iron-shod hooves of war-horses bearing lancers, and from seaside, the wail of an officer's horn. The thin snowfall had abated. A sky of flat white outlined the roofs, etched gray and pewter, and dull charcoal. Gulls wheeled and cried above the emptied fish market. Their circling flight changed direction too often, and the grind of the drays up the incline from the docks seemed diminished. The more sensible carters kept to their homes before braving the unrest in the streets.

A lone servant girl bearing an errand basket hurried by, head down, disinclined to share gossip or greeting.

Arithon tucked the plain wool hood against the tugging, damp clasp of the wind, then set off, brisk paced, for the ramshackle stalls of Beckburn Market. He did not choose the straight course, but ducked through courtyards and closes, passed on light feet through the dead stems of flower gardens and under rose trellises, where, in summer, young lovers met sweethearts. Now the dried canes shook to the sea winds, and ice choked the stepped ledges of the fountains.

Alone, the Master of Shadow moved fast. He knew the old city as well as the back of his hand. His bard's ear warned which lanes were obstructed and which ones offered clear passage. The sphere of loaned quartz always warmed to his touch where Koriani scryers swept the byways. Other searchers' activity seemed stiflingly muted, the morning's hysteria subsided into a poised and explosive apprehension. Tight-faced tradesmen clumped on the street corners. No matter how innocent each passerby seemed, they whispered, disturbed glances cast over their shoulders to take note of anyone watching. The shutters stayed barred on the mansions. Wrapped in Jasque's mantle, Arithon became what he seemed, an anonymous lackey sent out on an errand too trivial for high-ranking house staff.

Where he did not wish to be seen or heard, he masked his presence with shadow. As much as he could, he kept out of the thoroughfares. The back alleys and servant's gates, the footpaths across middens, and the dank, narrow gaps between buildings where the runoff from overlapping eaves spilled melodious droplets into the brick-channeled gutters; he knew the mazed byways which led to the twisting, hillside stairs and the weed-grown plots of the commons. There, in swift passage, he trod unpaved earth, and first noticed the queer note of resonance.

He paused, listening, teased by the feeling that something unsettled traveled through the ground. Yet if aught was amiss, its signature energy left too faint an imprint for a bard's ear to capture in sound. His blocked mage-sight, of course, told him nothing.

Arithon lingered, one sensitive hand pressed to a snowy outcrop where the stone of the hillside pressed through. The vibration he half sensed lay far outside hearing, more a breaking touch against intuitive instinct, there and then gone before mental logic could grasp it. Perhaps his own nerves had played tricks on him, with fickle rock casting back the high-frequency echoes of his own uneasy fears.

Despite the futility, Arithon stilled his mind. He suspended his will, sought the receptive quiet that had once opened the wellspring of his mage talent.

*Nothing* met his questing query. As always, the core of his trained mastery eluded him, the inner vision of refined perception swallowed into a bottomless well of blank blindness. Plunged into the familiar, searing pain, as his lifetime dedication to honed faculties rammed headlong against the slick, black wall of the blockage he had carried off the bloody field at Tal Quorin, he stamped back the bleak fury. Wrung through by fresh grief, he rejected entrapment in the clogging, numb bog of self-pity. All but running, he pressed through the dank close that opened on Beckburn Market. More imperative, now, that he find Dakar quickly; the spellbinder's knowledge could sound for the anomaly, and identify threat or dismiss his fleeting hunch as the phantom of overwrought fancy.

The stalls with their ramshackle gray boards and used wares were not closed, although foot traffic was scant. Arithon filled his needs with dispatch, his accent a southcoast sailhand's slack drawl, and his dark hair masked salt-and-pepper gray. The coin he had lifted from the dandy's purse bought him new boots for Fionn Areth. He chose also four warm shirts, a wool tunic and thick hose, and weatherproof cloaks in dull colors. Since a bow and flint striker would invite the wrong questions, he settled without, his purchases bundled and tied up in scrap twine as he set off for Threadneedle Street.

In the perfumed sanctum of the dress shop run by the aging Madame Havrita, he obtained the promised yard of yellow ribbon. Payment was made with his own honest silver, then all of his masterbard's glib tongue required to extricate himself from the gossip inveigled by her bevy of chattering seamstresses.

Outside, the thin snowfall had restarted. A party of armed horsemen clopped by, their saddlecloths sewn with a private house blazon. The slight, cloaked figure burdened like a servant was given no second glance, though the wood cart at the crossing was stopped and subjected to a thorough search at sword point. While the drover vented his scathing annoyance, Arithon s'Ffalenn ducked into the ice-rimed back alley that led him a crooked course, and let out on the brick paving of Dagrien Lane.

The tavern he sought, the Tin Flagon and Flask, overshadowed the street, its sagging half-plank balconies hung with flickering, soot-paned lanterns. Noise from inside could be heard through latched windows, and the usual drunks snored in heaps in the gutter, content to lie where they had been ejected for bingeing, obstreperous behavior. The seamier dives were Dakar's preferred haunts when he fell into scapegrace indulgence.

The sagging boards of the stair had not changed through the quarter century of Arithon's absence. He pushed open the refitted door, already scarred by rough usage and the odd gouges left by sailors who believed that carved marks on port taverns would ensure a safe return from sea voyaging.

The Flagon's clogged air hit his lungs like a steamed blanket, a miasma of overheated bodies in damp wool, and the gagging, grease-thick scent of meat stew. The trestles were packed, the ragtag of the streets jammed cheek by jowl with the overworked seamstresses from Threadneedle Street, drawn in for the halfpenny beer. Sky signs and portents, and the escape of the dreaded Spinner of Darkness made the drinking more serious than usual. Seated, sprawled, or tipsily standing, both sexes shouted and threw dice and argued. At the Flagon, a wastrel could collapse without harm. The floor was strewn with stale rushes that had likely not been changed in a year, bones and refuse picked out in the carmine light that bled from the smoke-filmed sconces.

Arithon blinked, eyes stung by the fug of exhaled breath and the rancid brown fumes from the tallow dips. When he failed to find Dakar's rotund frame propped upright among the garrulous roisterers, he continued his review of the lumpish figures dropped prone upon benches and floor. Marked out by distinctive, bullroaring snores, the Mad Prophet sprawled like a walrus on the settle, his ham pink hands crossed on his breast, and his legs stuffed calf deep in the woodbin.

He had evidently been a fixture for some time. Someone had parked a plate of stripped bones on his groin. By his head, three revelers sang off-key ditties. Curled in the straw underneath his slack bulk, two toothless derelicts grumbled in dispute over stakes to a game of mumblety-peg. To complicate matters, four of the mayor's stark-sober guardsmen bulled through the rear entrance with orders to toss the establishment for news of the morning's escaped fugitives.

Arithon's tactic to extricate Dakar was simple, direct, and expedient. He pinched the pooled dip from the nearest sconce and fired the unsavory rushes. Stepped back, masked in shadow, as the flames fanned and spread, he watched the shouted dismay of the Flagon's owner entangle with the bellowing squeals from singed patrons. He could have laughed for bright irony. To judge by the horde of rats that emerged to flee the disaster, he had no doubt accomplished a public service by purging a nest of breeding pestilence.

Retired to the street amid yelling pandemonium, Arithon caught the sleeve of a tavern maid with a rawboned build and the pursed lips of no-nonsense character. He offered a gold piece in smooth negotiation, while inside the roiled taproom, the garrison soldiers howled for buckets. They drew weapons at length, and by force, pressed every lout into service to douse straw before the blaze spread and ignited the planked timbers of the building.

The woman bit the gold, grinned with surprise, and rammed back into the smoke and confusion.

Arithon backtracked to Threadneedle Street. There, he mounted a loft stair with red-painted newels and knocked on a door fitted with a brass latch cast in the busty curves of a sea nymph.

Through the brief interval as the bar scraped inside, he altered the appearance of his face and dark hair with a deft, wrought illusion of shadow. Another man greeted the large, scented woman, painted and powdered, and clad in a gown roped in freshwater pearls. She planted her bulk in the entry, arms folded, and inquired after his business.

When he gave no answer, she surveyed him in turn, from his wide, hazel eyes and middle-aged crow's-feet, to hair of a lank, lackluster brown dusted iron gray at the temples.

His voice held an almost forgotten light music as he prompted her flagging memory. 'Meliane, you're magnificent. As always, we have a mutual old friend who's fallen facefirst into trouble.' He kissed her perfumed cheek, his mouth tweaked to a smile that caused the woman to squeal and snatch him headlong into her bosomy embrace.

'Medlir? Is it Medlir?' Twice his slim girth, and two fingers taller, Meliane thrust him at arm's length. Her ringleted hair chimed with amethyst dangles, and gold necklaces sparkled to her heaved breath as she beheld his wry, laughing features. 'Merciful fate! All these years, and I'd thought you a figment, crafted out of a Sorcerer's mischief to serve our fat mayor his comeuppance.'

'Do I feel like a figment?' asked the Master of Shadow, who, in the calm and reasonable persona of Medlir, had served the late Masterbard as apprentice twenty-five years in the past. 'I've paid one of the wenches from the Flagon to bring Dakar here. He's falling-down drunk and disorderly, as usual. Can we plead for your famed hospitality?'

'Oh, for him, I've a girl with a willing enough heart, provided you share all the gossip.' The comfortable, large woman flung her door wide, her smile all oyster shell teeth. 'You do still pay silver for the extra service in advance?'

Arithon, as Medlir, gave her laughter. 'Enough to slake the thirst of every soldier who comes searching.' He stepped into the incense-soaked air of a brothel that had changed not at all through the years. A stalking, sleek shadow against banks of lit candles, white and pale gold in brass stands, he stayed genial. 'Does the weasel I remember still keep your account books? If so, I could owe you a fortune.'

'Dearie, yes. Wulfcars still tends the ledgers. Will you sit?' She waved a plump hand toward a violet hassock, flanked by two muscled, bronze statues whose yoked shoulders supported carafes of spiced wine hung on chains. 'Serve yourself as you wish.' Her welcoming gesture encompassed the laden table of sweetmeats, all of them spiced, and infused with enspelled aphrodisiacs.

'You've that poor an opinion of my aging manhood?' teased the man she knew as Medlir.

Surprisingly graceful for her generous frame, Meliane snapped back a scarlet curtain. She shouted down a hallway spangled in light thrown by candles in pierced copper shades. 'Casley? Freshen the room in the annex. We've a customer.'

Her swept mass of hair like combed brass as she turned, Meliane studied her questionable guest, tucked in cat elegance on the hassock. She sighed, divided between longing and dramatized, mock disappointment. 'Your manhood was never in question, my sweet. Every girl I ever had who laid eyes on you has tried to breach your bastion of unshakable good taste. Or were my instincts in error? Has it been pretty boys all along?'

'It's been pretty trying,' Arithon confessed. 'Keeping Dakar's randy appetite supplied tends to limit the available partners.'

Meliane clapped plump hands in delight. 'Still kept the sauce on your tongue for evasions, I see. If you were the Master of Shadow, the Alliance at Etarra posts a price of five thousand gold royals on your head.'

'So little?' said Arithon , eyebrows raised, unconcerned. 'The army housed in Lysaer's barracks eats thrice that, over the course of one winter. Were I in fact the Spinner of Darkness wanted for acts of foul sorcery, believe this. You would never hold such a man long enough to collect.'

Her probing suffered a rude interruption as a commotion thumped up the outside stair. Meliane arose in a cinctured gleam of stitched pearls and peered through a spyhole in the window bay. 'Your prophet's delivered, but not by a wench. He's being lugged, hand and foot, by two of the heavies who toss drunkards out of the Flagon.'

'Well, give them an afternoon's frolic, at my expense,' said Arithon from his perch on the hassock. 'Keep them happy enough, they won't rush off to inform the mayor's overzealous pack of troops.'

Meliane measured him. Comfortable as he looked, his relaxation was illusion. The hand held beneath his plain cloak surely gripped a readied weapon, and the eyes were alert and too steady for a man who played for anything less than blood stakes. Experience had taught her when customers were most dangerous; this one lit her instincts to screaming.

At least resignation came tempered in coin. The whole day had been bad for business. 'Just warn the lugs they can't traipse their hobnailed boots over my spotless carpets.' Feeling all of her years, Meliane moved to the door and opened the latch by worn precedent. She had hosted the Mad Prophet through scurrilous excesses far more than once in the past.

The annex room where Casley installed them had a sloping low ceiling, two dormer windows curtained in garnet chintz, and a bed wide enough for a tournament. The two muscled men who plonked the Mad Prophet on the quilts were cozened away down the hall. Arithon, thoughtful, chose sweet tact with the nubile Casley: he bequeathed her a large denomination in silver, with his involved request for hot food and a rare vintage wine that required an effort to collect.

Left behind a closed door, in privacy that he knew could not last an hour without a betrayal, Arithon surveyed the Mad Prophet, limp as a beached whale in the ruby cast of the tinted lanterns. For a marvel, the spellbinder's comatose state did not include rattling snores. The fringed pillows instead made Dakar look wasted, eyes sunken into the blued orbits of his skull, and the white-streaked hair at his temples grown prominent. Set at odds by his bedraggled presence, the sweet scent of patchouli clashed with the seamier tang of pipe smoke and rotgut gin.

'Spirits are scarcely your usual style,' Arithon said in too quiet, opening observation. 'What went wrong at the jam seller's?'

'We're alone?' Dakar mumbled. He shed his playacted illusion of oblivious, drunken collapse, opened his eyes, pained, and rubbed pudgy fists to gummed sockets. The groan he dredged up shook the flab at his midriff, soul deep and resonant as a martyr's. 'Save us all, if you're wearing Medlir's identity, we must still be in Jaelot. Say I'm having nightmares, if you've got any shred of pity in your miserable heart.'

'We're still in Jaelot,' Arithon affirmed, in no mood to lighten the circumstance. 'I'm wearing Medlir's identity because even Meliane's grasping nature wouldn't accommodate for a stranger.' Not when armed searchers might toss her back rooms in hot search of the Spinner of Darkness.

'Meliane, bless her. She always did come to everyone's rescue in time.' Then, sharpened to edged accusation, 'She wasn't the one who fired the straw.'

'I'd hoped to entice you to walk.' Arithon's ghost step passed from washstand to window. His oddly blurred profile seemed to shimmer between forms as he peered through a gap in the curtains.

'I had a disaster,' Dakar confessed, then dropped the shattering gist, 'a collapse from a fit of tranced prescience.'

Deceptively cold nerved, Arithon raised his unbandaged hand and eased closed the small crack of daylight. 'Then you don't remember the vision you saw?' He faced into the room, the shuttered planes of his face washed in gaudy light from the lanterns.

'Why else would I drink?' Dakar said, peeved. 'The gift had to be stifled. All of us want out of this city, alive.' He let slackened wrists flop back on the quilts, anger dissipated into a puff of lavender and rose-scented air. 'Never mind I'd be worse than useless, dropped comatose in the streets spouting prophetic futures. That sort of behavior could send me to the faggots condemned as a lunatic seer.'

Arithon unearthed the chamber's close stool. He shut the fringed velvet cover, and sat, his expression wide-open and thoughtful. His linked hands and posture suggested a long wait, and a patience as forced as cranked wire.

From his purgatory of discomfort on the pillows, Dakar said, 'You know Meliane will sell us out to the first man who offers more coin than you have in your purse.'

'Tell me a fact I don't already know.' Arithon maintained his listening posture.

Dakar ejected a rude phrase, too sick for verbal evasions. 'All right, we're compromised. There's a problem, a big one. Something's upset the clear flow of the lane force. I can't say why. The prescience I had is utterly blanked from my memory.' *Which meant whatever he had dreamed would inevitably come to pass.* Nor were recriminations in hindsight much use, that an imbalance of such magnitude was *surely* the reason for Sethvir's failure to intervene with their meddling with the Sanpashir focus in the first place.

Arithon did not pass judgment, but said gently, 'We daren't attempt our planned escape by lane transfer from Jaelot. Is that the bad news you're evading?'

Dakar twisted his neck in the mire of pillows, sick for more than physical reasons. 'The difficulty can't be helped. To get you and Fionn

Areth clear of danger, we have no choice left. We'll have to cross through the city walls.'

Never slow to grasp setbacks, Arithon stood with the whiplash athleticism that too many opponents forgot could accompany small stature. 'You can't help, either. That's why you were drinking. *If you try to tap your inner resource for an act of grand conjury, your talent for visions will take precedence and overwhelm all of your faculties.*'

'Quite,' Dakar said, slack with an exhaustion that, this time, held nothing feigned. 'A stunning predicament, with a pack of Koriani and all the mayor's guards like howling demons at our heels.'

'My heels,' snapped the Master of Shadow in weary and acid correction. 'It's my life and liberty that make you and Fionn Areth desirable as enemy bargaining chips.' Poised by the doorway, rimmed in carmine light, he pulled the nondescript hood of Jasque's borrowed mantle over his head. 'I trust you're not too undone to arrange livery mounts? Good. Then we'll separate, for safety's sake. Bring horses, provisions, and gear for winter travel. I'll steer Fionn Areth out of this snake pit. Just manage to meet us before midnight at the abandoned sawmill three leagues north of the walls.'

His quick fingers tripped the latch, then paused. The Master of Shadow turned back and delivered his wry parting. 'Don't worry for your stomach.' Then, in jarring and genuine sympathy, when another in his position might have shown rage for the dangerous increase in stakes, he grinned. 'You can eat the feast Casley brings while you're waiting. Drink to luck with the rare vintage Cheivalt red you'll find to wash it down. On my way out, I'll make sure Meliane sees I won't play sitting pawn in her parlor.'

# Cogs

In the westlands of Camris, Lysaer s'Ilessid sits in a drafty campaign tent, poring over tactical maps by the guttering light of one candle and saying to the coiled whip presence of Sulfin Evend, 'Don't ask how I know. It's not instinct, but certainty. We'll cross into Rathain and discover that the Master of Shadow is once more abroad on the continent . . .'

At Althain Tower, under Luhaine's uneasy vigil, Sethvir shivers and mumbles in the grip of ill dreams, while across the breadth of the continent, in searing, patched flashes, his earth-sense shows him the pending pressure of the solstice tide that will crest in last passage at midnight, the song of the pulse still running dissident where the power lanes are left roiled from the malice of Morriel's masterstroke . . .

In Jaelot, Dakar the Mad Prophet arises after a replete hour of Casley's fine favors; he engages a simple cantrip of illusion and forges a writ of requisition, complete with the mayor's lion seal; the language grants him permission to draw supplies from the garrison stores, four horses from the stables and an unrestricted pass through the city's outer gate for the purpose of bearing dispatches on to Highscarp . . .

# XV. Crucible

J asque came to the lady in the late afternoon with soft word that Fionn Areth had awakened. 'He's rested, though the abuse he has suffered has left him surly and confused.'

In sad fact, the young herder's last recollection had been of a hot meal and a bath. The posset Arithon had mixed to ease pain through the restitching of his torn wrist had blurred any memory he had of being carried to bed.

'Well, he hasn't been through the most pleasant experience,' the lady agreed in shared empathy. One candle burned in her tapestried parlor. Set into a scene the golden hue of aged parchment, she sat sewing the yellow ribbon from the market onto one of her lace shawls by touch. Arithon sprawled in a cushioned wing chair, asleep himself, his hands fallen loose and relaxed in his lap, and his head tipped against a tasseled cushion in rare and artless abandon.

'Should I arouse him?' asked Jasque with a lift of his chin, his query a tentative whisper.

The lady shook her head, her sparse wisps of white hair pinned like combed shell against the ivory lace of her bonnet. 'That would demean what I think is a mark of his personal trust. Let his Grace be. No doubt he'll hear the step on the stair when the young man is ready to come down.'

'As you wish.' Ever deferent, Jasque retreated again. The door closed, the oiled latch fallen with a respectful click. An interval passed, where naught moved but flame-cast shadows and the lady's diligent needle. The coals in the grate threw off soporific heat and the aromatic spice of white birch.

In the chair by the candle, Arithon s'Ffalenn raised his head. His eyes flicked wide open, the transition from sleep accomplished without seam or stray movement.

Nor was the lady oblivious. As though she had sensed some minute shift of focus, she paused between labored stitches, her needle a scribed line in midair. 'You're back with us,' she observed.

'"*Know a man's truths by his unwatched arrivals,*"' Arithon said in quotation. His good-humored satire derived from a comedy that Jaelot's theater troop had performed on the green in her young years, when, unscarred and sighted, she had probably entertained suitors.

But no moment remained for kindly reminiscence. As though summoned on cue, Fionn Areth's halting step clumped in awkward descent from the stairway.

'No respite from melodrama,' Arithon quipped, then relapsed back into recitation, '"*Nor is the hour ever chosen to reveal the true self behind a man's spun mask of pretense.*"' An oiled silk ripple of movement saw him onto his feet.

The lady sensed rather than heard his soft footstep as he crossed the thin swath thrown by the candle and closed the few strides to the door. Quieter than Jasque, he reopened the panel to admit the spell-wrought person of his double.

The contrast between them showed most in that moment, when fate set them again face-to-face. Arithon poised, unthinking in balance as a cat, while the herder boy staggered, his reach for the latch caught unfinished as the panel whisked back and destroyed his last semblance of privacy. Moved to reflexive compassion for the disgruntled injury stamped in a frown of uncanny likeness, Arithon shot out a hand. Unasked, he braced the boy's halting step, sparing him further indignity.

Fionn Areth said a rude word in Araethurian dialect that meant scat of a gelded goat.

Arithon held on through the unsteady aftermath, his equanimity unmoved by the rancor. 'Freedom has done very little, I see, to improve your civil disposition.'

Fionn Areth shook off the helping grasp. Dressed in borrowed clothes, stiff-lipped and determined, he completed his marred entrance alone. Though the rich, patterned carpet damped the thump of his limp, the dim lighting withheld its kindness. Each step he took was a tortured achievement that left him drained white and shaking. Annoyed by his audience, and hackled against pity, he caught the arm of the chair that his royal-born double had just vacated. Hands gripped to white knuckles, he lowered himself into the cushions, all elbows and awkward, hard breathing. 'I'm not running anywhere,' he announced, his voice a drawn line of defiance.

'For the knee, or straight pride?' asked Arithon with a delicacy that jabbed. 'Or shall we consider how the lady would face the fire a second time, when the mayor's armed guards search house to house, and find her in polite company with a convicted Sorcerer?'

Fionn Areth swiveled and glared back at him, murderous. If his eyes were the same green, his fury was less artfully focused as he conceded in clipped capitulation. 'The knee. It's stiffened. I don't expect it's going to bear weight, no matter how many men Jaelot sends hounding down your accursed back trail.'

If Arithon was irritated, he reclosed the door panel with unruffled deliberation. He used the awkward interval that followed to build up the lagging fire. As the herder boy shifted in pained effort to find comfort, no witness could fail to note the stressed joint, poorly concealed beneath the knit hose just bought from Beckburn Market. In fact, the hot swelling had grown markedly worse, the mending Elaira had begun on torn sinews set back by the morning's rough flight.

The Master of Shadow knocked the loose ash back into the grate. Without airs or propriety he reclaimed his earlier seat on the hassock beside the lady's chair, that she not feel edged out of conversation. Then, very calm, he addressed his made double with the unswerving attention that sent Dakar into mute fits of dread.

'Do you want to be healed?' Delivered with a bard's incisive clarity, the inquiry cut like a razor. 'The Koriani sigils to bring regeneration are in fact still in place. With some effort on my part, they can be retuned. Yet the question begs asking: are you ready, Fionn Areth, to stand upon your own two feet? Are you prepared to carry yourself forward from here?'

All crossed arms and defiance, Fionn Areth glared at the open cuffs of his shirt. The lacings were too short to accommodate the sturdy, herder's bones of his wrists. He made that his excuse not to have to look up. The miserable awareness rode his tense shoulders, that he was outmatched before he even measured the challenge in the Prince of Rathain's sovereign stare.

The greater issue most tactfully unsaid yawned like a pit at his feet. *He saw himself stripped by that Sorcerer's regard. What was he but green youth, a bumpkin goatboy whose desires were an undefined snarl of dreams, a grandiose cloth of ideals not yet backed by the tested fiber of character.*

The unbending pressure of the Shadow Master's quiet became a statement beyond spoken word: that the living continuity of the s'Ffalenn royal line might hang on this hour's decision. A crown prince's destiny was entangled with his own. By Koriani machination, their fates had been paired, two lives cast headlong into jeopardy if the coil of an unwanted responsibility was not mastered with mature consideration.

Nor was the room, with its incense-soaked shadows and patina of wealth any comfort, despite the fire's snug warmth. Fionn Areth felt displaced in that setting as a rickle of hay straw and burlap. The Vhalzein pearl-and-lacquer table, the richly dyed tapestries, the untrustworthy, deep pile of the carpets felt unreal, their cosseting beauty a suffocating dream after bleak life on the moorlands.

'No one can speak for you,' the Teir's'Ffalenn prompted.

Fionn Areth unlocked his tense, sweating fingers from the linen that covered his forearms. His discomfort written upon angular features that had never been his born legacy, he stated, 'I can't accept your black principles.'

The corners of Arithon's mouth flexed and almost broke through to a smile. 'As the Alliance defines them, neither can I.' Then his irony gave way to that intent gravity even Fellowship Sorcerers respected. 'You don't have to like me. We need only come to a simple agreement. As you wear my face, my enemies become yours. Just cleave to an undisputed common ground whose only shared goal is survival.'

Frustration peaked, that the dictates of circumstance left no slack at all for refusal. 'How do I know I'm not being lied to?'

Forgotten amid her lace wrapping of shawls, the lady sucked in a fast breath. Braced as though she expected an explosive outburst of fury, she stilled. The volatile seconds crawled past in suspension, while the ribbon and thread that had kept her preoccupied crumpled between the scarred stubs of her fingers.

But Arithon s'Ffalenn no more than looked down. His recoil masked no act of duplicity, but became stripped response to a startling, deep pain that struck past his kept privacy to witness. 'Challenge me on even ground,' he invited the young man ranged like a crouched tiger against him. The schooled temper of his voice for a mercy allowed him the grace to appear conversational. 'But for your life's sake, and mine, forgo your hostilities until we're safely outside Jaelot's walls and past reach of the Koriani Prime's plotting.'

'Then do your work,' Fionn Areth said through locked teeth. He leaned forward, his rebound into eagerness transparent. 'On those terms, I would have my knee whole again.'

He would walk unsupported, if only to claim that later opportunity to enact the role of judge and savior. If a Sorcerer's glib tongue spoke him false promise, there would be redress. For the deaths at the Havens, and Dier Kenton Vale, and Tal Quorin, his young arm was prepared to strike for the Light. In the name of Lysaer s'Ilessid and the Alliance, he vowed he would rise to his chance to deliver the Spinner of Darkness to his long-overdue date with justice.

In frank unconcern for the watershed just crossed, Arithon arose from the hassock. The etched planes of his face stayed serene, and his temper, disarmingly content not to quibble with impassioned fancy and flawed idealism. He gave his neat bow to the lady as though she had not been maimed or blinded. On that moment, only a mage-trained perception might have guessed the degree of trepidation he held shielded behind genteel manners and clasped hands.

'You asked me for music,' he opened to honor her earlier request. 'As Masterbard, I am bound to repay the grace of your hospitality. Take this song as my gift. Though made to accomplish Fionn Areth's healing, in every way known, its artistry springs from my heart.'

Unable to plumb the veiled depths his performance might come to reveal, the lady set aside her mangled sewing. All innocent expectation, she spoke her permission for the musician to proceed at his pleasure.

Arithon bowed again, then faced the chair where Fionn Areth feigned gruff indifference. 'Are you ready?'

A curt nod. 'Sooner started, sooner finished. Will I need to remove my hose?'

'That's not necessary.' Arithon knelt. The opulent magnificence of the carpet framed him, rough-clad as a commoner, his carriage too unprepossessing to suggest his reputation as a killer who sent armies to wholesale doom. Settled on the floor at the young man's stockinged feet, he finished his unvarnished explanation. 'Sound transmits itself through all things of substance. Plain cloth will pose no impediment.'

Unself-conscious on his knees, he seemed too slight a presence to bear sanction as crown prince; too unimposing for a criminal Sorcerer; too meanly appointed for the title of Masterbard he had just made flat claim was his right.

And yet, there were depths not apparent to the eye. *Despite all appearance, he was not detached.* Some held, inner tension seemed to shimmer beneath his seamless veneer of calm presence. His green eyes stayed clear. No tremor marred his raised hands. The fingers were longer and slimmer than the herder's, tanned and well weathered from seafaring. Nor were the fine knuckles any less marked with abrasions from the morning's flight across rooftops. He sketched no arcane passes; fashioned no seals to wake magecraft, but only cupped his palms in the air on either side of Fionn Areth's wrapped knee.

His voice as he spoke seemed to jar the taut stillness wrapped at the hidden core of him. 'By tonal harmonics, I'll try to refire the Koriani sigils of healing. You may feel sensation, but I promise, there won't be any pain.'

Fionn Areth looked away, all but shrugged his nonchalance. Constrained by his inexperience and countrybred dignity, he strove to behave as if the trial to come was not cut from the cloth of the terrifying unknown.

Arithon angled his head to one side. The listening quiet he sustained while measuring the needs of an audience by its nature left him exposed. He must abandon self-command, lay bare the vulnerability that opened him to his talent. This time, as he let those inner barriers fall away, he sighed in soft surrender, conflicted by a queer, longing tenderness that made the very blood in his veins seem to burn.

As though air itself spoke a language he knew, the mild frown eased from his forehead. He captured a breath; hesitated. Suspended on the precipice of a step *he knew* must carry hard consequences, he engaged his will and let go.

In irrevocable commitment, he lowered poised hands, rested palms and fingertips against the hot, swollen flesh of Fionn Areth's torn knee. The touch was less substantial than the brush of a swan's feather, fallen. No force and no mystery resided in the contact. Yet as though an unseen dialogue had opened, Arithon flushed with a passion too forceful to bridle. A frisson ripped through him. As swiftly, he spent his reserves and contained it, though not without snapping his web of false peace to a turmoil akin to anguish. The flooding color ebbed from his face, until tensioned pallor described every angle of bone that stamped his ancestral bloodline.

From that moment, the room might as well have ceased to exist.

Become the tuned instrument of his high art, Arithon saw wholly inward, mind and talent aligned to a lens of absolute clarity. No man, now, but Masterbard, he gave over his whole being as sounding board for the frequencies sealed in the chained sigils a Koriani enchantress had left imprinted under his hands.

The seals were, heart and mind, the work of Elaira. Her signature rang through like dark water and moonlight, an essence of womanly mystery that transfixed his spirit and raised a cry all the hours of eternity could not answer. She was the one love he could never embrace; not without breaking her vow to the Koriani Order, which cold binding would bring her destruction.

Nor could he retreat, not now. Once before, Arithon s'Ffalenn had partnered her efforts to accomplish a difficult healing. The fusion of sound and spelled magic had left a link beyond time to erase. As his sensitized skill traced the map of the sigils that underpinned her fine spellcraft, stark dismay plucked his nerves like a dousing chill. No touch of his could be stealthy enough not to arouse her awareness. She knew him too well. Her song partnered his in a union that held the same need as life and breath. From the first instant Arithon touched her linked spellcraft, Elaira was simply *there* in his mind.

Nor could he spare her his pain in return, as the instinctive welcome that surged in response was jangled to recoiling fear, then a desolate, shared understanding. She knew why he must act. Once again his free choice, and hers, must become the string-tied puppet of circumstance.

'I'm sorry,' the words spoken, unthinking, aloud. His agonized headshake whipsawed the silence. 'Beloved, forgive me. May you be somewhere far removed from Jaelot, in a haven both sheltered and private.'

For a boy's life relied upon their paired talents. Fionn Areth's survival perforce must take precedence over the fury and blind pain, that the cast lot of fate forced them separate.

Then the agony, redoubled by the gift of her gratitude, that he had not been too proud to reach out, and ask help from her strength out of principle. Her love became the more poignant in renewal, for his trust, that she would not, now or ever, stint the needful burden of sacrifice.

'Oh beloved.' There were tears in his words, a bitterness of brine where the touch of her should have been honey.

Arithon wrenched in a shuddering breath. All the while, his hands had not shifted position. They trembled only slightly as he completed his mental sounding to find the tonal frequencies of the magelight that bound each drawn sigil to its chain of harnessed energy. That signature chord, lowered the exacting, requisite octaves, became accessible as sound he could replicate with the instrument of his voice. His whole body sheathed in the discipline of his art, he opened his throat and sang the first pure note to initiate the succession.

The lusterless sigil under his hands reawakened and warmed with shared resonance. He shifted the pitch, a sweet, gliding rapture of tuned force that spoke, and refigured the ritual magics which called primal power from the elements. Nor was that bright forging recaptured on a surgically precise intonation. His own vital humanity could do no less than color the pitch with emotion. His love for Elaira was caught like spun gold in the exacting grace of execution. His unadulterated regard, and its twin partner in pain, for the passion unshared between them, framed a tangible force. Melody poured from his heart, blazing and bright as the fractured light trapped in the planes of cut diamond: agony and joy that knew no limits, twined as one inseparable thread.

Arithon sang. His art was his master. He gave himself over to the demands of the moment, yielding and clear as a stream of fresh water poured formless, out of a jar. The notes of his making cascaded in phrases of a cappella simplicity, a beauty of sound shot warp through weft with words phrased in lyric Paravian. All over again, as he had once done in Merior, he became voice and instrument for the loom of Elaira's spellcraft.

The union this time came bittersweet with foreknowledge that consummation could not follow. *Every tie they had ever held between them remained, renewed on this hour, reinforced.* She was his, and he, hers, and no other's, no matter the obstacles between them.

His tempered voice broke the limits of passion and held strong, sustained, locked to the parameters of Fionn Areth's healing.

Had a mage of trained stature been present, in expanded perception the dark would have burst and blazed into lines of trued light. The powers called down to realign torn tissues razed dross from the mind and reforged muddled thought into ecstasy. No listener escaped. On her chair, sight-blind, the lady rocked with her arms folded over her breast, the yellow ribbon pressed to a cheek riven through by the lava red scars of old burns.

The Araethurian goatherd sat limp in his chair, paralyzed by a beauty that recast his bones in vibrations of unalloyed sorrow. He wept. The tears fell and fell off a face not his own, as if for that moment he became breathing surrogate for the bard whose concentration *must not snap* under the assaulting force of an insurmountable pressure.

And yet, one male voice clothed over in artistry was not enough to tear the necessary fissure through the veil. Cut off from access to the wellspring of true mystery that linked the full range of his mage talent, Arithon sensed his best effort fall short. Attuned as he was to the buildup of heat under the clasp of his hands, his trained instinct gave warning. The very air surrounding seemed weighted by friction, a pent-back torrent of raised flux that his bardic art could not fully access, or trigger, or release. He had called in the elements; but no sung note in his power could grant them permission to unleash.

Nor could Elaira release him the key to a conjury not of his making. Not through his mind, or their shared mental contact. Consummation demanded her presence.

'*Oh, beloved!*' his cry never spoken in words, but tapestried into the unalloyed flight of free melody.

She answered, her giving spirit the velvet that disarmed his drawn sword of denial. He could not stop her, not by plea, not by force. Elaira was herself. His love was not made to become the halter to compel her decision to stay safe.

'*I was called for this purpose,*' her assurance rang in his mind.

She would leave her body to stand at his side, spirit twined with spirit, as before, back in Merior, they had done still enfleshed to spare a young fisherman's limb from amputation. Her laughter resounded like the chime of small bells as she answered his peal of dismay. '*And how are the circumstances this time any different? Either we stay the same course of character that brought us together, or we become cowards, unworthy of all our shared intimacy.*'

He bowed to her wisdom, which cradled the root of the undying integrity between them.

The song from his throat could not then do other than soar, embracing the joy of her welcoming.

Her touch firmed, then melted him, crossing the threshold that entwined self-awareness with its dense-form housing of flesh. On a breath, she was there, unshielded spirit limned in a light his mage-blindness could never see. Yet her presence enveloped him, a tide of limitless tenderness that made him ache to the bone for a partnership snatched short of the exalted fulfillment of reunion.

His voice could not be kept separate from the tempest. Dark, minor harmonics described burning longing, until air itself lit like a brand for his sorrow.

Elaira touched him back in shared consolation. This time, unlike Merior, her resilience was the force that bolstered his strength to refocus his mind and reclaim the dropped thread of his purpose.

Time bent, stretched, became limpid, the anomaly sustained by the demand of high mystery, and a song that matched and held its true pitch through its shining edge of sharp temper. The spell seals rekindled, though the forge-fire forces that knit their waking were too refined for the mind to endure. Gifted the borrowed lens of Elaira's trained insight, Arithon extended his talent. He reached past the veil and recaptured the unseen, highest frequencies of electromagnetics that bound energy into form and substance. Then he downscaled that tapestry, remade its pattern in sound with a focused expectancy that, in turn, re-created the upper-range harmonics. Form followed function; the traumatized tissues stitched under the sigils had no choice but to refigure through the spelled template of regeneration.

Fionn Areth never noticed the precise moment when the pain dissolved from his torn leg. Immersed in the fabric of Arithon's singing, he felt the ache of enforced separation; of the shimmering dichotomy of transcendent love held earthbound by a restraint that must endure, deathless, a stripped nerve of killed hope and agony.

The flame-scarred lady who shared the performance was aware of the last sigil's closing. Sight-blind, but attuned to the low speech of stone, she sensed the descent, the slow, spiraled recontainment of forces as tonal harmonies were singly collapsed and dispersed. Although no light had impressed her maimed senses for a span that encompassed five decades, she dreamed. Her inner mind showed her, in flash-point-clear vision, a woman wearing a Koriani mantle reach out to touch her beloved's dark hair where he knelt.

Then the insight fled, the apparition erased like a gale-blown candle. The bard's last line ended. Crippled eyesight locked down, plunging her back into the irremediable prison of darkness the fires had left her.

Unwitnessed by any but the eyes of his double, the singer lowered his hands. His closing note quavered silent. Stillness returned to the heated, close chamber with the opacity of poured lead. All things seemed duller, the fine ivories and gold leaf somehow clogged in the spent tang of incense and the wan flutter of the single candle. The grand chords of high mystery faded and fled; the musician whose art had brought fleeting command was reduced to the framework of his humanity. The moment robbed him of trapping or title. He was no prince, no Sorcerer, no masterbard. Just a man, kneeling, burdened by a desolation of spirit no living being might lift from bowed shoulders. Fate's cruelty remained, written into his naked expression, and stamped on the forced, tired lines of his carriage.

For Elaira, the gradual, spiraling fall must end in the dusty, chill dimness of the vintner's shed. The transit plunged her through an ice bath of ink. Much like her past experience in Merior, her senses returned to her piecemeal. Hearing resurged first, snapped back into sharp, unpleasant immediacy by voices clashing in argument across the unseen space over her head.

The sluggish thought followed, not funny at all, that she had likely broken Lirenda's directive not to stray from her perch on the wine tun. By logical extension, she must have overbalanced in trance and fallen prone on the floor.

A patchwork of unhinged impressions confirmed: she lay sprawled on the fusty, damp cold of packed earth. Her left shoulder throbbed, most likely bruised in the limp tumble that resulted when she enacted her rash decision to spiritwalk. Her head ached as well, no less than she deserved for flitting out of body without making the most basic, sensible preparations.

Lirenda was screaming in unintelligible rage. A calmer voice answered, then rose on a fractured note of distress.

Whoever spoke for her, the protest gained nothing. The floor where the debated enchantress lay prone seemed to buckle and move with a violence that negated the staid, grounding properties of earth.

Elaira mumbled a fishwife's curse on the fool who was trying to move her. Raked through by nausea for that thoughtless unkindness, she curled into a protective knot on her side. Eyes open, she could discern nothing as yet but the star-punched black of the void. The tormentor she reviled clamped a grip on her shoulder. Fingers bit painfully into her collarbone, shaking and worrying as though the shock of harsh handling might speed her recovery into full consciousness.

The rage in her burned. Her crystal-bonded oath to the Koriani Order all but choked her, life and breath. Now, *even now*, she was not left her peace. No moment was given to cherish and sort what small memories she retained of her recent contact with Arithon. That, more than anything, tore out her heart, that she had seen and touched him outside of the veil, and could not snatch the chance to reflect and savor the bittersweet gift of the experience.

Then the mind reconnected to outward events, and hearing regained its lost linkage to reason. Lirenda's ranting came clear as a flask dropped on ice, spewing vitriolic frustration. 'Time is the one option we don't have left! She'll wake up if it kills her, and speak what she knows. If not, you'll be more sorry than tears. Morriel Prime won't be sanguine. Dare you send our Matriarch word that we had both Fionn Areth and the Shadow Master in hand and, through inept fumbling, have lost them?'

Elaira dragged in a breath. The effort fanned a dull ache that seeped down to the lead-weighted marrow of her bones. 'You can all stop fighting like starved dogs on a carcass. I'm awake, if about to be sick.' She shuddered. Her chilled hands broke into slick sweat as another cramp knifed through her stomach.

'She should have peppermint tisane and a warm bed to recover from your callous mishandling,' Cadgia scolded in undaunted sympathy.

What Elaira received instead was Lirenda's nailed finger, prodded into her exposed ribs. 'You were with him, weren't you?' Then, in whiplash interrogation she could not safely ignore by feigning fogged wits or vagueness, 'Where is Arithon s'Ffalenn?'

Shaking, torn by a misery beyond the simple discomfort of nausea,

Elaira shook her head. 'He's inside of a house. In a room with one candle.' Tears pricked her eyelids, born out of hopelessness. If only her talents could answer self-will, she raged in a desperate black wish. But she lacked the schooled strength to annihilate the disloyal, strong beat of her heart. She used words as she could to buy time, all the while enraged by the deficit: there was not enough rhetoric in the compass of human language to stall long enough to save anything. 'If there were windows, they were covered, or else masked by thick tapestries.'

The detail cut with unmerciful, cruel force, that Elaira remembered the sweet tang of used incense and citrus, but could not recover even the subliminal texture of the black hair she had touched as the song that had called her had faded.

'You were with him,' Lirenda persisted. The hems of her skirts slapped Elaira's turned cheek as she whirled and paced out her agitation. 'His mind and yours, they were paired. Our seeress *captured the event as it happened*. Deny what she saw at your peril.'

Elaira said nothing, caught as she was between ripping cramps and the knot in her throat caused by a desperately held urge to weep.

'How does Prince Arithon plan to leave Jaelot?' Lirenda pressed, inexorable. 'Don't pretend you can't access his intent.'

Elaira's voice as she answered was scarcely her own. Her outright betrayal of Arithon's trust was made worse by the fact he had known, *and had forgiven in advance*, the inevitable surrender she must make to the demands of her order. The exigencies of her oath were not mutable, nor his status as Morriel's mortal enemy.

Since the agony could only be pointlessly prolonged, Elaira made the distasteful task the brutal, brief work of one sentence. 'He plans to leave by way of the wall, through a small postern gate behind the back courtyard of a merchant whose fourth-generation grandfather made his family fortune by smuggling.'

Lirenda clasped hands to a triumphant clash of gold bracelets. 'There I will finally corner him.' Her jabbing vindication could have drawn blood as she promised, 'You'll be there, Elaira. You'll see his face when he's taken, and you'll hear his curse as he knows, for all time, *that your hand denied him his freedom.*'

# Last Rites

High on the slopes of the Skyshiel Mountains, the circle of twelve seniors who survived the night's conjury undertook the last rites for the departed. Mourning began for the Koriani Prime Matriarch and the one seeress left dead when her crystal sphere shattered under the stresses of uncontained backlash. The burden was shouldered despite rugged terrain and the louring threat of a storm front. The gravity of the matter allowed little choice. When ranking enchantresses passed the Wheel of Fate, their remains were inevitably riddled with spellcraft. Imposed sigils and bindings of longevity were entwined with entangling ties to a personal crystal, its imprinted matrix yet entrained to the signature Name of the departed. The seals which contained those disparate energies always became breached upon death; their concentric, layered circles would gradually erode as the fading charge of the life aura slowly trickled off and dispersed.

Worse, both elderly women had died unattended. Before their sad state was discovered by servants, the hazed phosphor of leaked spell force had winnowed and fanned through the forest. The circle of seniors had been immediately faced with the painstaking task of reeling in those questing tendrils and settling them into containment.

Their toil had extended past the hour of noon, with exacting work still to follow. Not only were the shades of the dead not released until each tie became cut by a banishment; here, in the open, beneath unwarded sky, each damaged link in those refined chains of conjury must be ritually dispersed. If the precautions were not complete before sundown, such uncoiling forces became as a magnet for stray iyats, or else bled off on the winds of high altitude to magnify discord elsewhere.

While the young initiate, Selidie, remained tucked in her pallet in the oblivious throes of drugged sleep, the bodies of the departed were removed from the palanquin. Warded circles were woven around the site, held and guarded by half the Senior Circle.

The oldest women, wise with experience, implemented the requisite next steps. From inside, they burned herbs and copal in a ceremony far older than man's inhabitancy on Athera. A blood ritual regrounded the ephemeral essence to earth, and a raising of fire consumed the last, lingering threads that might hamper the spirit's passage across the veil. By Koriani custom, eight levels of cleansing were enacted before the last, which nullified the patterned resonance from personal quartz crystals recovered from the hands of the dead. In the late afternoon, meticulously thorough, the sisters wrapped the bodies in silk bound with silver cord. They placed the bundled forms upon litters and began the arduous, uphill journey to an isolate ledge past the timberline.

There, on a windswept outcrop, the twelve Koriani joined hands in a circle and raised their thin voices against the bitter gusts and chanted the incantation of parting for each name. Throughout the hour of recitation, the palanquin's bearers cut deadfalls and cedar boughs and stacked the dry wood for two pyres.

As the hour of solstice sundown drew nigh, thin snowfall cast a milky veil over the fir-clad valleys. The peaks overhead were lost in torn cloud, the leeside ledges chalked in glare ice and a pillowed upholstery of drifts. Young Selidie still slept. Cocooned in her blankets, she breathed without stirring.

While the ripping blasts from the north snapped the palanquin's curtains and cracked the red-banded hems of the twelve sisters' mantles, the funeral rite proceeded without her. A gray silhouette in the premature gloom, the sixth-rank enchantress sprinkled the wrapped corpses in aromatic oil, then touched them alight with a pine torch. Sparks whirled and flew, chased through shredding rags of black smoke. The tormented flames flared and flattened. In silence, the mourners observed while the pyres were consumed, a drawn-out interval made brutal by the thin air and knifing cold.

At due length, the last sigil of closure was sealed. The twelve seniors shivered from chill and exhaustion. The storm closed around them with shrieking, wild force, lidding the mountains into false twilight and erasing the notch of the valley as worsening snow pelted the upper slopes in stinging, horizontal fury. The hour seemed a sorry, inauspicious time to turn weary thoughts to the future.

Yet time would not pause for the crisis that faced them.

'We must choose who will assay the burden of prime power,' said the sixth-rank elder, helped down the slippery slope on the arm of a spryer sister. Her wise, lined eyes were pinched with strain as she voiced her doubt in trepidation. 'Morriel's long illness seeded too much dissent. An abyss of peril will yawn at our feet if any opening is claimed for debate.'

'Who among us is qualified?' the third-rank seeress despaired. The facts in past record supported her grim outlook: forty-two hopeful candidates had failed to survive the last initiation, and they had been exhaustively trained to master the rigorous trial. 'Whoever we appoint could be facing a virtual death sentence.'

Yet whether or not Morriel's passing had upset the chain of succession, the order could not languish, leaderless. On the sundown lane surge, the seeresses on watch at each sisterhouse would learn of the late Prime's unexpected demise.

'Qualified or not, one of us must stand forward.' The rawboned speaker blotted her damp nose, her weary shrug fatalistic. 'Too late to wish differently. The torch has already been passed.'

Resettled in a hollow beneath gale-blasted firs, the enchantresses of the order's seniormost circle huddled around the thrashed flames of a campfire the servants had kindled in their absence. Faces burnished red by the terrible cold, the women pressed close for warmth and examined their critical predicament. Opinion differed over which enchantress should be named to undertake the perilous initiation.

Beyond any question, all agreed on one point: the Prime's untried young candidate was in no way prepared. Selidie had not yet achieved second rank, nor matured her self-control to harness deep access to the focus of a small crystal pendant.

Since no such green novice could survive the ordeal, or master command of the Waystone, the talk turned to Lirenda, who had borne the title of First Senior for decades, and who was the order's only verified eighth-rank.

Supporters were quick to argue her case. 'Despite the misdeed which caused her to fall from favor, the terms of her penance will shortly be settled in Jaelot.'

The crabbed, older seeress agreed. 'If Lirenda achieves Prince Arithon's captivity, we'll have proper grounds to reinstate her. Those terms were set by the late Prime herself.' She paused, while the snowfall cast a veiling pall over the firelit ring of hooded faces. 'As well, Lirenda's already mastered the Skyron aquamarine. Who else has the strength and experience to shoulder the test to subdue the Great Waystone?'

Yet other, respected voices disagreed. 'She's the only confirmed eighth-rank we have. If she dies, too much advanced knowledge will be lost.'

'A council of Peeresses should be called to deliberate.' The sixth-ranked senior jabbed the earth with her bone-handled walking stick, irritable from the effects of high altitude, which settled pain in her aged joints. 'The sisters at Whitehold have a seventh-rank initiate whose name isn't tarnished by disgrace.'

'The initiate at Whitehold would be doomed on the moment she opened her mind to grapple for control of the Great Waystone.' That incisive observation arose outside the circle, from a blanket-wrapped figure, emerged without sound from the shelter of the palanquin.

Heads turned in surprise. Selidie had listened in on their sensitive discussion, unnoticed until she spoke. The young woman had not troubled to dress. Under the gale-whipped fringe of wool blankets, her ivory shins were naked. She walked on rosy, bare feet in the snow, supremely untroubled by the buffeting punishment dealt by the winter elements. Her pale hair blew also, tangled and loose, flung by the howling, ice-barbed gusts across the cream skin of her features.

'Sister, are you daft?' The kindly old seeress offered her mantle in genuine consternation. 'Put on warm clothes before you catch cold or blacken your toes with frostbite!'

The sixth-rank senior, less tolerant, added, 'What gives you the right to criticize your betters? Morriel has died with your training incomplete. Every one of us here outranks you.'

'Morriel has died,' the young woman agreed. She paid no heed to rebuke, but came on, arms cradled around something bulky clutched under the folded blankets. She stood with raised chin and bright-eyed defiance just outside the perimeter of the circle. 'And I beg to differ. I outrank you all. The late Prime named me her successor.'

'What! You? Assume the Prime's powers?' The sixth-rank enchantress all but laughed, her finger stabbing in censure. 'The very idea is preposterous! Just yesterday, you scarcely managed to imprint a basic spell template in a cleared quartz!'

'Be silent!' Selidie snapped a second phrase in guttural, harsh syllables, then invoked the prime sigil of command.

The elderly senior fell quiet by force, compelled beyond will by the bindings laid down with her oath of initiation. Her pale face, and her gasping, choked fear lent the shocking declaration of rank a thread of convincing evidence.

'Further, I've had contact with Cadgia in Jaelot.' Selidie measured the Senior Circle's sudden, wary reserve, her lips turned in a settled, acidic smile too worldly for her unmarked features. 'You need not look stupefied. The wards guarding the city from outside prying by the Fellowship in fact remain sealed at full strength.'

Which implied she had scried through that barrier by wielding full command of the Prime's ciphers of prerogative.

Only Lirenda's supporter clung to her staunch disbelief. 'Show us proof.'

Selidie said nothing, but shifted the blankets. The hidden object in her clasped hands proved to be the Great Waystone, raised from its cradle and wrapping. Its focal matrix already blazed with the actualized forces of tuned power none held the hard-core experience to tap, except the former Prime Matriarch.

'Save us all!' cried one senior above the gasped murmurs of her peers. 'How has this miracle come to pass?'

The succession was fact. First-level novice to ninth-rank initiation, Selidie had survived and assumed the high office of Koriani Matriarch. Through her ran the knowledge and memories of every one of her predecessors, preserved to be accessed at need.

Though the precedence solved a desperate quandary, the circumstances raised dire questions which no voice among them dared ask. No senior alive had ever borne witness to a successful transfer of prime power. Morriel had been by lengths the oldest sister in the order, and the nature of such mysteries had remained her most guarded secret. Nor was her heir inclined to waste words explaining her mercuric rise to supreme authority.

'The conspiracy against Rathain's prince is still in play inside Jaelot. As we speak, Lirenda has taken charge and ventured into the streets. She's presently laying the final trap to take Arithon s'Ffalenn as our captive.' Her eyes as impenetrable as turquoise enamel, Selidie surveyed the circle of twelve left at her immediate disposal. 'I would know if her trial meets with success. Afterward, the rest of the order must be told of the change in our chain of command.'

'Your will, Matriarch.' The old seeress was first to open the circle and give due obeisance, as Selidie Prime stepped inside.

# Trap

Light snow changed to sleet as the afternoon waned. Glaze ice rimed the cobbles and pebbled the scalloped slate of Jaelot's gabled rooftrees. Inside town walls, the mansions of the rich quarter rose to high peaks that notched the wan sky like knifed pewter. The shadowed, closed shops and the steep slopes of back byways had emptied of citizens since a curfew enforced by the mayor's sealed writ called a halt to workaday commerce.

Set under enforced peace, the city was not calm, nor settled into complacency. The morning's raw turmoil had merely reshaped into a distressed and brooding expectation. Dogs barked in the lanes and the courtyards, upset by the shouting of officers. The ongoing hue and cry showed no sign of letup as compulsory searches were conducted house to house, with small regard for nuisance or propriety. The occasional ripe language of overstressed landlords stewed through lidded quiet, scored by the clang of the destriers' hooves as squads of lancers swept through the cleared streets.

Arithon and Fionn Areth began their harried passage to the walls in that ice-burnished climate of danger. Their presence, the only furtive shadows, crunching prints through the courtyard trellises. The windows of the mansions were tight shut and barred. No welcoming glow from interior candles leaked through to save two hunted fugitives from chance missteps. Yet the Master of Shadow showed no hesitation in the deepening twilight. He found his way through the blackest covered archway by touch. The chained mastiffs, he soothed with

554

his bard's gifted voice; where needed, he used masking shadow to blend their presence with their surroundings. The pair moved, swift and silent, their survival dependent on the stark simplicity of logic: that the mayor's guards would sweep last through the private gardens of the rich, who relied on fierce dogs or kept hired men-at-arms for security.

There were no forgiving havens to recoup from mistakes, no kindly benefactors who owned the rare grace of the lady's understanding. This was Jaelot's rich quarter, where grudges and distrust had inbred for generations, fermented to an ingrained intolerance. No blueblood family had forgotten the injury of Halliron's long-ago satire. Hounded by the sword, and by Morriel Prime's contorted conspiracy to dismantle the Fellowship's compact, Arithon and Fionn Areth eased through the wrought-iron gate of yet another sprawling mansion. The sleet fell straight down in the windless air, tapping an incessant, white noise tattoo. Against gathering gloom, the evergreen yew wore its red berries like pert buttons on mantles of spangles and frost.

Despite every care, there were mishaps.

As Arithon gently eased up the stiff latch, a flock of gray-and-black chickadees took wing and scattered, cheeping their strident alarm. Four pigeons exploded from the eaves of a carriage shed, all but flying in the faces of the mounted troop who jingled past at a vigilant trot.

The sergeant in charge raised his mailed fist and drew rein, his inquiry ringing against the main street facade, with its bow windows and pillars, crowned with black ivy and carved cherubs. A grumbling lancer dismounted under orders to investigate the private inner courtyard.

Arithon snatched the only available shelter, pressed against the dank stone of an ornamental archway set into the mortised wall as a lover's niche. Fionn Areth flattened beside him. For an interval of stopped breath, the pair froze into agonized stillness, while the rider thrashed snow-clad topiary and poked his sword through a winter-stripped arbor twined over with the knotted briar of climbing roses. The stab-and-slash assault of the garden continued, to the accompaniment of swearing, until the man reached the dwarf pear trees planted in rows along the west side of the house. The warmed slates on the roof shed droplets of melt off the gingerbread lip of the eaves. Constant runoff splashed the man's neck and shoulders. The small icicles he snapped off the branches in his blundering inflamed him to bursts of ripe language.

'No rats lurking here. Whole rotten business is useless as trying to milk the damned tits on a boar.'

The red-faced sergeant still astride in the avenue called back his nasal disagreement. 'Pigeons don't fly from their roosts for no reason.'

Sword steel screeled through stripped branches as the guardsman jabbed several more haphazard thrusts into a cranny, then peered behind a stone bench carved from the tails of two spouting dolphins. 'Since when does a scared pigeon's brain count for more than two-legged good sense?'

'Where a Sorcerer's concerned, good sense won't cut bait.' The sergeant tugged the curb on his restive charger, as fed up with the hours of extended patrol, but committed to the letter of duty. 'A wetting's going to hurt a lot less than docked pay if that sniping little criminal isn't found.'

The lancer sidestepped the brick rim of an herb bed, grumbling ill-natured obscenities. Another six steps would carry his search as far as the niche in the archway.

Fionn Areth shrank with stopped breath, his fist welded onto his sword grip. The odds were worse than unfavorable. If the first guard could be dropped by a swift, surprise lunge, Arithon did not carry enough throwing knives to fell the eight lancers still held in reserve. The mortared stone that presently shielded their backs would become a dead-end culvert to trap them. Steered on by fright, Fionn Areth began the inevitable last move, to ease his steel free of the scabbard.

Arithon's fingers clamped his wrist with bruising force. The curt toss of his head gave the emphatic command to watch and endure in steeled patience.

Caught short of brash panic, Fionn Areth surveyed the oncoming threat with fresh outlook.

The lancer advanced, oddly sidetracked by a gardener's handcart rimed with ice-crusted tools *that had not been there a moment ago*. At least, Fionn Areth did not recall avoiding the rakes and the outthrust, rusted mattock when he had traversed the same pathway. Nor were his footprints, or Arithon's, still visible, though the sleet fell too thinly to have masked their fresh tracks.

Cold fear threshed through Fionn Areth all over again, that an illusion wrought out of shadow could beguile sound eyesight with such consummate ease.

The lancer bypassed the apparent obstacle, none the wiser for the fact that he was the victim of sorcery. He stamped, crackling, through the browned stalks of last summer's flowering annuals. At next step, for no logical reason, he tripped and measured his length. The incised clay pot that had raked his shin bloody *should* have been too obvious to overlook, the blare of exposed terra-cotta a red flag on a walkway dusted dull gray in the falling winter twilight.

'Sithaer's coupling fiends!' Propped up on one fist, the downed man spat ice from his mustache, then winced and sucked his breath through locked teeth. 'I've turned my damnfool ankle.'

'Well, limp on it!' the mounted officer snapped. Although he could not see what had passed, he had small patience left for delays created by bumbling incompetence. 'We aren't going to have orders to stop searching courtyards until the mayor's convinced that shapechanging Sorcerer can't be found.'

The guard reached his feet, stumbled, then gimped purposefully onward, his mind distracted by pain. He swept the shallow archway with a cursory glance. Nothing suspicious caught his eye: apparently he discerned no more than blank gloom and shadowy, dank stone strung with runners of sun-starved ivy.

'Nobody here,' he concluded to his sergeant in disgust. Spurs jinked in staggered, uneven rhythm as he hobbled back through the street gate. 'I'll stake beer against hog wind, we don't find a damned thing.' He slapped the thin rime of snow from his saddle and scrambled awkwardly astride, his carping folded into the crack of departing hooves as his party retreated down the lane. 'Next time, someone else can grunt on foot, beating Ath-forsaken flower beds for criminals.'

Fionn Areth relapsed into shivering reaction. His clasp slipped, nerveless, from the wrapped grip of his sword. He tipped his head back to rest against icy masonry while the pounding fear drained out of him. Spared yet again by the veiling gift of the Shadow Master's trained talent, he tasted sharp guilt through his rush of relief. If in plain fact he was still safe and breathing, he must not lose sight of his true purpose by feeling beholden to the dishonest tricks of a Sorcerer.

'Not much farther,' said Arithon, every nuance of his bardic skill pitched to offer encouragement.

Fionn Areth shot him a loaded glance of resentment. His ongoing need for healing and protection left him vulnerable and self-betrayed. All the bright, shining dreams, all the fierce expectation that had ridden on the promise of his birth prophecy had become irremediably spoiled by discovery his fate was eclipsed by another man's weightier destiny. He could not accept the hand offered in friendliness. Not without feeling the sting of his worthlessness. What was he to become, if not a used pawn in the byplay to capture the Shadow Master?

Even as he moved through the gathering nightfall on the heels of his living nemesis, he swore afresh to reclaim his plundered identity. He would wait for his chance, then draw reckless steel and end the life that entangled his own in dark partnership.

If Arithon was aware of the blind hatred that stalked him, he displayed no sign of caring. His step on the sleet-dusted path stayed assured; his manner alert as a man who walked softly through enemy territory. The long, plain mantle veiled him down to his boot cuffs. His low hood shaded the distinctive angles of his features into disingenuous anonymity. Felted in gloom as he picked his way across the ice-locked beds of dead flowers, he was dangerous for the fact that his understated presence suggested nothing out of the ordinary. No sign or fell portent marked him out as the Master Sorcerer who had thrice brought wholesale ruin to Lysaer's valiant war hosts.

Presented that face of vulnerable humanity, his black arts and fell deeds could become deceptively easy to excuse and forget.

Fionn Areth moved, unforgiving, at Arithon's heels through the glazed tufts of dead chrysanthemums that rimmed the far wall of the garden. Failing light scribed the cover of ivy in jagged ink, snow-pocketed silver in the crannies. The Master of Shadow paused, ever watchful, as he explored the overgrown masonry with his fingers. In the street, a dog bayed. Horses clopped past to a jangle of mail, and a muffled whoop of male laughter. The troops that scoured the streets in massed force showed no sign of letup by nightfall. The oddity persisted, that in switched-back flight through the terraced maze of courtyards, the fugitives had encountered no sign of further Koriani pursuit.

Arithon answered Fionn Areth's concerned thought. 'They haven't lost interest.' His hands, still busy, dug under the ivy, apparently disappointed in the object of his quick search. 'No help for us; we'll have to go over.' The Shadow Master dried his reddened, wet hands and restored them to the warmth of his gloves. 'The hidden door's rusted shut. Evidently grandfather Tawis didn't bother to pass down his penchant for smuggling.'

Half-turned in inquiry, his face a pale blur against the backdrop of gathering gloom, Arithon regarded the unhappy presence of his double. 'Can you give me a leg up? I'll bear the risk if the street outside isn't empty.'

Fionn Areth made a stirrup of his hands, set his shoulder to the vine-clad brick. The slight, athletic body he assisted up the wall owned the climbing skills of a sailhand. A scuff of leather sole on the coping, a minimal rustle of greenery, and the prince gained clear vantage of the thoroughfare below. Suspiciously quiet, the twisty, torchlit avenue bordered the north bastion, overlooked by the high black loom of the battlement.

A pause of assessment, as Arithon weighed unease against a flat lack of viable options. He listened, strained and still. By the rustle of cloth at his back, he knew Fionn Areth wrestled the same crawling nerves. Despite his leashed patience, the Master of Shadow detected no trace of the subliminal chime of spellcraft he expected. Nor had he kept the gift of the lady's crystal through the risk of this last passage. 'Something's not right.'

The timing seemed too fortuitous, that this most critical crossing should conveniently fall in a lag between mounted patrols.

'You think we're expected?' Fionn Areth had to fight his strained whisper to keep his teeth from chattering outright.

'If we are, more delay will just work against us.' Arithon's etched word of decision floated down. 'I can mask us with shadow, provided we're quick. The pine brands in the sconces can be made to go out, but that's best done with finesse to look natural.'

Yet the night was dead windless. The sleet pattered down perpendicular, undeflected by so much as an eddying draft. Whatever sleight-of-hand sorcery Arithon concocted, the air would not serve him as ally. The best he could do under adverse conditions was hope the shadow-doused torches would be taken as an act of neglect by the lampsman who made rounds at nightfall.

'Still clear,' Arithon said. 'If we step into a trap, we'll make an ally of havoc. I hope you'll be sporting and help improvise.' Although every instinct jangled in mute warning, he extended his arm to the Araethurian herder who peered up from the gloom-shrouded garden.

Fionn Areth grasped the proffered wrist, felt his flesh clasped in turn by fingers that were firm and too humanly chilled. One wrenching heave drew him up mortised stone to a precarious shared perch on the wall enclosing the rich merchant's courtyard.

Near at hand, all was stilled. The hissed backdrop of sleet served as a lens to magnify the distant shouts of a matron, objecting to searchers invading an attic that no doubt held someone's stashed contraband. The echoes of discord bounced off the facade of Jaelot's high battlements, threaded through by a neighbor's crying infant.

'Now or never,' said Arithon, fired to unlikely humor. 'If the spitting mayhem concerns Dame Carrigan's loft, her shrieking will provide us as good a diversion as any.' He cast his leg over, then lowered himself from hooked fingers. 'The old woman keeps a still, and sells watered-down gin,' he cast back, his amused explanation accompanied by a brief rustle of ivy as he released and set down in the street. 'The town guard was bought off to leave her in peace. That's why she's busy maligning their mothers back to the sixth generation.'

'You knew her?' Fionn Areth dropped down alongside to a faint scrape of steel as his quillon clashed with a cloak button.

'No.' Arithon darted a swift glance right and left. 'But Dakar used to swill her rotgut spirits. That made him her bosom confidant. Come on.'

The pair sprinted across the narrow thoroughfare. Ahead, the rise of an octagonal battlement loomed against the gray screen of precipitation. A scant twenty paces distant, the arched portal at the base that housed the strapped postern which smugglers' bribes kept unlocked. If a garrison archer lurked in the corniced embrasure overhead, the fugitives could but pray the doused torches would impair the visibility required to snap off an accurate shot. Freedom nearly within reach, neither man dared rely on fool's luck, that the lag in patrols had extended too long to be trustworthy.

The moment held all of their desperate commitment, and no last-ditch avenue of escape when the Koriani snare overtook them.

The resonance of the spellcraft unfurled out of nowhere, inaudible to mortal hearing. A masterbard's extreme sensitivity sensed the vibration through skin and bone. Given split-second warning, but no time to act, Arithon slammed to a stop.

Fionn Areth skidded into his shoulder, his puzzled exclamation bitten off short as an explosive flare of light razed the gloom from the street. The facades of the mansions, stone battlement, and curtain wall vanished into an eye-searing glare and the whiteout dazzle of snowfall.

'Stand fast,' commanded a female voice. 'If you move, you'll find yourselves helpless, struck down by a seal of paralysis.'

The noose of flung spellcraft flickered and dimmed, leaving the fired runes of a circle of ward that held the look-alike fugitives surrounded. The hazed glare thrown off those hot lines of force unveiled the enchantress who had lurked under masking seals of illusion until her chosen moment of ambush. Her exquisite beauty was jet and fine ivory, a frost maiden's majesty cloaked in the amethyst purple worn by the Koriani Order. Cut sable against the moonstone silk lining of her hood, her pinned coils of hair crowned a carriage of aristocratic refinement.

'I know you!' Fionn Areth exclaimed. Betrayal rang through as cruel revelation unstrung the last, lingering thread of denial. 'You promised a sword in exchange for my trust.' He rammed forward, obstructed by the arm that Arithon raised in restraint. 'I remember your lies! *You* were the one who set meddling hands on my fate, long years ago in my childhood.'

'I meddled in nothing. You gave full consent.' The enchantress dismissed his accusation with a graceful, denigrating gesture. 'As for the sword, are you not wearing one? You've served your part well. Stand aside, boy. What better reward could you ask beyond this, to have helped with the capture of Arithon of Rathain?'

'That's pure arrogance!' The prince's hand rammed the herdboy aside. 'The blade was my gift, freely made without strings. And, indeed, have you accomplished anything near what you claim?' The quarry named as the enchantress's prize stepped forward, not cowed in the least by her spelled circle or its implied threat to his person. 'You've dared to address me by the s'Ffalenn royal title, madam. Will you deny that you stand in my kingdom, under my sovereign law?'

'Your law, as defined by the Fellowship of Seven?' Lirenda laughed in astounded disdain, the lit spark in her manner excited to passion by a challenge kept simmering for years. 'Our order predates them. We answer first to our founding tenets. Those give clear priority to humanity.'

'Now there, our points of philosophy differ,' said Arithon, conversational. One easy, neat stride carried him to the circle's edge, close enough that he could measure his Koriani antagonist in an unwanted, eye-to-eye intimacy. 'You've taken a boy, one of my kingdom's subjects, and made a mockery of his free will. For life, you have marked him. Wherever he goes, his face makes him bait for the unprincipled hate of my enemies. Where lies the humanity in the act of playing a live man as a decoy?'

'One detail altered without harm to life or limb,' Lirenda countered. Her bared fingers remained clasped to her quartz crystal, steadfast in contempt as she held the spelled circle in balance. 'For your intervention, today, six men have died. Four others lie beyond our sisterhood's powers to heal. Your liberty kills, prince. With Tal Quorin and Minderl Bay and Dier Kenton Vale as your testament, you have no defense left to argue.'

'Where are the friends at my back to speak for me?' Arithon's voice struck a note that, oddly, held truthful appeal. 'This is no fair trial of character, but only a raw bid to snatch power.'

'What friend could stand surety for the madness the Mistwraith's curse has engendered?' Lirenda replied, assured in her righteous judgment. 'You are taken prisoner by Morriel Prime's will. Your fate lies at her disposition.'

Arithon s'Ffalenn faced her, gone white to the bone. 'For my list of dead, I will answer to Daelion Fatemaster without anyone's appeal for intercession. Here, today, in Rathain, men have died for the cost of your political manipulation.' His bard's voice a textured tapestry of grief, he leveled his own accusation. 'As subjects of the realm suborned into treason, their offense becomes mine to answer. Beware, madam. If you act out your role as a Koriani cat's-paw, be careful of hardness of heart brought on by a flawed cause and shallow character. I swore a crown oath in mercy and compassion. Not even Morriel

Prime can call me to heel like a dog and expect to receive meek obedience.'

'You would resist?' Lirenda's surprise was a clear peal of scorn, raised to exultation for the stunning discovery that her wounding had struck to the core of him. 'Go on. Try and move.' The sensitivity of his bard's gift had once left her unmoored and helpless. Now, at long last, he would share that ignominy. 'See how far you get, belly down in the snow without control of your body.'

Yet Arithon chose not to challenge the seals that gleamed sultry scarlet, held tuned and ready to fell him. 'I should fear, do you think?' Without words, soft as breath, he unfurled a small shadow. The understated finesse of his gift blanketed the quartz matrix the enchantress employed to maintain the trap's spell-turned focus.

The circle that pinned him collapsed into sparks.

'Run for the postern!' he urged Fionn Areth. Burst into a sprint, he did not look back. If by misfortune the gate was barred shut, he knew no more options existed. He and his double would be trapped like small game, snagged in dire spellcraft, or else brought to bay by the zeal of the mayor's armed lancers.

No scrap of spun shadow could keep the enchantress cut off from the focusing properties of her quartz. He had bought but a handful of seconds. His tactic was surprise, and the shock of intervention, since the dampened vibration of the crystal would inflict dragging imbalance through even an instant of interruption. Longevity bindings would be held in abeyance; that debilitating upset at best might slow down the counterwards the enchantress required to dispel the masking veil of his gift.

Arithon flanked Fionn Areth in headlong flight to snatch back his last hope of safety. Faced ahead, thinking fast to match opportunity with circumstance if a garrison patrol should add threat of armed force to the setback, he plunged into the yawning gloom of the archway. The smuggler's gate loomed in the echoing dark, concealed in the stone of an archer's nook.

Exhausted, played to the end of an endurance that had seen him through twenty-four razor-edged hours of risk, Arithon was nakedly unprepared for the last, diabolical cruelty set by the order to break him.

Yet another enchantress awaited before the latched postern, and escape. For his sake, and in forethought, she had a torch ready when the flurried echoes of running feet pattered toward her, snatched through with the extended, fast breaths of two men pressing the limits of exertion.

She used a spelled sigil to ignite the pine brand. Its first, struggling flame cast her face in pale gold, the sweet curve of each feature remembered in love and framed by the wisps torn loose from a braid of unruly auburn hair.

The sight of her presence struck like a shot arrow, straight through to his unshielded heart. 'Ath, oh Ath, lend me mercy!' Arithon cried. *'You've been here all along as a game piece?'*

The impacting force of her living presence was too much, too soon, the nerve ends of separation ripped raw with the bonding renewed through the course of Fionn Areth's healing. Her name was wrenched from his throat, the galvanic, blazing joy of recognition transformed to a cry of drawn anguish, 'Elaira!'

Years and distance had not changed the unbearable quandary. He *still could not touch her*, could not lay claim to his freedom and pass. Not without breaking her life vow of obedience to the Koriani Order.

'Elaira, beloved.' Hands outflung, at a loss, he ran dry of words. Every stricken plane of his face matched her tormented dismay. She had been most ruthlessly used, Lirenda's spelled circle no more than an opening ploy of diversion. The wretched truth of his integrity imprisoned them both, that this, the insidious last coil of conspiracy, could not fail to unbind the magnificent strength of his will.

Of all things he could be asked to endure, he could not face himself as the cause of Elaira's destruction. Nor could she endure to let him stand steadfast. Arithon saw through to her most naked self, that neither could she shoulder the grim stakes her Koriani service had bequeathed her. He read like plain text the split-second hesitation that spanned her impulsive decision. She would move, *grasp the bar*, force the sacrifice herself. If he stopped her, *oh, he knew*, if he yielded to Morriel's captivity with Fionn Areth's life cast into the order's control as a pawn, Elaira could not withstand the burden of guilt. Her eyes pleaded. Clouded conscience came at too high a cost for her true woman's heart to support.

And so he must stop her, who loved her beyond the breath and life he had sworn his blood oath to the Fellowship Sorcerers to preserve, *no matter the means or the cost.*

'Don't speak,' he gasped, the necessity of plain speech an effort that required a reserve of deep strength he never knew he possessed. The tenderness he preferred resurged by reflex as, even under the extremity of pressure, he admired the straight honesty of her stance. 'No, don't speak.' Such courage could humble, that she did not shrink or flinch through the crux of harsh circumstance that could smash like glass the priceless trust held between them.

Unaware of Fionn Areth's presence as witness, Arithon found the bravado to match her. 'For my sake, sweet lady, I beg you! Don't raise the bar. If I pass through that door, on my word and my honor, we shall both share the moment in triumph.'

In the heightened fragility of the moment, Elaira dared not even blink. Her gray eyes held dammed rivers of tears; the torch in her closed fingers trembled. 'What other card is between us to play?' She swallowed, shaking harder, her fierce desperation cutting with pain to unman him. 'Don't presume I am innocent. Whose memory was used to transform Fionn Areth? Take the release I can offer. Go free. Let one less poisoned weapon reside in the Koriani arsenal.'

Arithon shook his head in violent rejection. *'Don't speak!* You can't turn my heart that way.' Mind within mind, they knew each other too well. Lies and half-truths made too lame an effort to blind and deceive and win distance; that gift, at least, he could grant her, born from the bonds of indelibly shared understanding.

'Lady, beloved, you are as myself. No matter what happened, there has been no betrayal between us.' In the confines of damp stone, pinned inside Jaelot's walls, Arithon stepped forward, that the light would fall on his features. 'Shall I prove out my faith in you?' She could not but look at him. In his wide-open eyes, by his self-contained dignity, she *must read* his forthright plea of intent.

His gaze matched to hers, that fought against tears, he gave her in snatched phrases the re-created template of logic that had framed her decision fifteen years ago. 'Between your life and the change to Fionn Areth's face, you weighed all the options. At the crux, *I believe this*, you chose for the best.'

The torch wavered in her tortured grasp.

'Oh, yes.' A hitch, a caught breath. 'Yes, I know you!' As the tears, too long held, spilled ribbons of lit gold down her cheeks, Arithon reined back the violent urge to press forward and gather her into his embrace. All he owned, he would give, just to lend her the warmth of his comfort. Wrung to the marrow by a need that matched hers to close final union between them, he poured heart and spirit into the words that were all he could give her in safety.

'Elaira, sweet lady, keep faith in my character. The boy's freedom of choice, in my hands, will stay sacrosanct. I swore a crown prince's oath to Rathain. His plight is the charge of his liege to redress! His maligned fate is the insult to my name and birthright, and a flagrant breach of charter law. *You were right to entrust me! I ask you, hold firm. On my own merits, I must be left my sovereign right to win free of this coil of conspiracy!'*

The blind hope held no substance. She would know, he was hamstrung; and yet, cornered, desperate, he was Torbrand's lineage. He would not back down. Even possessed by the Mistwraith's insanity, he had never yet conceded defeat in good grace.

Nor was Elaira without the stark grit to encourage, and receive the forgiveness he offered. Through salt tears, her mouth bent in that wry smile she saved to level his deepest defenses. 'You have boneheaded stubbornness. Is it true, what I heard, that Parrien s'Brydion once broke your leg to restrain you from misguided loyalty?'

'Well yes,' Arithon admitted, contrite. 'But let's not omit facts. I'd had the bad manners to make splinters of the salon in his brother's state galley, beforehand.'

Elaira laughed. 'The wasp hazing the bull? I ought to have guessed.' She mopped her damp chin with the back of her sleeve, then said in apology to Fionn Areth, 'This is a man who can't ever admit the hour he's been fairly beaten.'

'That's likely to change,' a chill voice intruded. Disheveled, short-tempered, no longer possessed of her seamless coiffure or composure, Lirenda arrived like the shadow of bane in the open mouth of the archway. 'Or will you see Elaira made into a mindless husk just to maintain consistency?'

Arithon whipped around like a wildcat to face her. 'Keep the lady's name out of this!' His eyes, brilliant green, matched that tone of chill hatred with a hot-blooded, furious challenge. 'If you would claim the victory for Morriel Prime, then sully your hands, bitch. *Come take me.*'

Lirenda flicked a fallen wisp of black hair from her face, her vindictive triumph made all the sweeter by years of deferred anticipation. 'What, no begging for me?' She advanced, the assured clarity of privilege etched into each mocking consonant. 'No princely gallantry? Shall I have no soft word of forgiveness? Or are my vows any less binding than Elaira's when enacting our Prime Matriarch's given will?'

Braced in vised stillness, prepared to draw steel, to use any and every unforgivable expedient to defer his inevitable defeat, Arithon s'Ffalenn ceased breathing. His head tipped a startled fraction to one side. As if through his bard's sensitivity, he could hear and interpret some subtext layered through Lirenda's fierce joy in his downfall, he suddenly straightened and laughed. 'You believe your heart's fiber is made sterner than hers? Oh, madam.' He flung off his cloak. 'Shall we take the issue to trial?'

'How far you have fallen, how desperately you grasp at straws.' Flushed to wicked enjoyment, Lirenda advanced. 'Will you stoop to try steel against spellcraft? A dog shown the collar and leash can but bark. Do go on. Discard all the pride of your training along with the manners of your royal birthright.'

Lit to reckless delight, Arithon did not appease her taunt with the obvious. His quick hands stripped off his gloves, then followed with sword and dagger. In a debonair abandon, he tossed the sheathed weapons and clothing into the startled arms of Fionn Areth. Still regarding Lirenda, he raised both dark eyebrows. 'Sword steel can but kill.' His expression was poured honey stirred through with malice, and his voice, the lightning bright cadence of satire. 'Madam, did you know Caolle?'

Thrown off her stride, Lirenda stiffened. 'What? Do you think to enact some petty revenge? Yes, I knew him. He died as my captive.'

As Arithon advanced, unarmed, toward her, she fell back an unthinking step.

'Caolle died free, avenged by his own hand.' Smooth in grace, possessed of a calm to outwear chiseled granite, Arithon s'Ffalenn raised his bare hands, palm upward. 'You once bound him like a calf, to draw me to slaughter. *What's wrong?* Can you not bear to shackle me in turn?'

Unprepared for the presence of him at close quarters, Lirenda retreated a second step on stunned reflex, her golden eyes wide in the flood of Elaira's held torch.

'Go on,' prompted Arithon. His smile opened into a genial invitation, he lilted a stunning, light phrase of clear melody.

Lirenda snatched a swift breath. Her hand closed in involuntary defense and shielded the quartz at her breast. 'Don't. Not again.'

'Oh, madam,' provoked Arithon in virulent good humor. 'Can it be that I know you?' He sang another line. His flexible voice used the acoustics of closed stone and magnified nuance to a spellbinding presence woven of unfettered sound. His intimate words fell too softly for any but Lirenda to overhear. 'What is a vow, after all, but a snippet of wind hobbled in words without meaning? Your heart knows a truth that your mind would deny.'

He reached her. Framed in the velvet shadow of twilight, he extended a bare hand and entrapped the fist she held cupped to her quartz. 'I'm no cipher, but a living man. Would you know me?' A tug drew her to him. His second, swift move snatched the bone pin that fastened the tightly bound length of her hair. The jet coils spilled free. The long, straight length cascaded down her back, catching small snowflakes like diamonds.

Lirenda could not pull free. His gentleness disarmed, waking passion and need where she had no armor of experience. No weapon she owned could match his compassion; no power of denial could heal the breach of a lifetime starved of affection.

The gift of his intimacy was no dry barb of intellect, but a breathing force that stripped away pretense and *cared*. Against the sure truth of his masterbard's empathy, she stood emotionally naked.

'What principle stands in the absence of love?' Arithon drew her closer, then stroked her cold cheek with a touch to wake fire from frost. 'Nor are you Morriel's bloodless instrument, after all.'

He caught her chin, turned her face. 'Lirenda?' He laid his lips upon hers, kissed her until he unchained the torrents of passion she had mistaken for the surrogate of ambition. She found the cradling support of his arm and gave way, swept into a spiraling sweetness of ecstasy beyond any dream to fulfill. When she lay in limpid surrender against him, he unclasped the hand tucked through her black hair.

The plea escaped before thought. 'Don't leave.'

'I must.' Then the parting line, shaped in a pity honed like a knife thrust. 'Tell me again, what's the worth of a vow? If you would use loyal hearts for your weapon, *pray don't forget how the experience feels.*'

Stunned beyond thought, beyond reason, beyond poise, Lirenda sensed nothing else but the surgically brisk withdrawal of Arithon's embrace. The impact of his absence left her unmoored. She scarcely heard his purposeful step, retreating back into the archway.

As though the script had been written and played behind a liquid shimmer of tears, she saw Arithon reclaim his cloak and his weapons from Fionn Areth's numbed hands. Then the Prince of Rathain stepped to the postern, where Elaira patiently waited.

He gave her a gallant's smile that burned for the gentle regard that was genuine. Nor was his voice either polished or suave as he stood inside arm's length, without touching. 'Beloved, forgive me.'

Elaira regarded him, her staunch pride expressed in the bracing wit that had never yet failed to salve the agony from his stripped nerves. 'Were you going to tell me you usually kiss your one-night trollops in private?'

He laughed. The free-ringing sound held a spark of pure pleasure, unforced and rich with surprise. 'I don't kiss them at all, that they don't wear your face in the sanctity of my thoughts. Now tell me the truth. Will your senior peer's profligate romantic indiscretion be enough to shield you from blame?'

For indeed, he had managed the miracle of creating a cunning double blind. Lirenda could not reveal Elaira's collaboration in Prince Arithon's escape. Not without laying bare the glaring weakness Morriel was least likely to forgive in a successor.

'Go safely, both of you.' Elaira stepped aside, allowing clear access through the postern.

Arithon gestured for Fionn Areth to pass first. While the herder set his strong shoulder to raise the bar, the Prince of Rathain paused, one hand raised. While the door hissed open with the oiled ease kept for Jaelot's wealthy smugglers, and sleet swirled cold through the gap, he traced the determined lift of Elaira's chin, then cupped her face with a tenderness no one else living could match. 'You are as my life, lady. *Never forget that.*'

The next instant, he was gone, and Fionn Areth with him, safely vanished into the gathering darkness. Elaira pulled the postern closed and dropped the bar back in place. Through the uplifting, bittersweet rush of pure gratitude, she ached for the memory left with her. The tiny impressions returned to haunt deepest, of his hands, which were chilled, and of clothing that had not been nearly sufficient to withstand the storm that rolled in off the waves of Eltair Bay.

# Aftermath

Surrounded by her circle of twelve tranced seniors, the newly invested Koriani Matriarch infuses the wakened focus of the Great Waystone with the sigils of prime command, that no witness will recall the past night's events, or question her unprecedented succession; then she sends word far and wide to each peeress, of Morriel's death, and of Lirenda's failure in her charge to take Prince Arithon captive . . .

After nightfall on the desolate, wild shore of Camris, Lysaer s'Ilessid broods over the latest news from High Priest Cerebeld, that his damaged plot has been salvaged by the unexpected miracle of Prince Kevor's intervention; now Tysan's traumatized guilds set their seal to new documents, promising a standing armed force for the Light, and expanded fortifications to rival the Alliance garrison at Etarra . . .

As cloudy darkness wraps the spire of Althain Tower, and the solstice tides rise toward the harmonic surge that will fire the sixth lane at midnight, Luhaine's worried vigil at Sethvir's side is relieved by the arrival of two adepts of Ath's Brotherhood; and with them, he gains news that Prince Arithon has successfully snatched Fionn Areth from the claws of Koriani conspiracy, and Dakar awaits with hot food and supplies to shelter them from the inbound storm front . . .

# GLOSSARY

AESHA—one of the volunteer women who assisted the crown healer at Avenor.

    pronounced: aye-ash-ah

    root meaning: *aeash*—a balm

AIYENNE—river located in Daon Ramon, Rathain, rising from an underground spring in the Mathorn Mountains, and surfacing south of the Mathorn Road.

    pronounced: eye-an

    root meaning: *ai'an*—hidden one

ALESTRON—city located in Midhalla, Melhalla. Ruled by the Duke Bransian, Teir's'Brydion, and his three brothers. This city did not fall to merchant townsmen in the Third Age uprising that threw down the high kings, but is still ruled by its clanblood heirs.

    pronounced: ah-less-tron

    root meaning: *alesstair*—stubborn; *an*—one

ALITHIEL—one of twelve Blades of Isaer, forged by centaur Ffereton s'Darian in the First Age from metal taken from a meteorite. Passed through Paravian possession, acquired the secondary name Dael-Farenn, or Kingmaker, since its owners tended to succeed the end of a royal line. Eventually was awarded to Kamridian s'Ffalenn for his valor in defense of the princess Taliennse, early Third Age. Currently in the possession of Arithon.

    pronounced: ah-lith-ee-el

    root meaning: *alith*—star; *iel*—light/ray

ALLAND—principality located in southeastern Shand. Ruled by the High Earl Teir's'Taleyn, *caithdein* of Shand by appointment. Current heir to the title is Erlien.

    pronounced: all-and

    root meaning: *a'lind*—pine glen

ALTHAIN TOWER—spire built at the edge of the Bittern Desert, beginning of the Second Age, to house records of Paravian histories. Third Age, became repository for the archives of all five royal houses of men after rebellion, overseen by Sethvir, Warden of Althain and Fellowship Sorcerer.

    pronounced: al—like 'all,' thain—to rhyme with 'main'

    root meaning: *alt*—last; *thein*—tower, sanctuary

    original Paravian pronunciation: alt-thein (thein as in 'the end')

AMA'IDAN—colloquial phrase in old Paravian for asking forgiveness for a blunder.

    pronounced: ah-mah-aid-an

    root meaning: *ama'idan*—please forgive

ANIENT—Paravian invocation for unity.

    pronounced: an-ee-ent

    root meaning: *an*—one; *ient*—suffix for 'most'

ARAETHURA—grass plains in southwest Rathain; principality of the same name in that location. Largely inhabited by Riathan Paravians in the Second Age. Third Age, used as pastureland by widely scattered nomadic shepherds.

pronounced: ar-eye-thoo-rah

root meaning: *araeth*—grass; *era*—place, land

ARAITHE—plain to the north of the trade city of Etarra, principality of Fallowmere, Rathain. First Age, among those sites used by Paravians to renew the mysteries and channel fifth lane energies. The standing stones erected are linked to the power focus at Ithamon and Methisle keep.

pronounced: like 'a wraith'

root meaning: *araithe*—to disperse, to send

ARITHON—son of Avar, Prince of Rathain, 1,504th Teir's'Ffalenn after founder of the line, Torbrand in Third Age Year One. Also Master of Shadow, the Bane of Desh-thiere, and Halliron Masterbard's successor.

pronounced: ar-i-thon—almost rhymes with 'marathon'

root meaning: *arithon*—fate-forger; one who is visionary

ARWENT—river in Araethura, Rathain, that flows from Daenfal Lake, through Halwythwood, to empty into Instrell Bay.

pronounced: are-went

root meaning: *arwient*—swiftest

ASANDIR—Fellowship Sorcerer. Secondary name, Kingmaker, since his hand crowned every High King of Men to rule in the Age of Men (Third Age). After the Mistwraith's conquest, he acted as field agent for the Fellowship's doings across the continent. Also called Fiend-quencher, for his reputation for quelling iyats; Storm-breaker and Change-bringer for past actions in late Second Age, when Men first arrived upon Athera.

pronounced: ah-san-deer

root meaning: *asan*—heart; *dir*—stone 'heartrock'

ATAINIA—northeastern principality of Tysan.

pronounced: ah-tay-nee-ah

root meaning: *itain*—the third; *ia*—suffix for 'third domain'; original Paravian, *itainia*

ATCHAZ—city located in Alland, Shand. Famed for its silk.

pronounced: at-chas

root meaning: *atchias*—silk

ATH CREATOR—prime vibration, force behind all life.

pronounced: ath to rhyme with 'math'

root meaning: *ath*—prime, first (as opposed to an, one)

ATHERA—name for the world which holds the Five High Kingdoms; four Worldsend Gates; original home of the Paravian races.

pronounced: ath-air-ah

root meaning: *ath*—prime force; *era*—place; 'Ath's world'

ATHIR—Second Age ruin of a Paravian stronghold, located in Ithilt, Rathain. Site of a seventh lane power focus.

pronounced: ath-ear

root meaning: *ath*—prime; *i'er*—the line/edge

ATHLIEN PARAVIANS—sunchildren. Small race of semimortals, pixie-like, but possessed of great wisdom/keepers of the grand mystery.

 pronounced: ath-lee-en

 root meaning: *ath*—prime force; *lien*—to love; 'Ath-beloved'

AVENOR—Second Age ruin of a Paravian stronghold. Traditional seat of the s'Ilessid High Kings. Restored to habitation in Third Age 5644. Became the ruling seat of the Alliance of Light in Third Age 5648. Located in Korias, Tysan.

 pronounced: ah-ven-or

 root meaning: *avie*—stag; *norh*—grove


BECKBURN—market located in the city of Jaelot.

 pronounced: beck burn

 root meaning not from the Paravian

BLACK ROSE PROPHECY—made by Dakar the Mad Prophet in Third Age 5637 at Althain Tower. Forecasts Davien the Betrayer's repentance, and the reunification of the Fellowship of Seven as tied to Arithon s'Ffalenn's voluntary resumption of Rathain's crown rule.

BRANSIAN s'BRYDION—Teir's'Brydion, ruling Duke of Alestron.

 pronounced: bran-see-an

 root meaning: *brand*—temper; *s'i'an*—suffix denoting 'of the one'; the one with temper

BRETA—one of Fionn Areth's sisters.

 pronounced: bret-ah

 root meaning: *bretah*—little sprout


CADGIA—Koriani seeress of senior rank who was temporarily assigned to Lirenda's service.

 pronounced: cad-jee-ah

*CAITHDEIN*—Paravian name for a high king's first counselor; also, the one who would stand as regent, or steward, in the absence of the crowned ruler.

 pronounced: kay-ith-day-in

 root meaning: *caith*—shadow; *d'ein*—behind the chair; 'shadow behind the throne'

CAITHWOOD—forest located in Taerlin, southeast principality of Tysan.

 pronounced: kay-ith-wood

 root meaning: *caith*—shadow—shadowed wood

CAMRIS—north-central principality of Tysan. Original ruling seat was the city of Erdane.

 pronounced: Kam-ris, the i as in 'chris'

 root meaning: *caim*—cross; *ris*—way; 'crossroad'

CAOLLE—past war captain of the clans of Deshir, Rathain. First raised by, and then served under, Lord Steiven, Earl of the North and *caithdein* of Rathain. Planned the campaign at Vastmark and Dier Kenton Vale for the Master of Shadow. Served Jieret Red-beard, and was feal liegeman of Arithon of Rathain; died of complications from a wound received from his prince while breaking a Koriani attempt to trap his liege.

    pronounced: kay-all-eh, with the 'e' nearly subliminal

    root meaning: *caille*—stubborn

CAPEWELL—city located on the south shore of Korias, Tysan. Home of a major Koriani sisterhouse.

CARITHWYR—principality consisting primarily of a grasslands in Havish, once the province of the Riathan Paravians. A unicorn birthing ground. Currently used by man for grain and cattle; area name has become equated with fine hides.

    pronounced: car-ith-ear

    root meaning: *ci'arithiren*—forgers of the ultimate link with prime power. An old Paravian colloquialism for unicorn.

CARRIGAN—matron who brews watered spirits in Jaelot.

    pronounced: carey-gen

CASCAINS—rugged chain of islets off the coast of Vastmark, Shand.

    pronounced: cass-canes

    root meaning: *kesh kein*—shark's teeth

CASLEY—prostitute in Meliane's house, in Jaelot.

    pronounced: caz-lee

CATTRICK—master joiner hired to run the royal shipyard at Riverton; once in Arithon's employ at Merior by the Sea.

    pronounced: cat-rick

    root meaning: *ciattiaric*—a knot tied of withies that has the magical property of confusing enemies

CENWAITH—great grandmother, and one of the eldest clan chieftains who maintain watch over Caithwood.

    pronounced: sen-wayth

    root meaning: *cian'waith*—shining smile

CEREBELD—Avenor's High Priest of the Light, formerly Lord Examiner of Avenor.

    pronounced: cara-belld

    root meaning: *ciarabeld*—ashes

CHEIVALT—coastal city south of Ostermere in Carithwyr, Havish. Known for its elegance and refined lifestyle.

    pronounced: shay-vault

    root meaning: *chiavalden*—a rare yellow flower which grows by the seaside.

CIANOR SUNLORD—born at Caith-al-Caen, First Age 615. Survived both the massacre of Leorne caused by methuri, or hate-wraiths out of Mirthlvain Swamp in the year 815, and led the Battle of Retaliation on Bordirion Plain (which by the start of the Second Age had been enveloped by the swamp). In 826, Cianor's forces were defeated at Erdane by Khadrim;

Cianor retired to Araethura, gravely wounded. Crippled but alive, he was on hand at the arrival of the Fellowship of Seven. Healed by the Sorcerers; appointed Keeper of Records in 902; stabilized the realm after the murder of High King Marin Eliathe in Second Age 1542. Crowned High King of Athera in Second Age 2545 until his death in a rising of Khadrim in 3651.

    pronounced: key-ah-nor

    root meaning: *cianor*—to shine

CILADIS THE LOST—Fellowship Sorcerer who left the continent in Third Age 5462 in search of the Paravian races after their disappearance following the rebellion.

    pronounced: kill-ah-dis

    root meaning: *cael*—leaf; *adeis*—whisper, compound; *cael'adeis*—colloquialism for 'gentleness that abides'

CILDEIN OCEAN—body of water lying off Athera's east coast.

    pronounced: kill-dine

    root meaning: *cailde*—salty; *an*—one

COREYN—road master of caravans, often hired by Reysald, merchant of Daenfal.

    pronounced: core-rain

    root meaning: *ciorain*—antique nail

CORITH—island west of Havish coast, in Westland Sea. Site of a drake lair, and a ruined First Age foundation. Here, the council of Paravians met during siege, and dragons dreamed the summoning of the Fellowship Sorcerers. First site to see sunlight upon Desh-thiere's defeat.

    pronounced: kor-ith

    root meaning: *cori*—ships, vessels; *itha*—five for the five harbors which the old city overlooked

COWILL—initiate priest dispatched to Alestron by Cerebeld.

    pronounced: cow-ill

DAELION FATEMASTER—'entity' formed by set of mortal beliefs, which determine the fate of the spirit after death. If Ath is the prime vibration, or life force, Daelion is what governs the manifestation of free will.

    pronounced: day-el-ee-on

    root meaning: *dael*—king, or lord; *i'on*—of fate

DAELION'S WHEEL—cycle of life and the crossing point which is the transition into death.

    pronounced: day-el-ee-on

    root meaning: *dael*—king or lord; *i'on*—of fate

DAENFAL—city located on the northern lakeshore that bounds the southern edge of Daon Ramon Barrens in Rathain.

    pronounced: dye-en-fall

    root meaning: *daen*—clay; *fal*—red

DAKAR THE MAD PROPHET—apprentice to Fellowship Sorcerer, Asandir, during the Third Age following the Conquest of the Mistwraith. Given to spurious prophecies, it was Dakar who forecast the fall of the Kings of Havish in time for the Fellowship to save the heir. He made the Prophecy of West Gate, which forecast the Mistwraith's bane, and also, the Black Rose Prophecy, which called for reunification of the Fellowship. At this time, assigned to defense of Arithon, Prince of Rathain.

    pronounced: dah-kar

    root meaning: *dakiar*—clumsy

**DAGRIEN COURT and LANE**—locations in the city of Jaelot, Rathain.

    pronounced: dag-ree-an

    root meaning: *dagrien*—variety

**DAON RAMON BARRENS**—central principality of Rathain. Site where Riathan Paravians (unicorns) bred and raised their young. Barrens was not appended to the name until the years following the Mistwraith's conquest, when the River Severnir was diverted at the source by a task force under Etarran jurisdiction.

    pronounced: day-on-rah-mon

    root meaning: *daon*—gold; *ramon*—hills/downs

**DAVIEN THE BETRAYER**—Fellowship Sorcerer responsible for provoking the great uprising that resulted in the fall of the high kings after Desh-thiere's conquest. Rendered discorporate by the Fellowship's judgment in Third Age 5129. Exiled since, by personal choice. Davien's works included the Five Centuries Fountain near Mearth on the splinter world of the Red Desert through West Gate; the shaft at Rockfell Pit, used by the Sorcerers to imprison harmful entities; the Stair on Rockfell Peak; and also, Kewar Tunnel in the Mathorn Mountains.

    pronounced: dah-vee-en

    root meaning: *dahvi*—fool, mistake; *an*—one; 'mistaken one'

**DAWR s'BRYDION**—grandmother of Duke Bransian of Alestron, and his brothers, Keldmar, Parrien, and Mearn.

    pronounced: dour

    root meaning: *dwyiar*—vinegar wine

**DEAL**—city located in Elkforest, principality of Carithwyr in Havish.

    pronounced: deal

    root meaning: *dayal*—moss grown

**DESH-THIERE**—Mistwraith that invaded Athera from the splinter worlds through South Gate in Third Age 4993. Access cut off by Fellowship Sorcerer, Traithe. Battled and contained in West Shand for twenty-five years, until the rebellion splintered the peace, and the high kings were forced to withdraw from the defense lines to attend their disrupted kingdoms. Confined through the combined powers of Lysaer s'Ilessid's gift of Light, and Arithon s'Ffalenn's gift of Shadow. Currently imprisoned in a warded flask in Rockfell pit.

    pronounced: desh-thee-air-e (last 'e' mostly subliminal)

    root meaning: *desh*—mist; *thiere*—ghost or wraith

DESHIR—northwestern principality of Rathain.
   pronounced: desh-eer
   root meaning: *deshir*—misty
DHARKARON AVENGER—called Ath's Avenging Angel in legend. Drives a chariot drawn by five horses to convey the guilty to Sithaer. Dharkaron as defined by the adepts of Ath's Brotherhood is that dark thread mortal men weave with Ath, the prime vibration, that creates self-punishment, or the root of guilt.
   pronounced dark-air-on
   root meaning: *dhar*—evil; *khiaron*—one who stands in judgment
DIER KENTON VALE—a valley located in the principality of Vastmark, Shand, where the war host thirty-five thousand strong, under command of Lysaer s'Ilessid, fought and lost to the Master of Shadow in Third Age 5647. The main body of the forces of light were decimated in one day by a shale slide. The remainder were harried by a small force of Vastmark shepherds under Caolle, who served as Arithon's war captain, until supplies and morale became impossible to maintain.
   pronounced: deer ken-ton
   root meaning: *dien'kendion*—a jewel with a severe flaw that may result in shearing or cracking
DYSHENT—city on the coast of Instrell Bay in Tysan; renowned for timber.
   pronounced: die-shent
   root meaning: *dyshient*—cedar


EARLE—Second Age ruin located in West Shand, south of the Salt Fens. Fortress where the Mistwraith's first incursion was fought, until Davien the Betrayer caused the uprising; also, where Seannory bound the four elements to conscious presence, in event Athera had need.
   pronounced: earl
   root meaning: *erli*—long light
EAST HALLA—principality located in the Kingdom of Melhalla.
   pronounced: hall-ah
   root meaning: *hal'lia*—white light
EASTWALL—city located in the Skyshiel Mountains, Rathain.
ECKRACKEN—king drake who died by the Salt Fens in West Shand; his bones are guarded by a grimward, and his mate's remains rest on the waste continent Kathtairr.
   pronounced: ack-rack-in
   root meaning: *aykrauken*—scorcher
EILISH—Lord Minister of the Royal Treasury, Avenor.
   pronounced: eye-lish
   root meaning: *eyalish*—fussy
ELAIRA—initiate enchantress of the Koriathain. Originally a street child, taken on in Morvain for Koriani rearing.

pronounced: ee-layer-ah

root meaning: *e*—prefix, diminutive for small; *laere*—grace

ELDIR s'LORNMEIN—King of Havish and last surviving scion of s'Lornmein royal line. Raised as a wool-dyer until the Fellowship Sorcerers crowned him at Ostermere in Third Age 5643 following the defeat of the Mistwraith.

pronounced: el-deer

root meaning: *eldir*—to ponder, to consider, to weigh

ELLAINE—Erdani woman affianced to Lysaer s'Ilessid.

pronounced: el-lane

ELSSINE—city located on the coast of Alland, Shand, famed for stone quarries used for ship's ballast.

pronounced: el-seen

root meaning: *elssien*—small pit

ELTAIR BAY—large bay off Cildein Ocean and east coast of Rathain; where River Severnir was diverted following the Mistwraith's conquest.

pronounced: el-tay-er

root meaning: *al'tieri*—of steel/a shortening of original Paravian name; *dascen al'tieri*—which meant 'ocean of steel,' which referred to the color of the waves

ENNLIE—a woman volunteer who assists the Crown Healer at Avenor.

pronounced: an-lee

ERDANE—old Paravian city, later taken over by Men. Seat of old princes of Camris until Desh-thiere's conquest and rebellion.

pronounced: er-day-na with the last syllable almost subliminal

root meaning: *er'deinia*—long walls

ETARRA—trade city built across the Mathorn Pass by townsfolk after the revolt that cast down Ithamon and the High Kings of Rathain. Nest of corruption and intrigue, and policy maker for the North.

pronounced: ee-tar-ah

root meaning: *e*—prefix for small; *taria*—knots

*EVENSTAR*—first brig stolen from Riverton's royal shipyard by Cattrick's conspiracy with Prince Arithon. Captained by Feylind.


FALGAIRE—coastal city on Instrell Bay, located in Araethura, Rathain, famed for its crystal and glassworks.

pronounced: fall-gair—to rhyme with 'air'

root meaning: *fal'mier*—to sparkle or glitter

FALWOOD—forest located in West Shand.

pronounced: fall-wood

root meaning: *fal*—tree

FATE'S WHEEL—see Daelion's Wheel.

FARIENNT TYR—Paravian invocation to make manifest.

pronounced: far-ee-an-teer

root meaning: *ffar*—to make; *ient*—suffix for 'most'; *tir*—to be

FELLOWSHIP OF SEVEN—Sorcerers sworn to uphold the Law of the

Major Balance, and to foster enlightened thought in Athera. Originators and keepers of the covenant of the compact, made with the Paravian races that allowed Men to settle on Athera.

FEYLIND—daughter of Jinesse; twin sister of Fiark; born in Merior by the Sea, and currently serving as captain of the *Evenstar*.

    pronounced: fay-lind

    root meaning: *faelind'an*—outspoken one/noisy one

FFEREDON-LI—ancient Paravian word for a healer, literally translated 'bringer of grace;' still in use in the dialect of Araethura.

    pronounced: fair-eh-dun lee

    root meaning: *ffaraton*—maker; *li*—exalted grace

FIARK—son of Jinesse; twin brother of Feylind; born in Merior by the Sea, currently employed as a factor by an Innish merchant.

    pronounced: fee-ark

    root meaning: *fyerk*—to throw or toss

FIONN ARETH CAID'AN—shepherd child born in Third Age 5647; fated by prophecy to leave home and play a role in the Wars of Light and Shadow.

    pronounced: fee-on-are-eth cayed-ahn

    root meaning: *fionne arith caid an*—one who brings choice

FIRST AGE—marked by the arrival of the Paravian Races as Ath's gift to heal the marring of creation by the great drakes.


GACE STEWARD—Royal Steward of Avenor.

    pronounced: gace—to rhyme with 'race'

    root meaning: *gyce*-weasel

GREAT WAYSTONE—amethyst crystal, spherical in shape, the grand power focus of the Koriani Order; lost during the great uprising, and finally recovered from Fellowship custody by First Senior Lirenda in Third Age 5647.

GREAT WEST ROAD—trade route which crosses Tysan from Karfael on the west coast, to Castle Point on Instrell Bay.

GRIMWARD—a circle of dire spells of Paravian making that seal and isolate forces that have the potential for unimaginable destruction. With the disappearance of the old races, the defenses are maintained by embodied Sorcerers of the Fellowship of Seven. There are seventeen separate sites listed at Althain Tower.


HALFMOON—tavern located in city of Innish.

HALLIRON MASTERBARD—native of Innish, Shand. Masterbard of Athera during the Third Age; inherited the accolade from his teacher Murchiel in the year 5597. Son of Al'Duin. Husband of Deartha. Arithon's master and mentor. Died from an injury inflicted by the Mayor of Jaelot in the year 5644.

    pronounced: hal-eer-on

root meaning: *hal*—white; *lyron*—singer

HALWYTHWOOD—forest located in Araethura, Rathain.

    pronounced: hall-with-wood

    root meaning: *hal*—white; *wythe*—vista

HAMHAND JUSSEY—see Jussey.

HANSHIRE—port city on Westland Sea, coast of Korias, Tysan; reigning official Lord Mayor Garde, father of Sulfin Evend; opposed to royal rule at the time of Avenor's restoration.

    pronounced: han-sheer

    root meaning: *hansh*—sand; *era*—place

HARRADENE—Lord Commander of Etarra's army at the time of the muster at Werpoint, still in power after Vastmark campaign.

    pronounced: har-a-deen

    root meaning: *harradien*—large mule

HAVISH—one of the Five High Kingdoms of Athera, as defined by the charters of the Fellowship of Seven. Ruled by Eldir s'Lornmein. Sigil: gold hawk on red field.

    pronounced: hav-ish

    root meaning: *havieshe*—hawk

HAVRITA—fashionable dressmaker in city of Jaelot.

    pronounced: have-ree-tah

    root meaning: *havierta*—tailor

HIGHSCARP—city on the coast of the Bay of Eltair, located in Daon Ramon, Rathain.


ILITHARIS PARAVIANS—centaurs, one of three semimortal old races; disappeared at the time of the Mistwraith's conquest. They were the guardians of the earth's mysteries.

    pronounced: i-li-thar-is

    root meaning: *i'lith'eans*—the keeper/preserver of mystery

ILSWATER—both a lake bordering the principalities of Korias and Taerlin; and the river which carries the water trade route from Caithwood to Riverton.

    pronounced: ills-water

    root meaning: *iel*—light

IMAURY RIDDLER—Centaur guardian who enspelled the foundations of the Second Age ruin beside Mainmere. Legend holds the stones will sing in the hour of Athera's greatest peril.

    pronounced: ah-more-ee

    root meaning: *imauri*—riddle

INNISH—city located on the southcoast of Shand at the delta of the River Ippash. Birthplace of Halliron Masterbard. Formerly known as 'the Jewel of Shand' this was the site of the high king's winter court, prior to the time of the uprising.

    pronounced: in-ish

root meaning: *inniesh*—a jewel with a pastel tint

INSTRELL BAY—body of water off the Gulf of Stormwell, that separates principality of Atainia, Tysan, from Deshir, Rathain.

    pronounced: in-strell

    root meaning: *arin'streal*—strong wind

ISAER—city located at the crossroads of the Great West Road in Atainia, Tysan. Also a power focus, built during the First Age, in Atainia, Tysan, to source the defense-works at the Paravian keep of the same name.

    pronounced: i-say-er

    root meaning: *i'saer*—the circle

ISHEAL—Paravian word to wish peace or calm.

    pronounced: ish-ee-all

    root meaning: *isheal*—to make quiet

ITHAMON—Second Age Paravian stronghold, and a Third Age ruin; built on a fifth lane power-node in Daon Ramon Barrens, Rathain, and inhabited until the year of the uprising. Site of the Compass Point Towers, or Sun Towers. Became the seat of the High Kings of Rathain during the Third Age and in year 5638 was the site where Princes Lysaer s'Ilessid and Arithon s'Ffalenn battled the Mistwraith to confinement.

    pronounced: ith-a-mon

    root meaning: *itha*—five; *mon*—needle, spire

IVEL—blind splicer who works under master shipwright, Cattrick; known for his spiteful tongue.

    pronounced: ee-vell

    root meaning: *iavel*—scathing

IYAT—energy sprite native to Athera, not visible to the eye, manifests in a poltergeist fashion by taking temporary possession of objects. Feeds upon natural energy sources: fire, breaking waves, lightning.

    pronounced: ee-at

    root meaning: *iyat*—to break


JAELOT—city located on the coast of Eltair Bay at the southern border of the Kingdom of Rathain. Once a Second Age power site, with a focus circle. Now a merchant city with a reputation for extreme snobbery and bad taste. Also the site where Arithon s'Ffalenn played his eulogy for Halliron Masterbard, which raised the powers of the Paravian focus circle beneath the mayor's palace. The forces of the mysteries and resonant harmonics caused damage to city buildings, watchkeeps, and walls, which has since been repaired.

    pronounced: jay-lot

    root meaning: *jielot*—affectation

JASQUE—servant of a blind spinster who lives in Jaelot.

    pronounced: rhymes with 'cask'

    root meaning: *jiask*—binding faith

JERIAYISH—initiate priest of the Light who has a seer's talent.

pronounced: jeer-ee-ah-yish

root meaning: *jier'yaish*—unclean magic

JIERET s'VALERIENT—Earl of the North, clan chief of Deshir; *caithdein* of Rathain, sworn liegeman of Prince Arithon s'Ffalenn. Also son and heir of Lord Steiven. Blood pacted to Arithon by Sorcerer's oath prior to battle of Strakewood Forest. Came to be known by headhunters as Jieret Red-beard.

pronounced: jeer-et

root meaning: *jieret*—thorn

JEYNSA—daughter of Jieret s'Valerient and Feithan, born Third Age 5653; appointed successor to her father's title of Steward of Rathain, or *caithdien*.

pronounced: jay-in-sa

root meaning: garnet

JUSSEY—Captain of the Guard in the city of Daenfal, Rathain; renowned for his mastery of the sword.

pronounced: juss-ee


KATHTAIRR—landmass in the southern ocean, across the world from Paravia.

pronounced: kath-tear

root meaning: *kait-th'era*—empty place

KELDMAR s'BRYDION—younger brother of Duke Bransian of Alestron; older brother of Parrien and Mearn.

pronounced: keld-mar

root meaning: *kiel'd'maeran*—one without pity

KELLIS—clan elder and Duchess of Mainmere.

pronounced: kell-iss

root meaning: *kiel'liess*—balm of grief

KEVOR—son and heir of Lysaer s'Ilessid and Princess Ellaine; born at Avenor in Third Age 5655.

pronounced: kev-or

root meaning: *kiavor*—high virtue

KEWAR TUNNEL—cavern built beneath the Mathorn Mountains by Davien the Betrayer; site of High King Kamridian s'Ffalenn's death.

pronounced: key-wahr

root meaning: *kewiar*—a weighing of conscience

KHADRIM—drake-spawned creatures, flying, fire-breathing reptiles that were the scourge of the Second Age. By the Third Age, they had been driven back and confined in the Sorcerers' Preserve in the volcanic peaks in north Tysan.

pronounced: kaa-drim

root meaning: *khadrim*—dragon

KHARADMON—Sorcerer of the Fellowship of Seven; discorporate since rise of Khadrim and Seardluin leveled the Paravian city at Ithamon in

Second Age 3651. It was by Kharadmon's intervention that the survivors of the attack were sent to safety by means of transfer from the fifth lane power focus. Currently constructing the star ward to guard against invasion of wraiths from Marak.

pronounced: kah-rad-mun

root meaning: *kar'riad en mon*—phrase translates to mean 'twisted thread on the needle' or colloquialism for 'a knot in the works'

KHETIENN—name for a brigantine owned by Arithon; also a small spotted wildcat native to Daon Ramon Barrens that became the s'Ffalenn royal sigil.

pronounced: key-et-ee-en

root meaning: *kietienn*—small leopard

KIELING TOWER—one of the four compass points, or Sun Towers, standing at ruin of Ithamon, Daon Ramon Barrens, in Rathain. The warding virtue that binds its stones is compassion.

pronounced: key-eh-ling

root meaning: *kiel'ien*—root for pity, with suffix for 'lightness' added, translates to mean 'compassion'

KORIANI—possessive form of the word 'Koriathain'; see entry.

pronounced: kor-ee-ah-nee

KORIAS—southwestern principality of Tysan.

pronounced: kor-ee-as

root meaning: *cor*—ship, vessel; *i'esh*—nest, haven

KORIATHAIN—order of enchantresses ruled by a circle of Seniors, under the power of one Prime Enchantress. They draw their talent from the orphaned children they raise, or from daughters dedicated to service by their parents. Initiation rite involves a vow of consent that ties the spirit to a power crystal keyed to the Prime's control.

pronounced: kor-ee-ah-thain-to rhyme with 'main'

root meaning: *koriath*—order; *ain*—belonging to

KOSHLIN—influential trade minister from Erdane, renowned for his hatred of the clans, and for his support of the headhunters' leagues. Assigned ambassador to Avenor's court.

pronounced: kosh-lynn

root meaning: *kioshlin*—opaque


LACHONN—Fionn Areth's brother.

pronounced: lash-on

root meaning: *lachonn*—goatherd

LAW OF THE MAJOR BALANCE—founding order of the powers of the Fellowship of Seven, as written by the Paravians. The primary tenet is that no force of nature should be used without consent, or against the will of another living being.

LIRENDA—former First Senior Enchantress to the Prime, Koriani order; now assigned to capture Arithon s'Ffalenn to reinstate her credentials as prime successor.

pronounced: leer-end-ah

root meaning: *lyron*—singer; *di-ia*—a dissonance—the hyphen denotes a glottal stop

LITHMERE—principality located in the Kingdom of Havish.

pronounced: lith-mere

root meaning: *lithmiere*—to preserve intact, or keep whole; maintain in a state of harmony

LUHAINE—Sorcerer of the Fellowship of Seven, discorporate since the fall of Telmandir. Luhaine's body was pulled down by the mob while he was in ward trance, covering the escape of the royal heir to Havish.

pronounced: loo-hay-ne

root meaning: *luirhainon*—defender

LYRANTHE—instrument played by the bards of Athera. Strung with fourteen strings, tuned to seven tones (doubled). Two courses are 'drone strings' set to octaves. Five are melody strings, the lower three courses being octaves, the upper two, in unison.

pronounced: leer-anth-e (last 'e' being nearly subliminal)

root meaning: *lyr*—song, *anthe*—box

LYSAER s'ILESSID—prince of Tysan, 1497th in succession after Halduin, founder of the line in Third Age Year One. Gifted at birth with control of Light, and Bane of Desh-thiere. Also known as Blessed Prince.

pronounced: lie-say-er

root meaning: *lia*—blond, yellow or light, *saer*—circle


MAENOL—heir, after Maenalle s'Gannley, Steward and *caithdein* of Tysan.

pronounced: may-nall

root meaning: *maeni'alli*—to patch together

MAINMERE—town at the head of the Valenford River, located in the principality of Taerlin, Tysan. Built by townsmen on a site originally kept clear to free the second land focus in the ruins farther south.

pronounced: main-meer-e ('e' is subliminal)

root meaning: *maeni*—to fall, interrupt; *miere*—reflection; colloquial translation: 'disrupt continuity'

MARAK—splinter world, cut off beyond South Gate, left lifeless after creation of the Mistwraith. The original inhabitants were men exiled by the Fellowship from Athera for beliefs or practices that were incompatible with the compact sworn between the Sorcerers and the Paravian races, which permitted human settlement on Athera.

pronounced: maer-ak

root meaning: *m'era'ki*—a place held separate

MATHORN MOUNTAINS—range that bisects the Kingdom of Rathain east to west.

pronounced: math-orn

root meaning: *mathien*—massive

MATHORN ROAD—way passing to the south of the Mathorn Mountains, leading to the trade city of Etarra from the west.

pronounced: math-orn

root meaning: *mathien*—massive

MEARN s'BRYDION—youngest brother of Duke Bransian of Alestron. Former ducal emissary to Lysaer s'Ilessid's Alliance of Light.

pronounced: may-arn

root meaning: *mierne*—to flit

MEARTH—city through the West Gate in the Red Desert. Inhabitants all fell victim to the Shadows of Mearth, which were created by the Sorcerer Davien to protect the Five Centuries Fountain. The shadows are a light-fueled geas that bind the mind to memory of an individual's most painful experience.

pronounced: me-arth

root meaning: *mearth*—empty

MEDLIR—an alias used by Arithon s'Ffalenn when he was Halliron Masterbard's apprentice.

pronounced: med-leer

root meaning: *midlyr*—phrase of melody

MELHALLA—High Kingdom of Athera once ruled by the line of s'Ellestrion. The last prince died in the crossing of the Red Desert.

pronounced: mel-hall-ah

root meaning: *maelhallia*—grand meadows/plain, also word for an open space of any sort.

MELIANE—madam of a house of ill repute in Jaelot.

pronounced: mell-ee-an

MENNIS—a guild minister in Avenor.

pronounced: men-iss

MERIOR BY THE SEA—small seaside fishing village on the Scimlade peninsula in Alland, Shand. Once the temporary site of Arithon's shipyard.

pronounced: mare-ee-or

root meaning: *merioren*—cottages

METHISLE—small body of land in Methlas Lake, site of Methisle fortress in Orvandir.

pronounced: meth

root meaning: *meth*—hate

METHSPAWN—an animal warped by possession by a methuri, an iyat-related parasite that infested live hosts. Extinct by the Third Age, their crossbred, aberrated descendants are called methspawn, found in Mirthlvain Swamp.

pronounced: meth

root meaning: *meth*—hate

METHURI—an iyat-related parasite that infested live hosts, extinct by the Third Age.

pronounced: meth-you-ree

root meaning: *meth'thi*—hate wraith

MIDHALLA—principality located in Kingdom of Melhalla.

pronounced: mid-hall-ah

root meaning: *maelhallia*—grand meadows/plain

MIN PIERENS—archipelago to the west of the Kingdom of West Shand, in the Westland Sea.

pronounced: min—to rhyme with 'pin,' pierre-ins

root meaning: *min*—purple; *pierens*—shoreline

MINDERL BAY—body of water behind Crescent Isle off the east coast of Rathain. Also reference point of a battle where Arithon tricked Lysaer into burning the trade fleet.

pronounced: mind-earl

root meaning: *minderl*—anvil

MIRALT HEAD—port city in northern Camris, Tysan.

pronounced: meer-alt

root meaning: *m'ier*—shore; *alt*—last

MIRTHLVAIN SWAMP—boglands located in Midhalla, Melhalla; filled with dangerous, crossbreeds of drake spawn. Guarded by the Master Spellbinder, Verrain.

pronounced: mirth-el-vain

root meaning: *myrthl*—noxious; *vain*—bog, mud

MISTWRAITH—see Desh-thiere

MOGG's FEN—marsh located in Korias, Tysan.

pronounced: mog's fen

root meaning: *miog*—cattail

MOIREY—landlady of the Halfmoon Tavern in Innish; also known as Fat Moirey.

pronounced: mow-ar-ee

MORFETT—Lord Governor Supreme of Etarra.

pronounced: more-fit

MORRIEL—Prime Enchantress of the Koriathain since the Third Age 4212.

pronounced: more-real

root meaning: *moar*—greed; *riel*—silver

MORVAIN—city located in the principality of Araethura, Rathain, on the coast of Instrell Bay. Elaira's birthplace.

pronounced: more-vain

root meaning: *morvain*—swindlers' market

NARMS—city on the coast of Instrell Bay, built as a craft center by Men in the early Third Age. Best known for dyeworks.

pronounced: narms—to rhyme with 'charms'

root meaning: *narms*—color

ODREY—a merchant courtier in Avenor.

pronounced: oh-dree

ORLAN—pass through the Thaldein Mountains, also location of the Camris clans' west outpost, in Camris, Tysan. Known for barbarian raids.

pronounced: or-lan

root meaning: *irlan*—ledge

ORLEST—galleymen's port on the coast of Korias, Tysan; also known for its salt harvest.

pronounced: or-lest

root meaning: *iorlest*—salt

OSTERMERE—harbor and trade city, once smugglers' haven, located in Carithwyr, Havish; current seat of Eldir, King of Havish.

pronounced: os-tur-mere

root meaning: *ostier*—brick; *miere*—reflection


PARAVIA—name for the fertile continent on Athera.

pronounced: par-ray-vee-ah

root meaning: *para'i'on*—great mystery

PARAVIAN—name for the three old races that inhabited Athera before Men. Including the centaurs, the sunchildren, and the unicorns, these races never die unless mishap befalls them; they are the world's channel, or direct connection, to Ath Creator.

pronounced: par-ai-vee-ans

root meaning: *para*—great; *i'on*—fate or great mystery

PARRIEN s'BRYDION—younger brother of Duke Bransian of Alestron, Keldmar, and older brother of Mearn.

pronounced: par-ee-en

root meaning: *para ient*—great dart


QUAIRE—a mountain peak in the Skyshiels, Rathain.

pronounced: kwear

root meaning: *quaire*—pyramid

QUARN—town on the trade road that crosses Caithwood in Taerlin, Tysan.

pronounced: kwarn

root meaning: *quarin*—ravine, canyon


RADMOORE DOWNS—meadowlands in Midhalla, Melhalla.

pronounced: rad-more

root meaning: *riad*—thread; *mour*—carpet, rug

RAIETT RAVEN—brother of the Mayor of Hanshire; uncle of Sulfin Evend. Considered a master statesman and a bringer of wars.

pronounced: rayett

root meaning: *raiett*—carrion bird

RATHAIN—High Kingdom of Athera ruled by descendants of Torbrand s'Ffalenn since Third Age Year One. Sigil: black-and-silver leopard on green field.

    pronounced: rath-ayn

    root meaning: *roth*—brother; *thein*—tower, sanctuary

REYSALD—a merchant in the city of Daenfal, Rathain.

    pronounced: ris-sald

RIATHAN PARAVIANS—unicorns, the purest, most direct connection to Ath Creator; the prime vibration channels directly through the horn.

    pronounced: ree-ah-than

    root meaning: *ria*—to touch; *ath*—prime life force; *an*—one; *ri'athon*—one who touches divinity

RIVERTON—trade town at the mouth of the Ilswater river, in Korias, Tysan; site of Lysaer's royal shipyard.

ROCKFELL PIT—deep shaft cut into Rockfell Peak, used to imprison harmful entities throughout all three Ages. Located in the principality of West Halla, Melhalla; became the warded prison for Desh-thiere.

    pronounced: rock-fell

    root meaning not from the Paravian

ROCKFELL VALE—valley below Rockfell Peak, located in principality of West Halla, Melhalla.

    pronounced: rockfell vale

    root meaning not from the Paravian


s'AHELAS—family name for the royal line appointed by the Fellowship Sorcerers in Third Age Year One to rule the High Kingdom of Shand. Gifted geas: farsight.

    pronounced: s'ah-hell-as

    root meaning: *ahelas*—mage-gifted

SANPASHIR—desert waste on the southcoast of Shand.

    pronounced: sahn-pash-eer

    root meaning: *san*—black or dark; *pash'era*—place of grit or gravel

SANSHEVAS—city located in Alland, Shand; known for silk.

    pronounced: san-shee-vahs

    root meaning: *san*—black; *cievas*—worm or grub

SARDS—pass through the Skyshiels on the trade route connecting Daenfal with Jaelot.

    pronounced: rhymes with 'shards'

    root meaning: *saardes*—whirlwind

SASHKA—a favored prostitute at the Fat Pigeon Tavern in the city of Southshire.

    pronounced: sash-kaa

s'BRYDION—ruling line of the Dukes of Alestron. The only old blood clansmen to maintain rule of their city through the uprising that defeated the rule of the high kings.

    pronounced: s'bride-ee-on

root meaning: *baridien*—tenacity

SCIMLADE TIP—peninsula at the southeast corner of Alland, Shand.
pronounced: skim-laid
root meaning: *scimlait*—curved knife or scythe

SEANNORY—Centaur guardian who bound the four elemental powers in the fortress at Earle for need of the world's protection.
pronounced: see-an-or-ee
root meaning: *saenniori*—enchanter

SECOND AGE—Marked by the arrival of the Fellowship of Seven at Crater Lake, their called purpose to fight the drake spawn.

SELIDIE—young woman initiate appointed by Morriel Prime as a candidate in training for succession.
pronounced: sell-ih-dee
root meaning: *selyadi*—air sprite

SELKWOOD—forest located in Alland, Shand.
pronounced: selk-wood
root meaning: *selk*—pattern

SETHVIR—Sorcerer of the Fellowship of Seven, served as Warden of Althain since the disappearance of the Paravians in the Third Age after the Mistwraith's conquest.
pronounced: seth-veer
root meaning: *seth*—fact; *vaer*—keep

SEVERNIR—river that once ran across the central part of Daon Ramon Barrens, Rathain. Diverted at the source after the Mistwraith's conquest, to run east into Eltair Bay.
pronounced: se-ver-neer
root meaning: *sevaer*—to travel; *nir*—south

s'FFALENN—family name for the royal line appointed by the Fellowship Sorcerers in Third Age Year One to rule the High Kingdom of Rathain. Gifted geas: compassion/empathy.
pronounced: s-fal-en
root meaning: *ffael*—dark, *an*—one

s'GANNLEY- family name for the line of Earls of the West, who stood as *caithdeinen* and stewards for the Kings of Tysan.
pronounced: s-gan-lee
root meaning: *gaen*—to guide; *li*—exalted, or in harmony

SHADDORN—trade city located on the Scimlade peninsula in Alland, Shand.
pronounced: shad-dorn
root meaning: *shaddiern*—a sea turtle

SHAND—High Kingdom on the southeast corner of the Paravian continent, originally ruled by the line of s'Ahelas. Device is falcon on a crescent moon, backed by purple-and-gold chevrons.
pronounced: shand, as in 'hand'
root meaning: *shayn* or *shiand*—two/pair

SHANDIAN—refers to nationality, being of the Kingdom of Shand.
  pronounced: shand-ee-an
  root meaning: *shand*—two
SHANDOR—city located on the coast of West Shand.
  pronounced: shan-door
  root meaning: *cianor*—to shine
SHIP'S PORT—city located on the coast of Eltair Bay, West Halla, Melhalla.
SHONIAN—a river in Falwood, West Shand.
  pronounced: show-nee-an
  root meaning: *shon'ien*—a unicorn's dance
s'ILESSID—family name for the royal line appointed by the Fellowship Sorcerers in Third Age Year One to rule the High Kingdom of Tysan. Gifted geas: justice.
  pronounced: s-ill-ess-id
  root meaning: *liessiad*—balance
SITHAER—mythological equivalent of hell, halls of Dharkaron Avenger's judgment; according to Ath's adepts, that state of being where the prime vibration is not recognized.
  pronounced: sith-air
  root meaning: *sid*—lost; *thiere*—wraith/spirit
SKANNT—headhunter captain, trained under Pesquil, now captains the Northern League.
  pronounced: scant
  root meaning: *sciant*—a lean, hard run hound of mixed breeding
SKJEND—a wineseller in the city of Morvain.
  pronounced: skinned
SKYRON FOCUS—large aquamarine focus stone, used by the Koriani Senior Circle for their major magic after the loss of the Great Waystone during the rebellion.
  pronounced: sky-run
  root meaning: *skyron*—colloquialism for shackle; *s'kyr'i'on*—literally 'sorrowful fate'
SKYSHIELS—mountain range that runs north and south along the eastern coast of Rathain.
  pronounced: sky-shee-ells
  root meaning: *skyshia*—to pierce through; *iel*—ray
SORCERERS' PRESERVE—warded territory located by Teal's Gap in Tornir Peaks in Tysan where the Khadrim are kept confined by Fellowship magic.
SOUTH SEA—ocean off Paravia's southern coast.
SOUTHSHIRE—southcoast port town located in Alland, kingdom of Shand; known for its shipbuilding and orange groves.
STRAKEWOOD—forest in the principality of Deshir, Rathain; site of the battle of Strakewood Forest.
  pronounced: strayk-wood similar to 'stray wood'
  root meaning: *streik*—to quicken, to seed

SULFIN EVEND—son of the Mayor of Hanshire who is appointed Alliance Lord Commander by Lysaer s'Ilessid.
   pronounced: sool-finn ev-end
   root meaning: *suilfinn eiavend*—colloquialism, diamond mind—one who is persistent
SUNCHILDREN—translated term for Athlien Paravians.
SUNWHEEL—blazon of the Alliance of Light, consisting of a gold geometric on a white field.
s'VALERIENT—family name for the Earls of the North, regents and *caithdein* for the High Kings of Rathain.
   pronounced: val-er-ee-ent
   root meaning: *val*—straight; *erient*—spear


TAERLIN—southwestern principality of Kingdom of Tysan. Also a lake, Taerlin Waters located in the southern spur of Tornir Peaks. Halliron taught Arithon a ballad of that name, which is of Paravian origin, and which commemorates the First Age slaughter of a unicorn herd by Khadrim.
   pronounced: tay-er-lin
   root meaning: *taer*—calm; *lien*—to love
TAL QUORIN—river formed by the confluence of watershed on the southern side of Strakewood, principality of Deshir, Rathain, where traps were laid for Etarra's army in the battle of Strakewood Forest.
   pronounced: tal quar-in
   root meaning: *tal*—branch; *quorin*—canyons
TAL'S CROSSING—town at the branch in the trade road that leads to Etarra and south, and northeastward to North Ward.
   pronounced: tal to rhyme with 'pal'
   root meaning: *tal*—branch
TALITH—Etarran princess; former wife of Lysaer s'Ilessid. Died of a fall from Avenor's tower of state.
   pronounced: tal-ith—to rhyme with 'gal with'
   root meaning: *tal*—branch; *lith*—to keep/nurture
TALVISH—a clanborn retainer in sworn service to s'Brydion at Alestron.
   pronounced: tall-vish
   root meaning: *talvesh*—reed
TAWIS—deceased grandfather who smuggled contraband into the city of Jaelot.
   pronounced: tow-iss
TEIR—title fixed to a name denoting heirship.
   pronounced: tayer
   root meaning: *teir's*—successor to power
TEIREN—feminine form of Teir.
   pronounced: tay-er-en
   root meaning: *teiren's*—'female successor to power'
TEIS—a poor commoner's child in Avenor.

pronounced: tea-iss

TELMANDIR—ruined city that once was the seat of the High Kings of Havish. Located in the principality of Lithmere, Havish.

    pronounced: tell-man-deer

    root meaning: *telman'en*—leaning; *dir*—rock

TELZEN—city on the coast of Alland, Shand, renowned for its lumber and saw millworks.

    pronounced: tell-zen

    root meaning: *tielsen*—to saw wood

THALDEINS—mountain range that borders the principality of Camris, Tysan, to the east. Site of the Camris clans' west outpost. Site of the raid at the Pass of Orlan.

    pronounced: thall-dayn

    root meaning: *thal*—head; *dein*—bird

THARRICK—former captain of the guard in the city of Alestron assigned charge of the duke's secret armory; now married to Jinesse and working as a gentleman mercenary guard at Innish.

    pronounced: thar-rick

    root meaning: *thierik*—unkind twist of fate

THIRD AGE—marked by the Fellowship's sealing of the compact with the Paravian races and the arrival of Men to Athera.

THREADNEEDLE STREET—a street in city of Jaelot.

TIDEPORT—trade port on the south shore of Korias, kingdom of Tysan.

TIENELLE—high-altitude herb valued by mages for its mind-expanding properties. Highly toxic. No antidote. The leaves, dried and smoked, are most potent. To weaken its powerful side effects and allow safer access to its vision, Koriani enchantresses boil the flowers, then soak tobacco leaves with the brew.

    pronounced: tee-an-ell-e ('e' mostly subliminal)

    root meaning: *tien*—dream; *iel*—light/ray

TIRIACS—mountain range to the north of Mirthlvain Swamp, principality of Midhalla, Melhalla.

    pronounced: tie-ree-axe

    root meaning: *tieriach*—alloy of metals

TORBRAND s'FFALENN—founder of the s'Ffalenn line appointed by the Fellowship of Seven to rule the High Kingdom of Rathain in Third Age Year One.

    pronounced: tor-brand

    root meaning: *tor*—sharp, keen; *brand*—temper

TORNIR PEAKS—mountain range on western border of the principality of Camris, Tysan. Northern half is actively volcanic, and there the last surviving packs of Khadrim are kept under ward.

    pronounced: tor-neer.

    root meaning: *tor*—sharp, keen; *nier*—tooth

TORWENT—smuggler's haven and fishing town in Lanshire, Havish.

pronounced: tore-went

root meaning: *tor*—sharp; *wient*—bend

TRAITHE—Sorcerer of the Fellowship of Seven. Solely responsible for the closing of South Gate to deny further entry to the Mistwraith. Traithe lost most of his faculties in the process, and was left with a limp. Since it is not known whether he can make the transfer into discorporate existence with his powers impaired, he has retained his physical body.

pronounced: tray-the

root meaning: *traithe*—gentleness

TYSAN—one of the Five High Kingdoms of Athera, as defined by the charters of the Fellowship of Seven. Ruled by the s'Ilessid royal line. Sigil: gold star on blue field.

pronounced: tie-san

root meaning: *tiasen*—rich


URAY—a man-at-arms in the city of Daenfal.

pronounced: you-ray


VALENFORD—city located in Taerlin, Tysan.

pronounced: val-en-ford

root meaning: *valen*—braided

VASTMARK—principality located in southwestern Shand. Highly mountainous and not served by trade roads. Its coasts are renowned for shipwrecks. Inhabited by nomadic shepherds and wyverns, non-fire-breathing, smaller relatives of Khadrim. Site of the grand massacre of Lysaer's war host in Third Age 5647.

pronounced: vast-mark

root meaning: *vhast*—bare; *mheark*—valley

VERRAIN—master spellbinder, trained by Luhaine; stood as Guardian of Mirthlvain when the Fellowship of Seven was left shorthanded after the conquest of the Mistwraith.

pronounced: ver-rain

root meaning: *ver*—keep; *ria*—touch; *an*—one original Paravian: *verria'an*

VHALZEIN—city located in West Shand, shore of Rockbay Harbor on the border by Havish.

pronounced: val-zeen

root meaning: from drakish, *vhchalsckeen*—white sands

VHANDON—a renowned clanborn war captain of Duke Bransian s'Brydion of Alestron.

pronounced: van-done

root meaning: *vhandon*—steadfast

VORRICE—Lord High Examiner of Avenor; charged with trying and executing cases of dark magecraft.

pronounced: vor-iss

root meaning: *vorisse*—to lay waste by fire

WATERCROSS—settlement in Caithwood sited at the intersection of the trade road and the Ilswater.

WARD—a guarding spell.
   pronounced: as in English
   root meaning: not from the Paravian

WATERFORK—city located in Lithmere, Havish.

WARDEN OF ALTHAIN—alternative title for the Fellowship Sorcerer, Sethvir.

WEST GATE PROPHECY—prophecy made by Dakar the Mad Prophet in Third Age 5061, which forecast the return of royal talent through the West Gate, and the bane of Desh-thiere and a return to untrammeled sunlight.

WESTWOOD—forest located in Camris, Tysan, north of the Great West Road.

WHITEHOLD—city located on the shore of Eltair Bay, Kingdom of Melhalla.

WORLDSEND GATES—set at the four compass points of the continent of Paravia. These were spelled portals constructed by the Fellowship of Seven at the dawn of the Third Age, and were done in connection with the obligations created by their compact with the Paravian races which allowed Men to settle on Athera.

WULFCARS—accountant at Meliane's brothel in Jaelot.
   pronounced: wolf-cars